AN
ECHO OF
THINGS
TO COME

By James Islington

AN
ECHO OF
THINGS
TO COME

The Licanius Trilogy: Book Two

JAMES ISLINGTON

www.orbitbooks.net

Copyright © 2017 by James Islington

Cover design by Lauren Panepinto
Cover illustration by Dominick Saponaro
Map © 2016 by Tim Paul
Cover copyright © 2017 by Hachette Book Group, Inc.

Orbit
Hachette Book Group
1290 Avenue of the Americas
New York, NY 10104
orbitbooks.net

First Edition: June 2017

Orbit is an imprint of Hachette Book Group.
The Orbit name and logo are trademarks of Little, Brown Book Group Limited.

The publisher is not responsible for websites (or their content) that are not owned by the publisher.

The Hachette Speakers Bureau provides a wide range of authors for speaking events. To find out more, go to www.hachettespeakersbureau.com or call (866) 376-6591.

Library of Congress Cataloging-in-Publication Data
Names: Islington, James, 1981– author.
Title: An echo of things to come / James Islington.
Description: First edition. | New York : Orbit, 2017. | Series: The Licanius trilogy ; book 2
Identifiers: LCCN 2017010723| ISBN 9780316274111 (hardcover) | ISBN 9780316274135 (softcover) | ISBN 9780316274128 (ebook)
Subjects: LCSH: Imaginary wars and battles—Fiction. | Imaginary places—Fiction. | BISAC: FICTION / Fantasy / Epic. | FICTION / Action & Adventure. | FICTION / Fantasy / Historical. | GSAFD: Fantasy fiction.
Classification: LCC PR9619.4.I85 E28 2017 | DDC 823/.92—dc23
LC record available at https://lccn.loc.gov/2017010723

ISBNs: 978-0-316-27411-1 (hardcover), 978-0-316-27412-8 (ebook)

Printed in the United States of America

LSC-C

10 9 8 7 6 5 4 3 2 1

For Mum and Dad.
Thank you so much for fostering my love of writing
and for the love you've always shown me.

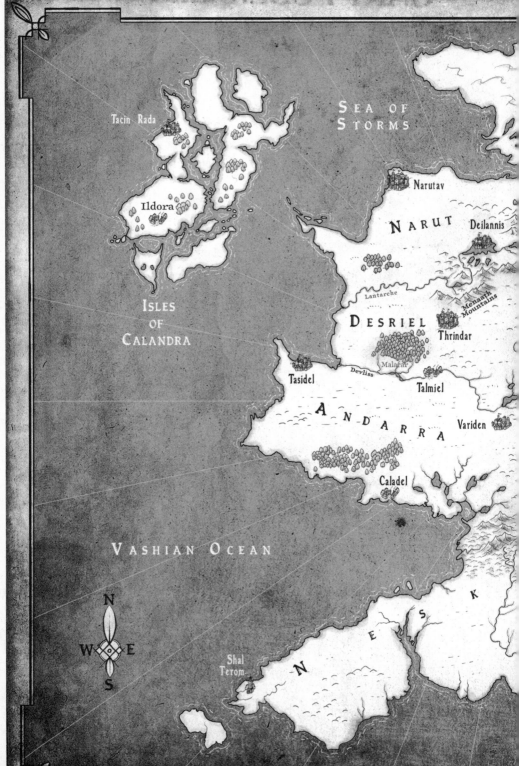

Tacin Rada

SEA OF
STORMS

Narutav

NARUT

Deilannis

Ildora

Lantarche

Menaah
Mountains

DESRIEL

Thrindar

ISLES
OF
CALANDRA

Malacar

Devliss

Tasidel

Talmiel

ANDARRA

Variden

Caladel

VASHIAN OCEAN

N

E
S
K

N
W   E

N

S

Shal
Terom

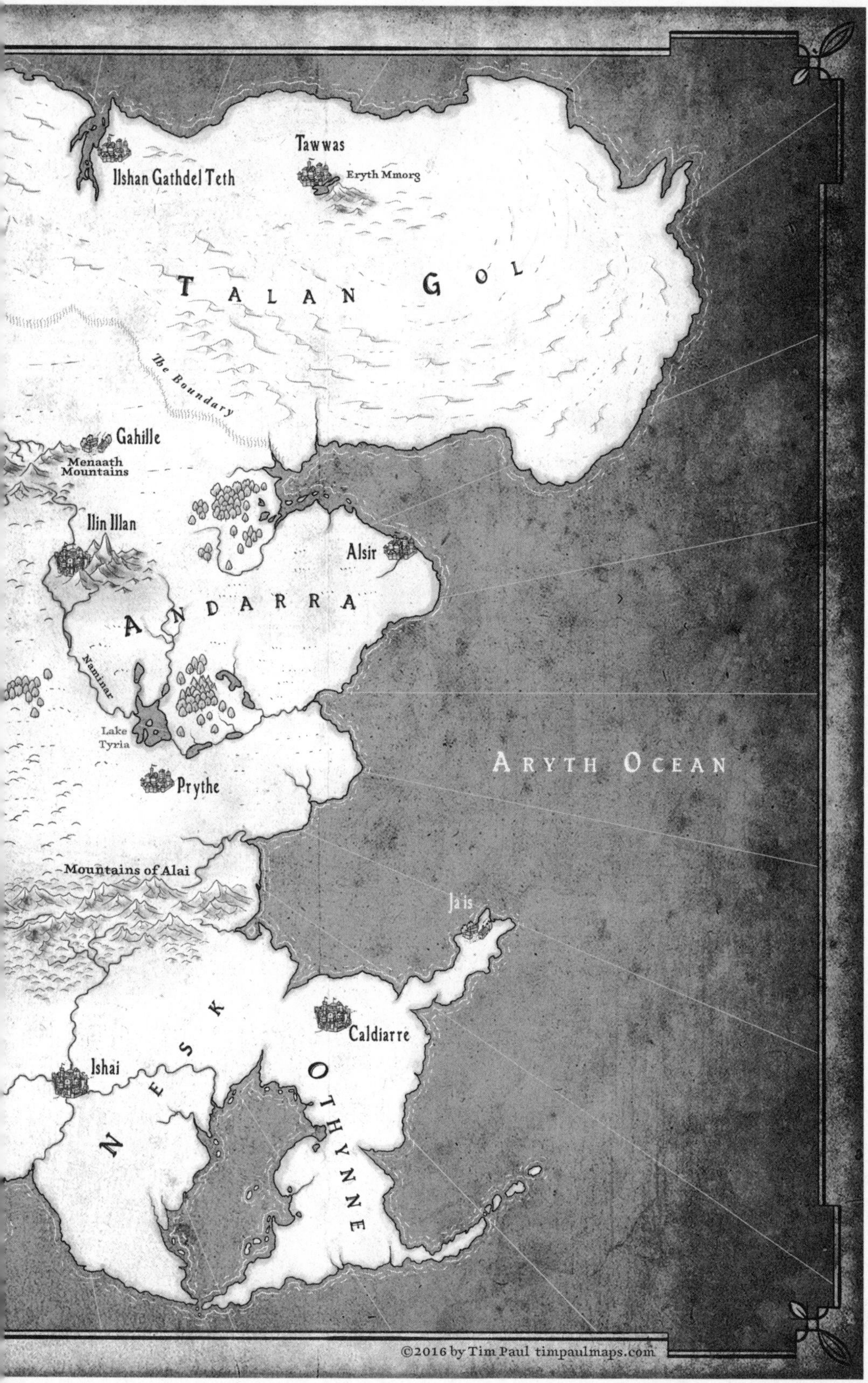

Ilshan Gathdel Teth

Tawwas

Eryth Mmorg

TALAN GOL

The Boundary

Gahille

Menaath
Mountains

Ilin Illan

ANDARRA

Alsir

Naminar

Lake
Tyria

Prythe

ARYTH OCEAN

Mountains of Alai

Jais

Caldiarre

Ishai

NESK

OTHYNNE

©2016 by Tim Paul timpaulmaps.com

The following is meant only as a quick, high-level refresher of the events in *The Shadow of What Was Lost*, rather than a thorough synopsis. As such, many important occurrences and characters will be glossed over during this recap, and some—in a few cases—are not mentioned at all.

THE PAST

Two thousand years ago, the **Boundary**—*a barrier of energy that separates the land of* **Andarra** *from the northern wastelands of* **Talan Gol**—*was erected. Though many details surrounding this event have been lost, religion holds that the Boundary was created as a prison for* **Aarkein Devaed,** *a terrifyingly powerful invader who commanded twisted monsters and sought the destruction of the entire world. During the same tumultuous period in history, the* **Darecians**—*a powerful race of people who ruled Andarra at the time of the invasion—mysteriously vanished.*

The Darecians' role was eventually filled by the emergence of the **Augurs:** *a new group of people able to use a power called* **kan,** *which (among other abilities) allowed them to see an immutable future. To assist in their governing of Andarra, the Augurs chose the* **Gifted**—*those able to manipulate a reserve of their own life force, called* **Essence,** *to physically affect the world around them.*

This hierarchy, once established, remained virtually unchallenged for hundreds of years.

A generation ago, that changed.

After several embarrassing mistakes, it became apparent that the Augurs' visions had abruptly stopped coming to pass. Refusing to openly admit that there was a problem, the Augurs instead withdrew from the public eye as they tried to determine what was happening, tasking the Gifted with controlling an increasingly nervous populace. Public unrest soon turned to anger as some of the Gifted began overstepping their new mandate, often violently. A schism in Andarran society quickly formed.

Eventually, things came to a head and a shocking, bloody rebellion overthrew the Augurs and the Gifted, with the uprising instigated by **Duke Elocien Andras**—*a member of the previously token monarchy*—*and fueled by the mysterious proliferation of new weapons designed to target those with powers. The Augurs were summarily killed, and of the five original Gifted strongholds (called* **Tols***), only two*—**Tol Athian** *and* **Tol Shen**—*held out against the initial attack.*

After spending five years trapped behind their Essence-powered defenses, the Gifted finally signed the **Treaty** *with Duke Andras and the monarchy, officially ending hostilities. The cost to the Gifted, however, was high. The* **Tenets** *were created: four magically enforced, unbreakable laws that heavily restricted the use of Gifted abilities. Commoners were also allowed to become* **Administrators** *of the Treaty, giving them even more legal and practical control over those who could wield Essence.*

Furthermore, any Gifted who broke any terms of the Treaty not covered by the Tenets were forced to become **Shadows***, permanently stripped of their abilities and horribly disfigured in the process. This applied most often to the unfortunate Gifted students who lacked the skills to pass their graduation* **Trials***, and who were therefore not vouched for by the Tols as able to adequately control their powers.*

Thus the Gifted, while technically free again, remained heavily policed and despised by most. Meanwhile, the powers of the Augurs were condemned under the Treaty. For any who were discovered to have such capabilities, a death sentence at the hands of **Administration** *awaited.*

THE SHADOW OF WHAT WAS LOST

Sixteen-year-old **Davian** is an intelligent, hardworking student at the Gifted school at **Caladel**—but as his Trials approach, he still cannot figure out how to wield his powers, despite having the **Mark** on his forearm that both binds him to the Tenets and indicates that he has previously used Essence. To make matters worse, Davian can unfailingly tell when someone is lying—something that only an Augur should be able to do. His closest friends, **Wirr** and **Asha**, are the only ones he has told about this unusual skill.

When **Elders** from Tol Athian arrive early to conduct the Trials, Davian is approached in the dead of night by one of the newcomers, a man called **Ilseth Tenvar.** Ilseth claims to have been a member of the **sig'nari**, the group of Gifted who served directly under the Augurs before the rebellion twenty years ago. He admits to knowing that Davian is an Augur, and urges him to leave before he fails his Trials and is turned into a Shadow. Ilseth also provides Davian with a mysterious bronze box, which he explains will guide Davian to somewhere he can be properly trained.

Confident the Elder is telling him the truth, Davian leaves the school that same night; Wirr, after discovering at the last second Davian's plan to flee, refuses to let him go alone and accompanies him.

Unaware of these events, Asha wakes the following morning to find that everyone in the school has been brutally killed. In shock and not knowing why she is the only one to have escaped the slaughter, she realizes that Davian and Wirr's bodies are not among the dead. However, when Ilseth discovers that Asha has been left untouched, he reveals himself to have been complicit in the assault. Assuming that Asha was deliberately left alive by his superiors (and being unwilling to kill her himself as a result), Ilseth instead turns her into a Shadow, thereby erasing her memory of everything she has seen that morning—including the knowledge that Davian and Wirr may still be alive.

Davian and Wirr head north, avoiding trouble until they are captured by two **Hunters**—the Andarran term for those who track down and kill the Gifted for profit. However, they are rescued by another Hunter, **Breshada**, who despite her profession mysteriously lets them go again, saying only that they owe their thanks to someone called **Tal'kamar.**

Continuing to follow Ilseth's instructions, the boys cross the border into **Desriel**, a country governed by a religious organization called the **Gil'shar**, who believe that all human manipulation of Essence is an abomination. In Desriel, the punishment for even being born with such an ability is death.

Navigating several dangers, Wirr and Davian are led by Ilseth's bronze box to a young man named **Caeden**, a prisoner of the Gil'shar. They set him free, only to be attacked by a creature known as a **sha'teth**. Caeden saves them from the sha'teth in a display of astonishing power, despite being physically weakened from his captivity.

Meanwhile, Asha is brought to Andarra's capital **Ilin Illan** by Ilseth, who continues to pretend that he had nothing to do with the slaughter at Caladel. The **Athian Council**—the group of Elders who lead Tol Athian—come to believe that Asha may hold the key to finding out more about the attack, but do not wish to share this information with Administration, who are also looking into the incident. The Athian Council decides to keep her at the Tol, hiding her true identity from everyone else.

After a traumatic encounter with a sha'teth that mysteriously refuses to attack her, Asha meets **Scyner**, the man in charge of a secret underground refuge for Shadows known as the **Sanctuary**. Scyner recruits Asha to find out why Duke Elocien Andras—head of Administration, and enemy to those in the Sanctuary—is showing such great interest in the attack on her school.

When Elocien hears that Asha is a survivor of the attack, he uses Tol Athian's need of a new political **Representative** in the ruling body of the **Assembly** to have Asha assigned to the palace. Asha soon learns that Wirr is Elocien's son; he may not only still be alive, but thanks to his birthright will one day be able to single-handedly change the Tenets. Despite Elocien's reputation as the driving force behind the rebellion twenty years ago, Asha also discovers that he has secretly been working with three young Augurs for the past few years—**Kol, Fessi,** and **Erran**. Knowing this, she realizes that she cannot betray Elocien's trust to Scyner, despite the deal she had previously agreed to.

In Desriel, Davian, Wirr, and Caeden meet **Taeris Sarr**, a Gifted in hiding who believes that Caeden is somehow tied to the recent, worrying degradation of the Boundary. Taeris also reveals that Ilseth Tenvar lied to Davian during their encounter at the school, and so exactly why Davian was sent to Caeden remains a mystery. Concerned that Ilseth's motives are untoward and that his bronze box may trigger something undesirable upon contact with Caeden, Taeris recommends that the box be kept away from him until they know more.

Davian and Wirr soon discover that Caeden has been charged with murder by the Gil'shar—but has no memories of his past, and does not even know himself whether the accusations are true. Taeris determines that they need to head back to Andarra, to Ilin Illan, where Tol Athian has a **Vessel** (an Augur-made device created to use Essence in a specific way) that may be able to restore Caeden's memories. However, with the Desrielite borders so carefully guarded, they decide that their best course of action is to enlist the help of **Princess Karaliene Andras**—Wirr's cousin—in order to get home.

When they finally meet with Karaliene, she recognizes Caeden as an accused murderer and refuses to risk a major diplomatic incident by smuggling him out of the country, despite Wirr's involvement. Their best hope dashed, Taeris determines that their only other option is to leave Desriel through the ancient, mysteriously abandoned border city of **Deilannis**.

In Ilin Illan, Asha forges new friendships with the Augurs, soon discovering that they have had unsettling visions of a devastating attack on the capital. Not long after, rumors begin to circulate of an invading force—christened "the **Blind**" due to their strange eye-covering helmets—approaching from the direction of the Boundary.

As she and Elocien try to determine how best to defend the city without exposing the Augurs, Asha makes the astonishing discovery that the Shadows are still able to access Essence, if they do so by using Vessels. This, she realizes, means that their abilities are only repressed when they are made into a Shadow, and not completely eliminated as was previously assumed.

After an abrupt, strange message from a seemingly older Davian, Asha becomes suspicious of Ilseth's version of events surrounding the attack on the school at Caladel, and has one of the Augurs restore her lost memory. When she finds out that Ilseth was complicit in the slaughter, she fools him into revealing his lies to the Athian Council, who subsequently imprison him.

As Davian and Wirr travel through the eerie, mist-covered city of Deilannis, they are attacked and Davian is separated from the rest of the group. He is caught in a strange rift, barely surviving his journey through the void; when he emerges back into Deilannis he meets **Malshash**, an Augur who tells him that he has traveled almost a century backward in time.

Disbelieving at first but eventually convinced of Malshash's claims, Davian spends time in Deilannis's **Great Library**, a massive storehouse of ancient knowledge. Under Malshash's guidance, he quickly learns to use and control his Augur abilities. Though Malshash's exact motivations for helping him remain unclear, Davian realizes that his teacher has been studying the rift in the hope that he can change something that has already happened.

Back in the present a devastated Wirr, believing Davian is dead, continues on to Ilin Illan with Taeris and Caeden. As they travel, they come across horrific evidence of the invading force from beyond the Boundary—strengthening their belief that they need to find a way to prevent it from collapsing entirely. Concerned that Caeden's memories may hold the key to exactly how to do that, they hurry to Ilin Illan before the Blind can reach the city.

Once in Ilin Illan, Taeris attempts to convince the Athian Council to help them, but the Council—having heard the accusations of murder leveled against Caeden and also influenced by their combative past with Taeris—refuse. With nowhere else to turn, Taeris and Caeden take refuge in the palace, where Wirr is able to convince Karaliene that Caeden is a central figure in what is happening.

In Deilannis, a training accident results in Davian experiencing Malshash's most traumatic memory: the death of his wife **Elliavia** at their wedding, and Malshash's desperate, failed attempt to save her afterward. Malshash, after conceding that this is one of the main reasons he wants to alter the past, sends Davian back to the present.

Davian heads for Ilin Illan but is briefly waylaid by another Augur, **Ishelle**, and an Elder from Tol Shen, **Driscin Throll**. The two attempt to convince Davian to join Tol Shen, but Davian has heard about the invasion by the Blind and is intent on reaching the capital in time to help.

Davian arrives in Ilin Illan, enjoying an all-too-brief reunion with Asha and Wirr before the Blind finally attack. Meanwhile Caeden and Taeris, understanding that the Athian Council is never going to help them restore Caeden's memory, plan to sneak into Tol Athian and do so without their permission. However, before they can use the Vessel that will restore Caeden's memories, Caeden instead activates Ilseth's mysterious bronze box, a flash of recognition leading him to leave through the fiery portal it subsequently creates.

As Wirr and Davian help with the city's defenses, Asha convinces Elocien to give Vessels from Administration's stockpile to the Shadows, as they are not bound by the Tenets and thus can freely use them against the invaders. After Asha and the Shadows join the fight, the Blind's first attack is successfully thwarted.

Despite this initial victory, Ilin Illan is soon breached and the Blind gain the upper hand in the battle. Elocien is killed as the Andarran forces desperately retreat, and Asha realizes to her horror that he has been under the control of one of the Augurs all along. She decides not tell a grieving Wirr, who, with Davian's help, hurries to Tol Athian and changes the Tenets so that all Gifted can fight. Even so, it appears that this new advantage may come too late.

Caeden finds himself in **Res Kartha,** where a man seemingly made of fire—**Garadis ru Dagen,** one of the **Lyth**—reveals that Caeden wiped his own memory, setting this series of events into motion in order to fulfill the terms of a bargain between the Lyth and someone called **Andrael.** This bargain now allows Caeden to take the sword **Licanius,** a powerful Vessel—but it also stipulates that he may keep the sword for only a year and a day, unless he devises a way to free the Lyth from Res Kartha.

Concerned about what he has agreed to but even more concerned for his friends, Caeden returns to Ilin Illan, utilizing the astonishing power of Licanius to destroy the invading army just as defeat for the Andarran forces seems inevitable.

In the aftermath of the battle—having revealed himself as an Augur during the fighting—Davian decides to take Ishelle up on her offer and head south to Tol Shen, where he believes he will be able to continue looking for a way to strengthen the Boundary against the dark forces beyond. Asha chooses to remain in Ilin

Illan as Representative, while Wirr inherits the role of **Northwarden,** head of Administration.

Still searching for answers about his past, and determined to help his friends fight whatever is beyond the Boundary, Caeden uses the bronze **Portal Box** again. He this time finds himself in the **Wells of Mor Aruil** and meets an Augur named **Asar Shenelac,** who appears to recognize him.

To Caeden's horror, Asar restores a memory that indicates not only that Caeden was responsible for the murders in Desriel of which he was accused—but that he is in fact Aarkein Devaed.

For I did not know which was harder to bear:
The echo of her passing, or the long silence that followed.

Prologue

The morning air was still as Caeden brushed his thumb against the axe's edge, nodding as a fine line of crimson blushed where the skin made contact.

He stared at the gently welling blood for a few moments, its momentary sting nothing against the sudden onslaught of memory the sight provided. Time—almost a year, now—hadn't dulled the edge of his guilt, hadn't helped his horror to fade.

Nor had it eased the inescapable ache of his loss. To Caeden's shame, that still hurt more than everything else combined.

Would this work? Surely it had to. He felt absently at his neck, probing at the welts from where the rope had twisted and scraped, tightened. He remembered the snap as he'd jerked to a stop.

And he remembered the tears as he'd woken, just dangling there, unable to breathe but his body refusing to fail regardless. Remembered his disbelief when his hands and legs had been able to move, as if nothing had happened.

He'd hung there for hours in a stupor, waiting for an end that refused to come.

Caeden inhaled sharply and steeled himself against the memory, handing the axe to the grizzled captain standing opposite. It was taken hesitantly, the burly man's uncertainty unmistakable.

"Are you sure about this, Lord Deshrel?" he asked quietly.

Caeden nodded once, then knelt. Placed his head carefully on the block.

"A clean cut, Sadien. All the way through. If it is not..." He

1

swallowed, then twisted slightly to look up. "A clean cut," he repeated, his tone firm.

Sadien hefted the weapon, expression bleak, then gave a single nod.

Caeden turned back toward the ground. He closed his eyes.

"I am sorry, Ell," he said softly as the blade fell.

Caeden gave a choking gasp as he came awake.

His hands flew to his neck, searching for the wound he knew had to be there. They came away clean of blood; even so it took several seconds to orient himself, to separate what he had seen from where he was.

Slowly the pounding of his heart began to ease and he lay sprawled on his back for a while, just breathing, staring vacantly at the black stone ceiling. Gently pulsing veins of Essence—Caeden thought that it was Essence, anyway—ran haphazardly across its surface, standing out jaggedly against the dark, smooth stone. Colors trickled through those veins in a constant, rhythmic, hypnotic waterfall of motion. Green here, a deep blue there. A soft yellow, then an unsettling red. The hues fluctuated and coalesced through the thin spiderweb of lines, not overpowering the clean light of the Essence lamp by Caeden's bed, but bright enough to consistently draw his eye.

He was still here—still in the same plainly furnished, perfectly circular chamber. Still deep underground, right where the Portal Box had sent him after the battle in Ilin Illan.

"You remembered something."

Caeden flinched, then rolled and scrambled weakly to his feet, stumbling a couple of steps away from the balding, white-bearded man standing in the doorway.

"Leave me alone." His voice was hoarse, little more than a whisper.

Asar stooped, carefully placing a plate of food and a cup on the ground between them. The motion was familiar now, well practiced. He straightened again, for a moment looking as though he was about to leave.

Then he touched the sword at his side, a gesture more than a warning.

"A year and a day, Tal'kamar," Asar said softly, the gently shifting lights from the wall reflected in his eyes. "And now you have two weeks less than that—two weeks less to stop the end of all we know. Two weeks in which you've barely eaten, barely drank anything. Barely slept, as far as I've been able to tell." The older man stared at Caeden for another long moment, then shook his head, looking bewildered. "Why do you still fight it? I knew it would come as a shock, but this...have you truly changed so much?"

"Yes." Caeden snarled the word, but he could hear the desperation in it. "I am not...*him*."

"How can you tell?" asked Asar quietly. "You do not even know who he is."

"I know enough."

"I doubt that. You know a couple of stories, a few grains of sand in the hourglass of your life. And out of context, at that." Asar's eyes showed his concern. "I cannot force this on you, Tal'kamar—for it to work, you must be willing. But you know I speak the truth. You still have the Portal Box, so you could have run. You could be a world away by now. Yet here we stand."

Caeden grimaced but didn't argue. The bronze cube with the mysterious markings—the Vessel that had brought Caeden here in the first place—*was* still in his pocket. He closed his eyes for a long moment, trying to shut out the anger, the fear, the despair. Every emotion told him to run, to ignore anything that might touch on what he'd seen. What he'd *done*.

But he knew, deep down, that it wouldn't change anything. He couldn't avoid his past forever. And the longer he waited, the harder facing it would be.

He wanted nothing more than to tell Asar to leave, as he had every other time the man had come.

But he didn't.

Slowly, he shuffled forward. Picked up the cup on the ground and took a few sips, letting the cool liquid slide down his raw throat.

"I remember dying," he said quietly. He gave an involuntary

shiver. "I remember the blade falling on my neck, and..." He trailed off.

Asar's expression didn't change, but what Caeden thought was pity glinted in his eyes. "That must be disorienting."

Caeden gave a humorless laugh, rubbing again at his neck. "Yes."

He hesitated. Part of him wanted to ask—ask how he could still be here, how he could remember something like that.

But the other part still didn't want to know.

Asar continued to study him, then took a seat opposite with a sigh. "Tal'kamar, we do not have time to just—"

"I didn't believe it at first." Caeden forced himself to maintain eye contact with Asar, but he couldn't keep the pain from his tone. "When you showed me...*that*...I thought you were trying to fool me, for some end that I didn't understand. I did consider running, using the Portal Box again. I considered finding you and trying to force a confession from you, too."

Asar watched him impassively, silent.

Caeden took a deep breath, but his voice still trembled as he spoke. "I knew that the memory was mine, though. I *knew*. Just like I know that I remember dying. I didn't dream that I died. I *remember dying*." He dropped his gaze, hands shaking as the torrent of emotions he had fought constantly over the past two weeks threatened to overcome him again. Shame. Fear. Horror. Rage. Crushing, soul-searing guilt. And threaded through it all, that ever-present, impossibly heavy cord of despair. "So you're right. I know the truth."

"And yet?" asked Asar softly.

Caeden gave another rasping laugh, spreading his hands. He was beyond lying, beyond subtlety. Honesty was all he could manage. "And yet I still fear it. I fear what knowing the rest will do to me. How it will change me." He raised his eyes so that they met Asar's again. "A friend of mine once told me that when I got my memories back, I would have a choice. That no matter what I'd done, who I'd been...that I had a decision to make, moving forward. That the man I have been since I woke up in the forest, the one I *want* to be, doesn't have to be erased by what I remember. *Shouldn't* be erased." He kept his gaze locked on Asar's, but he could still feel his hands quivering as unwanted echoes of memory crashed around in his head. "But I killed people. Murdered them. Fates, I was *Aarkein Devaed*."

Asar watched him for a long moment.

Then he nodded slowly.

"You did. You were. You want reassurance, but..." He gave the slightest of apologetic shrugs. "In some ways we *are* slaves to our memories. What you remember will change you. The knowledge you gain will change you. Understanding what is at stake *will* change you, change how easy it is for you to be the man you aspire to be. It will be easier to make choices you might believe unthinkable now. It will be harder to choose what is right over what is expedient, when you know how many times that has resulted in failure, and how important it is to succeed." He leaned forward, expression serious. "But all of us who live long enough face that problem, Tal'kamar. Sometimes it's what's right against what lets us win. Sometimes it's what's right against what lets us survive. But it is always a choice."

Caeden swallowed, clenched his fists. Nodded. The next line of inquiry was the hardest, the one that had been burning within him since the moment Asar had shown him who he was.

"I remember...I remember *renouncing* the name Aarkein Devaed," he said quietly, heart pounding. "I was glad that I would not remember the things I'd done as him." It was the only reason he was still here.

Asar leaned back, nodding slowly in response to the unasked question.

"Yes, Tal'kamar. You did. You rejected the name. You took the narrow road. You switched sides," he said gently, a surprising note of pride in his tone. "If it helps, you had stopped being Aarkein Devaed long before you lost your memory. We have been trying to stop what he started for a long time now. We are fighting everything that he once stood for."

Caeden breathed out, entire body going limp. He took a few seconds and allowed himself a long draught of water this time, a wave of emotion rolling over him.

Then he looked up at Asar, resolve beginning to return alongside the relief.

"And my memories," he said softly. "They'll help us stop the invasion?"

Asar was silent for a few seconds, and Caeden saw the answer in his hesitation.

"This is about so much more than that," the older man said eventually. "You are right to want to save the country, Tal'kamar, but this is about saving the world. We are at the brink of resolving a conflict that has raged for lifetimes, and sometimes we need to choose the greater good. We need to—"

"We need to do both. I haven't come here just so that I can leave my friends to their fate." Caeden cocked his head to the side, a flash of memory triggering. "The lesser of two evils, and the greater good. The most dangerous phrases in the world."

Asar studied Caeden, looking more taken aback than irritated.

"Even so, sometimes sacrifice cannot be avoided. If you would just let me restore your memories—*all* of your memories—then you would understand." Despite the words, Asar's tone held a note of uncertainty now.

Caeden leaned forward. "You said I wanted to change," he said softly. "Perhaps this is one of the reasons why."

Asar grunted. "Perhaps," he conceded, not looking pleased at the thought. He shook his head. "But that is a conversation for another time. For now, we at least need to restore the memories you wanted. You need to understand what we're trying to do, and why." He gestured. "Follow me."

Caeden hesitated, then reluctantly trailed after Asar, stumbling a little as he vainly tried to stretch muscles that were stiff from disuse.

The tunnel outside his room was lined with more of the strange, variegated veins of light pulsing in between its smooth black surfaces. It seemed to be the same everywhere on this lower level, but Caeden couldn't even begin to hazard what might be causing the strange phenomenon.

"What is this place?" he asked eventually, his voice echoing hollowly down the passageway.

"I told you when you arrived. The Wells of Mor Aruil." Asar said nothing for a moment, then glanced across and shook his head as if suddenly realizing that the name would mean nothing to Caeden. "Mor Aruil was once a Darecian outpost, a tiny island not far from the edge of the Shattered Lands. We didn't know for a very long time, but the Darecians were here because they had discovered a massive source of Essence. These tunnels were once all conduits, part of the system they used to draw that Essence to the surface." He snorted softly at Caeden's look. "No need to be concerned—the Wells went dry millennia ago. The Darecians used some of these tunnels as storage for a while after that, but the island never had much value from a tactical perspective. They eventually closed it all off. Abandoned it. Every tunnel connected to where we are is shielded, protected, impossible to break into. The only way in or out is by opening a Gate."

Caeden skipped a couple of steps to keep up with Asar. "A Gate?" The other man had said the word as if it were significant.

"A portal. A less...*fiery* version of what that bronze box of yours does," Asar elaborated wryly. "Very few people know how to make Gates, so even if the others somehow know where we are, none of them can get in here." He shrugged. "And even if they could—I am by far the strongest of the remaining Venerate. It would take all of them combined to beat me, here. We are safe enough." There was no boasting in Asar's voice, just a quiet, reassuring confidence that what he said was true. Caeden felt the tension in his shoulders relax ever so slightly at the words.

They reached the end of the tunnel, and Caeden blinked as they emerged into a large room. Like the upper level of Mor Aruil—the one on which the Portal Box had first deposited him two weeks ago—no shifting colors trickled through the walls here. Light was provided by smokeless yellow torches that burned low but steady, illuminating walls lined with bookshelves, each one filled to overflowing with tomes and loose paper. In the corner, a single bed was neatly made.

Asar gestured Caeden to a seat; after a moment Caeden slowly took it. "You live here?"

"I do."

Something in Asar's voice made Caeden pause. He glanced around again at the small bed, the shelves of books. "You said no one could get in *or out* if they could not create a Gate..." He gave Asar a querying look.

7

Asar inclined his head. "We all make sacrifices," he said quietly.

Caeden swallowed at that, nodding. There was silence as they settled into their seats, and then Asar leaned forward.

"This process—restoring your memory—it is...going to be difficult. Exhausting, even." Asar grimaced. "We couldn't just repress your memories, Tal'kamar. If the Lyth had been able to access them, they would not have accepted Andrael's deal as fulfilled. So you had to go through Eryth Mmorg—what the others call the Waters of Renewal." He gestured, expression twisted in distaste. "All but the faintest vestiges of your memories were wiped clean when you did that."

Caeden frowned. "I thought you said they were just hidden?"

"They are. Not inside your head, though." Asar held his gaze. "You are an Augur, Tal'kamar. You can go back to those moments in time, re-experience the things you've lived through. What I showed you, the day you arrived—I didn't know what you would see, not for sure. I just sent you back there."

Caeden shuddered at the reminder, but eventually forced a nod.

Asar watched him for a moment, then sighed. "Using kan to peer through time—even into the past—will be tiring. I'll guide you as best I can, and it will get easier as we go, but you're going to need to sleep in between the memories at first. A lot, probably."

Caeden hesitated. "Wouldn't it be easier to just...explain what's going on?"

Asar gestured, a hint of impatience to the motion. "I will explain some, certainly. I will answer the questions you know to ask. But some of it is too complex, some would simply take too long, and some..." He sighed. "Some you will not like. To understand—*truly* understand—what is going on, you need the context that only your memories can provide. And I will *not* waste time debating the right course of action with you as a parent would a precocious child."

Caeden scowled, shuffling a little in his seat. "Very well. If I'm not the enemy that half of Andarra seems to think, then let's start with who we're really fighting." He leaned forward. "At least explain what is waiting for us beyond the Boundary, should it fall."

Asar hesitated, clearly reluctant.

"Shammaeloth, Tal'kamar. Shammaeloth is who is waiting beyond the Boundary," he said eventually.

Caeden stared at him blankly. "*Shammaeloth*. From the Old Religion."

"Perhaps." Asar stared intently at Caeden, as if willing him to understand. "It is what we call him, at least. It is a name appropriate to his nature." He gave a small shrug. "But it would also not surprise me if he was Shammaeloth in fact. He is very, very good at using truth to lend strength to his lies, and he has used the core of that religion to lie to us from the beginning."

Caeden just stared for a moment, trying to come to grips with what the other Augur was suggesting, unable to keep the incredulous look from his face.

"What is he, then? A man? A creature? Something else?" He gave a nervous laugh. "So what actually happens when the source of all evil gets free?"

Asar sighed at the cynicism in Caeden's tone, not saying anything. Eventually, he just shook his head.

"It is a lot to take in. And I understand your doubt, Tal'kamar. Truly I do," he said softly, "but we do not have time for it. Perhaps it is better if I show you."

He leaned forward abruptly. Before Caeden could react, his fingers were touching Caeden's forehead.

Caeden screamed, but here he had no voice. Shrieking pain raked at him, but though he tried to twist away from it, he had no body. He tried to focus but there was no clarity here, just a constantly rupturing schism of consciousness. Every fiber of his being scrabbled desperately to get away from the raw, cold torment. He could not.

He thrashed in convulsive agony for longer than he could bear, and then more. Days? Years? There was a screeching cacophony until it could be borne no longer; there was an empty, swirling silence that left a desolate panic bubbling uncontrollably inside of him. There was searing pain and icy wretchedness. There was misery and anguish and bottomless loss.

There was no relief.

*   *   *

Caeden woke to the sound of screams.

It took him a moment to realize that they were his own. Tears streamed down his face; his throat was on fire and every muscle was taut as he lay curled into a tight ball, shivering uncontrollably.

Time passed; eventually he took some deep, shuddering breaths and forced his body to unwind. Still trembling, he rolled onto his side, looking up at Asar.

"What...what was that?" he gasped.

"The Darklands," said Asar quietly, leaning down and offering his hand. "It is where we think our enemy is from. His realm. And it is what this world may become if he succeeds."

Caeden hesitated, then grasped Asar's hand, letting the white-bearded man haul him back into his chair. "There was..." He trailed off, shuddering. His mind shied away from the memory. "I don't know how to describe it."

"Nobody does," said Asar gently. "The best I have heard it explained is that it is an absence. It is what it would be if there was no joy, no life, no light, no hope. If everything—*everything*—that made this world a comfort to us was stripped away, completely and utterly." Asar gazed at Caeden sympathetically.

Caeden just groaned. "How long was I there?"

"You were not *there*, Tal'kamar. I do not believe that is something which even we could endure. What you saw was a memory from a man named Alchesh. One that came at the cost of his sanity." Asar paused. "And it was only a moment. What I just showed you was a fraction of a second in that place, no more."

Caeden shivered, instinctively sinking back against the fabric of his seat.

"That is what we fight, Tal'kamar," continued Asar quietly. "That is what is coming if the Boundary should fall. We believe that Shammaeloth's goal is Deilannis—to reach the rift there and to tear it wide, so that he can escape this world. Escape time itself. And in doing so, allow the Darklands to consume what he leaves behind." He leaned forward. "So now you see. *That* is why we do not have time to deal again with the doubt and unbelief that you have already been through once. *That* is why it is so imperative that we restore your memories."

Caeden closed his eyes, still trying to steady himself.

"Why would I ever have fought for him, then?" he asked softly. "Why would *anyone*..."

"Because he fooled us." Asar's words were firm but gentle. "For a long time, we thought that we were doing the right thing."

"The right thing?" repeated Caeden, a hint of scorn returning some of the strength to his voice. "How could he possibly fool someone into believing that?"

"It's *what he does*." Asar's voice had turned sharp, and Caeden could see that he'd touched on a wound still not healed. "Do not assume that his intent was obvious, nor that we were simply stupid or naive. He gave us not only a compelling falsehood, but a compelling morality to go with it—something to live for and something to live by. Do not forget that he is older than even we can imagine. He spent *hundreds of years* proving himself, building trust, laying the foundation of his story and giving us a sense of purpose. He knows each of our weaknesses, and he exploits them in unimaginably subtle ways. He is more intelligent, more convincing, more clever, and more *patient* than any of us could ever hope to be. So much so that most of the others are not just still fighting for him—they *believe* in him, heart and soul."

Caeden subsided, shifting uncomfortably, not sure how to respond.

Eventually, he nodded.

"Very well," he said reluctantly. It was a hard thing to comprehend, let alone accept—but at least for now, he didn't seem to have a choice. He straightened, his heart rate finally slowing again after what Asar had shown him. "Who are these others you keep mentioning?"

Asar sighed again, impatience creeping into his tone this time. "There were eleven of us, originally. The Darecians called us the Venerate; in their language, it was a way of mocking us—both for the blind worship we received, and the blind worship we gave. But it stuck." He took a deep breath. "You and me. Gassandrid. Alaris. Cyr. Isiliar. Andrael. Diara. Meldier. Wereth. Tysis. Three and a half thousand years ago, Shammaeloth brought us all together. We were immortal before we ever met him, but Shammaeloth is the one who first showed us how to use kan."

Caeden opened his mouth, then shut it again. "So...these others are our enemies now, too?" he asked, thinking immediately of his previous encounter with Alaris.

Asar groaned, the sound one of pure frustration. "Shammaeloth's true nature started to show through. Some of us saw it, some of us didn't. Inevitably, we broke apart." He shrugged tiredly. "Look—we could keep going like this for days. I could spend precious hours explaining our past, recounting events you've already experienced, trying to train you again—and in the end, that is exactly how much wiser you would be. Hours, not the centuries you need to be." He rubbed his forehead. "Time is against us, and this will be a difficult process. Laborious. Every moment I spend giving you an overview of things that you have to remember regardless, is a moment utterly wasted."

Caeden shifted uneasily. "But I already know so much more than I did an hour ago. What if I can't remember at all? What if it takes too long and then you just have to tell me anyway?"

"I know that you are afraid of your memories, but do not let that fear dictate your actions," growled Asar, a clear rebuke. "Give me a month. One month to try and sate your curiosity by restoring what you already know, rather than me trying to teach you. After that, if you still do not have everything you need? I will talk until my throat is raw and your ears bleed. I will impart every piece of knowledge I possibly can." He leaned forward, gripping Caeden by the shoulder. "But Tal'kamar? If we get to that point, we have already failed. My words simply cannot replace your experiences. The truth is, I could talk for a hundred years and never bring you to where you need to be. So this *is* the only way forward."

Caeden swallowed, chest taut, but nodded slowly.

"Then let's begin," he said quietly.

Chapter 1

Davian spun smoothly past another slow-moving bolt of shimmering white Essence, not bothering to extinguish it this time.

He darted across the rain-slick courtyard toward his target, weaving nimbly between the bright slivers of energy inching across the open space, all the while focusing on the spherical mesh of dark, hardened kan from which the attacks were emanating. He gritted his teeth, blinking away the occasional droplet of rain that made its way into his eyes, continuing to force back the flow of time as he moved. Everything was much harder this far from Deilannis. It was less than a minute since he'd begun, but already he was nearing his capacity to keep this up.

He stepped to the side as more bars of molten light appeared; he diverted some of his focus and snatched a few of them from the air nearby with kan, redirecting them back at their source. They hit the spinning sphere and simply dissipated.

He grunted, not bothering to look around as the first of the bolts he'd ignored finally smashed into the tall stone archway behind him, accompanied by the muted roar of crumbling masonry as it began to collapse.

The Elders were *not* going to like that.

Brightening at the thought, he dodged between the two kan barriers in his path—similar in construction to the sphere ahead, but entirely static—and skidded to his knees as another stream of light, this one far stronger than anything he'd seen thus far, sliced through the air where his head had been a few seconds earlier.

His eyes widened a little. That was new.

Dangerous, too.

He growled, forcing himself up again and finally reaching the outer edge of the swirling sphere. He breathed deeply, the sharp cold of the winter's morning in his lungs helping him focus, clearing his head. He could do this. The barrier wasn't perfect—the hardened mesh confronting him was just a shell protecting active, malleable kan underneath, and he could occasionally spot the more vulnerable lines of dark energy writhing through the gaps.

The problem was that the mesh was constantly revolving. Even slowed though it was to his perception, the protective shell still moved too fast for him to accurately thread his own kan through it. And the moment any of his attacks touched the hardened, spinning outer layer, they dissipated like smoke in the wind.

Stepping into motion again he prowled the edge of the barrier, every nerve taut as Essence attacks flashed out at him, slowed but still requiring quick reactions at this range. In between the strikes he arrowed dark energy experimentally into the gaps of the sphere, probing for weaknesses. Each time, his threads were cut by the mesh before they could impact what was inside. He tried forcing the kan through faster, but to no avail. He tried matching his threads to the rotation; the shell somehow sensed what he was doing and jerked in response, changing direction, shifting savagely and unpredictably in order to slice through his attack.

He growled again, for a moment considering trying hardened kan of his own—but the memory of his last such attempt held him back. A kan blade would more easily disrupt the softer internal workings of the shield, but there was one firm rule when two constructs of hardened kan clashed: whichever was created first was stronger. Even if he succeeded in damaging what lay within, it wouldn't be fast enough to stop the mesh from rotating into his own attack.

And the last time he'd been manipulating hardened kan when it had been broken, he'd ended up bedridden for an entire day combating the resulting headache.

Davian's sense of urgency mounted as a faster-moving bar of Essence grazed his shoulder, and he felt time start to push against him again. He squinted. A portion of the sphere seemed to be only shell, with no active kan strands behind it at all. Was that right? Easier to maintain, he supposed, but flawed. Dependent on illusion for security. Hardened kan couldn't stop him from physically moving through it. And if he could place himself inside it without being hit by any of the active kan strands, the rest would be easy.

He waited three more full rotations of the mesh, batting away flashes of Essence, until the gap he'd spotted came toward him again.

He dove forward.

The world lurched as the active strands—rotating with the shell, hidden neatly between two close-set layers of hardened kan—caught him. He was ripped violently back into time, dropping to one knee and groaning, head spinning. His limbs felt weak and he swallowed, barely avoiding dry-retching. Behind him, he could hear the last pieces of the shattered archway still smashing to the ground.

When he'd recovered enough to look up, Ishelle's amused grin greeted him.

"You really thought you could just *walk* through it?"

Davian grunted. "I thought there was a gap," he coughed, rising unsteadily to his feet, quickly supported by Ishelle as he stumbled. "That was dirty."

Ishelle's smile widened as she gestured with her free hand, dismissing the barrier that had been whirling around her. "Because my shield actually did what it was supposed to do? Or because I outsmarted you?"

"Dirty," repeated Davian firmly, though he gave her a smile as he rubbed his head. He sighed, then politely disengaged himself from Ishelle's grasp, glancing around at the cloud of dust where the archway into the courtyard had once been. "And...hmm."

"Hmm," agreed Ishelle, giving him a stern look.

"That's not *my* fault," protested Davian. "There was no way I could have absorbed all of those bolts *and* kept myself outside of time."

"That was the point." Ishelle peered at him. "You need to be less competitive."

Davian snorted. "We won't mention that one blast that nearly took my head off, then." He sighed. "I still have no idea how to beat that shield of yours. You say you can maintain it while you're asleep, now, too? If mine was half as effective, I'd be ecstatic."

"A few years of constant nagging from Driscin helps get it

right," observed Ishelle. She paused. "And the fact I'm better than you, of course. That's relevant, too."

Davian barked out a laugh, then immediately regretted it as pain shot through his skull. "Of course. Not counting when we practice with Reading, or communicating mentally, or altering our passage through time, or drawing Essence, or—"

Ishelle cut him off with a loud sigh of mock sadness. "Better, Davian. *Better.*"

Davian grinned, but dipped his head slightly in acknowledgment. "Give me a few moments, then we can go again?"

"You don't want to try something a little less painful?" Ishelle glanced at the pile of debris. "Or, maybe, less destructive?"

"I *want* to." Davian shrugged. "But that's not why we're here."

Despite the light tone of the conversation, he couldn't keep an undercurrent of unease from his voice as he said the words. That was usually present whenever he talked about their training now, though. It had already been a month since the battle in Ilin Illan—three long weeks on the road, then the last one at Tol Shen itself.

And despite his best efforts, he was still none the wiser as to how they were supposed to seal the Boundary.

He sighed. These Disruption shields—designed to block any kan attack—were, apparently, the very first thing most Augurs were taught. That made sense, once Davian had thought about it. Given the importance they had placed on confirming visions, they would also have needed a way to be certain that those visions had not been artificially created or altered in any way.

More importantly right now, though, he and Ishelle had agreed that this was the best way to prepare for when they eventually did reach the Boundary. Though neither of them had any real idea what they'd be facing once they headed north, learning to circumvent the protection of hardened kan seemed like a logical move. It would be on an entirely different scale, of course—but assuming that the Boundary was protected from tampering, these types of barriers would almost certainly be involved.

It was all still speculation, though. Despite his hounding of the various Elders here—as well as spending every spare second that he could in Tol Shen's multiple libraries—information on what they were up against was even more scarce than Davian had initially feared.

Ishelle shrugged. "If you want to provide me with more entertainment, I won't complain."

Davian gave her a wry look, then stared up at the cold gray sky for a few seconds. "One more round. Just...give me a minute."

"I don't think a minute's going to help you." Ishelle slid smoothly onto the bench next to him—just close enough for him to feel uncomfortable, but not quite close enough for him to shuffle away without looking immature.

Davian leaned forward instead, twisting the ring on his forefinger absently and focusing on the courtyard. It was empty, as always. Reserved for the Augurs. Not just the yard, either—the towering buildings that surrounded it on all four sides, too. A large statue sat at each corner, each one holding pulsing, burning representations of weapons that lit the area brightly at night, as well as giving the Augurs a constant source of Essence with which to train. Grand balconies across multiple floors overlooked the wide but enclosed space, and pathways between buildings crisscrossed the air above. A hundred windows reflected back the cloud-covered sky. All were empty. All were silent.

His vision swam for a moment as he stared; he hesitated, then slowly relaxed his mental control, allowing his body to begin drawing Essence again from the nearest statue. He'd been consciously, periodically cutting himself off since leaving Ilin Illan—a somewhat risky proposition, perhaps, but it was more dangerous by far to remain ignorant of his limitations.

In the past month, he'd learned that he could comfortably survive for at least a few hours without Essence: even more when completely sedentary, but significantly less when training with kan. How long had this time been? An hour? He never pushed his experimentation too far—the moment that he started to feel tired or nauseous, he always stopped—but he tried to do it regularly and under varying conditions. The more he knew about his unusual condition, the better.

"No new visions last night, I take it?" he asked eventually as the tightness in his muscles began to ease.

"Nothing." Ishelle gave a languid stretch. "More terribly sad looks from Thameron later today, I fear."

"Wouldn't be an afternoon at Tol Shen without one or two of those," agreed Davian.

Elder Thameron—Tol Shen's appointed Scribe—had been one of the few people who had actually seemed excited by their arrival. But Ishelle's Foresight was weak at best; since leaving Ilin Illan she'd had only a few visions, and none had been of anything particularly important.

Combined with Davian's ability still being blocked after Deilannis—a problem Ishelle had been unable to detect, let alone fix—they had been a source of constant disappointment to the Council. In the last few days, Thameron had taken to looking a mixture of frustrated and depressed whenever he spotted them.

Davian pushed himself to his feet, dismissing the thought. "Ready," he announced, stretching a little. "This time I think..."

He frowned at Ishelle's expression, turning to see movement beyond the remains of the archway at the far end of the courtyard. Three red-cloaked figures were picking their way past the debris, and even at this distance Davian could see that they wore grim expressions.

"Be nice," he murmured, low enough that only Ishelle could hear.

"Always," responded Ishelle with a vaguely hurt look. She turned to the trio as they approached.

"I think your archway fell down," she called out to them, expression innocent as she indicated the rubble.

The Elders glowered at them as one, not excluding Davian from the glare. Normally the Council would have underlings relaying messages, but Davian suspected that they had very few willing volunteers when it came to dealing with the Augurs. Even the Elders themselves, when they visited, seemed reluctant to come alone.

Aliria, an attractive redheaded woman who was perhaps ten years Davian's senior, crossed her arms and ignored Ishelle's cheerful observation. "The Council has requested your presence immediately."

"Immediately?" Davian frowned. It was unlike the Council to summon them without notice.

"Immediately," confirmed Thil grimly, red cloak unable to hide his lithely muscular form. Like Aliria, he was closer to Davian's age than Davian had ever expected an Elder to be—in his midthirties, perhaps even younger.

"Requested?" Ishelle gave Thil a bright smile.

Thil met her gaze for a moment but then looked away. Davian shot Ishelle a reproachful frown, then grabbed his cloak from the bench.

"It's fine. We're coming," he reassured them. He glanced pointedly again over at Ishelle.

Ishelle glowered at him, but eventually sighed.

"Yes, yes. We're coming," she agreed.

Davian did his best not to react as the throng of Gifted ahead parted, almost brushing up against the walls of the buildings on either side in their eagerness to give the Augurs a wide berth.

"You'd think a week would be long enough for them to realize that we're not dangerous," he murmured to Ishelle. They had quickly become isolated as the Elders escorted them through the Inner Ward of Tol Shen, with every eye warily on them. Though the hubbub of cheerful voices still emanated from farther ahead, Davian and Ishelle left only muted murmuring in their wake.

"But we *are* dangerous." Ishelle abruptly veered off to the left, and Davian had to hide a smirk at the stuttering sidesteps and looks of sheer panic she elicited from those now in her path. She rejoined Davian after a few seconds, ignoring the glares of the Elders and not bothering to conceal her own amusement at the discomfort she'd caused. "See?"

Davian shook his head. "Now that I think about it, I can probably see why they get nervous around us," he said drily.

Ishelle shrugged. "I tried to be friendly. We both did. Fates, we tried the entire way here."

Davian sighed, but acknowledged the statement with a nod. They *had* tried to put the Gifted at ease—making sincere efforts to strike up conversation with their companions during the journey to Tol Shen, and then with plenty of others since their arrival. It seemed like each attempt had ended with the Gifted either rudely or nervously excusing themselves.

Half the Gifted here were clearly terrified of them. The other half, perhaps more worryingly, appeared to resent their very existence.

Doing his best to ignore the stares of the crowd as they passed, Davian instead focused on the still-unfamiliar surroundings. Like Ilin Illan, most of the structures in Tol Shen were the Builders' work; it showed in every smooth line of the fortress, every perfectly placed stone.

Even so, the massive network of interconnected buildings and walkways felt very different from the capital. Here beauty gave way to something geared more purely toward functionality, with hints of a militaristic design filtering through to everything from the arrow-straight layout of paths, to the flat-topped roofs, to the way that the buildings grew gradually taller the closer they stood to the center of the compound.

And, of course, there were the enormous walls that always loomed in the background. Almost as tall as the Shields at Fedris Idri, the walls were what divided Tol Shen into its three concentric circles—the Outer, Inner, and Central Wards.

Unlike the Shields, though, there was no one manning these walls; instead, blue lines of Essence pulsed constantly around their upper third. On their first day at the Tol, Ishelle had vividly demonstrated the purpose of that Essence by tossing an apple at it. Her projectile had turned to ash the moment that it had made contact.

The crowd thinned and the path began to slope gently downward as they approached the passageway beneath the wall that connected the Inner and Central Wards. Allowing for no more than five people abreast, the tunnel began fifty feet before the looming barrier. The red-cloaked guards at the entrance eyed Davian and Ishelle mistrustfully as they approached—most Gifted knew them either by sight or description now—but as soon as Thil flashed his dual silver armbands, they were reluctantly waved through.

They started through the tunnel. A few paces ahead, Elder Aliria murmured something to her two companions and dropped back, falling into step with Davian and Ishelle.

"Elder," said Davian politely, nodding. Despite the close confines, something odd in the acoustics meant that his voice didn't echo as it should have. The way the stone absorbed sound was still unsettling, even after having made this trip several times.

Aliria smiled prettily at him, and Davian suddenly knew what was coming next.

"I was wondering if you'd reconsidered your stance on Reading?" Aliria swept a lock of red hair back from her face. "I do understand your hesitation, but it really would be for the good of the Tol. And it would be a wonderful way to start working together." She paused. "In fact, working that closely with us, I'm sure we'd need to get you some accommodations in Central. It would alleviate the need for this nonsense of you having to be escorted every time you need to see the Council."

Davian and Ishelle glanced at each other.

"We have reconsidered," said Davian slowly. He almost laughed as Aliria's expression grew greedy. "There's just one problem."

"Most of the Gifted around here seem to have figured out how to shield themselves," chimed in Ishelle.

"We've been trying," continued Davian. "Really hard. But..."

"They're just really good at it," concluded Ishelle apologetically.

"Evidently had good teachers," said Davian regretfully.

"So even if more Augurs arrive, I'm afraid they won't be able to help you, either," observed Ishelle.

"Which is a shame because we really wanted to help," added Davian.

Aliria's expression had steadily darkened as they'd talked, until now her anger was unmistakable even in the dim Essence light of the tunnel.

"I see," was all she said. She increased her pace, rejoining the other two Elders without another word.

Davian watched her go, then sighed. "Perhaps we shouldn't have been quite so glib about it."

"We were exactly the right amount of glib." Ishelle gave an unconcerned shrug. "I'm more worried that we genuinely can't Read anyone now."

"Something which we were never going to do anyway," said Davian firmly. "If we want people to stop being terrified of us, we have to show them that we have some moral boundaries."

"Or at least pretend to have them," said Ishelle.

Davian snorted. "Either way. We're not spies."

"We're not," Ishelle concurred readily. "Besides—the second we let the Council start taking advantage of our abilities, there won't be an end to it."

Davian grunted in agreement. It had been Aliria who had approached them on their first day at the Tol, too; then, as with today, she'd strongly implied that the offer came from the Council itself. That had never been explicit, though, so there would no doubt be vehement denials if the Augurs ever claimed as much.

Davian nodded toward the three Elders ahead. "So what do you think this is about, anyway?"

Ishelle glanced across at him. "I can guess what you're hoping for, but I wouldn't wager it's anything to do with the Boundary. Driscin's still"—she paused, closing her eyes briefly—"at least a day away. Maybe two."

"And they won't want to discuss it until he gets back. I know."

"Driscin's the only one on the Council who was part of the sig'nari," Ishelle said, her tone taking on the slightest hint of defensiveness. "Ever since he found me, he's been the one they've turned to for advice when it comes to Augurs—and they probably did it long before that. You can't really blame them for wanting to wait for him."

Davian sighed but said nothing more. They'd already had this disagreement on several separate occasions, and right now wasn't the time to continue it.

They trailed after the Elders in silence after that, emerging from the other side of the tunnel and into the tranquil gardens of Central Ward.

Davian shook his head as he took in the bright, lush greenery and gently tinkling fountain in the distance, as was always his reaction when they came here. Central was home to the Elders and their likely successors, men and women either already in power or being primed for it. The buildings here were not just taller but better furnished, gardens were beautifully maintained even as they kept their clean, militaristic lines, and the streets and walkways were startlingly peaceful due to the exclusivity of the area. It reminded him more of the palace at Ilin Illan than anywhere else.

After a few minutes they reached the Council Chambers, a

tall tower with elegantly tapering sides that was situated close to the very center of Tol Shen. The guards frowned as they approached—a reaction Davian was growing accustomed to—but opened the doors for them without hesitation.

To Davian's surprise, the majority of the Shen Council were inside.

The Council's primary meeting hall was, in many respects, not dissimilar to the one at Tol Athian: a large room with the Elders' seats raised well above the main floor, on a balcony accessible only by an entirely different entrance. Just as it had in Tol Athian, it made Davian feel very much like a supplicant coming before a ruler. Which, he had no doubt, was by design.

The biggest distinction, though, was one that was hard to miss.

At the back of the Elders' balcony, contained behind an enormous glass wall, a torrent of Essence swirled and pulsed in constant, hypnotic motion. It silhouetted the Elders dramatically, making the entire upper section difficult to look directly at.

There were other differences from Tol Athian, too, though they were less pronounced. These chambers were richly adorned, with tapestries and gilt-framed paintings on the walls. Even against the bright light, Davian could tell that the seating above was plush, far more comfortable than the solid-looking benches he'd seen in Tol Athian. There were younger Gifted serving food and drink here, too, their ears glowing from the Essence that blocked their hearing while they were in the room.

The Elders—at least twenty of them up above, more than Davian had seen together since the day of his and Ishelle's arrival—were talking softly amongst themselves.

Davian shuffled his feet impatiently after a few seconds, exchanging a wry glance with Ishelle as their entrance was all but ignored.

"You'd think that if they were going to summon us, they'd at least show us the courtesy of realizing when we'd arrived," observed Ishelle loudly.

Davian found himself caught between wince and smirk as the voices above stopped, silence falling as red-cloaked men and women turned to glare down at them.

"Augur Ishelle. Augur Davian. Thank you for coming." Elder

Lyrus Dain led Tol Shen; his gray hair singled him out as one of the older Gifted on the Council. His words were polite enough, but as always, Davian sensed the sneer that was barely concealed beneath.

The soft-featured man paused as Aliria—Elder Dain's wife—and the other two Elders joined the Council members on the balcony. His expression darkened when Aliria gave him the slightest shake of her head as she sat.

Lyrus continued to frown in thought for a moment, then turned back to the Augurs. "I'm sorry to take up your valuable time," he added drily.

"You're forgiven, Elder Dain," said Ishelle politely, giving no indication that she'd seen the exchange with Aliria. "But perhaps we could get to why we're here?"

Lyrus didn't react, but Davian could almost see the irritation radiating from him. "As you say."

Davian sighed inwardly. Most of their dealings with the Council had gone this way, though not all of them had degenerated quite so quickly. Ishelle, for all her ties to Tol Shen, seemed to have little respect for anyone here aside from Driscin.

Lyrus glanced at one of the Elders sitting behind him—Nathyn, Davian thought was his name—and a silent exchange passed between them. Lyrus turned back. "I would like you both to confirm for me where you were last night." His tone was stern, containing a hint of accusation.

Ishelle and Davian exchanged a puzzled glance. "We were in bed," said Ishelle.

Davian flushed a little at the raised eyebrows. "Separate rooms," he emphasized.

Lyrus nodded absently, though he didn't look like he cared either way. "And can you verify that?"

"I was asleep," said Davian slowly. "So not really."

"Same," concurred Ishelle. She squinted up at the Elder. "Why are you asking?"

Instead of answering, Lyrus bent to the side, quietly discussing something with Nathyn and the other Elders within earshot.

Davian bit back a scowl. The ongoing battle to extract even
small amounts of information from the man—from any of the

Shen Council, for that matter—was a constant reminder of just how little respect he and Ishelle were afforded here.

Eventually, Elder Dain straightened again.

"Someone was seen skulking around Central a few hours ago, just before dawn. When the men on duty spotted them, the intruder just...disappeared. Vanished from right in front of the patrol." He gave them a pointed look.

Davian exchanged another glance with Ishelle, but he could see from her expression that she was as surprised as he. "You're sure they weren't mistaken?"

"Three men swear they saw the same thing." Lyrus shrugged. "I'm not accusing either of you of anything"—he paused, his tone indicating that wasn't entirely true—"but if it *was* one of you, now's the time to tell us. There will be no consequences if you admit it straight away, of your own free will."

"We've respected the rules and kept to the Inner and Outer Wards since we got here," Davian assured the Elder, unable to completely hide his exasperation at the suggestion. "And we're well aware that Central is off-limits without an escort. It wasn't us." He said the words with confidence, refusing to give Ishelle the querying look that he wanted to. He didn't *think* she would have gone exploring—not without at least mentioning the idea to him first, anyway—but it wasn't something he *couldn't* imagine her doing.

Lyrus sighed. "Very well," he said reluctantly. "I believe you."

Davian ignored the suggestion in Lyrus's tone that he had few alternatives. "Good." He kept speaking, not giving the Elder a chance to dismiss them. "Has there been any news from the Boundary?"

Lyrus frowned down at Davian for a moment, then shook his head impatiently. "No, Augur Davian. The same as yesterday, and the day before that, and the day before *that*. The Boundary, as far as we know, is still stable." He held up a hand as Davian opened his mouth to argue. "Undoubtedly decaying, else the Blind would never have been able to get through. But there have been no reports of further breaches, and we have certainly received no word of any other...threats. No monsters that need slaying just yet."

The last was met with a quiet ripple of laughter from the balcony, and Davian reddened.

His reaction wasn't just from this one ill-concealed mockery. After Ilin Illan, Tol Shen—along with everyone else—had finally accepted that the Boundary needed sealing; in fact, it was the entire reason the Augur Amnesty existed. The destruction in the capital had left everyone on edge about what further forces might be waiting in Talan Gol.

Yet. From the moment Davian had tried to bring up Devaed, or dar'gaithin, or Alchesh's visions...it had always ended like this. Despite their unusual armor, despite what had happened at Ilin Illan, everyone seemed intent on reassuring themselves that the Blind had been only men. That the threat from the north was ultimately coming from the descendants of the original northern Andarrans, trapped behind the Boundary two thousand years ago. It was a story that had caught on fast—something that was identifiable, quantifiable, easy to grasp for everyone involved.

After everything Davian had been through, he knew there was more to it—and yet no one seemed willing to listen. Aarkein Devaed and his Banes remained a dark legend from a disproven religion, while Alchesh was still just a mad Augur whose foretellings had been proven false centuries ago.

Davian knew, deep down, that he should just let the Shen Council's disbelief go. He'd managed to for the past week. A few months ago, he probably would have kept doing so.

But things had changed. *He'd* changed. He just didn't have the patience for this...narrow-mindedness.

"So when the Assembly's envoy comes to check on our progress, I assume I can tell them that you said that?" he asked, ignoring Ishelle's warning look. It didn't take a particularly sharp mind to know that Tol Shen would be doing the opposite of this in the Assembly—playing up the Boundary's weakness and their own role in training the Augurs to fix it, in order to solidify their political position in the capital.

Above, the laughter faded.

"Careful, Augur Davian," said Lyrus, all mirth gone from his tone. "I give you and Augur Ishelle some leeway with your lack of

respect. I won't with threats. The Amnesty places you under *our* direction. Remember, you're afforded protection from the law only so long as you do as we tell you to." He smiled again, and this time the cold, confident superiority of the expression made Davian's blood boil.

He stared up at the Elder.

"I'm not threatening you, Elder Dain," he said quietly. "I'm just trying to work with you."

He was sick of this. He'd only been here a week, but the Council weren't even *pretending* that they had a sense of urgency about the situation. That was likely because, at least in the short term, actually sealing the Boundary would prevent Tol Shen from capitalizing further in Ilin Illan—but he hadn't come here just to be a pawn in their quest for more power. Davian had left Wirr and Asha behind because the threat of what lay beyond the Boundary—what Caeden had warned them about—was something that couldn't be taken lightly. It certainly wasn't simply a risk to be balanced against improving Tol Shen's political standing.

And yet, that was exactly how the Elders here were treating it.

"Besides," he added.

He reached out, pushing through kan. Forced himself out of the flow of time.

He walked through the passageway to his left, past two sets of guards and up the steps to the Elders' balcony. Once there, he positioned himself behind and slightly to the right of Lyrus, in front of the other Elders present.

He placed his hand on Elder Dain's shoulder and leaned forward, letting time wash over him again.

"Augurs shouldn't need threats," he concluded quietly into Lyrus's ear.

Lyrus leaped from his seat as if Davian had physically attacked him; other Elders flinched away, gasping at his abrupt appearance in their midst.

Davian paused for a few seconds to make sure his point had been made. From Lyrus's blanched face and the deathly silence that followed his pronouncement, he suddenly wondered if he'd gone too far. He'd wanted to show Elder Dain that he was unintimidated, not make an enemy of him.

Still—his point had been made, and it was too late to take it back. A week of being polite had got him nothing but excuses. It had been past time to show the Elders that he and Ishelle weren't there to be pushed around.

He glanced down below at Ishelle, giving her a slight shrug before forcing back time once again.

He left.

Chapter 2

Asha held her breath and flattened herself against the smooth, Essence-lit wall of the corridor, heart pounding loud in her own ears.

She silently cursed her luck and stayed perfectly still as the three red-cloaked guards drew nearer. They were early today; she should have had plenty of time to reach the main level of the Tol before they'd even started the trek down here. A careful glance over her shoulder showed three of the half-dozen Gifted behind her were already in motion, one idly examining the Victor's Lament as he stretched, unintentionally blocking the entrance to the Sanctuary. There was no going back that way.

She screwed up her face in frustration, though careful to ensure it didn't cause her head to shift. She should have waited a few more minutes before leaving. Her impatience—and perhaps over-confidence after doing this so many times—was going to get her caught.

Moving deliberately, she turned her gaze back to the men walking toward her, trying to stay calm. Was the burly one on the left walking too close to her side of the corridor? The Veil rendered her invisible, but that hardly mattered if someone managed to blunder into her.

She tensed, ready to move swiftly if she had to; better to cause suspicion and confusion than to get caught outright. The guard's arm passed within an inch as he strode by, his cloak actually brushing against her legs as it flared out behind him.

Asha froze. That would have looked strange to anyone paying attention.

Nobody reacted.

Resisting the urge to exhale in relief, she forced her legs into motion and moved silently in the opposite direction, keeping to a quick walk. She had a minute or two, but the men being relieved wouldn't wait long before they started making their way back up to the Tol. There were two more sets of guards for her to navigate, and the last thing she needed in these narrow corridors was more people to avoid.

She hurried through the abandoned passageways of Tol Athian's lower level. As always, the dim lines of Essence emphasized the area's emptiness almost as much as the sound of her footsteps, which now that she was alone managed to echo no matter how softly she trod. At least it was a familiar journey; she made the myriad turns back to the main stairwell confidently, not bothering to pause and check the carefully sketched map she kept folded neatly in her pocket.

A few minutes and six guards later, and she was on the main level of the Tol again, stairwell behind her and out of sight. Checking that no one was around—nobody but the assigned guards ever came this way, but it never hurt to be cautious—she deactivated the Veil, slipping the smooth silver torc into her pocket and breathing out a slow sigh of relief.

That had been close, closer than any of her other sojourns down there. She had to be more careful in future.

She adjusted her fine red cloak and started walking, slipping smoothly from the side tunnel into Tol Athian's main passageway. A passing Administrator shot her a half-suspicious, half-sullen look, but otherwise nobody paid her entrance any notice; the crimson flow of traffic here was dense, close to that of a busy city street.

Even so, it wasn't hard to see that there were markedly fewer Gifted hurrying by than there once would have been. Those who did still wore anxious, vaguely haunted expressions, too. The month since the Blind's incursion had done little to ease the grim mood of Tol Athian's residents.

A few minutes later she was turning into the narrow corridor that accommodated the small study the Council had set aside for the Representatives' use. Her heart sank when she saw that the door was ajar.

Pausing and taking a deep breath, she pushed it fully open and strode inside.

"Taeris," Asha said politely as she entered the brightly lit but cramped room, affecting nonchalance. This was Taeris's study as much as hers, but he rarely used it, as evidenced by the close to complete lack of anything on his desk. Hers, by comparison, was a chaotic mess of paper, scribbled notes, and reams of reports hiding every inch of the scratched wooden surface beneath.

"Ashalia." Taeris sighed, making no effort to keep the wry disapproval from his scarred face. Asha noted with curiosity the new line of angry red that ran down his cheek, almost reaching his jawline. "Please shut the door. I think we need to talk."

Asha gave a slight nod, flicking the door shut and taking a seat at her desk, which was arranged in the narrow space facing Taeris's. "What brings you here?"

Taeris glanced toward the door to ensure it was closed, then just raised an eyebrow.

Asha grimaced. "Si'Bandin was upset?"

"*Lord* si'Bandin was *very* upset. Where were you?"

"You probably don't want to know." Asha didn't fully trust Taeris, but nor could she quite bring herself to lie to his face. The conversation she'd overheard between him and Laiman Kardai just after the battle a month ago had been unsettling—she still hadn't been able to find out anything more about "Thell," the name by which Taeris had called the king's adviser—but she didn't think either man was an enemy, either.

Taeris watched her for a few moments, then sighed again. "I probably don't. Even if I have my suspicions," he added significantly, rubbing his forehead. "But you need to tell Lord si'Bandin something better than "personal reasons," this time. He was amongst the first to publicly support you after the battle. He feels like you—*we*—have forgotten that."

Asha rolled her eyes. "Hard to do when he manages to bring it up every time I see him."

"And he's an insufferable bore to boot," agreed Taeris readily. "But he *did* help stop you from being thrown in prison."

Asha scowled at that, though she knew there was truth to the statement. She still occasionally had nightmares about that night at the Shields, but in some ways the days following their victory had been almost as bad. With most of Administration reeling from Wirr's ascension to Northwarden and his changing of the Tenets, Asha had become an easy, high-profile target at which to vent their fury. Demands that she be punished for giving Vessels to the Shadows had been loud and insistent. Veiled implications that she had somehow collaborated with the Shadraehin had soon followed.

"Torin would have stepped in if things had gone that far," she said, a little testily. Her friend had wanted to do so from the very start, in fact, but she'd insisted that he stay out of it unless things became dire. The other Administrators had already been doing everything that they could to undermine him; going out of his way to help her would only have made Wirr's own position less tenable.

It had been with some trepidation that Asha had approached the Houses for support, but she need not have worried. Michal, Asha's former mentor and Taeris's predecessor, had been nothing if not thorough in her training; it had been easy to target the Houses who could most benefit from an alliance with the rising political fortunes of Tol Athian. Si'Bandin had been one of the first to stand up in the Assembly and oppose efforts to sanction her, but he'd been far from the last.

"I'm not suggesting you owe him our vote," said Taeris gently. "But a meeting isn't much to ask, even if it's just to tell him no again. You should reschedule as soon as you can."

Asha nodded, doing her best to look properly chastised, though she'd chosen to skip that particular meeting for a reason. Lord si'Bandin was no doubt continuing to try to get their support for removing the Assembly-mandated limiting of grain prices, which had threatened to skyrocket after the Blind's rampage through the north. If she had to listen to his vague reasoning one more time— and stop herself from pointedly mentioning the man's extensive farmland holdings in the south—she wasn't entirely sure that she could stay civil.

"I'll try and speak to him tom—"

Darkness, and then she was blinking up dazedly at a concerned-looking Taeris. She groggily levered herself up from her prone position, gingerly touching the side of her head. No blood, thankfully, but it definitely hurt. "What happened?"

"You just...fainted, I think? You hit the side of the desk on the way down." Taeris helped her to her feet, looking at her worriedly and steadying her with his arm. "Should I take you to the physician?"

"No." Asha straightened immediately, forcing a smile. "I'm fine. Just tired. It's been a long month." She made the excuses quickly; she didn't want Taeris, or any of the Gifted for that matter, to know about these dizzy spells. Though a few of the Council now supported her as Representative, the rest were still looking for an excuse to replace her with someone of their own choosing.

Besides—she'd quietly visited a physician already, albeit one from Ilin Illan's Lower District. Not as good as those employed by the palace or the Tol, perhaps, but still competent, and infinitely less likely to recognize her. The man had been unable to find anything obviously wrong.

Taeris hesitated, but eventually acquiesced with a nod. "As long as you're sure."

"I'm fine," Asha repeated, though without any heat to the words. It was true enough; with the exception of an aching head from the blow it had sustained, she felt no different from how she had moments before the fall.

Still.

It was the fourth time this had happened to her in three weeks, and she hadn't been able to pinpoint a cause. It could be something to do with her trips down to the Sanctuary, she supposed, but the other episodes hadn't coincided with any of her previous visits. She never felt ill, before or after. She didn't even feel especially tired—no more so than she'd felt since becoming a Shadow, anyway.

"At least come and see me if it happens again," Taeris said gently, still looking concerned. He studied her. "I know it's been a hard month. I know you're frustrated with how things have gone here, too. Just...don't let that frustration lead you into pushing yourself too hard. Or throwing away your position here after working so hard to keep it," he added in a drier tone.

Asha nodded ruefully. Taeris wasn't wrong about that last part;

she'd fought hard to stay on as Representative, and she was risking throwing that away by angering men like si'Bandin.

Ultimately, though, no position was worth having if it meant being forced to sit on her hands and do nothing.

Taeris gave her a tight smile and stood, indicating he'd said his piece.

"Any word on the search?" Asha asked quickly before he could start for the door.

Taeris hesitated, then grimaced. "No. I believe Administration's still devoting a lot of resources to hunting them, but...no." He held her gaze. "You know I'm not going to say anything, but be very careful who else you ask about that."

"I know." Administration's concerns about Asha hadn't been entirely dismissed by the Assembly: she was now explicitly banned from having anything to do with, or any operational knowledge of, the investigation into the Shadraehin. Including, of course, having any access to the Sanctuary. "Doesn't it bother you, though? There were families living down there. Children. And they all manage to disappear without a trace, without anyone noticing?"

"Fates, Ashalia. Of course it bothers all of us, especially if what you've said about this 'Scyner' is true. But unless the Shadows have some direct connection to the Boundary that I'm missing..."

Asha hesitated, doing her best to hide her frustration. The Shadraehin was important; what Davian—the older version of him—had told her indicated that there was much more to her plan than simply arming the Shadows and disappearing. But she couldn't mention that to Taeris, or to anyone for that matter. Davian had said it was important not to, and she'd given him her word.

"I'm sure having access to a prewar Augur could help," she observed eventually.

"A willing, trustworthy one? Probably," said Taeris, a hint of impatience creeping into his tone. Asha could hardly blame him; they'd been over this ground before. "But those don't sound like qualities we can count on from the man you met. Besides..." He sighed. "I don't doubt Scyner's an Augur—you're too smart to be this certain about a fake—but nobody recognizes him from the name, nor the description you gave. The Council are convinced that the Shadraehin tricked you somehow, used the concept of her commanding an Augur to intimidate you into giving her access to the Vessels. My support for you in the matter is only making things worse, too, I'm afraid. They won't give Scyner another thought without some sort of proof."

Asha scowled, though it was hardly surprising news. She hadn't told anyone about her role as Scribe or about the other Augurs—Wirr's position was tenuous enough without stirring up more scandal surrounding his father, and while she hoped that Erran and Fessi were going to accept the Assembly's Amnesty, she hadn't seen them since the day of the battle. If they wanted to remain in hiding, she wasn't going to be the one to reveal their existence.

It didn't help that the Athian Council were also, for some reason, constantly at odds with Taeris. Despite what appeared to be a genuine effort on his behalf to work with them, they rarely listened to his opinion, and it often felt as though their decisions were determined more by what Taeris *didn't* recommend. Their animosity toward him seemed to go beyond mere dislike... but she still hadn't been able to ascertain why from anybody, and Taeris himself had been entirely disinterested in talking about it.

"So there's been no news about the Shadraehin herself, either?" Asha pressed.

Taeris rolled his eyes, looking exasperated.

"Nothing I'd consider news. Though there is one thing—probably nothing, so I suppose it doesn't hurt to mention it," he added, albeit reluctantly. "Her name was bothering me, so I looked into it."

"Her name?" Asha frowned. "Isn't it just Darecian for 'leader'?" She'd heard that somewhere, though she wasn't sure where. Probably someone had mentioned it in the Sanctuary—half of her time down there had involved listening to enthusiastic monologues about the Shadows' leader.

" 'Shadrian' is the Darecian word for leader," said Taeris, pronouncing it with less of a drawn-out *ee* sound at the end. "Which is *derived* from 'shadraehin.' Shadraehin is actually 'High Darecian.' "

"Ah. Well. My mistake," said Asha.

Taeris gave her a wry look. "The High version is more nuanced than just 'leader.' It speaks of . . . unity. It's a rallying cry, a focal point."

Asha brushed back a strand of blond hair from her face. "Seems appropriate, given what she's done with the Shadows."

"Which is why it's odd," Taeris explained. "There are very, very few people who would actually know the difference. High Darecian's not exactly common—I can barely cobble together the odd phrase myself. And given his ability to understand the sha'teth, the only person who I can think of that might have a better understanding of it than me, is Caeden."

Asha stared at Taeris. "So you think that the Shadraehin and Caeden are connected, somehow?"

"They *could* be." Taeris shrugged. "As I said, it's not much."

Then he frowned at her. "And that's now *everything* we're going to discuss on the matter. Someone overhears us, and I'm in almost as much trouble as you. Understood?" He watched her for a moment longer to ensure his point had been made, then gave a slight nod and headed for the door.

Just as he was about to open it, though, he paused.

"Ah. I should also let you know—I've had another inquiry from Iain Tel'An."

Asha stiffened, her scowl deepening. The rising political fortunes of Tol Athian, along with the now-public knowledge of her friendship with Wirr, had resulted in some unexpected—and unwanted—attention from some of the young men at court. "You know what to say to him by now, surely. Same as Lyannis, and Jadyn, and the rest of them."

"They might be more inclined to leave you alone if they hear a refusal from you personally, you know." Taeris sighed. "I know how you feel about Davian, but . . . don't you think it might be worth at least talking to some of these boys?"

"Not particularly." Asha shook her head. "It's nothing but awkward and embarrassing, Taeris. The Houses think I'm a prime target because I'm young, a Representative, and a Shadow. And what Shadow wouldn't be grateful for the attention, right?" She couldn't help but let a tinge of bitterness creep into her tone.

Taeris looked at her blankly. "Is that really what you think?"

Asha snorted. "Are you saying I'm wrong?"

"I'm saying you're wrong." Taeris smiled at her dubious look. "The lords of the Houses do sometimes push their sons in certain directions, but...even with the Tol's improved fortunes, I doubt any of them would be urged toward us. I really don't think any of these boys were forced to make an approach."

Asha frowned. "You expect me to believe they're genuinely interested?"

To her surprise, Taeris laughed. "I expect you to have a better grasp on your own reputation," he said with amusement. "A lot of people saw you fight at the Shields, and trust me, they haven't kept quiet about it. For many of them, you're the one who saved their lives. Fates, you're the Shadow who saved the *city*. I *still* can't get through a meeting without being asked for an introduction."

Asha blinked. "But there were girls from the Houses who fought, too," she pointed out. "And bravely."

Taeris rubbed his forehead, still smiling. "True, but none impacted the battle the way you did. Not to mention that after that the Houses rally behind you to stop Administration from throwing you in jail, it turns out you're a childhood friend of the prince, *and* you mysteriously ignore the attentions of some of the most eligible young men in Ilin Illan. Interested? Fates, Ashalia. Perhaps if you paid more attention to what's going on rather than chasing news of the Shadraehin, you'd realize you're considered one of the most intriguing women in the city right now."

Asha stared at him in silence for a few moments, flustered.

"It...doesn't matter," she said eventually, shaking her head. She *had* been refusing a lot more invitations than when she'd been studying under Michal, but she'd assumed that was due to Tol Athian's rising popularity and her relationship with Wirr rather than anything to do with her directly. "It doesn't change anything. If you and Wirr really think I should keep my connection to Davian a secret, then I will—but I'm not going to pretend that I'm either interested or available. It's a waste of my time and if what you're saying is true, would be unfair to them as well." She held Taeris's gaze defiantly.

The older man said nothing for a few seconds, then sighed.

"As you say," he murmured. He gave her a nod, the motion holding a hint of respect. "I will let Iain know."

He made to turn, then hesitated.

"And Ashalia? It would be remiss of me not to remind you that if you have somehow been making your way down to the Sanctuary again, you are risking both your safety and your position as Representative in doing so." His expression remained smooth as she began to frown at him. "And *particularly* remiss of me not to ask you to stay away from the detailed maps of that area that I happen to know are in the Athian library. The Council is done with them now, and I doubt anyone is keeping track of who accesses that sort of thing…but still. I trust that you'll do the right thing."

He gave a wry nod to Asha's grateful look and then opened the door, slipping out into the corridor and leaving her alone once again.

Asha hurried along the still-scarred street, drawing her cloak closer against the gray morning and ignoring the stares of passers-by as she made her way back toward the palace.

The walk was a short one across Ilin Illan's Upper District, but the reminders of what had happened here a month ago were still everywhere. Most of the Builder-made structures remained but several more recent ones lay in crumbling, charred heaps, the recent rain leaking lines of black onto streets still pockmarked from where blasts of Essence had gouged out stone. New frameworks were rising everywhere—Asha could spot a dozen at a glance as she looked out over the districts below—but for every structure being rebuilt, two still lay in ruins.

The crowds, too, moved differently than they once had. Ilin Illan's streets were busy but most of its residents were quieter, subdued. People still hurried everywhere, but uneasily rather than cheerfully, cautiously rather than with purpose.

Even now, it was as if those who had survived the attack couldn't quite accept that the Blind were truly gone.

She relaxed a little once she reached the palace, despite the still-blackened gardens harkening back to the battle as much as anywhere else. It was far from the beautiful landscape it had once been, but it was at least familiar.

Strange though it seemed, this was home now.

She made her way to her quarters, frowning as she spotted the muscular, redheaded man reclining against the wall by her door.

"Can I help you?" she asked cautiously as she approached. The stranger's clothes were finely made but bore no insignia, and she didn't recognize him as being from one of the Houses.

The stranger inclined his head politely. "Representative Chaedris? Prince Torin is waiting for you within."

Asha brightened. "Thank you."

She slipped inside. The study adjoining her quarters was entirely her own, larger and better appointed than the one in the Tol. It was also a Lockroom, ensuring that the conversations she had within were completely private, even from any Gifted or Augurs attempting to eavesdrop. The majority of the time that she was not assisting Taeris directly, she spent here.

"Representative Chaedris," said Wirr with mock formality as he stood, smiling. Despite the cheerful greeting, the blond-haired boy looked...older. Tired, more grim than he had even a month ago.

"Prince Torin." Asha grinned, then embraced him. "It's good to see you, Wirr."

"You too, Ash," said Wirr sincerely. "Sorry I haven't been able to come and visit these past couple of weeks. Things have been..."

"I know." They both sat, and Asha nodded to the door. "Assistant?"

"Bodyguard." Wirr shrugged awkwardly at Asha's sudden frown. "Just a precaution. I'm not the most popular figure in the city right now."

Asha stared at her friend worriedly for a few moments more, but eventually inclined her head, accepting the explanation.

Then she smiled slightly. "Actually, that's not *necessarily* what I hear."

Wirr gave her a blank look, then rolled his eyes as he understood. "Don't even joke about that. My uncle's already told me I can't refuse any more dinner invitations without looking rude, no matter how much work I have to do. I'm supposed to be dining with the Tel'Raths tomorrow night."

Asha's smile widened. "Along with the very eligible Iria Tel'Rath, I assume?"

"I assume," said Wirr heavily. He snorted as he saw her expression. "Don't laugh. You haven't fully understood the meaning of the word *awkward* until you've had to deal with..." He gestured as if trying to wave away the memory. "But I'll tell you about that another time. Maybe. I can't stay long, but I wanted to check if you've made any progress."

Asha's amusement faded, and she glanced around to make sure the door was shut.

"Still nothing," she admitted. "I've made five trips down there now—one this morning, in fact. A few hours each time. But it's a big place."

"Five?" Wirr's blue eyes held hers, concerned.

"I haven't seen anything to be worried about," Asha said quickly.

Wirr grunted, not looking convinced. "And yet both the sha'teth and the Blind know their way around down there. Look, Ash—I know you can take care of yourself, but even with your Veil, every minute you spend in the Sanctuary is a risk. What happens if you get injured? Trapped? It's not as if we can come searching for you if you don't come back."

Asha restrained a grimace at that. Wirr had a point—only Shadows could survive in the Sanctuary. She didn't like keeping her dizzy spells from him, but this was why it was necessary. He was probably the one person who could truly force her to stop her investigation...and she knew he would, if he found out what had been happening.

Wirr continued, oblivious to Asha's discomfort. "Not to mention the trouble you'd be in if anyone found out you'd been down there at all. Fates, or even if they found out you still have that Vessel. On that *alone*, Administration would be trying to put you in a cell."

Asha waited until he'd finished, then widened her eyes at him. "It really *is* dangerous, isn't it? Thank El I have you to tell me, Wirr. I would never have thought of all of that myself," she said

40   innocently.

Wirr glowered at her, though eventually a reluctant smile crept back onto his face.

"Fine. Point made. You're not uninformed." He scratched his chin. "You just make terrible, terrible choices."

Asha grinned at that. "Perhaps. But I'm the only one willing to look who actually can," she reminded her friend gently.

"I just want to make sure the risk is worth taking." Wirr held up his hand as Asha made to protest. "I'm not suggesting you stop, and you know I'll help in any way possible. But..." He looked at her seriously. "I don't want you to get yourself killed chasing after something that may not even exist."

"The Shadraehin knew about the Vessels, Wirr. Knew Shadows didn't lose their Reserves. She *has* to know more about how it all works."

"But that doesn't mean she can help you find a cure. Or that there even is one." Wirr rolled his shoulders awkwardly, evidently hating to be negative about something so important to her. "I *hope* there is. But..."

"I know." Asha couldn't be angry at Wirr for doubting. He didn't know about Davian's message; without that, Asha herself would have had reservations about this pursuit. "I'm not giving up, though. I promise I'm being careful, but that's the best I can offer you."

Wirr sighed, but eventually inclined his head.

There was silence for a few seconds, and then Asha straightened. "What about your inquiries? Have you figured out how Administration got their Vessels?"

Wirr grunted. "No," he admitted. "Elder Olin always said that he didn't know where Traps, Shackles, and the other Vessels used during the war came from—but I just assumed that he and the other Elders from Caladel simply didn't want to talk about it." He shook his head in obvious frustration. "Now, though...it doesn't seem to matter who I ask. I can't get a straight answer about it from anyone."

Asha's heart sank. "But surely *someone* knows. Things like that don't just materialize." She'd been hoping that if they could find out more about the origin of the Vessels used to create Shadows, they could perhaps learn more about their operation.

"And yet you'd think they did, the way everybody talks." Wirr leaned forward, expression serious. "Ash, I couldn't find a single person who remembers anything like them before twenty years ago. There's no documentation of them in Administration's files, and the Athian Council claims that they didn't even know that creating Shadows was *possible* until they agreed to the Treaty. The same goes for the Vessel that controls the Tenets, and the Oathstones that are used to bind Administrators. I can't find a single Gifted or Administrator who knows where they came from. Or at least, none who will admit it to me," he amended drily.

Asha gave him a sympathetic nod. Along with Administration's continued fury, half of the Gifted seemed to feel that Wirr had betrayed them by not removing the Tenets entirely. Despite his best efforts, his allies on either side of that divide right now were few.

"What about your uncle?" she asked eventually. "Surely he knows?"

Wirr grimaced. "He's only been back on his feet for a week, and he's had more pressing issues to worry about. I did ask, a few days ago, but…" The blond-haired boy shook his head in evident frustration. "He told me to leave it alone. Claimed that he didn't know, that my father had been in charge of it all—but he was adamant that the things that went on back then should be left in the past. He got a little agitated about it, actually." He sighed. "He *is* still recovering, so perhaps I'll let him calm down and ask again in a few weeks…but I'm not really expecting it will help. He's right—my father was the driving force behind the rebellion. If anyone knew where the Vessels to make Shadows came from, it would have been him."

He fell silent.

Asha felt a swell of sympathy for her friend, along with a brief stab of guilt. Would Erran know where the rebellion's stockpile had originated? She doubted it; it seemed like information the Augur would have shared, even if he'd had to do so while pretending to be Elocien.

She considered again whether to tell Wirr the truth about his father, and again immediately dismissed the idea. It wasn't her secret to share and even if it had been, it would hardly be fair to either of her friends. Elocien was gone. Revealing Erran's Control would only taint the good memories Wirr had of his father.

Eventually she sighed, nodding. "What about the connection between Taeris and Laiman?" After overhearing the two men's conversation the day after the attack on Ilin Illan, she had told Wirr everything she'd learned.

"No evidence of it that I've been able to find." Wirr shrugged. "I'm as curious about it as you, but Laiman's been friends with my uncle since before the end of the war. As for Taeris, he's one of the few people in the Assembly who actually believes that there might be worse than more soldiers in fancy armor waiting for us in Talan Gol. I think it's safe to say that they're both on our side, regardless of whatever secrets they're keeping."

Asha frowned but nodded, not pressing the point. She wondered again about the other secret Laiman and Taeris had mentioned—the one Wirr supposedly knew about Davian, but that Davian himself didn't know. She'd been sorely tempted to ask Wirr what it was...but after thinking about it, she'd decided that she should trust her friend and avoid putting him in an awkward position. If Wirr thought it was important for her to know, then he would tell her.

"How are you doing with everything else?" she asked, switching topics.

Wirr grunted. "Administration, you mean? They're angry I'm in charge, angry my father kept the truth from them, angry that I've agreed to the Augur Amnesty. Angry the Tenets have been changed. Angry about the Shadows. They're just..." He sighed.

"Angry?" suggested Asha.

Wirr gave her a tight, wry smile, though it quickly faded. "It's making it very difficult to do anything that actually makes a difference. I try to organize anything within Administration, and it's blocked. I put forward something to the Assembly, and my own people sabotage it. It's...not what I was hoping it would be, thus far," he concluded with a slightly self-conscious shrug.

Asha gazed at her friend sympathetically for a few seconds. "It will get better. It's only been a month; everyone's still in shock at how much things have changed. Give it time."

Wirr sighed, nodding. He looked like he was about to say something when there was a sharp knock at the door; Asha opened it to find Wirr's redheaded bodyguard standing outside.

"Apologies for interrupting, Sire, but you're needed," he said, peering past her at Wirr. The words were delivered mildly enough, but something in his tone indicated urgency.

Wirr grimaced, but inclined his head. He shot Asha an apologetic look. "The excitement never ends." He held her gaze. "Promise me you'll be careful?"

Asha gave him a slight nod of confirmation. "You know where to find me if there's any news. Or if you need an ear," she added softly.

Wirr gave her a quick, grateful smile, then followed his bodyguard out into the hallway.

Asha stared at the closed door for a few seconds, then sighed.

It had been good to see Wirr, but she wished they had more time to talk—more time to enjoy the moments of familiarity and normalcy that always came from catching up with her friend from Caladel. Those moments were too few, and when they were over, they usually only made her long for their times back at the school. Especially the ones that had included Davian.

After a few seconds, though, she pushed herself to her feet, heading to her desk and shuffling through the papers that had already begun piling up. There simply wasn't time for reminiscing.

She had a lot of work to get ahead on before her next trip to the Sanctuary.

Chapter 3

Wirr stifled a yawn as he closed the door behind him, then raised an eyebrow in his bodyguard's direction.

"So. What crisis needs averting now, Andyn?"

The redheaded man—perhaps ten years Wirr's senior—gave no indication of emotion or opinion as he spoke, maintaining the neutrally proper demeanor he always displayed. "Lady si'Danvielle just happened past, Sire. She seemed somewhat surprised to see me here, as she assumed that you would be attending the meeting between Administration and the newly arrived Desrielite ambassador."

"What meeting?"

"Exactly, Your Highness."

Wirr stared at the muscular man for a moment, then looked to the side and cursed. "Pria."

"Lady si'Danvielle did mention Administrator si'Bellara was attending," confirmed Andyn. "She took the ambassador into the Blue Hall ten minutes ago."

Wirr gritted his teeth. Administrator Pria si'Bellara was his second-in-command only because the three Administrators ahead of her had resigned rather than work for Wirr, but that didn't mean that she made any effort to keep him informed. "I don't suppose Lady si'Danvielle happened to mention what this meeting was about, seeing as you two seem to be on such good terms?"

"Only that the ambassador appeared rather agitated when he arrived, Sire," said Andyn, Wirr's irritation seeming to slide right by him.

Wirr groaned, rubbing his forehead. "Wonderful." He sighed, then gave his bodyguard a rueful smile. "Very well, Andyn. Let's go and have a polite conversation with our newest Desrielite friend."

⚜

"Ah. The gaa'vesh. Now we come to the heart of the matter," sneered Ambassador Daresh Thurin, the large, muscular man's finger pointed directly at Wirr as he walked into the hall.

Wirr glanced around and adjusted his long coat, waiting for the men outside to shut the heavy double doors behind him before responding. Despite its name, the Blue Hall displayed mostly the same pure white walls found everywhere else in the palace; instead, its moniker came from the distinctive swirling design over the southern door that was made entirely of inlaid lapis lazuli. Today the hall's occupants consisted mostly of the ambassador's retinue, though a couple of men in blue cloaks also stood over to the side, no doubt there in order to officially witness whatever was going on.

Pria herself sat opposite Ambassador Thurin, her curly black hair neatly tied back. The willowy woman met Wirr's cold gaze calmly, with no hint of either surprise or guilt. Probably, he realized, because she was experiencing neither.

Once the doors had thudded closed behind him, Wirr took a deep breath.

"I apologize for my tardiness, Ambassador," he said smoothly, walking over and dragging a chair across to the table. He made himself ignore the uncertain looks of the ambassador's men, as well as the way their hands slid unconsciously toward where their weapons would be, had they not been disarmed upon entry.

He sat, nodding for Andyn to stand a little to his left, between himself and the Gil'shar soldiers. Unarmed or not, it never hurt to be careful.

Then he turned back, smiling cheerfully at both Pria and Daresh as they glared at him. "What have I missed?"

The ambassador's lip curled. "You have missed nothing meant for your ears, gaa'vesh."

46   Wirr sighed. "Please, Ambassador Thurin. I am the North-

warden. If you have business with Administration, then you have business with me."

Daresh looked over at Pria, jaw clenched. "By the Nine, Administrator si'Bellara, I will say no more until we are able to speak in private."

There was silence, every eye in the room now on Wirr.

Wirr just shook his head, more exasperated than angry. An obvious test. The ambassador had to have known that he would need to deal with Wirr eventually.

"Such...bluntness," mused Wirr. "An interesting choice, but it hardly seems very ambassadorlike. Ambassadorish. Ambassadorial?" He turned and gave Andyn a querying look.

"It is a word, Sire," Andyn confirmed.

"Excellent. Not very ambassadorial," concluded Wirr cheerfully. "Perhaps the Gil'shar picked the wrong man for the job? Because the wrong man for the job probably wouldn't be welcome here. In this *country*," he clarified.

Ambassador Thurin's face darkened. "Are you suggesting—"

"*Yes*, Ambassador. If we are going to dispense with pleasantries, then let us dispense with pleasantries. You are a *guest*—a guest of both my land and my family. No matter how you feel about me personally, if you cannot behave in a civil manner when representing your own country, then you have no place here, and I will be more than happy to see you on the road back to Thrindar. Immediately. *However*. If you would like to discuss the problem *at hand*—whatever that may be—then I am willing to listen."

Wirr kept his voice calm, steady. As little as a month ago, confrontation like this would have made him more than uncomfortable. Now? He coaxed, argued, dealt with people blinded by their irrational fears and prejudices on a close to daily basis.

And as both Laiman and his uncle had drilled into him mercilessly, he was the prince. Insults were not something to which he could simply turn a blind eye.

Still, Ambassador Thurin blinked, clearly taken aback by the ultimatum in Wirr's response. Even Pria, normally unreadable, glanced at him with undisguised surprise.

There was silence again, this one longer than before.

Then the ambassador inclined his head. It was the slightest

of acknowledgments from the powerfully built man, but it was enough.

"Very well. Firstly, and most importantly, I am here to discuss the surrender of your spy into our custody," said Daresh, his tone as if nothing unusual had transpired.

"Spy?" Wirr ignored the ambassador's refusal to use his title—there was no point pushing his luck—and shot a glance over at Pria, who just shrugged.

"The one you managed to plant within the Gil'shar. The one who was chosen to be amongst my bodyguards for the journey here." Daresh's expression was grim. "Unfortunately for you, our guards at the Talmiel crossing are thorough. Your agent set off a Finder."

"You had a Gifted hiding *within the Gil'shar*?" Wirr stared at the man for a few seconds and then shook his head, dazed at the thought. "Ambassador, surely you must know that he's not one of ours."

"There is no point in denying it," said Daresh, his tone hardening. "Meldier knows, it is impossible that a gaa'vesh could have gained entry into the Gil'shar without significant, well-resourced assistance. Had they not been chosen to accompany me, it is possible that they would never have been discovered."

Wirr rubbed his forehead. "Do you really think that we would send one of the Gifted to Desriel? And if we did, do you think that we would send someone foolish enough to allow themselves to be tested by a Finder right in front of you?" He gestured. "What did this supposed spy say when you questioned him?"

The ambassador watched Wirr with narrowed eyes. "They tried to deny it, at first—acted surprised, demanded that they be tested again. When they failed a second time, they cut their way free. Escaped." His face darkened at the memory. "Three Desrielites were killed."

Wirr grimaced, softening his tone a little. "Then I am sorry for your loss, Ambassador," he said genuinely. No wonder the man was furious. "But again, I tell you that I have no knowledge of any Gifted in Desriel, let alone inside the Gil'shar."

"Do I have your word, in front of these witnesses and the

Nine Gods, on this?" Daresh leaned forward. "This is your only chance to avail yourself of Desriel's mercy, *Northwarden*. Concede involvement, work with us, and we will negotiate the proper reparations in good faith. Should your word be proven worthless, though, the matter will not be so easily resolved."

"You have my word," said Wirr, ignoring the sneer in the other man's use of his title. He had no idea how any of the Gifted could have possibly infiltrated the Gil'shar—or why they would even have wanted to. "If you give me this man's description, I can let my Administrators—"

"That will not be necessary." The ambassador continued to watch Wirr but appeared convinced, at least for now. "It seems I spoke in haste. Let us just…forget this unpleasantness."

"Thank you, Ambassador. Perhaps we should move on to the purpose of your visit," Pria interjected smoothly before Wirr could say anything more.

Wirr barely avoided glaring at her. Both the ambassador and Pria knew that Wirr would have used the spy's description to protect him, try to keep him out of the hands of the Hunters who were undoubtedly already searching for him. Not to mention, of course, that getting to this Gifted first would mean that he could find out how in El's name they had managed to avoid detection within the Gil'shar.

Eventually, though, he hid his irritation beneath a smile and polite nod, and they began the meeting in earnest.

Wirr exhaled as he watched Ambassador Thurin leave the hall, retinue trailing behind him.

The last two hours had felt like ten. Wirr had forced himself to be calm, polite and methodical as he'd guided Daresh through the minutia of the new Tenets, carefully navigating each of the sharply observed hypothetical scenarios that the ambassador had posed. The man's questions had been often rudely phrased, but the course of the meeting had eventually driven most of the venom from his tone. By the end, Wirr felt as though he'd at least held his own against the Desrielite.

"I think that actually went better than it did with Ambassador Aganaki," he observed quietly to Pria as the door finally shut, leaving them alone. "And Ambassador Whylir."

Pria began straightening the papers on the table in front of her. "Probably because, unlike the Eastern Empire and Narut, Desriel don't have any citizens who can now use their powers 'in self-defense or to protect Andarra,'" she observed drily.

Wirr flushed. Though Andarra had by far the largest population of Gifted—even after the war twenty years ago—his wording of the Tenets had *not* gone over well with their neighbors.

He scowled, then shook his head, suddenly remembering how the meeting had begun. "You should have let me know that the ambassador was here, Pria."

His second-in-command gave a small shrug, unfazed by his tone. The woman was perhaps ten years older than Wirr—young for her position, but that was no longer uncommon. Many of the Administrators who had worked closely with his father had been replaced over the past month. Some had abruptly resigned, some had been demoted after reports of substandard work or sudden revelations of supposed indiscretions. It wasn't hard to see the connection, though.

"I thought it prudent to have the meeting without you, Your Highness. I don't believe I was wrong, given the ambassador's initial reaction."

"An option we could have discussed, had you let me know about it." Wirr kept his voice calm and even, despite the aching tiredness pressing against his eyeballs. "We need to communicate, Pria. If we do not, it will only cause embarrassment to Administration."

"I apologize, Your Highness. It won't happen again."

Wirr nodded, restraining a sigh. Like many Administrators, Pria chose very specifically to address him as "Sire" and "Your Highness," but never as "Northwarden." It was perfectly acceptable for them to do so, and he knew he couldn't ask them to change without sounding petty. But it was one of the many little acts of defiance that had plagued him for the past month.

"How goes communicating the new Tenets?" he asked, changing the subject.

Pria grimaced, sweeping back a strand of curly black hair that had come loose. "A good portion of our people now know. Most realized that something had changed when their Marks renewed themselves, and the rest figured it out fairly quickly when they heard that the Gifted had fought at the Shields. They've been proactive in finding out the details, for the most part." She shook her head, and Wirr could see her latent anger in the motion. "And those who haven't been are discovering fairly quickly that something's changed, regardless."

"But no one has been able to circumvent them?"

"No, Your Highness. Not that I've heard."

Wirr nodded an acknowledgment, as always feeling a vague sense of relief at the confirmation. Until a month ago, he'd considered the Tenets to be akin to subconscious rules; certainly his own experience had shown him that there was no way to consciously disobey them. Administrator Ionis's twisting of the Third Tenet during Wirr's attempt to change them, though, had badly shaken that belief.

Fortunately, the last month appeared to be proving that his fears were for naught. All reports said that the Administrators were bound to the new rules, regardless of whether they knew their wording. It meant—at least, Wirr fervently hoped it did— that Ionis had been a unique case, empowered only by his specific, unhinged perspective. In trying to have Wirr kill all of the Gifted, the Administrator had seemingly truly believed that he was helping rather than harming them.

Even now, the thought still made him shiver.

"Good," he said eventually, shaking himself from his dark thoughts. "Any new reports from the north?"

Pria kept her face smooth, but something in her eyes reflected her disdain for the question. "Nothing to indicate any threat, Sire."

Wirr sighed. "You know that's not what I'm asking. This is important, Pria." He held her gaze. "Have there been more sightings?"

"More panicked farmers claiming to have seen monsters? A few, but nothing that we haven't already heard. Nothing from reliable sources," Pria said dismissively. "Our people stationed up there have reported nothing unusual."

"The three of them living twenty miles south of the Boundary, you mean?" Wirr didn't bother keeping the irritation from his tone. He had tried to have Administrators assigned to the Boundary itself, but Pria and others had argued—fairly, to an extent—that it was not within Administration's mandate to be there. Their purpose was civic rather than military; Administrators were not soldiers, had not joined with the expectation of having to man a hostile border. And while there *were* some Gifted at the Boundary now, the new laws passed by the Assembly meant that those Gifted did not specifically require oversight. With Administration in Ilin Illan already decimated after the attack, Wirr had known from the start that he was facing an uphill battle to send any of their few remaining people away.

He rubbed his forehead tiredly. The eventual compromise had been to have the Administrators from Taenir—Administration's northernmost outpost—make the journey to the Boundary once per week, to inspect and report back. Unfortunately, the trio stationed in Taenir had appeared less than enthusiastic about the assignment, and their updates had been a frustrating combination of brief and dismissive.

Pria just shrugged at the cynicism in his voice. "The Administrators up there are still in a good position to observe, Sire, and we have to trust what our own people are telling us. An overreaction to the news that the Boundary is weakening was to be expected, but we must ensure that we do not get caught up in it. The size of our army was more than halved only a month ago, and we have already sent enough soldiers north to prevent another attack from easily breaking through. Sending more men as a precautionary measure would only weaken our borders with Desriel, Nesk, and anyone else who might be taking notice of our already tenuous position."

She held up a hand, forestalling his evidently expected protest. "The Augur Amnesty"—Pria's face twisted at the mention—"was passed for this very reason, Sire. Tol Shen has repeatedly indicated that they have the situation well in hand. And I know what you've said in the past about your…theories…on what else may be in Talan Gol, but you cannot expect the rest of us to believe the same without evidence. So argue for sending more soldiers north all you wish in the Assembly, Highness, but unless our own people up there say it is necessary, Administration will continue to stand behind what it feels is best *for the country*."

Wirr grimaced. Despite Pria's minor outburst—unusual, for her—he still considered pressing the issue once again. The Administrator's dour expression, though, suggested that there was little point in trying.

He sighed, frustration beginning to well up again before he hurriedly pushed it back down. He'd already presented his case to the Assembly weeks ago, explaining the horrors he'd seen, covering the mysterious events surrounding Caeden in exhaustive detail. Then Taeris had come forward to verify everything, adding what Wirr had felt were eloquent and legitimate concerns to how the defense of the north was being handled. For a few hopeful minutes, Wirr had thought that the Houses might be swayed to action.

But then Pria and the other Administrators present had spoken up, forcing Wirr to concede that his position did not reflect the official one of Administration. Dras Lothlar had pressed an obviously frustrated Taeris, who had admitted that the Athian Council were also not convinced about the nature of the threat. Taeris's claims of having seen a dar'gaithin were questioned by some, openly mocked by others. Aarkein Devaed was referred to as a myth, a religious legend.

And just like that, any momentum they'd had was gone.

Wirr took a deep breath. "I can only encourage you to go and read those other reports again, Pria," he said calmly. "Refusing to believe evidence is not the same thing as lacking it."

Pria scowled this time. "Then perhaps, Sire, it is time for you to finally address some of the reports we've been receiving regarding the Augurs? To raise them as a serious issue to the Assembly? Because if I am understanding you correctly, then those accounts are 'evidence,' too."

Wirr closed his eyes for a moment in frustration. As soon as the Augur Amnesty had been announced, the claims had begun. A shopkeeper turned murderer from Variden, who said he didn't remember anything about his crime. A seamstress from Alsir caught having an affair in which she insisted she hadn't been a

53

willing participant. Representatives from somewhere he'd never even heard of, alleging their entire village had been Controlled for months. They were intent on denying responsibility for their wrongdoings, of course, but often equally intent on getting what they assumed would be seen as justice—sure that their words would cause the Assembly to rethink the Amnesty.

He shook his head. "That's different, Pria, and you know it. Those people may be being honest, but they have too much incentive to lie. If we take everyone saying 'Augurs made me do it' at their word, then we give a free pass for anybody even thinking about committing a crime."

Pria stared at him. "How unfortunate for anyone actually telling the truth, then," she eventually observed stonily. "I have other work to which I need to attend, Sire. May I go?"

Wirr just inclined his head, too tired to argue further.

He gazed after Pria as she left, standing there for a few moments, lost in thought until a gentle cough interrupted his reverie. He turned toward Andyn, who had been standing a discreet distance back throughout the conversation.

The bodyguard hesitated, and then nodded to the nearest window.

"I thought you might like to be reminded of the time, Sire."

Wirr gave him a puzzled look, glancing out the window. The sun was high; it was noon, perhaps a little after.

"Oh. Fates." Wirr started walking, beckoning for the man to follow. "I…" He paused, then gave Andyn a curious look. "I forgot something."

"Of course, Sire," said Andyn smoothly.

The man's face remained expressionless, but Wirr could have sworn he saw the faintest glimmer of amusement in his blue eyes.

Wirr made a few more turns, restraining a smile as he and Andyn came to the corridor outside the Great Hall.

Dezia looked relaxed as she leaned against the sill of the east-facing window, gazing down onto the gardens below. She glanced up as she sensed Wirr's approach; though she didn't overtly react, her blue eyes lit up when she saw who it was.

The hallway was long and full of people at this time of day—servants, guards, the odd lord hurrying about their business—and so Wirr made sure to keep his nod of greeting polite and formal.

"Dezia! What a coincidence."

Dezia gave a curtsy appropriate to their respective stations. "Your Highness. It's been a while."

"Too long," agreed Wirr, sincerity in his tone. He paused. "Did Karaliene speak to you earlier?"

"No, Sire. What did she want?"

"I'm not sure." Wirr shrugged. "I'm about to go and find her myself. You could accompany me, if you wish."

Dezia inclined her head, only the smile in her eyes giving away her amusement. "I'd be honored."

They started off, but quickly came to a halt again as Andyn gave a pointed cough. Wirr glanced over at him with a raised eyebrow.

"Highness. I thought it might be worth pointing out that Princess Karaliene's quarters are the other way?"

Wirr shook his head. "I have a feeling that she might be in the gardens this afternoon, Andyn."

"Still the other way, Sire."

"The *west* gardens."

"Of course, Sire." Andyn gave the faintest hint of a sigh. "My mistake."

Wirr exchanged a glance with Dezia, then turned back to the redheaded man. "It's a long walk over there, and I really should be safe enough here in the palace. I can meet you back in my rooms when I'm done."

Andyn didn't hesitate. "The answer is the same as three days ago, Sire. And three days before that. My job is to protect you, regardless of location." His eyes flicked to Dezia. "Or whom you are with."

Wirr just gave a resigned shrug.

Andyn hesitated. "I *should* drop back a little as you walk, though, Sire. Not so far as to let you out of sight, but…it's wise for me to avoid routine. Predictability is as good as an invitation to assassins."

Wirr cocked his head to the side, genuinely surprised at the stolid man's suggestion. He gave his bodyguard an approving look.

"That sounds like a sensible plan, Andyn. I...commend your initiative."

Andyn dipped his head, hiding whatever expression was on his face. "Thank you, Sire."

They began walking, Dezia close enough to talk to quietly, but not so close that they looked...together. They arranged these walks far enough apart, and in different areas of the palace, that it was unlikely anyone rushing through the hallways would take much notice of them—but only so long as they acted with absolute propriety while together.

Wirr waited until Andyn had dropped back, then sighed. "I'm late. Sorry."

"I was beginning to worry you weren't going to show up. You can only pretend like you're interested in looking at an utterly destroyed garden for so long, you know." She grinned at him, though she quickly hid the expression again. "Trouble this morning?"

Wirr nodded ruefully. "Just had a delightful chat with the Desrielite ambassador—he accused me of trying to use one of the Gifted to infiltrate the Gil'shar, of all things. Which I guess means he assumes I'm not only underhanded, but incompetent."

"You're definitely not underhanded," said Dezia.

Wirr shot her a wry smile. "Ha. Ha. And of course Pria kindly tried to save me from that conversation by failing to mention that the ambassador was here at all."

"That was thoughtful of her." Dezia shook her head wonderingly. "She really doesn't understand the whole 'hierarchy' thing very well, does she?"

"I think she understands it just fine. She just has a different idea of where I should fit into it."

Dezia gave him a sympathetic nod. One of the few people in whom he felt able to confide his struggles, she'd already heard plenty about his difficulties with Administration over the past month. "And the Assembly?"

"Still won't pay attention unless at least either Administration or one of the Tols officially change their position." Wirr shook his head grimly. "I can hardly blame them. If I can't convince my own organization to support sending more soldiers north, I can hardly expect the Houses to."

There was silence for a few moments as they came to the stairs leading down into the western gardens. Work had already begun in earnest to restore the foliage here, and only a few spaces still showed the dark splotches where Davian had drained the life from the plants during the battle. The day had turned sunny and a few people had emerged to enjoy it, but the pleasantly green expanse was mostly empty.

"You haven't heard anything else about this threat against you?" Dezia eventually asked quietly. She kept her eyes forward as she spoke, but Wirr could hear the concern in her tone. She'd been waiting to ask, as she did every time they met.

Wirr forced a cheerful expression. "Still narrowed down to 'someone doesn't like me,' I'm afraid."

The rumor of a plan to assassinate Wirr had come to light two weeks ago. It hadn't really come as a surprise—even after their efforts in defending the Shields, plenty of people still harbored a deep-seated hatred of the Gifted. Now that one had abruptly taken charge of the very organization meant to keep them in check, some backlash had been inevitable.

Dezia nodded slowly. "At least they're taking it seriously," she said softly, stealing a glance back at Andyn, who was still trailing at a discreet distance. "I much prefer knowing someone's watching out for you."

Wirr's smile faded but he nodded, heart swelling a little as he glanced across at Dezia. He hated only being able to see her every few days, pretending to run into each other as they did. It was necessary, though. Anything more and word would quickly get back to his uncle, one of the Houses with an eligible daughter, or worse—his mother. The king was a good man, but he was also politically savvy and far from sentimental. If it meant doing what he thought was right for the kingdom—or if Geladra demanded it—Kevran would have Dezia sent away in a heartbeat.

As if reading his thoughts, Dezia cocked her head to the side. "So. All I've heard anyone talk about today is how you have a rather important dinner tonight?"

Wirr snorted. "Not of my own free will," he assured her. "Apparently it's my mother's doing, despite her not having spoken to me since the funeral. And Uncle told me it was either go, or risk offending Lord Tel'Rath and endangering our relationship with him in the process."

"To be fair, your uncle *did* try and organize a few dinners prior to this, and you always managed to have an excuse," Dezia observed, a slight smile on her lips.

Wirr looked at her with narrowed eyes. "You almost sound as if you think it's funny."

"The picture of you being forced into a formal dinner with Lord Tel'Rath and family? With the sole purpose of him trying to get you interested in his daughter?" Dezia's eyes sparkled. "I would pay *gold* to see that sort of awkwardness. Real, actual gold."

Wirr tried to give her a dirty look, but couldn't help laughing softly. "To be honest, when I think about this supposed assassin and dinner tonight, I'm not sure which is worse."

Dezia shook her head, still smiling. "At least you'll have Andyn with you. I'm sure he can protect you from Iria if need be."

Wirr glanced back at his bodyguard, who was still maintaining a polite distance. "Wonderful. I didn't even think about that. He'll never show it, but I'm beginning to suspect that Andyn takes perverse pleasure from my suffering."

Dezia's smile widened. "I knew I liked him." The expression lingered, though her tone became more serious. "Speaking of your family—have you organized to visit your mother and sister yet?"

Wirr coughed. "Ah. Not yet. There's just been so much to do around here, and…" He shrugged uncomfortably.

"You really should think about it," said Dezia, tone gently reproachful. "I know the funeral was awkward, but you can't avoid them forever. And the longer you leave it, the worse it will get."

"I know." Wirr nodded, sighing heavily. "I know."

They talked for a while longer as they walked through the gardens, not obviously strolling, but taking the most circuitous route possible. The rest of the conversation revolved mostly around inconsequential things, allowing them to simply enjoy each other's company in the bright afternoon sunshine.

Eventually, though, they reached the end of the gardens, and the regret in Dezia's eyes acknowledged that it was time to part ways.

"East courtyard in three days? Say, third bell after noon?" she suggested quietly.

"Third bell it is." Wirr held her gaze for a few seconds, wishing he could show more affection. "Looking forward to it."

"Me too." Dezia gave him a serious look. "And tonight, just remember—Tel'Rath's fortune is based mostly on trade and agriculture. You should talk about how you're hoping to increase taxes on both those things, in as much detail as possible. Iria will be fascinated and Lord Tel'Rath will no doubt appreciate your honesty, and be glad he asked you around."

Wirr narrowed his eyes at Dezia. "Good advice."

"Of course it is." Dezia walked away with a casual wave. "I look forward to hearing all about it."

Wirr grinned after her, then headed back over to Andyn. Without talking, they began walking back through the gardens.

"You seem to be running into the young lady Shainwiere quite a bit, recently, Your Highness," noted Andyn, his tone imparting neither approval nor disapproval. "From my count, that's three times. Three times since I was assigned to you ten days ago."

Wirr glanced at his bodyguard, shrugging. "We both live in the palace. It's bound to happen."

Andyn simply nodded. "Of course. It's just that I need to be on the lookout for threats, and I was just thinking that someone coincidentally running into you so often seems...odd. I should probably report it to the king."

"No!" Wirr faltered and turned to Andyn, trying not to let panic show on his face. "There's no need..."

He trailed off. His bodyguard's expression remained an impassive mask, and yet Wirr couldn't help but sense amusement radiating from the man.

"I take your security very seriously, Highness," said Andyn

smoothly. "But if you don't feel there's a need to report these meetings, I suppose I can overlook them."

Wirr stared at him for a moment longer, then chuckled, shaking his head ruefully.

"Come on, Andyn," he said resignedly. "Let's go and prepare for dinner."

Chapter 4

Caeden blinked blearily as Asar removed his hand from Caeden's forehead, the other Augur settling down in his chair opposite with a mixture of wonder and frustration in his expression.

"You are a puzzle, Tal'kamar," Asar muttered, half to himself. His piercing blue eyes bore into Caeden's. "Still nothing?"

Caeden rolled his shoulders uncomfortably, leaning back. They were in Asar's quarters again, the room feeling plain next to the pulsing, multicolored beauty of the tunnels and chambers elsewhere in Mor Aruil. "I catch glimpses. Names, places. Images. Little bits of information here and there. But...nothing major. Still nothing like what you said to expect."

He sighed. It had been two weeks since they had started this process, two weeks since Caeden had finally accepted the memory that Asar had first shown him. Every morning he'd left his sparsely furnished chamber, walking the surreal passageway with the rippling veins of light to Asar's quarters. Every day Asar had tried to coax out his ability to see into his past, all the while strengthening him with a constant flow of Essence—an indescribably exhausting process for both of them.

And each night, Caeden had collapsed back into bed, unease settling deeper into his chest each time. Asar was trying. Caeden was trying.

But they were getting nowhere.

He swallowed, heart sinking at the expression on Asar's face. "Perhaps you're just going to have to teach me after all," he concluded quietly.

Asar sighed, shaking his head. "We have had this conversation, Tal'kamar," he said irritably, the dark circles under his eyes making him look even more tired than Caeden felt. "I can talk for months, talk until the air in my lungs gives out—it could never replace thousands of *years* of memory, of skills you have learned and context you have gained."

Caeden hesitated. He'd already accepted what Asar was saying—the memory of the Darklands still flickered uncomfortably in his head sometimes, a reminder of what he was really fighting against—but that didn't make it any less frustrating.

"You have told me why we're doing this," he acceded, trying to keep his voice calm and even, though tiredness was shortening his temper. "But what about *that*?" He gestured to Licanius, where Asar had it strapped to his side. "I still don't understand why I would erase my memories, risk so much just to get it. I know the stakes, Asar—but clearly not everything important. Perhaps if you just—"

"Tal'kamar, the more I explain, the less motivation you have to remember." Asar's voice was a tired growl. "I understand your fear of facing the man you once were, but you cannot put this off forever. Our plan relies on you *remembering*."

Caeden flinched at the rebuke, scowling. "But what happens after I remember? What is our next step? How do I fulfill this bargain with the Lyth? Perhaps if you just *explained* the plan, I would feel a little more comfortable. Why won't you just tell me?"

"For El's sake, Tal'kamar. I'm not telling you because *I don't know*."

There was silence for a moment, Asar's features set in a snarl, the admission clearly coming hard. Caeden stared at him in disbelief.

"You don't *know*? Two weeks of this, and you don't *know*?"

Asar looked to the side. "Not all of it, anyway. I know you are intending to use the Lyth's power to strengthen the ilshara somehow, to buy us more time, but...the fact is, you didn't feel the need to share the details with me. You didn't *trust* me. You didn't trust *anyone*, Tal'kamar, because that was who you were. And so instead, I was forced to trust you." He gave a bitter laugh. "Your plan had almost been uncovered once before; I think you were afraid that by telling it to me, you risked that happening again. And if you were the only one who knew how to hold off the Lyth, it meant that no one would dare try to stop you, once you'd started. You wanted that security. You wanted that control." He leaned forward, meeting Caeden's gaze. "So now it's time to *earn it*."

Caeden swallowed, subsiding a little, though the frustration remained. Asar's reaction seemed genuine.

"Very well," he said eventually, a little more calmly. "But you can at least tell me what happens if the Lyth get Licanius—you wouldn't be so worried about it if you didn't know. Is it really that bad?"

Asar hesitated, looking again like he was about to deflect the question.

Then he sighed, nodding slowly.

Caeden shivered at the certainty in his eyes. "How? Why?" He forced aside his exhaustion and leaned forward, encouraged by the first real response he'd had, though he knew that he was trying Asar's patience. Licanius lay on the table next to Asar and from where Caeden was sitting, it looked...unremarkable. He knew that it was more than just a sword—remembered how much easier his holding it had made accessing and controlling kan, how delicately it had let him manipulate the dark energy. But that was all. He'd felt powerful, godlike next to those he was fighting against—and fighting for, if it came to that—but it was still just a weapon. Asar had defeated him while it was in Caeden's possession, seemingly with no more trouble than it would have taken to swat a fly.

"What could it *possibly* do?" he continued. "Back in Res Kartha, Garadis said that the Lyth would use it for that which it was made. For its original purpose. What did he mean?" Those words, uttered after Caeden had finally taken Licanius, had plagued him over the past month.

Asar stayed silent throughout the minor outburst, just watching. Once he was satisfied that Caeden had finished, he hesitated.

"I don't know a lot about where the Lyth came from—none of us ever did, except for perhaps you and Andrael. And you were always reluctant to talk about it," he said eventually, slowly,   63 resignation thick in his tone. "We only discovered their existence not long after you raised the ilshara. For a while after that, our history with them was... combative, shall we say. Bloody, on both sides, until Andrael struck his deal. But what we learned from that period is that their bodies are made up almost entirely of Essence, and it's that fact that keeps them trapped where they are. Unlike us—unlike people—they're not shielded from the Law of Decay. From the effects of kan. They can use Gates to travel anywhere in the world, but if they stay away from Res Kartha for more than a few minutes, they simply... fade away. Dissipate." After checking that Caeden did not look too lost, he kept going. "You understand the Law of Decay?"

Caeden nodded; Davian had explained it to him once, and even as his friend had spoken, the details had come back. "Essence needs a Vessel. Outside of a Vessel, it erodes."

Asar grunted, sounding almost amused. "More complex than that, Tal'kamar, but close enough." He sighed. "And do you know the cause of Decay?"

Caeden shook his head mutely.

"Kan," said Asar simply. "Its mere presence within the world. As long as there is kan, the Lyth are trapped. And kan exists here because it is drawn through the rift between our world and... there."

Caeden frowned for a moment longer. "The rift in Deilannis that you believe Shammaeloth is trying to reach," he said slowly. "You're saying kan comes from the Darklands."

"Yes."

Caeden frowned, suddenly uncomfortable. The power they were using came from *there*? "So this rift... Licanius can close it, somehow? Isn't that what we want?"

"It is—which is why you went to such lengths to get Licanius. But if the Lyth take possession of it, we don't believe that they will close the rift entirely. We think that they want to control it instead. Use it." He gestured. "We want to erase it from existence. They want to make it into a door that they can open and close at will. They'll free themselves, but they won't fix the bigger problem."

"Why?"

"Does it matter?" Asar's face showed his frustration at having to engage in the conversation. He held up his hand as Caeden made to ask another question. "Can you not see where this is going, now? The more answers I give, the more questions that will follow. You know more, and none of it *matters* if you cannot do anything about it. We need to try again, or you need to rest so that you have more energy for our attempts tomorrow. Which should it be?"

Caeden licked his lips, then nodded with a sigh. He wasn't done with this line of questioning, but he'd learned *something*. For now, it was enough.

"One more try," he said, a little reluctantly. He was exhausted, but they were here now.

Asar inclined his head. "Very well." He took a deep breath, leaning forward to place his hand against Caeden's forehead once again. "This time, I'm going to try and send you back to Kharshan. Your first meeting with Gassandrid. Concentrate, Tal'kamar. *Concentrate*."

Caeden closed his eyes. At first there was nothing, and he began bracing himself for another failure.

And then everything suddenly...blurred.

The sun beat down upon the baked-clay streets of Kharshan, its constant heat merciless even at this late hour of the day.

Caeden shaded his eyes against the sinking ball of flame, studying the Citadel as he approached. It was larger than all the other structures in Kharshan, though the multi-tiered building with its flat-topped roofs was still made of the same uniform, sandy-colored brick as everything else here. It stood out as the peak of this isolated desert city, but it was not as impressive or palatial as he'd expected for the abode of a revered leader.

The guards at the entrance reported his arrival promptly, and a minute later a traditionally attired attendant appeared, his torso as clean-shaven as his face. It was uniform for any who might engage in manual labor, practical but also an indicator of status.

Caeden bowed low. Servants were venerated here, in their position because of their willingness to put others above themselves.

It was not easy to become a servant in Kharshan; there were only a few dozen of the official positions, and those were vied for constantly.

"It is an honor to be served," he said formally, carefully pronouncing the words in the strange tongue.

The man blinked at him in surprise but quickly regained his composure, bowing smoothly in return. Lower, as was the custom. "It is an honor to serve." He straightened, looking at Caeden for a moment. His expression was carefully subservient but his eyes were sharp, appraising. "Please, follow me. My master has awaited your arrival eagerly."

They moved into the main structure. Caeden had half expected to walk inside and discover that the outer shell was nothing more than a ruse, but the inside was just as plain, just as simply adorned. Perhaps more so, in fact. The walls were bare of art, the furniture utilitarian at best. The only thing of note, other than the lack of finery, was the enormity of the rooms and hallways. The narrowest passage Caeden saw could easily accommodate five men across—understandable, though, given that the Zvael considered the body sacred. Even an accidental touch against another would at the least cause embarrassment here, and at worst have the offender thrown in jail for their carelessness.

He did note one oddity as he was guided through the roomy interior: a man chained to the wall. He did not look abused or uncared for, but he was clearly a prisoner. Why here though, within these walls, Caeden was uncertain.

It took a full minute of walking before they reached the room in which Gassandrid sat. Caeden had seen him earlier during the victory celebrations, even managed to gain an invitation here, but this was the first time he had actually seen the man up close. He looked young—though as Caeden had already determined that they were alike, that would be in appearance only. His short-cropped black hair and immaculately trimmed goatee were common to the Zvael, but his hazel eyes were unsettlingly perceptive as he watched Caeden enter.

A long table laden with food split the middle of the room. Caeden eyed it, vaguely disappointed. This was more like what *he'd expected. Food was not scarce, exactly, but what was on the table was easily enough to feed ten.*

"Gassandrid," said Caeden politely.

Gassandrid inclined his head. "And you are Tal'kamar."

Caeden nodded back, hiding his surprise. He'd kept his endeavors mostly quiet over the past hundred years; he was not accustomed to his reputation preceding him.

Gassandrid turned to the servant. "Please tell the others that it is time to eat."

The servant bowed, then disappeared through a nearby door.

Caeden frowned. "Others?" He'd imagined this conversation would be private.

"My attendants. There are a dozen or so of them. Do not worry—they will eat at the other end of the table for the sake of our privacy."

Caeden looked at him curiously. "You eat with your servants?"

"Am I any more a man than they?" Gassandrid frowned at him. "Are they not my people, my friends? Why should I not dine with them?"

Caeden shook his head in surprise. "I meant no offense," he said, words slow due to the strange language. "It is not the custom elsewhere. Rulers fear that it lessens their authority."

Gassandrid sighed. "If a builder and an architect sit at the same table, does one role become more like the other? Or do they work better together because of it?" He waved Caeden into the seat next to him. "We are all servants, Tal'kamar—just with different roles. They serve me so that I may serve the people. We have different jobs, but we are equals nonetheless."

Caeden conceded the point with a nod; it was not so simple elsewhere, but the customs and beliefs of Kharshan were different enough to make such a statement true.

Gassandrid watched him for a long moment, then smiled slightly. "But you did not come here to talk about who sits at my table," he said quietly. "I have been expecting your arrival for some days now."

Caeden raised an eyebrow. "Days? How—"

He cut off as the far door opened and a burst of chatter filtered into the room, followed by a train of men and women. They each bowed politely in Gassandrid and Caeden's direction before taking a seat, keeping to the other end of the table as Gassandrid had said they would. They began serving the food, their conversation and laughter low, just enough to fill the room with the pleasant sound.

Gassandrid watched Caeden with amusement. "You may speak, Tal'kamar," he said. "None can overhear."

Caeden coughed, a little disconcerted, but nodded. "How did you know I was coming?" he asked eventually.

Gassandrid smiled. "It was shown to me. It is happening exactly as I saw."

Caeden frowned. "A prophecy?" he asked dubiously.

"Nothing so vague." Gassandrid leaned forward, lowering his voice. "I have seen these moments, exact and clear. Like a memory, but of something that has not yet happened. Played out in perfect detail. No signs, no interpretation like the charlatans would have you believe is necessary. Only what will be."

Caeden stared at Gassandrid, suddenly uncomfortable. Was the man insane? In all his travels, in his hundreds of years, Caeden had not heard of anything like this beyond the vague claims of soothsayers.

"That...sounds useful," he said eventually. "Can you tell me something? Something about my own future?"

Gassandrid shook his head. "I said it was shown to me. I did not say it was my own power."

"Oh." Caeden gritted his teeth. Was he being toyed with? "Who showed it to you, then?"

"The one who sent you here," said Gassandrid, watching Caeden's expression closely.

Caeden opened his mouth to say that no one had sent him here, that he had come of his own volition.

Then he understood.

"The creature of light?" he said softly.

Gassandrid nodded. "He has been seeking out those like you and I, those who will live long enough to make a difference in this world. There is much I have to tell you." He glanced across the table, toward his servants. "But after the meal. Some matters are too sensitive to discuss over food."

Caeden was tempted to protest. He'd waited for so long, looked so hard for even a hint of the creature he'd seen four hundred years ago. He couldn't begin to estimate how many times he'd doubted himself, doubted what he'd experienced. Wondered whether it had been a powerful figment of his imagination, a way to give himself hope where there was none.

But he restrained himself. He had learned patience the hard way, sitting in a cell for eighty years. Better to wait a little longer than risk offending the source of his information.

"How old are you, Tal'kamar?" asked Gassandrid suddenly, his hazel eyes curious.

Caeden hesitated.

"Four hundred and fifty years. Give or take," he said eventually.

Gassandrid's eyebrows raised. "So it is true."

Caeden frowned. "What is true?"

"That we cannot die."

Caeden stared at Gassandrid, taken aback. He'd felt certain that they were the same, regardless of the other claims Gassandrid had been making.

"How old are you?" he asked slowly.

"I am thirty-five."

Caeden almost choked.

The man looked closer to his midtwenties than midthirties, but that was beside the point. This was not Alarais, someone who had had years of experience at this existence. This was someone who hadn't yet lived through even a single lifetime.

"There are stories about you in battle," said Caeden eventually, after he'd recovered. "Men say you're impervious to Essence."

Gassandrid inclined his head. "The Zvael do not lie. Blades and arrows cut me, but Essence—any Essence—dissipates. And I can control my own Essence well enough to ensure that those blades and arrows never get close enough to touch me." He looked at Caeden curiously. "You?"

Caeden shrugged. "I heal quickly. But that is all." He decided not to go into too much detail. He didn't trust Gassandrid with the knowledge of his weakness.

Gassandrid accepted the statement with a nod, and the talk

turned to smaller things for a while. Gassandrid spoke a little about the war against the Shalis, confirming or denying rumors that Caeden had heard along the way. At times he appeared modest, deflecting credit for victories onto others, pushing the idea that he had done it to serve his people. At others he seemed almost childishly pleased that rumors of his exploits had reached so far across the lands, no matter whether they were perfectly accurate or wildly exaggerated.

Finally, though, the dinner came to an end. The servants rose one by one and began filing out, cleaning up their dishes as they went. Eventually Gassandrid stood too, beckoning Caeden to do the same.

Caeden frowned, but stood and followed Gassandrid into a small antechamber. It was furnished with two chairs facing each other, nothing more.

Caeden's frown deepened as he sat. "Why are we in here?"

"I had this room designed especially for such conversations," said Gassandrid easily as he took the seat opposite Caeden. "We cannot be overheard, either accidentally or otherwise. There are certain aspects of this discussion..." He gestured apologetically. "You will understand soon enough."

Caeden acceded the point with a nod, though he was still unsure of how rational Gassandrid actually was. The man evidently believed everything he said, but that hardly made it truth.

He forced himself to appear relaxed, at ease. Sometimes those who believed in something strongly enough were the most dangerous, too.

"Which religion do you follow, Tal'kamar?" asked Gassandrid once they were both comfortable.

Caeden shook his head slowly. "None, particularly."

Gassandrid frowned at him. "Come now. Of course you do."

Caeden blinked, not expecting the response. "I do not believe in gods," he said slowly.

"But you do not believe this with passion," observed Gassandrid.

"There is only one reason to be passionate about a lack of faith—and that is fear," said Caeden quietly. "Fear that you are wrong. An innate need for others to share your opinion, so that you can be less afraid." He shook his head. "I do not feel the need to argue, to cajole, to threaten or accuse. If others wish to believe differently, that is no business of mine. I simply do not think that there are gods."

"Then your religion is one of the self," observed Gassandrid, his tone holding neither judgment nor surprise. "You believe that you are a god."

Caeden snorted. "No. Of course not."

Gassandrid leaned back, crossing his arms. "What is a god but a being with more power than those below them can comprehend? With understanding more vast than others can imagine? If you do not believe such a being exists above you, then surely you are a god, Tal'kamar. You are immortal. You are more powerful than any normal man could ever dare dream of becoming. Your knowledge and experience is more vast than other men can even imagine."

Caeden smiled slightly. "But without the moral imperative, perhaps."

"Not at all. A parent has moral imperative over their child. What do your added years of experience not enable you to understand better than those who have lived a fraction of your lifetime?" He gestured out the door, toward one of his servants. "If I told Sola there that you had lived more than ten times his age, if I described the powers you possessed and the things you have seen. Do you not think that he would listen to you? Respect you? Revere you, even?"

Caeden shifted, becoming uncomfortable. "I am not a god, Gassandrid. We are not gods."

Gassandrid studied Caeden for a moment. Then he nodded.

"I agree, Tal'kamar," he said quietly. "But if you do not believe it is possible for a higher power than ourselves to exist, then you must concede that we are."

Caeden scowled. "If there were a higher power than us in this world, Gassandrid, I would know of it by now."

"Would you?" Gassandrid nodded to Sola. "Do you think he knows of you?"

Caeden hesitated for a moment, then sighed, waving his hand tiredly. "Very well. Continue," he said, though he couldn't keep the dubiousness from his tone. "Which religion should I believe *in, Gassandrid? Derev? Mekrahk? The six hundred gods of Thilian Mar, perhaps? The animal gods of Suza? The God Who Does Not Speak? The Blind God? The Gods of the Elements?"*

Caeden could hear the irritation entering his voice, but he didn't care. *"I have seen more bad gods than good men venerated during my travels, Gassandrid. I have seen the Three Gods of Rel worshipped—one for mind, one for body, one for spirit— where men take three wives and force each one to embody those aspects, on penalty of death. I have seen the people of Drash deify the Field of One Hundred Statues, each icon a different god for a different purpose. That field is filled with mounds of gold and silver where people throw their offerings, within sight of the slums where the poor live in squalor until they starve.*

"I have seen religions that sacrifice animals. Religions that sacrifice humans, children. I have seen the City of Portaeus, where they worship the No God, where only the worship of self is allowed." He leaned forward. *"I have seen mankind making up stories to make themselves feel safe at night. Or for power. Or for glory. Or for respect. Or for control. But I have never known a god, Gassandrid. The wise among us understand that they are fantasies. That they do not exist except in our own minds."*

Gassandrid watched impassively while Caeden spoke, seemingly unperturbed by his outburst. When Caeden had finished he gave a small nod, as if having expected just this response.

"You are right to doubt, of course," he said quietly. *"But I was not talking of religions—things created by men in order to control other men. I was talking of gods."* He stretched. *"You have heard of El, then?"*

Caeden felt his mouth twist into something close to a snarl. *"I have,"* he growled. *"Those particular lies were taught in my place of birth. In my youth I believed the myth, right up until the moment I realized that if the One God existed, he hated me more than any other man on this earth."*

Gassandrid looked at Caeden appraisingly. *"Of all the religions, it is actually closest to the truth."* He held up a hand as Caeden opened his mouth to protest. *"And also the furthest from it. You are not wrong in describing it as a lie, Tal'kamar. If anything, it is perhaps the worst lie that has ever been told."*

72

Caeden stopped, frowning a little. "How so?" he asked eventually.

Gassandrid took a deep breath. "The account of how this world came into existence—its creation by El, the fight between El and Shammaeloth—is, essentially, true," he said quietly. He shook his head slightly as Caeden made to argue. "It is true, until it talks about who won."

Caeden blinked. "What?"

"When El created the world, He gave some of Himself into it. Part of His power." Gassandrid's tone was calm, matter-of-fact. "Shammaeloth, in his jealousy, took advantage of that weakness and trapped Him here, within the bounds of time. El had intended for the world to be free, but Shammaeloth needed control in order to contain El. So he created fate. A single path, when there were supposed to be infinite possibilities. A complete lack of free will." Gassandrid spread his hands. "In short, Tal'kamar, we are puppets. We live in a prison of inevitability. A mirage of choice."

Caeden shifted, looking for any sign of doubt in the other man's eyes.

There was none.

He grunted, suddenly regretting his decision to come here. "Then Shammaeloth has already won," he observed tiredly. "A cheerful religion indeed."

Gassandrid shook his head, either missing or ignoring Caeden's wry tone. "Not a religion, Tal'kamar. Religion is the following of rules and rituals in the hope that they will somehow garner the favor of a higher power. This...this is fact. A true history, albeit one rarely told." His voice became quiet. "And you are wrong about Shammaeloth having won. Visible or not to those beneath them, even gods have limits. Even gods make mistakes. Once El was within the bounds of this world, Shammaeloth could no longer risk touching it directly. He'd set the world on a path, but could not prevent El using the last of His power to make a final, small change."

Caeden shifted. "Which was?"

"Us." Gassandrid looked Caeden in the eye. "Immortals. Shammaeloth chose to make El suffer, to spoil the thing He loves most—and that pain and destruction is not something we can fully prevent. But our presence has bent the path. Our choices are still predestined, still made within the limits of Shammaeloth's corruption of time... but they are not choices for which he originally planned. And that means that there is a chance for something more." He leaned forward. "Through us, El can steer the enemy's design toward a particular outcome. We can fix it. There is a way to make the world a place where we truly make the decisions, not Shammaeloth. A way to change everything that has ever been, in fact."

Caeden stiffened, his skepticism momentarily fading.

It was what he had been told, all those years ago. One of the driving forces that had kept him searching, that had led him to Gassandrid in the first place.

"A way to make all things right," he said softly.

"A way to make all things right," affirmed Gassandrid. "A way to change the past and break Shammaeloth's prison. A chance to save the world from fate itself."

Caeden shook his head slowly. He wanted to believe—thought that maybe he could, after everything he had seen.

And yet something held him back.

"You still have no proof," he said softly. "You are no different from any other fanatic. We may share the same longevity—I will grant you that—but it makes you no less likely to lie. Or to believe falsely, for that matter."

"What if I could give you proof?" Gassandrid said the words eagerly. "What if I could show you, beyond all doubt, that what I say is true?"

Caeden shook his head. "Impossible."

Gassandrid, though, didn't look dissuaded. "I was the same as you, Tal'kamar," he assured him. "But I met Him—as you already have. And He showed me."

Caeden didn't comprehend what Gassandrid was saying for a moment. As soon as he did, though, he scoffed before he even realized what he was doing.

"The being from the forest? You're saying that was El? The creator of all things?" He shook his head. "I'm sorry, Gassandrid. That was no god."

Gassandrid took out a sheaf of paper, neatly bound. He handed it silently to Caeden.

"What is this?" asked Caeden, taking the bundle with a mildly confused frown.

"Your proof," said Gassandrid quietly. "Your future, just as El has shown it to me. He may be weak, but He is less affected by time than we. He can see into the inevitability of what is to come. He can see how we will shape Shammaeloth's plan away from the ruin it was meant to be."

Caeden snorted. "Vague warnings of what is to come will not sway me, Gassandrid."

"These are not parlor tricks." Gassandrid smiled slightly. "I do not ask you to join us now, because I know that you will not until you are ready. Read what is within at your leisure, Tal'kamar. Read it, and try to prevent it if you wish. Regardless of what you do—no matter how you strive—what is written on those pages will come to pass." He settled back, a glint in his eye. "I do not care if you return in one year or a thousand. Once you believe— once you are certain—then, and only then, come and find me again."

To Caeden's surprise he stood, indicating that the conversation was over. Before Caeden could recover enough to decide if he wanted to ask more questions, he found himself being gently but firmly ushered outside.

Gassandrid turned as if to leave him, and then hesitated.

"You saw the man in chains on your way in?" he asked quietly. When Caeden nodded he continued. "He lost his temper over a small matter of coin, and ran his neighbor through with his sword. These facts are undisputed. He awaits only my judgment." He looked Caeden in the eye. "The law demands death for death. So which should I throw to the cleansing fires of the inferno—him, or his blade? Which do you think would be justice?"

Caeden stared at Gassandrid, more certain than ever of his insanity. "You know the answer."

"But do you, Tal'kamar?" asked Gassandrid softly. "Something to ponder in the coming years."

Before Caeden could respond, he had closed the door.

Caeden scowled for a moment, then glanced at the bundle of pages in his hands. He almost threw it away in disgust.

Almost.

Shaking his head in disappointment, he headed back toward the square. There was nothing for him here except a madman, clearly.

It was time to leave.

Chapter 5

Caeden's vision cleared, and he took a deep breath as the sparse furnishings and overflowing bookshelves of Asar's quarters came back into view.

Finally.

So that had been Gassandrid—one of the Venerate. Intense, confident. So sure of his beliefs, even back then. The memory was an old one, though Caeden knew straight away it was not nearly as old as his memory of being beheaded. During that meeting with Gassandrid, he'd been perfectly comfortable with the concept of his own immortality. It had been a different body, too—lighter skin, taller and slimmer than when he'd been called Lord Deshrel. But it hadn't felt strange, either.

He frowned as he straightened, giving a slight nod to Asar's querying look. There were still things he couldn't place. He knew that he'd found Gassandrid after searching for him—searching for others like him—but he couldn't remember what had driven him to do that. He recognized phrases in the memory, but couldn't pinpoint the context.

It was something, more than he'd had in a long time. But in the big picture, it was still just a glimpse.

"Is that really what you all thought?" he said slowly, feeling his brow furrow as he put together the pieces. "That Shammaeloth—this thing behind the Boundary—was actually *El*?"

"It's what *we* thought," Asar corrected quietly, though there was more than a hint of relief to the words. He'd been trying not to show it, but Caeden could tell that the other Augur had been getting nervous about their lack of progress. "We take it for granted now, but imagine a world without kan—one where no one knew that the future was inevitable. And then imagine that you were suddenly shown the truth, and that the only compelling explanation came from the one who showed you."

Caeden shook his head, thinking back on the memory. "But I didn't believe him," he pointed out.

"You did after two hundred years of trying to prove his Foresight wrong," said Asar. "You were the hardest to convince, and then the most fervent to believe." He rubbed eyes that were red-rimmed from tiredness and strain. "This is good, Tal'kamar. This is very good. We are beginning to make progress. Not a moment too soon, either."

Caeden acknowledged the statement with a wry nod, the weight that had been on his shoulders for the past two weeks just a little lighter, despite the myriad more questions the memory had raised in his mind. He opened his mouth to speak, but was sabotaged by an enormous yawn.

"You should rest." Asar gave him an encouraging nod. "It won't always be this exhausting. The more you go back, the easier it will be."

Caeden hesitated. "You don't think we should keep going, then, while it's working?"

"You can barely keep your eyes open—and that's despite all the Essence I've been feeding into you. Even our bodies have their limits. So go." He picked up a tome from the table next to him and motioned to the door in a clear dismissal.

Caeden smiled at the almost affectionate action as he rose. "What do you read in here all day, anyway?" he asked, gesturing to the bookshelves. "What is all of this?"

Asar's expression turned serious. "It is everything we know about Shammaeloth. Every theory, every rumor, every religious teaching. Every scrap of knowledge that we were able to save." He crooked another smile, though this one looked more forced. "We're not all-knowing, Tal'kamar, even when we have our memories. Sometimes we actually have to do research."

Caeden snorted, nodding a wry acknowledgment before exiting and heading back to his room. For once, the long, smooth black tunnel with the gently pulsing veins of color didn't unsettle him.

Tired though he was, he and Asar were making progress.

Caeden stretched as he gradually came awake, gazing up contemplatively at the jagged lines on the roof as they morphed smoothly from one hue to the next.

For the first time since he'd arrived, he felt the faintest flicker of anticipation—of *hope*—at the coming day. Restoring his memories this way was hard, perhaps even harder than Asar had first suggested. But it was *working*.

"Tal."

Caeden started, rolling to his feet with alacrity at the unfamiliar voice. A young woman stood in the doorway to his room, calmly smoothing back her waist-length black hair as gently shifting colors played across her perfectly formed oval face.

He gaped for a few seconds, silent, gaze locked with hers. Her eyes were a startling blue, even in the multihued light. There was something about them, too—they held a fierce hunger as she looked at Caeden, a strange joy that he did not understand. He found himself flushing beneath their intense emotion.

"Who are you?" Asar had assured him that they were alone in the Wells, and nobody else was supposed to be able to get in. "Where is Asar?"

The woman's eyes flicked around the room, cool but evidently wary. Apparently seeing nothing to perturb her, she glided toward him. "The Keeper is in his quarters, Tal," she said. "It's just us."

Caeden took a step back. "Who are you?" he repeated, this time more firmly.

The woman sighed, a sudden sadness in her eyes. "When you told me that you were going to erase your memories, I assumed you were lying," she said softly. "You truly do not recognize me?" She gazed at him. "Your wife?"

Caeden barked out a disbelieving laugh. When the woman's expression didn't change, the room tilted a little, and Caeden swallowed as he grasped at the top of his bed for balance. "No," he muttered. Whether it was in answer to her question or a refutation of the statement, he wasn't sure.

The stranger opened her mouth to say something more, but whatever it was, he didn't hear it.

Everything blurred.

Caeden glared suspiciously at the plate in front of him, unconvinced that anything on it was edible.

"Not drunk enough," he muttered to himself, pushing the black-and-pink mass disdainfully to one side.

He tried to rise but instead slipped on the grimy, ale-sodden floor and staggered ungracefully back into his chair again. A few of the tavern's patrons glanced over, but none laughed. Hardened to a man and always looking for sources of amusement, yet not one of them dared even to smirk.

It was because they all knew him, or at least knew the tales. Not the truth, of course—not the reason he drank until he couldn't see straight, not the things he spent such a vast portion of his considerable income trying to forget.

If they knew about those, they would not have dared turn their heads.

Still, the tales were enough. In this sodden, dirty corner of Elhyris, nobody was willing to risk raising the ire of Tal'kamar the Blessed.

He leaned forward and laughed blearily into his cup at the thought. "Blessed" was the word they murmured every time he returned with more Vaal, every time they watched with wide, greedy eyes as heavy bags of gold changed hands for just a single one of the creatures.

If they'd ever seen him a few hours before those exchanges— ever seen the vicious, suppurated puncture marks all over his body—they wouldn't believe that he was touched by Talis. No. They would realize how very much, in fact, the opposite was true.

But Caeden knew not to let them see. He didn't enjoy this life, but at least it was rote. Waking up in another unknown land, ignorant of location or language or customs, remembering who he'd been but trapped in a body not his own…he couldn't do that again. Wouldn't.

His gaze shifted from the dregs of his ale to his hands, still strangely square and unfamiliar even after five years. That wasn't the worst of it, of course. He was shorter than he had been. Stockier. His skin was lighter, almost white. His eyes were green, not brown. His black hair was curly, not straight. He was a little younger, perhaps, and more muscular.

But he was not himself. He was no longer Lord Tal'kamar Deshrel.

The only part of that man still surviving was the guilt.

He grunted, forcing his gaze up again and gesturing to the barkeep, indicating that he required a refill. The man nodded without complaint. He knew Caeden's gold was good—and knew not to try telling Caeden that he needed to stop, too. After the first few...disagreements, every man here was aware of that rule.

Caeden's eyes slid blurrily past the barkeep to the sight of a woman seating herself at the corner table. She was alone, which was unusual in and of itself—even women who could handle themselves rarely traveled these parts without significant protection—but there was something else, something that made his heart constrict.

The long, straight black hair. The set of her shoulders, even facing away from him.

It was too familiar.

Caeden stumbled to his feet, attempting to use the back of another chair for support. There was a crash as it slid sideways and he fell clumsily on top of it.

He barely noticed the pain. The woman had heard the commotion, was looking around at him.

He stared at her, wide-eyed.

The tavern went silent.

"Get out!" Caeden was still on his knees, crawling away in confusion as he shouted the words at the woman. "Please, away from me! I see your face too many times in my nightmares to see it here, too. This is my place!"

The woman just looked at him, her deep blue eyes filled with alarmed bemusement. Caeden vaguely heard the scrape of chairs as some of the other men stood; afraid of him though they might be, this was a disturbance they could not ignore.

It was too much. Too much. Caeden's vision blurred one last time, the woman's face sliding from his sight.

"My *place*," he whispered as his head sunk to the floor, body curling into a tight ball, the alcohol and emotion finally combining to overcome him. "Oh, fates. I'm so sorry, Ell. I know it's not you. I miss you."

She was gone, gone forever. He needed to stop seeing her everywhere he looked. He needed to wake up...

Caeden stumbled as his vision cleared again and he shook his head, taking some deep breaths as the woman across from him looked on with a vaguely concerned expression.

Another memory. He still shook from the emotion of this one. Even now—even as his own thoughts took hold once more and the memory became more distant, easier to press down—he found it hard to believe that anyone could feel such pain. Could feel so *broken*.

Worse, though, was that he recognized the woman standing across from him this time.

It had been her whom he'd seen in the tavern. He was certain of it.

"You were dead," he whispered. He didn't understand what was going on, but he knew he'd believed that much.

"Obviously not," the woman corrected him gently. "We need to leave. Now."

Caeden shook his head, still trying to come to grips with what was happening. "I'm not leaving."

"You cannot trust the Keeper. He will only show you what he wants you to know—not what you *need* to know." She held out her hand, and something about her eyes—shining as they looked at him—made Caeden hesitate. "Tal. Please. There isn't—"

A blast of Essence ripped across the room, lifting the woman up and slamming her hard against the rock wall, a good twenty feet away from Caeden. The blow elicited a cry of surprised pain from the stranger.

Caeden spun to see Asar in the doorway, hand outstretched. The older man's expression was grim.

"You cannot torment him anymore," he growled. He stared at the woman, intent, as if Caeden did not even exist. "You made a mistake coming here. I don't know how you found us, but I knew you were here from the moment you opened the Gate. And you were never strong enough to face me." He held her gaze. "This time, I am going to send you back."

Caeden shifted, watching the woman's face. From Asar's tone, she should have been terrified.

Instead, her lips curled into a slow smile.

"The problem with hiding away where you think no one can find you, Keeper, is that you never know what's happening in the outside world."

Suddenly the river of Essence pressing against her body appeared to...shift. Not ease, but somehow part a little. She slid slowly down the wall until her feet were firmly on the ground again.

Then she walked forward.

Caeden's eyes widened as she pushed through the Essence as if wading against the flow of a torrential river, slowly but surely, step by deliberate step making her way toward Asar. It was clearly an effort, but equally as clearly she was overpowering the white-bearded man, whose eyes had gone wide with shock and effort. Asar's cheeks were flushed, and beads of sweat stood out on his brow.

"Tal'kamar," he gasped. "Stop her."

Caeden hesitated.

It took him only a second to make his decision; Asar had been trying to help over the past month, no matter what the woman said.

But in those few precious moments of doubt, the stranger acted.

Caeden found himself flying backward, the base of his skull slamming into the wall behind him. It was enough of an impact to leave him dazed; even as he recovered enough to grasp at Essence, he saw the woman reach Asar.

Saw her stretch down and draw Licanius from the scabbard at the older man's waist, Asar powerless to stop her.

Saw her thrust forward with an almost disdainful motion, sliding the blade smoothly and carefully into Asar's chest.

Caeden shouted, dashed forward desperately, but he knew it was too late. There was horror in Asar's eyes as the blade went in.

Asar slumped to the ground, and everything stopped.

The silence was eerie as Caeden skidded to his knees beside the older man, ignoring the woman standing over them. Asar's head lolled limply as Caeden shook him, then tried to put pressure on the wound as it pumped heart's blood onto the floor.

"You'll be all right," he muttered as he pressed desperately downward, ignoring the hot, sticky liquid spurting between his fingers. "You're like me. You'll be all right."

"He won't. He is dead, Tal." The woman was breathing hard and flushed, as if herself surprised. She tossed Licanius to the ground beside Caeden. "Make certain no one ever takes that from you again." She turned her back on him and began studying the room, as if deliberately indicating how little a threat she considered him to be. Whether it was arrogance or an attempt to convince him that she trusted him, Caeden wasn't sure.

The Portal Box, Tal'kamar. Use it. Get Licanius and get out of here.

Caeden almost made a sound, so startled was he by Asar's voice in his head. He glanced down at the man in his arms, but the body hadn't moved.

"You need to listen to me now," the woman continued, still a little breathless as she examined their surroundings, oblivious. "Your plan doesn't work without Asar—but I know how to fix that, *and* keep you alive and free. I have spent the last twenty years making sure it is possible. Even after what you did to me." There was a tremor to her voice, and it suddenly occurred to Caeden that she might not be trying to prove a point by facing away from him. The woman simply didn't want to meet his gaze.

She was nervous.

She is not your wife, Tal'kamar. I don't know how she has become so powerful, but do not trust her. Never trust her. The voice was weak, but insistent.

Caeden looked back over at the stranger again and felt his jaw clench.

Then he slipped his hand into his pocket, drew out the Portal Box. Closed his eyes and funneled Essence into the next face in sequence.

With a roar, the vortex of fire sprang to life.

The woman whirled at the sound, eyes widening, but whatever she said was lost to the thunder. Caeden dove for Licanius, snatched it up and set off for the tunnel.

An impossible blast of Essence caught him again, pinned him to the spot.

"There is no point in running, Tal!" The stranger's voice barely carried to him, but he caught the words this time. "You cannot stop them without the Siphon!"

Caeden reached for kan through Licanius; with the blade in his grasp, he should have easily been able to manipulate enough of the dark energy to absorb the pulsing white torrent holding him in place.

Nothing happened.

Before Caeden could panic at his failure, the woman was suddenly stumbling and then slipping to her knees, eyes wide as she took in Asar's hand around her ankle. The white-bearded man was weak, though. Caeden could see that he was doing all he could.

The Essence vanished from around Caeden.

Asar locked eyes with him, and his expression pleaded with him to flee.

Caeden ran.

As he passed, he grabbed one of Asar's arms and strengthened his own body with Essence. He knew the action was futile, that the motion alone would probably finish the wounded man. But he couldn't leave him alone to face...whoever she was.

With a mighty heave, he threw Asar through the portal, then leaped after him.

"No!" The scream was desperate, somehow heartrending. "Tal, no! It's taken me so—"

The portal closed behind them.

Gasping and cold from shock, Caeden forced himself to focus and scrambled over to where Asar lay. The man's skin was ashen and his breathing shallow. He may have survived longer than a normal person would have against such a wound, but his time was clearly drawing to a close.

Caeden hurriedly tapped into his Reserve once more, pressing his hands against Asar's chest and letting the energy flow into the older man's body.

Nothing happened.

"Stop," rasped Asar, his tone resigned rather than urgent.

"Why aren't you healing?" Caeden asked desperately after a few moments, sitting back helplessly. "What can I do?"

Asar gave a wracking cough, which Caeden suspected was meant to be a laugh. "Nothing. There is nothing you can do for me now, Tal'kamar. She used Licanius." He groaned. "I had no idea she had gained access to so much Essence. You did well. She has ever been a weight around your neck."

"Who was she?" asked Caeden pensively. "She said she was..."

"She isn't." Asar's voice was becoming quieter. "Forget about her, Tal'kamar. *Caeden.*" He grasped Caeden's hand, the last of the light in his eyes dimming. "This will change things, but you must still focus on remembering. You sacrificed everything for this. Just...stay the course." He gave Caeden a last grim smile. "Be the man you aspire to be, and this...this will all be worthwhile."

He didn't say anything after that. His breaths became slower and slower, more labored, until there was only silence.

Caeden sat there for a while, hands and shirt soaked in blood, dazed. Still not entirely certain whether he should be grieving for a friend, or lamenting an enormous mistake.

Finally he stood, shakily taking in his surroundings for the first time. The sun beat down viciously from overhead. There were a few lonely trees on the ridge to his right, but otherwise everything looked dry and cracked. Lifeless.

He turned to go, then paused.

The grave took him less time than he'd thought, once he put his ability with Essence to good use. It was a shallow one, but better than leaving Asar to whatever animals roamed these parts.

When he was done, Caeden straightened, giving the small, lonely mound a final glance.

"Be the man I aspire to be," he murmured to himself.

He started walking.

Chapter 6

Davian sat at the edge of the fountain, staring pensively down the narrow street toward the pulsing blue peak of the Central Wall, for once barely noticing the concerned stares of the Gifted as they passed in an arc around him.

It was afternoon now, a couple of hours since the meeting with the Council. Though two men standing some distance away had clearly been assigned to keep watch over him, no one had actually approached to escort him out of Central Ward yet. He didn't really know if that was a good sign or not.

He sighed. His reacting to Elder Dain like that hadn't been a *wise* move... but he wasn't sure that he regretted it, either. If he hadn't drawn the line somewhere, the Council would have become increasingly difficult to deal with.

He glanced up as Ishelle slid onto the stone beside him; he'd been too deep in thought to notice her approach.

She stared at him for a moment, expression inscrutable. "So. What was *that*?"

"That was me losing my temper." Davian rubbed his neck. "Sorry."

"Sorry? Nonsense. It was *magnificent*." Ishelle beamed at him. "Honestly, I didn't think you had it in you. I'm not sure any of the Elders back there did, either. If you could have seen Elder Dain's face when he realized who was standing behind him..." She snickered, grinning uncontrollably at the memory.

Davian couldn't help the slight smile that crept onto his face.

"He did seem a bit startled." He looked at her cautiously. "You don't think I went too far?"

"Oh, you *definitely* went too far," Ishelle assured him cheerfully. "I doubt Elder Dain has had anyone act like that toward him publicly since before the war. Maybe ever. He still looked half-confused when I left; there's no way he'll forgive you for that sort of defiance." She shrugged. "But all it really means is that he'll dislike us with marginally more intensity than before. Which hardly matters; you saw his reaction to what you said. He needs us as much as we need him. Given how they've been treating us, it was probably time to remind him that we know that."

Davian inclined his head; Ishelle's take on it was much the same as his own. He'd have preferred to keep the peace, but if this meant that the Council would take them more seriously, perhaps it had been worth it. "I hope you're right."

"Of course I'm right," said Ishelle, turning and locking eyes with a red-cloaked man hurrying toward them. The man had probably been asked to finally chaperone them from Central Ward, but his determined expression wilted under Ishelle's steady gaze. He stuttered to a stop several feet away, inclining his head to indicate that he would wait. "So what do you think they're hiding from us?"

Davian shook his head. "Something," he agreed grimly. Lyrus had seemed genuinely concerned that they might have been here in Central Ward unsupervised, far more so than a simple breaking of the rules would account for. The gathering of so many Council members at once had only reinforced the impression that the issue was somehow important. "Honestly, though? I don't really care. They can keep their fates-cursed secrets if they would just let us deal with the Boundary."

"It *will* get better once Driscin's back, you know."

Davian glanced across at her. "You really trust him to change things?"

"I do." Ishelle's tone, for once, was entirely serious. "The rest of the Council will listen to him." She looked at him for a moment, hesitating.

"He's not Taeris," she added softly.

Davian grunted, nodding a reluctant acknowledgment. He knew that some of his mistrust of the Elders—*any* Elder—was stemming from his discovery that Taeris had been lying to him since the moment they'd met. That the man had actually *set up* the encounter in Caladel three years earlier, in which Davian had been attacked, badly beaten and scarred.

To make matters worse, Ishelle hadn't been able to tell Davian anything more than he already knew about that incident. She'd only been able to Read Taeris briefly in Thrindar, and so the reasons *why* the man had done what he had remained a mystery.

Ishelle studied Davian for a moment, then sighed. "Why don't you spend some time in Prythe while I take the Augur interviews today?"

Davian came out of his reverie. "Really? Why?"

"It's not as if being at the interviews is hard work; it's literally sitting in a corner and Reading people." Ishelle shrugged. "And I'm thinking the Elders might be a little more…*relaxed* if you weren't there today."

Davian snorted, acceding the point with a nod.

The interviews were part of their daily routine—sitting in and Reading anyone who was claiming sanctuary under the Amnesty. Some people did it to try to get the small monetary reward the Assembly had offered for coming forward as an Augur. Some showed up because they genuinely thought that they might have abilities—they'd had premonitions, or vivid dreams, or sometimes would swear that they "knew" what other people were thinking.

But a few always came with hidden weapons, too, intent on getting close enough to the Augurs to do them harm. None had come close to succeeding, of course, as Davian or Ishelle always Read their intentions long before they had the chance to act. It was still a far from pleasant task, though.

"As long as you're sure, I suppose I could use some time away from this place," he eventually conceded. "Thanks." He glanced up at where he approximated the sun was hiding behind the clouds. "More training when I get back? Or should we try the library again?"

"Training, I think." Ishelle nodded to herself cheerfully. "Wouldn't want to deprive you of another chance at abject humiliation."

Davian sighed. "Perhaps if we practice something other than Disruption shields…"

"It's nothing to do with you losing. It's the face you make when you concentrate." She screwed up her features into as ugly a contortion as she could manage.

Davian stared at her for a moment, then felt the corners of his mouth curl upward as he shook his head in amusement.

It was a genuine smile and it felt good, a release from the pressure that had been building up since their meeting with the Council. He didn't always feel comfortable around Ishelle, but it was times like this that he was grateful she was around. Having to deal with all of this by himself could easily have been a burden too heavy to bear.

They stood and started walking, their red-cloaked chaperone vanishing gratefully as soon as they reached the tunnel to Inner Ward. Once through, they headed straight for the nearest passage to Outer Ward.

Davian found himself gazing around in fascination as they strolled, still finding the differences between the wards remarkable. On the surface, Inner—where he and Ishelle had been housed, much to Ishelle's ongoing irritation—looked similar to Central, but the atmosphere was distinctly different. The streets were busier, both in volume of people and how rushed those people looked as they went about their business. And whereas everyone in Central moved with a cool sense of superiority, most of those here just seemed...tired. Ishelle said that there was constant competition to move up to Central, and that underlying tension appeared to run through every glance and conversation.

"So has anybody recognized you?" Davian asked casually as they made their way through the streets.

Ishelle shook her head. "When I was here before, I mostly worked in the kitchens. Driscin did put me in Shadow classes for a couple of months, but even then I was just another Gifted student. It was easy enough to blend in."

Davian nodded at that; Shen didn't have any outlying schools like Tol Athian, so every one of their students boarded here. "Shadow classes?" he asked curiously.

"It's what we called classes in the Outer Ward. One step away from—"

"I get it," said Davian quickly. "So the classes are split up between Wards, too?"

"Same as everything else here. The students with the most potential live and take classes in Central. Those showing some promise live in Inner, and the rest..." She shrugged. "Most are in Outer. There's a high turnover and the teachers there barely notice anyone who's not distinguishing themselves enough to move up."

Davian grunted, unsurprised. "Sounds awful."

Ishelle shrugged again. "It's effective. It means that those with potential actually strive to fulfill it. The teachers try to produce great students because when they do, it's a chance for them to move up themselves. And the ones already in Central work hard to make sure that they're not pushed back down. It's not necessarily a system that encourages great friendships, I suppose, but it sure as fate makes everyone strive to be better."

"Not awful at all, then. My mistake," said Davian drily.

They kept walking, chatting quietly, eventually coming to the tunnel to Outer Ward. Once again they were let through with barely a second glance, though Davian noticed that the guards were fastidious in checking the bands of people going in the opposite direction. Worn around the right wrist, those bands were the primary indicator of where each Gifted belonged in the Tol—two bands meant access to Central, one to Inner, and none for those restricted to Outer Ward.

Davian adjusted the single band on his wrist irritably, still not accustomed to it. In a lot of ways it reminded him of wearing a Shackle, despite his ability to take it off whenever he wanted to. The band was apparently linked to a small amount of his Essence, something called a Trace, which the Shen Council had insisted on taking from him when he'd arrived—meaning that he was the only one able to wear it. Anyone else putting on Davian's band would do so at the expense of severe burns to their wrist.

Not that he had any intention of flouting the Tol's rules and giving it away, anyway. The Council took the segregation of their wards very seriously; according to Ishelle, Gifted had been expelled for braving the pain of a stolen armband and sneaking into more central areas than they were allowed. For students, that punishment would have resulted in their being turned into Shadows.

"So you really don't think Elder Dain will take any action over this morning?" he asked absently, following the train of thought.

Ishelle shook her head confidently. "No. We're too valuable for that. Besides, you showed him up, but you didn't really do anything *wrong*." She glanced at him. "Did I ever tell you about the time I first met him?"

Davian shook his head.

Ishelle smirked. "Driscin had already been teaching me for about a year when he introduced us. Lyrus insisted on meeting with me one-on-one, so that he had a chance to really emphasize what I could and couldn't do while I was at the Tol. He wanted to make sure that I understood what was expected of me. I think that he thought it would be intimidating for me."

She shrugged. "I was learning Control, and he was taking *forever* to go through all the different things that I could be punished for. Driscin wasn't around, and Lyrus's shield was *much* weaker than he thought it was. So I figured I would... practice on him."

Davian stared at her. "You practiced on *Elder Dain*?"

Ishelle grinned. "It was only meant to be something small—every time he went to tell me how I would be 'punished' I made him say the word 'cuddle.' It was just the two of us, he didn't realize it was happening, and it made the whole boring thing a lot more entertaining to listen to."

Davian sniggered as he envisaged it. "And you got away with that?"

"Well." Ishelle's smile widened. "What I didn't realize was that I hadn't undone the Control properly before he left... and that he had a big speech in front of the entire Central Ward the next day. All about discipline."

Davian felt his eyes widen. "You're serious?"

Ishelle put on a deep voice, pretending that she was addressing a large crowd. "The next person who looks the other way when standards drop, I will personally cuddle. *Anyone* who does not perform to the level expected in Central Ward will be *severely* cuddled."

Davian stared at her in open-mouthed, grinning disbelief, then guffawed more loudly than he'd intended, drawing curious glances from passers-by.

"What happened when someone told him?"

"That was the best part. Everyone was so intimidated by him, he went through the *entire speech* like that. No one wanted to be the one to speak up. Driscin figured out what I'd done and made me undo it straight after, but..." She giggled. "As far as I know, he never found out. That speech was two years ago, and I *still* hear it referred to as the Cuddle Speech whenever Lyrus isn't around."

Davian put his hand over his mouth, muffling another laugh. "That's amazing. And terrible. But amazing."

Ishelle shrugged modestly, looking pleased at his reaction.

As Davian continued to chuckle, they finally emerged into the crowds of Outer, which despite the lack of space still managed to ripple away uneasily as people recognized them.

Outer Ward was completely different again from the other two wards. Physically the largest of the three concentric rings, it was the only ward into which all the Gifted were allowed, and thus also by far the most congested. It housed not only the majority of people in the Tol, but also its own marketplace, storage buildings, the common-access library, and a hundred other facilities. It was raucous and chaotic most of the time, the extra bodies making everything cramped, loud, and uncomfortable.

After a couple of minutes they came to the Entrance Hall, and Davian glanced at the structure, wondering just how many claimants were waiting for an interview today.

"You're sure you—"

"I am." Ishelle made a shooing motion. "Go. Do... whatever it is you do to relax."

Davian flashed a grateful smile and inclined his head, splitting off toward the Tol's eastern gate. Despite the quickly parting crowd and sullen stares, he found himself with a spring in his step at the prospect of getting away from everything for a while.

He exited the Tol, even managing a cheerful nod in response to the suspicious glare of the guards at the gate. Despite the gray afternoon sky overhead, he headed into Prythe with a smile on his face.

The walk into Prythe was a short one.

Unlike Tol Athian, Shen—the fortress being above ground, not to mention the size of a large town itself—was located beyond the city's walls, but it still essentially adjoined Prythe, and   93 the journey took only ten minutes. It was a pleasant excursion; the clouds were finally beginning to clear, and a hint of spring was in the air now that the worst of winter had passed.

Davian, for once, didn't feel the need to hurry. He'd made this trip a couple of times already since their arrival, despite having nothing specific to do in the city. As one of the Gifted, he'd always had to wear both a Shackle and a red cloak to identify himself in public—but as an Augur, there were no such restrictions. Not *technically*, anyway; he wasn't sure if it was an oversight due to hastily drafted laws, but he intended to take full advantage of the situation while it lasted. The ability to blend into a crowd and just disappear was something he hadn't truly been able to experience in years.

He let his mind drift as he wandered through the streets, enjoying the anonymity. Prythe had neither the breadth nor beauty of Ilin Illan—the houses and shops here were constructed from a melange of materials and styles old and new, made by hands far less skilled than the Builders'—but the city made up for it with sheer *bustle*. The main streets were alive, energetic, the crowds a noisy, colorful maze of moving parts as people weaved out of the way of carriages or veered toward a stall they'd just spotted.

Musicians—something Prythe was renowned for—stood at every corner; the moment one tune threatened to become soft in Davian's ears, another picked up somewhere ahead. A young blond woman singing a bright tune made him think of Asha; as he often did, he wondered how she was getting on in the aftermath of the battle with the Blind. Hoped, idly, that things were going better for her than they were for him.

He twisted the silver ring on his finger as he paused to listen, struck by a sudden bout of melancholy. It had been one of the hardest things he'd ever had to do, leaving Ilin Illan to come here. Leaving her. It had been the *right* thing to do, of that he still had no doubt.

It didn't mean he missed her any less.

Word from the capital had been scarce, too. He thought Wirr was still Northwarden, at least. When he'd arrived at Tol Shen he'd been bemused by how few Administrators there were, only to discover days later that the vast majority had left in the preceding weeks, heading for Ilin Illan to protest after the Tenets had been changed. There *were* some still around—three had been present for his and Ishelle's official acceptance of the Amnesty—but in the week since his arrival, Davian could count on one hand the number of times he'd seen a blue cloak amid all the red.

He stood listening to the music for a while, standing among the small crowd the woman had gathered on her corner. Her voice was crystal, beautiful and clear, cutting through the hub-bub of the city. A smattering of applause sounded when the last note of the song faded and she curtsied, face flushed from the performance.

Davian, along with several others, paused to toss a coin into the bowl in front of her. It wasn't much, but the Tol took care of his needs, and he had more than enough to spare after his compensation for accepting the Amnesty.

The singer gave him a bright smile of acknowledgment. Then, as he was about to walk past, she leaned forward and put a hand on his arm.

"Excuse me," she said quietly as the rest of the crowd began to drift away. "I know this is none of my business, but you may want to keep one hand on that purse of yours."

"What?" Davian stared at her in confusion.

"You've wandered past this corner today, what—three or four times? Every time, there's been a gentleman not far behind who seems intent on keeping you in sight, but staying out of yours." She shook her head wryly. "I only noticed because he's painfully obvious, so I'm not sure how much of a danger he is—but then, you're evidently not used to being in the city, so…" She shrugged apologetically. "He must have seen you have some coin, sensed you were an easy target. I thought you'd like to know."

Davian swallowed a sudden surge of unease, nodding his thanks. Had someone recognized him? There had been no reason to think that Prythe would be dangerous; no one outside the Tol should even have his description, let alone know him by sight. "What does he look like?"

"Short, stocky. Brown cloak with a hood that he keeps pulled over his face." She shook her head. "You'll know him if you see him. Fates, he looks suspicious enough that I'm surprised the city watch hasn't pulled him aside yet."

Davian thanked her and started apprehensively down the street, resisting the urge to look over his shoulder. If there was someone after him, he needed to know who.

He made himself keep a steady pace until he came to the mouth of a narrow alley, then turned down it and broke into a sprint, rounding the next corner before stopping and closing his eyes.

He pushed through kan.

Sources of Essence sprang into view around him, pulsing and flowing everywhere he looked. He focused, sharpening his image of the sources until they were distinct from one another, identifiable at a glance. Though the Essence outlines were never much more than silhouettes, every source pulsed at a slightly different rate, glowed with a different hue or at a different intensity. It was subtle, but he'd been practicing hard over the past month. He could recognize one from another now.

He stretched his senses out back along the alley that he'd just run through, examining the crowd in the street. At first there was nothing, the ebb and flow of people seeming no different from before.

Then a source separated from the mass of bodies, pausing at the entrance to the alley; though Davian couldn't see walls using kan, he suspected his pursuer was peering around the corner of a building.

Davian frowned. The man's Essence glowed significantly brighter than those around him.

He was Gifted.

Before Davian could wonder at the fact, his pursuer evidently realized that there was no sign of his quarry, losing all pretense of stealth and breaking into a sprint. Davian waited until the figure was almost at the corner and then stepped smoothly into its path, ready to draw Essence if the need arose.

The brown-cloaked man skidded to a halt, blue eyes wide as he realized who stood in his way.

Davian scowled, relaxing somewhat as he took in the familiar features under the hood.

"*Elder Thameron?*" Davian rubbed his forehead. "What are you *doing* here? Why are you following me?"

Elder Thameron licked his lips, looking caught between irritation and embarrassment. Eventually, the former appeared to win out.

"Did you really think the Council would let you wander the city alone?" he snapped, keeping his voice low. "Without supervision? Without *protection*?" He rolled his shoulders uncomfortably, glancing around. "And keep your voice down. I'm in a lot of trouble if an Administrator finds me out here without my robe and Shackle."

Davian stared at the Elder in disbelief. "Why not just tell me?"

"Because you made such a fuss about it when you got here." Thameron sighed, tone softening. "We don't want you to feel like a prisoner, Davian—but you *are* our responsibility. With all that entails."

Davian said nothing for a few moments, though he was seething inwardly. He'd been surprised at how easily the Council had acceded to him and Ishelle being allowed to leave the Tol, but had assumed it was a conciliatory gesture—an attempt to compromise a little after all the other restrictions they'd placed on the Augurs. He should have known that it wasn't without caveats.

A gamut of insults ran through his head, but he made himself breathe deeply instead of releasing them. Eventually, he calmed enough to simply shake his head in disgust. The pleasure of his time away from the Tol was now a distant memory.

"I'm going back." He started walking, but stopped immediately as Thameron started alongside him. He turned to face the Elder, staring at him stonily. "If you need to follow me, you can keep doing what you were doing. I'm not interested in company."

Thameron flushed but when Davian started walking again, he didn't try to fall into step. Davian didn't look to see how far back the man was keeping, but the mere knowledge of his presence was a knot between Davian's shoulders.

He headed in the general direction of the Tol, hesitating as he went to walk past the singer who had warned him. The blond woman was still taking a break so he turned and veered over to her side, giving her a brief, albeit forced, smile of greeting.

"I just wanted to say thanks for the tip. It wasn't a cutpurse after all." He glanced over his shoulder, glaring toward the brown-robed shape of Elder Thameron as it emerged from the alley. "Just someone being a nuisance."

The singer frowned, staring at him in bemusement. "What?" She took an uncertain half step back. "Who are you?"

Davian blinked. "Um. We spoke a few minutes ago?"

The woman gave him a hesitant smile. "Sorry, friend. I think you have me mistaken," she said, her careful tone suggesting that she wasn't entirely sure of Davian's mental stability.

Davian frowned. "No—no, I'm quite sure it was you. You warned me about..."

He trailed off.

There was genuine confusion in the woman's eyes, and no hint of recognition.

"Never mind," he said quietly, swallowing, anxiety suddenly arcing through him. "Sorry to disturb you."

He hurried off before she could respond, his mind racing, Thameron temporarily forgotten.

The singer hadn't lied to him, and there were only two reasons for her not to have remembered him after such a short period of time.

Someone had taken her memories of him, or—more likely—she'd been Controlled, and it hadn't been she who had warned him about Thameron in the first place.

Either way, an Augur had been there.

He shivered, the memory of what Asha had told him about Scyner flashing through his head. If there was an Augur in Prythe, why would they not yet have gone to the Tol? Why warn Davian about Thameron? How had they even known Davian was an Augur?

More questions occurred to him as he walked, but none of them had obvious answers. Davian gritted his teeth and continued pushing through the hubbub of Prythe, angling back toward Tol Shen as dusk began to settle on the city. He needed to talk to Ishelle.

For the first time since he'd arrived, he found himself feeling genuinely uneasy.

Chapter 7

Wirr tugged irritably at the fine shirt he was wearing.

It wasn't so much the material; he was getting accustomed to that again, even if it galled him to think of dressing up for dinner while people in the city were trying to rebuild their homes. It was more that he'd been all but manhandled into wearing it. His uncle had insisted that he look not just presentable, but *good*. He'd forced the royal tailor on Wirr for just this occasion.

"You look very nice tonight, Your Highness," observed Andyn as the carriage moved along the streets of the Upper District.

Wirr shrugged. "Not through any fault of my own," he assured his bodyguard drily.

"Knowing your usual appearance, Sire, I assumed as much."

Wirr blinked in surprise, then snorted and shook his head, allowing himself a small smile at the unexpected crack. It seemed that Andyn was finally beginning to relax a little around him— not to the extent of any impropriety, but enough that Wirr found himself glad for the redheaded man's company tonight.

The ride to the Tel'Rath residence was short; all the Great Houses had residences in the Upper City, as close to the palace as they could manage. Even so, Wirr couldn't help but fixate on the aftermath of the battle, still evident in the scarred streets and crumbling walls where blasts of Essence had torn them apart. It was too easy to recall his own wild flight down this road, away from the Shields and back toward the Tol, certain that he would die and still trying to comprehend the loss of his father.

A month on, and the memory still made him feel ill.

Soon enough, though, Wirr found himself gazing around at the Tel'Rath grounds as the carriage rolled through the tall outer gates. He'd never been here before, only walked past the high gray walls that kept passers-by from peering inside.

Despite knowing how wealthy the family was, he was still surprised to find the grounds were nearly as impressive as the palace's. The immaculately kept lawns and gardens had been untouched by the invasion, and a dedicated road wound its way up to the enormous house—verging on a castle—that sat with its back firmly against Ilin Tora.

Wirr grimaced as the carriage came to a stop, noting the throng of people waiting outside the front door for him. Not just Lord and Lady Tel'Rath, along with Iria. All the servants had come as well.

"Quite the welcome, Sire," observed Andyn cheerfully.

Wirr kept his face smooth, fighting the urge to glare at his bodyguard.

The next half hour passed in a mildly awkward, stiffly polite blur of pleasantries and small talk, followed by another hour of equally polite one-on-one political discourse with Lord Tel'Rath. Wirr had assumed part of the evening would go this way; Wirr's influence was significant regardless of his current conflicts within Administration, and Lord Tel'Rath was hardly the kind of man to pass up a chance to further his various agendas.

Still, by the time dinner was announced, he had more than had his fill of the conversation. Lord Tel'Rath was civil enough, even outwardly friendly, but Wirr couldn't help but get the sense that every word out of his mouth was guarded. Considered. *Tactical.*

It was almost a reprieve when he was seated next to Iria at the dining table.

The meal passed pleasantly enough, much to his relief. Lady Tel'Rath, a statuesque woman whose long hair had begun to show signs of silver, was clearly skilled at diverting her husband's attempts to discuss politics at the table—even if she managed to find a way to heap praise on Iria every few minutes instead.

For her part, Iria seemed more embarrassed than anything else by the attention. She was a pretty woman of around twenty years, only a year or two older than Wirr himself, but more shy than he'd expected from a daughter of one of the Great Houses. Her long black hair was simply bound, and she wore a green dress that was form-fitting but still on the side of modesty. She was friendly toward him but far from pushy, engaging him in light, albeit awkward conversation here and there over the course of the meal.

As dinner began to wind down, Lord Tel'Rath was fetched by a servant, and he nodded politely to Wirr before hurrying off after the man. A few minutes later, Lady Tel'Rath murmured an excuse and disappeared as well, leaving only Wirr, Iria, and Andyn in the room.

Wirr did his best not to look irritated. He'd known this moment in the evening would come—some casual excuse to leave him and Iria alone, with only Andyn standing discreetly in the corner to ensure there were no suggestions of impropriety. Iria was proving to be sweet-natured, occasionally even funny—certainly not what he'd expected—but that, of course, didn't change anything.

After an awkward pause, Iria shook her head, looking vaguely embarrassed.

"So here we are." She glanced at the door, then gave him a shy half smile. "I apologize for my mother, Your Highness. Anything she said that sounded too good to be true? Assume it was. She's... not exactly a master of subtlety."

Wirr returned the smile with a rueful one of his own. "I'm not sure she was trying to be, just then."

Iria laughed, the sound only slightly nervous. Wirr suddenly felt a wave compassion for her. It wasn't her fault that they were here, any more than it was his.

As he already had several times, he considered explaining to Iria that his romantic interests lay elsewhere—without revealing any specifics—but as before, he dismissed the idea straight away. Perhaps Iria was as pleasant as she seemed and wouldn't use the information to her advantage, but if her father caught wind... Wirr didn't even want to think about the consequences.

They chatted for a while, Wirr polite but carefully distant, not wanting to convey the wrong impression. Slowly, he began to relax. The evening had been awkward, but not nearly so bad as he'd imagined. And it was close to over.

Suddenly he frowned, whatever Iria was saying fading into

the background. Nothing had noticeably changed, but the air abruptly felt...heavier.

There were no incidental noises from outside the room now, either.

He glanced across at Andyn, whose brow was furrowed. More than anything else, the bodyguard's tense posture told Wirr that something was amiss.

Wirr held up a hand to Iria, indicating that she should stop speaking. Iria stared at him in confusion, flushing, and he realized she probably thought that he was being rude. Ignoring her, he cautiously reached for Essence.

It was there...but sure enough, when he tried to draw some of it, nothing happened.

He turned to Andyn, his voice low and urgent. "Someone's activated a Trap."

As if to punctuate the words, there was a sharp shout of alarm from somewhere outside the dining room. Andyn drew his blade as the far door to the room crashed open, two men and a woman in dark clothes striding through.

Andyn immediately moved toward them; the woman pointed a crossbow in Wirr's direction, but Andyn had positioned himself to block the shot.

She fired anyway.

Wirr's bodyguard staggered backward from the impact and then crumpled to the floor, a dark-red patch spreading rapidly across his shirt, bolt embedded in his stomach. The woman who had shot him swept forward barely without pause, reloading the crossbow almost absently, eyes fixed on Wirr.

Wirr and Iria both yelled for the guards, but Wirr knew even as they did so that anyone who responded wouldn't get there in time. He glanced around; fortunately the hall was long and the attackers had entered from the far side. There were no weapons at hand, though. Iria snatched up a knife from beside her dinner plate, but Wirr knew that even if she somehow got into position to use it, it would be useless.

He pushed Iria toward the closest door, and headed there himself.

Before he could move two paces it opened, another three men

entering with blades drawn. Steel glinted in the candlelight only where it did not have dark blood smeared on it.

Iria was ahead of Wirr, her momentum taking her directly into the newcomers. The one closest to her shoved her aside, his target clearly Wirr. There was a crashing of plates and cutlery as Iria ricocheted off the table; she cried out, falling to her knees.

She still had her knife, though. As the last man went to walk past her she leaned over and swung viciously.

The bald man roared with pain and anger as the knife dug into his thigh, collapsing on one knee and twisting toward Iria, violence in his eyes as he raised his sword. Wirr snatched up a dish from the table and hurled it at the man, the pottery shattering as it hit him in the face, causing him to fall backward with a snarl.

"Get help!" shouted Wirr to Iria. His path to the doorway was still blocked, but hers was not.

Iria didn't need encouragement. Gasping, she scrambled around her assailant and fled.

Wirr snatched another plate from the table and threw it, but this time his target was watching and ducked it easily, sneering as he did so. Wirr backed away, but he was caught between the two groups coming toward him, and he was unarmed.

Even if Iria found help, it was not going to be in time.

He leaped across to the other side of the table, buying himself a few extra seconds. "I don't suppose we can talk about this?" he said shakily, unable to keep the panic from his tone as his attackers adjusted with slow but confident steps, hemming him in.

Then the tip of a sword appeared through the chest of the closest assailant to Wirr's right.

Wirr gaped as the man's eyes rolled into the back of his head and he slid to the ground. Everyone froze; there was a shocked silence as the attacker standing next to him lowered his blade, staring at the body of his comrade, confusion quickly turning to horror.

"What in all fates?" snarled the woman with the crossbow. "What are you—"

She cut off with a choking sound and Wirr turned to see her clutching at her neck, beads of red dribbling between her fingers. The man who had slit her throat tossed aside his blade; before anyone could move, he calmly picked up her weapon from where she'd dropped it and fired.

The bolt flew past Wirr's face and took another assailant in the eye.

There were three bodies on the floor now, and the fourth attacker, whom Iria had stabbed, appeared to have retreated. It had all happened in a matter of moments.

"He's doing something to us," snarled one of the two remaining men, fear thick in his voice as he broke the stunned silence. He stepped forward, raising his sword.

Then spun and slashed it across his still-confused-looking comrade's face.

Wirr finally recovered enough to force his limbs to move, diving for one of the fallen assassin's swords and holding it out in front of him. His hand was shaking. He'd seen violence, seen more death than he'd ever expected to over the past year, but *this* . . .

"The danger has passed, Prince Torin." The sole remaining attacker lowered his blade and held up his free hand in a calming gesture. "My name is Scyner. I wish only to talk."

Wirr frowned for a moment, still dazed at the turn of events. Then comprehension set in.

"You're the Augur," he said softly. "The one working for the Shadraehin." He swallowed, staring around at the bloodied corpses. "You . . . you did all of this?"

"Yes." Scyner said the word without emotion.

Wirr stared at him. "Why?"

"Your well-being is important. Let that be enough, for now." Scyner sighed as he saw the doubt in Wirr's expression. "Very well. My time here is limited, so listen carefully. I know of your investigation into how the weapons against the Gifted came to be in Administration's hands twenty years ago. How the Tenets came to be. Ultimately, I have been watching you because I was waiting for an opportunity to give you the answers you are looking for. I hadn't considered this to be one," he added drily.

Wirr clenched his fists, though it was to prevent them from continuing to shake rather than from anger. "And in return?"

"In return, we begin building a trust." Scyner held his gaze steadily. "No matter what you have heard about me, we want the same thing—the restoration of the Boundary, and the final defeat of the forces behind it. You and I will be working together soon enough toward that end. It is important that you understand what we are dealing with when that happens, as well as the role you will need to play."

Wirr licked his lips, forcing himself not to scoff. Scyner had murdered all of the old Augurs—had admitted as much in front of Asha. And he'd killed Asha's friend.

Wirr had no intention of ever working with this man, but now did not seem like the time to mention it.

"Then tell me. Tell me how Administration came by the weapons," he said.

Scyner smiled, though it was mostly a baring of teeth. "I do not need to Read you to know that you would not trust a single word that passes my lips, Prince Torin—and besides, there is nowhere near enough time to explain everything so that you would understand." He glanced at the door as distant shouts began to filter into the room. "I am hoping that you will believe your father, though."

"My father is dead," said Wirr, anger and frustration and dazed confusion burning only just beneath the surface.

"Go to his study at the Tel'Andras estate. There is a safe hidden there behind the wall, accessible only to the Northwarden. You will know it when you see it." Scyner gave him a small, encouraging nod. "You will find your answers there. Once you do—once you understand—I hope that you will be willing to hear me out in full."

He raised his sword again, and Wirr took a step back, tensing.

Scyner turned the blade and plunged it into his own stomach.

Wirr watched in frozen horror as the man collapsed silently to the ground, mouth opening and closing as the light died from his eyes.

The shouts from outside the room were louder now, and then suddenly there were people crowding around him.

He barely registered them, unable to take his eyes from the carnage in front him.

Someone gently took the sword from his hand, guiding him to a seat. Iria, he thought; the young woman was surprisingly calm 105 given the circumstances. Was that impressive, or suspicious? Suddenly he didn't know where to look, who to trust.

"Torin!" It *was* Iria, shaking him gently by the arm, sounding concerned. "Torin, are you injured?"

Wirr turned, bemusedly taking in what was happening. He and the Tel'Rath family were surrounded by tense-looking guards. Lord and Lady Tel'Rath were staring at the bodies on the floor with a mixture of fear and horror; whether it was because of the corpses, or because they were thinking about what this would do to their reputation, he wasn't entirely sure. Iria's eyes were fixed on him—concerned, but there was something else in her expression, too.

He focused, snapping back to the present.

"Fates! Andyn!" He shoved his way past the startled-looking guards and rushed over to his bodyguard, dropping to his knees. Andyn was unconscious but still drawing uneven, rasping breaths. The injury was a bad one, the crossbow bolt still embedded in Andyn's stomach, but the attackers' Trap was no longer in effect.

Wirr shrugged off halfhearted efforts to pull him away and closed his eyes, letting Essence flow out of him and into Andyn's wound, simultaneously using another strand of energy to gently draw the bolt out of his body. It was a strain—wounds this bad took an enormous amount of Essence to heal—but when he eventually sat back, drained, Andyn's breathing had become more regular.

This time he didn't resist the hands that looped under his arms and gently lifted him to his feet.

The next few minutes passed in a blur. He was being asked and asked again if he was injured; then he was rushed away past even more bodies in the corridors leading outside, vaguely understanding that he needed to be taken back to the palace as quickly as possible, that he couldn't stay any longer because there was an ongoing threat.

His carriage and driver were still waiting where he had left them out in front. The situation was quickly explained to the driver, who looked uneasy but was reassured that four of Tel'Rath's guards would be packed inside the carriage, and another eight would be escorting it outside.

Before Wirr could even bid the Tel'Raths farewell, he was away, the carriage moving steadily along the wet, darkened streets of Ilin Illan, more slowly than usual to account for the men jogging alongside. There was silence inside, those assigned to protect him looking out the windows watchfully and not inclined to conversation.

That suited Wirr just fine at the moment. He needed time to calm down, to think. Scyner clearly hadn't just committed suicide: he had to have been Controlling the man Wirr had been speaking to, just as he'd Controlled the others to make them turn on their allies. What he'd told Wirr about his father's study, though... Wirr didn't know what to make of it.

Scyner had been right about one thing, though. Wirr didn't trust a single word out of the Augur's mouth, no matter what he'd just done to save him.

He closed his eyes, breathing deeply, letting the silence of the trip calm him. By the time the carriage had pulled up outside the palace, his head was clearer and he felt close to in control again.

King Andras and Karaliene were waiting to meet him as he alighted.

"Torin!" Karaliene enveloped him in a hug, and his uncle soon followed.

"I'm all right," he assured them after a few moments. He frowned. "How did you...?"

"Lord Tel'Rath sent a runner ahead of your carriage." Kevran frowned. "I wish he'd waited. I would have sent more men to accompany you."

Now that he was home and among familiar faces, Wirr felt his tensed muscles finally beginning to relax. His uncle's towering figure was nothing if not reassuring; the king had always been a large, powerfully built man, but the illness he'd suffered before the Blind's attack had robbed him of a lot of his presence. That was finally beginning to return, now that he was close to full strength again.

"I'm here safely. That's all I care about right now," Wirr admitted, a wave of exhaustion washing over him.

"We're just glad you weren't harmed," said Karaliene quietly, squeezing his arm.

They went inside, finding a convenient room where they could talk privately.

"Assassins," muttered the king as he sat, the word a curse on his lips. "Even after the threats, I didn't really think..." He sighed. "Do you have any idea who they were?"

"None. Plain clothes, plain weapons." Wirr quickly shook his head to the king's questioning look. "And no—I don't think the Tel'Raths were involved. Iria was lucky not to get killed." He hesitated, considering mentioning Scyner's involvement but immediately discounting the idea. His uncle had been vehemently against the idea of him looking into the Vessels that had facilitated the war twenty years ago. Wirr hadn't decided if he was going to pursue what Scyner had told him, but he at least wanted the opportunity to do so.

Kevran grunted. "I'll still be asking how armed men made it into their dining room," he said grimly. "One was caught, apparently. Hopefully he can lead us to whomever was behind it."

Karaliene opened her mouth to add something, but suddenly there was a disturbance outside the room. Wirr stiffened, for a moment fearing the worst, but then restrained a weary smile as he recognized the raised voice outside.

"I am aware of exactly who is in there." Dezia's words were loud and firm. "If you would just go in and ask—"

Wirr moved over to the door and opened it a crack, peering through and shooting Dezia a tired grin. Then he raised an eyebrow at the guard. "She can come in."

Dezia rolled her eyes, but accepted Wirr's motioned invitation to enter, glaring at the guard on her way past. Once the door was shut, she turned to Wirr and examined him with narrowed eyes.

"So I hear your dinner didn't go too well," she said eventually. The words were delivered lightly, but Wirr heard the strain in her voice clearly enough.

"It was a little more exciting than I thought it would be. But everyone's all right." Wirr gave her a slight, reassuring nod.

Dezia breathed out, the tension in her shoulders easing.

"Well. As long as the Tel'Raths are safe," she said. "I was worried for them when I heard."

There was a cough from across the room. Wirr and Dezia

turned to see Kevran watching them with a mixture of concern and amusement, with Karaliene standing a little behind him. Her expression was similar, but with markedly less concern.

"Dezia," said the king, giving her a wide, dangerous smile. "I had no idea you knew my nephew so well."

Dezia flushed. "I...we traveled together from Desriel, of course," she stammered, suddenly remembering who else was in the room. "When I heard about the attack, I wanted to make sure he...that everyone was all right for myself."

"Your concern is touching," said the king, his expression not changing.

Karaliene spoke up. "And you must be quite well informed, too, 'Zia. I mean to say—you heard about it very quickly. Almost as quickly as we did, and we were the first ones to know. And *we* were waiting to hear how the dinner had gone," she added.

Dezia reddened further, then glowered at Karaliene. "I'm well informed about a lot of things, you know," she said, a little ominously.

Karaliene, still standing behind her father, blushed and subsided. Fortunately for her, the king didn't notice the exchange, instead looking between Wirr and Dezia thoughtfully.

He said nothing, though, for which Wirr was grateful. He knew he might be summoned for a frank discussion later, but now—tonight—all he wanted to do was go to bed and get some rest. He was suddenly, awfully tired.

"Not everyone got away uninjured," he said quietly, knowing that he was dampening the mood again, but too tired to care. "Andyn took a crossbow bolt to the stomach."

Dezia gave him a sympathetic look. "How is he?"

"I healed him; he should be fine. I'm about to go and see if he's back now, though, and check on him."

"You'll do no such thing." Kevran frowned at Wirr. "If Andyn's condition changes, I'll make sure you're informed. But you need to rest, Torin. You can barely keep your eyes open, let alone stand."

Wirr made to protest, but was sabotaged by a wide yawn in place of words. He grunted. "First thing in the morning, then," he said, a little sheepishly. "The man got hurt because of me, Uncle."

"He did his job." Kevran said the words without cynicism, but Wirr could hear the rebuke. "He did it well, and you're right to be grateful. But it's what he's paid for." He rubbed his chin. "In light of what has happened tonight, I'm wondering if it might be a good idea for you to get out of the city for a while. Easier to give you increased security without raising any questions, and…"

"I can go and see my mother." Wirr said the words without thinking. His mother and sister were currently living at the Tel'Andras estate, where his father's old study was.

Kevran nodded, looking vaguely surprised at Wirr's suggestion. "Good; it's probably time that happened anyway. I know things have been awkward between you two—they're awkward between her and myself, too, to be honest—but you're her son. You're going to have to speak with her eventually."

Wirr didn't protest, and the king inclined his head. "Then it's settled. You'll leave in the morning, stay with your mother and sister for a few days. It's not unusual, and it should give us a little time to investigate without constantly needing to worry about your safety. I'll send men ahead of you tonight; with them as well as your family's regular guards, that estate is all but a fortress. I doubt there's anywhere safer you could be right now."

They spoke for a little longer, but Wirr's yawns soon grew uncontrollable and he was eventually pushed out the door. Once he reached his room he collapsed onto the bed, too tired even to undress. The tension of the attack had finally worn off, replaced by a sheer, deep exhaustion that he hadn't felt since after the battle a month ago.

He lay back, for the briefest of moments wondering if he was taking Scyner's bait. It was a fleeting thought, though.

He slept.

Chapter 8

Ten days on, and the fires continued to burn.

Caeden stared out from the upper-floor window over the devastated city of Silence, wondering idly how there could possibly be enough fuel to sustain such furious carnage. From his vantage point, it appeared that still nobody was trying to douse the flames. Still no one dared incur his wrath.

Eventually he turned away. Pushed down the grief, the guilt, the horror at what he had ordered. This was the last of them. The Darecians had nowhere left to run except to where he wanted them.

"I see you haven't changed much."

The voice came from the doorway; Caeden spun to see a young man standing at the entrance to the enormous, broken hallway, eyes meeting his without flinching. The stranger moved carefully around several chunks of shattered marble, gesturing at a low pool of fire that blocked his path. Immediately the flames died, and Caeden watched as Essence drifted away from where they had been before dissipating into the ether.

Caeden closed his eyes, registering the man's Essence signature.

"Andrael," he said softly.

The man nodded, not pausing as he came closer. "It's been a long time, 'Kein."

Caeden found himself caught between smile and grimace at the familiarity. The name Aarkein Devaed had been chosen for the fear it was meant to strike into the hearts of his enemies. Andrael, of course, had always delighted in turning it into an affectionate moniker.

111

"It is good to see you," said Caeden, voice thick with emotional sincerity. He swallowed, gesturing to a relatively undamaged block of stone, then sitting opposite. "Three hundred years is a long time to bear the hatred of a dear friend," he added quietly.

Andrael paused halfway into his sitting motion, obviously moved by the comment. He nodded, then sat carefully. Though his unfamiliar features were youthful, his eyes looked tired beyond measure.

"Hatred? No, 'Kein." Andrael gave him a sorrowful smile. "Anger? Disappointment? Perhaps. But El knows it was never once hatred. I will swear that to you right now."

Caeden stayed silent, a lump in his throat at the words.

Andrael gestured at the city beyond the window. "So does Cyr know?"

"Cyr helped. Said that if his city was to fall, it should be by his hand." Caeden watched Andrael closely. "He likes it as little as I, but we both accept that it needs to be done."

He waited for the remonstration, the protests. To his surprise, they did not come.

Encouraged, he went on. "You should speak to the others. They know they can trust me now." He leaned forward, unable to keep the eagerness from his tone. "I know you don't believe me, but—"

"I believe you, 'Kein." Andrael's quiet voice cut through Caeden's words. "I know it was not madness. I have believed you for a long time now."

"That's wonderful!" A smile split Caeden's face, and only something in Andrael's body language kept him from leaping to his feet in delight. "The others will be so excited, Andrael. So relieved! Tysis is here somewhere, you know. We should find her and let her know the good news!"

Andrael waited for Caeden to finish, his expression unmoving. When there was silence again, he sighed.

"I am not back, 'Kein," he said gently. "Your actions may have shattered the Venerate, but they were merely the final blow. We were weakening for centuries before that. There is no force in this world that can now mend what has been broken, my friend." He swallowed, looking sad at that last part. "The others…they are well? Where are they now?"

Caeden sank back onto his makeshift seat, heart wrenching at the words.

"Cyr and Gassandrid are in Loec. Alaris is off searching for suitable commanders for Telesthaesia. Isiliar and Wereth are organizing the Ironsails down at Mosharis." He shrugged. "The others…you probably have a better idea than I. Of everyone who left, you are the first I've seen again."

He paused, then exhaled heavily. "I am sad to hear you are not back to stay, but…that does not mean we shouldn't celebrate the reunion. Come. Let's at least find Tysis, and she can find out all that has been happening as well. She misses you, too, you know." He crooked a sly smile. "I think she may still hold a torch, actually." He got to his feet, gesturing for Andrael to follow.

The other man shook his head slowly, the long brown strands falling over his eyes unable to hide his look of regret.

"Tysis is dead." He whispered the words, barely loud enough for Caeden to hear.

"What?" Caeden frowned at the other man. "How? Her weakness is Deprivation. It would take…"

He trailed off, sighing as he understood what Andrael was saying. "You did it? El take it, Andrael. She's not going to be happy when she gets back."

"She's not coming back, 'Kein."

Caeden snorted. "We both know how she reacts to dying. I'll take any wager you're willing to make that she'll be back within the year."

Andrael turned to face Caeden fully. "No," he said softly. "I mean she's not coming back. At all. She will not wake up in another body."

Caeden opened his mouth, then blinked as Andrael's words finally struck home. "What do you mean, she won't wake up in another body?" he asked slowly.

"I mean she won't go through the Chamber. She is gone, my friend. Ended. Forever. She. Is. Dead." Andrael said the words gently, as he would if explaining a frightening concept—a frightening truth—to a child.

Caeden gave a short, confused laugh. Then he looked into Andrael's eyes, saw the rock-solid belief there.

"That's not possible," he whispered, blood suddenly cold.

Andrael reached down to the sword at his hip, drawing it slowly and holding its tip away from Caeden to indicate it was not meant as a threat.

"When I left, I was... broken," said Andrael quietly. "I didn't know what to believe. I thought you were a liar. I thought you were mad, and the rest of them were mad for following you. But I wanted to know for sure. So I traveled, back to places we had not been in centuries. I saw the Shattered Lands, found out about the past Alaris refuses to talk about. I even visited your homeland for a time."

Caeden stiffened at that, but said nothing.

"I made five Vessels. Swords, because... well, because I anticipated that you would not let me use those Vessels willingly." He scratched his head. "The first, I made so that I could Read you... but as I researched, I came to understand that that was not necessary. There were only hints to begin with," continued Andrael softly. "Rumors. Stories passed down. That's all that was left, sometimes, after we departed. Do you know how many libraries we destroyed, over the years? How much knowledge we took?" He waved away Caeden's anticipated protest. "It doesn't matter. The point is, I went looking for a way to prove you were lying. And instead came away convinced that you were telling the truth."

Caeden frowned. "And this is the blade you forged?" he asked pensively, indicating Andrael's weapon.

"No. That sword is with another." Andrael sighed. "This blade... this is the culmination of three hundred years' worth of toil. After the first, I made three others, but none of them worked quite as I needed them to. This one does." He said the words sadly rather than with any sense of triumph.

"What does it do, Andrael?" asked Caeden softly, already knowing the answer.

Andrael stared at the blade for several seconds. "It ends us, 'Kein. Permanently. This will pierce Alaris's skin, drain Gassandrid's source, cause your mind to cease before it can heal you. But as it does those things, it also prevents us from coming back."

114

Caeden shivered, feeling like nothing but scrambling farther from the other man, despite there being at least a twenty-foot gap between them. "But why?" he whispered. "What could lead you to make such an abomination, Andrael? We are the only hope for this world. If you believe me, you must surely believe that."

Andrael laughed, and the hairs on the back of Caeden's neck raised at the sound. It was tinged with mania.

"That's where you're wrong, 'Kein," he said eventually. "The only hope for this world is to remove kan from it completely. To stop it from being drawn through the rift, so that the rift may then be sealed."

He sheathed the blade.

"The only hope for this world is for all of us to die."

Caeden groaned as the yellow light of dawn pried open his eyes.

He lay there for a few moments, taking some deep breaths and getting his bearings. Another memory. Details continued to trickle through his mind, incidental and yet nothing he'd specifically seen. He knew he'd found Tysis afterward, a single wound to her chest, arranged in dignified fashion on her bed. He knew Andrael had left again before Caeden could decide what to do with him. He knew now that the Ironsails were ships powered by Essence, great metallic instruments of war that the Darecians had created long ago.

He knew, too, that this memory was one of his most recent ones thus far. Still from before he'd come to Andarra, so at least two thousand years old—but after he'd met Gassandrid. After the breaking of the Venerate, in fact.

Caeden went cold as he sat up, suddenly registering what the memory meant. This was why Asar hadn't healed. And...was this why Asar had been so reluctant to tell him everything? That they had gone to all this effort to get Licanius, in order to eliminate anyone who could use kan...the Venerate, the Augurs? *Themselves?*

Garadis had said that the Lyth would use Licanius for its original purpose, and it had clearly been meant as a threat. Plus, Asar himself had said that the plan was to close the rift completely. If Andrael had been telling the truth...

It all fit. There were still plenty of unanswered questions, and the thought made his stomach turn...but it all fit.

He shivered as he cautiously touched the blade at his side, suddenly more wary of it than he had been a moment ago. Death didn't terrify him, but the realization that Licanius was the only thing that could give it to him was deeply unsettling.

He thought for a moment, and then pushed the troubling concept aside. Whatever his plans for Licanius, they would have to come after he had dealt with the Lyth. He had no intention of killing himself—or Davian, or anyone else for that matter. If his plan had involved anything like that, it was a concern for another time.

Eventually he sighed, then climbed slowly to his feet and surveyed the way forward.

His decision to stop last night had been a wise one; he'd been aware of the steep drop ahead but dusk had hidden the scattered shale and loose rocks that littered the path downward. Now, in contrast, dawn had brought enough light to see for miles.

Everything below was much the same as the hillside in front of him—just rock, dirt, and dust—and yet somehow, the farther he looked, the more unsettling the sight became. Where the light approached the barren ground in the valley it was as if it just...*faded*. Not completely, but the longer he stared, the more certain he was that the plain was somehow absorbing far more light than it should.

He squinted grimly at the expanse of lifeless earth for a few moments, then turned his frown to the thick, lush, tangled forest to his right. As it had for all of yesterday as he'd followed the tree line, the dense foliage looked all but impenetrable.

And just as he had yesterday evening when he'd reached the crest of this hill, Caeden couldn't help but notice how that profuse, vibrant green just...ended.

It was as if the forest had been cut cleanly in half, the east-facing edge stretching away in an unnaturally straight line for as far as he could see. Past that border—down into the plain—there was no hint of life. No trees, no plants, not a blade of grass. An invisible boundary beyond which nothing appeared able to survive.

Shaking his head, Caeden let his gaze wander down the hill and into the enormous valley it overlooked. There *was* something else out there, barely distinguishable. A distant, dark shape rising from the ground.

Tentatively, he moved forward. He *could* turn south, continue to follow the edge of the forest—but he didn't think that was where he was meant to go.

Muscles tensed, he stepped off the soft grass and onto the desolate earth, ready to leap back at the first sign of danger.

He felt...something. Not pain, exactly, but a downward tugging at his body, as if his weight had suddenly increased. His squeezed his eyes shut, concentrating on the sensation.

He shivered as he realized what was happening.

Essence had begun trickling out of him, wisps of energy sucked from his body and draining away into the barren ground.

He quickly checked his Reserve. It seemed untouched—still an immense ocean of light, not noticeably dented by the sapping. The whole thing made him more than a little uneasy, but it didn't appear to be an immediate cause for alarm.

He took another step, then another, cautiously moving farther away from the greenery behind him. Nothing more happened.

He glanced uncertainly over his shoulder, then steeled himself and began picking his way down the hill.

The dark mass Caeden had spotted was taller than he'd thought; it took at least an hour of brisk walking before he got a sense of the structure, and another hour before he neared its base. He paused when he finally got close enough, staring apprehensively.

The five enormous pillars of polished black stone ahead, set in a circle, stretched hundreds of feet into the sky. They were perfectly straight and square—perfectly smooth, too, from what Caeden could tell at this distance. No joints, no indication stones had been fitted together. Just sheer, reflective black columns of pure hewn rock.

There was something about the pillars that unsettled him, more than just their incongruity in this place. They had a sheen, untouched by the layer of dust that coated everything else. And there was a...*hum* as he approached. Not loud, but just at the edge of his hearing. A vibration on the air that disoriented him a little, made him nauseous.

He closed his eyes for a moment, both to steady himself and to once again monitor the drain on his Essence.

He froze.

He'd been checking his Reserve at regular intervals, but five minutes ago it had been well over half full. More than enough for the journey back.

Now...now what had been an ocean of light was little more than a lake. For the first time that he could remember, he could see the edges of his power. See the limits of his Essence.

A sudden wave of tiredness washed over him and he dropped to his knees, light-headed. Panic threaded through the haze. What was happening? The light in the west was beginning to fade. But that was wrong. Sunset shouldn't be for hours.

He gritted his teeth, forcing his gaze upward to the ring of columns. There were no specific memories, but something told him that the area within was safe—that if he could simply reach that circle, the drain on his Essence would stop.

If he couldn't...

Fear drove him back to his feet and he stumbled onward for what seemed like an age. Just when it felt as though his legs would no longer hold him, the dusty ground turned to shallow, black stone steps; he dragged himself forward, up the mild incline, and between two of the enormous black columns.

Immediately it felt easier to breathe, as if an enormous pressure had been released from his chest. He slumped to the ground, gasping, quickly checking his Reserve. Still drained—frighteningly near empty, in fact—and yet, the leakage had stopped.

Even with the respite, he knew that he was far from safe. His tenuous grasp on consciousness threatened to slip away; he fought the exhaustion, wary of what might happen if he fell asleep here.

He took a few deep, steadying breaths and raised his head, taking in his surroundings. It was dusk and the last of the light across the plain was dying, though where the day had gone he couldn't fathom. He straightened, frowning. The circular stone plateau set amid the columns—slate gray rather than black, perhaps a hundred feet in diameter—was not as empty as he'd initially assumed.

Set to one side, up against the inside of one of the pillars, was a hulking mass of jagged steel and stone. Twice Caeden's height and three times as wide, it was incongruous, clearly not part of the design of this place, despite the gleaming black segments that looked made from the same obsidianlike material.

Caeden studied the strange, serrated object curiously. At first the twisted protrusions from its core looked haphazard, as if thin slivers of metal and rock had been forced together at random. But as he stared, he began to see something more. An order to the mass, a logic.

He released the column he'd been leaning against for support and made his way cautiously toward the object, still a little unsteady on his feet. His brow creased as he drew close enough to examine it. There was a shelf affixed to the side, barely noticeable amongst the bladelike extensions, holding a collection of unremarkable items. Some clothing. A long blade and dagger. Three rings made of a metal Caeden didn't recognize.

He came to a stop in front of the mass. Made up not only of stone and steel but also of glass, it glinted in the fading light, its pieces interlocking in ways that were both puzzling and yet somehow made perfect sense to him.

He shifted uneasily, then leaned forward as he spotted a pane set into the side. Unlike the rest of the glass he'd seen, this was smooth. Clear.

A window.

Caeden squinted at the pane, trying to see through to the inside, but it was utterly dark beyond. As he edged closer another wave of dizziness struck; he grunted in frustration, laying a hand against one of the smoother sections of the object to steady himself.

He felt the Essence draining from him too late.

He stumbled back, staring in shock as the mass whirred to life, a low thrum filling the air as Essence ran around its edges, lines of cold blue breaking the fading light. Pieces of blade began to shift, some slivers withdrawing from the core, others pushing into it. Sections began to rotate and slide, grinding into place with heavy groans.

After several seconds the motion stopped and silence fell again, though the device continued to glow ominously.

Caeden felt a chill as he stared up at the new formation of stone and steel and glass. The bottom was smooth, capsule-like now, but the top was something else entirely. Jagged teeth set along an elongated jaw, bared in a snarl. Two eyes staring down at him, blazing with blue light. It was stylized, all sharp edges and angles, but unmistakable.

A wolf's head.

He shivered. Essence lit the inside of the device now, too, and he could finally see its contents.

The man inside, perfectly preserved, had clearly been tortured to death. Vicious, needle-like blades protruded through his skin everywhere—through the neck, the arms, the hands. Some of the blades remained straight and clean, while others were hooked, as if designed to keep the body perfectly in place.

Caeden had only a few seconds to react; though he'd snatched his hand away from the device immediately, this final drain on his Reserve had been too much. He sank to his knees, only barely registering that the forward section of the capsule was beginning to ripple, warping and melting away to expose the body to the open air.

He couldn't be certain, but as consciousness faded, Caeden could have sworn that the eyes of the man in the coffin began to open.

Chapter 9

Asha slipped into the library.

The darkness of the Decay Clock in the corner indicated the lateness of the hour—well past midnight—but even so, Essence lamps emitted a soft light above every desk. No one was manning the entrance, though she assumed that the librarian was in among the books somewhere. Since the burning of Tol Thane, the Gifted treated their knowledge with a care bordering on obsessiveness. The library was always open, but it was never unattended.

Still, she released a small sigh of relief at the emptiness of the silence, relaxing. She was allowed to be here, but since the battle it sometimes felt as though her every movement was scrutinized—and the less attention she got while she looked for the maps Taeris had mentioned, the better.

"Representative Ashalia."

She jumped, spinning to see a young blond-haired Shadow reclining in the corner, an open book in his lap. He was trying unsuccessfully to hide his amusement at her reaction.

"Brase?" Her eyes narrowed. "Don't do that."

"Sit here or greet you?"

Asha just made a grumbling sound, though she smiled as she did it. Brase was one of the youngest Shadows at the Tol—one of the youngest Shadows anywhere, in fact. He'd failed his Trials last year, but hadn't come to Ilin Illan until after the battle. With the abrupt shortage of Shadows in the city—and a sudden, distinct lack of interest in hiring from the Houses—he'd had no trouble finding a position at the Tol.

121

He was also, Asha had discovered over the past couple of weeks, unintimidated by her. Most of the Shadows—the ones left behind, anyway—treated her the same way that they treated the Gifted, or even Administrators. Their unconditional respect-bordering-on-servitude attitude made her deeply uncomfortable, which in turn made it all but impossible to strike up any friendships.

Brase, though, showed no signs of the weight that seemed to constantly bear down on the others' shoulders. He refused to take a cue from them, too, much to Asha's relief.

She made to continue on into the library, then hesitated.

"How well do you know where everything's shelved now, Brase?"

Brase straightened. "What are you after?"

"Maps. Probably very old." Asha hesitated. "Specifically, of the lower levels of the Tol."

Brase squinted at her. "Planning an adventure?"

"Wanting to be better informed the next time someone tries using those catacombs to invade the city," said Asha firmly.

Brase frowned. "Didn't you block everything off down there, though? Locks, guards, that sort of thing?"

"Just want to be thorough."

Brase cocked his head to the side. " 'Officially' or 'unofficially' thorough?"

Asha coughed. "Let's say unofficially?"

"My favorite kind of thoroughness," announced Brase cheerfully. "I think I know the ones you're talking about. Follow me, Representative, and be dazzled by my map-finding skills."

He started down the main aisle, Asha trailing after him. After a few moments, she realized that Brase was walking with a slight but distinct limp.

"Did something happen to your leg?" She wasn't just asking from politeness. She was all too aware of how badly the Shadows could be treated, even here in the Tol—and she could only imagine how much worse that might have become since the battle. Her position as Representative shielded her from the worst of it, but she knew that the few Shadows who had stayed in the city were far from benefiting from their role in the victory.

"It's nothing," said Brase quickly. His tone indicated embar-

rassment.

"Did someone attack you?" Asha pressed.

"What?" Brase looked back at her, startled. "No. Fates no. Nothing like that." He gave a self-deprecating shrug. "My own clumsiness. I was walking down some stairs this morning and I got a little light-headed. I fell." He sighed. "Right in front of one of the girls from my old school, too—you know, one who actually *passed* the Trials. So not my finest moment."

"Oh." Asha frowned contemplatively as they walked.

Then she swallowed.

"That was this morning, you said?" She glanced across at the young man. "Do you get light-headed often?"

Brase rolled his shoulders again. "Now and then, I suppose. It's actually happened a few times, this past month." He gave her a quizzical look.

Asha didn't respond for a few seconds. It could be nothing.

"The other Shadows," she said. "Have any of them mentioned getting dizzy, too?"

"No," said Brase slowly. "But there's only Dastiel and Reubin working in the library, and I don't really speak with them much. They're not terribly social—by which I mean they never talk to anyone, ever, about anything. Unless one of the Gifted tells them to, of course." His brow furrowed. "Why? Has the same thing been happening to you?"

Asha hesitated. She liked Brase and thought he could be trusted not to spread word of her strange infirmity, but she also didn't want to say too much. "I had something similar happen this morning. Probably just a coincidence." She shrugged, trying to keep her smile light and disinterested. "Still, it might be worth asking the others if they've experienced the same thing. And let me know if it happens to you again, too. No harm in keeping an eye on it. Just between us, though—no need to worry anyone else," she added significantly.

Brase nodded. "Good idea." He didn't press, for which Asha was grateful, though from his expression he understood that there was more to it.

The young man stretched, then indicated a nearby wall, lined with drawers. "Now. Those maps."

Asha refocused. She could investigate this further at a later time.

For now, she needed to concentrate on finding out more about the Sanctuary.

⚭

Asha held her breath as she approached the great steel door.

None of the guards looked around from their mostly drowsy conversation as she stepped carefully past them. The door to the Sanctuary was open—it always was, now, as no one could seem to close it—and Asha slipped into the roughhewn tunnel, focusing on the ground ahead.

Despite her increasing familiarity with this journey, she still found herself nervous every time she entered the Sanctuary. It wasn't just the danger—though that played a part, certainly. The Blind were likely long gone, but at least one of the sha'teth had frequented this space.

Rather, it was more the sense of emptiness that left her unsettled. As she moved along the darkened tunnel toward the distant speck of light, there were no sounds. Not a breeze, not the distant echo of voices, not the scuttling of rats. Only her own breath and quiet footsteps reached her ears.

She carefully skirted the last of the wards she'd helped place, the ones meant to forewarn the Tol should anyone ever try to enter through these tunnels again. It was difficult—the Essence, generated by a Vessel, was whisper-thin and impossible to see—but she'd helped Taeris set them up, and memorized their locations carefully. The last thing she wanted to do was cause a panic upstairs.

She shivered, checking her Reserve wasn't too far depleted from using the Veil. It rarely was and yet a couple of times recently, she'd been surprised to discover that she had less Essence stored than she had expected. She'd been pushing herself hard, though, this past month—harder than most Shadows ever pushed themselves. It stood to reason that her body had been drawing on Essence to keep her going.

She walked through the tunnel, treading carefully; though she could see the glow of the Conduit at the end, she had to trust the smooth floor underfoot for the most part. Her footsteps made little noise, but even the slightest scuffing of her shoes echoed down into the darkness, making her flinch. When she'd come here with

Jin, there had been plenty of other sounds. Conversation, both between them and in the distance. Laughter. Tools at work. The general hubbub of life.

That was all gone now. The silence was dead, grim and oppressive.

Asha blinked as she emerged onto the platform overlooking the Sanctuary, squinting against the initially blinding light of the Conduit. The power flowing through the cylinder was as torrential and terrifyingly beautiful as ever. Even accustomed to the sight as she now was, Asha took a few moments just to watch.

Then she made her way down the stairs, toward the eerily abandoned structures sitting a small distance from the pillar of light. She'd been through each of those houses several times, but there had been no indication of where the former occupants may have gone. The same went for the tavern, the school...everything was simply empty.

She frowned as she studied the school, a squat building big enough for a single class. Of everything, the absence of the children bothered her most. How had they gotten away without anyone noticing? Had they left before the Blind had come through here? There were no bodies, she had been relieved to find—which seemed to indicate that the Shadraehin had moved everyone in time. But exactly *how* she had done that remained a mystery.

Asha pulled out the copy she'd made of the maps Brase had found for her, studying them carefully. They were from a time long past, of course, and didn't show any of the buildings the Shadows had built. But the Conduit—marked as *Cyrariel*, though she had no idea what that meant—was indicated clearly, as was the tunnel she'd just entered through.

She flipped the page, studying some of the other plans. Her map of the catacombs showed just how complicated the warren of tunnels truly was; paths diverged and intersected and twisted everywhere, with many on the map simply ending. Whether that was due to a dead end or a lack of knowledge on the cartographer's behalf, she didn't know.

She was so lost in thought that she nearly didn't register the movement in the corner of her eye.

When she did she spun toward it, stifling a sharp intake of breath.

Two figures walked along no more than a hundred feet away,

silhouetted against the blinding light of the Conduit. A man and a woman.

At first she assumed that they were Shadows, and she took a couple of quick steps toward them.

Then she registered the sinuous movements, the black cloak and hood of one. As her eyes adjusted, she realized that the other had no black marks on her face, either.

She faltered to a stop.

A sha'teth. And...someone talking to it. A woman. Someone not a Shadow, but able to get as close to the Conduit as Asha herself would have dared go. Unafraid of both her surroundings and her company, too, from what Asha could gather from her body language.

Asha froze for several seconds, not taking her eyes from the pair.

She should retreat. Leave. She was hidden by the Veil, and there was no reason to suspect she'd be detected if she simply headed back to the Tol. It was the safe thing to do. If Wirr or Taeris were here, they would be telling her to do exactly that.

But there was a conversation going on. She couldn't hear it, exactly; the voices were low and the two were enough of a distance away. But listening might tell her who the woman was, or what the sha'teth was doing back down here.

It could give her insight into what the enemy was planning next.

Her heart pounded, and she licked her lips nervously. It was a risk, but it was also too good an opportunity to pass up.

She quickly slipped the map back into her pocket, careful to minimize the sound of crinkling as she steadied her breathing, making sure it was as even and silent as possible. Then she crept forward, carefully placing her feet so as not to make any sound. The dead silence meant that the stranger's conversation with the sha'teth would be easy to overhear.

It also meant that any sound Asha made would likely draw attention.

She inched closer, studying the stranger in particular. The woman was young—older than Asha, but not by more than five or six years. Her shoulder-length red hair was arranged in a style Asha hadn't seen before, and her clothes looked finely made.

There was something about her, though. A set to her features, the way she carried herself. Motions jerky, eyes too wide, fiercely intelligent one moment and then glassy the next.

As terrifying as the sha'teth was, it was the stranger who filled Asha with a deep, unsettling sense of dread.

Shivering, she forced herself closer, until the words passing between the sha'teth and the woman became clear.

"...still no sign." The sha'teth's rasping, whispery voice was just as disconcerting as Asha remembered. The way it was speaking, the way it held itself around the woman, seemed...deferential. "You are certain that the Trace you gave us is real?"

The woman gazed directly into the blinding light of the Conduit for several seconds without answering, without blinking. Asha thought she hadn't heard, but eventually she cocked her head to the side.

"Certain?" She gave a laugh, low and throaty, and Asha flinched at the sound. It was raw, tinged with madness. She continued, in a voice that would have been a whisper anywhere except in the deathly silence that surrounded them. "Yes. Certain. As certain as the high tide. As certain as the moon. Certain, certain, *certain.*"

She finally turned to study the sha'teth, leaning in close and peering up under its hood in a childlike motion. "Certainty is a funny thing. Because *you* were certain that you could perform this task as ably as Aelrith. A wish from the mindless, a flight of fancy from the thing that does not breathe? Surely not. And yet you were not made for this purpose. Are you *certain*, Vhalire?"

Asha felt a chill as she processed what had been said, recognized the name from her very first visit here. *When the time comes, do not let Vhalire suffer.* Aelrith's words to her seemed like forever ago now, but those awful moments after it had so casually killed Jin were etched indelibly on her memory.

Ahead, the woman continued to just stoop and stare under the creature's hood, smiling wildly, her face inches from the sha'teth's.

Then, when there was no immediate response, she straightened again with an odd sigh, her gaze sweeping beyond the creature and around the Sanctuary. The action was absent rather than suspicious, but Asha froze even so.

The woman's gaze was about to pass over the space in which Asha stood when the sha'teth rasped again, drawing her attention back.

"Yes." The response was flat, lifeless. It contained neither concern, nor any indication of offense. It was a statement, nothing more or less than that.

The woman stared at the creature silently for several seconds.

Then she screamed.

Asha recoiled instinctively at the sound. It was a shriek of rage, of frustration, confusion and fury and terror all rolled into a single note. The woman turned and as Asha watched wide-eyed, she plunged her hand deep into the Conduit. Within moments she was a pyre of pure energy, as hard to look at as the Conduit itself.

"Lies!" She flung her fist at the nearest building; there was a roar and every stone in the structure exploded, raining debris on the nearby houses. Asha took a stuttering step backward. The point of impact had been some distance away, but it was clear that the woman was unhinged.

"Lies!" Another roar, another building crumbled. "Lies! *Lies!*" Another. Another.

The destruction was away from Asha but she still stood with every muscle tense, prepared to run if it came to it. Thunderous echoes crashed around the cavern as pieces of wall and roof still collapsed; an enormous cloud of dust rose from the area the woman had targeted, thick and slowly billowing outward. Asha kept a close eye on that cloud, too. Dust landing on her would naturally be absorbed into the Veil's protection—she knew this from her tests—but it would make it difficult to breathe. And a single cough could give her away as easily as becoming visible.

Finally the light had drained away from the stranger and Asha could see that she had collapsed to the ground, cradling her hand. There was a choking sound and after a few moments, Asha realized that the woman was sobbing.

"El take it, Vhalire. Are you truth, or another falsehood? El, it hurts. It always hurts, but this feels worse. Sharper. Is this really real?" She shook her head violently as if to pry loose demons from it, even as more tears rolled down her cheeks. "Meldier couldn't craft a good enough version of him, you know. He tried. El knows he tried. It all held up until the end, and I would find him, and the things I would do to him would never be enough. He was my friend, and I did those things, and the dok'en couldn't sustain the fantasy, and it would break, and I would be back again screaming and begging and writhing and the pain would be all I knew and..."

She kept sobbing into the silence for a while.

"This is real, Isiliar. You are free."

The sha'teth's rasp cut through the silence, and Asha blinked. Was she imagining something different in its voice? The slightest softening of tone?

The woman—Isiliar; the name sounded familiar for some reason, but Asha couldn't place it—sniffed, wiping her eyes furiously. She glanced up at the sha'teth.

"I will never be free," she said softly. She slowly uncovered her hand, and it was all Asha could do not to make a sound. It was glistening red, burned; the white of bone showed through in places.

Isiliar closed her eyes and as Asha watched, the flesh began to knit back together. Within moments, the woman was flexing her hand again as if nothing had happened.

"We need to stop him, Vhalire. We *need* to. By El and sun and stars and moon and all the oceans and all the fates, we *need to stop him.*"

"I understand."

"Do you, though? Do you, Vhalire? Can a monster truly understand why another monster must be stopped?" She stared bitterly at the creature, apparently unafraid of insulting it. "Can you truly see how Tal'kamar is deluded, and exactly how his delusion will tear this world asunder? His actions will imprison *every creature* that lives. That *has* lived. That *will ever* live. I know you can *know* that, Vhalire, but do you appreciate it? Does the concept freeze you in your tracks? Do you wake up at night sweating over the consequences of this one man's actions?"

The sha'teth said nothing. Isiliar glared at it for a moment and then her gaze went glassy, focus lost again as she stared blankly into the Conduit.

Suddenly there was movement off to Asha's left; she turned her head to see a small form walking toward the pair. She nearly cried out a warning when she saw who it was.

A little boy—no older than six, she thought—wandered toward the sha'teth and Isiliar with no hesitation, no concern whatsoever.

Asha's warning died in her throat. Something about the stride of the child was off. It was too . . . balanced. Too confident.

No six-year-old walked like that.

Her fears were confirmed when both of the two standing beside the Conduit turned, unsurprised.

"You see," said Isiliar, softly enough that the child would not be able to overhear, shaking her head so that her red locks swayed. "The worst part is that in fighting for the world he wants, he has turned us into monsters, too. He has crafted us into monsters and thieves and death itself . . ." Her eyes were filled with horror as she watched the boy approach.

The child stopped a few feet from Isiliar and the sha'teth.

"Lord Alaris is asking for you. He says that you should not be unprotected until you have your full strength back." The child's voice was eerily calm, too mature for the mouth out of which it came. "He also says that it is dangerous here. Too close. Exposed."

"Which is why I am traveling to Ilshan Gathdel Tir," said Isiliar, sounding close to lucid for once. "Vhalire will send me, and I will use the Cornerstone to return. A day only, creature. Tell him that it is for a day only, and then I shall return."

"He insisted. He says Tal'kamar stored Knowing with you for a reason."

Isiliar did not answer straight away, staring off into the distance again. Just when Asha thought she would not respond at all, though, her attention snapped back to the present.

"I tell you as I told him: I do not *know* the reason. Besides, Alaris should be concentrating on finding one of the others—one more and the ilshara will come down. So I am leaving, abomination. You will simply have to explain to Alaris that you could not stop me. Unless you actually wish to try, of course. If you desire to end your two years early, you are welcome to do your best." She licked her lips, eyes suddenly wide and wild, daring. "In fact, I think I would *like* you to try."

The boy simply inclined his head. Asha shivered as she watched him. His eyes were . . . empty. Lifeless.

Asha wasn't certain, but she suspected that he was an Echo.

"He will be angry, Lady Isiliar. But I shall tell him," said the child.

Isiliar held her pose for a moment longer and then sighed, turning to the sha'teth. "Do you have anything more to tell me? A clue, a hint, a shadow of an idea?"

"No," said the sha'teth.

"Nothing he is *willing* to tell you." The Echo stared at the sha'teth challengingly. "She has been sighted in the lower levels again. The one you asked about."

Isiliar turned toward the child. "The one whom Tal'kamar is protecting?"

"Yes." The boy continued to gaze at the sha'teth intently. "You should not trust this one. He has been tainted; his release was not unconditional. We all know it."

"At least I am imperfect by design. You are imperfect by nature." The sha'teth's rasp was as flat as always.

The Echo hissed as if burned, but said nothing in response.

The woman gave the sha'teth a rebuking look. "Vhalire, Vhalire," she said ruefully. "A point, regardless of whether it is your fault. I do wish that the others hadn't let Tal'kamar turn you. The blindness of friendship encompasses all, sometimes." She turned back to the Echo, evidently not expecting a response. "It matters not. If you get the opportunity—if you are certain that it can be done—then kill her. Otherwise, assume as we have: that Tal'kamar has Seen her future, which means that our attempts will fail. And a failed attempt will only forewarn her, and those around her. So make no foolish moves."

The Echo scowled at that, but eventually nodded.

Isiliar glanced across at the sha'teth. "Come, Vhalire. Real or imagined, we go home." A dreamy half smile slid across her face, somehow more terrifying than her usual expression. "Home."

Vhalire stepped forward, gesturing at the Conduit. Essence began to spin and weave itself out of the cylinder and into what looked like a doorway.

Immediately, the groan and grind of stone against stone filled the air, and Asha's angle allowed her to see through the opening and into ... somewhere else.

An enormous room lay on the other side of the doorway but everything glinted, made of steel and black polished stone. As

Asha watched, massive pieces of the floor began to shift, the seemingly random pattern slowly replaced by a thin strip of black stone leading away from the portal, with steel squares on either side. There was a crackling sound as some of the steel snapped neatly together, an escape of some form of energy.

Isiliar stepped through onto the black stone, followed closely by the sha'teth. The doorway vanished.

Asha continued to stare wide-eyed for a few moments, eventually recovering herself enough to turn her attention to the young boy. He gazed at the Conduit for a while, then calmly turned and began walking.

He was reporting to someone else—so there were clearly others down here.

She still wanted nothing more than to leave, but Asha knew that she had to follow him.

She trailed after the Echo, trying to keep a safe distance; though the creature was only inhabiting a child, she'd seen how dangerous they could be. She frowned to herself as she watched the boy clamber over some of the debris Isiliar had created, movements far too sure for someone of that age. Was it one of the Shadows' children? She didn't recognize him, but it would make sense. Her stomach churned at the thought.

Before long, she realized where the Echo was heading.

Directly for the catacombs.

Asha swallowed, vacillating as the young boy reached the pitch-black entrance, pausing to light a lantern it had evidently hung after its inward journey. She had to make the choice. She had maps but they were incomplete, old. It was still a big risk.

The Shadows could be down here, though—hostages or worse. Their children, too.

She came to a decision.

Heart pounding, she crept after the Echo.

At first, she found that it wasn't too difficult to follow the creature; it moved at a slow enough pace, and she needed only to stay close enough to be able to use the light of its lantern. The first few tunnels they traveled through were wide and straight, easy enough for Asha to hang back without fear of being detected.

132   Then they reached the first junction.

The tunnel had been growing tighter and tighter as they'd progressed, until the passage walls were too close for two people to walk side by side. The development concerned Asha a little—if the Echo decided to turn around and head back toward her, she would have to keep ahead of it or risk it bumping into her.

Then they emerged into a room, no more than twenty feet wide on each side. There were seven exits, identical dark holes in the wall.

The Echo turned unerringly for the third one along.

Once they began down this new tunnel, Asha finally understood that *this* was truly the beginning of the catacombs. The claustrophobically tight passageway twisted and turned every ten paces or so; suddenly there were entrances to new tunnels every half minute. The twists meant that Asha had to walk closer to the Echo now, otherwise the corners hid the light from her, and she risked stumbling over ground that she could not see.

She crept along as quietly as she could, holding her breath half the time, resisting the urge to pull out a map to try and figure out exactly where she was. If she was still on the maps at all, of course. She'd given up trying to remember each of the turns they'd taken.

For a while, the Echo seemed focused forward. It moved at a slow but steady pace, never looking behind, never making a sound.

Then the tunnels became even narrower, even more winding. Asha was fearful of letting the young boy's lantern out of her sight now, despite the danger of being so close. The Echo had already made so many turns into side passages that Asha knew, beyond any doubt, that if she lost her quarry—if she were left alone here—then this place would become her tomb. Even *with* a light, there was no way that she could find her way back.

It was thirty minutes into their journey when her foot caught a stray stone, sending it skittering across the ground. A small thing, but to Asha it sounded like thunder itself.

Her stomach clenched and she froze, holding her breath. The Echo kept walking as if it hadn't noticed, but Asha saw the slightest hesitation, the tiniest clenching of muscles in the neck.

It had heard.

Gritting her teeth, she forced herself to keep creeping after it, allowing herself as much distance in between as she dared.

They walked on for another minute, and Asha began to wonder whether she'd imagined the Echo's reaction to her mistake.

The child rounded a corner up ahead and without warning, the lantern went out.

The sudden darkness was utterly, completely blinding. Asha bit back a gasp of surprise, forcing her body into motion despite the sudden spike of terror that threatened to freeze her to the spot. She took a swift, silent step to the side and then lay flat on the ground, positioning herself against the wall as best she could. The passageway was too narrow for anything else.

A moment later, she heard the faintest sound of fingers brushing against rock coming toward her.

"Are you here, flesh?" That youthful voice, not a body's length from her position, sent a shiver of cold horror down Asha's spine. "Surely you are not so brave. Surely you are not so foolhardy. If you are, I think the odds are now even, yes? If I find you, there will be no mercy."

Asha stopped breathing, closing her eyes. Her vision was useless to her here anyway, and it helped her to focus only on sounds.

The soft brushing of skin against rock came slowly closer, moving at chest height along the wall opposite. Asha compelled herself to remain motionless as it passed by her position. It might have been her imagination, but she fancied that she felt a slight breeze against her face from the child's footsteps.

The sound continued for a few more seconds, then stopped. Asha bit her tongue, focusing on the pain to prevent herself from panicking.

The noise started again—this time on her side of the wall. For a mad second, she considered rolling to the other side of the passageway, pushing herself up against the wall that the Echo had already gone along.

She resisted the urge, knowing that the sound would give her away as surely as crying out. The boy was brushing his hand against the wall, but Asha was lying on her side, flat against it. So long as the Echo didn't nudge her with its foot, she would be all right.

"Are you here, flesh?" It was a whisper, but so close that it almost made Asha flinch. Right above her, in fact, as was the sound of brushing fingers.

Suddenly there was a spark and the lantern flared to life again, burning like the sun even behind the lids of Asha's eyes. She didn't dare open them, didn't dare move, but it couldn't have been more than a couple of feet from her face.

"Hmm." The young boy sounded dissatisfied.

Then the light was moving away from her again.

Asha opened her eyes, her relief nearly as hard to keep silent as her terror had been. The Echo was pressing on; already it had rounded a corner, the glow of its lantern fading.

Asha scrambled to her feet as silently as she could and hurried after it, heartbeat so loud that she was a little concerned that the Echo would somehow be able to hear it.

For a few more minutes they continued as before, and Asha began to calm. The Echo appeared more cautious than it had been, was moving more slowly. But it didn't say anything more.

Then, as abruptly as the first time, the light vanished.

Asha froze, holding her breath and immediately closing her eyes this time, concentrating on sounds once again. Rather than footsteps coming toward her, though, there was a slight receding scuffling, and then . . . nothing.

Asha's brow furrowed, then her heart dropped as she understood what had happened. The Echo hadn't stopped being suspicious at all.

It had killed the light, then hurried ahead in order to lose her.

And it had succeeded. She couldn't move in the darkness, not without making a significant amount of noise. The Echo had undoubtedly waited for its moment, too, ensuring that there was one of the rooms with branching pathways up ahead. There could be as many as a dozen exits from it, and she would have no way of knowing which one the creature had taken.

She leaned against the wall, taking a few slow, deep breaths to keep the fear at bay. Quietly, though. It was entirely possible that she was wrong and that the Echo was waiting for her to panic, to rush blindly after it and make noise in the process. She had no intention of taking that risk.

She made herself assess the situation. She was lost—there was no getting around that. She couldn't even see her maps in the pitch black, and she wouldn't be able to determine her location on them anyway after taking so many turns. The catacombs were vast and tangled; she could wander aimlessly for weeks in the maze down here without finding an exit.

Asha had made a mistake following the Echo, but there would be time enough to berate herself once she was out.

For now, she had two real options. The first was to try and find her way back; her eyes were adjusting, and she could see that there was the faintest light being emitted from the walls, so there was a chance—a very slim chance—that she could recognize enough twists and turns to make her way back to the Sanctuary. It was a tempting option, the one that would allow her to be proactive, to distract herself from the realities of the situation. The one that would make her feel like she was *doing* something.

But she knew, as soon as she considered it, that the alternative was better. Stay where she was. Be patient. Whatever the Echo was doing down here, it clearly wasn't working alone. In fact, now that she thought about it, Isiliar and the sha'teth had indicated that they would be joining the Echo and whomever else was down here soon enough. It was logical that they would then take the same route.

If Asha moved, if she tried to find her own way and became lost, she would miss the opportunity to follow them.

She gritted her teeth. She had the food she'd brought down for a meal: rationed carefully, that was enough to last at least a couple of days. She hated the idea of just sitting there in the dark, waiting and hoping, constantly afraid both of being found and of not seeing anyone. But at least this way, at worst, she still had the option of a last-ditch attempt to find her way back.

She listened for another few moments, squinting into the near darkness of her surroundings for any sign of movement.

Then she deactivated the Veil.

When nothing happened, she squeezed her eyes shut in relief, exhaling heavily.

Moving slowly, she made her way forward until she reached the next junction, a careful traversal of its edges revealing nine different exits from the room. Like most of the other such junctions, there was also more space at the sides—a more secure place for Asha to sit, without having to worry about being tripped over if someone took her by surprise.

She wedged herself into the most out-of-the-way corner, nestling the Veil in her hands. She wouldn't use it for now—not while she was so alert, anyway. The drain on her Essence wasn't a necessary one, and she could activate it the moment that she heard or saw something. She would have to use it again if she became sleepy later on, but she would deal with that if and when the time came.

Trying to keep the terror at bay, she released a few steadying breaths into the darkness, and settled down to wait.

Chapter 10

Davian exhaled as he walked through the Tol's Essence-lit eastern gate and onto the wide but busy pathways of Outer Ward.

The trip back from Prythe had been a nervous one, filled with hesitant pauses to check whether anyone was trailing him through the steadily encroaching darkness. He'd seen nothing, but if he was right—if an Augur had truly Controlled someone simply to speak with him—it wouldn't take much for them to remain hidden. The somewhat familiar surrounds of Tol Shen had never felt friendlier, even the passing glances from the Gifted suddenly seeming less hostile than usual.

He didn't loiter before heading for Inner Ward though, hurrying through the connecting tunnel with a wave of his silver armband. A few minutes later, after a surprisingly polite and helpful conversation with the guards outside the Augurs' residence, he found himself headed for the Inner Archive.

The Inner Archive was a large library that, while not close to the size of the Great Library in Deilannis, still rivaled anything else Davian had seen. Each ward had its own Archive, he knew, but the breadth and depth of knowledge available varied greatly between them. He had been largely unimpressed with his sole visit to the Outer Archive, which appeared focused more toward basic texts and theory for the newer Gifted students. And he and Ishelle hadn't been inside the Central Archive yet, though an eventual visit had been promised. Much to his frustration, Davian suspected that any truly useful tomes—anything relating to the Boundary, or even Augurs for that matter—would be stored there.

Soon reaching the Inner Archive, he hurried beneath its towering archway of an entrance and inside, breathing out when he finally spotted Ishelle, who was reclining at a table in the corner and reading by the gentle light of an Essence globe.

"I need your help," he said as he slid into the chair opposite her.

Ishelle didn't look up from her book. "I know."

Davian grunted. "Very funny. I think there might be another Augur in Prythe."

Ishelle straightened, shutting the tome she'd been reading and sliding it to one side. "What?"

Davian quickly related what had happened, eliciting an unsurprised eye roll when he revealed that Thameron had been following him. When he described the singer's odd memory loss, though, Ishelle leaned back.

"Fates," she murmured. "Two in a day." She smiled slightly, watching Davian's reaction.

Davian opened his mouth to respond, then caught himself. He stared at Ishelle for a few moments in confusion, then slowly matched her expression.

"Someone came forward?"

"You chose the wrong afternoon to take a break. Only two troublemakers...and our first genuine Augur." Her smile widened at the excitement in Davian's expression.

"You're certain?"

"He let me Read him. I'm certain."

Davian gave a short, loud laugh, pushing back his chair eagerly and ignoring the irritated looks from the Gifted studying in the Archive. "So where is he?"

Ishelle waved him back into his seat. "His name's Rohin, and he's in a meeting with the Elders—which I said we wouldn't interrupt," she said firmly. "We went through some basic tests, though. He doesn't seem particularly strong in any one area—he's got some talent Reading people, but I wouldn't say he's better at it than you or I. And he says he's only had about a half-dozen visions in the past year. All minor, personal things." She shrugged. "No training. No experience. He only figured out what he was a few months ago, and he's been busy hiding it from everyone ever since. So don't expect too much from him."

Davian nodded; it was hardly surprising that the newcomer wasn't especially skilled. Davian's time in Deilannis had given him a strong foundation in all the Augur abilities, and Ishelle had been training for years. They'd both known that new Augurs would need nurturing. It didn't detract from his excitement.

"So he was here while I was in Prythe. He definitely wasn't the one who spoke to me," he mused. "If Rohin won't be available for a while, do you feel like a trip into the city?"

Ishelle hesitated, then shook her head. "The Council has called everyone to the Great Hall this evening, to introduce him formally to all the Gifted once they're done with their meeting. At least one of us should be here when that happens."

"When?"

"Could be an hour, could be three." Ishelle shrugged. "They weren't specific."

Davian grunted. He was eager to meet the new Augur, but he didn't want to let the one in Prythe slip away, either. He'd come back because he'd wanted Ishelle's presence in the event that he was attacked. But if getting rid of Thameron had been the first step toward the Augur in the city making contact, Davian wanted to provide them with another chance soon—before whomever it was decided that the risk wasn't worth it and left again.

"You're going back, I take it?" said Ishelle, though it was more statement than question.

Davian inclined his head. "I think I should. You'll have to pass on my apologies," he added with sincere regret. He sighed, standing; there was no point in delaying. "What's Rohin like?"

Ishelle shrugged. "He's our age, of course. He seemed . . . nice, I suppose. I didn't get much of an opportunity to talk to him, and I *did* go into that meeting half expecting another would-be assassin, but . . ." She grinned. "I'm sure we'll all get along. Fates, believe it or not, even the *Elders* seemed to like him."

Davian felt his eyebrows raise a little. "I don't know whether to be impressed or worried." He smirked. "Or wonder whether all the Elders have suddenly stopped using their shields."

Ishelle snorted, glancing around surreptitiously. "Don't even joke about that." Her smile faded. "Don't leave yourself open to whomever this is in the city, either. Be careful out there."

Davian nodded a grim acknowledgment, then set out for Prythe once again.

Davian set down his empty cup, trying not to look exasperated as he surveyed the bustling, noisy tavern.

It was late, and both his patience and confidence were rapidly running thin. He'd been here, alone at a table, for close to an hour; preceding that he'd walked the torchlit streets of Prythe for closer to two, retracing his steps from earlier that day and giving anyone who wanted to approach him plenty of opportunity.

Thus far, no one had even looked at him twice.

There was no one from the Tol following him this time to scare them off, either. He suspected Thameron had related the afternoon's incident to the Council—or, possibly, everyone was too distracted by news of the new Augur to worry about what Davian got up to for an evening in Prythe. Either way, he was confident that he wasn't being watched by one of the Gifted.

Unfortunately, it didn't seem to have made a difference.

He sighed, silently berating himself. The longer he'd been here, the more foolish this idea had seemed. He had no idea how the Augur had recognized him earlier, and there was no telling if they'd realize he was back in the city. If it had *been* an Augur. With so much time to think, his doubts over even that much had been steadily growing.

He braced himself against the table and stood, pressing a coin onto its surface and nodding politely to the barkeep as he headed for the door. There was no point in staying; he'd checked the tavern's customers several times for any sign of Control, and even briefly Read each of them to ensure that the Augur hadn't come to follow him in person. He should have stayed at the Tol to meet Rohin. This had been a waste of time.

The crush of people in this section of the city, despite the late hour, immediately enveloped him when he hit the street; he moved slowly through the crowds in the general direction of the Tol, deep in thought.

There *was* one last thing he could try—the same thing that he'd done to Thameron that morning. It felt like it was probably not worth the effort, but he was here now. It couldn't hurt.

He made the decision abruptly and moved to the side, ducking into a dimly lit side alley and then hurrying as quickly as he could without drawing attention. Halfway along he slipped into an even narrower alley, this one entirely empty and dark, little more than a couple of feet of space between two buildings. He stopped just inside and turned, closing his eyes.

He pushed through kan, extending his senses, carefully focusing as bright silhouettes became sharp all around him. Other sources of Essence—the flame from the fire in a nearby kitchen, two cats stalking along the roof, flowers in the garden over to the right—he mentally filtered out, leaving only the people in his immediate vicinity. Within moments he'd isolated the images of the crowd and was able to watch their movements.

One silhouette immediately stood out. It was cutting its way directly toward his position, weaving around others with a definite sense of purpose.

Davian's heart skipped a beat. He let the other figures fade from his mind, giving this one his full attention. It paused when it came to the mouth of the alley, and Davian knew his pursuer was peering down it, no doubt trying to determine where he'd gone. They were close—close enough that Davian could probably emerge from his hiding spot and see their face, perhaps even catch them—but he held back.

There was something else, almost imperceptible. Certainly impossible to see if he hadn't been studying this one person with such intense focus.

A minute thread of kan stretched away from the silhouette.

The person following him was being Controlled.

He took a steadying breath. The Augur had known where he was for a while, presumably . . . but they hadn't taken the opportunity to approach him, didn't seem to want to talk.

He quickly made himself invisible as whoever was being Controlled started down the alley. The mesh for invisibility used very fine strands of kan, and someone being Controlled wouldn't be able to look for it anyway. Unless the Augur was close by, there was no way they would be able to spot him.

A few moments later someone appeared a few feet in front of him, pausing to peer down the narrow gap in which he'd concealed himself. Her features were difficult to make out beneath a tightly drawn hood but it was clearly a young woman, one he thought looked no older than he. For a moment Davian worried that she was going to walk toward him—he couldn't move from beneath the mesh of kan without revealing himself, and he wouldn't be able to physically avoid her in this narrow space—but she gave a slight, puzzled frown and then moved on.

Davian waited until she'd exited the alley and then sprang into motion, ducking back the way he'd come, carefully tracing the line of kan he'd spotted back through the crowd. It was difficult, maintaining his awareness of what was around him while following the thread—he earned more than a few irritated stares from people as he bumped into them—but for the most part, he avoided notice.

Before long, he found the source.

The Augur was standing at the mouth of a narrow gap between two buildings, alone, leaning against the wall and watching those going past with keen interest. The light here was dim, but enough for Davian to see that it was a young man with no black marks on his face—not Scyner, then, whom Asha had described as a Shadow in his forties.

Davian studied him for a moment and then circled around the building, coming up behind the other Augur. He carefully prepared a kan blade, then gripped the stranger's shoulder.

"Stay calm," he growled, leaning forward so that he could murmur the words into the young man's ear. "I just want to have a chat about why you're following me."

The stranger flinched away and tried to use Essence, but Davian was ready; he slashed out with the kan blade, ending the attempt to draw energy before his stalker could utilize it. Davian followed that by slamming down a Disruption shield. It was nowhere near as good as Ishelle's, but it would do what he needed it to.

"I doubt you want Administration on top of us, so don't try that again," Davian muttered impatiently. "We're both Augurs. Let's talk."

The stranger's shoulders slumped. "Fine," he said, not turning. He rubbed his forehead. "Fates. You're better than I realized."

Davian grunted. "You can stop Controlling that girl you had following me, now, too."

Then he frowned. The line of kan hadn't dissipated, so he knew that the Augur hadn't broken the connection. But the direction of that line had changed.

Now it led behind him.

"I'm flattered that you think I'm in charge," said the young man wryly.

Pain blossomed at the base of Davian's skull, and everything went black.

Chapter 11

The voice seeped through the pain, a whisper among screams.

"Wake up, Devaed," it growled again, quiet yet hard as stone.

Every nerve felt like it was firing in exquisite agony; Caeden's eyes fluttered open and he began to jerk desperately, manically, panicking as he took in the hundreds of razor-edged needles that pierced his body. Trying to extricate himself only made it worse, though, if that were possible. He gave a clawing, rasping groan and forced himself to still.

His gaze lifted slowly from the quivering black slivers protruding from his chest, his vision tinged red.

A man stood in front of him, watching impassively. He was tall, his skin a deep brown, eyes gray and cold and focused calmly on his. He did not look like he was taking pleasure in Caeden's situation, but neither did he seem sympathetic.

"You...you were in here," Caeden gasped, mind finally fitting the pieces together.

"Still," agreed the man quietly. "Even after all this time. And every time I woke up, every time I went through the Shift, I thought about what you said when you put me in there." He leaned forward, expression going as still and cold as ice. "*I would take your place if I could.*"

Caeden gave a sobbing moan in response, unable to formulate anything except the most basic thoughts. The man knew him. The man hated him. He was helpless.

"Why did you come here? Why did you release me?"

Caeden closed his eyes. He needed to lie but his thoughts were fragmented, torn apart by the pain before they had a chance to fully form.

"I need your help," he gasped.

The man laughed, a genuinely surprised sound. "My help? My *help*?" He stared at Caeden in bewilderment. "Have you switched sides yet again, old friend? Why in the One God's name would I help you?"

Caeden drew a shaky breath. "Lyth," he whispered.

His torturer's smile faded.

"Ah," he said, nodding to himself. He leaned over; when he straightened again he was holding Licanius, examining it with fascination. "So this is it? This is the last sword Andrael ever forged?" He turned it over in his hands, but Caeden could see the care with which he handled the blade. He knew of what it was capable. A ripple of panic ran through him.

"I never saw it, you know," the stranger continued, tone almost conversational as he looked it over. "We talked about it so much, but this is the first time…" He squinted, spotting the inscription. " 'For those who need me most'? He was never shy about wanting it to end, was he? You, on the other hand…"

He waved his hand dismissively, as if suddenly realizing that he was talking mostly to himself. "And there's the trap. I use Licanius on you, and I have no idea how to stop the Lyth coming for the rest of us. Which I can only assume that you do, if you agreed to Andrael's binding. Because even in your madness, Devaed, you were never a fool. More's the pity." He tossed the blade aside, looking half-amused and half-disgusted. "So where is Asar, then? Waiting on the edge of the Plains like a frightened child, I suppose?"

Caeden was unable to hide a flicker of emotion at the name; the man saw his grimace and froze, eyes narrowing as he studied Caeden's expression.

"He's dead?" He glanced back at the sword on the ground. "You *killed* him?" His face transformed into a mask of pure anger. He moved as if to retrieve the blade and from the sense of purpose to his stride, Caeden could guess on his next course of action.

"Not me," gasped Caeden quickly. "A woman." He shook

his head, but the movement sent blinding torture through every nerve. "She...not my wife," he murmured hazily, knowing the words would be close to unintelligible.

It was enough, though. The man stopped dead.

"Ah." The stranger's shoulders slumped, the tension draining from his stance. "I see."

He said something else, but that was the last Caeden heard.

The voice faded.

Caeden paused in the doorway, not wanting to interrupt Ell as she sang softly to herself.

He recognized the tune after a few moments—sad and slow, the haunting melody had always been one of her favorites. He closed his eyes as Ell's voice drifted through the room, clear and beautiful as always, each note shimmering in the air.

The dead know not on what they lay
The dead fear not the silent ground
The dead hear not what people say
The dead care not if they are found

The dead feel not if bones are set
The dead think not of battles lost
The dead dwell not on their regret
The dead remember not the cost

The dead have now their struggles ceased
The dead long not for what may be
The dead are gone, and now know peace
The dead live on in memory

He opened his eyes again, sighing as the last strains faded. Those words took on a very different meaning for him now.

"I never asked why you liked that song so much," he realized softly. "Most people only sing dirges at funerals, you know."

Ell looked over her shoulder, smiling and giving a slight shrug.

"It makes me . . . feel, I suppose," she said. "It's what any good song should do."

Caeden just nodded.

Ell noticed his expression and stopped, her eyes searching his. "Are you all right?" Suddenly she grimaced, closing her eyes as she understood. "Ah, Tal. Of all the El-cursed things to sing, after what you've been through. I'm so sorry."

Caeden swallowed the emotion again and gave a half-laugh. "It's not sadness," he assured her. "It's . . . amazement. As if this is a dream." His hands shook a little. "A dream I'm terrified of waking from."

Ell stepped forward, taking his hands in hers. "There's no need to be afraid," she said with a gentle smile.

It had been a day since he'd woken from his drunken stupor to find Ell sitting pensively at his side, just as beautiful as in his memories. At first he'd thought he was hallucinating; he'd simply gaped at her, mute, desperately grasping for ways to explain what he was seeing.

Then she'd asked him how he'd known her name. She was cautious of him—afraid, even, given how different he now looked— but she'd heard him calling out to her, and her curiosity had led her to stay despite his apparent insanity.

So he'd haltingly explained as they sat there in that grimy, deserted tavern, still not quite believing that he was talking to his wife. In the end, he'd related almost everything. Her apparent death, though he couldn't help but omit what he'd tried to do—what he'd done—directly after. His attempts at suicide, the last of which had led to his waking up a few days from this village in a body not his own, unable to speak the language, and with no idea of how much time had passed or where this continent was in relation to home.

Ell had listened silently, her skeptical look turning to disbelief and then cautious excitement as she heard details that only Caeden could have known. And when he'd finished, she'd embraced him, weeping for joy.

It had been only at the feel of her arms around his shoulders, the scent of her hair in his nostrils, that Caeden had finally under-
stood that it was real.

He'd wept then, too.

After a while Ell had told him her story, simple though it was. She remembered what had happened at the wedding, but only up to leaving him at the wedding table in Caer Lyordas. After that she'd woken up here, in Elhyris, though perhaps a hundred miles to the north.

She'd wandered ever since. She would arrive at a village, stay for long enough to work odd jobs, earn some money, and improve her understanding of the language. She would ask about her homeland, about even rumors of Ilshan Gathdel Syn or the Scion War or the Crystalline Palaces. And then, when she was certain that no one knew anything, she would move on.

For five years, she had done this. All searching for a way back to him.

He smiled at her and she smiled back, though like everything else since he'd woken it was…different from how he remembered, somehow. Hesitant, though he couldn't put his finger on exactly how. He shook his head to himself. It was his imagination, trying to find fault in order to comprehend the miracle, to try and force it into a perspective that he could more easily grasp.

And perhaps some of it was him, too. He knew he'd changed. Maybe Ell was cautious because she saw that every time he looked at her, he couldn't help but remember what he'd done. Remember what it had taken to bring her back from the dead.

Would she act the same if she knew what he'd sacrificed to keep her alive? He assumed that it had been his actions at the wedding that had somehow saved her, brought her here. He would tell her, eventually—he had to—but for now, all he wanted was to be with her. To not have to think about anything else but her, alive and well and with him.

Ell watched him for a moment longer, his hands in hers. Then she kissed him lightly on the cheek and stepped back again, gesturing around.

"This is a nice house," she observed. "But why no mirrors?"

Caeden rolled his shoulders uncomfortably. "I…had them removed."

Ell nodded slowly, studying his face. "Of course." She smoothed back her hair, frowning up at the intricately detailed vaulted ceilings. "I assume being reincarnated didn't come with a lot of gold, though, so—how did you afford all of this?"

Caeden grinned, shaking his head. "I've been hunting Vaal," he explained.

"Vaal? Aren't they...? Oh."

Caeden nodded. The Vaal were creatures of the night, roughly four feet long and scorpionlike. Their armored backs sprouted three long tails when disturbed, each one with barbs coated with poison that could kill a man within a few minutes. They were completely black, virtually impossible to see in the darkness, and moved in packs of up to twenty. Thankfully for the local populace, they also kept to their own section of forest.

A Vaal's blood could cure any sickness, which is why a single one of the creatures could fetch a year's wages. But nobody was foolish enough to actually hunt them—not unless they were desperate beyond measure.

Caeden unconsciously rubbed at his arm, though there were no puncture marks there now, nor any sign of the wounds that inevitably covered his body each night. He died often during the hunt—less on each subsequent trip, but still many times over. He was becoming a better and better woodsman, able to flit so silently through the forest that often not even the sharp-eared Vaal heard him before he first struck.

Even so, there was no way to attack one of the pack without the others sensing it—and once they knew that he was there, there was no recourse but to ignore their barbs for as long as he could. He'd move from creature to creature as they swarmed him, flipping them and snapping their necks as fast as possible before the poison did its damage, trying to ignore the unsettling feeling of his heart constricting, slowing, and then finally stopping altogether.

He would wake again a few hours later, the remaining Vaal gone along with his wounds, the bodies of the creatures he had killed scattered nearby. Returning with them each morning had made him a legend within the township—one even more mysterious thanks to the days he spent barely able to walk in the tavern.

It was only when he'd realized that he was earning more coin than he could spend on drink that he'd bought this house. Lav-

ish though it was, it had been practically an afterthought; after a year or two of sleeping by the road, he had become accustomed to hard beds and cold nights. Since he'd arrived here, he had found himself caring little for things like comfort.

Ell looked at him, a little worriedly. "I know your...ability means that they can't kill you," she said. "But there must be less painful ways to make a living."

Caeden nodded slowly. "Perhaps I'll do something else now," he acceded, trying to keep the reluctance from his voice. He didn't try explaining that he hadn't done it for the money, hadn't done it to "make a living."

He'd done it because those blessed few hours, after the poison had taken effect, were the only times that he got anything close to something resembling sleep.

He grimaced. Looking at Ell now, so beautiful in the afternoon sun, he suddenly understood that that wasn't going to change. He was fiercely happy that she was alive, but it didn't alter what he'd done five years ago.

He had to tell her the truth. It would hurt her, but there were some lies that were too big, too poisonous for a relationship to survive. He could drive her away with another lie—that he didn't love her anymore, or something equally trite—but he knew that she wouldn't believe it. She would pursue him to the ends of the earth until she had the truth.

"Ell," he said heavily. "I have something to tell you. About the night...about the night of our wedding."

The light in Ell's eyes died, and she suddenly looked nervous. "No." She walked forward and stood up straight, meeting his gaze firmly. "Not yet."

Caeden frowned. "Ell, I have to tell you. It's important."

Ell paused, then reluctantly nodded, sweeping a strand of her long, straight black hair from her face as she sat again. It was a familiar motion, one Caeden recognized all too well. For some reason, his heart ached to see it.

Slowly, haltingly, he told her of what had happened that night. How he'd found her. How he'd chased the priest responsible, killed him, filled with so much rage and pain that he could barely understand what he was doing.

153

And then how he'd tried to bring her back. How he'd tried to use that strange power—the one he hadn't been able to tap again since—to buy her life with countless others.

There was a long silence after he had finished, and he stared at the floor, unable to watch Ell's reaction. He knew her, knew that she could not let this pass.

Then there was a hand gently cupping his chin, lifting his face. He looked up in surprise to find Ell gazing at him.

Her eyes were sad, but they were not shocked. Not filled with disgust or fear or rebuke.

"I know, Tal'kamar," she whispered. She swallowed, leaning forward so that her eyes were level with his. "I've known since I woke. I remember the bodies. I remember you, standing there like some ancient god, terrible and wonderful, giving me life again."

Caeden blinked back tears of relieved confusion, heart suddenly twisting in unexpected directions. Ell knew?

"I'm...I'm sorry," he choked out. Ell held him close, smoothing back his hair as tears started to trickle down his cheeks. "I'm so, so sorry."

They stayed like that for a long time.

The pain was everywhere, burning, hot and sharp and all-encompassing.

Caeden began to shake again and he tried to force open his eyes but couldn't, tried to order his fractured consciousness, but the excruciating crash of emotions and sensations was too much. He opened his mouth to moan, but no sound came out.

He scrabbled to focus amid the nightmare, grasping desperately at fragments of realization. The woman from the Wells, the one who had killed Asar...it had been Ell. His wife. She hadn't been lying. Somehow, she hadn't been lying.

He tried to understand what that might mean, but his thoughts were drowned out by the thundering roar of blood in his ears.

"Do you have to go?" asked Ell quietly.

Caeden pulled on his boots, forcing a smile as he watched the last of the sunset fade through the window. "We could use the gold," he said, deflecting the question. "I spent too much and saved too little, I'm afraid."

It was true, but not really the reason he had decided to hunt Vaal tonight. Despite having had Ell back for close to a month, he still couldn't sleep. Every time he tried, he went back to Caer Lyordas, took his friends' and family's lives all over again. Only this time, at the end, he'd saved Ell...and when she awoke and saw what he'd done, she couldn't look at him. And he was left alone.

That was what he had expected Ell to do, when he had told her. Even after discovering that she had somehow known all along—had had five years to process it, five years to come to terms with it—she still wasn't acting the way he'd thought she would. He saw none of the pain he had caused when he looked into her eyes. Only the joy of seeing him, and...an absence. Those perfect pools of deep blue were most certainly Ell's, and yet sometimes it felt as though he were looking at a different person.

And so he hunted at night still, to clear his head, to get the dreamless rest from reality that he could not seem to find elsewhere.

Ell looked at him for a while, and Caeden got the distinct impression that she knew there was more to it. Eventually, though, she nodded. "I hope it goes well," she said quietly. She sighed. "And be careful, Tal. I know you're invincible and immortal and so on, but that doesn't mean I'm not terrified of losing you again."

Caeden smiled at that, meeting her blue-eyed gaze. Then he stood, stretching.

"I will. Don't worry. I'll be back before dawn," he promised.

He slipped out the door, exhaling as he felt the cool night air on his face. The days in Elhyris were hot and damp, tropical; his skin always felt clammy while the sun was out. The nights, though...the nights were fresh and clean, crisp, every trace of moisture vanished from the air. He didn't understand why; the weather here was still beyond his comprehension, even after five years. But night was by far his favorite time. It woke him up. Made him feel alive again.

Still, he quickly found his thoughts weighing on him as he walked down toward the dingily torchlit streets of Ashmal. He'd felt—more and more, over the past couple of weeks—that he was 155 doing Ell a disservice. That perhaps she was staying with him out of a sense of obligation, because he'd saved her life and her leaving him would mean it was for nothing. Perhaps she was afraid of what he would do, too, if she left—remembered how he had been when she'd found him, and couldn't bear the thought of him returning to that wretched state.

He knew her well enough to know that that would be something Ell would do. Sacrifice herself, her own happiness, because someone she cared for needed it.

His dark thoughts were evidently reflected on his face, for the few people still out in Ashmal scurried away as he approached. Some gave him a respectful nod and one even went so far as to bow slightly, but he barely noticed. These people eked out a living here, some legitimately, but most through criminal endeavor. He took neither pleasure nor pride in their awe.

Soon enough he was through the town and into the Everwood. The moon was bright tonight, making navigation easier, though the close-growing, gnarled trees with their enormous leaves still blocked out most of the light. He had a regular path now, a trail he'd beaten over countless journeys just like this. Even in pitch black, he could usually make his way with a minimum of effort.

Eventually he waded through the small, murky stream that marked the Vaal border, grimacing as the tiny fish that swam there at night nipped at his ankles. The Vaal did not like water, he'd discovered—probably the main reason that their territory hadn't advanced right into Ashmal itself. Unlike the locals who pretended education in such matters, he doubted their reticence was from a fear of humans.

Vaal territory was different from the rest of the forest. There was very little undergrowth here; the Vaal liked to use their armored tails to crush or uproot anything growing lower than three or four feet from the ground. It gave them better vision of their surroundings and let them move faster in packs. It also left any growth over that height alone, meaning that Caeden's vision was still obscured half the time.

He stood still, closing his eyes, listening for the strange clack-clack sound the Vaal liked to make with their silvery, forked tongues when they gathered in a pack. Sometimes he wondered if it was a language of some kind, wondered whether the monsters had more intelligence than anyone gave them credit for. Every time he had the thought, though, he ignored it. He didn't care to find out either way.

Eventually the faint sounds of a pack filtered through the whispering forest; he pinpointed the direction and began walking, careful not to make a sound. Surprise didn't necessarily matter—the pack wouldn't run—in fact if he yelled now, they would likely come to him. But it was a challenge he liked to set himself, a way to determine if he was improving. Even in his darkest moments he'd always needed some sort of motivation, some sense of achievement and progress.

He crept along as the clack-clack sound increased, eventually lying on his stomach and worming forward until he could see the group of Vaal, sitting together in a clearing and facing one another. Their vision was sensitive to movement so it was always better to move slowly, edging forward until he was within striking range of the first one. If he was lucky, that one would be dead before the others even reacted to his presence.

He was ten feet from the nearest Vaal when the clack-clacking suddenly stopped.

He frowned, freezing as the Vaal shifted, turning to face the opposite direction. He'd never heard them just fall silent like that.

The clack-clacking came again. Quieter but higher pitched, urgent.

Then the Vaal were off as fast as their centipedelike legs would carry them, moving at an angle away from Caeden. He let out a mental curse; whatever had just happened had cost him a good hour of hunting.

He shifted, squinting through the foliage. There was something coming. Nothing moved, but suddenly the moonlight was more... intense. A gentle, warm glow bathed the clearing, rapidly becoming brighter and brighter until Caeden had to look away for fear of hurting his eyes.

Behind the intense light was... something, moving toward him. A presence at the center of that blinding glow. It paused as it drifted through the trees, and Caeden had the distinct impression that it was searching.

He felt its gaze focus on him.

Caeden held his breath, willing himself to melt into the ground. For the first time since he'd died, he felt fear—true, blood-chilling, mind-numbing fear.

The light crept closer, its warmth touching his skin now, moving lazily. Caeden knew that the presence was focused on him, suddenly understood that he could run for a thousand years and still be no farther from the being in front of him. It knew what and who and where he was, and it did not need to rush to get to him.

The light settled only feet in front of him, its presence like the sun itself, throwing the forest around him into painfully sharp relief. He forced himself up into a kneeling position, hands shaking with inexplicable terror. Even with his head turned to one side, the light still burned; his one attempt to face the presence resulted in him immediately having to look away again.

He shivered, despite the beads of sweat collecting on his brow. He hadn't been able to make out any details, but there had been a vaguely humanoid figure in the midst of that light.

Then there was a voice, filling Caeden's head with quiet intensity.

"Tal'kamar," it whispered. "She is not yours. She is not...true."

Caeden said nothing for a few long moments; that terrible voice echoed in his mind, crashing around inside his skull, nearly unbearable. He took a few deep breaths; this...being, or whatever it was, did not seem to be threatening him.

"What do you mean?" he gasped. "What are you talking about?"

"She is not true," repeated the voice, sounding frustrated. "I have...traveled far...risked much to warn you. To help you. The woman in your house...is not the one you knew five years ago."

Caeden rocked back under the words, though this time it was as much from what was being said as from the intensity of the voice in his head. "Elliavia?" He swallowed, trying to calm himself. To grasp what was happening. "She has changed, I suppose. We both have. But—"

"You understand not," the thunderous voice interrupted, somehow managing to be both a growl and completely unemo-

tional. "I speak not of change. The woman you knew...died. Another now...inhabits her body. She pretends to be the one you knew, but she...*is not."* *It emphasized the last two words, as if frustrated that Caeden was not comprehending its meaning.*

A sudden flush of anger ran through Caeden and he struggled to his feet defiantly. "Who are you, to make such a claim? What *are* you?" *He shook his head.* "It does not matter. I do not believe you."

"Yes you do." *The light watched him.* "You knew it was true...before I ever spoke. You have known it to be true since... the moment you looked into her eyes." *It drifted closer, its heat unbearable, and Caeden imagined that he could feel its breath.* "I am not here to...reveal, Tal'kamar. I am here to confirm...what is in front of you. To allow you...no excuse. I am here because without me, you might have been...willing to pretend. And that would mean that you never tried to find...the solution. The way to...make all things right again."

Caeden squeezed his eyes shut, heart pounding. Could it be true? Ell had changed, but...wouldn't anyone have changed after five years, after what she'd been through? Of course they would have.

"You are lying. You are lying and even if you weren't, there is no solution," *he gasped.* "You can try to forget, but you can never go back. Never truly fix things."

"You *can*, Tal'kamar," *the light assured him.* "I swear it by... my name. I swear it by Truth."

Caeden clenched his fists and faced the radiance, eyes closed, though it took every ounce of willpower he had to do so. The heat tore at his face. "I do not know what or who you are, but you are lying. About Ell. About everything," *he said, voice shaking despite his best efforts.* "If you want to harm me, then do your worst. But I have heard enough from you."

The light sighed, a sound full of regret. "Harm you? Tal'kamar, I am...here to save you," *it whispered.* "You will see. If you truly want to know if...your beloved is who she says, tell her...about tonight. Tell her I name her...Nethgalla, the Ath. Tell her I name her a citizen of...Markaathan, the Darklands. And tell her that she is...warned of consequences, should she not tell you the

159

truth." *The warmth began to recede, withdrawing through the trees.* "Tell her, Tal'kamar, and then...think on what I have said. There is a way to make...all things right. *All* things. When you believe that, come...and find me."

The heat, the searing light, faded. Vanished.

The presence was gone.

Caeden stood there, trembling, for a long time. After a while he heard the cautious clack-clack of the Vaal returning, but tonight he felt nothing at the sounds. Not excitement, not fear. Just the cold decision to leave, now, before their stinging barbs put him to sleep.

A way to make all things right.

An impossibility, something he knew without having to even think about it. There was no way to make right all the things he had done. There was no way to change him back into the person he had been five years ago, revive his friends and family, stop himself from being a murderer and a monster and a broken shell of a human being.

And yet...

There had been something in the creature's voice. A certainty that Caeden couldn't shake.

His stomach churned as he made the trip back across the stream and toward town. Ell. How could the creature possibly expect him to believe that she wasn't "true," wasn't who she claimed to be? He shivered. It hadn't been wrong about everything, he conceded; he had been feeling that something wasn't quite right. But it was the time they'd spent apart, his change in appearance, everything they had both been through. It was never going to be just as it was.

When he slipped through the front door, he was vaguely surprised to see Ell still awake, reading by the fireplace.

She looked up as he entered, her smile brightening the room. "Changed your mind?" *she asked eagerly, putting down her book and standing.*

She walked toward him for an embrace, and he hesitated.

"Not exactly," *he said softly.*

Ell faltered, a frown clouding her features. "Is something wrong?"

Caeden cleared his throat. "I ran into someone...something...tonight," he said slowly. He looked up, holding her gaze, heart pounding. "Who is Nethgalla?"

He saw it—small, gone in an instant but unmistakable. A flicker of shocked recognition.

Ell shook her head. "I don't know," she said casually. "Why?"

Caeden squeezed his eyes shut, as if that alone could block out the knowledge. He felt a tear trickle down his cheek, then another.

"It said to warn you of consequences if you did not tell me the truth," he said, voice cracking. He opened his eyes again, Ell's beautiful face blurring through his tears. "She's dead, isn't she."

Ell's eyes were wide, and he saw the beginnings of tears filling them, too. "She's not dead, Tal," she whispered. "She is standing right in front of you."

"Tell. Me. The truth." Caeden whispered the words, pouring every ounce of emotion he had into them. The pain, the horror, the shame, the fear.

Ell held up her hands, the tears falling now, and nodded. "Sit down. Let me explain," she said unsteadily.

Caeden wanted to refuse, to remain standing, but it felt wrong under the circumstances. Ell seemed upset and scared, not dangerous or angry. Still, he couldn't help but seat himself well away from her, perching at the edge of his chair and ready to spring up at even the hint of a threat. Whatever else was going on, he'd already been fooled. He had no way of knowing this woman's true intentions.

Ell took a seat opposite, swallowing, composing herself before she began.

"You are right. My name is Nethgalla," she said quietly. "I come from a place known here as the Darklands. It is..." She gestured, looking frustrated. "The best way to describe it is that it is another world. A world very much unlike this one."

"Another world," repeated Caeden dully.

Ell—Nethgalla—shook her head. "I cannot imagine how hard it must be for you to even conceive of it, Tal. I—"

"Do not call me that," Caeden growled.

Nethgalla winced, but inclined her head. "As you wish. Trying   161 to explain where I come from is . . . it's difficult. The natural laws that govern this world are either different, or do not apply there at all. It is a place of many horrors, Tal'kamar. A place of endless pain." She shivered, and Caeden somehow knew that it wasn't an act. "A place it is near impossible to escape."

She looked over at Caeden, but he didn't respond. Just watched her coldly.

Nethgalla swallowed. "There are certain people in this world with . . . with a gift. A power that few others have. One of those people is you, Tal'kamar," she continued. "The ability to draw power from beyond this world." She held up her hand as Caeden made to protest. "I know you don't believe this—not yet. But it is what you used at our wedding. It is how you drew Essence not just from yourself, but from everything around you." She hesitated. "And it is how you made the gateway for me to enter this world."

Caeden stared at her for a long time in silence.

"Through Ell," he whispered eventually, his voice hoarse with emotion. "Ell's body was the gateway."

Nethgalla looked at her hands, unable to meet Caeden's gaze. "Yes," she whispered. Then she looked up, her expression determined. "But when I entered Elliavia's body . . . I gained all of her memories. She became a part of me." She leaned forward, her tone earnest. "I still have each and every one of those memories, Tal. I feel the same love for you that she felt. I didn't realize it at first, but when I did—that's why I came to find you. Because I love you. Because I have always loved you. I love you as fiercely as she ever did." She stood, taking a hesitant step toward him. "I am Nethgalla, but I am Elliavia. I am your wife, Tal'kamar."

Caeden stared into those beautiful blue eyes he knew so well, and a wave of nausea drew bile into his throat. It was all he could do not to throw up.

"No," he said softly, standing and backing away. It was all so clear now. All the small things, all the things he'd been surprised that she had accepted. "My wife is dead. You are . . . you are an abomination."

"You don't mean that, Tal," said Nethgalla, a tremor in her voice. She looked at him pleadingly, and it broke his heart because her

162

expression was one he had seen Ell wear countless times. "I have her body, her memories, her love for you."

"You are different." He was shaking like a leaf, but he still managed to put a few more feet between him and the creature that had stolen his wife's body. "You are nothing more than an echo of her."

"How can you tell?" asked Ell pleadingly.

"Because she would not have forgiven me." Caeden whispered the words. It was true. He'd known it was true from the very beginning. He looked up into those familiar eyes, letting all of his pain, all of his frustration, all of his disbelief congeal into the one undeniable truth.

"Because she could never have loved the man I have become."

There was a deafening silence at that and it was too much, too much to take. He couldn't look at her anymore. Couldn't be in her presence a single second longer.

He left.

He strode from the house in a daze, heedless of Ell's calls for him to wait, to stop. He walked almost absently through the town, into the forest. He barely noticed as he walked past the Vaal-controlled lands, walked until his feet ached and then blistered.

He walked numbly until his legs gave out from under him and he collapsed into the cold, dewy grass. He couldn't move now and his feet burned as if he'd been standing on hot coals, but it was still insignificant next to the sadness that felt as though it were ripping his chest apart anew each moment.

He wept, then. Wept until the dawn came.

He didn't know how long had passed afterward, but eventually he dragged himself to his feet.

A way to make all things right.

Slowly, inch by inch, he started forward again.

He didn't know where he was going or what he was looking for, but it was all he had left.

Chapter 12

Asha flinched as a distant echo reached her ears.

She held her breath, heart pounding as she strained for another sound, another indication that she was not alone down here. How long had it been since the Echo had vanished? Hours? A day? Every moment stretched in the cold and the close, oppressive dark. Every second left her more nervous that she'd made the wrong decision, more inclined to jump up and start trying to find her own way out.

She exhaled softly as the sound came again. Footsteps. Definitely footsteps. Relief and tension flooded through her at the same instant; she activated the Veil and started silently stretching her stiff muscles, anticipating having to spring into motion at any moment.

A flicker of movement caught her eye, a glow that bobbed and grew in strength as the echoing footfalls came closer. Asha steeled herself, carefully shielding her eyes from the entrance to the room.

Even with the precaution, the light from the lantern was painful at first after so long in the darkness.

Asha squinted, able to make out two forms walking side by side. One seemed to glide rather than walk; even if it had not been cloaked in black, it was hard to mistake the presence of a sha'teth. The other she quickly recognized as Isiliar.

Despite her excitement, she couldn't help but restrain a shiver as they passed by, not ten feet from where she stood.

"...must tell them, Lady Isiliar," the sha'teth was saying in its odd, rasping voice, little more than a whisper. "Your suspicions are more than they have."

"Again, and again, and again you bring this up," snapped Isiliar as she stopped short, giving the sha'teth a black look. She appeared calmer than she had in the Sanctuary, but even so, when she shook her head the motion was too quick, violent and twitchy. "The point, Vhalire, the *point*, is that I am the only one left who knows. The only one who remembers. Wereth and Andrael and Tal'kamar and I. The first two are dead. The third left this when he left me." She tapped the blade at her side, face twisting for a moment. "We both know why. We both. Know. Why. I knew even before Alaris told me."

Asha focused. There was that name again—Tal'kamar. The one whose location Davian had asked her to relay to the Shadraehin. She hadn't recognized it at first, but after hours of sitting in the darkness and thinking back over what Isiliar had said, she had made the connection.

There was a long silence. "So you are set on forcing him to come for you," the sha'teth rasped eventually.

"Yes. Yes, yes, *yes*, Vhalire." Isiliar laughed but it came out wrong, high-pitched and close to maniacal, completely lacking in humor. "You *do* understand! How delightful. How wonderful."

Isiliar abruptly started forward again, forcing Vhalire to trail after her. Asha carefully followed, staying as far back as she could. Though the unsettling pair sent ice through her veins, she was still glad that they were both present; any small noises that she made had a much better chance of being masked if there was conversation.

"You are so certain he will come, but what of the Ath?" Vhalire's tone continued to be flat, but there was a hint of insistence to it now. "You say she took this device, and there is more than enough evidence that she knows how to use it."

"Took the device and *left me there*." Isiliar's voice was vague, but it suddenly had an edge to it, too. "Left me there in madness and blood, all so that she could try and dabble in the affairs of her betters. More heartless than Tal'kamar, though less to blame. More like you in many ways." She glanced across at the sha'teth. "I will remind them both of what screaming is before this world is done. But no, Vhalire. Tal'kamar will not seek Nethgalla, not while he believes me still captive, still easily accessible. Even if he didn't, in fact. He will always prefer my screams to her whispers, and think them easier to believe."

"Deilannis, then." Asha could barely hear Vhalire, he was talking so softly. "I have seen him venture there once already. If Serrin's story is anywhere, it is there."

"His story, perhaps, but not how to replicate the horror he wrought. Not how to bend it to fulfill Andrael's task." Isiliar shook her head as her voice echoed crazily through the stone passageways. "No. He will come for *me*."

They had made their way through several new twists and turns by this point, and now entered a corridor that was wider and straighter. Asha dropped a little farther back, intrigued by the conversation but unwilling to risk discovery, especially as the discussion between Isiliar and the sha'teth appeared at an end for now.

After a few more minutes of tensely creeping along after the pair, Asha spotted a new source of light up ahead. For an irrational moment her heart leaped, thinking it was daylight. Soon, though, the illumination revealed itself to be Essence, a bright and pulsing globe set into the wall.

Below it sat a door that closed off the end of the passageway; Isiliar opened it and with an exaggeratedly polite gesture, motioned the sha'teth through in front of her. Beyond the doorway Asha could see a well-lit space, furnished and distinct from the sparse corridors they had been traversing thus far.

Asha hesitated, then silently hurried forward and slipped in behind them, careful not to make a sound. She barely made it inside before Isiliar closed the door again.

There were no other visible exits from this new area, Asha quickly realized. They were in a massive hall, the vaulted ceiling at least thirty feet high, the thick pillars of stone that towered every ten feet or so decorated with intricate friezes. At the far end of the enormous room, a crystal clear waterfall fell gently into a narrow pool, though where it drained away to she could not see.

Asha swallowed, then stepped carefully over to the nearest column, well out of the way of any conceivable path the other two might take.

"So, Vhalire," Isiliar said quietly as she pocketed the key to the door. "We come to the end of our journey."

"We are not yet at Alkathronen, Lady Isiliar."

"No, Vhalire. We are not."

Isiliar didn't move but suddenly Vhalire shrieked. It was a terrible, stomach-churning keen; Asha clapped a hand over her mouth to stifle a gasp of horror, eyes wide as the sha'teth stumbled, flailing as though it had suddenly lost control of its limbs.

Isiliar gestured and suddenly Vhalire was being lifted into the air, then slammed with enough force against a pillar to shake dust from the ceiling. The scream cut off abruptly, replaced by ragged gasps.

Isiliar moved forward, her face a blank mask. She stopped only inches from the still-struggling sha'teth, then reached up and drew back its deep hood.

Asha's stomach twisted. The scarred white skin of Vhalire's face was puffy in some places, limp in others; the entire thing was a disfigured mess, a parody of what a man's face should be. And yet the eyes staring out from it, full of pain, were blue and clear and intelligent as they watched Isiliar.

The redheaded woman examined Vhalire, apparently unfazed by the unpleasant sight.

"The others may be blind, creature, but I am not. Tal'kamar is still using you somehow. It is evident in the way you move, you speak, you react. I can smell his stench on your breath." As Asha watched in horror she drew her sword, holding it up to the light. A low thrum filled the room. "I have been told that things have changed. Suspicion, Vhalire! Suspicion everywhere, and here most of all. Tal'kamar *believes*. It doesn't matter how wrong he is, so long as he thinks he is right. A man who believes is the worst of enemies. A man who believes is more dangerous than anything. As our enemies get smarter and more insidious, so must we react harder and more swiftly. This is now a world where only the ends matter. Once, this would not have been necessary." She shook her head. "But then, once, *you* would not have been necessary."

She stepped forward and plunged the sword into Vhalire's stomach, a slight, muffled clang as it sliced clean through and hit the stone beyond.

The sha'teth didn't scream this time but just writhed silently, mouth opening and closing like a newly caught fish.

Then something odd happened. Its face began to change; a measure of color flushed its cheeks, and the pallid, drooping skin tightened a little. Its eyes were not just intelligent, now, but also pleading.

"Please," Vhalire whispered, and Asha felt a chill. The voice coming from the creature's mouth wasn't low and rasping anymore. It was . . . *human.*

If Isiliar noticed the change, she either expected it or didn't care. She gestured; bands of Essence snapped the sha'teth's arms and legs into place against the pillar, hanging it off the ground. The sword still quivered in its stomach. "Lower those mental barriers and let me in, monster."

Vhalire forced his head up so that he could meet Isiliar's gaze, the motion evidently an enormous effort through the pain. "No. It would release some of the meld into you." Again the voice was human, though strained with agony.

"A risk I am willing to take."

"I am not."

"Then I estimate you have . . . an hour, perhaps, before I have the information I need anyway?" Isiliar shrugged. "Be it on your head, Vhalire. The choice is yours entirely. I'll return soon to see whether you've changed your mind."

She spun and walked back to the door, flicking the latch and exiting the room.

Asha just stood where she was for a long few moments, breathing softly, wide-eyed as she stared at the disfigured monster pinned against the column. Dark blood—blacker than it should have been—dripped incessantly from the wound in its stomach. There was less than Asha would have expected, though it was impossible to tell how much was being soaked up by the sha'teth's jet-black clothing.

Then the creature was turning its head.

Looking straight at her.

"Caution, marked one." The sha'teth's rasp had returned and its struggles eased somewhat, as if the pain was less. "This is no place for mortals. Isiliar has been asleep long enough that her 169 senses are dulled, but you cannot go undetected around one of the Venerate forever. She will know you are here when she returns."

Asha felt a chill; there was no one else in the room, no one Vhalire could possibly be talking to. Still, she didn't move. Didn't lower her Veil.

Vhalire's eyes suddenly changed. Became sharper.

"Kill…kill me." It was the more natural voice again, desperate and strained, somehow made all the more disturbing coming from that horrific face. "Please…do it. Too dangerous…to let Isiliar know. You must take…and hide the sword. Do not keep it. She will track you if…you hold it for too long…" Vhalire suddenly gasped and twitched, muscles spasming in evident agony.

Asha moved silently toward the door but Vhalire's gaze followed her with eerie accuracy, though the creature's mouth hung agape now, wordless.

When the time comes, do not let Vhalire suffer.

Asha bit her lip, squeezing her eyes shut for a long moment. Aelric's words, uttered to her after the other sha'teth had killed Jin what seemed like a lifetime ago, were impossible to ignore. She didn't understand what was happening, didn't know what to do.

"I don't know how to get out," she said softly. "Tell me how to get out, and I'll do it."

The sha'teth just stared at her, blue eyes wide. Pleading. Frantic. It moved its mouth but only rasping came out, followed by a hacking cough and a thick dribble of jet-black blood.

Asha put her hand to her mouth, partly in horror and partly in panic. Leaving Vhalire seemed the smart choice. If she killed him—as he apparently wanted—Isiliar would know that someone else had been there as soon as she returned. But the sha'teth appeared to think that she'd realize Asha was there anyway.

In the end, it was the one thing that Asha couldn't ignore that pushed her to a decision. For all his monstrosity, Vhalire's pain was evidently real. He was genuinely suffering, more than she had the stomach to watch.

More than she had the stomach to walk away from.

She swallowed and then turned away from the door, moving slowly toward the sha'teth, eyes locked on the protruding, quivering sword. With a trembling hand she reached out, resting her hand on its hilt.

She nearly snatched it away again.

There was something unsettling about touching the weapon, a sense of sudden revulsion that went even beyond the reality of the situation. She shivered and gritted her teeth, forcing herself to grasp it firmly.

The sha'teth's eyes met hers.

Its head dipped. The slightest hint of a nod.

Asha yanked backward, grimacing at the wordless shriek that accompanied the steel sliding out of Vhalire's body. She gasped and staggered backward as the blade finally pulled free, oozing blood and black bile onto stone.

A tremor ran through Asha's arm and for a moment a strange resonance filled the air, like a hum just beyond the range of her hearing. The sha'teth commanded her attention, though. Its screams quickly died but its body still thrashed and convulsed in obvious pain.

Resisting the urge to vomit, Asha steadied herself, grasping the hilt tightly in both trembling hands. She hesitated. The sha'teth was moving around too much, too violently. She couldn't get a clean strike in at its chest.

She almost faltered, almost ran from the sight. For a moment she half turned, her instincts to flee becoming close to overpowering.

"Neck."

It was the too-human voice again; Asha twisted back to see that Vhalire's eyes were squeezed tight against the pain. Asha thought that she could hear his teeth grinding.

She took a deep breath, steeling herself.

Before she could change her mind, she swung as hard as she could.

She'd expected more resistance than Vhalire's neck provided; the sword sheared through flesh and bone cleanly, making a wet clanging sound as it struck the stone beyond. Vhalire's head toppled to the ground in a spray of black, and his body stilled.

Asha stood there for a moment, panting.

Then the hum she'd heard before intensified. At first she thought it was the reverberation of metal against stone but it quickly filled the room, quivering, resounding, *thrumming* in her head.

Followed by darkness.

⚜

Asha woke on cold stone illuminated by pulsing Essence, inches from the pool of black blood that had seeped down the wall and across the floor.

She lay there for several moments, disoriented, fear arching through her as she took in Vhalire's sightless eyes and disfigured, pallid face on the ground a few feet away. Memory flooded back. How long had passed? Isiliar was nowhere to be seen; she evidently hadn't yet returned.

But it surely wouldn't be long before she did.

Asha propped herself up weakly, unsteadily. What had happened? The act of executing Vhalire had made her sick to her stomach—sha'teth or not—but she was quite certain that her unconsciousness hadn't been merely a reaction to that.

For a strange moment the reason was there, right at the edge of her mind. As she paused and tried to focus on it, though, she felt a trickle of something on her face. She wiped at it absently.

Her hand came away stained bright red.

Asha froze, panicking for a moment, probing her face gingerly for an injury. There was nothing though. Her eyes ached as if she'd been awake for too long but otherwise she felt...not fine, exactly, but well enough. Despite the hot, sticky blood, she didn't think that there was an open wound.

She stumbled over to the pure, glasslike shimmering waterfall at the end of the hall, peering into it at her surprisingly clear reflection.

With a wave of nausea, she saw that the trails of red down her cheeks had originated from her eyes.

She kept checking for a few more seconds but when she couldn't find a specific injury amid the smeared blood, she realized that there was little more she could do right now. Her use of the Veil had apparently ceased when she'd fallen unconscious; she activated it again, breathing easier the moment she was concealed.

She hesitated, then hurried back and picked up the blade that lay next to Vhalire's body on the floor. There was still a strange, unsettling sensation at the first touch, but nothing like the revulsion she'd felt before. The Veil immediately adapted to the weapon, extending its invisibility around the steel.

She drew another calming breath, shaking her head as she finally took a moment to survey the scene. As few options as she had, she didn't think Vhalire had been lying when he'd said that Isiliar would be able to see through the Veil sooner rather than later.

She had to leave. Now.

She moved with purpose, first snatching up her canteen out of her satchel and filling it from the pool beneath the waterfall, taking a few quick mouthfuls and splashing her face to clean it of blood. Then she headed for the exit and shut the door carefully, reluctantly behind her. The Essence bulb lighting the hallway outside was still glowing, but it didn't cast light far.

Asha faltered to an indecisive halt.

Fear suddenly raked at her muscles, turning every movement into one of stuttering indecision. The long, quiet terror she'd felt waiting for Isiliar and Vhalire to return came flooding back as she stared down the passageway into the darkness. She would barely be able to *see*, let alone find her own way out.

She compelled herself forward again, step-by-step leaving the light behind. At worst she needed to get to the first intersection, to be certain that she wasn't leaving herself somewhere Isiliar could easily sense her presence. She wasn't sure how the woman would be able to detect her, exactly, but it seemed far more likely to happen if Asha was in her direct line of sight.

She walked for a full minute before slowing once more, frowning and casting an uncertain glance over her shoulder, measuring the distance back to the Essence bulb on the wall. It was little more than a dot now.

She turned forward again, pausing to let her eyes adjust. As before, the walls here gave off a very faint illumination, revealing at least a vague outline of the way ahead. The odd light was almost nothing, less than a crescent moon on a cloudy night... but it was enough.

Asha suddenly registered the faint sound of muttering coming from up ahead, and a burst of nervous energy took her into a side passage just as the first hint of bobbing torchlight brightened the tunnel.

"...shouldn't struggle, Vhalire. Shouldn't, shouldn't." Isiliar's murmurings were unsettling, somewhere between perplexed and agitated. "Nothing more the meld can do to me. Tal already did it. Far too late..."

The muttering softened to incoherence again and Asha turned, glancing along the passageway she'd ducked into.

She grimaced. This wasn't the way back to the Sanctuary.

Her breath caught.

This *wasn't the way back to the Sanctuary*. She wasn't sure how she knew, but she *knew*.

A high-pitched scream reached her ears, long and loud, though she could tell it had been muffled by the closed door. Isiliar had found Vhalire.

Asha hesitated.

Then she sprinted back into the main passageway, turning away from the sound of Isiliar's anger. Following the hallway that was now bizarrely, miraculously, familiar.

She heard the door crash open behind her but she didn't stop, didn't pause for even a moment.

The wild shrieks of rage chased after her into the darkness.

Chapter 13

Davian groaned as he came awake.

He shook his head, eyes adjusting to the dim room. It was still evening; he was propped up on a bench against the wall, with a table in front of him. Another tavern, he thought, though oddly empty.

He touched the back of his head gingerly. A lump had formed there, still tender to the touch.

"Sorry about that," said a female voice to his right.

He turned to see the young woman who had been following him, seated alongside the young man Davian had confronted.

He stumbled to his feet, wincing at the sharp pain ricocheting through his skull. "Who are you?" He quickly forced himself to concentrate but as far as he could tell, no lines of kan joined the two now.

"Sit down, Davian," said the young man wearily, waving him back into his seat. "We mean you no harm."

"You were following me and then you attacked me," retorted Davian.

"He has a point," observed the teenaged girl, sweeping back a lock of short black hair. She didn't smile; something about her eyes suggested that she rarely did. "My name is Fessi, and this is Erran. We're friends of Asha's."

Davian stared for a long moment as the names registered.

"Oh," he said eventually, slowly lowering himself back into his seat. "So...you're *both*...?" He left the last word unsaid, peering around, still uncertain as to exactly how much privacy they currently enjoyed.

"Augurs," finished Erran cheerfully. "It's fine. I've Silenced the room."

Davian thought for a moment, then sighed as he understood. "You weren't Controlling her. You were *communicating* with her."

"Can't blame you for the assumption. It looks similar," admitted Erran. "To be honest, I didn't think anyone else would be able to spot it."

Davian just shrugged. Erran was probably right; most Augurs wouldn't have been able to detect a strand of kan that thin. Ishelle certainly wouldn't have. The more Davian had practiced with her, though, the more he'd come to realize just how easily sensing the dark energy around him really came.

"I was looking for it, after the singer you Controlled this morning didn't recognize me when I went back to thank her."

"Fates," muttered Erran, shaking his head irritably and then shrugging at Fessi's I-told-you-so look.

Davian glared at them. "Asha *did* tell me about you," he acceded. "But that doesn't mean I don't want to know what you're doing, following me around like this. You had plenty of chances to introduce yourselves today."

Erran, at least, had the good grace to look abashed. Fessi just shrugged.

"You're bait." She shot a frown in Erran's direction. "Or you were supposed to be."

"*Useless* bait with that Elder stumbling around after him," rejoined Erran defensively. He coughed, looking as though he'd suddenly remembered that Davian was still there. "Uh. Useless bait that we would *never* have put in any real danger," he added with a hopeful smile.

Davian stared at the two of them disbelievingly. "Danger from whom?" he eventually growled.

"Scyner." Fessi's voice was flat as she said the name, not sharing in Erran's attempt at levity. Her eyes were dark pools, intense. "Did Asha tell you about him?"

"She did, but..." Davian frowned. "You think he's after me?"

"We think he might come here," corrected Erran with a vaguely reproving look in Fessi's direction. "He wanted us, back in Ilin Illan. Wanted Augurs to help him with something." He paused, a flicker of emotion altering his expression. Asha had told Davian what had happened to Kol; the impact of his death was clearly still fresh for these two. "And unless he's been shunning all human contact since the battle, he'll know about the Amnesty. If it's Augurs he wants, here's where to find them."

Davian sighed, putting it together. "So you were following me, hoping that he would turn up." His head was still pounding, and he couldn't summon enough energy to be annoyed. "You wanted me to get rid of Elder Thameron, because you figured that he might scare off Scyner. And you couldn't show yourselves because Scyner would recognize you if he spotted you."

Erran gave a half-approving, half-apologetic nod. "Essentially."

Davian studied the two of them for a moment. Despite his first impressions, Asha had spoken well of them.

"So what happens next, then?" he asked quietly. "I'm sure Scyner is dangerous, but the possibility of the Boundary collapsing is more so. And you've made contact with me now—if Scyner was keeping an eye on me, he already knows that you're here." He leaned forward. "Why don't you accept the Amnesty? If you come in, we can—"

"No."

There was silence for a moment as Davian waited for Fessi to expand on her emphatic statement, but it was Erran who eventually jumped in.

"We've been watching Tol Shen for a few days," he explained quickly. "Not just looking for Scyner, but to see what's happening there. What sort of people we'd be putting ourselves at the mercy of." He shook his head, exchanging a glance with Fessi. "I dealt a lot with Shen when I was at Ilin Illan, and...honestly, I don't trust them. Only a certain type of person rises through their ranks, and so long as the situation at the Boundary benefits them, I cannot imagine it will be high on their list of priorities to fix. No matter what they say in the Assembly." He held Davian's gaze steadily. "Tell me you think I'm wrong."

Davian shifted uncomfortably in his seat.

"It's been a struggle to get them to even talk about the Boundary," he admitted eventually. "But that doesn't mean your coming in isn't our best shot at restoring it. I've learned a lot, training with Ishelle this past month, and there's another Augur who arrived just today. That would make five of us. *Five* Augurs. If we all stood together, there's no way that the Council could ignore us."

Erran and Fessi exchanged silent glances, and Davian frowned. He closed his eyes for a moment, quickly pressing through kan.

Sure enough, a thin line ran between Erran and Fessi. They were communicating again.

It was irritating, but he hid his feelings. No point letting on that he knew.

"It's not just their delaying that we're worried about," said Fessi eventually. "We think that they're actively hiding something."

"We suspected that the Tol might have information on Scyner," Erran explained to Davian's querying expression with a slightly embarrassed shrug. "But we also figured that the Council wouldn't just hand it over. So we may have...invited ourselves over to the Central Archive."

"You broke into *Central* Ward?" said Davian incredulously. That would have been no easy feat, even for Augurs.

"Harder than we expected after you and that other Augur decided to teach everyone in there how to shield themselves. Thank you for that, by the way," added Erran drily.

Davian rubbed his forehead, groaning as he made the connection. "This was last night?"

Erran just gave him another rueful shrug.

Davian sighed. "So why do you think they're hiding something?"

Fessi leaned forward. "We were seen before we could take a look, but there's something below Central Archive. There are stairs leading downward with, what—a dozen Gifted guarding it?" She glanced at Erran, who nodded confirmation.

"And—we think—there's some sort of kan barrier at the entrance," the young man added. "That's how we were spotted. We went to investigate, and suddenly Fessi couldn't keep us outside the flow of time." He shook his head grimly. "I don't know whether the barrier's just part of the structure, or whether the Council has a Vessel that's creating it, but you don't employ that sort of security because you're worried about one of the Gifted sneaking in."

Davian frowned, but nodded. Erran had a point.

"We may be wrong, of course," said Fessi quietly, watching his face. "But if we are, the Council should have no problem showing you whatever's inside. If they have nothing to hide, then they have nothing to hide."

"And if they do show me?" asked Davian.

"Then we'll reconsider the Amnesty." Fessi met his gaze calmly. "Don't worry. Either way, we agree that the Boundary's important—when you go north, we'll go, too, even if we don't let the Council know about it." She paused. "And once the Boundary's no longer a threat, we're hoping that you'll help us find Scyner."

"Our coming north isn't contingent on that, though," clarified Erran quickly.

Davian nodded slowly.

"That's fair," he conceded. He stood. "I'll speak to the Elders either this evening or tomorrow—and I'll figure out a way to bring all of this up without letting on that there are other Augurs around. I can meet you back here and let you know their response in . . . say, two days?"

Erran inclined his head. "We'll keep watch," he assured Davian. "If you need to contact us sooner, just head into Prythe again. Even if someone's following you, we should be able to speak without anyone ever knowing we're in touch." He tapped his head, indicating what he meant.

"Even if I'm shielded?" asked Davian.

Even if you're shielded.

Davian flinched, then gave him a wry nod, not letting on how impressed he was. Asha had said mental communication was a talent of Erran's. She hadn't been exaggerating.

"No matter what happens, we're going to need as many of us as possible to fix whatever's going on up north. So I'm glad you're here," said Davian.

"Even after we tried to use you as bait?" asked Erran cheerfully.

Davian stretched. "You failed pretty spectacularly, so no harm done."

Erran cocked his head to the side for a moment, then grinned, though Fessi looked less amused at the jibe.

"See you in a couple of days." Erran's smile faded. "And…keep an eye on the Elders. I can't imagine that they're going to be happy when you start asking about whatever's under Central Archive."

Davian acknowledged the cautioning statement with a nod, then left the tavern and began heading back out of the city. Erran and Fessi had given him plenty to think about, but he put it all temporarily to the back of his mind as he approached the Tol's walls.

It was time to meet the new Augur.

∞

Davian sighed with something approaching relief as he finally spotted Ishelle standing outside the Great Hall.

The well-lit Outer Ward—at least in this eastern section—was packed, more so than he'd ever seen it before. He pushed his way through the unusually thick press of bodies, waving as he caught Ishelle's eye.

"Why are there so many people here?" he said a little breathlessly as he finally got within earshot. He turned and put the wall to his back, surveying the crowd bemusedly.

"I told you. The Elders called everyone together to introduce Rohin."

Davian blinked. He'd assumed that the Elders had meant to introduce Rohin to those in Inner Ward, not everyone all at once. From the size of the crowd—he could see others still streaming out of the hall, now that he had a good view of the entrance—nearly every Gifted in the entire Tol must have given up their evening to cram inside.

He shook his head, examining the throng. Some were hurrying off to sleep but many others just stood around in small groups, chatting and enjoying the atmosphere. Most looked cheerful, even vaguely excited. "Where is he now?"

"Still inside. The Elders thought it would be a good idea if he made himself accessible to the Gifted afterward," said Ishelle. She nodded toward the entrance. "We should probably wait until the crowd thins a little before trying to get back in, though."

Davian opened his mouth to point out that people would just get out of their way, but closed it again with a mild frown. The

Gifted passing by clearly recognized he and Ishelle, but their reactions were actually... *pleasant*. Many nodded politely, one or two even smiled in his direction.

"I know everyone knows how to shield themselves now, but you're sure..."

"I checked. No Control," confirmed Ishelle.

Davian gave a relieved nod, relaxing. He'd been surprised at the Elders' change in direction—making such a big deal of Rohin's arrival, introducing him so publicly—but it appeared to have already made a difference. Perhaps by acknowledging the Augurs in this way, the rest of the Gifted felt more informed, and thus less as though their presence was something to be feared.

Ishelle nudged him with her elbow. "So what about you? Find anything?"

"I'll tell you once we're somewhere a bit quieter."

Ishelle gave him a friendly push. "Tease." She nodded, though. She understood the need to be circumspect about what they talked about in public, even if she sometimes pretended not to. There was always the chance someone was listening in.

They chatted idly for a few minutes, Ishelle enthusiastically running through the events of Rohin's introduction. Davian listened absently until the crowd had dissipated to a more manageable stream of bodies, then nodded toward the entrance.

"It looks like we can get in now."

They started weaving their way through the throng. Those leaving the Great Hall were talking excitedly among themselves, Davian idly noting that most of them were female.

He stopped short for a moment as they entered the main hall, staring.

Ahead, a tightly packed crowd blocked their view of the new Augur—almost all of them women. A male voice said something indistinguishable, and there was an eruption of laughter from the group.

"You're *sure* he's not using Control?" Davian asked drily.

Ishelle shot him an amused look. "Jealous?" She gave him a gentle shove forward.

Davian snorted but kept walking, politely pressing his way through the crowd until he got to the front row.

The young man sitting at the edge of the Essence-lit dais glanced up, smiling when he saw Ishelle. He was, perhaps unsurprisingly, handsome, with short jet-black hair and the faint beginnings of a beard on his cheeks and chin. He slid his athletic frame into a standing position, azure eyes bright as he turned his examination to Davian.

Davian barely prevented himself from rolling his eyes. He suddenly knew why Ishelle had been so excited by the new Augur's arrival.

"Rohin," the young man said with a wide, friendly smile, extending his hand to Davian.

"Davian." Davian shook the outstretched hand warmly.

Rohin inclined his head, then glanced around at the crowd. "I'd like to speak with the other Augurs now. We need some privacy. I'll be available to speak with you all again in the morning."

Davian frowned at Rohin's bluntness, but the Gifted began to disperse, looking disappointed but not unhappy.

Davian trusted Ishelle, but he still couldn't help but check for any tell-tale lines of kan stretching from Rohin to those around him.

It was just as she'd said, though. Nothing. He wasn't using Control.

"Looks like your welcome has been somewhat warmer than ours," he said wryly once the Gifted were out of earshot.

Rohin's smile slipped a little. "Ishelle was telling me about that earlier. The Council's behavior toward the two of you sounds inexcusable."

Davian sneaked a sideways glance at Ishelle. She didn't seem to think anything of the comment, though.

He coughed, then decided to let it be. There would be a time to talk about their relationship with the Council—in particular, about how much they needed them—but now wasn't it. "So when did you realize that you were an Augur?"

Rohin gave him an odd look, his chiseled jaw clenching for a moment.

Then he shrugged.

"It's a boring story, to be honest. Not really worth telling."

There was a sharp pain in Davian's temple, and a pitch-black burst of smoke erupted from Rohin's mouth. Davian flinched, taken aback. He couldn't remember seeing such a strong indication of a lie before.

Rohin didn't notice his reaction, instead glancing across at Ishelle. "Did I not mention that already?"

"You did," Ishelle assured him, "but Davian wasn't here. He was in town. Finding another Augur, hopefully," she added cheerfully.

"It's . . . complicated," said Davian, issuing an apologetic look to Rohin's suddenly curious one. Fessi and Erran had asked him not to reveal their presence, and he simply didn't know Rohin.

"Ah," said Rohin, nodding slowly as if suddenly understanding something. He focused on Davian. "You should know—I'm completely trustworthy. Likeable, too. I'm sure soon enough you'll happily tell me all your secrets."

The black smoke that erupted from Rohin's mouth was even stronger this time, and now—though it had never happened before—the substance didn't dissipate. Tendrils crept toward Davian; he took a hesitant half step back, but before he could do more they were curling around his arms and legs. He opened his mouth to cry out but the smoke was suddenly filling it, choking off his air.

He coughed violently, gasping and swaying a couple of times before dropping to his knees with a groan.

As Rohin watched on with a mildly confused frown, the black cloud enveloped him.

Davian lay on his side, staring in bemusement at the bars of his cell.

He rubbed his eyes, hazily trying to recall how he'd got there. He remembered the conversation with Rohin . . . and then being carried by multiple sets of hands, his breathing strained, vision blurred and hearing muffled by the persistent dark smoke. He had done his best to stay conscious and not panic, but at some point, he must have passed out.

He had assumed that he was being taken to someone who could help, though. Not to a prison.

The black tendrils were gone, now, at least; he winced as he sat up, head pounding, every small movement making his brain feel like it was crashing against the sides of his skull. There were no windows here but there was light filtering through from the other side of the bars, hurting his eyes, too bright against the rest of the darkness.

"Hello?" he called out, steadying himself against the bed before standing. He was weak, weaker than he felt he should have been. The cell was no more than ten feet across and a similar depth, pure white stone, smooth and apparently unbroken by cracks or joins.

"Where am I?" Davian muttered to himself, as much puzzled as concerned. The cell had the distinct look of the Builders' work, so he was probably still inside the Tol. Dazed, he moved across to the bars and leaned his face against them, trying to see what lay beyond.

Outside was a hall, windowless and lit by the bright yellow Essence that pulsed through each of its four thick pillars. Cells the same as his own lined the far wall perhaps thirty feet away, though he couldn't see any other prisoners through the bars. At the end of the hall was a large archway with something inscribed around its edges, though it was far enough away that he couldn't make out the symbols.

"Is anyone there?" he called as loudly as he could. His voice was weak, thready. He coughed, squinting against the light, dizziness flooding over him.

He instinctively reached out for the Essence in the nearest pillar, thinking to steady himself.

He froze.

There was nothing. He could still sense kan . . . but he couldn't access it.

Davian closed his eyes, breath constricting as he tried to fight back a sudden wave of panic. There was no Essence in the room, and apparently no way for him to draw on it even if there had been.

But he'd been practicing for this—he didn't need to get anxious just yet. He had time.

Of course, there was also the consideration that he didn't have any idea how long he had been in here, let alone how long it might be before the cell door was opened again.

He compelled himself to calm, quickly studying the edges of the cell. The room was lined with kan, some of the constructs vaguely similar to the Disruption shields that Ishelle had taught him to create.

This wasn't her work, though. This was both refined and self-sustaining. The threads were delicate, minute, layered upon one another.

Seamless.

He opened his mouth to call out again, but was saved the effort by the sharp echoing of footsteps outside. His heart sank as Rohin strode into view, the dark-haired young man watching him with something approaching caution, despite Davian's captivity.

"Davian," said Rohin quietly when he saw him standing at the cell door. "You're awake. Good. We need to talk."

"Why am I in here?" Davian growled.

"You seemed to have an adverse reaction to me, last we spoke. Ishelle thought this was prudent, and I agreed."

Davian stared at Rohin, remembering again the black smoke that had erupted from the other boy's mouth. A lie, but unlike anything Davian had ever seen before.

"You were trying to Control me, somehow, but it didn't work," Davian guessed.

Rohin made a disdainful gesture. "Control? Please. My ability is something else entirely. Unique." He smiled, though it was an unsettling expression. "My words are *truth*, Davian. It's not deliberate. It just...is."

Davian didn't respond for a few moments. What Rohin had said was tickling at something in the back of his mind. In Deilannis, he'd read about many of the different natural abilities an Augur might have—there were dozens, hundreds if you accounted for minor variations, and he certainly hadn't gone through them all...

But when he'd read about his own, there had been another that was directly related. An opposite, of sorts.

Very rare. Very dangerous.

"Of course it's Control, Rohin," he said quietly. He shook his head, trying to concentrate. Everything was hazy, and it wasn't improving. "All our innate abilities are a form of one of the major powers. When you say something, it's not 'truth.' You're just fooling people into believing that those words are true."

Rohin sighed. "You *do* take the fun out of it," he said chidingly. "But you're right, of course. So—I'm assuming that my ability conflicts with yours, somehow. Your mind was telling you that what I was saying was both true and false at the same time." Rohin smiled slightly at Davian's look of surprise. "The lovely Ishelle has been *most* talkative."

Davian felt his expression darken, a sudden flash of anger energizing him. "If you've touched her..."

Rohin chuckled, though the sound was humorless. "No, no. It was tempting, but...no. Messing more than is necessary with another Augur is a little too dangerous for my tastes." He gestured aimlessly. "Besides, it's not like I don't have options."

Davian just stared at Rohin in disgust, not knowing what to say to that.

Rohin didn't react to his disdain. "You know, you're only the second person I've met with whom I can have an actual conversation?" He sounded almost rueful. "For the past year, I've simply learned to...enjoy what I can. But now? I would like us to be friends, Davian." His eyes were bright with anticipation. "I know you don't think much of me right now—fates, I can hardly blame you—but we could do a lot of good together."

Rohin crossed his arms, leaning against the pillar outside Davian's cell. "You should also know: I had a very enlightening discussion with Graybeard. You know—the one who was in charge of the Tol," he elaborated with a lazy wave at Davian's confused expression. "He's dead now, but before he went, he had some very interesting things to say about us Augurs. For example. Did you know that half of the Elders here were aware that the attack on Ilin Illan was coming—*years* before it happened—and used that time to arrange for themselves to take charge of us, rather than preparing the city to defend itself?"

Davian swallowed, pushing down his initial reactions: horror, fury, disdain, a sense of disbelief at Rohin's words. Elder Dain was dead? Davian wasn't sure how much, if anything, to believe of what Rohin was saying—but he also didn't know how long he'd already been in this cell, and angering Rohin would only extend his stay. At some point, without kan—and thus without Essence—his body would simply stop functioning. Shut down.

Rohin didn't know it, but Davian needed to get out *soon*.

"If that's true, then I'm listening," he said, hating the words but doing his best not to show it. "You say you want to be friends. What did you have in mind?"

"A truce." Rohin stretched. "I know you're angry now, but I'm sure that you can see how valuable I could be here. The Amnesty dictates that Augurs have to do as the Shen Council says, but now the Shen Council does as *I* say. We can work together, try and get the Augurs back to their rightful position in society. And we can do it with impunity—because any actions we take, the Council will say were at their behest."

Davian nodded slowly. He wasn't actually tempted but for a moment, he wondered whether Rohin might have a point. "We could force them to finally send us to the Boundary."

"*No.*" Davian blinked at the vehemence of Rohin's response. The other boy immediately calmed, but Davian knew that he hadn't imagined the reaction.

"Why not?" Davian hesitated. If he wanted Rohin to believe that he was interested in what was being offered, he had to sound like he was at least trying to negotiate. "I know it probably seems irrelevant right now, but the danger is very real. If you'd seen Ilin Illan—"

"We can't leave." Rohin rolled his shoulders uncomfortably. "We're safe here."

"We won't be if the Boundary falls," pressed Davian.

"It's not as simple as that." Rohin scowled. "I've Seen things, Davian. I've *Seen* what happens at the Boundary when it collapses. However bad you say Ilin Illan was...you cannot *imagine* what it will be like." He said the last in close to a whisper.

Davian stared at him in unfeigned horror for a long few seconds.

"*When* it collapses?" He swallowed. "What have you Seen, exactly?"

"It doesn't matter. We go north, we die."

Davian was silent for a moment.

"Perhaps...perhaps you're right, then," he said eventually, trying to sound reluctantly convinced. He didn't believe it for a second—regardless of what Rohin had Seen, they had to *try*—but his goal here wasn't to argue.

Rohin gave him a relieved nod. "It wouldn't have mattered, anyway. The Council would have made far too much trouble for us after we left."

Davian made certain not to outwardly react, but his breath caught. "Can't you just convince them that they want us to go?"

Rohin hesitated and then scowled again, though mostly to himself. "It's irrelevant."

Davian let the matter drop, concealing his relief.

From the sounds of it, Rohin's Control wasn't permanent.

He studied the young man for a moment, trying to keep his head clear. Rohin was eager to talk, and that made him prone to giving away information. Davian supposed that was understandable. Having everyone agree with you sounded nice in theory, but it probably meant that Rohin hadn't had an honest conversation since the ability had manifested itself.

Still, Davian didn't know how much longer he had before his lack of Essence became a serious problem. He couldn't waste time trying to wheedle more from Rohin. If he managed to get out of this cell, there would be time enough for that later.

"I'm willing to give this a try, Rohin. It's not as if I have a lot of options, and you're right—perhaps with your ability, we can actually do some good." He scratched his head. He couldn't seem to accede too easily. "I'm not convinced about the Boundary just yet, but I won't cause trouble over it, either. We can have that discussion another time."

Rohin nodded slowly. "Excellent." He didn't seem overly suspicious of Davian's capitulation, but perhaps that was a side effect of his being accustomed to others' obedience. "Now. All you need to do is drop your shield so that I can Read you, and we can let you out of there."

Davian's heart sank. "What? How can I trust you not to Control me?" he asked, trying not to panic. "Without a shield…"

Rohin frowned. "How could I possibly trust you not to betray me, otherwise? And you're the one in the cell," he pointed out.

Davian squeezed his eyes shut; it was getting harder and harder to mask his weariness. "Fine," he muttered.

Rohin began unlocking the cell, then hesitated. "I can't Read you without this door open, but you need to stay back until I'm done. No tricks, or it will go poorly for you."

Davian grimaced but nodded, feeling his energy slipping away. It was becoming difficult to breathe. He sat on the far edge of the room and closed his eyes, waiting until he heard the sound of the door opening.

The moment it did, everything became...clearer. The pulsing pillar from outside was blinding with Essence, as was Rohin himself as he stood in the doorway. Davian could suddenly sense the other pillars in the hall, too, as well as another source not far behind Rohin that he didn't recognize.

Davian's body had started sucking hungrily at Essence already, but he knew that he didn't have long. He augmented the draining process, focusing on Rohin, trying to keep the lines of energy thin enough that the Augur wouldn't notice.

"You still have your shield up, Davian," he could hear Rohin saying in the background. "You need to...wait. What are you doing?"

Davian didn't stop; the pillars began to dim out in the hallway behind Rohin, plunging the cell into deep shadow. He began drawing harder from Rohin, watching as the young man's source began to shrink. It wasn't difficult, and he felt the strength flowing back into his limbs, sharpening his mind.

And suddenly, he realized how easy it would be just to end this.

One sharp, violent drain would kill Rohin, just as it had Ionis. It was safer. More reliable. To take the right amount to simply render Rohin unconscious meant a constant draw, which the other Augur could cut off if he was quick enough.

Davian almost did it.

Something held him back, though. A nagging sense in the back of his mind that making that choice, when it was expedient rather than necessary, was not a step that he could come back from.

He breathed deeply and then began stumbling toward the exit. Rohin shook his head as if to clear it, gripping the frame of the door to steady himself. His eyes were wide, but his understanding had come too late to stop Davian. Every moment that passed, Davian grew stronger and Rohin became weaker.

Then there was a rush of kan slicing through his lines of Essence, and a Disruption shield abruptly materialized around Rohin, blocking the doorway.

In the hall behind the young man, Ishelle had dropped her invisibility.

Davian stuttered to a stop, heart sinking as he saw her expression. "Ishelle," he said urgently. "He's Controlling you. Controlling everyone. You heard him."

"Kill him," choked Rohin.

Ishelle hesitated. For a moment, no one moved.

Davian gathered all his concentration and tried to step outside of time, but he was still too dizzy; time stuttered for barely a moment before washing back over him. Ishelle came to a decision and moved toward him.

Davian changed his focus and lashed out with Essence instead, trying to push her out of his way without causing her injury. Ishelle blocked the attack easily, then simply dragged Rohin back into the hallway and began to shut the cell door.

Davian acted on instinct, hardening a sphere of kan within himself and sucking all the extra Essence he'd gathered into it.

The door clanked shut.

"I said kill him," snarled Rohin, stumbling to his feet.

"I am," said Ishelle quietly. "A fight is an unnecessary risk. No food or water will do the job just as effectively."

Rohin shook his head in disgust, though the action was directed more at Davian than Ishelle. "Why? Why try and escape when I offer you so much?"

Davian squeezed his eyes shut, trying to think of something to say that could help his situation. There was nothing, though.

"What you're doing is wrong, Rohin," he said softly. "Surely, deep down, you know that. Surely you can see..."

He trailed off as Rohin simply walked away, gesturing curtly for Ishelle to follow. Within moments, Davian was alone once again.

He swallowed, forcing down a sudden swell of panic. He hadn't anticipated Ishelle helping Rohin—an oversight, in retrospect, but there was nothing to be done about it now. At least he'd bought himself some time.

He slumped to the floor, his back against the smooth white wall, and began to nervously examine the hollowed-out ball of kan he'd created. He could *sense* it well enough—just couldn't touch it, couldn't modify it in any way. If there was a flaw in what he'd done, there was no way to fix it now.

He'd made the sphere instinctively, desperately, even though he knew that it was incredibly dangerous to do so. A container of hardened kan, within which he'd stored all the Essence he'd drawn but not used. Then he'd left the tiniest gap that he could manage in the shell, allowing a faint trickle of Essence to constantly filter out, directly into his body.

He shook his head dazedly as he studied it. Against all odds, it *did* seem to be working. That wasn't supposed to be possible, though—everything he'd read in Deilannis, as well as what Ishelle had been taught, said that the presence of a kan construct within the body could cause any number of problems. Side effects were meant to range between nausea and a sudden, violent death, and yet he felt...fine.

Perhaps it was something to do with not having a source, or perhaps the consequences were not yet revealing themselves—but for now, it appeared he'd drawn enough to survive for a while longer. A day or two, perhaps?

A sliver of hope blossomed in his chest. He'd been scheduled to meet Erran and Fessi, and they would know something was wrong when he didn't show. Would it be enough for them to come looking for him, though?

And even if they did, they wouldn't know about Rohin's ability, wouldn't realize that they needed to avoid him at all costs. Davian's flicker of excitement died again. The last thing he wanted was to hand Rohin more Augurs to control.

Sighing, he settled down in the corner of the bare cell, doing his best to clear his mind. He couldn't panic.

There would be a way out of this.

He just had to figure out what it was.

Chapter 14

Caeden awoke to the crackling of a fire, and no pain.

He moved slowly, cautiously, testing each limb with care. He was lying flat on the ground. Nothing was piercing his body, nothing was restraining him.

He'd been released from the capsule.

There was a brief, sweet moment of relief, though that was quickly swept away as the things he'd remembered while imprisoned came flooding back. Elliavia. Nethgalla.

The same woman who had killed Asar.

He swallowed, just lying there, grief suddenly heavy against his chest again.

He knew it was just a memory—in a lot of ways, still detached from whom he currently was—and something that had happened a long, long time ago. And yet the emotion of the discovery rocked him as if it were brand new. It *was* brand new. He'd experienced the impossible hope of discovering that the woman he loved was still alive—and then the despair of understanding that not only was she dead, but that he'd created the mockery that had taken her place.

Caeden's breath caught, and his mind shied away from that last thought. He didn't remember the details of his wedding, but that...*that* was something that he knew he didn't want to relive.

Suddenly recalling where he was again, he forced down the sadness and focused, propping himself slowly up onto one elbow. The man who had originally been in the torture chamber was sitting opposite, staring meditatively into the flames between them.

He didn't react to Caeden's motion, and at first Caeden wasn't sure he had even noticed it.

"How long, Devaed?" The stranger's voice was quiet, but it carried clearly across the stone plateau.

Caeden hesitated, then took a deep breath and sat upright. "How long...?"

"How long was I in there?" The man finally moved, turning his head to face Caeden. He was calm, but something in his eyes smoldered as they looked into his. "Decades? Centuries?"

Caeden didn't answer for a moment. Honesty was easiest, but honesty could also get him killed.

So too could lying, though.

"Does it matter?" he asked quietly.

The black-haired man stared at him in disbelief for a few moments, then looked away. "I suppose it does not," he said with a soft, bitter laugh. "I just thought you might tell me. For the friendship we once had."

Caeden opened his mouth to respond, but a sudden flash of familiarity ran through him.

Another of the walls in his mind cracked, then crumbled.

Caeden slid gracefully along the grass behind the low wall, releasing his time bubble so that he appeared midmotion to Isiliar.

"Show-off," murmured the redheaded woman.

"Don't pretend like you're not impressed," whispered Caeden, moving smoothly and pressing up against the stone barrier. He closed his eyes, reaching out with kan. "There's only ten of them. Why bother waiting for me?"

"I'm building habits. Part of the team. You should try it." Isiliar smiled. "And if you bothered to look with your eyes, you'd see that there's twenty. They got some Telesthaesia from somewhere."

Caeden raised an eyebrow. "More? Alaris really needs to learn to keep an eye on his belongings. Especially the things that make our job harder." He risked a quick peek over the wall, taking in the distant group of black-armored men. "They're far enough away that we can deal with the others before they get here, at least. And just one commander. He's either pretty good, or has absolutely no idea what he's in for. Nine connections at once can be brutal."

"I've seen you manage at least two dozen."

"That's because of my vast intellect," observed Caeden.

"Well." Isiliar crooked a mock dubious smile at him. "Vast capacity, at least. There's clearly plenty of room in that pretty head of yours."

Before Caeden could respond she was moving, leaping and sliding over the wall.

With a soft laugh he followed, running a dozen paces before easily evading the first sword that sliced in his direction. The man who had swung it went down, Caeden breaking his leg without even needing to alter his momentum.

He continued forward, flashing between two more blades before disarming the man to his left and delivering a brutal blow with his elbow. The man's nose crumpled beneath the impact, its owner unconscious before he hit the ground.

Caeden tossed aside the steel he'd confiscated, taking a moment to watch in appreciation as Isiliar spun and whirled and dealt maiming blows at every turn. She was a dervish of pain, efficient and terrible. Much better than he, if he were being honest.

Then there was a furious chorus of shouts, and their first real test rushed toward them.

Telesthaesia drank in the clean light of the morning, absorbing rather than reflecting it. Caeden knew that was due to the Absorption endpoints that occurred naturally in the dar'gaithin scales, making them immune to both kan and Essence.

"You want the pawns or the commander?" Caeden asked as Isiliar downed the last of the regular men.

Isiliar thought for a moment, ignoring the rush of black armor coming her way.

"Which way did we do it last time?"

Caeden shrugged. "I think I got the commander. I think. Ladicia is a bit of a blur, to be honest."

"Sounds right. The usual stakes?"

"Of course."

The black-clad soldiers were almost upon them. Isiliar gave a slight nod and vanished, altering her passage through time to much better effect than he had. He gave a jealous sigh, then turned his attention to his attackers.

"I really should be making Alaris do this," he muttered to himself. Then, in a louder voice, he addressed the men coming toward him.

"Those helmets look awfully uncomfortable," he called as he was quickly surrounded. "Don't suppose you'd like to just... take them off?" He sighed again as the men formed a tight circle around him. "Seriously, though. Easier for all of us if you just take them off. You don't get hurt, I don't have to lose another bet."

Nine swords swung at him all at once.

Caeden had known exactly what was coming; he jumped, his legs already infused with Essence. The leap took him a dozen feet into the air; he somersaulted—he didn't think Isiliar would be watching, but the flair was worth it just in case she was—and landed gracefully outside the circle, one of the men's helmets in his hands.

He shook it at the attackers sternly. "You see? If you take the things off, it will not be anywhere near as bad." He paused. "Well, I suppose most of you don't see, as such. Which is a shame. Because what I just did... it was pretty impressive. That was not easy."

The man whose helmet he had ripped off was staring at him in shock, eyes glazed over. Caeden felt a wave of sympathy for him; breaking the connection like that was unpleasant at best, dangerous at worst. Not many minds were permanently damaged by it, but still.

"So. Surrender?" asked Caeden hopefully. "Last chance."

Eight men came toward him, much faster than the average soldier. Their commander was certainly doing an impressive job, activating the Time endpoints in the armor at the same time as fighting Isiliar. That gave him a modicum of hope of winning his bet, at least. He brightened at the thought.

Then he created a time bubble again. Telesthaesia made it less effective, but it was still good enough.

196   "No helmet for you. Or for you. Or for you," said Caeden

cheerfully as he darted between the men, removing their eye-concealing helmets one by one and tossing them to the side. He let time crash back into him for a few seconds, panting a little at the effort, then activated the bubble again before the remaining soldiers could react.

"Five, six, seven, eight. Nine," *he finished with satisfaction as the last helmet came off, its former wearer crumpling to the ground. He stood with his hands on his hips, observing the dazed men lying all around him.* "Now isn't that better? Fresh air. Seeing with your own eyes. Not having to share a mind with nine other people. You have to admit, I did you a favor."

"I don't think they can hear you," *came Isiliar's voice from behind him.*

He turned. "I won."

"No." *Isiliar sighed.* "Sorry, Tal. Connection was still active when I took him."

Caeden narrowed his eyes. "You lie."

"Normally. But not right now."

Caeden groaned. "Fine. I'll pay later. Let's go and find the others and get this over with." *He scowled across at her as they started walking back toward the town.* "You're really no fun to be paired up with, you know?"

"Not my fault you're not very good at all of this yet," *observed Isiliar, smiling.*

Caeden gave her a playful shove. "Next time, Is." *He looked toward the center of the town.* "Think this Paetir fellow is going to be tough?"

"He'll be tough." *The familiar gravelly voice came from behind them; Caeden didn't break his stride but grinned cheerfully as Meldier fell into step with them, followed quickly by Diara.*

"Pessimist," *said Isiliar.*

"Quite the opposite. Been a while since we've had a good challenge," *said Meldier happily.* "Telesthaesia was a good warm-up, but hardly a fair fight. And knowing what we know about Paetir, I would like to take some measure of enjoyment in taking him down."

Caeden's smile slipped a little, and he nodded. "El knows that's true." *He'd been one of the ones given Vision, this time.* 197

Paetir hadn't been anything special—a powerful mage, another would-be despot on their list to deal with—until he'd come across some old Shalis artifacts.

Then he'd gone on a rampage.

His army was small, but in this relatively quiet region of Rinday, they were unstoppable. Killings and rapes were the norm whenever Paetir took a new town. As he had this town yesterday. Caeden and the others had been too far away to be able to stop it—not that they could have, given that it had been Seen—but they intended to ensure that this was the last time it would happen.

Caeden smiled again as another figure joined their group, limping slightly.

"Alaris." Caeden slapped him on the back, then nodded to his leg. "Getting careless?"

"There were twenty of them in my sector. All with Telesthaesia. Three commanders. All subdued, no casualties. By myself."

"Bah." Meldier made a dismissive noise. "All I hear is excuses."

"Unimpressed," agreed Caeden.

"You're getting old," Isiliar chimed in.

Alaris allowed a small smile at the jibes. "Aren't we all," he said drily. He studied the compound up ahead. "He's going to be strong. Do we want to actually . . . plan something?"

The other four exchanged glances. Caeden shrugged.

"I suppose. As long as it doesn't take long," he said. "I'm kind of hungry."

They sketched out a quick plan of attack, coordinated by mental communication. Alaris and Caeden would take the front, providing a distraction for—hopefully—the bulk of any remaining soldiers wearing Telesthaesia. Meldier, Isiliar, and Diara would all come in from the sides and back, staying as quiet as possible until they sighted Paetir.

"What if this doesn't work?" asked Meldier.

Isiliar gave him a dry look. "Then we're back to the way we usually do things?"

"Right." Meldier gave an exaggeratedly slow nod. "Punch everyone that's not us until they stop moving."

"See?" Isiliar grinned at Alaris. "We didn't need to come up with a plan. We've got Meldier."

Alaris rolled his eyes. "See you in ten minutes."

Caeden's stomach rumbled. "And then food."

"And then food," agreed Alaris.

The others dashed off to take their positions. Caeden and Alaris waited a few moments, then started toward the compound.

"I can't believe Andrael and Gass wanted to sit this one out," said Caeden conversationally as they approached. "Feels like they would have enjoyed it."

Alaris gave him a reproachful look, and Caeden sighed dramatically but fell silent. Alaris had changed a lot over the past five hundred years. Grown more serious, less joyful.

"Just like old times," Caeden observed.

Alaris eyed him dubiously. "Old times involved you being in prison for eighty years, and me still king. This feels different."

"Don't get hung up on the details." Caeden glanced across at his friend. "Do you miss it?"

"Being king? No," said Alaris absently. "I'm embarrassed when I think back on it, to be honest."

Caeden looked at him in surprise. "I thought you were a pretty good king."

Alaris shrugged. "I did as well as I could. But I was one man, making decisions for an entire country. Doesn't the arrogance of that stagger you? When Gassandrid showed me the truth, it was... hard. I'd felt like I was making a difference, prior to that. Now..." He gestured. "This is how we make a difference. We are the only ones who can. I hate what happened to the Shining Lands, but we need to use our gifts responsibly. We need to see the bigger picture."

Caeden nodded slowly. He knew that the Shining Lands were no more—that once Alaris had left, their enemies had swooped. Alaris himself had tried to reclaim some of it, but even then its occupants had rebelled against him, accusing him of abandoning them when they had needed him most. It had affected Alaris more than the man cared to admit, Caeden thought.

They were at the compound now, in sight of the four guards at the entrance. Caeden and Alaris walked forward calmly; they

199

were both clearly unarmed, and the guards did not look particularly perturbed as they approached.

The first soldier stepped forward. "What business do you have with Lord Paetir tod—"

Alaris blurred around the man, attacking the three men behind him with quick, efficient punches. They were unconscious before the guard had time to turn.

"We'd like to talk to him about all the murdering and the raping and the torture," said Caeden calmly as the last of the three men slumped to the ground. "Specifically, about how we'd like him to stop."

"We don't really expect there will be much talking involved," said Alaris.

"Actions speak louder and all that," agreed Caeden cheerfully as the bemused guard watched them with an increasingly terrified expression. He clapped the man on the shoulder. "But you, my friend? For you, words are going to be better. Tell us where Paetir is. And how many inside with the black armor."

"Second floor. Third room on the right after the stairwell," said the man immediately, voice shaking. "Maybe thirty men in armor, another dozen without."

He crumpled to the ground as Alaris hit him from behind—not hard, just with enough force to render him unconscious.

"Paetir doesn't inspire much loyalty, does he?" observed Caeden as they walked through the archway and into the complex. "Thirty men in Telesthaesia. Five commanders, maybe?"

"One for each of us. Not as bad as I'd thought," said Alaris. "I'll be glad to get that armor back."

"Is and I were talking before about that. You know, you really ought to take better care..."

He trailed off. They were on the path to the main building, and outwardly nothing had changed. But that last step forward...

"I felt it, too," said Alaris with a frown, cocking his head to the side. "No kan."

Caeden quickly experimented; sure enough, when he reached out for kan, there was nothing there. He switched to Essence, relieved to find that he could still access his Reserve without issue.

200   "Annoying," he observed.

"It makes things a little trickier," agreed Alaris. He stepped back out of the kan-dampening field, evidently communicating the problem to the others before rejoining Caeden.

"This is why I don't like plans," complained Caeden quietly as they sneaked toward the door. "They never work."

"Your plans never work," corrected Alaris. "Mine are just flexible."

Caeden coughed. "I assume this flexibility has turned into 'everyone attack at the same time'?"

Alarais peered through a nearby window. "But at least it's from a few different directions. The core of the plan is still intact."

Caeden grinned. "I take it back. Alaris, strategic mastermind."

Alaris smiled, though his attention was still focused on what was inside the building. "Hallway. Two guards, both wearing Telesthaesia. Fools aren't wearing their helmets though, so they're hardly going to be threats. Can't see anything beyond that."

Caeden rolled his shoulder. "They're going to be quick." He glanced at Alaris's leg. "You going to be all right?"

Alaris gave him a withering look, then opened the door and strode inside.

The fight was short. Without the increased skill set and mental presence of a connection, the two men were no match for Caeden and Alaris's combined thousand years of fighting experience. Soon both guards were unconscious, and Caeden was peering through the doorway behind them. Elsewhere in the compound, there were flashes of Essence as the others began to deal with the men not wearing armor.

The compound was a winding maze of hallways and rooms; Alaris and Caeden hurried along, dealing swiftly with any Telesthaesia opposition and even more quickly with anyone else. Despite Alaris's minor injury, the entire process was surprisingly easy.

Finally they came to the main hall, bursting in to find that they were not the first to arrive.

Diara stood in front of what could only be described as a throne, atop which a young man lounged, seemingly unperturbed by their appearance. Diara glanced behind her when she heard the doors crash open, nodding to them calmly. A dozen men armored in Telesthaesia were arrayed in a protective circle around the man on the throne; two more stood a little farther back, evidently commanders.

"This is him?" asked Alaris, striding forward.

"I am Lord Paetir," affirmed the man, his gray eyes watching them with cool disinterest. "And you are the ones I've heard so much about. The ones venerated everywhere for your fight for justice." He said the words mockingly, disdainfully.

Diara turned to Caeden and Alaris. "That sounds about right, doesn't it?"

Caeden nodded. "I think that's us."

"Probably us," agreed Alaris. He looked at the young man, and his expression hardened. "Which means that we're going to have to put you on trial, Lord Paetir. Sorry."

Paetir's scowled at the flippant tone of his attackers. "It will be satisfying to watch you die."

"He really *doesn't know us very well*," said Diara.

Caeden nodded. "It's a little embarrassing to watch." He sighed, glancing up at Paetir. "We did *beat a good deal more of your men on the way in*, so we're not too concerned," he observed. "But don't worry. At least it means you won't be alone at the trial."

Paetir stood, drawing his sword.

"Going to fight us yourself?" asked Meldier in amusement as he strode in. He gestured to the men in black armor. "I mean, I'm all for doing this the easy way. But come on. If you want to make things interesting, at least consider *letting them help*."

"I don't need their help," said Paetir calmly. He inclined his head slightly. "But I'm not a fool, either."

The men in Telesthaesia moved as one, sprinting forward.

The next minute passed in a blur as Caeden swept among the soldiers, spinning around and between blades, ripping off helmets where he could. He took injuries to the arms, the legs, one to the face; each time he tapped his Reserve, healing the wound before it could slow him down. It was hard, painful work without access to kan, but he was making progress. They were winning.

It wasn't until he heard the roar of anger from Meldier that he knew something was wrong. He dealt with the last of the attackers near him and then turned, heart sinking.

Diara's body lay sprawled in front of Paetir, a gaping wound in her chest despite the Resonance chestplate she always wore. Caeden cursed. Diara was the weakest of them: a blade through the heart was all it took to send her to the Chamber. She always took precautions, though. How had Paetir hurt her?

Meldier was effectively blocked by a wall of Telesthaesia, but Caeden had no such obstacle. He leaped across the remaining space, sliding smoothly to a stop in front of Paetir.

Paetir smiled toothily at Caeden, swishing his blade confidently in front of him. "I told you I didn't need the help."

Caeden felt a chill as the air reverberated in time with Paetir's motion. His blade wasn't ordinary steel, though it had looked it from a distance. It thrummed with energy.

Caeden didn't feel the need to say anything in return; he leaped forward, faster than Paetir could possibly respond.

And gasped as he felt cold steel slide between his ribs and into his heart.

A second later, Paetir thrust his blade into the wound.

Caeden's mind went numb as he tried to understand what had just happened. He blinked at Paetir as the man rammed the steel home, agony coursing through Caeden's body as the wicked edge cut flesh and organs.

"Everyone dies," whispered Paetir, his face only inches from Caeden.

Caeden drew a deep, rasping breath. Closed his eyes. Concentrated.

His body was already reacting, already pulsing Essence to the wound. There was interference there; the kan scaffolding on the blade was hampering the healing. Caeden focused, drawing more Essence. More. He felt flesh begin to heal. Painful though it was, he could even feel his heart pumping around the blade, cutting itself anew with each beat, but forcing blood through his veins nonetheless.

He opened his eyes, energy igniting inside of him.

"Not true," he whispered back.

He placed both hands on Paetir's shoulders and pushed with Essence-infused muscles; the man went flying backward, rolling along the floor awkwardly for several feet. Paetir had kept *his grip on the blade, though. Now it was out of Caeden's chest, muscle and ebony skin knitted itself back together immediately. It hurt, and Caeden went down on one knee, weaker for the blow. But he knew immediately that he would be all right.*

Then Alaris was there, crouching beside him with a hand on his shoulder, concern etched on his features. "What happened?"

"He stabbed me."

Alaris grunted. "I can see that." He straightened as he saw Paetir climbing to his feet a short distance away. "How?"

"Vessel blade. Nullified Diara's Resonance armor, and..." He hesitated. "I think it's bending time. Cutting a second or two ahead, somehow. Be careful. No telling what else it does."

Alaris stared at him for a moment as if to confirm he wasn't joking. When Caeden gave him a tired nod, he sighed.

"Doubt it will make a difference on me. Just stay back." He glanced at Diara's body. "I'd hate to have two of you to look for."

"So glad you care," coughed Caeden.

Alaris grinned, then turned to face Paetir. The other man was still doing his best to convey an aura of control, but his eyes betrayed his concern now.

"You know you cannot best me," he said to Alaris. "You can still leave."

Alaris smiled at him sadly.

"We're past that point, Paetir. It's over."

He darted forward.

Alaris winced; a moment later Paetir's sword caught him in the stomach. Rather than cutting his skin, though, the blade just stopped; Paetir's eyes widened as Alaris knocked it aside with his bare hands. Then Alaris was shoving the would-be warlord up against the wall, quickly striking the man's wrist to send his blade clattering to the stone floor.

Alaris glanced back at Caeden. "Done?"

Caeden took a moment to look around. Black-clad men everywhere were either unconscious or moaning in pain, but none still fought.

He slowly lay on his back, relaxing, exhaling heavily and closing his eyes.

"Done," he confirmed tiredly.

Caeden touched his mug lightly to Meldier's as they sat in the tavern, listening to the sounds of celebration outside.

"We did a good thing here today," said Caeden, watching his friend's expression.

Meldier nodded. "I know," he said softly. He rubbed his forehead. "I wonder how long until we see her again?"

Alaris shrugged. "Depends where she comes back, and whether she's been there before or knows where it is. Could be months. Could be years." He winced as he shifted, touching his stomach gingerly, evidently still hurting from the blow he'd taken. That injury, along with the one to his leg, wouldn't heal until he slept. "We can't wait for her. Gass has sent word; he's already had another Vision. She'll have to find us."

"I know." Meldier sighed. "First time we'll be shorthanded in, what...thirty years?"

"More like forty," agreed Isiliar.

There was silence again and Caeden hesitated, not sure whether to bring up what they were all thinking. Eventually, he took a deep breath.

"So. Are we going to talk about it?"

The others shifted uncomfortably, evidence enough they had been pondering the same thing. Meldier didn't look up, but he nodded slowly.

"Where do you think he got it from?"

"Shalis artifact?" suggested Isiliar.

Alaris shook his head. "The only thing I ever saw them use kan on was their Forge, and even that was a relic of their past." He glanced at Caeden. "You knew them, though. Do you think—"

"No." Caeden shook his head firmly. "The Shalis using kan would go against everything that they stood for."

"Could it have been someone like us?" asked Meldier quietly.

They looked at each other uncertainly. "Surely El would have shown us," said Isiliar.

"He can only do so much," observed Alaris.

"But something like that..."

"We cannot assume," agreed Caeden quietly. "He shows us   205 what we need to know. We all have faith in that. But it may be that this is something that we do not yet need to know." He hesitated. "Besides, there is one other possibility."

Alaris nodded, even as the other two looked at him in confusion.

"One of us," Alaris said quietly.

Meldier stared at him blankly, then snorted. "You're joking. You think one of us created a Vessel blade, then gave it to a monster like Paetir?"

"I don't think it," said Alaris levelly. "But we cannot discount it, either."

"He's right, Meldier," said Caeden gently as Meldier opened his mouth to retort. "Think about Geraldon, or the Spires. Things happened there that seemed odd, but we passed it off as coincidence. Particularly as it's never been much more than an inconvenience before."

Meldier subsided and across from him, Isiliar looked thoughtful.

"We've traced mages using their Essence," said Isiliar suddenly. "Could there be a way to do the same with kan?"

There was a short, considering silence from the group, and then Alaris nodded contemplatively. "We're still only beginning to scratch the surface of how to use it," he conceded. "Gass or Andrael might know. They've been studying it the longest. If there's not a way, then perhaps we need to find one. A method of making us all accountable for what we do with this power." He carefully brought Paetir's blade out from its sheath at his side, laying it on the table. "Cutting the future is impressive enough," he said quietly. "But the way it sheared through Resonance armor…"

"You think it was made to fight us," said Meldier.

"Exactly." Alaris looked each of them in the eye. "Until we know more, this should stay between us, Gass, and Andrael. If we need to make inquiries to anyone else, let's keep it subtle." He peered pointedly in Isiliar's direction.

Isiliar arched an eyebrow in response. "I know how to be subtle." She was immediately met with a round of exaggerated coughs and amused grins, but her retort was cut off as a flood of locals abruptly poured into the tavern, making a beeline for their table.

It had happened several times already in the past hour, word spreading that they were the ones who had liberated the town from Paetir and his men. Alaris slid Paetir's blade carefully back into its sheath, out of sight.

A deluge of congratulations and blessings were accompanied by much shaking of hands; Caeden accepted the adulation as graciously as he could, giving the others a wry smile when the strangers weren't looking. It was awkward, sometimes... but it was also nice. Seeing that they were making a difference. Seeing that they were making people's lives better.

He leaned back, enjoying the banter and the sounds of jubilation still ringing from outside.

For the first time in years, he felt content.

Chapter 15

Caeden blinked as his vision returned.

He focused quickly this time, aware that the man opposite was watching him intently. Disorienting though these abrupt memories were, he was finding them less exhausting, easier to recover from now—finding it easier to make connections with other memories, too.

This one had been of the Venerate, before the split. They'd been more like brothers and sisters than friends. It had taken Gassandrid a long time to gather them together, but once he had, they had thrown themselves into the work. It had given them purpose—and it had been *good*. It had felt as though they were finally fighting for something real, actually making a difference in the world rather than just drifting through it. El had given them visions of atrocities, and they had done their best to right them. To bring justice where they could.

Except…it hadn't been El. It had been whatever it was that lay beyond the Boundary. The being that Asar had called Shammaeloth.

He swallowed, suddenly realizing that he now recognized who was across from him.

"Meldier," he said softly.

Meldier—it was undoubtedly him; the mannerisms, sharp features, even his steel-gray eyes were just as Caeden had remembered them—cocked his head to one side, examining Caeden curiously. "Where did you just go, Devaed?"

"I…" Caeden trailed off, the initial rush of warmth and affection fading as he recalled their current circumstances. "I was… just surprised. You let me go."

"Much faster than you did for me," observed Meldier darkly. He leaned forward, and Caeden could see that his hands were shaking slightly. With anger, probably. "Unlike you, I can make personal sacrifices when the world is at stake."

Caeden didn't know how to respond to that, so he said nothing. Meldier's expression blackened further at the silence.

"Why did you do it?" he asked softly. "Will you answer me that much, at least? I cannot say how often I wondered. Thousands of years of proof. Your friends, all warning you, all trying to help you stay on the right path. I know you weren't the first to lose faith, but you were by far the most unexpected. The others were all weak, unable to do what was needed for the greater good. But you…" He gave a soft laugh, gesturing around them. "That was never something that you struggled with. So what made you change your mind?"

Caeden shifted uncomfortably. He had no idea of the answer.

Meldier sighed, toying idly with something in his hand. It was a small, flat metal disc with a notched hole in the center. "It doesn't matter. Events move forward. The deal with the Lyth has been activated, just as Andrael wanted. And I assume that this"—he held up the disc—"is part of your plan to stop them from killing us all."

He looked up, noticing Caeden's blank expression and mistaking it for surprise. "It wasn't *that* hard to find your hidden compartment," he said with a satisfied look. He turned his attention back to the object. "Figuring out what this does, though, is another story entirely. I've spent the better part of a day trying to analyze it, but the kan scaffolding is so fine that it's hard to properly see. And what I *can* see…it has more endpoints than a Lance, *plus* two Connectors. And no signature." He'd been talking mostly to himself, but after the last sentence he glanced again in Caeden's direction. "So I know it's a companion piece, at least. To what, though? What in El's name could need to handle power like this?"

Caeden managed to keep his face smooth, hiding his bafflement.

Meldier stared back at him and then grunted, looking irritated but unsurprised by his silence. "I cannot help you if I don't know what the El-cursed thing does, Devaed."

"I don't need your help. I just need that." Caeden nodded calmly to the disc, though his stomach churned. If Meldier didn't know what it was, then there was no point in continuing to risk this charade. He'd trapped the man in a device that could only have been meant for torture, and left him there for fates knew how long. How that hadn't driven Meldier utterly insane, he had no idea—but if Meldier discovered that Caeden had lost his memories, there was no way that Caeden could trust anything the other man said.

"Then why in El's name release me?" Meldier growled, shaking his head and touching the sword at his hip. Caeden barely stopped himself from flinching at the motion; Meldier seemed under control on the surface, but there was something much darker and wilder lurking beneath his every gesture. "You *will* tell me the plan. I hold all the cards now—and last I saw you, Devaed, you were intent on imprisoning the entire world. So you'll have to forgive me for making sure you're not just going to let the Lyth do so in your stead."

Caeden repressed a shudder at the cold certainty of his tone. "I would never do that."

Meldier stared at him, then sighed. "At least tell me why you freed me, then. You evidently haven't realized your mistakes and come to make peace, else you'd be telling me what's going on. So why now? The Nexus is still stable, despite my concerns. The dok'en was still operational, and I assume that your entry keys over there"—he nodded toward the shelf off to the side—"are still working, too. So what has changed, that it doesn't matter whether your El-cursed Cyrarium gets fed?" He leaned forward. "You would not have let me loose without purpose. We know each other too well for that. So *why?*"

Caeden shook his head silently. He didn't know what a Cyrarium was, but he recognized the term dok'en—it was how he had spoken to Alaris on the road to Ilin Illan, what seemed like forever ago now. A place constructed in the mind, seeming almost real while you were there. Meldier's ability to mentally survive his imprisonment made a lot more sense now, even if the purpose behind it was more unclear than ever.

Meldier gave him a puzzled look.

"You seem...unaffected by being here," he said suddenly.

Caeden shrugged, trying to conceal his discomfort in not knowing what the other man was talking about.

Meldier watched him for a few moments in silence. "When last you were here, you were more broken than any man that I have ever seen." He held up his hand to forestall an argument he obviously expected Caeden to make. "You did not see me, and I did not show myself. I apologize for that. But... we all know what this place means to you. You do not need to pretend otherwise. It was quite cunning, actually, hiding the Tributary here." He grimaced. "And brave," he added reluctantly.

Caeden's mind raced. He knew he needed to respond.

"It was a long time ago," he said eventually.

The man studied him again, this time with a frown.

"No," he eventually said slowly. "No. *Eternity* is not long enough to heal those sorts of wounds. Not completely." His frown deepened as he tapped the sword at his side. "How *did* you get Licanius? How did you overcome Andrael's stipulations? We always assumed that he had Seen the one he wanted to wield it being there for another purpose, but..." He leaned forward. "Tell me, Devaed. What is your worst memory of this place?"

Caeden exhaled ruefully.

It had been worth trying, but Meldier knew.

"I have none," he said simply. "I erased my memories to get Licanius. Asar was meant to restore them, but he was killed before he could finish the process. Though, do not think I will not fight back if you attack. I remember some. Enough." He paused. "And my name is Caeden now. I've changed. The man I was before is gone."

Meldier shook his head. "No. Here, your name will always be Devaed," he said quietly, bitterness in his tone.

Caeden grimaced at that, glancing away.

Meldier said nothing for a while, just watching him.

"El take it," the other man muttered eventually. He gave a soft laugh. "I have no idea whether to believe you."

Caeden hesitated.

"Read me, then," he said reluctantly. "I'm being completely honest. And I truly do wish to stop the Lyth, not let them loose."

Meldier's frown deepened. "We cannot Read or Control each other," he said slowly, studying Caeden even more intently than before, his eyes burrowing into Caeden's skull. "We can share memories, but Reading another of the Venerate's thoughts is impossible." Sadness flickered across his face. "That is why, above all else, we needed trust."

Caeden heard the sorrowful rebuke in the words, and didn't know how to respond. He knew as soon as Meldier said it that it was true, though.

"You're still fighting for the wrong side, Devaed," continued Meldier, his voice quiet. "I don't know if you remember your madness, but El knows I do. *You* are in the wrong here." He leaned forward, gesturing at their surroundings. "Before... everything, that would have meant something to the man I knew. To my friend."

Caeden scowled. "No—I know what's going on, Meldier. And even if I hadn't had it explained to me, I have seen what your 'right' side does. You're the aggressors, the invaders. I've seen your soldiers desecrate the bodies of women and children, just to draw out a city's defenders. I've seen the monstrosities you use." He straightened. "Nothing you say can change that."

Meldier frowned. "I cannot speak to the specifics," he conceded, "but a soldier's responsibility is to his men and his mission; if he can use the tools at hand to gain victory and spare even one of his own people's lives, then he will—he *should*—repugnant though those tools may be. That does not mean that he revels in his actions, nor can it ever be the arbiter of whether he is actually good or evil." He sighed. "War is the very definition of ends justifying means, Tal'kamar—on both sides. When we fight for the greater good, it is a reality that we must accept... and you of all people believed that to be true. In many ways, you are the embodiment of the very thing that you are trying to condemn."

Caeden's scowl deepened. "That is a lie."

Meldier just exhaled heavily in response. "You don't even know what this place *is*, do you?"

Caeden glowered but remained silent, unable to refute the point.

Meldier stared out into the gathering gloom. "These are the Plains of Decay," he continued softly. "They were once the center of the Darecian Empire. Buildings more beautiful than you can imagine, and a people more loving and peaceable than any I have ever known. Centuries ahead in philosophy, art, all kinds of knowledge…" He swallowed a sudden lump in his throat. "This land was once a single city. An enormous, connected metropolis. It housed millions of people. *Tens* of millions."

Caeden shifted uncomfortably. He knew a little about the Darecians, and Meldier's words tickled at the edges of his memory, but not enough to recall anything specific. "What happened?" he asked, knowing that it was the question expected of him.

"You did. This…this was all your doing."

Caeden shivered, but shook his head firmly. This was why he hadn't wanted the man to know about his memories. Meldier was trying to worm his way inside his head, to feed into his fears.

"I don't believe you," he said, voice flat.

Meldier was silent. Then, abruptly, he stretched out his hand.

A sliver of black arrowed toward Caeden's head; he tried to avoid it but it moved with him, striking him in the forehead.

"Then let me show you," said Meldier grimly.

Caeden moved through the crumbling hallway, numb with shock and grief and fear.

He caught a glimpse of the outside world through the window, and the sight caused him to stumble, to retch in the corner before moving on. The beauty of Dareci was decaying at a horrific rate; the first thirty miles of the city were now little more than a gray, shattered stain on the face of the earth. The crystal buildings of the middle rings still held, as well as the stone of the outer—including the one in which he now stood—but they wouldn't for long.

Two thousand years. Two thousand years of life, and he had never seen death or destruction such as this.

Tears streaming down his face, he leaned his shoulder into the door at the end of the hallway and burst through it.

The man at the far end of the room was standing at a window, watching. To his right, the machinery of a Gate lay ready to be activated, though Caeden could see the warping of the lines of kan even now. They had minutes. Less, maybe.

The man turned at the sound of Caeden's entrance. He was tall, his pale skin stark against the shadows cast by the moonlight.

Caeden paused when he saw his expression. There was none of the madness he'd expected, none of the wild, jittering schism of consciousness that surely must have occurred for him to do this. Just hands that were shaking, and rivulets through the dust on his face.

Sadness and guilt. Only sadness and guilt.

"Meldier," said Tal'kamar softly. "I did not know that you were here."

"Tal." Caeden leaned against a nearby pillar, suddenly trembling himself now that there was a lack of forward momentum. His heart broke as outside the window, behind Tal, he saw another tower silhouetted in the moonlight silently crumble to dust in the distance. His voice cracked. "Why?"

"You know why. It has to be this way." Tal drew a deep, shuddering breath. "And it's Aarkein Devaed now."

Caeden felt sick. Aarkein Devaed. He recognized the language, though few would. "The fate of all that could be," in the Shalis' tongue. They were long-extinct now, their Furnace used only to rebuild dar'gaithin, but Tal'kamar had always thought well of them.

"Aarkein, then," said Caeden. "Listen to me. This is…madness. Beyond madness. You need to stop it. This is not what we do. You can still stop it." The last was plea more than statement.

Tal shuddered, the motion noticeable though he'd never stopped shaking. "I cannot," he whispered. He rubbed his arms, a nervous gesture. For the first time since Caeden had known him, he looked…lost. Broken. "And even if I could, it is inevitable. What was meant to be. I did it, and did it now, because we can use it for our own ends. But with or without me, it was going to happen. He showed it to me." He coughed, a dry, rasping sound. "We are the blade, Meldier. Just the blade."

"And yet none of us knew. No one else was told. This was all on you, Tal." Caeden crept forward, hand outstretched in a calming gesture, approaching as one might approach an easily startled animal. One that could attack at the slightest provocation. "Just think for a moment. Think. Why would this burden be yours alone to bear? Why for this, and for nothing else?" He took another step. Another. "But if you were fooled, somehow. By your mind, by Shammaeloth, by some enemy of the Darecians…"

"I am certain, my friend. El gave me this task," said Tal quietly.

It was too much for Caeden to take, too hard for him to listen to.

"Can you hear yourself?" Caeden roared the words, rage overtaking fear. "You have just murdered millions of people, Tal! It is the very opposite of what we stand for, what we have been trying to do. We're here to protect these people! We're trying to save them!"

Tal didn't reply for a few moments.

"We are," he said softly. "I know that it is hard to hear, but we are."

He gestured to his right; the Gate flickered, blue fire whirling into existence. The flames were muted, drawn toward the center of the shattered city as kan scrabbled hungrily at the Essence within.

"Go," said Tal. "The Gate cannot withstand for much longer. Nor can we." Fresh tears slid down his cheeks.

Caeden watched his friend—or the man who had once been his friend—and his heart broke. This was not the Tal'kamar he knew. Despite the calm exterior, this version was unstable. Dangerous. Utterly mad.

Caeden could not save Dareci, but he could ensure that its destroyer was not allowed to escape its fate.

He stepped slowly toward the Gate, then turned to Tal before he went through.

"I pray the Chamber cures you, Tal," he said softly. "And I pray that we will meet again when it has."

He formed two kan blades, angling them to the side and just behind him.

He stepped through.

He felt rather than saw the blades slash through the Gate's machinery; there was a brief cry of horror from Tal, cut off as the Gate collapsed in upon itself, barely before Caeden had made it through.

He stood on the other side for a few moments, silent.

Then he fell to his knees. Sobbed. Wept for what had happened.
Wept for the friend he'd lost.

Caeden gasped, tears streaming down his face.

That had been *him*. Him, as seen by someone else. The body was different, the voice, the reactions... but he knew. Meldier's memory had been painfully clear, as clear as if it were his own.

He stared into the fire for a few moments in numb disbelief, trying to fully grasp what he'd just seen. The memory didn't have the same visceral impact of what he'd done in Desriel, nor did it have the same gut-wrenching emotion of the one from Elhyris.

This was far, far worse. This was murder on a scale that he couldn't comprehend. This was...

He shook his head. It was beyond his emotional capacity to process. Not just the horror inherent in his actions, but... it was as if the sliver of faith he'd still had in his past self, the one he'd been nurturing since that first day in the Wells, had finally died.

He drew a shivering breath, then turned to see Meldier watching him.

"So. You see now? I could not be in this place and have a conversation with you, without you understanding what you did here. To do so spits on the people you murdered. The millions who died for your selfishness. The great civilization that you burned to the ground." Meldier held Caeden's gaze steadily, but his voice seethed with pent-up emotion. He'd clearly just relived it as well. "To this day, that memory haunts me above all others. To this day, I think of the friends I lost here and I *do not forgive you*."

He shuddered. "And despite that? Despite that, Devaed? I understand what you did more than I understand what came after," he said softly. "You once told me that conviction is nothing until it is tested. Though none of us ever accepted your actions here, we at least grasped *why*, and we worked with you to make them *mean* something. You shattered the Venerate, but many thought that your doing so was a necessary step. That you acted in secret to protect us. That you sacrificed your soul for the good of all." He ran his hands through his hair. "But in turning your back on us after that, you made what happened here worse by far. You strove to make these deaths *meaningless*. For that alone, I should take Licanius and I should strike you down."

Caeden swallowed, heart wrenching with every word. This wasn't what he'd expected from his enemies. What Meldier was saying made sense. He sounded like a man who wanted only justice.

He sounded...*right*.

"But you won't," said Caeden, voice shaking slightly as he forced down the horror.

"No. Not now, because I understand what it is to sacrifice for the greater good." That was clearly directed at him, a bitter jibe. "Because better to let a monster live than to condemn the world."

Caeden closed his eyes, and silence fell as he took a few deep breaths. Forced himself to calm.

Some distant part of him was still reeling from what Meldier had revealed.

Another part—a part that he was slowly forcing himself to acknowledge—had already known.

Not the specifics, perhaps. Not the scope of the evil he'd perpetrated. But from the moment he'd discovered that he was Aarkein Devaed—discovered that his very name had been synonymous with all that people feared—he'd been heading toward an uneasy understanding that his memories would be something to endure, not welcome. An acceptance that there was nothing he could now do to truly make up for whatever had gone before.

He took another breath, and then another. It hurt, it sickened him, but all this memory had truly achieved was to confirm the worst.

And even if he'd done those things—even if redemption was truly beyond him—that didn't mean that he shouldn't *try*. He'd left these memories behind for a reason. He'd left that *path* behind for a reason.

So he pushed down the shame, the disgust. Buried them deep.

Those were Aarkein Devaed's to bear, not his.

He opened his eyes.

"I believe you." Caeden said the words clearly and calmly, even as his emotions still roiled. "And you're right. The man that you just showed me? He was a monster."

Meldier blinked, his brow furrowing. "But?"

"But that wasn't me." A surge of determination ran through

him. "You can call me Aarkein Devaed all you like. You can show me my past—things that turn my stomach to even think about. But that *isn't me now*."

Meldier frowned, shaking his head. "You're simply telling yourself that to give yourself comfort. To dissociate yourself from what you just saw. But when your memories come back, you'll start to justify your actions. You'll—"

"My memories *have* been coming back," insisted Caeden. "Asar said something to me once that I didn't think anything of at the time. He said that it was unfortunate that our plan didn't go as it should have, and that I took a year to find him when I should have taken days. He acted as if it were a terrible thing, my meeting others and being influenced by them, forming a personality before trying to get my memories back."

He nodded slowly, confidence building. "He was wrong. I don't know whether I knew that it would happen this way, but he was *wrong*. Perhaps things would be different if I hadn't met other people, *good* people, and spent time with them. Perhaps if I'd gone to him a blank slate, you would be talking to a very different man. But I didn't. Instead, I see these memories and . . . yes, they become a part of me. But I reject them, too. They will stay with me always, but I will *not* let them take away who I already am."

Meldier listened in silence, the heat of his initial emotion gradually dissipating. When Caeden was finished, the other man looked more sorrowful than angry.

"You have the confidence of a mortal," he said eventually, quietly. He gave a tired smile. "And the failings of one. I know that this is hard to hear, but pushing down the pain will not make it go away. Better to face your sins, Devaed. Better to own them. When you live as long as we do, it is the only way forward."

Caeden gritted his teeth, saying nothing. He *was* different. In many ways, what Meldier had just shown him was easier to accept than the other memories. Not because it was less horrific, but because it was *so* unthinkable, *so* foreign to him that he could easily identify it as something that he could never now do.

Eventually Meldier sighed, shaking his head. "But perhaps you have changed. In truth, I *hope* you have," he said quietly. "Only time will tell."

"It always does," murmured Caeden, an automatic response.

He frowned as he realized what he'd said, saw the recognition of the phrase in Meldier's eyes. Before he could say anything further, though, a soft, eerie whispering began from outside the circle of black columns.

Caeden glanced around past the reach of the fire at the now-complete darkness, but Meldier didn't seem to notice the sound, digging something from his pocket and holding it up. Caeden's eyes widened as he recognized the bronze of the Portal Box.

Meldier hesitated, then irritably tossed the cube to him, followed a few seconds later by the steel disc. Caeden juggled the two Vessels, nearly dropping them in his surprise.

"Take them, then," Meldier said resignedly. "There is nothing more for us to say."

Caeden's heart pounded, but he kept his face smooth. "And Licanius?"

Meldier scoffed. "You think that I would give it back to you?"

"I cannot defeat the Lyth without it," said Caeden calmly, meeting Meldier's gaze.

Meldier shook his head. "Explain why, and I will give it to you."

"I'll not tell you my plans." Caeden pocketed the disc but held on to the Portal Box, quickly checking his Reserve. It was close to full again. "But I cannot leave here without it." He hesitated. "Do you remember Paetir? That warlord we took on in Rinday?"

Meldier blinked, then reluctantly nodded. "When Diara died. The first time we found one of these." He lifted Licanius slightly. "In a lot of ways, it's where all of this began."

"We were doing good, then." Caeden's heart pounded, but he didn't let his nervousness show. He was gambling here—working with incomplete information—but it was all he had. "I want that feeling again, Meldier. I want to help people. But I *need* Licanius to do it."

Meldier gazed at the sword for a long, tense second.

Then he grunted.

"Truth be told, Devaed, I'm not sure how far you can go without it anyway," he said ruefully. "Andrael's agreement with the Lyth means that it's bound to you, and you to it." He sheathed the blade. "You will get it when you are ready to leave. Not a moment before."

"I can leave straight away," said Caeden.

Meldier gave an exasperated sigh, and some of the tension went out of him as he gestured at the whispering darkness that surrounded them. "Not until dawn, you can't. Trust me."

Caeden frowned, but something in Meldier's voice rang true. He nodded, unwilling to reveal the extent of his ignorance by asking further questions. "Dawn, then." He did his best to keep the relief from his face.

Meldier turned away, the conversation evidently finished in his mind. Caeden breathed an inaudible sigh of relief. He needed the silence, the chance to catch his breath.

It wasn't long though before his thoughts returned, however unwillingly, to Meldier's memory. He chewed over it for a while but no matter how he approached it, there was no getting around what Devaed had done. What *he'd* done. Trying to comprehend *anyone* doing that was... beyond him. The evil was so great that it felt more an abstract concept than reality.

Devaed had been a monster—Meldier wasn't wrong about that much.

But Devaed was also the past.

He clenched his fists. Meldier didn't know him anymore. Caeden might not have all his memories, and he might not know what lay ahead—but he knew who he was, and who he wanted to be.

For now, tonight, that would have to be enough.

He settled down in front of the fire to wait.

Caeden gazed into the flames, trying to ignore the constant, unsettling susurrus from beyond the columns.

The sun was still some time from rising, and everything outside the ring in which he and Meldier stood was utterly dark. The fire illuminated the smooth stone plateau well enough, but that light did not extend an inch past the surrounding pillars. The whispering moans that emanated from the black drifted around them, unceasing since they had begun.

"What *is* that?" he asked abruptly, unable to restrain his curiosity any longer. When Meldier made no response—the man had been silent since relinquishing the Vessels—Caeden stood, took a few steps toward the nearest gap between columns, and squinted, trying to see out into the inky black.

"Stop." Meldier's voice was sharp, authoritative.

When Caeden turned to give him a questioning look, he sighed. "You don't want to go out there, Devaed. El, even *I* don't want you to go out there. Stay within the Nexus, and you will be fine."

Caeden took a hesitant step back, trusting the concern in Meldier's voice more than his words. He gave a final stare into the darkness, then retreated back to the fire.

"Another effect of what I did here," he said quietly, not needing Meldier's slight nod of acknowledgment to know it for truth.

"Effect or means, I have never been entirely sure," said Meldier quietly. "The Darklanders have always been tied to the Columns."

Caeden went cold. "Darklanders?" A disquieting flash of the memory Asar had shown him played through his mind, dizzying him slightly.

Meldier said nothing for a moment, and Caeden thought he was ignoring the question. Then he sighed.

"It's what you called them. Shades from the other side. I don't think they have much agency here, but if they sense life out where they can reach it, they will swarm. I've seen it happen." He saw Caeden's expression and snorted. "Don't worry, Devaed. There's no rift to the Darklands out there. Just…them. Drifting, aimless, so long as there is not enough Essence to burn them."

Caeden nodded silently and held out his hands, letting warmth seep into them. Silence fell again for a time.

"How much do you really remember?" asked Meldier abruptly.

Caeden didn't reply. He wanted answers, but revealing just how little he knew…it would be worse than foolish. He wasn't about to disclose a weakness like that.

"El take you," said Meldier in exasperation when it became clear that Caeden wasn't interested in conversation. "Just talk to me. We *were* friends, you know, and…part of me still holds out hope for you, even now."

Caeden glared over at him. "If you know about the Darklands

and the rift, then I don't see what there is to say. What you're doing is going to unleash that horror on the *world*, Meldier."

Meldier snorted. "Is that what Asar told you? Because you clearly don't have all of your memories, so I do not see how you could possibly be doing more than just parroting that claim."

"I know the story that you believe," pressed Caeden. "I remember Gassandrid telling me that it was really El trapped here in this world, and that he wanted to set us all free—free from fate."

Meldier scowled. "And do you remember meeting El? Do you remember the proof He showed us? The undeniable *logic*? You mentioned Rinday. What about back then? What about all the good we did together?"

Caeden glared, though he couldn't help the shiver of uncertainty that ran through him. The memory of Rinday had been confusing; there was no denying the sense of peace, of *rightness* he'd had back then.

Meldier leaned forward, perhaps sensing his doubt. "Let that guard of yours down for just one second, and let your friends help. Look at what you did to me here—shutting me in the Tributary, using me as you would use an animal, an object. I can show you the *truth*. If we can just work together to—"

"No." Caeden said the word calmly, but he felt his jaw clench. "You've made it clear that we are on opposite sides, Meldier. The truth of an enemy is not something I want to hear."

"Sometimes that is the truth we need," observed Meldier quietly. "Because the truth, Devaed, is that even if you are right? It *doesn't matter*. You cannot deny that we are prisoners of whatever force has burdened this world with inevitability—and what is the point of living if we cannot truly make our own choices? What is the point of living without *possibility*?"

Caeden was silent for a moment, thinking. He couldn't help but remember a similar conversation with Nihim, what seemed like forever ago.

"Even if our choices are inevitable, it doesn't mean that they are not our own," he observed eventually.

"That is like saying that if I throw you from a cliff, you are choosing to fall." Meldier leaned forward. "And whether it is thanks to Shammaeloth, or El, or some other force entirely, is irrelevant. Fate is the master of everyone in this world, and no one with a master is ever truly free. So I fight for the only side that offers me hope."

Caeden closed his eyes. "Hope?" he repeated softly. This had the feel of an old argument, something they had debated many times, but he had no idea of how best to respond. He pushed down another uncomfortable flutter of doubt in his chest. "What you showed me? I was on *your* side when I did it. And as much as you admitted to hating it, you also said that you understood it." He shook his head slowly. "Argue all you want, Meldier. I'll never be on the same side as someone who *understands* something like that."

Meldier's expression faded to a scowl, and for a moment there was a dangerous anger in his eyes.

"Very well," he said, sounding as though he were forcing out the words. "Never let it be said that I did not try. I suppose for now, all that matters is that you find the other part of that Vessel. Fail in that, and it won't matter whose side you are on."

Caeden frowned. What had Ell...Nethgalla...screamed after him as he'd escaped the Wells? It was all a blur, but he was sure that she'd said that he couldn't stop the Lyth without something she had. The Siphon, she'd called it?

He grimaced, putting the concern to the back of his mind, at least for now. Even if she'd been referring to the other piece of the device, he knew that the creature who had stolen his wife's form couldn't be trusted. He would worry about Nethgalla only if he found himself with no other option.

A hint of yellow crested the eastern edge of the valley, and the whispering surrounding them abruptly dissipated.

Caeden and Meldier exchanged a glance, a silent understanding passing between them. They both stood.

Meldier unbuckled Licanius, then tossed it on the ground to the side. Caeden hesitated, then moved over to the blade and picked it up, keeping a mistrustful eye on Meldier as he did so.

"Use that on one of us, Devaed, and our past will mean nothing. I will come for you, and I will make you suffer," said Meldier quietly. There was no heat to his words. It was a promise, not a threat.

Caeden swallowed, but nodded. He could hardly blame

the man.

"When I find whatever goes with the disc you found," he said quietly, buckling the sword to his waist, "do you have any idea what the completed Vessel might be? What it might do?"

Meldier stared at him for a moment, eyes going from Caeden's face, to the sword at his side, then back again.

He shook his head sheepishly.

"Something that allows the Lyth to leave Res Kartha without Decaying, and yet prevents them from going to war with us again—with you? No. The others and I have pondered the problem enough over the years to be quite certain. There's nothing I know of that could achieve such a goal."

Caeden nodded grimly. "Have you ever heard of something called a Siphon?"

Meldier stared, looking chagrined. "You really don't know your own plan, do you?" he eventually said ruefully. He shook his head. "I have never heard of it. Perhaps one of the others will recognize the name, but I am just as in the dark as you." He glared at Caeden. "Well. Perhaps not *quite* as much in the dark."

Caeden gave him a vaguely apologetic look, then held the Portal Box in front of him and tapped his Reserve. He carefully funnelled Essence into the next face in sequence, suddenly pensive again as yet another leap into the unknown loomed.

For a moment nothing happened.

Then the blazing tunnel opened with a familiar roar, though the sound was...muted, somehow. Not muffled but more warped, as if it were not traveling correctly through the air.

"I hope that what you say is true," Meldier yelled over the sound. "I hope you are a new person. Someone better." He paused. "But either way, the Lyth *must* be prevented from getting Licanius—because if they do, they *will* kill us all. Even if you trust nothing else you have learned thus far, trust to that."

Caeden locked gazes with him for a moment, seeing the quiet certainty in the other man's eyes.

He gave Meldier a grim nod, then walked once again into the vortex of flame.

Chapter 16

Wirr breathed in the early-morning air, feet dangling over the balcony as the first hint of dawn began to lighten his surroundings, silhouetting Ilin Tora against the sky.

He yawned a little as he gazed out over Ilin Illan, which spread out like a living map below. Despite his initial weariness, he hadn't been able to sleep much. He was sitting just outside Karaliene's rooms, flanked on one side by his cousin and on the other by Dezia; they'd been like that for much of the night, just talking, enjoying the relative hush and privacy that accompanied the early hour.

"Any idea where Aelric is?" he asked idly, suddenly realizing how long it had been since they'd seen him. Dezia's brother had joined them to begin with—the only reason Andyn's replacement had agreed to give him some privacy—but had hurried off after a while with a brief, muttered explanation and never returned.

"Probably asleep. He finds all of this new responsibility exhausting." Dezia smiled to show she was half joking, then shifted slightly as she glanced at him, her hip touching Wirr's as they watched the city below slowly come to life. Wirr could still see buildings in need of repair after the devastating fires of the Blind's attack, but a pleasing amount of progress had been made toward getting the city back in good order.

"I know how he feels."

"Poor Torin," murmured Karaliene. "An entire *month* of being responsible. However have you survived." She exchanged a good-natured eye roll with Dezia.

Wirr elbowed his cousin amiably, then sighed as he noticed the eastern horizon starting to become obviously lighter.

"Almost time," he said heavily.

There was silence for a while—not an awkward one, but more contemplative. Dezia turned to Wirr, and Wirr was abruptly aware of just how close their faces were.

"You'll be careful, won't you?" she said, expression serious. She looked him in the eye. "There's no way Scyner has your best interests at heart."

Wirr gave her an appreciative smile, but shook his head. "I don't think he'll hurt me," he said. "He could have killed me—all he had to do was not intervene. And I hate the thought, but I'm fairly sure that he could get to me at any time."

"Do me a favor? Be careful anyway," said Dezia. Her tone was light, but Wirr could see the concern in her eyes.

Wirr nodded. "I will." They stared at each other for a long moment, faces not more than a foot apart.

Then Karaliene gave a loud cough, making both Wirr and Dezia jump. Wirr turned to glower at his cousin, only to notice the man climbing the spiral staircase toward them. Wirr straightened, modifying his glare to include a hint of gratitude.

"Master Kardai," he said as the man approached, dragging himself to his feet and offering a hand to each of the girls. They accepted graciously, allowing themselves to be pulled up.

Wirr frowned as he caught the expression on Laiman's face. "Is something wrong?"

The king's adviser hesitated, glancing at Wirr's companions. "I hear that you will be taking some time at your family's estate in the country, Sire. Leaving this morning. A well-advised move, if I may say so," he said carefully. "But first, I wanted to...discuss something with you. Show you something, actually." His second glance at Karaliene and Dezia indicated that he preferred to do so privately.

Wirr turned away from Laiman, giving the girls an apologetic look. "I suppose we should do that sooner rather than later, then," he said regretfully. He kept his focus on Dezia and Karaliene. "You'll see me off in a couple of hours?"

228   "Of course," said Karaliene, and Dezia nodded with a smile.

Wirr smiled back, then reluctantly followed Laiman down the winding staircase. "What is this about?" he asked once they were out of earshot. "I thought I'd already made all the necessary arrangements for the next few days."

"It's about last night, Sire," Laiman said quietly. "I'm sorry for interrupting."

"It's fine." He was accustomed to being dragged away in the middle of personal conversations now. "What are you showing me?"

Laiman hesitated. "I want you to have a look at the men and woman who attacked you. I know you said that you didn't recognize them, but I felt that it was worth having a try while they weren't in the process of trying to kill you."

"So we're going to look at some corpses." Wirr gave Laiman a flat look. "Perhaps I accepted your apology too quickly."

"Probably, Sire," said Laiman cheerfully.

Wirr allowed a wry smile at that, though it quickly faded. He liked Laiman; the man had been a good teacher when he'd returned to court. Whenever he saw him now, though, he couldn't help but think about the mysterious conversation that Asha had overheard after the battle.

"I was surprised to hear that there were six of them, Your Highness," Laiman observed after a while, casting a sideways glance at Wirr as they walked. "It must have been quite a fight."

Wirr hesitated, then shook his head.

"I'm not exactly sure what happened. It was all so fast, but...they ended up turning on one another. I barely had to do anything."

"Not according to young Iria Tel'Rath."

Wirr blinked. "What?"

"She says that you single-handedly saved her, and then took on the rest to let her escape." Laiman gave an amused cough. "The way she puts it, Sire, the one left alive fled from the sheer force of your heroism."

Wirr rubbed his forehead. "That's not even close to how it happened. Iria stabbed one of them in the leg, and I threw a plate at him to distract him. After that..."

He trailed off, not knowing how to describe the rest. Laiman, fortunately, assumed that he was just surprised at Iria's description. "It's not how she tells it, Sire," he reiterated to Wirr with a slight smirk, "and she's been telling it a *lot*. So if I were you, I'd be careful about making a Tel'Rath a liar. Especially given how well you come out of the entire thing."

Wirr sighed, shaking his head. Just what he needed.

Soon enough they had reached the room in which the bodies were being kept. Wirr noted, much to his surprise, that it was one of the palace's more out-of-the-way Lockrooms.

"You're keeping them in here?" he asked in bemusement.

"Temporarily. I wanted to ensure that no one had opportunity to tamper with any evidence before I inspected them." Laiman shrugged as he produced a key and inserted it into the lock. "And while there are already rumors about what happened last night, the less that prying eyes can discover, the better. Not even an Augur could see what's in here without either having this key, or breaking down the door."

They entered; the room was cold, probably a deliberate choice considering its contents. Wirr's stomach turned a little as he saw the five pale figures lying side by side on the long table, their wounds exposed. His fortitude had increased significantly over the past year, though. He stared at the corpses without flinching, studying each face closely.

"I definitely don't recognize them," he assured Laiman.

Laiman inclined his head, walking over to the nearest man and pulling back the corpse's right sleeve.

Wirr felt his brow furrow. The majority of the man's arm was covered in an old scar, possibly a burn.

"Strange injury," he observed slowly, not seeing the significance.

Laiman nodded, then proceeded to pull back the woman's right sleeve. A near-identical scar lay beneath the cloth, stretching from wrist to elbow.

"The other three don't have them," said Laiman quietly. "But the man that was captured does, too."

Wirr was silent for a few moments, processing.

"A Mark?" He rubbed his chin. "You think they did that to themselves to hide a Mark. You think that they're Administrators."

"Did any of them with that scar actually attack you?"

Wirr thought for a moment. The woman had shot Andyn; at the time he'd assumed it was because he was blocking her line to him, but now...

He shook his head slowly. "Not that I can think of. It happened fast, though," he prevaricated. He'd told Dezia and Kara the details of the attack—he'd felt the need to tell *someone*—but he didn't know Laiman well enough to elaborate.

He shifted uncomfortably as the implications of what Laiman was showing him started to hit home. He understood that he was unpopular; his position as prince gave him a lot of protections from people's anger, but he'd still had to endure plenty of furious Administrators during the first couple of weeks after the battle.

Still—strangely, it hurt to think that the threat might be coming from within his own organization, almost as much as it unsettled him.

"At least we should be able to identify them," he said eventually. "Administration keeps detailed records on everyone who takes the Oath."

Laiman shook his head. "Take another look at those scars."

Wirr did so, brow furrowing again as he stared at the disfigured forearms, and tried to ascertain what his uncle's adviser was getting at.

"These are old. Healed years ago," he said suddenly.

"Which means that these Administrators didn't burn off their Mark specifically for this," concluded Laiman. "You may not be able to find any documentation on them at all."

Wirr gave him a blank look. "That shouldn't be possible."

"There are, what—fifteen Oathstones held at Administration's outposts around Andarra?" Laiman shrugged. "There have been rumors of Administrators 'borrowing' Oathstones for almost as long as there's been an Administration. And except for a recent spate of concern over the past couple of years, I don't believe your father ever particularly pushed for it to stop."

"But why?" Wirr scratched his head; he'd never heard this before. "The Oathstones are tied to the Tenets. Whether someone gets their Mark officially or unofficially, they're still bound by the same rules."

"The same *limitations*. Not the same *rules*." Laiman shrugged. "Administrators might act unpleasantly toward the Gifted, and I know that infractions often go unpunished—but ultimately, they are still constrained by the law. The old Fourth Tenet allowed them to issue commands, but there was always a recourse for anyone who was truly being taken advantage of that way. Always oversight, however light. And real consequences for those actually found guilty of abusing their power."

Wirr's stomach churned as he understood. "So there were people out there with the ability to make the Gifted do whatever they said—with their only restriction being that they couldn't make them violate the other Tenets," he said slowly. "And if the Gifted reported it, Administration would have no record of whomever was responsible. If they even believed them."

"Exactly." Laiman sighed. "The thing is, though—I doubt any of those 'unofficial' Administrators could have organized such a coordinated attack. Someone with inside knowledge had to have helped them, or at least passed them information." He looked Wirr in the eye. "If you were not already leaving, I would be strongly advising you to do so. And if you felt like staying away from the city for a little longer than planned, I wouldn't blame you."

Wirr swallowed, then shook his head. "No," he said softly. "I can afford a few days away to see my family, especially as it's something that I already should have done. But if I'm absent for too long, what little authority I have will be eroded completely— and the longer I'm away, the more likely Administration are to try and revoke the Augur Amnesty. I can't let that happen."

Laiman gave another nod, this time a hint of respect in the motion. "You're right, Sire," he acceded. "But that's even more likely to happen if you're dead. At the least, I would urge you to keep your movements quiet and your bodyguard close for a while."

Wirr nodded morosely, staring at the still forms of the people who had tried to kill him. He didn't feel afraid, exactly. More a deep sense of unease, a sense that further violence was inevitable—but that he had no idea when it might occur.

Laiman watched him for a few more seconds, then sighed. "I've said my piece, Sire," he said gently. "There's probably a carriage waiting for you by now."

Wirr gave Laiman a nod, then slipped out of the Lockroom and went to ensure that everything he needed for the journey ahead was in place.

It was time to leave.

⚜

Wirr hid a grimace as he saw the tall figure spot him and change course.

Lord Tel'Rath's expression gave nothing away as he approached; Wirr came to a reluctant stop, barely restraining a sigh as he acknowledged that the man wanted to speak with him.

"Lord Tel'Rath," he said politely, bracing himself for whatever remonstrations were coming.

"Northwarden Torin," said Lord Tel'Rath, to Wirr's surprise the greeting containing more than a hint of respect. "I'm glad I caught you before you left." The older man hesitated, looking somewhat uncertain. "I . . . just wanted to . . . express my gratitude. To thank you," he finished awkwardly.

Wirr stared at him. Perhaps for the first time since Wirr had met the man, he appeared to be genuine. "For . . . ?"

"For saving Iria. She told us what you did." Lord Tel'Rath's tone was different from the previous night, different from how Wirr had ever heard it before. Gone was the careful intonation, the sense that he was guarding every word. This was unaffected. Honest.

"It was what anyone would have done. And Iria was far from helpless," Wirr observed. "She helped me as much as I helped her."

"You saved my daughter," repeated Lord Tel'Rath firmly, as if Wirr wasn't understanding what he was trying to say. "Whatever you may think of us"—he held up a hand as Wirr made to protest—"my family is important to me. I owe you a debt. I won't forget this."

To Wirr's astonishment, he held out his hand.

A little dazedly, Wirr took it; Lord Tel'Rath shook it warmly, then nodded and left.

Dezia, much to his relief, was waiting for him when he reached his carriage. She raised an eyebrow when she saw his expression.

"Running from something?"

"Lord Tel'Rath," said Wirr dazedly. "He was being . . . *grateful.*"

Dezia's lips quirked upward slightly. "That doesn't surprise me," she admitted. "You wouldn't believe what I've heard about you this morning."

Wirr rubbed his forehead. "I suspect I would, actually. How bad is it?"

Dezia bumped him with her shoulder. "Well, you saved Iria. And the Tel'Raths. Held off a dozen assassins with your bare hands, and looked dashing the entire time. So now, not only are you the most eligible bachelor at court, you're also the most desirable one." She grinned, unable to hide her amusement. "I think that about covers it."

Wirr nodded slowly. "Well, at least they got the facts straight."

Dezia's smile widened. "I'll be sure to tell anyone who asks that you confirmed it was all true, then."

Wirr gave her a gentle return bump of his shoulder in reproof, then glanced around with a small frown. "Before I go—I don't suppose you've seen Asha this morning?" Everything had been a blur since last night and he hadn't had time to seek her out, but he'd been vaguely surprised that she hadn't heard the news and come to check on him yet.

"Representative Chaedris?" Dezia shook her head. "Sorry. Not recently."

Wirr sighed; he'd just have to fill her in on everything when he got back. He nodded an acknowledgment and turned reluctantly toward his transportation.

"I hate carriages," he said grimly.

"Depends on where they're taking you, I suspect." Dezia's smile faded, and she laid a hand gently on Wirr's arm. "Look—I know you don't think this is a trap, but . . ."

"I know." Wirr gave her a reassuring nod. "I'll see you when I get back in a few days."

Wirr allowed the carriage door to be opened for him, then frowned sternly at the sole occupant.

"You *really* shouldn't be here."

Andyn shifted uncomfortably, though whether because of what Wirr had said or because of lingering pain from his injury, Wirr couldn't tell. "I know I failed you last night, Sire," he said quickly, "but I still feel I can be—"

Wirr cut him off with a laugh, swinging up into the carriage to sit opposite his bodyguard. "I didn't mean because of what happened. Fates, man. You saved my life." He shook his head in amusement. "I meant that you should be resting, not back on duty so soon. Just because you were healed doesn't mean that your body has fully recovered. Besides—the escort there will be protection enough, and my uncle has sent men ahead, in addition to the security my mother already has at the property."

Andyn grunted, though Wirr thought he saw a hint of relief in the man's expression. "I feel fine, Sire. You will be gone for several days, and assassins do not tend to be easily dissuaded."

Wirr thought for a moment, then sighed. He didn't really mind Andyn's insistence. After the previous night, a familiar face on this journey—one that he knew he could trust—would be welcome. "Seems an odd way to reward you, but if it's what you really want..."

Andyn gave a satisfied nod, and settled back into his seat.

Soon enough Wirr had said his good-byes, and they were moving. He rubbed his hands together nervously as they passed through Fedris Idri and began circling around Ilin Tora. It wasn't the threat of assassination that concerned him at the moment, though, but rather the sudden recognition of landmarks as the lush hillsides south of Ilin Illan rolled by. He'd taken this route from the city many times as a child.

He had no idea what sort of welcome would await him at his family's estate in Daren Tel. He had spoken with his mother and Deldri at his father's funeral, of course—even the instability in the city following the Blind's defeat hadn't kept them away from that—but the conversation had been brief, terse, and tearstained, barely more than an acknowledgment of their shared pain.

Since that day, he hadn't seen his mother or sister at all. They had retreated once more to the family estate, both to avoid the new dangers within the city—there had been some scattered lawlessness and looting after the invasion—and to grieve. Wirr hadn't objected. He'd grieved, too, but it had been in short bursts;

his duties demanded more of him than he could possibly have imagined, and he'd owed it to his uncle and everyone else to keep his mind focused on the tasks at hand.

That had all been normal, as far as these things went—nothing unusual in the events themselves. But that meeting with his mother at the funeral...

He shook his head at the memory. It might have been his imagination, or perhaps simply the emotion of the day, but she'd seemed cold and close to expressionless as she'd all-too-briefly spoken with him. And then he'd been allowed to do little more than embrace his sister before she'd been whisked away again.

So though he had tried not to dwell on it too much, he silently feared the worst. His mother had always shared Elocien's disdain for the Gifted... but his father had ultimately changed his views once he'd learned about Wirr.

Wirr just hoped that meant that his mother could, too.

Soon enough they were winding their way up the road to the house and through a tall gate, which had opened as soon as their carriage came into view. Wirr stared around the grounds, shaking his head a little at the sight. Unlike the ruined vegetation of Ilin Illan—much of which had either been burned or drained for Essence by Davian—everything here was a lush green, all immaculately kept gardens and neatly trimmed lawns within the stone walls of the property. He knew that it wasn't anything unusual, not compared to some of the properties the other Great Houses kept. Still, after all the suffering he'd seen over the past month in the city, it felt uncomfortably opulent.

Andyn suddenly leaned out the window, staring back the way they'd come with the slightest frown on his face.

"What do you keep looking at back there?" Wirr asked curiously. His bodyguard had done the same thing several times over the past few hours.

Andyn shook his head, but the puzzled frown remained. "Probably nothing, Sire."

"Out with it."

Andyn grunted, looking mildly embarrassed. "Dust. I think." He shrugged at Wirr's querying expression. "Not much, and I only see it occasionally, but enough that it could be someone on horseback following us. Walking some, then galloping in spurts to keep up, perhaps."

"I see." Wirr peered through the window himself, but couldn't see whatever Andyn had spotted.

"Once we stop, Sire, with your permission I'd like to take a look. Just for my own peace of mind."

Wirr nodded his acquiescence. Andyn was likely being overly cautious, but he could hardly blame the man after last night.

They pulled to a stop, and Wirr frowned out the window. Nobody was emerging from the main doors to greet them, however there were two men positioned either side of the entrance. They didn't wear the livery of House Andras, but they were clearly guards.

They could be a couple of the men his uncle had sent, he supposed... but if they were, they should have been in uniform.

Wirr disembarked from the carriage as Andyn began negotiating with the carriage driver for the use of one of his horses. He strode toward the front door, but his step faltered as the two men stepped smoothly into his path.

"I'm Torin Andras," said Wirr as he approached. "This is my family's house."

The man on the right, a brutish-looking fellow with a nasty scar stretching along the left side of his neck, regarded him flatly. "Please wait here, Sire. Someone will be along shortly."

Wirr stared at the man in disbelief and then glanced back over his shoulder at Andyn, who was holding the reins of a horse but not yet moving, watching the scene with a puzzled frown.

"Everything all right, Sire?" he called.

Wirr shrugged. "I'm sure it's fine." Whatever this was, there was no point in making a scene just yet.

Andyn inclined his head in acknowledgment, but made no move to mount his horse.

Wirr turned back to the guards. "Who are you?" he asked, not bothering to hide the irritation in his tone.

"We work for your mother," replied the burly man who had spoken earlier.

"Then you work for my family," said Wirr calmly. "Which includes me. Now let me in."

He didn't get to see whether the men were going to budge because a moment later, the doors opened and his mother emerged, squinting as she walked out into the sunlight. She glanced at the guards.

"It's all right, Markus," she said to the big man, waving at him to stand down.

Wirr cast another glance back toward the carriage. Andyn still hadn't moved. Wirr gave him a reassuring nod; Andyn hesitated for a moment longer and then nodded back, swinging up onto his horse and starting down the road.

Geladra was tall and slim, carrying herself with a grace born of her many years as duchess. Wirr stepped toward her, smile nearly faltering as he saw the hesitation in her body language before she embraced him.

"Torin. I heard about last night," she said, quickly stepping back to inspect him. "I'm so glad you're all right. What happened?"

Wirr shook his head as they started walking inside. "Six men attacked the dinner with the Tel'Raths." He frowned as he noticed Markus following them at a discreet distance, but his mother appeared to expect it, so he said nothing. "That's really all I know at this point."

Geladra cast a sideways glance at him. "The report that I received said that you beat them on your own. Did you use...?"

Wirr shook his head. "They had a Trap. I was just lucky that they didn't coordinate very well." He looked around, frowning. "Where are the men Uncle sent?" He hadn't seen any sign of them since arriving.

"I'd already taken it upon myself to hire Markus and a few others," said Geladra, indicating another pair of men without uniforms standing a little farther down the hallway. "Captain Rill already felt as though there were too many men to easily coordinate, and I knew Riveton still needed some spare hands to help rebuild, so I sent them there for a few days instead."

Wirr's frown deepened. Captain Rill was in charge of the Tel'Andras guards, but Wirr's memory of him said that he was hardly the type to refuse extra help.

They reached the sitting room and Wirr collapsed onto the big, soft chair in the corner that he always chose when he was here. He looked up to see his mother eyeing him speculatively.

"What is it?"

"Nothing." Geladra sat, for some reason looking a little more relaxed than she had a moment ago.

Wirr shrugged, then glanced at the door. "Does Del know that I'm here?"

"Deldri's away, I'm afraid. Visiting some friends."

Wirr's heart sank. His trip *had* been at short notice, but something in his mother's tone indicated that Deldri's absence was not a coincidence.

Sighing, he stood again, walking over to the open door and peering out at the big man standing just outside.

"Please let Andyn know where I am when he returns," he said politely. Before Markus could react, he shut the door firmly in his face, then returned to his seat. He wanted some privacy for this conversation.

He took a deep breath as his mother watched with a frown. It was better to come straight to the point rather than awkwardly dance around the subject.

"So Father didn't...he didn't tell you about me?" he asked quietly.

Geladra hesitated, then shook her head. "No. Not once. He never even hinted at it."

She looked at him, and he saw it clearly for the first time. Saw just how much that deception had hurt her.

Wirr swallowed. "I'm sorry."

There was an awkward silence for several seconds, neither quite knowing what to say to the other.

"Why are you here, Torin?" asked Geladra eventually.

Wirr grimaced. "Uncle thought it would be a good idea for me to get out of the city for a few days after..." He shrugged. "And I've been looking into something—the lead-up to the rebellion twenty years ago. How Father got hold of the Vessel that created the Tenets. How he found the Shackles, the Traps, figured out how to create Shadows. That sort of thing." He gestured aimlessly. "There's no documentation in Administration, and even some of the older, higher-ranked members don't seem to know anything."

Geladra stared at him, something approaching concern in her eyes. "I'm not sure that I can help you, I'm afraid. You know I didn't meet your father until after the war began, and he always avoided talking about how it all started."

Wirr inclined his head, deciding not to press, at least for the moment. "It occurred to me that there might be some answers in his study, though."

Geladra gave him a puzzled look. "His study? Administration cleared it out weeks ago."

"*What?*" Wirr stared at her in horror. "Who came?"

"I don't really remember," said Geladra apologetically. "They were younger, I think—nobody I recognized from my time there. It was just after the funeral. Everything's a bit of a blur, I'm afraid."

Wirr groaned. Geladra had been an Administrator herself until she'd retired to concentrate on raising him and Deldri, so he shouldn't have been surprised. Still, he'd made some quick inquiries just before he'd left—and as far as he had been able to tell, nobody in Administration had even thought to check Elocien's office here. *He* hadn't even thought to check it until Scyner had brought it up.

"Perhaps I can have a look around anyway?" he asked heavily. It was possible that Administration didn't know about the safe— if there even was one—but Wirr had been hoping to find something useful in his father's notes and files, regardless.

Geladra shrugged. "If you want to."

She stood, indicating that he should follow, and issuing a slight shake of the head to the concerned look from Markus as she opened the door. Wirr scowled to himself. More and more, it felt like everyone was acting as if *he* were the threat.

They walked through the house, only the occasional creak of a floorboard breaking the silence. Soon enough they reached Elocien's den; Geladra fished a key from her pocket, unlocking the solid oak door and swinging it wide.

Wirr grimaced.

The room was bare. There was still the old desk that he remembered, and a few other pieces of furniture that remained untouched. But the shelves were empty, the desk clear. He walked over to a cabinet and opened a drawer, knowing even before he looked inside that it slid out too easily to contain anything.

Wirr clenched his fists. If someone from Administration had come and taken everything without reporting it, Wirr doubted that he would ever see even a scrap of what had been in here.

He scanned along the wall, and a flicker of hope suddenly kindled in his chest. Behind the desk, a large metallic representation of the Administrator's Mark was inlaid into one of the wooden panels on the wall.

"It doesn't look like they missed anything," he said to his mother, "but give me a few minutes?"

Geladra shrugged again as if to indicate that she didn't know why he wanted to bother, but nodded.

As soon as the door was closed again, Wirr moved across the room to stand in front of the panel with the metallic inlay. Holding his breath, he pressed his Administrator's Mark to it. For a moment, nothing happened.

Then the panel slid to the side soundlessly, revealing cold steel with a single keyhole in the center.

Wirr stared at it with a mixture of relief and consternation. He recognized the design of the safe—he'd seen plenty of identical ones in Administration's main building in Ilin Illan, and there was even something similar installed in his own rooms in the palace. It was a type of Vessel, reinforced and Essence shielded. Common enough, but there was no way for him to break into it without the key.

He stared at the safe for another minute or so, trying to come up with a way to open it. In the end, he pressed his Mark to the panel a second time, relieved to see it slide shut again. He would have to figure out another way to break in; until then, he didn't particularly want his mother to know that the safe existed.

Geladra was waiting for him outside, as well as Andyn, who had finally returned from his reconnaissance. The redheaded man gave Wirr a slight shake of the head, indicating that he'd found nothing of interest.

Wirr turned to his mother. "So there's nothing at all left? They took everything?"

Geladra nodded. "Perhaps if you ask around Administration, you may be able to find out where they're keeping it all." She hesitated.

"Though I did hear one of them talking about destroying anything that they didn't feel was useful, so…I'm sorry, Torin."

Wirr stared at her, anger and frustration bubbling to the surface despite his best efforts. "Are you? Because you don't actually *seem* sorry."

Geladra's expression darkened. "Perhaps that's because I think Administration has every right to what they took."

"And I don't? I'm the *head* of Administration, but I'm never going to see anything that was in there now." Wirr's scowl deepened. "But it's clear that you don't approve of my position, so perhaps that's irrelevant to you."

Geladra stared at him for a few moments.

"You're right. I don't approve," she said softly. "Not of your position, nor the course of action your father took to get you there, nor the way that you rewrote the Tenets." She locked gazes with him. "You should be stepping down, Torin. Resigning. This attempt on your life last night just proves that being Northwarden isn't the right place for you. So long as you remain in charge of Administration, people will be upset and you'll be in danger. Besides—surely it has become obvious to you, by now, that Administration simply cannot function the way in which it was intended if it has someone like you at its head."

Wirr flinched; the words *someone like you*—delivered with disdain, however unconsciously—hit home harder than he had expected. In the corner of his eye, he saw Andyn shifting uncomfortably.

"Perhaps the way Administration was originally designed to function was flawed," said Wirr, trying to contain a flash of anger. "Or perhaps you're not remembering why it was created in the first place. Because it was *meant* to act as a way to let the Gifted live their lives, while ensuring that there were still checks and balances on their power. That was what Father always said." He did his best to keep his expression short of a glare as he spoke. "So who better to do that than me?"

Geladra said nothing for a few moments, but two spots of red on her cheeks showed that she was becoming angry. "Anyone, Torin," she said. "*Anyone* but you. Can you hear yourself? Checks and balances? You're *Gifted*. Are you so far above other men now that you believe that you alone can, and should, set your own limits? Aside from which—surely you've seen the effect that you're having on the Administrators. Surely you understand that you can't run the organization effectively when those under you don't respect or trust you."

Wirr scowled, all pretense that this wasn't an argument now abandoned. "I'm hoping that they can eventually behave like adults, and maybe give me the chance to earn those things over time."

"That's not something that will happen, given the decisions you've been making. This Augur Amnesty, this nonsense about the Boundary...it makes me *sick*, Torin. I know that you've come to trust the Gifted—it's only natural after living amongst them for so long—but surely you *must* see how everything that they've done has been for their own political gain."

"You think that the threat of the Boundary collapsing is *nonsense*?" Wirr closed his eyes, breathing deeply. He had to deal with these sorts of things within Administration all the time, but hearing the words from his mother felt worse by far. "So you would...what? Have things go back to the way they were? Should I be hunting down and killing my friend because he was born a certain—"

"*Yes*, Torin!" Geladra's frustration was on full display now, too. "You can't be making decisions based around your friendships—that's not what being a leader means! These people are *dangerous*. Do you think that the war started because everyone simply disliked them? Because they were jealous? People *gave their lives* to remove them from power. Your father risked *everything* to do it. And now you're just...holding the door open for them. You *spit* on his memory by acting the way you have been."

Wirr stared at her, pale, stunned by the outburst. Geladra had always been against the Gifted and the Augurs—it was one of the reasons she had fit so well with his father—but this was something else. There was raw *anger* in her tone.

He said nothing for several long seconds, trying to regain his composure. This wasn't what he'd wanted, wasn't what he'd envisaged at all when he had decided to come here. He could continue to argue but it was clear that the conversation had degenerated   243 into insults. If he kept talking, he was only going to say something that he would later regret.

"I'm sorry you feel that way," he said as calmly as he could. "I'm going for a walk. After that...I think perhaps I should leave."

He paused to let his mother protest but when she didn't, he nodded to Andyn and walked out without another word, ignoring the looming stare of Markus as he passed.

The grounds were well lit by lanterns, despite the late hour.

Wirr wandered, lost in memory, trailed a short but respectful distance by Andyn. Though an occasional liveried guard patrolled nearby, the men his mother had hired had not bothered to follow him out here, which was a relief. The gardens hadn't really changed over the past few years; he still comfortably knew his way through them, still knew exactly what to expect when he rounded a corner. The opposite of what he'd just been through with his mother, in a way.

He eventually sat on a bench, then glanced up at Andyn and gestured wearily to the seat next to him.

Andyn shook his head. "I may not have found anyone earlier, Sire, but there *were* fresh tracks. If someone's been following us, this would be the perfect spot to attack. Lots of cover, far enough away from the rest of the guards..."

"Honestly, Andyn? I'm almost tempted to let them at the moment."

Andyn's expression didn't change. "I'm fairly certain that would make me unpopular, Sire. And bad at my job. I'll stay where I am."

"Good to know that you're doing it for the right reasons," said Wirr, allowing himself a small smile. "Now if you'd only—"

"Sire." Andyn whispered the word, suddenly stock-still. He placed his hand on his sword, peering into the bushes to Wirr's left.

Wirr snorted. "Really?" He twisted, unconcerned, staring at the spot upon which Andyn's gaze was fixed. When nothing happened, he shook his head in amusement. "Nice try, Andyn."

"You can come out," said Andyn in a strong, clear voice. His sword was out of its sheath now. "I know you're there. Come out, and I won't kill you."

There was nothing for a few moments, and Wirr opened his mouth to chide Andyn again.

Then two hands appeared from behind a bush, fingers out-spread to show that they were not concealing anything. They were soon followed by a body, hard to see in the dim light, edging slowly toward them.

Wirr sprang to his feet, heart suddenly thumping in his chest.

"That's close enough," said Andyn calmly.

"I am not here to hurt anyone. I wish only to talk." The voice was a woman's, familiar to Wirr, though he couldn't immediately place from where. He squinted at the stranger, trying to make out her features.

"Then you may want to think about working on your social skills," observed Andyn tightly. "Most people don't need the ele-ment of surprise to start a conversation."

The woman laughed, low and soft, though the sound was as full of desperation as amusement. "Special circumstances," she replied. She shifted, stepping sideways so that the nearest lamp illuminated her face more clearly.

"Hello, gaa'vesh," the woman—little older than Wirr himself—said with a tired smile.

Wirr stared at her for a few moments, not sure that he could believe what his eyes were telling him. The woman's hair was short now, dyed black, but it didn't prevent him from recognizing her immediately.

Eventually he nodded back, though he didn't feel any less wary.

"Hello, Breshada," he said quietly, taking a half step back as Andyn positioned himself between them.

"You know this woman, Sire?" Andyn asked casually, never taking his eyes from the Desrielite.

"Yes." Wirr noticed Andyn's muscles relax slightly. "She's a Hunter." He nearly chuckled as the muscles tensed up again. "And she saved my life back in Desriel. Though I never really knew why."

Andyn's posture had changed enough times during the course of Wirr's explanation that he eventually gave up, scowling. "Is she a friend?"

Wirr grunted. "Breshada?"

"I am not here to kill you," Breshada said, making the statement sound like an act of generosity. She glanced coolly at Andyn. "If I were, you would both already be dead."

"I don't think I like her, Sire," said Andyn quietly. Wirr noticed that he hadn't sheathed his sword. "Perhaps it would be best to disarm her before we go any further?"

Breshada's face darkened. "Try to take Whisper, and—"

"Stop." Wirr heard the exasperation in his own tone, but he didn't care. "Breshada, keep your sword, but stay where you are. Andyn, don't start anything unless she does first." He turned to Breshada, ignoring the outraged stares of both her and his bodyguard. "Why in all fates are you here, Breshada? What's going on? How did you find me?"

Breshada stared defiantly at Andyn for a few more moments, then wilted.

"It is something of a long story. But the truth...I am in need of your assistance." She said the last as if it were the most distasteful thing that she could imagine. "I was following Ambassador Thurin, and I saw you. Recognized you, eventually—we had heard about the prince returning but I had not thought..."

She faltered. To Wirr's surprise, her hands began to tremble and she sat abruptly on the bench, abandoning any pretense at bravado. "I have been cursed, Prince Torin."

"Cursed?" Wirr exchanged a confused look with Andyn.

Breshada's face twisted and she drew up her left sleeve to reveal the black tattoo, barely visible in the lamplight.

"I am like you," she whispered. "I am gaa'vesh."

Chapter 17

Davian stiffened as he came awake, suddenly aware that he was no longer alone.

He rolled onto his side, flinching as he saw Ishelle sitting across from him against the smooth white wall of the cell, watching him silently. He quickly levered himself into an upright position.

"Why are you here?"

Ishelle grimaced, the emotion of the expression not hard to recognize.

She was ashamed.

"Rohin threw me in here because he didn't trust me after I..." She sighed, then gave an awkward shrug. "His ability must not work in here, because I started to realize what was going on as soon as he shut that door." She swallowed. "Davian, I...I'm sorry. You know I would never—"

"I know." Davian gave her a reassuring smile.

Ishelle released a long breath, inclining her head gratefully.

"Why didn't you kill him?" she asked eventually. "You could have."

Davian stared at the ground, debating how honestly to reply. He'd had plenty of time to ponder that same question in the long, silent hours after Rohin's visit. It was actually the first opportunity he'd had to slow down, to actually *think* about everything that had happened, in a while. He hadn't had the chance since Ilin Illan, certainly. Not really since Deilannis.

It had been hard to do.

There had been a maelstrom of emotions sitting just beneath

the surface for far too long now—things that he'd forced down, deliberately ignored in favor of focusing on what needed to be done. With everything that had demanded his attention recently, it had always been too exhausting, too intimidating to properly sift through those feelings.

"I've killed people before." He said the words hesitantly, hating to admit it even to himself, though it was hardly a secret. "In Desriel. In Ilin Illan. Not just the Blind, either." *Even at my wedding* he couldn't help but add silently; Malshash's memory still felt all too personal. "I was going to do it. I was going to take his life. And then I realized..." He shivered.

Ishelle frowned. "What?"

"That I thought that it was a choice." Davian swallowed. "That I was thinking about it in terms of odds. A higher chance of escaping, and all I had to do was end him." He shook his head, eyes wide as he said the words. Out loud, they sounded even more horrible. "Who thinks like that? I'm *comfortable* with it, Ishelle. It's like... it's like I used to be afraid of heights. Then one day Asha decided that she liked the view from the west wall of the school. After a few times of forcing myself to go up there I just..."

"Got used to it," said Ishelle quietly.

"It didn't bother me anymore," agreed Davian. "Not anywhere near as much as it had, anyway." He shrugged. "And in that moment, when I realized, I just... I couldn't. It made me sick that I considered it an option. I feel like... like I've lost my way, recently. Morally speaking. Like I've become someone I would have been terrified of a year ago." He was surprised to find himself saying it all out loud, especially to Ishelle. But the time alone had compelled him to confront these things, and talking about it felt... right.

Ishelle was silent for a few seconds.

"What you're describing, though—isn't that what being moral *is*? It shouldn't be about how you *feel*, it should be about what you *do*." She looked at him steadily. "I don't know, Davian. I think people can adapt to a lot of things, and sometimes we just... shut off the part of us that knows, deep down, what's right and wrong. But you didn't do that." She smiled at him, something inscrutable in her expression. "Honestly, that probably makes you better than anyone I've ever met."

Davian stared at her for a long moment.

Then, despite himself, he grinned.

Ishelle flushed at his amusement. "I'm serious."

"I know," said Davian quickly. He shook his head, still smiling. "I just don't think I've ever heard you *be* serious before. It's weird."

Ishelle snorted, then walked over to where he was sitting against the wall and slid down next to him.

"I really am sorry, you know," she said awkwardly.

Davian shook his head. "You have nothing to be sorry for," he said firmly. "He was Controlling you."

"Except it's not Control."

Davian frowned. "How do you mean?"

"It's more...subtle, I suppose. He says something, and your mind adapts to it. It's not like someone else is doing the thinking for you, and you have no say over it. He says to do something, and you...you *justify* it to yourself."

Davian thought for a moment.

"That's still Control," he eventually said gently. "More insidious, maybe, but he's still making you act in a way that you wouldn't normally. Any guilt lies with him, not you."

Ishelle nodded, but it was a halfhearted agreement.

"Well. At least you couldn't justify killing me," Davian observed brightly, trying to lighten the mood.

Ishelle, though, didn't smile. "But I could. I *did*. What I said to Rohin about leaving you in here was the truth." She hesitated. "The thing is...I started thinking about how you've been obsessing over that girl in Ilin Illan. About how she doesn't have anything I don't have except a thousand miles of distance, and yet you act as if you're married to her. I just had to think about how *frustrating* that is, and..."

Ishelle looked across at him, eyes meeting his, and Davian's smile faded.

She wasn't joking. Her face was only inches from his.

Davian swallowed. Did Ishelle really have those sorts of feelings for him? She was beautiful, and he wasn't immune to that fact—nor to her suddenly disconcerting proximity.

But she wasn't Asha.

He deliberately turned, facing forward again.

"She's my best friend." He said the words quietly, almost surprised to hear them coming out of his mouth. "She's my best friend, and I'm in love with her. That's what she has, Ishelle."

There was silence and then Ishelle was standing abruptly, facing away from him. For an uncomfortable moment, Davian thought that she was crying.

"You *do* know how to kill the mood," she said, and to his surprise the cheerfulness in her tone didn't sound forced. When she turned back to him, her usual bright smile was in place, with no trace of disappointment or embarrassment. "So how are we getting out of here?"

Davian said nothing for a moment, trying to figure out how to respond. It seemed odd to just leave it at that, and yet it was obvious that Ishelle didn't want to talk about it any further. Perhaps, at least right now, that was for the best.

"I haven't figured that one out yet," he admitted.

"So there's no rescue on the way, then?" Ishelle rubbed the back of her neck, meeting his gaze worriedly. "What about the Augur that you were looking for in Prythe?"

Davian opened his mouth to tell her about Erran and Fessi, then hesitated.

If the other empty cells he'd seen in the hall outside were the same as this one, it was odd that Ishelle had been put into Davian's. And her behavior since she'd been in here with him had been…strange. She'd always flirted with him, but that was in her nature—she did the same with plenty of others. The serious conversation, the heartfelt revelation…it all felt off.

His heart sank. He couldn't see if she was actually lying without access to kan, but it didn't feel like the real her.

"No," he said quietly. "If there really was an Augur following me in Prythe, they were good at staying hidden."

Ishelle just nodded, though there was a flicker of disappointment in her eyes. Whether it was from the lack of imminent rescue or her inability to gain information from him, he had no idea.

They tried a while longer to think of a way out, but soon enough Davian's eyelids began to droop again. Though the makeshift store
of Essence he'd been able to gather was still working, it didn't give

him a great deal of energy. And despite Ishelle now being in the room with him, he couldn't draw from her without access to kan.

Eventually, he slept.

When he awoke, it was to the sound of the cell door swinging open.

He leaped to his feet, relief loosening his constricted chest when he saw Fessi standing outside.

He glanced around. He was alone in the cell.

"Time to go," Fessi said encouragingly, beckoning, clearly not wanting to step inside. Davian stumbled over to the doorway, keeping one hand on the wall but getting stronger with each step. By the time he exited the cell, he was able to walk without the need for support.

"I can see why you and Asha make such a good pair," Fessi murmured. She glanced with distaste at the cell. "I shudder to think of what kind of trouble I'd have to get you out of if you two were together, though."

Davian gave her a wry look, relieved enough to enjoy the moment of levity.

"Good to see you," he said softly, breathing deeply as his sense of kan returned, funnelling Essence into his body. He put his back against the wall as he recovered, noting that they were alone in the wide white hall. "Is Ishelle with you?"

"The other Augur?" Fessi shook her head. "I haven't seen her. As far as I can tell, you're the only one down here." She put her hand on Davian's arm, and there was an abrupt shift as time bent around them. "Now. What in fates is going on out there? We tried Reading people to find out where you were—unsuccessfully—but it was like everyone had this...thick, liquid kan over their minds. A kind of black sludge that was seeping into their thoughts." She shuddered. "I know that sounds strange, but I can't think of any other way to describe it."

Davian winced at the description, then quickly filled Fessi in on what he knew about Rohin. "What you saw must be how his influence stays active for so long," he concluded grimly. "I'm immune because of my ability, but I don't think anyone else is."

Fessi gave a thoughtful nod. "We'll have to figure out how to deal with that once we're out of here."

Davian glanced around at the row of cells that lined the hall, frowning as he took in the inscription-covered archway at the far end. Beyond the opening, he could now see another door, this one twice as tall and wide as those elsewhere. "Where *is* here, exactly?"

"We're in the section of Central Archive that Erran and I couldn't get into a few days ago. I'm guessing this is one of the reasons the Council didn't want you knowing about it," Fessi added with a dark look at the cells.

Davian rubbed his forehead. "How did you know where I was?"

"I didn't," admitted the other Augur. "I've been here for almost two hours, wandering around trying to find you. When I noticed the kan barrier was gone from outside, it seemed sensible to at least take a look."

Davian nodded slowly. "Rohin must have found out about these cells from the Council, then had them remove the barrier so that he could come and go as he pleased."

Fessi hesitated, glancing toward the archway. "Speaking of which. Now we're here…"

Davian shook his head. "We should go." He knew that Fessi was keeping them outside the flow of time—only a few seconds would have passed since they'd begun the conversation—but every moment that they remained was a risk.

"I just want to see what's in there," said Fessi, nodding toward the mysterious opening at the end of the hall. "The Council wouldn't have put all that security in place just to hide some cells—and we may not get another chance to look."

Davian shook his head again, but swallowed further protests and allowed Fessi to drag him toward the end of the hall. She was right—there had to be something more than just cells down here—and it was clear that the dark-haired girl was not to be dissuaded anyway.

He studied the archway as they approached. Just as artful as the rest of the Builders' work, it was large, easily wide enough for several people to pass through at once. The angular symbols inscribed around its edges were unfamiliar to him, but Davian couldn't help but feel uneasy as he looked at them.

"Let's do this quickly," he said nervously. "We don't want to—"

They passed beneath the archway into the antechamber beyond, and everything *lurched*.

Davian stumbled as Fessi lost her grip on his arm, staggering farther into the room. She recovered her balance, then turned to Davian with a bemused expression.

"Sorry. Must have been another barrier," she said dazedly. "I thought I checked, but it..." She shook her head, frowning. "I checked, but..."

Her eyes rolled up into the back of her head, and she crumpled to the floor.

Davian rushed forward, ignoring his own sudden dizziness and dropping to his knees beside Fessi. She was still breathing but it was coming in shallow gasps; otherwise, Davian couldn't see anything physically wrong with her. He closed his eyes and reached out for kan.

There was nothing there.

He grabbed Fessi roughly under the armpits and dragged her hurriedly back out into the hall, feeling a chill as he realized that more symbols had appeared on the walls of the room—the same as those he'd seen over the archway, but these ones pulsing with blue Essence.

A warning. He didn't know what they said, but they were clearly a warning.

He returned his focus to Fessi once they were out past the arch again, quickly pushing through kan. Fessi's source was unusually dim—dangerously so, he thought—but there didn't appear to be anything actively attacking her. Whatever had been affecting her must have been restricted to the antechamber.

He quickly snatched more Essence from the nearest pillar, letting it flow into her. After a few moments, Fessi groaned and stirred.

"What happened?" she asked blearily.

"I'm not sure. You collapsed after going through the archway." He glanced over his shoulder at the room. The glowing symbols on the walls had vanished. "But I think if you're up to it, we should get out of here now."

Fessi staggered to her feet with Davian's help. "Not going to argue this time." She took a few deep, steadying breaths, then closed her eyes.

Once again, Davian felt time begin to bend around them, slipping by almost without touching them. Fessi gave a slight nod, then—one hand still firmly gripping his arm—led him to the other end of the hall and swung open the door.

Eight red-cloaked men stood in the space beyond, the way in which they were arrayed around the entrance clearly marking them as guards. At first they appeared frozen but as Davian watched, he could see the miniscule changes in their positions that betrayed their current motion.

Davian glanced at the young woman holding his arm, speechless. This was so far beyond his own ability as to be laughable. Fessi was keeping *both* of them almost *completely* outside of the flow of time—and she was doing it while undoubtedly still recovering from whatever had just happened.

Fessi caught his glance, then looked around at the near-statues and shrugged. "Practice."

She gently closed the door behind them, then proceeded to pull Davian through the crowded room, moving slowly and careful to avoid touching any of the figures. Davian followed her lead. Even the air of their passing at this speed could give them away, and he didn't like to think of what sort of injury he might inflict if he accidentally bumped one of the Gifted.

Soon enough they were outside, into the tranquil gardens of Central Ward. Davian gazed at the almost-frozen stream to his left in astonishment. It was evening but the moon was out, highlighting the eerily slow water with silver.

He expected Fessi to stop and rest once they were clear—he couldn't even imagine the amount of concentration that this would be taking, especially after what had happened inside—but she simply dragged him on matter-of-factly, neither rushing nor casual in her pace. They walked in silence past the men guarding the tunnel beneath the Central Wall, then through the near-empty streets of Inner Ward and beneath the Inner Wall.

By the time they were walking out of Tol Shen's eastern gate—still moving at the same pace, with their altered passage through time never once faltering—Davian's mind had gone numb from trying to conceive of how Fessi was managing to maintain the ability. By his estimate, the entire journey had taken them close to twenty minutes.

Outside of the bubble she'd created, he doubted more than ten seconds had passed.

They rounded a corner and Fessi finally slowed her grimly determined walk, glancing behind them before breathing out. There was a rush of air and suddenly the world sprang back into motion, trees by the road swaying in the same night breeze that now pressed against Davian's face. He blinked, coming to a halt as Fessi took her hand off his arm, stumbling a little.

He reached out to help her. "Are you all right?"

Fessi held up her hand, indicating that she didn't need assistance.

"She'll be fine." Erran's voice, coming abruptly from the darkened tree line, made Davian flinch. He turned to see the other Augur emerging from the foliage where he'd evidently been waiting for them. "She usually pushes herself harder than that before I wake up in the morning." Despite his cheerful tone, Davian couldn't help but notice a flash of concern in Erran's eyes as he looked at Fessi.

Erran turned back to Davian. "You didn't turn up to our meeting."

Davian gestured back at the Tol. "Busy trying not to die. Sorry."

Erran sighed. "Still a little rude." He gave Davian a slight grin and then paused, turning his attention to Fessi as she straightened. Davian didn't need to see the line of kan to know that they were communicating again.

After a few seconds, Fessi gave a reluctant nod, and Erran turned back to Davian.

"So. Let's figure out a way to make sure it doesn't happen again," he concluded quietly.

Chapter 18

Caeden paused in his descent, studying the vast, snow-covered city stretching away below him, highlighted red by the last light of the dying sun.

It had been an hour since the Portal Box had deposited him onto the mountaintop, the tallest peak of a range that filled the horizon intimidatingly in every direction. He shivered in the frigid air, unspoiled snow crunching underfoot as he struggled forward through knee-high drifts once again, continuing to angle downward. He'd known as soon as he'd spotted the smooth, clean outlines of the thousands of structures below that it was where he was meant to go next—where he'd find his reason for coming here.

Hopefully, where he'd find the answers he needed to stop the Lyth.

He squinted. The closer he got, the more remarkable the sight became. Lines of Essence bordered every road, every pathway, the snow that capped each building not anywhere in evidence along the lit streets. There were no adornments on any of the structures below, no outlandish design or particular flair to the architecture. Yet despite the obfuscation of powdery white, he could also see how intricately each building interlocked with the next, the entire city meshing into something far more than the sum of its parts. Every street managed to be both utilitarian and unique, functional but distinct. It was simple, but there was also an unmistakable beauty and artistry to it.

There was something else that constantly drew his eye, too—something he had noticed the moment he'd reached his vantage point.

The center of the city was utterly dark.

It wasn't simply as if there was no Essence flowing to the half-mile-wide area. Instead, the lines of energy running toward the darkness grew increasingly dim as they approached, flickering rather than pulsing, steadily weakening as they drew closer to the city center until they were eventually completely extinguished. It was hard to see in the fading light, but snow clogged the streets where the Essence began to dim, only melting away where it would have otherwise sat directly atop the faint illumination. The glow closest to the black vortex blinked and stuttered, giving the empty streets there a wild, eerie quality.

Caeden studied the sight grimly. After what he'd just been through in the Plains of Decay, he knew he'd need to keep a close eye on his Reserve while here.

He shook his head, pressing on despite his exhaustion. The journey downhill was cold, wet, and treacherous; he'd slipped multiple times, twice having to heal himself from a badly sprained ankle, as well as constantly drawing Essence to add warmth to his body. It didn't help that he hadn't slept in over a day, either.

Tiredness was better than stopping for too long, though. The utter silence here, the vast solitude, left him only his thoughts for company.

That was something that he didn't feel like dealing with right now.

So he forced his legs to keep moving, trudging through the deep white and slowly drawing closer to the city perched at the mountain's edge. After a while he found himself funnelled into a deep canyon, the gushing of water beginning to intrude on the silence. In the distance, along the path ahead, he could see a multitude of fountains and water features littering the entrance to the city— including two massive waterfalls that flanked the path into the city itself. Blue streaks of Essence lit the smooth, glasslike sheets, the energy darting along it at random intervals, moving as if alive.

Caeden paused, gazing at the falls for a moment. Each ran the length of the canyon for at least a hundred feet, perfectly symmetrical and completely sheer. The shimmering walls of water emerged from jutting rock overhead, continuing well past the level of the path and down into the inky chasms that lined the way ahead. Only a very distant roar indicated that there was any bottom to the dual abysses.

Despite the sound, Caeden recognized the sense of emptiness in the city beyond—an air of desolation, of things made by man and then abandoned, forgotten. It had been the same in Deilannis.

Whoever had lived here, they didn't any longer.

He started walking, entering the corridor of water. The air was actually slightly warmer here and moved gently, but there didn't seem to be any spray from the twin waterfalls. The road itself was smooth, dry, and generously wide; unlike the buildings and streets up ahead it was not made of white stone, but rather carved from the gray-brown rock of the mountain. Strange symbols were inscribed at intervals along both edges of the path, though Caeden had no inkling as to their meaning.

Despite his curiosity and the apparent safety of the road, Caeden kept to the middle. It was near completely dark now, and the strange blue energy sporadically darting along the curtains of water made him uneasy.

He reached the edge of the city without incident, hesitating in front of the white stone archway that marked its entrance. Now that he could see the buildings up close, everything looked so... *new*. Despite the rooftops laden with snow, nothing bore signs of age or wear; even the well-preserved structures in Deilannis would have felt derelict next to these.

He checked his Reserve again as he walked along the snow-free street, but there didn't appear to be any drain. For a few minutes he luxuriated in the appreciable increase in temperature, but his relief began to fade as he started scanning the buildings for any points of interest. He might be safe, but he also had no hint as to where he was supposed to go. From the stunning but now barely visible vista out over the edge of the city, to the warm lines and well-lit roads, the entire place was mocking in its vast, unfamiliar emptiness.

He eventually stopped, perching at the edge of a fountain and cupping his hand beneath the flowing water, wondering idly at how it was still operating in this climate. It was clear and clean, if icy; after a cautious first sip he drank deeply, taking a few moments to try and get his bearings.

Why was he here? Had he hidden the second part of the Vessel somewhere nearby? Or was he looking fruitlessly for the Siphon, when in fact Nethgalla already had it? He grimaced as he stared around. He needed a memory, needed *something* to point him in the right direction. He knew from what he'd seen from his bird's-eye view that the city was immense. If he'd hidden something here, he could potentially spend a lifetime searching for it.

He peered down the long, straight street to his left that ran toward the city's center. Farther along he could see where the Essence began to dim, and on the horizon was pure black.

Was what he needed somewhere in there? Even if his Reserve remained stable, that vortex of darkness made him more than a little uneasy. Anything could be lurking within.

And yet, some small part of him knew that it was where he was going to have to look.

He sighed, then stood and began walking, purposefully this time, toward the darkness.

It took five minutes for his surroundings to become noticeably dimmer, and another five before it was difficult to see. Ice now crunched underfoot again, and the chill was back in the air as a light snowfall drifted from the darkened sky. Shadows across the street merged in and out of existence everywhere as the Essence here flickered wildly and unevenly, pulsing bright for a moment, then blinking out entirely the next. The fluctuations appeared to be random, affecting different lines at different intervals, making it difficult to concentrate on any one thing. Occasional beams of starlight from above compensated a little, but still let him see far less than he was comfortable with.

There was still no drain on his Reserve, though. Cautiously, he closed his eyes and tapped into the ocean of energy within. A small ball of light sprang to life in front of him, clear and steady, banishing shadows and casting the area around into sharp relief.

He nodded slowly. The drain was on the Essence powering the city, then—not anywhere else. He was safe from what had happened to him at the Plains, at least.

He pressed on into the darkness, his illumination enough to see the buildings on either side of him but nothing more. He didn't want to attract the attention of anything lurking in here.

It wasn't long before he came to a stop outside a tall, thin tower. The structure was square and smooth, as oddly both distinctive and unremarkable as every other building in the city. Even so, this one felt important. He knew that he had to be close to the epicenter of the Essence drain; his ball of light still shone but it had begun to flicker and wane, strands pulling from it and drifting out toward the tower's doorway. He frowned for a few moments and then drew Licanius, closing his eyes and concentrating.

Kan was suddenly there—far easier to grasp, to manipulate, so long as he held the sword. He acted on instinct, stretching out with the dark energy, sending tendrils ahead into the silent tower. The action came as naturally as breathing.

Immediately, though, he flinched back.

There was other kan at work within the building, but to Caeden's senses it felt…broken. Wild. Not *dangerous*, necessarily, but uncontrolled. Wisps lashed about spasmodically, tethered to a central point but thrashing, as if struggling to break free. Wherever Essence came into contact with kan it was torn apart; other threads of the dark power seemed to be feeding along the lines that should have lit the building, as if seeking out energy to destroy.

Caeden opened his eyes again after a minute, considering the tower and letting his ball of Essence decay. Something within had broken into the lines of Essence that ran around the city, and the kan he'd sensed was devouring that exposed energy. He wasn't sure how he knew, but protected Essence—such as that contained within his body—*should* be safe.

He tapped into his Reserve again, rekindling the light but instinctively making it looser this time. Rather than a solid ball, he strung several strands of Essence into smaller spheres, separating them from one another.

He considered the result with a small frown. The illumination was much the same strength as before but if it was hit by a strand of wild kan, only a few balls would Decay. It took a little more concentration to maintain, but it meant that he wouldn't be abruptly left without light.

He just wished that he could remember how he'd known to do that.

He slowly moved forward, pushing open the door and letting the spheres of Essence drift into the room in front him. 261

Immediately lashes of kan began slicing through them but Caeden hardened kan of his own, pushing back against the majority of the thrashing tendrils.

Once confident that his light wouldn't be extinguished, he turned his attention to the single large room in which he found himself.

The part of the space that he could see was completely bare, with no furnishings or anything to distinguish it. As he shifted forward though, toward the source of the wild kan, a large object in the corner resolved itself from the shadows. He squinted, moving closer.

Something hard crunched underfoot.

He frowned, pausing to examine the tiny shards of metal and glass that littered the stone floor. As he saw the larger pieces of black rock mixed amongst the debris, he extended his Essence a little farther, illuminating the origin of the rubble.

A giant lump of twisted metal and stone was all that remained, but Caeden recognized it nonetheless. Half of the wolf's head had sunk and merged as if melted by a blacksmith's forge. The capsule below was open but misshapen, the wickedly edged needles inside blackened and bent. There were ashes at its base—though what they had once been, Caeden had no idea.

A torture device, just like the one from which he'd freed Meldier.

He stared at the wreckage for a long moment, wide-eyed. If someone had been inside when this had happened...

His strands of Essence vanished, plunging the room into darkness.

Caeden blinked. The kan shouldn't have been able to—

"Tal'kamar."

It was a woman's voice, low and slow with pent-up fury. Caeden flinched, heart pounding as he hurriedly tried to light the room again. There was a second's illumination; a woman holding a short sword now stood next to the shattered machine, staring directly at him. Her red hair was unkempt, her eyes sunken.

She gestured, and the light was gone again.

"Isiliar." Caeden took a step back, boots grinding against more of the shattered glass. She'd changed from his memory of her in Rinday when they'd fought together, but it was definitely her.

"We need to—"

There was searing light, followed by an enormous force crashing into his chest. He felt his ribs creak agonizingly and then break as he was lifted off his feet and smashed against the nearest wall; something cracked with a meaty snap, though whether it was bone, the stone wall, or both, he didn't know.

Pain arced through him as utter darkness fell once again. He wheezed and tried to move, moaning as he realized that his arm wasn't responding as it should. He didn't know how badly the limb was broken, but it felt like the jagged end of a bone was penetrating out through his skin.

He gritted his teeth and concentrated, remembering what he'd done when Paetir had stabbed him. Unleashed Essence began to flow from his Reserve to the damaged areas of his body; he felt his arm straighten and chest expand, bones and organs and flesh knitting together again as pure energy poured into the injuries.

It all took only moments. He started to scramble back to his feet, hearing the crunch of footsteps too late.

The kick caught him squarely in the stomach.

He felt something rupture as he tumbled, disoriented by both darkness and agony, landing on his shoulder at least twenty feet from where he'd started. Bright spots danced along his vision but his instincts took over more quickly this time; by the time he'd come to a complete halt Essence was already at work, forcing itself into the injury, keeping him conscious.

"Stop," he gasped into the black, scrabbling at his side to draw Licanius.

There was a flash of memory and he acted, throwing out a delicate mesh of kan to extend his senses. Dim shapes around him began to register in his mind, minute traces of Essence in the stone and air echoing back to him in faint, hazy outlines. It was far from visibility, but it was something.

He recoiled as he looked around. Black tendrils of absolute darkness still lashed out from the broken machine, leaving swathes of emptiness in their wake which were slowly filled again as motes of drifting Essence sought out the newly formed voids. Emerging through the snaking, writhing wisps strode Isiliar, her image burning bright as the sun itself as she stalked toward him.

Caeden focused and reached out, trying to drain some of the

Essence from the oncoming figure, hoping to slow her. Nothing happened; Isiliar didn't even flinch at the attempt. There was something impassable there, a barrier around the woman that Caeden's kan could not penetrate.

"Two thousand years." Isiliar's voice was high-pitched now, edged with madness. "Two thousand *years*, Tal'kamar."

One moment Isiliar's pulsing form was ten feet away; the next it was filling his vision, her brightly outlined features twisted in fury. He balked, slowing time and ducking as an Essence-enhanced punch barely missed his head.

The wall near his skull exploded at the impact, and he could hear crumbling stone bouncing away into the empty street behind him. Isiliar struck again, and again he dodged. More stone disintegrated, this time a section close to four feet wide.

He threw himself backward through the narrow hole and into the snow, rolling and coming to his feet, this time balanced enough to snatch Licanius from its sheath. His grasp on kan instantly became firmer, easier; he pushed himself outside of time and then refined the kan that allowed him to see in the darkness. Immediately Isiliar's outline—currently climbing through the hole in the wall after him—became clearer. She had a sword of her own drawn now.

Isiliar began moving purposefully through the barely moving snowflakes in the air toward him, and to Caeden's horror he realized that she was moving just as fast as he. Despite Licanius, her manipulation of time was as effective as his own.

He had only a second before Isiliar was upon him; he brought up Licanius and blocked her first strike, his arm shivering from the impact. He quickly fed more Essence into his limbs, defending desperately as his attacker rained blow upon blow down on him.

Caeden's eyes widened as Isiliar's sword flashed again and again, faster and faster and faster, each attack creative and unpredictable and relentlessly efficient. He poured every bit of concentration he had into stopping the furious blows, and he knew within ten seconds that it was not going to be enough.

Finally a quick flick of Isiliar's wrist sliced her blade along his fingers; he gasped, losing his grip on Licanius. The blade sank into the snow several feet away.

Caeden dove for it but without the sword, he wasn't able to maintain his time bubble. Isiliar was already standing there as he started to move, holding Licanius in her left hand and her own sword in her right.

She sheathed the latter blade and then blinked forward, backhanding him in the mouth so hard that he spun, falling hard again and sliding in the icy wetness. He rolled as he fed Essence into his broken jaw, fully expecting to see Isiliar's outline plunging Licanius into his chest.

"Do you know? Do you *know* what it took for me to stay *me*?" To his momentary relief, Isiliar hadn't moved. "Do you have any idea what it is to fear sleep? And then to fear waking?" He couldn't be sure while using kan to see, but he thought there were tears rolling down her cheeks. "El take you, Tal. I can't sleep without the pain now. I can't sleep if I'm *not in pain.*"

Caeden stumbled to his feet, holding a shaking hand out in a defensive posture. "Isiliar," he gasped. "Please. Stop. I'm here to keep Licanius from the Lyth."

Isiliar whispered her reply, so that Caeden could barely hear it. "I don't care."

The next minute passed like years. Without Licanius, Caeden was all but helpless against Isiliar's attacks; every punch cracked bone, every kick damaged organs and sent him skidding helplessly along the frozen ground. He lost his grip on kan entirely, plunging the street into complete darkness again. Every moment held the anticipation of more pain and the unknown of which direction it was coming from. Essence flowed in a steady torrent from his Reserve into his body now, but before he could do more than heal, Isiliar would be upon him once again.

Then Isiliar struck him one last time, and something changed.

Suddenly the pain and fear and cold and confusion...dimmed. They were still there, but distant.

He was calm now. Focused.

He reached out for kan, stepped outside of time. Isiliar was a force of nature when she attacked, but she had never had strong defenses. If he wanted to survive, he needed to take the offensive.

Caeden gestured, barely aware of what he was doing as an impossibly fine net of hardened kan sprang up around his body, each strand whisper-thin. He extended his time bubble outward as far as he could.

Then he opened his Reserve and unleashed a wave of Essence in every direction.

The energy decayed slightly where it struck kan but mostly twisted in on itself, intensifying, forcing its way through the minute gaps in the net. What started as a single, solid wave quickly became thousands of individual, razor-sharp needles bursting from his body, exploding in a shower of deadly light.

There was the crashing roar of crumbling masonry as buildings nearby caught the brunt of the force, the stone shredded by Essence, entire walls vanishing in clouds of angry dust, piles of snow from the rooftops collapsing into the street. To his left he caught the image of Isiliar desperately raising a kan shield, but by extending his time bubble he'd left her virtually no time to react. She absorbed some of the projectiles but not all; hair-thin blades of energy spiked into the left side of her face, her arm, both her legs. She gave a scream of pain, flesh ruined where his attack had struck, stumbling to her knees as the dazzling light quickly faded again.

He knew that the injury wouldn't slow her for long, though. His moment of odd, calm clarity passed and he stood stock-still for a moment, stunned by the destructive power of whatever it was he'd just done.

Then he ran.

He allowed his time bubble to shrink again as he dashed as best he could through the drifts of snow, heading toward the faint, flickering glimmer of Essence in the distance. The streets were straight and smooth, and he didn't waste time trying to augment his vision with kan again. Within a minute he could see the faint shimmer of white in front of him, and after a few more, the wildly fluctuating Essence was once again all around him.

He risked a glance over his shoulder, but behind was only shadow. Isiliar could be twenty feet away, or not coming after him at all.

He dashed down a side street, taking several quick turns before ducking through an open archway and collapsing against a wall, panting. He'd taken too much of a beating; his body might be whole but it was sapped, exhausted well beyond its limits.

His rest was short-lived. To his horror, outside in the street he could hear the distant scraping of metal against stone. He held his breath.

The sound paused for a moment, then came again. Closer this time.

He closed his eyes, reaching out with kan, extending his senses into the main street. Isiliar was walking slowly toward his position, dragging Licanius along the wall as she did so. She cocked her head to the side as he watched, looking straight at him.

"Tal'kamar." Isiliar's voice, edged with madness, boomed and echoed all around him, projected and magnified somehow. "You know that walls do nothing to hide you."

The stone ceiling above him cracked, then began to fall.

Caeden spun and dove back through the archway, rolling into the street as the building collapsed behind him. He struggled to his knees, coughing from the dust and debris.

He looked up to see Isiliar standing directly in front of him. The redheaded woman grabbed him by his shoulder, Essence-strengthened hand crushing muscle and bone as she lifted him to his feet and then beyond, holding him aloft as if he weighed nothing at all.

"You said that you would return to check on me. You *swore*." Isiliar's voice trembled as she watched him. Tears began to run down her cheeks.

She punched him in the head, hard enough that Caeden heard his skull crack, could feel the hot, sticky blood as it started to run down his neck. Isiliar barely noticed as she wept. She punched him again. Again.

Again.

"Isiliar. Stop."

Caeden's vision was nearly gone now, the fading world tinged with dark red. He tried to get his blurred gaze to slide in the direction of the newcomer, but to no avail.

"He left me."

"I do not believe...willingly. Once the ilshara...restrictions that he could not have anticipated...already explained this." The words were hard to make out in the haze. There was motion, and the vaguely familiar male voice came again. "You...not fully recovered, Is...give me Licanius before...better than him...not let Tal's sins become your..."

There was more that he couldn't understand; Isiliar eventually let go of Caeden's shoulder as she responded, letting him drop limply to the cold ground. He couldn't make out her words either, now, but her tone was defiant.

Not a good sign, he conceded absently. It didn't matter, though. This time, even the Essence flooding to his skull wasn't going to be enough.

He let the blackness take him.

Caeden guided Isiliar in front of him, taking care to move at a slower pace so that she wouldn't stumble and fall due to her restraints.

"We're almost there," he told her softly as they crossed the Bridge of Travail and into Alkathronen, the warm glow of the Builders' last city making navigation easy.

Isiliar shook her head, her auburn tresses bouncing with the movement. "Why are you doing this, Tal?" she asked hoarsely, not for the first time. "You cannot possibly hope to gain anything. The others will find me, or I will die and tell them in a year or two. Either way, they'll know you for a traitor." Her voice broke and she said nothing for a moment, as if waiting for Caeden to respond. When he didn't, she kept talking, though this time in close to a whisper. "Why now, Tal? Why, when we are so close to the end? So close to saving..." She trailed off, shaking her head. "You want this more than any of us. I know you do. So for the love of El, tell me why!"

Caeden considered not replying. Trying to explain to Isiliar—to any of them—was a lost cause.

And yet, Isiliar was his friend. Given what he was about to do, he owed it to her.

"What is the definition of a god, Is?" he asked quietly.

Isiliar cocked her head to the side, evidently taken off guard by the question.

"A god is...someone so much more powerful and knowledge-able than another being, that they are beyond their comprehen-

sion," she said slowly. "This makes them not just worthy of the lesser being's respect, but of their devotion—their faith."

Caeden nodded, pulling Isiliar to a gentle stop so that he could open a door for her. "So to many, we are gods. And yet we are far from perfect. We act in anger, in jealousy. We make mistakes. We fight amongst each other." He hesitated. "We lie."

Isiliar stiffened. "We have had this discussion a thousand times, Tal. Andrael was wrong. Mad. El has never misled us. You know that. We all know that. We established this before the Venerate even existed!"

"And yet I have doubts," said Caeden. "Doubts that after what we did to Andrael, I have not felt able to voice. We established only that the things that El was asking us to do were good. Or appeared to be good, anyway." He rubbed his forehead. "I am not trying to prevent Him from reaching the rift, Is. El knows I want to go back. I want the world that He's promised us more than anything. But I just…I also want more time. I need to be sure. And everybody else is so focused on the goal, they won't stop and listen."

Isiliar didn't reply for a few moments.

"I can understand that," she said eventually. "We all feel that way sometimes. But…we aren't El. We're not omniscient. At some point, we have to decide to trust. To believe." She sighed. "That is another mark of being a god, Tal. Lesser beings cannot fully comprehend them or their plans, and therefore must choose to have faith instead."

"That doesn't mean that we shouldn't think for ourselves, though."

Isiliar shrugged. "It's irrelevant—you have to know that. This will all be over in a few months. A year at most, depending on whether the Darecians have anything left up their sleeves."

Caeden didn't meet her gaze. "It will be longer than that," he said softly, leading her into the building.

Isiliar frowned as soon as she saw the Tributary, and Caeden could see her quick mind turning over the possibilities. He was stifling her ability to examine it with kan, but he knew it wouldn't be long before she figured out its purpose anyway.

It was subtle, but he saw it, even sooner than he'd expected. 269

The slight stiffening of the shoulders, the half-drawn breath, the minute widening of the eyes. For a normal person, it might not have been noticeable. For one of the Venerate, it was virtually a scream of horror.

"Who told you?" Isiliar's voice held the faintest edge to it now, the slightest tremor.

"I figured it out on my own. You hid it well, erased most of the evidence. But there was a monastery outside of Silvithrin. You stayed there once, before you met Gassandrid, and—"

"I got caught in the fire. For two days," said Isiliar softly. "I told them not to write it down."

"It was a miracle, for them. They had to."

"So that's why we're here." Isiliar shook her head. "What… what in El's name are you powering?"

Caeden hesitated. "An ilshara." He almost smiled at Isiliar's quirk of the eyebrow, though the grimness of the situation quickly reasserted itself. "A big one. Something of Andrael's design."

Isiliar nodded slowly, and though Caeden could feel her trembling beneath his grasp, she managed to keep her voice remarkably calm. "You believe Andrael's theory, that El will not be able to pass. You will be sorely disappointed."

"I hope I am."

"The others will know it's you," said Isiliar, a little desperately now. "Your signature will be all over it. Everyone knows that wolf symbol now."

"I will tell them that Andrael fooled me into helping make it, and then gave it to the Darecians. They will be suspicious, but they will believe that before they ever believe that I am against them." He shrugged, albeit uncomfortably. "And if El is truly who He says, then perhaps He will know. Perhaps He will reveal my treachery. There are many ways for this to fail, Is, but only if you are right."

Isiliar twisted slightly, glancing back at him. "Don't do this. Please."

Caeden gently adjusted his grip on her shoulder. "You know I don't want to," he said, heart breaking with the words. "But you and the others haven't given me a choice."

He tried to move Isiliar forward, toward the Tributary, but she

270

resisted this time. Caeden swallowed his emotions and gave her a steady push, forcing her onward. Isiliar was a wonderful fighter but bound as she was, she had little choice but to obey. She was too old, too wise, and too proud to beg. She knew that he was past the point of having his mind changed, too.

Still, accustomed as she was to keeping her emotions in check, her body language spoke volumes. It was the equivalent of another person screaming in frustration, outrage, and terror.

"How many of the others, Tal?" she asked, voice now clearly shaking as they approached the coffinlike box. "Am I the only one whose Essence you're going to leech, or do you think it will take more to stop him?"

"It doesn't matter. It had to be you, Is. You shouldn't have used Knowing on me." Caeden guided her carefully into the box, laying her flat and facing outward, her hands folded over her stomach. He hesitated, then gently shifted her slightly to the left. The needles would hold her in place once they began to drain her Essence, but it was important that he get the initial positioning right.

He met her gaze briefly, then looked away again. "Alkathronen itself will prevent you from ever being fully drained. The dok'en might get boring, but at least you won't feel pain except during Shifts." He indicated the three rings he'd placed on the shelf to the side. "And I'll check in on you when I can. You have my word."

He unbuckled the sword at his side and laid it at her feet, careful to ensure that it wasn't touching her. It was too dangerous to keep around the others, and too valuable to leave anywhere else.

Then he took the Siphon from his pocket, set it next to the blade. He still hoped that the crystal sphere was something that he would never need...but he could not shake his suspicions about El now. If what he feared was even close to true, then this could well be his only option.

He placed a hand on the maw of the wolf's head, preparing to activate the endpoint.

"Wait." Isiliar looked up at him, emerald eyes pleading. "That time at the monastery. I didn't sleep, Tal. Not once. I was aware the entire time." Her whole body was trembling now. "I don't think that the dok'en will work if I'm in that much pain."

Caeden frowned at her. "You're lying," he said, though he could hear the uncertainty in his own voice.

"You have Knowing right there." Isiliar held his gaze. "Cut me and see."

Caeden felt sick. He hesitated.

"I'm so, so sorry," he said softly. "It doesn't make a difference."

With the beginnings of tears in his eyes he shut the lid, muffling Isiliar's terrified screams.

Chapter 19

Wirr exhaled as he quietly shut the stable doors and gestured Breshada forward, still wondering if he was making the right decision.

It had taken a while to sneak the Hunter in here, unnoticed by any of the serving men still working or the patrolling guards, but Wirr thought they had made it undetected. He had considered forcing her to leave immediately; even given their past, he felt deeply uncomfortable letting Breshada stay nearby. Despite her age, despite her supposed situation, she was a murderer. A *mass* murderer. One who not too long ago had believed in her cause, heart and soul.

But her appearance, and her outlandish claim, were simply too strange to ignore.

When they had finally made their way into an empty, clean stall, Wirr pulled up a bucket and turned it over, using it for a seat. After a couple of uncomfortable moments, Breshada did the same. Andyn chose to remain standing, his sharp gaze never leaving the young woman opposite.

"You should be safe in here, at least for the night," said Wirr as a horse in the next stall over whickered softly. "Now. Explain what you meant, when you said that you were gaa'vesh." He frowned. "Why would you say that?"

"Because I *am*. I have touched the power that should only be touched by the gods," said Breshada, the words sounding like they made her want to throw up.

"That's not possible," observed Wirr. "People are born with a

Reserve, or they're not—and the Gil'shar would have found that in you long ago. I don't know why you think you're Gifted, but—"

"I *am* gaa'vesh!" Breshada snarled, gesturing angrily.

A blinding, twisting bolt of energy flew past Wirr's face, smashing into the hay bales behind him and setting them ablaze. Wirr stared at Breshada wide-eyed for a long moment, stunned, as Andyn quickly set about beating out the flames.

Breshada gazed at the charred straw, refusing to make eye contact, clearly ashamed. "So. You see it is true. I do not know how it is possible, but we were crossing the bridge into Talmiel, and..."

Wirr groaned as he finally made the connection.

"You? *You* were the one in the ambassador's party?" he said in disbelief.

Breshada looked up in vague surprise, inclining her head. "Yes. The Finder went off, and..." She swallowed, the memory evidently painful. "I thought it was a joke, a coincidence. Some Gifted using Essence nearby just as they checked me. Everyone did. We all laughed, talking about how funny the timing was. Joking about how I would have to be put down."

Wirr listened in silence, not knowing how to respond to the emotion in Breshada's voice. If he were being honest, part of him felt a savage satisfaction at the woman's horror. Certainly, the image of her laughing with her friends about killing Gifted was more than just distasteful.

But he couldn't deny the pain written clearly on her face, either, or the hopelessness that wearied her gaze. Breshada wasn't just upset...she'd discovered that she was everything she despised, the exact type of person she'd been trying to cleanse from the earth.

She was broken.

"When they understood that it wasn't a mistake—three different Finders, perhaps a dozen tests—they tried to take me. I could see it in their eyes when they finally realized. They thought that I was a traitor. An abomination." Breshada's gaze was still firmly on the ground, and her voice shook at the memory. "So I used Whisper. Ran. I even took one of the Finders, because I couldn't believe it was me setting it off. I assumed it was a trick. But..."

Wirr rubbed his forehead, barely believing what he was hearing. "How, though?" he asked quietly. "Don't the Gil'shar test—"

"Every year. Every year until we come of age, we are tested," said Breshada angrily. "And I passed. Always, I passed. Gaa'vesh aren't born in Desriel anymore, but still they test."

Wirr exchange a glance with Andyn. "But if your ability hadn't shown itself by the time you turned eighteen—"

"You think I *do not know this*?" Breshada hissed the last words in sudden fury; she gestured and another bolt of Essence burst forth, fizzing to the side and punching a divot in the hard-packed dirt. She quieted immediately, loose black hair swinging as she stared at the scarred ground with a mixture of fascination and disgust.

She raised her hand in apology at Wirr's stunned look. "An accident," she assured him, looking sick. "I do not use it deliberately."

Wirr buried his head in his hands. "This is..." He groaned. "They think that you were acting on our orders, Breshada. They think we sent you amongst them as a spy."

"What?" Breshada was on her feet, the intensity of her response having Andyn's sword half drawn before the bodyguard realized that her anger was not directed at Wirr. "They cannot think..."

"They do," Wirr assured her bitterly. "And they are searching with everything they have for you. Keeping a close eye on us, as well, in case we speak to you." He gestured tiredly. "Like, say, *exactly* as we are doing here." He doubted that the Gil'shar would be keeping a terribly close eye on him personally—he'd have to be worse than careless to meet with his own spy after she'd been unmasked—but even if he were only under casual observation, it could spell disaster.

Breshada balled her hands into fists. "I cannot believe that they would think that of me."

"Can you blame them?" asked Wirr quietly. "What else *could* they think, but to assume that the reason you hadn't been discovered before was because you were hiding your ability? And that if you were hiding your ability well enough to fool the Gil'shar, you couldn't have been doing it alone?"

He took a deep breath. "So. Here we are. Putting aside the question of exactly *how* this happened, for now—let's say that I believe you. What do you want of me, Breshada?"

Breshada grimaced, saying nothing for a few seconds. Then her shoulders slumped just a little farther.

"I...I cannot control this. I get angry and it just..." She gestured at the hole in the ground for emphasis. "I need to understand how this could have happened, so that I might undo it. At worst, I need to know how to avoid using it. Knowledge of the power is normally forbidden, but..." She trailed off brokenly.

Wirr sighed, deeply and heavily. The easiest thing to do would be to give Breshada up to the ambassador. It would solve a range of problems—not only would he not have to worry about a Hunter at his family's home, but the gesture would surely convince the ambassador that he wasn't working with Breshada, too.

He hesitated. He could all but hear his mother telling him that as Northwarden, it was his best option...but he couldn't do it. Political ramifications aside and regardless of what she'd done in the past, Breshada was Gifted now. And part of being a leader—the most important part, as far as he was concerned—was doing what was *right*, not just what was *best*.

He thought for a moment. "We could make you into a Shadow."

"No." Breshada's face twisted at the suggestion. "Living on in shame, marked by the displeasure of the gods? Better to die honorably than that." She held his gaze. "When I was told to spare you in Talmiel, I did not understand—not until I saw you again in Ilin Illan. Now I do. I must learn, gaa'vesh. I do not know whether this is a plot begun by one of my rivals in the Gil'shar, or whether it is a divine punishment for what I did to Renmar and Gawn. But either way, you and I are evidently tied together, and I must learn."

Wirr grunted. "First lesson? You may want to stop calling us gaa'vesh," he said drily. "Second? My name is Torin. And if others are around, it's 'Sire' or 'Your Highness.'" He raised an eyebrow at her scowl. "Unless you want the Gil'shar taking you back to Desriel sooner rather than later? Changing your hair might help you avoid the notice of anyone who doesn't know you, but it's only going to go so far. A mysterious, young, armed woman accompanying me and refusing to use my honorific? They'll spot you in a heartbeat."

Breshada continued to glower, but nodded sharply.

Wirr sighed. He hadn't said it explicitly, but he knew he'd just agreed to help her. *How*, exactly, he wasn't sure. But the decision had been made.

"Talmiel," he said suddenly. "You say that you were told to spare us." That night was all a bit of a blur; with everything else that had happened straight after, he'd barely even thought of it since. It seemed an age ago—but now that Breshada was there, he had to admit to more than a twinge of curiosity. "Why?"

Breshada hesitated.

"It was an exchange I made," she said eventually. Her eyes unfocused for a moment as she remembered, and her hand strayed absently to the hilt of her sword. "Tal'kamar gave me Whisper, and all I had to do was save you and your friend."

Wirr frowned for a second as he processed what Breshada was saying. She'd been given *Whisper* in exchange for saving them?

"This Tal'kamar," he said eventually. He remembered the name now; Breshada had mentioned it when they had first met, but it still didn't mean anything to him. "Who was he? How did you meet him?"

Breshada looked to the side, frustration evident in her expression.

"It is an old form of the name, written only in the histories of the Gil'shar," she said softly. "Tal'kamar is what he called himself, but...most of my people know him as Talkanor."

Wirr blinked, glancing across at Andyn, who gave him a wry shrug.

"As in, Marut Jha Talkanor? The *god*?" He couldn't keep the incredulity from his tone.

Breshada scowled. "Yes." She drew Whisper and suddenly everything seemed to hush. "I doubt every day—how could I not?—and then there is this. From whom else's hand do you believe I would have been given a blade such as this? Whisper feeds on the very life of those he cuts. Would you not claim that a myth, too, had you not seen it with your own eyes?"

She sneered at Andyn, who had stepped between her and Wirr, but when he did not move she reluctantly sheathed the blade again. "I had not long been accepted as a Hunter—the youngest to have achieved such an honor in decades—and Tal'kamar..." She swallowed. "There had been reports of others of the gods appearing amongst us, more and more over the past century. Akran, who trained me and two generations before me, claimed that he had been visited by Gasharrid once as a very young man. A friend of mine called Sek said that he had seen Diarys herself emerge from the Untouchable Tomb as he worshipped." Breshada's words were flowing now; she stared at the ground as she spoke, as if she'd forgotten Wirr and Andyn were even there. "As strange as it was, when Tal'kamar revealed himself to me— showed me the secret signs and the divine marks written on his flesh—who was I to doubt?"

"And he gave you Whisper so that you could save us?" Wirr asked gently. It had to have been an Augur—someone with fore-knowledge of their predicament, who had perhaps been able to Read Breshada and determine what was necessary to convince her of his divinity. Nothing else made sense, though Wirr had no intention of saying as much to her.

"He said that the blade had a great purpose, and that the only way that purpose could be fulfillled was through me. Then he told me what Whisper would cost—what taking it would mean. He is the God of Balance. He offered me the choice." She looked Wirr in the eye. "But mortals do not give away blades like Whis-per, Prince Torin, nor do they refuse them."

There was silence after that last pronouncement; Wirr just stared at the Hunter, not knowing what to make of what she was saying. Someone had given her a sword—a *Named* sword—to save them. That, for now, was probably the only thing that he could safely take away from the conversation.

He shuddered to think of how many Gifted lives had been lost because she'd accepted that blade, regardless of whether his and Davian's had been spared as a result.

He glanced across at the stable doors. They were far enough away from the main house, and from Captain Rill's patrols, that any noise they'd made shouldn't have drawn any attention. Still—his mother was clearly uneasy about his presence. If he stayed out here for too long, she could easily end up sending someone to look for him.

He was curious to learn more from Breshada, but it would have to wait.

"If you want my help—whatever form that might take—there is one condition. No matter the outcome, I need your word that no more of the Gifted will die by your hand." He leaned forward, meeting her gaze unflinchingly. "Ever."

Breshada licked her lips, and Wirr could see the frustration in her eyes. But there was something else there, too.

Resignation. She'd known that this would be something he'd stipulate.

"Agreed," she growled.

Wirr shook his head. "I want to hear you say the words. Swear it by the Nine Gods." Desriel was a barbaric place at times, but oaths were deeply important to them.

Breshada looked at the ground, silent for a long moment.

"In exchange for your help, I will not kill another gaa'vesh. I swear this by the Nine Gods," she eventually said softly, sounding as if Wirr had just ripped away something dear to her.

And perhaps he had. Killing the Gifted was probably the only thing Breshada had ever known.

Wirr nodded and stood; he'd risked staying here longer than he should have already. "Thank you," he said, trying to make his tone gentle. Whatever her sins, Breshada had not had it easy for the past few weeks. "I'm in your debt for Talmiel, no matter why you did it—so if you decide you don't want my help, you're free to leave, and I will never mention that you were here. Otherwise, just stay out of sight. I'll figure out what to do and find you again before anyone comes this way in the morning."

Breshada inclined her head; while she didn't look pleased, exactly, Wirr thought he saw at least a hint of relief flicker across her features.

He left the stables and started back toward the main house, lost in thought. Eventually, a polite cough from Andyn brought him back to the present.

"Are you certain about this, Sire?" his bodyguard asked cautiously.

"Not even slightly." Wirr shook his head grimly. "I haven't the first idea of what I'm going to do with her."

"What about the Tol?" asked Andyn.

Wirr shot him a wry look. "I'm not sure how welcoming the Council would be to a former Hunter." He glanced back. "Particularly when I can't really vouch for how much the 'former' part applies, despite what she just said."

"Don't put the Gifted killer in amongst the Gifted," acceded Andyn. "Politically savvy as always, Sire. But if I may ask, then— why help her?"

Wirr shook his head slowly. "She mysteriously becomes Gifted, when everything I've ever heard indicates that shouldn't be possible. She gets sent to save Davian and I in Desriel by someone who knew we'd be there well in advance, and who gave her that fates-cursed sword as motivation. Who's to say that she's not right—if they foresaw we'd meet in Desriel, how do we know that they didn't See that we would meet again, here and now? How do we know that we're not being pushed together for a purpose?"

"Even if true, there is still the matter of what that purpose might be, Sire," observed Andyn quietly.

Wirr nodded. "I know. But—I think—as long as she is this way, she won't try to harm us. She needs our help. And if she'd wanted our deaths, she wouldn't have bothered talking."

Andyn just nodded thoughtfully, saying nothing. They continued on toward the main house in silence.

Wirr wearily climbed the wide, curving stairs from the entryway and then started along the hallway toward his old room.

His mother, it seemed, had already retired for the evening. One of her hired men had greeted Wirr and Andyn at the door and then tried to escort them for a while, but his presence had irritated Wirr to the point that he had ordered the man to leave. The guard had looked reluctant—clearly Geladra's orders had said that he should do otherwise—but whether because Wirr was the prince, or because Andyn's posture had suggested that he would happily reinforce the command, the man had eventually slunk away.

Wirr had visited his father's study again after dismissing Andyn for the evening, examining the safe for more than half an hour before eventually giving up. It was frustrating, but Wirr would have to go back to Ilin Illan and see if he could find a way to circumvent the protections on it.

"Tor!"

Wirr dragged himself to a halt, head snapping around at the familiar voice, which had reached his ear in a low whisper. He stared, stunned, when he saw the face peeking out from behind a half-open door.

"Del?" He slipped into the room, wrapping his younger sister in a tight hug. "It's good to see you!"

Deldri hugged him back, then glanced warily out into the hallway, clearly wanting to be able to conceal herself again should someone else happen by. "You don't look surprised to see me here."

"Mother said that you were visiting friends," Wirr said, lowering his voice to match Deldri's. "But...it's a big house. After the way she made you leave at the funeral, and the way she's been acting, I did wonder." He frowned. "I'm surprised she convinced you to stay away for this long, though."

"There wasn't much convincing involved. She's had a man posted outside my room since about midday."

"*What?*" Wirr stared at his sister in horror. "She actually *locked you up?*"

"Well..." Deldri shrugged. "Basically."

"Uh." Wirr shook his head in disbelief. "I'm so sorry, Del. That's...horrible. How did you get away?"

Deldri smiled. "They either don't understand how windows work, or they think that girls can't climb. I'm not sure which."

Wirr chuckled, then sighed and rubbed his forehead. "Well. At least I'm left in no doubt as to how she feels about me, then. Not that there was much to begin with," he added heavily.

"She's being stupid." Deldri's expression darkened. "I knew she was angry, after she found out—I think more at Father than at you—but she's been acting so strangely over the past few weeks, Tor. Things have been..." She shook her head. "I've been wanting for us to go back to the city—you're there, and Uncle and Kara, and all my friends—but she won't even think about it. It's like she wants us to stay out here forever."

Wirr studied his younger sister for a moment. She was nearly fourteen, more adult every time he saw her, and it appeared that the past month had changed her even more. The innocent girl he'd met after returning from Caladel was gone—replaced by someone just a little older, a little more world-weary. It saddened him...but in many ways it made him trust her more, too.

"She's certainly upset about me taking over father's position," he agreed ruefully. "I came here to get some things from his study, but she let someone else from Administration clear it out first. She had to know I'd be interested in what was in there."

Deldri peered at him. "Ah. That's . . . not true. About Administration clearing it out, I mean."

Wirr frowned. "What do you mean?"

"I mean that I helped mother take everything out of that room *this morning*," said Deldri. "That was why she originally said that those men were here. She told me that she wanted the room for something else . . . but everything in there just got shifted to one of the back rooms. It's a mess, but it's all still there."

Wirr's heart leaped. "I don't suppose you want to show me?"

Deldri leaned across and peered cautiously out the door. "I'll make you a deal. I show you, and you take me with you."

Wirr blinked. "Back to Ilin Illan?"

"Please." Deldri looked at him imploringly. "She *locked me up*, Tor. Things have been horrible here. She doesn't really talk to me anymore; she's been preoccupied with something, and I feel more like I'm in the way than anything else. It's not as if there's any danger now, and I can go back to my old room and keep up with my studies in Ilin Illan. With my friends. And you and Kara and Uncle will all be there to look out for me." She widened her eyes at him, a look that she knew he'd always had a difficult time resisting. "*Please*." Despite her deliberately obvious attempt at softening him up, Wirr could hear the desperation underpinning her words.

Wirr ran his hands through his hair. It wasn't an unreasonable request, and it appeared that his mother had no intention of returning to court anytime soon. Normally he'd have suggested that Deldri stay—he didn't like the thought of his mother being out here with only the staff to keep her company, no matter how she was acting toward him—but if Deldri's account was accurate, things were worse than he'd imagined. It was hardly fair to his sister to just leave her here.

"Show me this room first," he said eventually. "I can't just take you with me, but I promise I'll speak to Mother about it before I leave. I'll push for it to happen." His expression darkened. "It seems that we're going to have some . . . controversial things to speak about anyway, so I may as well add it to the list."

Deldri gave him a brief, impromptu hug, abruptly looking much cheerier. Wirr smiled. For some reason, he'd known that Deldri wouldn't have cared about him being Gifted. It wasn't something they'd ever talked about—she'd been too young for such serious conversations, before he'd left for Caladel—but his little sister had always been a bright spot for him.

They made their way cautiously back down the stairs and toward the back end of the mansion. This area was sparsely furnished, the rooms used more for storage than any day-to-day purposes. Deldri eventually located the door she was looking for and opened it wide, admitting Wirr.

Wirr sighed as he entered. Loose papers spilled everywhere on the ground, while wobbly-looking piles of books were stacked unevenly against the wall, some having already fallen down. The floor of the small room was barely visible beneath the chaos.

"Still haven't figured out the whole 'neatness' thing, I see," he murmured as he stepped inside. "Is there *any* order to this?"

Deldri gave him a stare. "If you're going to be like that…"

Wirr felt the corners of his mouth curl upward. "That's a no, then." He scratched his head. "So…where would you advise we start, Del? I'm looking for a key, but I'm not sure where Father would have kept it."

Deldri scratched her head. "I wasn't exactly paying attention when we were putting—"

"Throwing?" interrupted Wirr.

"*Putting* everything in here," continued Deldri emphatically, "but I think I remember seeing a key in one of his desk drawers. We put everything like that over there in the corner. Placed it there. Very carefully," she added, sticking out her tongue.

Wirr just grinned in response, stepping over some detritus to the shambolic pile that Deldri had indicated. He began sorting through some of the papers—now that he was here, there was no point wasting the opportunity—and felt a stab of sadness as he recognized the familiar, flowing handwriting that his mother had always complained was neater than hers.

There was nothing much of interest at first. Run-of-the-mill orders to Administration that Elocien had never gotten around to sending. Some notes on how to improve the rotations of the

Administrators, so that there were fewer personal conflicts with the Gifted in outlying areas. A list of those who were excelling in their fields and were in line for promotion; that one Wirr carefully folded and pocketed, resolving to look into those people's performances. Assuming that they were still alive, of course. Plenty of Administrators from the city had died in the fighting a month ago.

When Wirr picked up the next notebook, though, something small and metallic dropped with a small thud onto the carpet and bounced away. Heart skipping a beat, he stepped over a pile of haphazardly strewn paper and snatched it up, examining it closely.

Etched into the metal was the symbol of the Tenets—a man, woman, and child, enclosed in a circle.

"Found it," he said, exhaling. He shot his sister a relieved smile. "Looks like this might not be a wasted trip after all."

"Why wouldn't Mother want you to have that?" asked Deldri.

"I don't think she even knows about it," admitted Wirr. "I suspect this was all just a way to...inconvenience me. She *really* doesn't think I should be in charge of Administration." He sighed heavily, glancing at his sister. "It's not just time, is it. She's never going to support me in this."

Deldri shrugged awkwardly. "You're probably right. It's been...it's been bad the past few years, Tor," she admitted, voice catching a little. "Ever since you left, whenever she and Father were together, it would end up in a fight. She was always saying that he'd changed, that he'd stopped standing up for what he believed in."

She glanced to the side. "He'd started telling me not to hate people like...you. Like the Gifted and the Augurs," she added softly. "He never said anything about you, specifically, but it made sense to me when we found out." She swallowed. "When Mother heard what he'd been telling me, it all but ended things between them. After that, I don't think he spent another full night here."

Wirr listened in silence, wanting to offer comfort but knowing he couldn't. He was responsible—the reason his parents had grown apart. He understood now why Elocien had chosen not to tell Geladra the truth...and he also understood what a toll that must have taken on his father. On both of his parents, and his sister as a result.

"I'm so sorry," he said quietly, meaning it.

Deldri gave him a small smile. "I'm old enough to think for myself, Tor. I know it's not your fault, and I know it wasn't Father's, either." She fell silent, her omission clearly indicating whom she thought *was* at fault.

Wirr grimaced. "Don't be so quick to judge her," he said gently. "She's been through a lot."

Deldri snorted. "Tell me you think I'm wrong."

Wirr hesitated, but he wasn't able to lie to his sister. "Just... don't hate her for it, Del," he said softly. "If this was a few months ago, I might have felt differently, but... I see people like her every day in the city. The problem is that she remembers when a lot of people with these abilities did bad things, so she assumes that there's a connection. She's *scared* there's a connection."

Deldri shook her head. "If you say so," she said, clearly unconvinced.

Wirr sighed, gesturing to the door. "We should keep moving. I need to see whether this is actually the key I'm after."

They started toward Elocien's office, twice having to duck into rooms as they caught glimpses of their mother's men, who were seemingly patrolling the house. There was no indication that they'd been spotted, though, and soon enough they reached their destination.

For a moment Wirr considered asking his sister to give him some privacy—he didn't know *what* he was going to find in the safe—but as much as Deldri had grown up, he still risked a commotion if he tried to leave her out of this now. He waited until she had shut the door behind her, then carefully pressed his Administrator's Mark against the symbol on the wall. Deldri watched in wide-eyed fascination as the panel slid back and Wirr produced the metallic key, slotting it into the lock.

It turned with a well-oiled click.

The door to the safe swung open silently and Wirr peered inside, heart pounding. Part of him—the part that remained suspicious of Scyner and his intent—wanted there to be nothing. It would be disappointing, but undoubtedly simpler.

When he saw the thick leather-bound notebook sitting inside, though, he breathed a sigh of relief. As much as he'd wanted Scyner to be wrong, his desire for answers was stronger still.

He carefully drew the heavy book out. It looked old but in good condition, with the pages sealed inside the cover the entire way around by what appeared to be thick red wax. He examined it curiously for a moment, then stuck his hand back into the safe, feeling around to make sure that there wasn't anything he'd missed. He was just about to give up when his fingers brushed against something hard and sharp in the back.

Frowning, he reached in farther and pulled out a black shard of stone no longer than his thumb. It was rounded, mostly smooth, but tapered to a jagged point at the end.

"What is it?" asked Deldri.

Wirr's brow furrowed as he recognized the object. "An Oathstone." One of the Vessels that were used to swear in Administrators. It wasn't *awfully* strange that his father had had one, he supposed...but then, they were rare. Rare enough that keeping one hidden away from Administration like this was at least a little odd.

Then he thought of what Laiman had told him before he'd left, about the 'unofficial' Administrators. His father wouldn't have been involved in anything like that, surely?

"Deldri!"

Wirr snapped out of his reverie, heart sinking as he turned to see his mother in the doorway, staring at the two of them with deep disapproval. Someone must have seen them coming back here after all. For a brief, panicked moment he considered trying to conceal the open safe and the book in his hand, but even as he had the thought, his mother's gaze took all of it in. He kept his right fist closed, hiding at least the Oathstone from view.

"What is that?" Geladra's tone hardened as she spotted the hefty leather-bound tome. "How did you..."

"I was told about it," said Wirr calmly. "I need it for my research."

"It's not yours. You need to hand it over."

Wirr stared at her in disbelief. "What? No."

"Those belong to Administration, Torin." His mother's tone was firm.

"I'm the *Northwarden*." Wirr growled the words. "And he was my father. Those two things give me more right to these than anyone."

Geladra scowled at that, but seemed to understand that her son was not to be dissuaded. She turned her gaze to Deldri. "And you disobeyed me. I was very clear in my—"

"I don't care," snapped Deldri, much to both Wirr and Geladra's surprise. "You kept me *prisoner*, and he's my brother. There's no reason I shouldn't have been able to see him." She moved a step closer to Wirr.

"She has a point," said Wirr quietly, not wanting to anger his mother further but unable to keep silent. "I'm *Gifted*, Mother. Not ill. Not a monster. Not one of the ruling class from twenty years ago. I'm *exactly the same person* I was before you found out. I can almost understand why you lied to me about Father's study—but lying to me about where Del was? Setting strange men to keep her locked up in her room? That's *horrible*."

Geladra flushed, but didn't back down. "That's *your fault*, Torin. I didn't like doing it, but can't you see? Your being Gifted is one thing, but it's the way it *influences* you—and those around you—that's the problem. You're *not* the same person who left three years ago. And you're not someone whose influence I wish to expose your sister to!" She all but shouted the last part, every word laced with angry defiance.

Wirr reeled back under the barrage, the blood draining from his face. This, evidently, was what his mother really thought of him.

He resisted the near-overwhelming urge to shout back, closing his eyes for a moment.

"I'll go. It's clear I'm not welcome here." He met his mother's gaze. "I will head back to Ilin Illan tonight. But I *am* taking the book."

"And I'm going with him."

Wirr grimaced as Deldri lifted her chin defiantly. Geladra stared for a moment, not quite understanding what her daughter was saying, and then gave a short, unamused laugh.

"You are not," she said bluntly. She looked at Wirr. "She cannot go with you. You may be Northwarden, but you have no say over what your sister can and cannot do, nor what is best for her." She held out her hand. "And you have no right to come in here and take something that doesn't belong to you." She glanced over her shoulder, out the door. "Markus. Please let your men know that if my son tries to leave with my property, you are to detain him."

Wirr stared at her in disbelief as Markus's looming form filled the doorway, blocking his exit. He felt his face grow hot, and anger burned again deep in his chest. If he handed over the book to his mother, he'd never see it again.

"This has gone too far. You *will* let me take it," he said grimly, calling her bluff. He hesitated. "And you *will* let Deldri come with me, too. Tell Markus that he and his men are to let us leave. I will not let this slide if you don't," he added quietly.

His mother gaped at him silently for a long few seconds. Then, looking as though it made her sick to her core, Geladra turned to Markus.

"Let them leave."

The brutish man stared at her, looking as surprised as Wirr felt at his mother's abrupt backing down. Still, eventually the man stepped aside with a scowl.

Wirr didn't linger; assisted by an impatient shove from Deldri, he hurried out into the hallway.

"What was that?" he muttered to Deldri.

"I told you she's been acting strange." Deldri cast a glance over her shoulder. "We shouldn't stay around for too long, though."

Wirr grunted an acknowledgment. "Grab only the things you need. I'll get Andyn," he said quietly. "Meet me out front as soon as you can."

His sister nodded at the urgency in his tone and dashed away.

Wirr hurried upstairs, flinching every time he saw one of his mother's men in his path. None of them moved to stop him, though, and soon enough he was shaking Andyn by the shoulder.

"Sire?" Andyn peered up at him blearily, then came awake with alacrity as he registered the tension in Wirr's expression.

"We're leaving." Wirr glanced behind him at the door. "Things got...ugly. My mother threatened to use force to stop me from keeping this." He indicated the book, still in his hand.

288   "I'll have the carriage brought around," said Andyn, sliding

into a standing position. The man apparently slept in clothing appropriate for such abrupt occurrences; once he'd buckled his sword to his side, he looked ready to go. "What about your other guest?"

Wirr blinked at him for a moment, then scowled. "Fates." He had forgotten. "If she's still there, tell her to meet us down the road, out of sight of the gates. She'll have to come with us."

"As you say, Sire," said Andyn, only a slight flicker of reluctance in his tone. He slipped out the door without another word.

A few minutes later they were pulling away; Markus and his men had watched their every move, but no one had tried to stop them. Wirr let out a long breath as the house began to recede.

"So what was that all about, Sire?" asked Andyn quietly, giving Deldri a meaningful glance as he said the words. "How did things escalate so quickly?"

Wirr shook his head, peering back at his mother. She was just...standing there in the lamp-lit entrance, surrounded by her men as she watched them depart.

He couldn't be sure, but he thought that she was weeping.

"I don't know, Andyn." Wirr sighed, settling back into his seat, a sick feeling in the pit of his stomach. "I have no idea at all."

Chapter 20

Darkness.

Not even darkness, just an utter absence of light. Fire all around, though the flames were shadow, black against the nothing, emitting no light. Pain. Asha whipped her vision around, trying to find somewhere, anywhere her gaze could fall that did not cause her agony. Loss. No physical body here, but she wasn't floating along—rather ripped from one location to the next, shreds torn from her at every movement. The act of quickly healing was as agonizing as the wounds. Sadness.

Rage. Depression. She was exhausted, she was furious, she was terrified, she was as alone as she could ever be. She reached for something good but good was merely a word now, an abstract concept. Not even her memories could touch on anything that felt tinged with something right.

"There's too much blood, Thell!" The words screamed through the void.

"Necessary, Taeris." Tension in the reply, but calmness, too. "Necessary."

Light. Blinding, beautiful light. Pain but a physical one, something exquisite and wondrous in and of itself.

Two faces, one vaguely familiar, one not.

"Evatha, tu terreth," said the unfamiliar one.

Asha knew the language, though this man's pronunciation was rough, barely understandable.

Obey, or go back.

She struggled to grasp the things that she was experiencing. Air against her face. Warmth. Light against her eyes. The physicality of everything around her as it came into focus.

She paused.

"Evatha," she rasped.

Asha's eyes snapped open and she sat bolt upright in her bed.

She just stayed like that for a few moments, staring, trembling at the intensity of the dream. Sweat dripped from every pore, and her nightclothes and sheets were sodden with it. Gradually, her mind recovered, focused, accepted that she was who she was and that it had all been in her head.

She rose, muscles aching from where they had tensed for too long, and mechanically changed into fresh clothes. Light was showing at the edges of the curtains; she drew them back to reveal a sunny early morning outside. All was quiet. Peaceful.

She closed her eyes, steadying herself. She'd just been through a traumatic experience, knew the terror of her time in the catacombs had probably been fuel for a rough night.

But that had to have been more than just a nightmare.

One of the men she'd seen had been Taeris, though she almost hadn't put that face together with the man she currently knew. He'd been younger. Without scars. Handsome, despite the fear in his eyes.

The other—the one Taeris had called Thell—*hadn't* been Laiman Kardai. That man had been heavyset, broad, with hazel eyes and jet-black hair.

She shook her head, trying to decide if this affected her plans for the morning. It had taken her upward of an hour to get out of the catacombs—though how she'd known the way back to the Sanctuary, she still didn't understand. Whenever the passageway had branched, she'd just been *certain* of which way she needed to go.

After sneaking back past the Tol Athian guards and arriving at the palace in the dead of night—only to discover that Wirr was no longer there—Asha had settled for sleeping, fully intending to go to Taeris in the morning with what she'd seen. She wasn't entirely sure how long she'd been gone, but she didn't think it was long enough for anyone to be looking for her. Sleep had seemed the best option.

She washed the sheen of sweat from her face absently as she pondered what she'd seen, then squared her shoulders and walked out the door, at first failing to register the two uncomfortable-looking young men sitting on the hallway couch opposite her room.

"Representative Chaedris." The handsome boy on the left leaped to his feet first, straight black hair looking unkempt from where he'd evidently been running his hands through it. "I'm glad to see you're well."

"Iain." Asha stared at him blankly for a moment, then groaned inwardly when she understood why he was there. "I'm terribly sorry, but perhaps we can talk later? I'm in something of a rush," she explained hurriedly.

"Ah. I won't take much of your time." Iain gave her a winning smile. "I was just wondering if you had dinner plans for this evening."

Asha barely restrained a sigh. She'd spoken in passing to Iain a few times during Assembly—he was pleasant enough, and shared her tendency to quietly mock the Houses' constant political bickering. But Taeris either hadn't passed on her message or hadn't been emphatic enough, because she had absolutely no interest in going down this road.

Before she could speak, though, the other young man who had been waiting stood and coughed politely. Lyannis Tel'Rath was smaller than Iain, wiry rather than muscular. His sharp, bright blue eyes stood out even more on an otherwise plain-featured face, which was slightly flushed.

"Actually...I'm hoping the Representative is already occupied tonight," he interjected with a small, nervous smile, speaking more to Asha than to Iain. "Representative Sarr suggested you might be interested in—"

Asha groaned, the act of opening her eyes far more painful than it should have been.

Lyannis was kneeling over her with a concerned expression, looking lost. He breathed an audible sigh of relief when he saw her stirring. "Good to see you, Representative," he said, giving her a wry smile. "If you wanted an evening to yourself that badly, you should have just told us so."

Asha gave a soft laugh, though it was quickly cut off by another groan. Her head felt as though it would split open. "What happened?"

"You...fell." Lyannis gestured, indicating that he was as mystified as her.

There were voices farther down the corridor and a moment later Iain's face joined Lyannis's above her, expression just as worried. "You're awake. Thank fates for that." He nodded to Lyannis and they positioned themselves either side of her, gently helping her up onto the couch. "I've sent for the physician—"

"No need." Asha quickly forced herself to straighten, a rush of apprehension helping. She didn't need more questions surrounding this. "I'm feeling fine. I didn't sleep well—just a little light-headed."

"You really should see *someone*," said Iain with a frown.

"She says she's fine, Iain," Lyannis replied firmly.

"The physician's already been fetched," argued Iain.

Asha sighed, though softly enough that the two boys glaring at each other didn't notice. She stood, forcing both of them to stand back a little.

"I'm feeling much better now. Thank you for your help, but I really have to be on my way." She hesitated. She didn't want to be rude, but she didn't have time for this, either. "And thank you both for the invitations—I'm honored you asked—but I'm afraid I'll have to decline." She gave them what she hoped was an apologetic smile, then turned and hurried off before either boy could protest.

She needed to talk to Brase.

Asha faltered as she caught sight of the red-cloaked figure up ahead.

For once she hoped that it was Dras; unpleasantly oily man that he was, at least she would need to do no more than force a smile and nod as she passed. It didn't take more than a moment for her to recognize Taeris's confident gait, though, and it was already too late to duck off to the side.

"Ashalia!" There was genuine relief in Taeris's voice as he called out to her, a smile splitting his horribly scarred features.

"I've been looking for you," he added, mild rebuke in his tone as she got closer. "I tried to find you last night and was told that you hadn't been seen for some time. If you weren't around this morning, I may have started to worry."

Asha hesitated, then came to a decision. What she'd seen in the Sanctuary was too important to withhold—and of everyone who she could currently talk to, Taeris was by far the best qualified to assess the information.

"That's something that we should discuss," she said quietly, glancing around the crowded hallway. "Probably in a Lockroom."

Taeris's eyebrows rose a little but he nodded immediately, gesturing for her to lead the way. Asha knew the locations of all the Lockrooms in the palace by heart now, and she and Taeris were soon seated in the closest one, the door closed.

Without preamble, Asha began explaining what had happened. Her investigation in the Sanctuary. Her encounter with Isiliar, Vhalire, and the Echo. The catacombs. She carefully modified the story at points, omitting mention of her Veil, but otherwise relating everything she thought was important.

Taeris listened in silence, his expression initially one of vaguely unsurprised concern, but by the end more thoughtful than stern. He sighed.

"Well. I suppose given the circumstances, we can leave exactly *how* you've been managing to get down there for later," he said drily. "You're quite certain about the names you heard?"

"Yes." Asha leaned forward. "You recognized some of them, didn't you?"

Taeris inclined his head.

"Alaris was the name of someone who tried to fool Caeden, to have him killed not long before the battle with the Blind," he said quietly. "The others..." He scratched his head, frowning. "Isiliar. Wereth. Alaris. When grouped together like that they all seem vaguely familiar, but fates take it if I can place from where. I'll look into them, anyway. See what I can find."

"What about Tal'kamar?" pressed Asha. She'd seen the glimmer of recognition in Taeris's eyes at the name, and it was by far the one that she was most curious about. *Tell her that Tal'kamar is taking Licanius to the Wells.* She'd delivered Davian's message to the Shadraehin, but she still had less than no idea of what it had meant.

Taeris hesitated. "You really think that this woman—Isiliar—was not in possession of all her faculties?"

"Fairly certain," said Asha drily.

Taeris nodded, looking vaguely relieved. "Tal'kamar, I think, is Caeden's real name. His name before he lost his memory," he explained. "Alaris called him that—as did the sha'teth, though it was using High Darecian at the time, and I don't think that the others ever picked up on it."

Asha stared at him, horrified. "The things Isiliar said about him—"

"Sound like the ramblings of a madwoman. Someone consorting with the sha'teth. An enemy of ours if there ever was one," said Taeris firmly. "You were there a month ago. You *know* that Caeden is on our side."

Asha subsided, acceding the point but still not entirely convinced. Caeden was the reason that the Blind had been defeated—there was no arguing that. But then, remembering Isiliar's words—the complete and utter conviction in her tone, how she had described him as a *monster*—Asha couldn't help but feel a sliver of uncertainty.

"So Vhalire is dead," said Taeris quietly, changing the topic slightly. "And he told you to hide the blade after you used it?"

"He said Isiliar would be able to track me if I kept it," affirmed Asha. She'd been reluctant to leave herself without a weapon, but Vhalire's warning about the sword had been clear enough. With Isiliar's screams still ringing in her ears, she'd concealed it under some rubble in a side passage, not minutes after beginning her flight.

Taeris nodded slowly. "And afterward, you say you suddenly knew the way out?"

Asha frowned at the Representative's expression. "You think that was connected to the sword, somehow?" She'd considered the possibility herself—though she had been more inclined to think that it was some strange side effect of her killing Vhalire—but in either case, she didn't know enough to even theorize how the two could be related.

"Perhaps," acceded Taeris thoughtfully, though he appeared to be talking to himself more than to her now. He shook his head, then focused on her again. "Do you think that you could find your way back to where you hid it?"

Asha hesitated. "Probably not." That was a lie; she knew those tunnels now, knew the exact spot where she'd buried it. But even if she thought that retrieving the unsettling blade was a good idea—which she didn't—right now, the idea of going back down into those darkened passageways wasn't something she could face.

"Hmm." Taeris looked disappointed, but didn't press. "The information alone is certainly valuable, anyway. I will let the Deilannis expedition know about these names you overheard—if they have time, they can look them up while they're there."

Asha nodded, relieved that he was letting the matter drop. "When do they leave?"

"Tomorrow. Later than I'd hoped, to be honest." Taeris rubbed his forehead tiredly. "It's been hard, finding the right people to go. Most who believe that the Boundary collapsing is actually a serious threat have already gone north. Of the rest, half think that a trip to Deilannis is a waste of time, and the other half—the ones who actually know something about it—think that it's a suicidal waste of time."

Asha winced. "I'm glad to hear that it's finally happening, anyway," she said quietly. "From Davian's description of it, there would have to be something in that library that could help the Augurs figure out how to seal the Boundary." That was the official reason the expedition had been formed—though from what she had overheard of the conversation between Taeris and Laiman, Asha privately suspected that there was more to it.

"Let's hope so." Taeris grunted. "Though to be honest, it may not even matter if the Augurs don't start moving soon."

"What do you mean?"

The Representative sighed. "They're still in the south. Fine, but still at Tol Shen."

"Oh." Asha's heart sank. "I didn't know that there had been any news."

Taeris shrugged. "I have my sources."

Asha frowned, but nodded. Shen had been frustratingly silent   297 over the past couple of weeks, and their promised updates to the Assembly had failed to materialize more than once. She had no idea where Taeris was getting his information, but he had no reason to lie.

She stood. "I'm glad to hear that they're well, at least," she said sincerely. She glanced out the window. "If you'll excuse me though..."

"Of course." Taeris peered at her. "Just don't forget about our meeting with Lord si'Veria in a few hours."

Asha rolled her eyes, but nodded. "I'll be there."

She left, then headed straight for the palace gates.

Tol Athian's library, as always, was quiet at this time of the evening.

Only a few Gifted were reading tomes in private, well-lit corners, and they ignored her entrance. Much to Asha's relief, Brase was sitting behind the desk at the door. He brightened when he saw her.

"Representative," he said jovially. "Just the person I wanted to talk to. I have an enormous headache. Would you like to know why?"

"Because you fell down and hit your head...perhaps three hours ago?"

Brase grunted. "Well. That takes the fun out of it. Can I assume that you're not basing that guess on my natural lack of coordination?"

Asha shrugged slightly, face carefully neutral.

Brase narrowed his eyes, even as the corners of his mouth curled upward. "Can I take it that the fresh scrape on your hand is also from a natural lack of coordination, then?"

Asha grinned in response to that, though the smile quickly faded. "So it affected both of us at about the same time," she said quietly. "What about the others?"

Brase sighed. "In my constructive and lively discussions with them, I've managed to extricate that they have been experiencing something similar. Nothing more than that, though. Nothing so exciting as specific times. They're terrified that someone will find out and...I don't know." He shook his head, looking caught between amusement and disgust. "They only told me once I promised not to tell anyone else."

"Good thing you're so untrustworthy, then," Asha observed wryly.

Brase smiled cheerfully in response. "So what's next? I've looked in every book I can think of, but..." He shrugged. "I'm not sure that there's anywhere we'd be able to find out more about something like this."

Asha thought for a long moment, chewing her lip.

"Actually," she said slowly, thinking back to her conversation with Taeris. "I can think of at least one place."

Chapter 21

Caeden opened his eyes, surprised to find himself without pain.

He was still lying in the street but he'd evidently been moved to the outer edge of the snow-bound city; it was warmer again and the buildings stretching away above him were well lit, with none of the wild flickering that marked the area closer to the center. All was silent.

The memory of what he'd done to Isiliar came flooding back, sending an acidic trickle of bile to his throat. He'd done that to his friend. He'd shut her in that device and left her there, even knowing how terrible it would be for her. He'd done that to his *friend*.

Suddenly, the way she had attacked him seemed perfectly reasonable.

He took a deep breath. He understood what the machines—the Tributaries—that Isiliar and Meldier had been in were now. Their purpose was not torture after all, though no less unpleasant for it.

He swallowed. The needles in a Tributary caused persistent injuries; when the occupant's body tried to heal itself with Essence, that energy was instead drained away into a storage construct called a Cyrarium. Thanks to their immortality and immense power, sealing one of the Venerate in a Tributary would provide a constant, uninterruptable flow of Essence for as long as they were in it. Millennia, if need be.

Isiliar's and Meldier's Tributaries, specifically, had been helping to sustain the Boundary.

Now, they weren't.

Caeden breathed out at the terrifying thought, lying perfectly still and just listening. When he couldn't detect any movement nearby he stirred, raising his head cautiously.

"Welcome back, Tal," came a deep voice from off to the right.

Caeden flinched, then turned and swivelled into a seated position. A man sat atop the low wall that ran alongside the road, watching him absently.

Caeden tensed with immediate recognition.

The man he'd been friends with. The man who had set him up to be killed.

"Alaris," he said quietly, carefully shifting into a more mobile position. The tall, muscular man didn't look about to do him violence, but Licanius sat atop the wall at his side, within easy reach.

Alaris gave him a tired, mildly amused smile. "You're safe. Isiliar left. Not *willingly*, exactly, but..." He shrugged.

Caeden didn't relax.

"What?" Alaris stared at him blankly for a second, then rolled his eyes. "Oh. You're not still upset over me sending you to Havran, surely."

"You tried to have me killed."

"You're *immortal*," pointed out Alaris, sounding more exasperated than anything else. "Even Telesthaesia wasn't going to be enough to contain you for a journey back across the ilshara, regardless of your... limited state. If they'd succeeded in taking your head, you would have come back soon enough. I was just trying to stop you from making a mistake, before you started something that none of us could stop." He gave the sword by his side a rueful glance. "In which, of course, I utterly failed."

Caeden was silent for a long moment. Alaris was right—Caeden hadn't known at the time and hadn't really registered the fact since, but there was no way that the Blind attack in Ilin Illan could have killed him.

"What about after that—the assault on Ilin Illan, on Andarra?" he asked quietly. "Was that you?"

Alaris's grimace was answer enough.

"We had no other way to stop you, Tal," the other man said eventually. "I hated giving Mash'aan and his men that armor, but they were the only ones who were capable. The only ones who volunteered, too." His eyes hardened. "But I do not apologize for trying. I was desperate but you *made* me desperate, and where we are now is proof that I had to do what I could. The Lyth are beyond dangerous—you've set in motion events that could destroy the *world*. Tell me you truly believe that I went too far."

Caeden felt his jaw tighten. "Your men slaughtered innocent people, violated their bodies, just to draw out soldiers from Ilin Illan."

"Innocent people whom your actions would have condemned regardless. Despise the methods, Tal, but not the intent. Just as you've always argued that what you did to Is and the others was justified." Alaris was still speaking quietly, but there was iron in his voice now. "Do you even know why she attacked you? Do you remember what you did? Because her time in the Tributary was...not kind to her, and she blames you for that." He looked at Caeden sadly. "Not unjustly."

Caeden swallowed.

"I didn't want to hurt her," he eventually muttered.

"I know. She knows, too, somewhere deep down," said Alaris calmly. "That's why she didn't use Licanius on you straight away, and it's why we're still here talking. For all your faults, Tal, you would never *want* to do that to one of your friends."

Caeden bowed his head, brow furrowed, silent for a while. Even more than with Meldier, something didn't feel right here. Alaris's words were...reasonable. The words of a man hurt by a friend but desperate to forgive him—not one bent on the destruction of an enemy.

Another memory tickled at the back of his mind, then suddenly came on in a flood.

Caeden yawned, stretching as he woke.

He rolled off his bed, rubbing his face as he stared around the cell. It hadn't changed much in the last eighty years. There was a nicer bed, a desk with material for writing, a few books, and a smokeless torch to read by...but the bigger things remained the same. No sunlight, no breeze, no way to tell whether it was day or night outside.

He looked down at his hands, still smooth despite the years they'd seen. He was glad for that. He hadn't known that his immortality would mean a complete lack of aging, not for certain, despite Alarais's assurances. The cell was dry and warm enough and he was always well fed, but it still wouldn't be an easy life for someone with an older body.

There was the clanging of a door down the hallway, and Caeden straightened in anticipation. He was the only resident of these cells at the moment, and it wasn't mealtime.

He brightened as Alarais's form came into view. "How did it go?"

Alarais sighed, slumping into the chair he'd had brought down, the one that sat permanently on the other side of the bars facing toward Caeden. "Well enough," he conceded after a moment. "Ulttar is more insistent than his father, but they have agreed to renew the treaty. There will be peace in the north for another generation."

Caeden gave a wide, approving smile. "Well done," he said sincerely. Alarais had worked hard to ensure that the hostilities between the Quar and Agrhest clans came to nothing. It was a small thing, small enough that most rulers would not have given it their attention at all. But Alarais was dedicated to peace, and even this squabble was not beneath his notice. "Why aren't you celebrating?"

Alarais's gloomy expression cleared, and he smiled, nodding slowly. "Ignore me. I was thinking of something else." He held up his hands, displaying a bottle and two glasses that he'd brought with him. "I am, in fact, about to do just that."

Caeden raised an eyebrow. "You need two glasses to celebrate?"

Alarais gave him a wry look. "I thought, perhaps, that you might join me."

Caeden stared at his friend. "I... of course," he said, lost for words. "What about the Law, though?"

Alarais poured wine into both glasses, then proffered one through the bars, which were spaced just far enough apart to allow the crystal to pass through.

"Just drink," he said. He raised his glass. "To peace."

Caeden echoed the sentiment, then took a cautious sip of the

wine. It was delicious, startlingly so to taste buds that had so long been deprived of all but the most basic nourishment. He shook his head, smiling in disbelief, and took another sip. He would savor every last drop.

Alarais watched him with a smile. "Good?"

Caeden laughed, a little giddily. "Objectively? No idea. But to me, it tastes like something El himself made."

"Probably an overestimation of the vintage," Alarais allowed, "but it is quite good." He sighed, setting aside his glass and leaning back, looking contemplative. "Sometimes I wonder whether all of this is worth it. These... extensions of peace."

Caeden looked at him in surprise. "I never thought I'd hear you say that. You made the Law for a reason, Alarais—a good one. From everything I hear, and everything I saw before I came to be here, your lands are blessed by your rule." He smirked. "Though whether my most recent source is entirely reliable..."

Alarais gave him a halfhearted smile. "Probably not." He rubbed his forehead, then gestured to Caeden. "Are you sure you're a proponent of the Law? It hasn't done you any favors."

Caeden leaned forward, frowning. His friend should have been delighted at the events of the day, not in a mood like this. "Alarais, I have said this to you many times before, but I need you to believe it. I have been in this cell for near eighty years, and you know something? I'm glad," he said sincerely. "I was out of control when we met. I was a wreck. I miss freedom, true, but that doesn't mean that I didn't need imprisonment."

He paused. "And ultimately, I deserved it," he added quietly. "You could have made my time in this cell unbearable, as probably would have befit my actions. But you didn't. You chose to befriend me. To help me. You've taught me politics, history, religion, mathematics, philosophy..." He shook his head. "Friendship. Morality. Trust. Belief. You are the best man I know, the best man I have ever met and the best man I am ever likely to meet. Your punishment for my evil was to change my life immeasurably for the better, Alarais. I can never repay the debt I owe you for that."

Alarais coughed, looking embarrassed. "I helped remind you of the good man you are, Tal—nothing more. Remember that." He sighed. "And I did not succeed in every area. You still believe that this thing you're searching for, this being, is out there somewhere."

Caeden nodded slowly. "I do. That night in the woods... whomever or whatever it was spoke the truth, and not just about Nethgalla. It's more than just wishful thinking, Alarais. I felt it. I won't pursue it as I did before—you have my word on that. But I will not give up, either."

"I wish you would," said Alarais softly. "When we first met, the idea had driven you almost to madness."

"I would like to think that if eighty years of listening to you hasn't done it, nothing will."

Alarais allowed a grin at that, though the smile quickly faltered. "I'm serious, though. You would have a place here in the palace. I trust you; I could use someone like you to help rule. You wouldn't need to leave."

Caeden laughed. "Why do you persist, even after all these years? I would love to stay, my friend, but I know what I know. This is a battle you cannot win."

Alarais smiled sadly. "Some battles are important to fight regardless." He stood, moving forward until he was at the door to Caeden's cell.

He motioned, and the door suddenly swung wide.

Caeden stiffened. He stared at the open door for a few seconds in stunned silence.

"What are you doing?" he whispered.

Alarais stepped to the side. "Today was the last day, Tal. Your sentence has been served, as demanded by the Law." He gestured, a small smile on his lips as he watched Caeden's reaction. "You are free to go."

Caeden didn't move. The open door, something he'd dreamed of a thousand times, was suddenly terribly intimidating. "Why didn't you say anything?"

"Because I know you too well," said Alarais sadly. "If you had been counting down to your release, you would have been making plans. Looking at maps. You would have fallen back into obsessing."

Caeden grimaced, but inclined his head. Alarais was right, and
they both knew it.

He took a hesitant step forward. "Why now?" He frowned. "I didn't think that the Law prescribed a length of imprisonment for what I'd done."

Alarais peered at him. "And the purpose of punishment under the Law?"

"Justice. A deterrent. And, where possible, redemption," said Caeden slowly.

Alarais nodded. "Eighty years, Tal. A lifetime down here. That is all the Law ever intended a man to lose." He smiled. "And in my estimation, you are not the man whom I first locked in here. That man was imprisoned because he was dangerous. His incarceration was justified. Yours is not."

Caeden's stare moved to the half-full wineglass on his table, and he suddenly understood. Alarais wasn't unhappy about the treaty being signed.

He took a hesitant step forward, then another, until suddenly he was across the threshold and outside. He breathed in sharply as a flood of sensations hit him, and he knew without checking that his Reserve was once again accessible to him. It felt like walking out into the snow straight after waking from a long, heavy slumber.

He turned to Alarais. "I . . . I don't know what to say." He swallowed a sudden lump in his throat. He was going to leave—he had to. He had served justice, here in this dungeon, for what he'd done. But he would not be redeemed until he could actually make things right.

Still, it wouldn't be easy to go. Alarais was more than just a friend. He was Caeden's savior, wrenching him back from a precipice that Caeden by himself would have plunged over. He was a mentor, the reason that Caeden now knew so much more about the world than he could ever have imagined.

He was a brother. A man like whom Caeden could only aspire to be.

Alarais saw his expression, and nodded.

"I will miss our chats, my friend," he said softly. He smiled, though his eyes were still sad. "And beating you at Rel'vit."

Caeden peered at him. "You've missed that for some time now."

Alarais laughed. "Perhaps," he conceded. He glanced down

the hall. "Can I at least tempt you to stay the evening? For a meal?"

Caeden shook his head slowly.

"A meal turns into a night. A night turns into a week." He gave Alarais an apologetic look. "It would be too much of a temptation."

Alarais nodded, unsurprised.

"At least promise me this much," he said quietly. "When you tire of your search, you will come back."

Caeden smiled. "On that, you have my word."

He stepped forward, and the two men embraced. Then they headed for the exit, Caeden a little unsteady, unused to walking in one direction for such an extended period of time.

When they reached the top of the stairs and Alarais opened the door, Caeden nearly fell to the ground in shock.

The sunlight seared his eyes, which had grown unhealthily accustomed to dim torchlight. He swayed, quickly supported by Alarais.

"Sorry," his friend said, a little sheepishly. "I probably should have thought of that."

"No. It's all right." Caeden steadied himself, then turned his face toward the sun. It was morning, but late enough that the sun's rays held a good deal of warmth. He kept his eyes closed, basking in the sensation despite the pain that still seared his eyeballs. "It's wonderful."

He stood like that for several seconds, then forced his eyes open. It hurt for a while, but eventually the landscape began to resolve itself from pure white glare into recognizable shapes. He turned to Alarais, who was watching him silently.

"So this is it," he said quietly. He gripped Alarais's arm. "Don't change, Alarais."

Alarais returned the gesture, his expression serious. "We will see each other again, Tal'kamar. I know it."

Caeden swallowed, then turned and headed off down the hill without another word, away from the shining palace that overlooked the surrounding countryside. He glanced over his shoulder at it one last time. It was crystal and white marble and gold, a thing of unique and remarkable beauty. His gaze switched to the *retreating form of Alarais and for a moment, he wondered if he'd made the wrong decision.*

Then he squared his shoulders. He didn't have the luxury of making the choices that he wanted to. Not when there was still so much that needed to be done.

He deliberately turned away, putting the rising sun at his back. It was time to resume his search.

"Alarais," Caeden said quietly as the memory faded.

Alaris stared at him, clearly taken aback—though whether by the sudden switch in conversation or the name itself, Caeden wasn't sure.

"Once," he said eventually with a small, puzzled shake of the head. "It's just Alaris now." He squinted at Caeden. "Did you just remember that name?"

Caeden licked his lips indecisively. Alaris was on the other side of this fight, of that he was quite certain. And yet Caeden's memory of their friendship, of the deep love and respect he'd felt for this man, was impossible to ignore.

"I remembered being in prison," he said quietly. "When you let me out."

Alaris cocked his head to the side. "El, I haven't thought about that in years. I put you in there to begin with, too, you know." He smiled at Caeden with something approaching affection, but quickly sighed and shook his head, as if suddenly recalling their current situation. "I was given the name Alar by my father. In the Shining Lands, common men ended their names with *is*, princes with *eis*, and kings with *ais*. I was Alareis, then Alarais." The brief light that had been in his eyes as he spoke dimmed. "But I have not been a prince or a king for a very long time, Tal."

Caeden nodded slowly, still trying to sort through his feelings. There was an openness to Alaris, a simple and direct honesty. And yet this was the man who had sent the Blind to Ilin Illan. The man whose actions had threatened the lives of Caeden's friends.

Alaris sighed, oblivious to Caeden's thoughts. "As much as I would like to reminisce, we cannot linger. If Is comes at me with a clear enough head, with anything even resembling a plan, then

309

she'll win. I'm stronger, but she has always been a better fighter. And you…" He gestured. "Don't take it personally, Tal, but from what I saw earlier, you're more or less useless right now."

Caeden grunted, oddly feeling mildly offended. "I brought down a building."

"The building wasn't the one trying to kill you," observed Alaris drily.

Caeden acceded the point with an involuntary half smile, though he hid it quickly. He glanced around at the empty city. "You think she's coming back?"

"Do you feel like she was in the mood to let things go?" Alaris held Caeden's gaze. "I assume that you have a plan to stop the Lyth from getting Licanius, and I assume that you're here because of it. Is certainly seemed to think so. So out with it."

Caeden hesitated, his gaze traveling involuntarily to the sword sitting beside the other man.

Alaris saw where he was looking and sighed, rolling his eyes. "El take it, Tal. Really?" He grabbed the sword and before Caeden could react, tossed it irritably at Caeden's feet. "Better?"

Caeden stared at the blade for a few moments, suspecting a trap even though he couldn't see how it could possibly be one. Eventually he stooped, picking up the sword. Licanius thrummed in his hands, and kan was suddenly everywhere.

"Why trust me with this?"

"Because I know that you know, deep down, that we're friends," said Alaris vehemently, an edge of affectionate exasperation to his tone. "Despite all that's happened, despite everything, we're *friends*. And I don't care what memories you do or don't have—you, Tal'kamar Deshrel, would *never* kill a friend."

Caeden said nothing for a long time, watching Alaris's face for any sign that he was being anything except genuine. He'd spoken with passion and though Caeden knew he should ignore everything that this man said, he found himself beginning to believe him.

"I'm looking for a Vessel," he said eventually. "I left it with Isiliar. When I…" He trailed off.

Alaris nodded, looking unsurprised. "The glass sphere with the Darecian markings, I assume? Is mentioned it. She says it was taken years ago. Though I have no idea how accurate her concept of time really is right now," he admitted.

Caeden's heart sank, and he asked the question despite already knowing the answer. "By whom?"

"Nethgalla." Alaris gave Caeden a glance that could only be described as pitying. "Is swears it was her."

Caeden closed his eyes for a long moment, but eventually nodded.

"How do I find her?" he asked quietly.

"She'll be looking for you. Watching your allies, your friends. She always is." Alaris's tone was gentle. "But if she has something that you need, she's probably intending to meet you in Deilannis."

Caeden frowned. "Why there?"

"It's the one place where you cannot kill her. Anywhere else, and her strength is not even close to ours." Alaris frowned as he said the words, squinting in Caeden's direction. "Exactly how much *do* you remember, Tal?"

Caeden glanced up at Alaris. Even holding Licanius, even with his latest memory, Caeden couldn't bring himself to trust the man. Not after the last time he'd done so. He had to remind himself that no matter how pleasant he seemed, Alaris *was* on the other side.

He held his tongue.

After a few seconds Alaris sighed again, though with more regret than irritation.

"Not enough, evidently. I understand. Trust is earned over time, not just by actions." He chewed his lip for a moment and then stood, nodding toward the waterfall-lined entrance through which Caeden had arrived. "I hope that one day you'll trust me again, Tal, but Is could return at any moment. If there's any other way I can help you right now, just tell me. Otherwise you need to get moving."

Caeden slipped a hand into his pocket, touching the Portal Box. None of the destinations on it would place him anywhere near where he needed to go. "Can you get me to Deilannis?"

Alaris gave a brief, wistful chuckle. "No. You, Gass, and Nethgalla are the only ones who know how to open a Gate. And even if I did, too, I've never been there."

Caeden grimaced but inclined his head; he didn't see that Alaris had any reason to delay him. "So where are we now?"

"Alkathronen." Alaris glanced around at the silent buildings. "Last city of the Builders. Last bastion of their race."

"The Builders?" Caeden didn't doubt Alaris's word, but... "It's certainly different from Ilin Illan."

"Ilin Illan? A gaudy mess," Alaris said deprecatingly, giving Caeden a reproachful look. "A city meant to distract the masses. *This* was their true achievement. Alkathronen exists because the Builders understood beauty more deeply than most—they understood when simplicity should trump detail, functionality should trump form. Ilin Illan came from their talent for understanding what *others* see as beauty. Distraction and seduction for those who think a thing is beautiful merely because it draws the eye, because it has a pleasing aesthetic."

Caeden glanced around again, considering. There *was* something special about this place, beyond even that of Ilin Illan. In Andarra's capital, there was always a new sight to dazzle. Here, nothing stood out... and yet the *sense* of Alkathronen was somehow more. As if the parts were less when compared to Ilin Illan's, but the whole was greater.

He shook his head. "Regardless. I should have asked where I need to *go*. I don't know how to get to Deilannis from here."

Alaris frowned at him.

"Did you not come from Ilin Illan? I assumed that Is..." He trailed off, sighing. "Walk with me. I will show you the way."

Caeden's brow furrowed but he nodded, falling into step alongside Alaris.

The silence pressed for a long few moments, and then Caeden took a deep breath.

"How can you possibly be fighting for them?" He couldn't help it; the question just burst out of him. "How can you be on their side?"

Alaris's step faltered.

"How can I not?" he eventually replied softly. "My side is hope, Tal—hope that things can be changed. Your side is despair, an acceptance of slavery. No matter how you look at it, no matter how you argue, *that* is the truth."

Caeden frowned. Meldier had claimed the same thing, almost

exactly. "Hope is one thing, Alaris, but Asar showed me the Darklands."

"Asar showed you the mind of a madman." Alaris glanced across at him, then raised an eyebrow at his expression. "Didn't he tell you? Alchesh was never supposed to have our powers. It utterly destroyed him, and that memory...that memory is hardly what I would call reliable."

Alaris continued, his tone that of a man who had had this conversation a hundred times before, and was exasperated by it. "The Darklands are a strange and terrible place, Tal—I know that better than anyone—and yes, certainly, dangerous. But this idea that El reaching the rift will somehow unleash it, unleash eternal suffering upon the entire world...there is no proof. You have only the ramblings of soothsayers from before anyone had even heard of kan. The tortured confessions of the shape-shifter who has lied to you more than any other being in this world. And the feverish memory of a broken man." He shook his head. "You were always operating just as much on faith as I. More so, I would argue."

Caeden was silent for a few seconds, processing what Alaris had said. "You're just trying to make me doubt."

"I'm telling you that you *should* doubt—as I do my own beliefs. The day on which you decide not to question what you believe, is the day that you start making excuses for why you believe it." Alaris spoke with a quiet intensity, a certainty that only deepened Caeden's sense of unease.

Eventually, Caeden grunted. "Perhaps if your side was less intent on destroying my friends, I would be more inclined to take that advice."

Alaris snorted, shaking his head. "In some ways, you have not changed at all—you still make assumptions when you do not have all the facts. *You* are the only one who actually wants a fight, Tal. We won't shy away from the conflict if you force it on us, and El knows that if you try to stop us when the ilshara does finally fall, we have the army to do what we need to. But it's never been our purpose to destroy anyone. If you stood aside now, no one else would get hurt."

Caeden gave a short, bitter laugh. "I'm more than happy to doubt *that*."

Alaris sighed as they passed through the large archway at the entry to the city, leaving the silently lit buildings of Alkathronen behind them. "I can understand how it must have seemed to you, watching Mash'aan invade, seeing the actions of his men. But as I have already explained, they only crossed the ilshara to stop you." His expression hardened as he spoke, his frustration and anger seeping through. "And do not forget that it was you who trapped Isiliar here. You—not someone acting under your direction, but *you*—trapped her here in a living hell for two *millennia* and drove her mad. So if you are going to judge a cause based only on the actions of its proponents, then neither of us can claim to be on the side of what's right."

Caeden just grimaced. He didn't have a response to that.

Alaris subsided again quickly as he glanced around into the city now behind them, not nervously, but evidently checking for signs of movement. "El take it. If we had a few hours, I'd happily continue this. It's been too long since we've talked." He rubbed his forehead in frustration. "If you really want to have this discussion—if you're genuinely interested in understanding both sides of this fight—then when the Lyth have been dealt with, come back here. I'll set some wards to let me know that you've returned. Don't let the others know. We'll speak as friends, and if you remain unconvinced, you have my word that I'll let you go."

Caeden grunted. "You don't want my word that I'll let *you* go?"

Alaris gave him a sudden, affectionate grin. "Said the mouse to the lion."

Caeden responded with a wry look, but nodded slowly. "I may take you up on that offer." He didn't let his gaze waver. "But no matter what you say, I won't abandon my friends."

Alaris's look was pained. "And I'd never ask you to," he said softly.

They had entered the canyon now, the two enormous, sheer waterfalls on either side, so close to the edge of the path that Caeden couldn't quite believe that there was no moisture on its surface. The air was perfectly still here but this was more than just the lack of a breeze. The water was clear as crystal, *perfect* in form.

314   Alaris walked a little farther and then suddenly paused, crouch-

ing and placing his hand over one of the roadside symbols that Caeden had noticed earlier.

The strange character flashed blue; there was a hum and Caeden flinched back as stone abruptly snapped upward from the abyss, forming a wide, smooth pathway leading directly into the curtain of falling water.

"This is the way," said Alaris quietly. "Step through the water, and you will find yourself in Ilin Illan. Well. Beneath Ilin Illan, anyway," he amended. "Follow the lines of kan and they will lead you out."

Caeden stared at the waterfall. "I just . . . step through it?"

Alaris nodded. "This was the Builders' home," he said quietly. "They connected each of their wonders to here."

Caeden didn't question further. A faint spark of memory said that Alaris was telling him the truth.

Alaris watched him for a few moments, then held out his hand.

Caeden considered it silently. This was the man who had sent the army against Ilin Illan, who had deceived him into walking into a trap. This was his enemy.

But this was his friend. He knew it, knew as he looked into Alaris's eyes that this was not a ruse, not a trick. It was a genuine gesture.

He clasped Alaris's hand.

"Stop the Lyth, Tal," said Alaris quietly. "Stop the Lyth, and then we can worry about everything else."

Caeden inclined his head in acknowledgment, then turned and stepped along the newly formed path and into the crystal clear water.

Chapter 22

Davian peered cautiously around the corner again, scanning the long road ahead for any sign of his target.

Still nothing? he thought, directing it toward where he knew Erran and Fessi were. He wasn't accustomed to communicating mentally, but Erran's expertise at it made the effort minimal on his side of things. The young Augur kept the connection between their minds open with enviable ease.

No one who even looks like the man that you described, asserted Erran, sounding mildly bored.

He wouldn't have noticed. There's a young woman selling bread across from him, and he can't stop—

I'm paying attention, growled Erran, interrupting Fessi. There was a pause. *And how would you know that, anyway? Aren't you covering the back?*

I did a quick circuit of the Tol. I'm fairly sure there was actually drool on your chin.

Davian sighed. *We need to stay at our posts, you two. We only have one shot at stopping Driscin before he goes inside.*

You should listen to him, Fess. A pause. *She really does mean quick, though,* Erran's voice reassured him. *Too quick to notice something like—*

Davian stiffened, suddenly tuning out Erran's easy banter. A figure was making its way along the road and though Davian had only met him once, it took only a moment to recognize Driscin.

He's here. Davian forced his voice through whatever Erran was saying. He glanced around. *Erran?*

Almost as he thought the name, the raised voice of a man a little farther toward the eastern gate of the Tol echoed down to him. His companion was staring stock-still, looking a mixture of confused and shocked as he was gesticulated at with what came close to violence. Within a few moments, every eye in the vicinity had been drawn to the commotion.

I don't think any of the Gifted standing watch are looking at him right now. Fessi, do you…

He trailed off as in the distance, Driscin vanished. Fessi appeared in front of Davian a split second later, the dazed-looking Elder grasping her arm.

"Driscin," said Davian, recovering himself quickly. "Good to see you again." He glanced from the older man to Fessi, then back again.

"We have a few things to talk about."

Davian paused at the foot of the hill, staring grimly up the slope toward the bright beacon in the darkness ahead.

Fifty feet high and sheer, the outer wall of Tol Shen was bathed in white Essence, revealing the shadowy shapes of what appeared to be hundreds of guards as they patrolled along its base. Davian swallowed nervously at the sight, raising his gaze to watch the occasional menacing flicker of blue along the top of the wall. There was no getting inside that way.

Movement, came Erran's voice in Davian's head. *A dozen, coming your way. She knows you're here.*

Davian shot Fessi a glance, who nodded confidently and grabbed both his and Driscin's arms. "Let's go."

There was a subtle lurch, and suddenly the gently swaying trees away from the road froze, the soft sigh of wind against Davian's cheek vanishing. Davian glanced at Driscin, whose eyes were wide as he gazed around. *How long?*

At least a minute.

Davian took a few deep breaths, calming himself and focusing on the way ahead. He doubted that Ishelle would be able to redirect any of the Gifted quickly enough to intercept them, but they had to be prepared for the possibility. They started forward, angling away from the road and keeping parallel to the Tol, just close enough to use the illumination from the walls to see the way ahead.

His heart pounded as he thought about what they were about to attempt. He glanced across at Driscin, whose grim expression reflected his doubts.

It had been a long, tense few hours since they'd explained everything that had been happening to the Elder. The older man had at first been incredulous that the entire Tol had been affected by Rohin's ability—and then, once convinced, had proceeded to argue in favor of the Augurs simply heading north, rather than mounting any sort of rescue attempt.

He'd been right in a lot of ways, too, much to Davian's irritation. Ishelle would know that Davian wasn't just running now, and that Driscin was with him—that was presumably why the defenses at Tol Shen had been so significantly boosted. And as important as it was to save the Tol, the benefit hardly outweighed the danger of risking the autonomy of even more Augurs.

But they were also the only ones who could stop Rohin. Davian couldn't walk away from that fact—and despite Erran and Fessi's vacillating, he suspected that they felt the same way.

Eventually, Driscin had conceded that he couldn't force them to leave; the rest of the afternoon had consisted of trying to figure out how to get to Rohin, now that he had Ishelle and an entire Tol full of Gifted to act as his bodyguards.

"You're *sure* Ishelle doesn't know about this entrance?" asked Davian again as they hurried through the forest that surrounded the Tol.

"As certain as I can be." Driscin's dry tone indicated that he was becoming tired of the question. "Ishelle's always been...difficult to keep an eye on, I suppose you could say. I didn't *particularly* feel like telling her about an entrance that only she could open."

Davian snorted. "I can see the logic in that." He hesitated. "It doesn't mean the other Elders won't have told—"

"They don't know about it, either." Driscin gave Davian a wry look. "Secret entrances aren't of much value when everyone knows about them."

Davian peered at him in surprise, but eventually shrugged his acknowledgment. Given the situation, he couldn't really argue the point.

Their decision to intercept Driscin was proving to be even more beneficial than Davian had anticipated. Rohin had what seemed like the entire Tol on guard against an incursion, but Driscin—thanks to his former role in the sig'nari—knew of entrances that, apparently, no one else was aware even existed.

Even more interesting, though, had been his admissions regarding the cells and the strange archway that Davian and Fessi had seen.

The Elder had been understandably reluctant to talk about it, but the area beneath Central Archive had apparently been set aside as something of a "contingency plan" for the Augurs. It was, Driscin claimed, one of the main reasons that the Council had felt comfortable accepting responsibility for them in the first place. Builder-made, the cells were the only ones known to be able to contain kan; according to Driscin, the Augurs themselves had sometimes secretly made use of them before the war.

That made sense, after Davian had thought about it for a while. As Rohin had demonstrated in ample measure, Augurs were not any better or worse than most people. It stood to reason that they would have needed their own prison, even if they hadn't broadcast that fact to the world.

Driscin's revelations about the archway, though, were what had been most useful.

It was the entrance to Tol Shen's vault. .

Like the cells, the Builders had designed the vault to account even for Augurs. Kan was completely inaccessible once through the archway, and the vault beyond was keyed to only specific people's Essence signatures—allowing some to unlock the vault door, and others to actually enter without triggering the vault's defenses. One ability was useless without the other, ensuring that at least two authorized people had to be present in order to access the vault's contents.

And if anyone else even entered the antechamber and wasn't recognized by the vault's defenses, their source was immediately targeted and drained.

"So you're sure this weapon will still be there?" asked Davian quietly as they walked.

"As certain as I can be." Driscin scowled, evidently annoyed at being asked the same questions multiple times. "Lyrus was the only one able to enter the vault. If what you say is true and he's dead, I cannot see how Rohin could have taken anything." He sighed, shaking his head. "I still think that there has to be another way, though. There *has* to be a way of separating Ishelle from Rohin. If we just can do that, we can use the amulet I told you about instead. It's a much better solution. It wouldn't just disable Rohin—it would hide him from Ishelle's ability to track him, too. I'm almost certain of it."

Davian blinked, then glanced across at the older man. He'd worn the same look of worry and pain since they'd settled on this plan, and Davian wasn't sure that he could blame him.

"There isn't a way," he said softly. "Not if the amulet needs physical contact. Rohin knows how easily another Augur could get to him now. I hate the thought, too, Driscin, but as long as he keeps Ishelle nearby and she's maintaining her Disruption shield, none of us have a chance of getting close enough to put it on him." He shrugged. "As much as I despise the idea of this Vessel you've told us about, it's our only choice."

Fessi grunted at that, shooting Driscin a dark look. Of everything kept in the vault, there was only one Vessel that Driscin thought would be effective through a Disruption shield—something he knew about, because it had been specifically stored there for use in the event that one of the Augurs residing in Tol Shen became hostile.

A stone dagger that he said could drain anyone's source, from anywhere, simply by feeding it a matching Trace.

"I still don't see how you can justify keeping something like that on hand," muttered Fessi, echoing the concerns that they had already raised when Driscin had admitted to the Vessel's existence. "*Nobody* should have access to a weapon that powerful."

Driscin raised an eyebrow. "The current situation is how we can justify it," he said quietly. "It's in the vault because it's the safest place it can be, and we stored it there for *exactly* this eventuality."

Fessi grunted again, still looking displeased, but said nothing further.

They walked without incident for about five minutes—Fessi once again showing no sign of tiring, despite the intensity at which she maintained her ability—before Driscin suddenly nodded to the right, toward a thick copse of trees. "Down there."

They angled away from the Tol's wall, heading for where the Gifted had indicated. The undergrowth was thick here, the view of the wall completely concealed by a tangle of bushes and close-growing leafy trees. Davian grimaced at the twigs and branches scratching his arms as they pushed their way into the foliage.

"You're sure this is the right way?" he muttered after fighting his way forward for a few seconds, not seeing an end to the thick brush.

Driscin squinted. "It's been twenty years," he conceded, "but I'm fairly certain...ah. Here we go."

The way ahead finally opened up again to reveal a small clearing, in its center a grass-covered mound with a rocky base. A dark shadow in the stone marked a narrow, muddy, dank-looking hole, about Davian's height and overgrown with weeds.

"We have to go in there?" asked Fessi dubiously.

Driscin glowered at her. "I'll try and find a nicer secret entrance for you next time. Now stop wasting time and get inside."

The three of them squeezed one by one through the dirty, claustrophobically tight opening, Driscin going first so that he could light the way with his ball of Essence. Davian was relieved to see that the passageway widened once they were inside; soon there was a corner and the tunnel—much longer than it had appeared from the outside—began to angle sharply downward.

Within a minute they had arrived in front of a single, large stone door. Davian strode over to it and pushed.

Nothing happened.

"How do we open it?" he asked with a frown.

Driscin shrugged. "I told you—this was the entrance that the Augurs used when they wanted to avoid notice, back before the war. The sig'nari knew *where* it was, but that was the extent of it."

Davian sighed, nodding. He closed his eyes, feeling his way toward the door with kan, sensing that Fessi was doing the same.

"The door is a Vessel," said Fessi abruptly, coming to the conclusion at the same time as Davian. "The left half already has Essence in it. The right half looks like it could be activated."

She glanced around, then shrugged and drew some Essence from Driscin's illuminating globe, ignoring his annoyed look as she fed the energy into the right-hand side of the door. The stone sucked in the light, glowing white for a moment.

Then it faded again. Nothing happened.

Davian frowned as he considered the entrance. The Essence had done *something*.

"If this was meant only for the Augurs, just using Essence to open the door wouldn't be enough," he realized abruptly, addressing the observation more to Fessi than Driscin. He pointed to the left part of the door. "What if it's a double lock? One Vessel that won't move without Essence, and another—the left-hand side—that won't move while it *contains* Essence." He closed his eyes without waiting for affirmation of the theory, placing his hands on either side of the door. He carefully extracted the Essence from the left, then let it flow through him and into the right.

The door shimmered again.

There was a click, and it swung silently open.

"Clever," murmured Driscin appreciatively. "Leave the left lock drained if you want the Gifted to have access as well, or make it Augur-only by filling it."

They headed into the passageway beyond. Unlike the narrow, dark stairwell that they had just come down, here clean, bright lines of Essence lit the way ahead. The stone underfoot was smooth, the path was wide, and the walls were neatly hewn.

Davian made to push on immediately, but Driscin held up a hand. "The door," he said quietly.

Davian gave him an objecting look. "We don't have time to waste. Every second gives Ishelle longer to react."

"We're not going to leave a way into the Tol just...open like this." Driscin's expression was sober, and something about his tone suggested that he found the very thought offensive.

Davian just inclined his head, not prepared to argue. *You in?*
Of course.

He swung the door shut and then refilled the locking mechanism with Essence. "Done."

Despite the urgency of their mission, Driscin tested the lock himself before giving a satisfied nod. "Let's go."

They walked for several minutes, the tunnel straight and wide, with only the occasional flight of stairs to climb. At a few points the path split, but it was always clearly in the wrong direction— once into a section that had evidently collapsed years ago, once jagging back in almost the same direction from which they'd come, and once downward into a tunnel that emitted the faint sound of falling water.

There was no conversation as they climbed a final set of stairs, finding themselves facing a door identical to the one through which they'd entered. Davian hesitated, then at a nod from Driscin drained the lock, feeding the Essence back into the door.

The door swung open, and he breathed a sigh of relief as he peered into the room beyond. It was dark, but clearly empty.

They slipped inside, Davian watching in fascination as Driscin pushed the stone door closed again behind them. It sealed seamlessly with the wall, nothing to indicate from this side that there was an entrance there at all.

"We're in Central Ward now. Probably only five minutes from the Archive," murmured Driscin, walking over to the door outside and opening it a crack. Evidently not seeing any threats, he swung it wide and gestured them through.

The next few minutes were tense as they kept to the shadows, twice having to skirt what appeared to be makeshift checkpoints along the streets. Davian could see the strain beginning to show on Fessi's face as they walked—extending the time bubble to include three people was something Davian didn't think he would be able to do for more than a few seconds, let alone minutes at a time—but her ability never once faltered.

Big group coming your way, and quickly, came Erran's voice in Davian's head. *I think they've figured out where you're*

going.

It's all right. We're already there, replied Davian, breathing out as they came within sight of the Central Archive. The large, silent building wasn't locked, and they encountered no Gifted as they hurried inside. Whether that was because Rohin didn't think there was anything worth guarding here, or simply because he didn't think that they would be able to break into the vault, was impossible to say.

The three of them finally entered the large hall—Davian rolling his shoulders uncomfortably at the memory of his incarceration—and came to a stop in front of the archway into the vault. Time swept back over them and Fessi stumbled, shaking her head and grasping Davian's arm tightly to steady herself.

He looked at the dark-haired girl. "Will you be all right?"

"I'll be fine." Fessi looked at the closest cell with obvious distaste. "Are you sure this next part's necessary, though?"

Davian nodded grimly. "We have no idea how Rohin's influence works. This is the safest way."

Fessi grunted a reluctant acknowledgment, then slipped inside the cell and shut the door, experimenting a few times to make sure that she could still open it from the inside.

"If anyone opens that door . . ."

"I'll use a time bubble and get out before they can see me." Fessi gave Davian a grim nod, then slid down so that she couldn't be seen through the bars.

Davian exhaled, turning to face the archway as Driscin gave him a worried look.

"You're certain this trick of yours will work?" The older man continued to peer at Davian uncertainly. "Because I'm not heroically coming in to get you."

Davian paused, examining the hardened shell of kan he'd carefully created within himself. It was larger than the first one he'd made, but he still appeared to be suffering no ill effects.

"I was fine when I was in there with Fessi." He shrugged awkwardly. "The vault targets any source that it doesn't recognize—but I don't have one. I'm guessing even the Builders didn't anticipate a dead man breaking in."

Driscin studied him for a long moment, then shook his head, clearly still fascinated by the concept. Davian had been more than a little reluctant to admit his condition to the others, but it had been necessary. After Driscin had described how the vault's security worked, there was no other way to explain how he had gotten around it when saving Fessi.

"And you're certain that the vault won't simply target the Essence you've got stored instead?" Driscin asked, not for the first time.

"It's inside hardened kan. It's no different to it being stored inside a Vessel, as far as I can tell. The logic is sound. It worked before," he reiterated.

Driscin nodded reluctantly. "I'll take your word for it. But once we're inside..."

"I know," said Davian quietly.

He swallowed, rechecking the Essence stored in his body. There were plenty of things about this plan that could go wrong, but this was by far the riskiest part.

He followed Driscin into the antechamber.

The change was immediate as he stepped through the archway, Davian's sense of kan vanishing completely. Unlike in the cells, he couldn't even *sense* the power here. It was just...gone.

He forced down a sliver of panic. Not being able to check on his self-made Reserve was unnerving, but after a few seconds he breathed out, nodding in response to Driscin's questioning look. He didn't have long, undoubtedly—even now he felt a little light-headed—but he wasn't collapsing, either. It seemed like it would be enough.

"I'm fine," he said grimly.

Driscin looked at him dubiously but inclined his head, aware that time was now even more against them. The older man strode forward and placed his hand against the next door.

Blue and white light began to pulse across the door's surface as Essence poured out of Driscin, entwining with the symbols in the stone. The outline of the door glowed blindingly bright for a moment and then went completely black, darkness rippling inward, eating away at the light until it was completely gone.

Driscin took his hand—which was trembling slightly—away from the door's surface.

It swung open.

Driscin gestured for Davian to move. "Remember—don't touch anything except the stone dagger," he said quietly. "We store things in here for a very good reason."

Davian gave him a grim nod, exhaling slowly, steadying himself.

He strode into the darkness.

Chapter 23

Davian blinked as his eyes adjusted to the inside of the vault.

He'd expected everything to be stored here, immediately inside, but it appeared that this was little more than an entryway. Ahead, a set of wide, smooth stairs led straight down, though he couldn't see the end of the tunnel into which they disappeared.

He paused for a few moments, holding his breath, waiting for . . . something. Some indication that the vault's defenses were going to try and kill him.

There was nothing, though. Davian glanced behind, a sudden wave of uncertainty rippling through him. The door was still open but Davian knew that if it closed, he would be utterly dependent on Driscin to open it again.

He frowned at it for a few more seconds, then sighed and turned to the stairwell. He couldn't afford to delay.

He moved onto the first step.

At once a low sound thrummed in the air; Davian faltered, heart sinking as the step he had touched began to glow—and then the next, and the next, until the entire staircase was shining with a glimmering white. Lines of blue flickered to life on the walls, tracing several unusual, complex patterns. He stepped back quickly, feeling a faint tug of dizziness.

It quickly passed, though; Davian hesitated and then started forward at a brisk pace, not letting himself be tempted into turning back. The vault had evidently registered his presence, but he felt no worse than before. As long as he hurried, he should be fine.

The stairwell was not as deep as it had first appeared, and

within a minute Davian could see the bottom. The stairs flattened out into a long, wide hallway, which was lined with multiple small recesses containing shelves that held texts, Vessels, or other items. Everything was lit with a mixture of sharp white and cold blue Essence, a decidedly unwelcoming illumination.

Davian rubbed his forehead, staring down the line of storage alcoves in bemusement. Driscin had warned him that what he was after was not the only thing stored down here, but he hadn't expected there to be so much.

He hurried on, scanning the shelves as he passed but not seeing anything like the stone dagger that Driscin had described, making himself ignore the urge to pause and examine some of the objects more closely. There was an enormous globe balanced on a slender stand, taller than he was, made of dark metal and with unfamiliar continents etched onto it. A golden helmet with Darecian words covering every inch. What appeared to be a wooden goblet, unadorned, but three times a usable size and with edges as thick as his fist. A black bracer that looked suspiciously like the ones the Blind had worn, though he didn't have time to more than glance at it before moving on. A set of five copper rings, three of them tarnished green. More. Each was positioned meticulously, as if each shelf were a tiny shrine.

Davian hurried past them all, his curiosity strong but still far from overpowering his sense of urgency. Though he tried not to think about it too much, he could sense his energy receding. Already his movements were slower, a little more sluggish than they had been a few minutes earlier.

Finally he reached the end of the hallway, the sound he had first heard upstairs now an almost physical presence in the air, a deep hum that felt as though it was pressing against his skull and trying to burrow its way into his brain. Was that normal, or was it the vault recognizing that he shouldn't be here?

He took stock of the items in the final set of alcoves, fighting down his steadily increasing sense of dread. To his right were two swords, completely different in design and yet somehow similar. The first had a sleek, curved blade, shorter than average but still wicked-looking. The second was straight and long but with a notched edge, giving it a barbaric, darkly bloodthirsty look.

To his left was a miniature stone dagger, little more than a letter opener in size. Beside it was a golden amulet in the shape of an eagle, emanating its own soft glow.

Davian released a breath that he hadn't realized he'd been holding, stepping up to the shelves upon which the Vessels sat. The dagger was a deep-green marble with black flecks throughout the stone. The amulet, on the other hand, was smooth gold; the eagle's widespread wings curled upward, designed to be worn just below the throat. It was incredibly detailed, shaped by a more artistically skillful set of hands than any Vessel Davian had ever seen.

He hesitantly, carefully leaned forward and picked up the dagger. Waited for something to happen.

Nothing did.

He released a breath, snatching up the amulet as well and dropping them both into the leather satchel he'd brought for the purpose. He turned to go.

Then he glanced at the two swords. He had no weapon of his own, and there had to be a reason that the blades were locked away down here.

He'd seen Breshada's sword, Whisper, in action. If these were other Named swords...

He stretched out a hand toward the curved blade, then hesitated again. He could all but see Driscin's disapproving glare.

In and of itself, the memory of the Elder's warning didn't dissuade him—but it was too much of a risk. There was a good chance these swords were valuable weapons, and taking one could well help Davian. But if they weren't—if they harmed him somehow, hampered his efforts to stop Rohin in any way...

He sighed, letting his hand drop to his side. He couldn't risk it. *Wouldn't* risk it, despite the temptation.

With a last, regretful glance at the weapons, he started back. The thrumming sound faded a little as he pushed himself up the stairs again, now acutely aware of just how tired he was. His limbs felt heavy, and even his thought processes were seconds slower than they should have been.

Davian stumbled a little as he came to the entrance, swallowing as he caught sight of Driscin's expression through the doorway.

"We have company." Driscin gestured to the hall beyond the archway, eyes taut with concern.

"A lot of company."

⚘

Davian scowled through the arch at the sea of red-cloaked bodies that had assembled in the hall.

"Driscin, listen to me." It was Elder Aliria standing at the front of the crowd, her tone urgent. "You're being influenced by Davian. He's jealous of Rohin, wants to kill him. He's using you to do that." She was echoed by a multitude of other voices, many of them desperate. Davian heard several other members of the Council in the chorus.

Driscin glanced across at Davian. "That true?"

Davian stared at him blankly.

Driscin turned back to the Council, shaking his head. "Davian says that's not true," he called.

"I'm not sure that's helping," murmured Davian.

Driscin shrugged. "Nothing we say is going to change their minds." More quietly, he added, "How long do you think until they get here?"

As if in answer to his question, the mass of red cloaks suddenly parted and Ishelle and Rohin walked into view along the wide hallway, Rohin with a dark expression. The handsome young Augur studied Davian silently for a few moments.

"So. Graybeard was wrong about him being the only one who could get in there," he said eventually, shaking his head in disgust. He glanced at Ishelle. "Seems like killing him was a waste."

Davian could sense Driscin's expression darkening at the words, but he said nothing.

Rohin sighed. "It's over, Davian." He nodded to the satchel slung over Davian's shoulder. "Whatever you came for, you can't use it from in there."

Davian leaned against the wall, studying him. He couldn't see the kan but he assumed that Ishelle would be maintaining her Disruption shield around the two of them. If Ishelle had been prudent—and he knew that she would have been—there would also be a similar barrier right in front of the entrance to the vault.

Not as effective as something actively maintained, perhaps, but unavoidable if he couldn't see it. Enough to stun him as soon as he exited.

"You know you can't get away," added Ishelle, as if reading his thoughts. "Just come out here with that bag, and we can talk."

Davian slowly unslung the leather satchel from around his neck, feeling the weight of the two Vessels within. He grimaced as a wave of tiredness washed over him, and he barely avoided staggering.

His artificial Reserve was running out.

Driscin turned away from the door, a deliberate act of disregard, but also so that only Davian could see his mouth move. "Take your time once you're out there," he said in a low voice. "The longer it takes for them to realize—"

"You. Big Nose," called Rohin suddenly, his impatient voice ringing across the square. "You need to kill yourself."

Davian and Driscin both spun, wide-eyed, just in time to watch as Elder Narius—a wiry, silver-haired man with a prominent nose—produced a hard, thin sliver of Essence in his left hand, and then calmly drew it across his right wrist.

As Davian and Driscin cried out in horror—their voices the only ones in the silence—Elder Narius switched the Essence blade to the other hand and proceeded to slit his left wrist, too. He let the energy dissipate and then stood there, frowning down in mild confusion at the blood gushing over his fingers and onto the stone.

A few moments later, he was slumping to the ground.

"Redhead," said Rohin calmly, glancing at Aliria before his gaze locked again with Davian's. "You—"

"Stop!" Davian shouted, his dizziness no longer entirely from the lack of Essence. They'd anticipated threats, maybe injuries, but hadn't thought that Rohin would escalate things so quickly.

"Wait," muttered Driscin. "If he's willing to do that—"

"No choice. I'm almost out of Essence anyway," said Davian between gritted teeth. He adjusted the satchel so that it hung on his hip, then held up his hands in a sign of surrender.

"I'm coming out now," he said loudly.

He stepped out of the antechamber.

He stumbled immediately as pain lanced through his mind; 333

everything spun and he went to his knees with a groan, despite Essence beginning to flood back into him. He couldn't even attempt to grasp kan, let alone try to escape.

Still, he caught the flicker—a fraction of a fraction of a moment—when the cell door to his left seemed to move slightly, and then the bag slung over his shoulder felt lighter. He breathed a silent sigh of relief.

"You should stop struggling," Rohin said to him grimly.

Davian gasped, the momentary hope forgotten as dark smoke snaked from Rohin's mouth, arrowing toward him and burrowing into his head, clogging up his nose and mouth, wrapping itself around his mind. He collapsed to the cold stone floor, rasping, struggling for air.

Then there was someone in a red cloak at his side, ripping the satchel from him.

"Empty," a male voice snarled.

"What are you playing at, Davian?" It was Ishelle's voice, urgent, accompanied by a low murmur of concern rippling through the gathered Gifted. "Where is whatever it was you took?" Anger entered her tone and she moved closer to him, though still near enough to Rohin to protect the other Augur. "*Where. Is. It?*"

Davian continued to cough, pretending for a few extra moments, though the worst of the pain from Rohin's ability had passed. He saw Rohin open his mouth again, but Ishelle put a restraining hand on the other Augur's arm.

"Left it with Driscin," Davian choked out eventually. "No way I'm letting you have it."

Ishelle stared into his eyes, then suddenly paled, swivelling to stare around the room.

"He's delaying." Davian could see the gears of her quick mind whirring. "Fates. The cells. He could have had another Augur hiding in there, and we wouldn't have been able to sense them. They've taken whatever he got from the vault."

"*What?*" Rohin scowled, then turned and spoke loudly. "Anyone listening should show themselves."

Nothing happened.

"Check the cells," snarled Ishelle to the Gifted, though she turned back to Davian straight away, clearly not expecting them to find anything. "What did you take, and where did your Augur friend go?"

"I don't know what you're talking about," coughed Davian.

Rohin scowled, then turned back toward the archway. "Time to come out of there, Elder."

"No thanks," called back Driscin cheerfully.

Rohin shrugged. "Davian. You should kill yourself."

Davian was braced for the impact but it still hurt. His vision receded as darkness tore at his head, tendrils of kan stabbing into his mind but unable to take hold. He screamed, writhing, for what felt like minutes.

After a time the pain finally eased and he just lay there, panting, tears streaming down his face.

"Very well," said Rohin quietly, seeing that Driscin was simply watching, apparently unperturbed by Davian's pain. "Ishelle. On the count of five, if Driscin has not come out, you should kill Davian."

Ishelle nodded, drawing a dagger from somewhere beneath her cloak and crouching, placing the blade across Davian's throat. He stared up into her eyes, but he saw no mercy there.

She would do it.

"One," said Rohin calmly. "Two. Three."

Davian swallowed, forcing himself not to flinch as the motion pressed the blade a little deeper. He was fairly sure that there was blood trickling down his neck now. "Driscin…" He licked his lips nervously.

"Four," said Rohin. Davian saw the muscles in Ishelle's arm tense; he briefly thought about trying to attack her, but knew immediately that he was still too weak to do anything before she slit his throat. What was Driscin doing?

There was a long silence, then Rohin grimaced. "Fine," he muttered. He glanced across at Ishelle. "That was 'fine,' not 'five,' by the way. You shouldn't kill him," he added absently, chewing his lip.

Ishelle immediately put the blade away and Davian closed his eyes for a moment, breathing a deep sigh of relief.

"You don't care about him," mused Rohin, sounding more thoughtful than angry. He turned to Ishelle.

"Ishelle. If Driscin has not come out of there within the next ten seconds, kill yourself."

Ishelle gave a short nod, turning the blade toward her own heart.

Before Davian could even call out for her to stop, Driscin was walking out under the archway.

"I'm sorry," he said softly to Davian, defeat on his face.

"*There* it is," said Rohin with a wry smile. "Now, Driscin. You should do everything you can to help me. You should tell me the plan, backup plans . . . anything I need to know."

"Don't!" choked Davian.

"We're working with another Augur. Fessi. She's the one who has the weapon," said Driscin calmly, ignoring Davian. "It's a small stone dagger."

Ishelle glanced at Rohin with a frown. "Elder Dain told us about that," she said slowly. "But it needs a Trace to work. You don't have Rohin's Trace."

Driscin met her gaze, but Davian could see the pain in his eyes.

"I never said that we were targeting Rohin," he said softly.

Ishelle paled as she realized what he was implying, glancing down at the silver band on her wrist. "Fates. The Council Chambers." She turned to Rohin. "They have my Trace there. If they kill me, you won't be able to stop another Augur."

"She'll try not to kill you," said Driscin softly, "but I'm not sure that anything less is possible. Once you're out of the way, she'll come for Rohin. Her ability to step outside of time means that he won't be able to command her before she gets to him."

Ishelle hesitated, then looked at Davian with a frown. "I wouldn't have thought—"

"Fates, just go!" snarled Rohin, gesturing desperately. "Stop her! I have everything here under control!"

Ishelle blinked away, Davian's vague impression of her Disruption shield vanishing at the same time. He breathed a sigh of relief.

Now, Erran.

Erran appeared behind Rohin, calmly reaching around and placing the golden amulet against his throat before anyone was even aware of his presence.

Rohin screamed.

Every motion in the hall came to an abrupt, shocked halt at the sound. Rohin collapsed to the ground, writhing in agony and tearing at his throat as the gold melted quickly around his neck, forming to his skin just as a Shackle would have done.

Davian struggled to his feet, a little stunned at the reaction himself. He'd expected surprise and outrage, certainly resistance. But not agony.

He barely had time to worry about it, though. Flashes of Essence filled the room as the Elders recovered and began to attack him and Erran. There were a few moments of real concern as Davian dove away from a couple of blasts, struggling to regain his grasp on kan. Erran, fortunately, had been prepared and blocked the attacks that would have otherwise struck him.

Things moved quickly after that. Once Davian was able to focus, he carefully drew Essence from those nearby, just enough to render them unconscious. Before long, only he and Erran remained standing, though both of them were breathing hard, hands on their knees.

Davian's gaze flicked back to Rohin. The Augur's screams had rapidly dampened to moans, but seemingly only because his throat had started to close up. He looked at Davian, wide eyes filled with pain. "Please," he wept, hands beating feebly at his neck. "Please. It's killing me."

Davian hesitated, a sudden seed of doubt entering his mind. Driscin had admitted that there were some assumptions surrounding the amulet, and that he didn't know *specifically* what it was supposed to do—only that it was meant to disable an Augur.

He reached out with kan, trying to see what was happening, and immediately recoiled.

Darkness was pouring from the amulet and slashing into Rohin with a fury such as Davian had never seen. It didn't seem to be doing any *physical* damage, but wisps of torn kan floated up from Rohin's face—from his nose, his mouth, his ears, and his eyes. Davian's stomach churned.

This wasn't just a Shackle for Augurs. This was actively hurting Rohin, even if Davian couldn't tell exactly how.

But he didn't think it was killing him, either.

"You brought this on yourself, Rohin," he said quietly.

Rohin tried to speak, but nothing came out of his mouth; his eyes rolled upward in his head as he finally went limp.

Erran glanced up at Davian, still a little winded. "So. That went well."

Davian nodded wearily. "Tell Fessi that she doesn't need to activate that dagger, and to get back here. Ishelle's not great at altering her passage through time, but if this amulet really does hide Rohin from her ability, she'll realize something's wrong and be on her way back here at any moment." He gazed around the room grimly. "Any luck getting rid of Rohin's influence?"

Erran's lip curled as he shook his head. "We'll just have to wait for it to wear off." He glanced down at Driscin's prone form. "He's not going to be pleased about what I did, is he?"

"We can always tell him that your wiping his memory of you was his idea." Davian forced a grin. "It's not like he can claim otherwise."

"I'm just glad it worked," said Erran. "I know Fessi would have activated that Vessel, but..."

Davian nodded grimly. They'd known that Rohin wouldn't let Ishelle leave his side without a good reason—and not without believing that he already knew what they were planning. Ishelle's need to move quickly had meant that she couldn't take Rohin with her, but thanks to Driscin, Rohin had felt as though he'd had every threat accounted for anyway.

Davian breathed out, still barely believing it had worked. They'd done everything they could to ensure that events would play out this way, but there had been no guarantee that it would work. If they hadn't been able to get the amulet on Rohin— if Ishelle hadn't taken the bait, or if Rohin had insisted on going with her at the expense of slowing her down—then the next step had been for Fessi to use Ishelle's Trace, activate the dagger she'd taken from Davian, and hope that it wouldn't kill Ishelle.

It still unsettled him that that had been their next best option.

Fessi appeared abruptly beside Erran, scowling down at Rohin. "She's slow, but she's on her way back. We need to go." She glanced at Erran. "Can you carry him?"

Erran sighed but stooped, slinging Rohin unceremoniously over his shoulder.

"We're going to have to rest now and then," he grunted, the strain of the other Augur's weight evident.

Fessi nodded and placed a hand on Erran's other shoulder, then hesitated.

"What about you?" she asked Davian. "Once Ishelle realizes that she can't find Rohin, you're her next best bet. And she can track you. It won't be easy getting back to the passageway."

"I'll be fine," said Davian quietly, nodding at Rohin's unconscious form. "Just get him hidden for a few days. I'll wait for you to make contact back at the tavern."

Fessi inclined her head, and the three Augurs vanished.

Davian took a deep breath, staring around at the carnage in the hall. Remarkably—aside from the bloodied form of Elder Narius—everyone appeared to be still breathing. It was as good an outcome as they could possibly have hoped for.

He nodded grimly to himself, and hurried toward the exit.

Chapter 24

Wirr stared absently out the carriage window at Fedris Idri.

Save for the men on guard, the pass through Ilin Tora was empty at this time of night. The polished-smooth brown walls reflected the dancing torches placed both along the road and atop the First Shield, the light bouncing and coalescing to make the narrow passageway into Ilin Illan seem bright as day.

"I will give you one thing, prince. It is beautiful here."

Wirr turned to Breshada, who was sitting opposite and also peering outside the stationary carriage. He watched her for a moment, then inclined his head, though she couldn't see the gesture. He supposed she was right. Fedris Idri was always a striking sight, but even more so when accentuated through the lens of a hundred gently flickering torches.

He pulled back, letting the heavy curtain drop again, glad to let the scene disappear. He doubted beauty was something that he would ever see in this place again.

"Desriel must have its wonders, too," he observed. "The Builders vanished long before our two countries split."

Breshada nodded distractedly, still peering through the glass. "But those, I will never see again," she said softly.

Wirr nodded silently again, not knowing how else to respond to the Hunter's statement. He glanced over at Deldri, whose eyes were still closed, her slumped position against the side of the carriage barely having changed since she had fallen asleep halfway through the journey. His sister had readily accepted Wirr's explanation that Breshada was another bodyguard—just one whose job was to keep mostly out of sight. The Hunter's permanent scowl, unwillingness to talk, and generally threatening demeanor had sold the lie well enough. Wirr was confident that Deldri wouldn't mention her presence to anyone once they arrived at the palace.

The door suddenly opened and Andyn swung back inside, eyes flicking suspiciously to Breshada for just a moment before he settled back into his corner. The carriage jerked into motion again, starting its passage beneath the First Shield.

"Any trouble?" asked Wirr. Normally they wouldn't have been stopped, but the lateness of the hour meant that most travelers were expected to check in with the city watch before proceeding.

Andyn shook his head. "No, Sire. They recognized both me and the carriage. The captain was a little irritated that he wasn't allowed to check inside, but I just told him you and Miss Deldri were both resting. Once I pointed out how...*protective* the nobility can be of their sleep, he agreed that it was best not to risk disturbing you."

Wirr snorted, catching a flash of amused approval on Breshada's face as he shook his head.

They moved on slowly through Fedris Idri, the gentle rocking motion of the carriage almost enough to lull Wirr to sleep. He only had to glance across at Breshada to regain his alertness, though. Ilin Illan would be crawling with Desrielite spies right now. Of the entire journey, this part was by far the most dangerous.

Ten minutes passed without conversation; everyone knew the plan and were content to keep the restful silence. Eventually they emerged from the pass and into the city itself, taking one of the smaller roads into the Upper District. When the carriage finally slowed to a halt again, Wirr gave Andyn a slight nod; his bodyguard slipped out the door, reappearing a few seconds later with a tired-looking Aelric.

"Your Highness," said Aelric sleepily, peering inside. His black hair was uncharacteristically unkempt, and the clothes he was wearing were rumpled.

Wirr stared at him. "Were you sleeping out here?"

"Your message was very specific about waiting for you here. Not so much about the time you'd arrive. Or why I needed to be here." Aelric gave him a baleful look.

Wirr restrained a chuckle. "I wasn't sure if we'd be delayed—and I didn't want to put too much information in the note. Sorry," he said, mostly meaning it. "Thank you for coming."

He glanced out the door. They had pulled to the side of the narrow street, or perhaps more accurately simply stopped; the road was barely wide enough to accommodate the vehicle. It was also, he was pleased to see, completely deserted at this hour. That wasn't a surprise—the Upper District saw little lawlessness and was only lightly patrolled, plus its residents were fewer and less inclined to be out late than in the other districts—but it was still a relief.

Wirr glanced across at Deldri. She appeared to be sound asleep, but he didn't want to risk her overhearing anything. He slipped out of the carriage, quickly followed by Breshada.

"Who's this?" Aelric nodded politely to Breshada.

"This is Breshada. She's why you're here," said Wirr cheerfully. "She's a Hunter who saved my life in Desriel, and now has somehow become Gifted—don't ask, we're not sure how," he added as Aelric opened his mouth. He continued, "The Gil'shar are convinced that Andarra—or more specifically, I—have been using her as a spy. And before knowing that she was here, or that she was the 'spy' that they were talking about, I explicitly denied any connection between us to the ambassador. So if we're associated, it will mean... well. Bad things. War, maybe?"

"Probably war," agreed Breshada as she straightened her clothes.

Aelric gaped at them for a good few seconds in silence, clearly fully awake now.

Eventually, he recovered enough to shake his head. "And you brought her here... *why*?" Breshada glared at Aelric, but the young man stolidly ignored her.

"She needs to be taught how to control her use of Essence." Wirr had strongly considered dropping her at one of the small towns they'd passed through on the way there—it wasn't as if one of the Gifted couldn't have gone out to meet her—but he had nowhere private to leave her and as long as she had Whisper, Breshada would stand out to anyone with eyes. Plus, Administrators in smaller towns weren't accustomed to their Finders going off, so any slip by Breshada would have led to her immediate discovery. 343

At least here in the city—where lots of people still went about armed after recent events, and with Tol Athian in the Upper District—none of that would be quite so much of an issue.

Aelric thought for a few seconds, then reluctantly inclined his head, evidently coming to the same conclusions. He held up a key, the one that Wirr had instructed him to retrieve from his office. "So where am I taking her?"

"The Administration building behind Upper Market. Two streets over from where we are now." It was currently empty; the last month—the battle, followed by Wirr's becoming Northwarden—had taken a massive toll on the number of Administrators residing in the city. He turned to Breshada. "Make sure no one sees you go in, shutter any lamps, and lock the door behind you. Don't open it for anyone except myself, Aelric, or Andyn. There are comfortable couches there, and we'll organize for some food."

Breshada nodded impatiently; they'd been over this several times on the way here. Wirr was only repeating himself from nervousness. "I will remain hidden," she assured him. "It is hardly in my interests to—"

She froze as faint voices trickled across to them—muffled, probably at least a street over, but too close for comfort. Aelric exchanged a look with Wirr and then ducked down a nearby alley to investigate, walking with a slight limp.

There was silence for a minute, Wirr holding his breath. Then, suddenly, the faint scuffing of footsteps on stone from behind him.

"Prince Torin? Is that you?"

Wirr's heart sank as the call rang out across the empty street. He recognized the distinctively scratchy, gravelly voice straight away. Lyon was the captain of the city guard—a good man, one who had worked willingly with Wirr on plenty of separate occasions over this past month. Wirr had known that he took it upon himself to do late-shift patrols, but the chances of him happening upon them here, now, had been slim. Lyon would have at least another man with him as well, probably two.

"This is going to be awkward," he murmured to Breshada, not turning but listening helplessly as footsteps began echoing toward them.

344

Before he could react or resist, Breshada was suddenly grabbing and kissing him.

He went stiff with shock, both at the act and the passion with which Breshada had planted her lips on his. In the background he thought he could hear a couple of soft, uneasy chuckles; after a stunned second he instinctively jerked away but by the time he was able to look around, Lyon and whomever had been with him was gone.

He staggered away from Breshada, putting his hand to his mouth in bewilderment. "What in fates…" He stared at the Hunter, shaking his head. "Why?"

Breshada wasn't looking at him, her eyes instead on the road. When there was no movement, she turned and gave Wirr a satisfied nod.

"Your people find public displays of passion…embarrassing," she observed, looking for all the world as if nothing odd had happened. "It's something we Seekers know to take advantage of, now and then. A lover's embrace already hides the features, and your people tend to avoid looking too closely into the bargain." She jerked her head toward the main street. "They will not remember my face. We are safe to proceed."

"Safe?" Wirr stared at Breshada, wide-eyed. "Safe?" He ran his hands through his hair as he thought through the consequences of what had just happened. He groaned. "In less than a day, every House in Ilin Illan is going to know that I was in a back alley in the darkest hours of the night, kissing some mysterious dark-haired girl. And they're going to want to know *who it was*."

"But I very much doubt that the Gil'shar will make the connection." Breshada sighed at his expression. "You complained to your sister for a full quarter of the journey here of the vapid women pursuing you. Would this not dissuade some of them?"

There was motion to Wirr's left and Aelric emerged from the shadows, still slightly favoring his left leg, a vaguely puzzled expression on his face. The look only deepened when he saw Wirr's scowl. "What happened?"

Wirr shook his head. "Remind me next time that you're a much better swordsman than scout," he said drily. "They came from the other direction."

"Oh. The acoustics must have..." He frowned. "Someone saw you?"

"They saw only two lovers locked in an embrace," said Breshada cheerfully.

Wirr rubbed his forehead, waving away Aelric's confused look. "It was Lyon, of all people. He recognized me, so Breshada here decided that kissing me would be the best way to avoid being identified and make him go away."

Aelric stared at him for a long moment, then abruptly guffawed. "You're serious. Did it work?"

Wirr glowered at him. He wasn't sure what reaction he'd expected, but that certainly hadn't been it.

"It did," said Breshada with satisfaction.

"Then what's the problem?" asked Aelric, still grinning.

"Bah." Wirr just shook his head. "You know where you're going. Try not to let anyone know you were even out of bed tonight—the fewer questions, the better. I'll speak to you in the morning." He hesitated, then gave Aelric a serious look. "Be careful."

"Of course." Aelric gave Wirr a casual mock salute, then nodded to Breshada and started down the road.

Breshada gave Aelric an appraising look as they walked off. "Perhaps there are other patrols around?"

Aelric's sudden look of panic as Wirr shut the carriage door again was just enough to redeem his mood.

Wirr collapsed onto his bed, the tension of the past day easing a little now that he was back in a familiar environment.

His arrival at such a late hour had caused a minor stir, but he'd eventually convinced the guards that no one needed to be woken or immediately made aware of his arrival. Deldri had woken up enough to make her way to her old rooms, and Wirr had gladly headed straight for his own. Though the journey itself had been easy—riding in a carriage was hardly a great exertion—the constant strain of having Breshada there as well had taken its toll. He was ready to sleep.

Still, as he began putting the few things that he'd brought on the trip back in their places, and the Oathstone from his pocket into his personal safe, he couldn't help but stare at the thick notebook he'd taken from his father's safe. Curiosity had been eating at him for close to the entire journey, but with Breshada there, he'd felt the need to stay fully aware of his surroundings the entire time.

Plus—though he didn't want to admit it to himself—he felt a good deal of trepidation about actually reading it. Scyner had pointed him in this direction, and Wirr couldn't help but wonder why.

He reached over, moving to open the leather-bound book, and then brow furrowing when it remained shut. He turned it to its side, remembering the red wax that sealed the tome. It was still completely intact.

He poked at it to no avail, eventually fetching a letter opener from his desk and carefully piercing the seal. It was harder than he'd thought, and a couple of moments after finally making the first incision, he hesitated. The red surface looked as if it were rippling.

Then he dropped the letter opener and nearly the book, too, as the wax abruptly melted away, seemingly into the book itself.

He stared at it, frozen, hand shaking a little and unsure how to react. Eventually, cautiously, he opened the heavy tome and slowly began flipping through it.

Nothing else strange happened. The pages were filled with his father's familiar, neat lettering.

After a few seconds, he went back to the first page, frowning as he saw the red writing. It was dated close to twenty-two years ago—before the beginning of the war—but the handwriting, unlike the rest of the book, was not Elocien's.

He tentatively touched the lettering with a fingertip. The letters were raised, dully reflective.

Written in the same red wax as the seal.

This confirms that the contents of this notebook have been independently assessed and verified by Elocien Tel'Andras, in the presence of Mirin Siks and Jakarris si'Irthidian. During the assessment, at no point did Elocien Tel'Andras display indicators of deception or have any external influences affecting his judgment.

There were three signatures beneath, again all in slightly raised red wax—his father's and then two others, presumably those named in the text. Frowning, Wirr carefully flipped forward to the next page, where his father's handwriting began in regular ink.

I am recording here the events that have culminated in my being brought before the Augurs tomorrow, so that I might again know the truth of our efforts once my Reading has taken place.

Hello, Elocien.

By now, presumably Jakarris has guided you to the safe and will likely also have told you some things that are difficult for you to believe—confusing, even, given that you will not have any memory of what has led us to this point. It was necessary to take those events from your mind as well, I am afraid. Given the situation and the suspicion that has fallen upon you, even a hint of rebellious thought during the Reading could be dangerous.

Because of this, I know that you will be wondering how you could have possibly chosen to start down the drastic and distasteful road of organizing a coup.

The short answer is: though they have been hiding it, something has happened to the Augurs. New visions are scarce compared to last winter. Three weeks ago, Eleran even took the extraordinary step of retracting a vision—despite it having gone so far as to be confirmed in their Journal and publicly announced by Therius. They have explained the decrease as a sign of generally calm times ahead, and the latest embarrassment as a miscommunication in the chain of verification.

Do not listen to them. You have already been able to confirm that both problems are far more serious than they are letting on.

Though these events being kept from you and Kevran is disturbing, more so is the subsequent rise of criminality amongst those wielding Essence. With the Augurs now focused almost entirely inward—seemingly isolating themselves as they search for a solution to their issues—the Gifted have realized that they are now all but without oversight. I have collated reports of public humiliations, beatings, even rapes and killings by Gifted who now believe themselves above the law. Despite my efforts to bring this to the Augurs' attention, no justice has yet been administered.

Because of this, away from the false calm of the palace, you will find that there is great civil unrest. Deranius's recent speech to the Assembly has apparently become infamous amongst the people and has already earned the Gifted a new nickname; his refutation of the claim that some of the Gifted are abusing their powers—declaring that they use their power for Andarra alone, and that they all but bleed for the good of the people—has been widely mocked. Now, when one of the Gifted is said to be bleeding for his countrymen, it is commonly taken to mean that they are using their power for their own gain.

The Gifted, needless to say, have started to realize that this is not a compliment. Outbreaks of violence over the term have been reported.

To indicate the extent and severity of the problem, the following is a list of crimes perpetrated by Gifted individuals that I have independently verified occurred and that went unpunished over the past year. It is hard reading, but I urge you to be thorough, as each one provides motivation for the difficult choices that we have made, and that we will continue to have to make. If you need further proof after reading this, pick any of these crimes at random and quietly verify the details that I have noted. You will quickly discover that they are accurate.

Wirr paused, frowning at the page. He'd heard plenty about the war and the reasons behind it, of course—but always framed a certain way. His father had told him stories of what it had been like before the rebellion, but after three years at Caladel…he'd found them difficult to believe.

Yet his father's words here—written to himself, apparently—were clearly not rhetoric. He seemed to be recording the facts, nothing more.

He flipped forward, scanning page after page with steadily increasing horror. His father had been right—they were hard to read. Massive corruption, oppression, rapes, and murders by the Gifted, all unpunished. There had even been two violently suppressed riots in the Lower District—described initially to Elocien and Kevran as "minor disturbances"—and scattered others throughout some of the other major cities in Andarra.

Soon enough, Wirr's father had painted a clear but graphic picture of the collapse of the rule of law—and the way in which the Gifted had taken advantage of it—during the period leading up to the war.

Eventually, Wirr's vision began to blur from tiredness and he pushed the thick notebook away, trying for a moment to envisage what it must have been like. The political structure of the day had been so similar to what it was now—and yet completely different. Currently, the Houses made up most of the votes in the Assembly; otherwise, the king held two votes, Administration held two, and the two Tols had only one each. Back then, *each Augur* had been given a vote, as had each of the five Tols. The Great Houses and the king had had a single vote each, with the minor Houses having had none at all.

Despite what Elocien had been accustomed to by the end of his life—the system that Wirr had grown up knowing—the circumstances in which he had written this account were as different as they could possibly have been.

Wirr rubbed at his eyes again, wanting to keep going but reluctantly conceding that he could not. Judging from the size of the book, he had hours upon hours of reading still ahead. This was something important, clearly—exactly what he'd been looking for—but the words were beginning to blur together, and he was already having to read sentences three times over in order to comprehend their meaning.

He needed to sleep.

Reluctantly, he stood and crossed to his safe, tucking the book inside next to the Oathstone. He didn't imagine that anyone would be so desperate for his father's journal that they would break in—but Scyner, not to mention his mother and thus probably half of Administration by now, knew of its existence. There was no reason to take chances.

He lay back, fully intending to at least ponder the implications of what he'd just read for a few minutes before preparing for bed.

He was asleep within moments.

Wirr came awake with a start as someone coughed loudly in his ear.

He flinched up into a sitting position, only relaxing slightly when he realized that it was Dezia who was standing by the side of his bed, arms crossed. He stared at her sleepily, trying to think why she might look so angry. Then his gaze transferred to Aelric, who was over by the door with an inscrutable expression.

"Is something wrong?" he asked in bleary confusion.

Dezia's frown deepened. "I just thought you'd like to know about the rumor going around the palace this morning." She watched Wirr's face without smiling. "The one about you having been spotted last night with a girl. Being more than just a little friendly," she added quietly.

"What?" Wirr frowned, then snorted as he registered what she was saying. "Oh. Fates no. It wasn't like that."

"So you weren't kissing her?"

"Uh." Wirr rubbed his eyes, trying to force his brain into motion. "Well...yes, but it wasn't..." He shook his head, then gestured at Aelric. "Easier if you tell her."

"I don't know what you're talking about. I was in bed all night," said Aelric. Behind Dezia's back, he gave a nonchalant, slightly smug shrug.

"*What?*" Wirr growled. He rubbed his forehead dazedly, a mild panic entering his tone. "He's joking. You have to believe me. It was..."

It was only then that he saw Aelric's expression begin to crack into a smile. Eyes narrowing, he turned back to Dezia, finally seeing her barely restrained amusement.

"Urgh." He groaned and collapsed back onto the bed as Dezia

burst out laughing. "You are both horrible people," he said to the ceiling, shaking his head.

"Probably," said Dezia cheerfully. She took a seat on the side of the bed, her smile fading to a sympathetic expression. "Aelric told me everything. It sounds like you got more than you expected on your trip."

Wirr grunted. "Breshada was certainly something of a surprise." He sighed. "And my mother... wasn't exactly pleased to see me, either. She tried to keep me from seeing Deldri—locked her in her room to avoid it."

Dezia nodded, all amusement gone now. "I saw Deldri earlier with some of her friends, and Aelric mentioned that she was in the carriage with you last night. I assumed that things must not have gone well, but still..." She laid a hand on Wirr's arm. "I'm sorry."

Wirr gave her an appreciative smile. "It is what it is." They locked gazes for a few seconds.

Aelric coughed loudly from the doorway. "I'm not sure this is what the king meant when he said that you should look in on his nephew," he said drily.

Wirr started, then looked questioningly at Dezia. "My uncle knows you're here?"

"He suggested that I come, actually," said Dezia with a small smile. "He wanted me to tell you about how, now that Aelric's of age, he was considering putting him forward for a position in the Assembly."

"Wanted *us*. Wanted *us* to tell him," said Aelric from the corner, but Wirr was barely listening. He stared at Dezia for a long moment, trying to process the implications.

If Aelric joined the Assembly, then he would need a title. House Shainwiere had been well regarded prior to Dezia's father's death, with a proud history, but lacking the land and wealth that would encourage one of the Great Houses to sponsor their application for entry into the Assembly.

As the king's wards, Aelric and Dezia had the upbringing to manage the responsibilities and pressures that came along with a title, so that wouldn't be a problem. And Wirr's uncle owned plenty of land—them being granted some would be unusual, but not unheard of.

There were obstacles, but none that couldn't be overcome. In a year, maybe two, there was no reason that Dezia couldn't be Dezia si'Shainwiere.

Dezia's grin widened farther as she saw him follow through the logic.

"That..." Wirr mirrored her expression dazedly, heart leaping. "That sounds like a *wonderful* idea." It wasn't just an exciting prospect, either. After everything that he'd just been through with his mother, the reminder that his uncle was still supportive of him meant more than he could say.

"It does mean that Aelric would have a say in the running of the country," observed Dezia.

Wirr laughed, a little giddily. "Still worth it."

"I'm *right here*, you know," Aelric grumbled. Despite his tone, he had a slight smile on his face, too. He shook his head. "We can talk about all of that later. Right now, I'm more interested in whether you found whatever Scyner sent you after?"

Dezia shrugged at Wirr's glance. "I assumed that you wouldn't mind him knowing."

"I don't." Wirr stretched, still grinning at the potential of Dezia's news. "There was a safe, exactly where Scyner said it would be—and it had a notebook in it. I started reading it last night, and..." He shook his head, smile fading. "It was strange. My father seemed to be writing it to himself, sometime before the war. He was saying that his memories of the rebellion were about to be removed, because he was due to be Read by the Augurs— and that the notebook was his way of remembering everything afterward. But there was some kind of seal on it. It didn't look like he ever got around to reading it again."

Aelric and Dezia stared at him in silence for a few moments. "What do you think that means?" asked Dezia eventually.

"I'm not sure yet. But...I think Scyner may have been telling me the truth. That notebook probably has at least some of the answers we're looking for. I'm intending to read the rest of it as soon as I can." Wirr sighed as he considered his schedule for the next few days. "There's a lot in it to get through, though."

Dezia nodded. "I'm glad the trip wasn't a complete disaster, at least," she said softly.

Wirr grunted in agreement, then glanced over at Aelric. "Speaking of disasters. Did our guest settle in all right last night?"

Aelric snorted. "*Settled in* is probably the wrong word. That woman is *jumpy*," he said drily. "But yes. She's safe."

They spoke for a little longer, but too soon Andyn arrived and Wirr had to shoo Dezia and Aelric away so that he could prepare for the day ahead. Even after only a couple of days out of the city, he had too much to catch up on to be able to idly chat.

The morning passed in a dull blur of meetings, beginning with an obsequious but thoroughly unhelpful Dras Lothlar, and capped by a trip to Administration's main building in the Middle District and yet another long, argumentative session with Pria as they went over Administration's official position on a variety of subjects. When Wirr finally returned to the palace to find Taeris waiting for him outside his study, he almost turned around. Despite the good news earlier in the morning, he was frustrated, hungry, and in no mood for further conversation—even with someone with whom he actually needed to speak.

Forcing himself to breathe, he instead offered the Athian Representative a polite greeting, and they entered Wirr's study.

Wirr collapsed into his chair as Taeris shut the door. "No news on the assassination attempt, I assume?" He knew Taeris well enough that he couldn't summon the energy to open with small talk or pleasantries right now.

Taeris blinked. "Not really, Sire. We're doing our best to find out more, looking at all the people who might be behind it, but..."

"It's a long list," finished Wirr heavily.

Taeris nodded. "Sorry. The man we captured isn't talking, either, I'm afraid." He rubbed his neck, watching Wirr with a mildly concerned frown. "How are you, Sire?"

Wirr gave him an awkward shrug, still unaccustomed to Taeris addressing him so formally. The scarred man had insisted on following proprieties after his position as Representative had been made official, though. "Tired," he admitted. "My trip out of the city didn't exactly go as planned."

He told Taeris the entire story, from his encounter with Scyner through to finding the safe and his clash with his mother.

"It sounds as though the book was Notarized," said Taeris thoughtfully after Wirr described to him what had happened with the seal.

Wirr looked at him blankly.

"It was a way of authenticating important documents," Taeris elaborated. "Not commonly used, though. Expensive. Two Augurs needed to be present in the room either while the document was being written, or while it was read by the person who had written it. The Augurs would check for signs of deception while that was happening, without Reading anything specific. It was a way of certifying the author's intent—that what they had put to paper was genuinely what they meant. The document was then specially sealed, so that whomever broke the seal could know that it hadn't been tampered with since the Notarization." He shrugged. "It was used mostly for treaties, trade agreements, large business deals, that sort of thing."

Wirr frowned. "So...my father never read it after it was sealed, then?"

Taeris shook his head. "It doesn't sound like it." He stared at Wirr for a few seconds. "Thank you for letting me know about this," he added. "If you have no objection—after you have read it, of course—I would be very interested to take a look at this notebook myself."

Wirr inclined his head, somewhat surprised that Taeris had asked so respectfully. "Of course." He sighed. "Something else happened while I was away that you should most definitely know about, too."

He proceeded to tell Taeris about Breshada. Taeris listened in silence, looking grim.

"Fates," he muttered once Wirr had finished. "I can't say whether I think it was wise or foolish to help her. But if what you say is true, and she really has become Gifted somehow..." He rubbed his chin. "I don't believe we've ever had access to someone so deep within the Gil'shar before. There has always been an assumption that they have weapons hidden away—two thousand years of hating the Gifted, they've certainly had plenty of time to collect them—but we've never had an idea of how many. Or where they're stored. Or under what circumstances the Gil'shar would actually decide to use them." He nodded thoughtfully. "She could be an asset."

"I'm not sure that she's quite at the betray-everything-she-knows stage just yet," observed Wirr.

Taeris grunted. "If she wants our help controlling Essence, she may have to get there."

Wirr hesitated, then shook his head.

"I'm not suggesting that we don't try and get the information, but I made a deal with her. Perhaps I could have pressed for more—but I gave her my word that we would help," he said quietly. "I don't know Breshada well, but I'm fairly certain that if we try holding out for more, we'll never get anything out of her. Except for maybe our throats cut."

Taeris looked unconvinced, but eventually sighed. "It's going to be awfully hard to convince anyone at the Tol to teach her in exchange for 'not dying,'" he observed wryly, "but there are some people I know who can be trusted, and who *may* be willing to assist. I'll see what I can do." He massaged his forehead. "I have to say, though—I'm not sure that your bringing your sister back here was the wisest choice."

Wirr frowned. "Deldri? Why?"

"Because while she was away from the city, most people had forgotten about her," said Taeris. "Now she's back? She's next in line to be able to change the Tenets. Possibly the only one who could be convinced to, too."

"Only if I'm dead," observed Wirr.

Taeris just looked at him.

"Oh." Wirr grimaced. "You really think it increases the danger to me?"

"I think it's a reminder that the new Tenets don't have to stay this way," said Taeris. "Anyone serious about removing you would already have remembered it, but I can't imagine that her presence will help."

Wirr ran his hands through his hair. He'd been caught up in everything else, but Deldri getting sucked into the politics and dangers of the city should have been something that had occurred to him already. "I'll speak to her. And to my uncle, too," he said ruefully.

The discussion moved on to other matters for a while. To Wirr's irritation there had, apparently, been new reports from the north—ones that Pria had again failed to mention to him—describing new sightings of dar'gaithin. Three men on patrol had been found dead near one of the outposts, too, their bodies ripped apart to the extent that they were barely identifiable. Yet according to Taeris, the Athian Council continued to side with most of the Assembly; they remained skeptical of the sightings, suggesting that they were unreliable and that the reported attack had likely been wild animals. Combined with Tol Shen's ongoing rhetoric surrounding the Augurs' ability to seal the Boundary, it continued to create a general sense throughout Ilin Illan that the situation was well in hand.

Taeris's frustration at that showed through more and more as he spoke. Many of his strongest allies within Tol Athian had left for the north weeks ago, and though he had at least thought to send one of his Travel Stones with them—so that they now had a way to quickly transport soldiers and supplies to the Boundary, if need be—it had only seemed to make his strangely combative relationship with the Council worse.

There was clearly a bitter history there, though neither side had been willing to speak of it to Wirr. In other circumstances, he would have seriously considered replacing Taeris as Representative; half the time Taeris spoke in the Assembly, Wirr knew that he was saying the exact opposite of what the Council would want him to.

But he was also one of the only people in power pushing to send more soldiers north. Right now, that was far more important than the Tol's antagonistic attitude toward him.

After talking for a while and ascertaining that there was no other important news, Wirr eventually made his excuses; there was a break until his next meeting and he was eager to get back to his rooms and read more of his father's notebook. When he opened the door to Taeris's study, however, he was surprised to find Aelric waiting outside.

"Can I have a word?" asked the young man quietly.

Wirr frowned but nodded, and they began walking. "Is everything all right with our guest?" he asked nervously.

Aelric inclined his head. "As far as I know."

"Good." Wirr breathed out. "So what did you want to talk about?" He noted Aelric's limping gait with a sidelong glance. "What *did* happen to your leg?"

Aelric grunted, looking vaguely embarrassed. "Training accident—nothing too bad. It's just stiff." He licked his lips. "I wanted to let you know that I will be heading out of the city to Variden for a few days."

Wirr looked at him in surprise. Aelric had no family, no connections outside of Ilin Illan that he knew of. "Why?"

"Just visiting a friend."

Wirr frowned. "And you're telling me this because..."

Aelric hesitated. "I...wanted to ask you a favor. If she mentions it, tell Dezia that you asked me to go and do something there. Sent me on an errand."

"So you don't want her to know why you're really going? She doesn't approve of this...friend?" Wirr felt his frown deepen. "Aelric, what's really going on?"

Aelric scowled, though the expression didn't hold much heat. "It's a personal matter. Just one I'd *really* prefer that Dezia didn't get involved in. It might be dangerous, and..." He gave a short laugh. "You know her, Torin. If I told her that I was staying anywhere except Ilin Illan, she'd press and press until she found out what was going on. And then she'd get herself involved."

"Dezia's rather capable of protecting herself," observed Wirr.

Aelric smiled. "I know." The expression faded. "But this is my problem to deal with. And I couldn't forgive myself if she got hurt because of it."

Wirr thought for a moment, then nodded slowly. "I'm not going to lie to her for you," he said quietly, "but I do need to send a letter to the Administrator in charge in Miorette. That's about halfway there. If you're happy to deliver it..." He shrugged.

Aelric nodded with alacrity. "Of course."

Wirr sighed. He still didn't like the idea of keeping something from Dezia, but Aelric was right—she'd get herself involved, no matter how dangerous whatever it was Aelric was up to. "I'll expect a full explanation for all of this as soon as you can give me one. And I'll be mentioning this to Dezia the moment that you're

back." He came to a stop, grabbing Aelric gently by the arm until the other man was facing him. "But, Aelric? If you're in trouble, you can ask for help. You know that, don't you?"

Aelric inclined his head wryly, but Wirr thought he saw a flash of appreciation in his eyes, too. "I know," he said. "But there's nothing to worry about. I can, and need to, deal with this on my own."

Wirr nodded, not entirely satisfied but acceding that Aelric wasn't going to tell him anything more. "Just remember that the offer's always there."

Aelric nodded a grateful acknowledgment, then made his excuses and hurried off. Wirr looked after him worriedly for a few moments, but eventually started moving in the direction of his own rooms. He didn't like what had just happened, but ultimately, Aelric was a grown man. All Wirr could do was offer his help, and hope that Aelric was smart enough to know when to accept it.

He got back to his room and unlocked his safe, vaguely relieved to find the thick notebook still in its place. He settled into his chair and opened it to where he'd left off.

He had a lot of reading to do.

Chapter 25

Caeden wandered slowly toward the palace, his hesitation growing with each passing step.

It had taken him a few hours to traverse the catacombs in which he'd found himself, a thin trail of kan leading him out to the hidden entrance at the base of Ilin Tora, just as Alaris had said it would. It had taken another two to skirt the base of the mountain and enter the city via Fedris Idri. That had all given him time to think about everything he'd learned since the Wells, about the things Alaris had claimed. About his best course of action.

Deilannis, he knew, was it—in fact, it was realistically his only option. He'd vacillated several times on whether he should trust what Alaris had told him; part of him wanted to ignore every word that the man had uttered, but another part—the stronger part—was confident that it was the truth. Alaris didn't want the Lyth to get Licanius. If nothing else, Caeden felt that he could trust that.

What he had yet to decide, though, was whether to see his friends before he went there. It was probably better just to leave, to keep everyone else out of it. Wirr, Davian, Taeris. Karaliene. None of them *needed* to be involved. None of them *needed* to know that he'd even been here.

He idly kicked a stone along in front of himself. He could be putting them in danger by making contact. Isiliar was probably still hunting him, and he doubted in her current state that she'd bother waiting until he was alone.

But he knew that wasn't the real reason he was hesitating—not the only one, anyway.

Alaris's words had shaken him more than he cared to admit, more than even the brutality of Isiliar's attack.

Neither of us can claim to be on the side of what's right.

It was easy for him to say, an easy lie. It should have been equally as easy for Caeden to dismiss.

But it wasn't.

He *had* been the one to imprison Isiliar—his *friend*. He remembered doing great things with these people, fighting side by side and defending what was *right* with them. And far from the enemy that Caeden had once envisaged, Alaris had seemed genuine in his regret over the invasion, over what had happened.

Worse—though it still sickened him—Caeden even understood the motivation for it now. The Venerate thought that by agreeing to the Lyth's bargain, Caeden was risking everything.

And, perhaps, he was.

He stared morosely at the sword hanging by his side. The only thing in the world that could kill Alaris, and the man had given it to him as if it were nothing. Given it to him because he believed that it was more important for Caeden to deal with the Lyth... and because he believed that Caeden was truly his friend.

Perhaps he'd been confident that Caeden couldn't beat him, even with Licanius. Perhaps it was a bluff. Alaris was thousands of years old; Caeden doubted that it would be easy to spot if he were lying.

He shook his head in frustration. It didn't *feel* like that exchange had been anything except genuine.

And he hated the thought of seeing his friends again while those doubts remained.

He swallowed, gritting his teeth against the indecision. He was making excuses to himself now. He knew, deep down, that some of his hesitation came from shame. He hadn't spoken to any of them since he'd found out who he was. Even now, standing in the middle of the Upper District, he hadn't decided whether he could. He wanted to tell them everything, and he wanted them to never know. He wanted to share the burden, and he wasn't sure if he could ever face them again if they knew.

Caeden paused as he came within sight of the palace gates, rolling his shoulders uncomfortably both at his memories of this stretch of road, and what lay ahead. Much had happened since the battle, and the worst signs of it had already been cleaned away.

His jaw tightened. What he'd done here hadn't been a mistake.

He was close enough now that the guards were watching him. He nodded to himself, his stride becoming more determined. He hadn't been on the wrong side of that fight. If he hadn't been here, hadn't fought, his friends would now be dead.

"You're him." One of the guards had frozen as he watched Caeden, who was close enough now to be within earshot. It was said quietly, but there was awe in his voice.

The other men with him frowned, studying Caeden for a couple of moments. One by one they straightened, eyes going wide as they realized to what their companion had been referring.

Caeden inclined his head awkwardly, unsure how he felt but at least relieved that he didn't have to spend too long trying to find someone who would let him in.

"I need to speak with Princess Karaliene," he said quietly. "Please let her know that Caeden is here."

There was no motion for a full five seconds, then one of the guards snapped into action, giving an awkward half salute and dashing through the gate into the palace grounds. The others just stood there, gawping at him.

Caeden gave them as friendly a smile as he could. There was respect in their eyes, certainly.

But there was also fear.

Not five minutes had passed before there was movement from within the palace grounds. Caeden turned to see Karaliene walking toward him, a wide smile splitting her face.

He smiled back.

And then the memory hit.

Caeden swept into the room, smiling broadly.

"It's done!" he announced triumphantly, glowing with the feeling of success. He brandished the Siphon aloft; as if at the motion, more cheers began raining down from the streets outside. He closed his eyes for a moment, listening to the joy in those voices.

After far too many years, it was actually over. He'd broken the bond of the Siphon, freeing the Shadows. Freeing Silvithrin from its tyrant. Serrin was gone, fled. Wereth and his Shadowbreakers were safe, and he had thwarted their final plan in time.

He took a deep breath, finally allowing himself to feel. Feel the joy of the moment, but also the pain of loss, the pain that had drawn him into this conflict in the first place. He'd called Thavari a fool for trying to do the impossible, to fix something that could not be fixed. It had been the last thing he'd said to his friend. And yet Thavari had tried anyway—an attempt which had ultimately led to this success. She would have been proud of Caeden, of what had just been accomplished. Caeden knew it.

His smile widened as he was enveloped in a warm, fierce hug, followed by a long and passionate kiss. He eventually broke away, smiling into Astria's bright blue eyes. Almost, they reminded him of Elliavia. Almost, he felt that old familiar sadness tug at his chest.

But instead he laughed, allowing the warmth of Astria's presence to spread through him, calming him and exciting him at the same time. That she was still here, still waiting for him, was the greatest miracle on a day of many. Before he'd left he had told her who he was, what he'd been, what he'd done. Everything he could think of to make her understand what she was tying herself to.

And despite all of that, she had stayed. Through his absence as he had trained with the Shalis, and his uncertainties afterward. Through the explosion of the Lightspire. Through the Desecration of the Three Bells, and the riots that had followed.

"How is Wereth?" she asked eventually.

Caeden sighed, still smiling. "Wereth is…happy. I think. I've never really seen him that way before, so it's hard to tell." He shook his head, glancing at the sphere of crystal in his hand. "He still blames himself for creating this, and particularly for letting Serrin get his hands on it. But now…I think he will return to Saran'geth. His job here is done, and for all the wonders that he created there, that city could still use a strong hand at the helm."

Astria smiled, sweeping a lock of her short brown hair aside. She was tanned from the Silvithrin sun, petite. Not the porcelain beauty of Tyrithia du Carr, nor the cold perfection of Evanarra

Gathius, both of whom had attempted to woo him over these

past few months. Astria was far more than that. She was bright, truly alive, full of energy and wonder and the purity of joy.

And somehow...she also understood him. Understood his moods, understood what he needed and when he needed it. He just hoped that he was half as good at knowing those things about her.

"So is the danger over?" she asked.

Caeden wavered, but eventually nodded. "For the most part. There will be a few weeks needed to sort out the new government, and nobody's decided what to do about the Shadowbreakers just yet—even Wereth. They didn't get to complete their plan, but the things they did prior to that were bad enough." He scratched his head. "We can leave, if you want. I'm not needed anymore; if anything, I suspect that my presence may cause more issues than those it solves. We could go to—"

"No." Astria laid a hand on his arm, her voice calm but firm. "No more running. Remember?"

Caeden hesitated, but inclined his head. She was right. If they moved on, he would only feel the need to press forward again, to keep looking to disprove Gassandrid's odd prophecies. But that way was madness. Even if some unseen force was somehow in charge of his life, even if these decisions were somehow not his own, he was happy here. *For the first time in as long as he could remember.*

"Good." Astria smiled at him, a relieved expression, then nodded toward the kitchen. "I need to go and tell Thera that she's safe now, but"—she waved him back into his chair as he made to rise—"she's safe now, *so you should relax. I'll get Amos to fix something for you on the way out." She smiled at him again, and this time it was a sly look of promise. "We'll have to celebrate tonight."*

"I look forward to it," Caeden said with a return grin.

He settled back in the armchair, closing his eyes and just... relaxing. How long had it been since he'd done that? Nowhere to go. No one to save, or find, or hunt, or escape from. The sounds of celebration still drifted in through the window, laughter and cheering and even joyful weeping audible from the street. He revelled in it, drank it in. Finally, he'd done something good. Something right.

After some time had passed, there was a knock on the door.

Caeden waved lazily to indicate that Amos, bearing a tray on which sat a single half-full glass, should enter.

"Amos!" He smiled at the older man. "You've heard the good news?"

"I have indeed, Master Tal," said Amos, as always refusing to shy away from propriety, even in this momentous hour and with people dancing in the street outside.

Caeden cocked an eyebrow at him. "And you are...pleased?"

Even Amos's exterior, it turned out, was not immovable. The hint of a smile crept onto his face.

"I am pleased, Master Tal. You could even say that I am very pleased."

"Glad to hear it, Amos." Caeden winked at the man. "Thank you for the drink. What is it?"

Amos began rattling off the mixture, and for a few moments Caeden barely listened, having not particularly cared about the answer.

Then he registered what was being said, and he stiffened.

"Amos," he said, speaking slowly as he interrupted the man. "I'm sorry...can you please repeat that?"

Amos repeated the ingredients, a small frown on his face at Caeden's tone. "Is there something amiss, Master Tal?" he asked after he was finished. "It is exactly as Mistress Astria requested that I prepare it. She was very specific."

Caeden closed his eyes, nodding slowly. "Nothing is amiss. You may go, Amos. Thank you."

He waited until the man had left the room, then stared down into his glass. Tried to remember.

Had he told her, at some point? This mix...it was his favorite. The one that he only made on special occasions, when he was celebrating something. When he felt like he'd won a great victory.

He hadn't felt that way in the last century. Longer, probably.

He went cold, hand trembling as he pushed aside the drink and leaned forward, head in his hands. It could be nothing. It could be a coincidence, or perhaps he'd simply told her at some point. Or maybe he'd written it down somewhere one time, somewhere she'd seen without him knowing. This could be her effort at springing a surprise on him.

But it didn't feel that way. He closed his eyes, imagining her eyes, picturing the way that she looked at him. Thought again about how it reminded him just a little of Elliavia.

She knew him, could read him like no one else could…

Time passed.

He wasn't sure how long he'd stayed like that, just staring at the wall, but when the sound of the door creaking open finally snapped him back to awareness, it was dark outside. The sounds of celebration still echoed up to him; that would likely continue for much of the night, if not the next few days.

"Tal?" Astria's voice came from the doorway. "Are you in here?"

"I am," said Caeden quietly.

The sound of footsteps, and then Astria's silhouette appeared in front of his chair, frowning down at him. "Tal? Why are you sitting here in the dark?" She moved to the side, lighting one of the lanterns, then returned to look at him with a puzzled, mildly concerned smile. "Are you all right?"

He leaned forward, looking into her eyes.

"I'm all right," he said. He held her gaze. "Not as good as that time I won the competition at Dianlys, but all right."

Astria put on an appropriately bemused smile, but he saw it. That moment of recognition, the flicker that meant that she understood what he was talking about. That *she* remembered what he was talking about.

"What competition was that?" she asked.

Caeden smiled tiredly, though it was only to force down the lump in his throat. "Or that time Mayden Caan was trying to claim birthright to Caer Lyordas. When we beat her…I was happy that day."

Astria said nothing, her smile fading.

"Or when I asked my wife to marry me, and she said yes." He gazed at her, light-headed, chest aching. "When I asked even though I knew that she was going to say no, because it was the stupidest thing that she could possibly do. Because she was so much better than me, so much better than I deserved. And she said yes anyway. She had to say it three times before I realized what she meant. Before I could believe it." He laughed at the memory, even as he blinked back tears. "The wife that you are not, Nethgalla. The wife that you could never be to me."

Astria opened her mouth to protest, then shut it again silently. She looked away, as if ashamed. Her gaze alighted on the glass sitting by Caeden's chair, untouched.

She groaned.

"You figured it out just from that?" she whispered.

"When did you kill her?" Caeden's voice cracked. "How much of her was her, Nethgalla?"

Nethgalla said nothing for a long time. There were tears in her eyes, too, when she finally spoke.

"While you were with the Shalis," she whispered. She leaned forward, her tone desperate. "She was going to leave you, Tal. She stayed for a few days but after you told her everything, she—"

"Enough." Caeden snarled the word as he came out of his seat, hand shooting out to grab Nethgalla by the throat. He needed to end this creature. He needed to be rid of her blight on his life, once and for all.

Beneath his grip, Nethgalla began to change.

Within moments, he found himself choking his wife. Choking Elliavia.

He released his hold, eyes wide with fear and rage and sorrow.

"You are a monster," he whispered. He drew his sword, leveling it at Ell's heart. "I should end you now."

"Tal. Please."

His heart wrenched to hear that name being said in that voice. He stepped back as if from a physical blow.

"Why do you do this? Why do you pursue me? Plague me?"

"Because I love you, Tal," said Nethgalla softly. Her eyes glistened. "Because I won't give up until you understand that it's me. That this thing you're trying to do...it's not necessary. It's wrong. I don't want you to do it, and you know that's something that your wife would say."

Caeden let the sword drop to his side and collapsed back into his chair, head bowed. "My wife would not have killed an innocent woman to trick me into loving her, either," he whispered. "She was the gentlest soul you could..." He trailed off, swallowing, trying to keep his emotions in check. "Just…leave. Leave and never return. The next time I see you, I will kill you, Nethgalla. It will pain me, but I promise you that I'll do it anyway."

When he looked up again, he was alone.

He sat there for some time, staring at the wall. The jubilant noise from outside was grating rather than exciting now. He knew that the victory he'd helped win here was still something good, something pure. It didn't stop it from turning to ash in his mouth anyway.

He eventually turned and produced a trickle of Essence, enhancing his voice. "Amos," he called.

A minute later the wrinkled man was by his side.

"How can I help, Master Tal," he asked quietly. He hadn't heard anything, but somehow he knew that something was wrong. His demeanor was as calm as ever, but it was…gentle. Sad.

"Please pack my things. I will be leaving in the morning."

"Alone, Master Tal?"

Caeden stood, staring out the window. The Broken Palace still burned in the distance against the night, its flames red and angry.

"Alone, Amos," he said heavily.

"Caeden?"

Caeden blinked, coming back to reality. Karaliene was in front of him, her smile replaced by a concerned expression. "Are you all right?"

Caeden froze, his heart sinking. It had been a mistake to come here—he should never have exposed Karaliene to this kind of threat. He inwardly cursed himself, cursed his weakness. He'd known Nethgalla was a danger, and Alaris had warned him that she would be watching his every move, watching his friends. It shouldn't have taken the pain of this memory to drive that point home.

It was too late now, though.

"I shouldn't have come here," he said in frustration.

Karaliene peered at him. "Glad to see you're alive and well, too," she said primly, though her blue eyes flashed at the words. She gave him a dangerous smile. "It's good that you're here, because we have a lot to discuss."

Caeden winced. "Sorry—I didn't mean it like…" He sighed. "I've put you in danger. We need to get inside, out of sight. Now. Does anyone else know I'm here?"

Karaliene frowned, shaking her head. "I was about to send someone to fetch—"

"Don't tell them. Don't tell anyone." Caeden rubbed his forehead, mind racing. "Can these men be trusted not to talk?"

Karaliene's frown deepened, but she nodded. "If I speak to them." She indicated that he should wait, then moved to the gate and murmured to the four men there. They listened intently, and nodded as one when she finished.

"They won't breathe a word," said Karaliene as she came back, glancing over her shoulder at the men, who were already facing back out into the street. "And we can get to my rooms without attracting too much notice." She shot an inquisitive look at him. "But then you're going to explain what's going on."

Caeden gave her a small, relieved smile. "Agreed."

The palace grounds were reasonably quiet as they wound their way toward the main building, and those few who glanced at him appeared to be doing so out of curiosity as to who was accompanying the princess, rather than from any recognition. Some here would have seen him fight, but not many had done so up close.

Soon enough they were alone in Karaliene's quarters, and the princess was indicating that he should sit. He watched her silently for a few seconds, wrestling with his emotions. As dangerous as he knew he was to her, now that the decision had been taken out of his hands, he felt…excited. Happy. He hadn't realized how badly he'd wanted to see her again, even with how much things had changed since they'd last been together. She had a way of lightening his burdens when no one else could.

He was also acutely aware of how selfish that feeling was.

"Now," said Karaliene after she'd composed herself. "This 'danger' that you mentioned." She leaned forward expectantly.

Caeden closed his eyes. He knew that what he felt for Karaliene wasn't love—not yet, anyway. But there was *something*, and it went beyond attraction. Something that, given time, had the potential to become more. She'd made him smile when it had seemed that everything else around him was crumbling. She'd believed in him when she'd had every right not to. She had befriended him, seen something in him that he wasn't sure anyone else had.

He swallowed. She'd seen the good in him—seen him as the man he wanted to be. He knew now, looking into her eyes, that he desperately didn't want that to change.

But he didn't want to lie to her, either. Hers was the one relationship he could remember that had felt truly open, truly without fear or deception. The only one in which he'd felt that he could truly be himself.

"I'll get to that," he said quietly, more playing for time than anything else. "How are the others? Davian, Wirr, Taeris?"

"Tor's away—he's gone to visit his family in the country. Taeris is at Tol Athian right now. Davian . . . Davian's gone to find other Augurs, to help seal the Boundary. He left almost as quickly as you did." There was a mild note of accusation in the last sentence.

"Ah." Caeden sighed. Perhaps it was for the best. The more people he saw, the more he could potentially drag into danger. None of them were in the same sort of peril as Karaliene, of course, but with Isiliar still out there . . .

Karaliene smiled, but there was sadness in her eyes as she watched him. "You're not staying, are you?" she said quietly after a few moments of silence, a statement more than a question.

Caeden shook his head, the action laden with regret. "I can't," he said softly. "There's so much happening that I need to—"

"I know." Karaliene gave him a small smile, her eyes understanding. "Tor told me what you said, before you left after the battle. There's more to it than just the Blind, isn't there?"

Caeden swallowed. He didn't want to make the situation seem hopeless to Karaliene—to anyone—but he couldn't deceive her, not about this.

"If the Boundary falls, I think we'll be facing worse than the Blind," he admitted. "There's another threat, too. Something I'm the only one able to stop." He said the words miserably, feeling their weight as he spoke them.

Karaliene placed a comforting hand over his, not saying anything. Caeden tried to give her a grateful smile, but the effort died on his lips.

"I've remembered things, Kara," he said suddenly. He knew it was the wrong move, knew how much it could jeopardize everything. Yet in that moment—gazing into Karaliene's eyes—he didn't care. He just wanted honesty. He needed truth with her, even if he had it with no one else. "Not everything, but...enough. Things about who I was. The things I've done. I'm not the—"

"Has it changed you?" Karaliene cut him off.

Caeden blinked. "No. I...no, I don't think so," he said slowly. "It's been confusing, but I'm trying not to let it."

"Then it doesn't matter." Karaliene's tone was calm but firm. She looked at him, and he saw that the sentiment was genuine. "You're on our side. You fought for us, saved us. *That's* what's important. *That's* what I care about."

Caeden stared at her for a few moments, then swallowed a lump in his throat. She meant it.

"Thank you." He met her gaze steadily, trying to convey the gratitude he felt and knowing he was failing. "Still. There are some things I need you to hear."

Karaliene studied him for a moment, then nodded slowly.

"Then tell me," she said quietly.

❧

Dawn was close to breaking by the time silence fell between them again.

Kara had done most of the listening, allowing Caeden to wander his way through the information he'd gleaned since he'd left, skipping back and forth as he remembered one detail or another. Occasionally she prompted him to explain something further, but otherwise just nodded along to indicate that she was paying attention.

Caeden had told her almost everything, in the end. Not the fact of his being Aarkein Devaed, or what he'd done to the Darecians at the Plains of Decay, or that he was responsible for the murders in Desriel—Kara had said that his past didn't matter to her and though part of him still wanted to come completely clean, the excuse made it too easy to keep those to himself.

But he told her about the Lyth. About Licanius, and the events that he had set in motion by taking it. About the Venerate, and Shammaeloth, and his apparent inability to die.

And then, though it made him sick to do so, he'd told her about Nethgalla. Explained, awkwardly, that he'd been married. That the Ath had stolen his wife's form—that Caeden had essentially created her, had let her into this world because of his desire to save Ell. He again skimmed over the details; though he had no specific memories of the wedding, he knew enough of what he'd done. Knew that he had sacrificed lives to try and bring Ell back.

When he was finished, Karaliene sat for a few moments, staring at the steadily brightening horizon to the east. She shook her head, eyes wide.

"Caeden, that's..." To his surprise she reached over, took his hand. A comforting gesture rather than a romantic one, but still. "I'm so sorry. That is more horrible than anything I can imagine."

Caeden let her hand rest on his for a few precious seconds.

Then he stiffened. Was sympathy, this implied acceptance of what he'd just told her, how Karaliene would normally react? He knew immediately that it was an irrational thought; even so, his memory of Astria was still painfully fresh, and the seeds of doubt it had planted were now hard to ignore.

He reflexively drew his hand away, more sharply than he'd meant to.

"Oh." Karaliene blinked at him in confusion, abashed. "Sorry."

"No. It's not..." Caeden gritted his teeth.

Karaliene's frown deepened as she watched him.

"Fates, Caeden," she said softly. "I'm me. You can ask me anything."

Caeden shook his head, flushing. "I shouldn't have to. I'm sorry." He rubbed his forehead. "I just...I remember what it was like. I remember how good she was at pretending to be someone else. And how it felt when I realized that the person I'd been talking to, confiding in, laughing with all that time—that they had been dead for..." The emotion of those moments suddenly hit him again and he paused, a lump in his throat. Old wounds, he knew, but still.

There was silence for a few seconds and then Karaliene switched positions, coming to sit next to him.

"There's a group of Gifted leaving soon for Deilannis," she said abruptly. "You should go with them. You could look out for

373

them, and . . . I'm sure it wouldn't hurt to have other people watching your back." She looked at him hopefully.

Caeden hesitated, then shook his head. "It's too dangerous. Isiliar may still be after me, and I'm not sure I can protect myself from her, let alone anyone else." He sighed. "I don't think I can delay even for that long, either. As much as I'd like to," he added quietly.

Karaliene looked disappointed, but nodded her understanding.

"You have changed, you know," she said suddenly. Caeden's heart sank, but she waved away his concerned expression. "You're more . . . confident, now, I think. You know your purpose." She smiled. "My feelings for you are the same, though."

Caeden's heart skipped a beat but he said nothing for a few moments, mentally turning the words over to make sure that he hadn't misunderstood.

"Even after what I've just told you?" he asked eventually.

"Even after whatever you haven't," said Karaliene quietly.

She brushed back a strand of flaxen hair and leaned in, smiling almost hesitantly at him as she drew closer, green eyes fixed on his. Her kiss was slow and passionate, and it took a moment for Caeden to allow himself to believe that it was really happening.

He lost track of time after that.

When they finally, reluctantly stood, the sun had well and truly raised itself above the eastern horizon outside the window. He and Karaliene walked side by side toward the gate, Karaliene occasionally leaning in and gently touching his shoulder with hers, resting on him for a few moments at a time.

Caeden pulled up short as they approached, just out of sight of the guards.

"You need to be careful. To protect yourself," he reiterated. "I have no idea what information Nethgalla might have. She may not know anything about you, but if she does . . ."

"I understand," Kara assured him soberly. She shifted. "What will you do in Deilannis? To her, I mean. Will you . . . ?"

Caeden grimaced.

"I don't know yet," he admitted softly.

Karaliene sighed, nodding. "It seems almost pointless to say, but still. Be careful."

Before he knew what was happening, she was kissing him again.

They eventually parted, Caeden flushed and slightly breathless. He stared at the princess with wide eyes.

Karaliene grinned at him. "Just wanted to make sure that you don't forget me." Before he could respond, she was walking away, disappearing between the columns at the edge of the courtyard and leaving him alone.

Caeden stared after her for a few moments longer, then felt a slow grin of his own spread across his face. He shook his head, wondering at how light he suddenly felt. It was the first time he'd felt this way, this happy, since...

Since the last time he'd seen her. He almost laughed aloud at the realization.

Filled with renewed vigor, he left, nodding to the guards cheerfully as he passed them on his way out of the grounds. Once on the road, he turned toward Fedris Idri, determined to make a good start of it despite the late hour.

It was time to go back to Deilannis.

It was time to face Nethgalla.

Chapter 26

She's coming, said Erran's voice inside Davian's head.

Davian straightened in his seat. Moments later, Ishelle's familiar figure walked into the tavern.

He kept his face smooth, making eye contact and nodding briefly to her from his table in the corner. Ishelle hesitated, glancing around before coming over.

"So," she said as she slid into the chair opposite. "This is awkward." Despite the lightness of her tone, the young woman looked more worn down than Davian had ever seen her, with dark circles under bloodshot eyes betraying her exhaustion.

He gave her a tight, sympathetic smile. "There's only one person to blame for everything that's happened, and it's not you."

Ishelle snorted. "I know that. I was talking about you outsmarting me."

Davian stared at her for a moment, then chuckled.

Everything all right? Erran's voice intruded in Davian's head.

I think so.

Ishelle sighed, oblivious to the exchange as she stared at Davian appraisingly. "Let's get this over with." She grimaced, reluctance and distaste heavy in her expression. "I'm not Shielding myself. Do what you need to."

Davian inclined his head, grateful that he didn't have to insist. They both knew that this was the only way to ensure Rohin's influence was gone, and there was little point discussing anything else until it was confirmed.

He reached out with kan and touched Ishelle's mind lightly,

breathing out in relief as he saw that there was no trace of the oozing, oil-like influence Fessi and Erran had described. He swallowed, trying to withdraw as quickly and gently as he could, but unable to avoid feeling some of Ishelle's roiling emotions through the connection.

She was calm on the outside, but touching her mind was like hearing a long shriek of horror. He was doing his best to avoid Reading anything specific, but Ishelle's thoughts were...jumbled. Disturbed. Saturated with shame and rage.

Davian didn't know what Rohin had done to her, or made her do. But she remembered, and it was tormenting her.

He met her gaze, trying to convey sympathy but not really knowing what to say.

"All right," he said softly. "It's gone. Nice to have you back, Shel." He hesitated. "I'm sorry you had to—"

"Let's not talk about it." Ishelle's tone brooked no argument, and Davian inclined his head. He would be there if Ishelle wanted someone to talk to, but it wasn't his place to press the issue.

"Have the Gifted recovered?" he asked eventually.

"Some. Most seemed to be back to normal yesterday, but there are still a few who won't do anything they think is 'disloyal' to..." She shook her head.

Davian nodded; it was much as he and the others had guessed, then. "Does Driscin have any theories?"

"He wouldn't say much to me." She sighed. "No one's saying much to me right now."

Davian winced, hearing the frustration in Ishelle's voice. "I take it you haven't been Reading the Gifted?"

"I'm not even willing to suggest it," Ishelle said soberly. "Things are...not great at the Tol right now. To be honest, there aren't many Gifted who are willing to be in the same ward as me, let alone the same room."

Davian grunted. "How's Driscin?"

For the first time, the hint of a genuine smile crept onto Ishelle's lips. "Still miffed." She raised an eyebrow at him. "I can't believe that he agreed to your messing around with his memories. Neither can he, I think."

Davian smiled slightly. "There wasn't any other way. We knew that we couldn't reach the vault without you knowing where we were. We knew that there was no way to get to Rohin if you were near him, and no way to get you away from him unless you both truly, absolutely believed that it was for a good reason." He shrugged. "It made sense that once you knew where we were, you'd wait for us outside the vault. And it made sense that Rohin would want to hear our plan from Driscin rather than from me."

"Yes. I figured all of that out. Eventually," said Ishelle drily. She tapped at the table absently for a few moments, studying Davian. "Driscin said to come back and see him once you'd verified that I was all right. I imagine he's got an idea of what should happen next."

Then she paused, shifting uncomfortably. "So what...what did you do with him?" The heaviness of her tone left little doubt as to about whom she was talking.

Davian paused, reminding himself that he'd checked Ishelle. It was safe to trust her again.

"Fessi's been keeping him hidden—I'm not even sure where, to be honest. But he's nearby." He gazed at her curiously. "You can't sense him?"

Ishelle shook her head. "I tried, believe me. Driscin told me what you did—told me all about that amulet. It was one of the few ways that he felt he could actually help Rohin, before Rohin's influence wore off. Trust me, the amulet works."

Davian was silent for a few moments, then leaned forward.

"What Rohin said to me. About Elder Dain and the Council having known about the attack on Ilin Illan," he said quietly. "Was that true?" He'd all but forgotten Rohin's accusation in the madness that had immediately followed, but these past couple of days had given him plenty of time to wonder about it.

Ishelle hesitated.

"I don't know," she admitted, looking uncomfortable. "I wasn't there when he forced Elder Dain to tell him all of that."

Davian sighed. Rohin could have been lying to him—there had been no way to tell either way, locked up in his cell—but it hadn't *felt* like he was.

"We should talk to Driscin about it," Ishelle added. "If he knows something, you'll soon figure it out."

"Good point." Davian levered himself to his feet. "No reason to waste time, then, I suppose."

Ishelle glanced around. "The others?"

"Nearby." Davian met her gaze steadily. "I want to know what's going on in the Tol before we let the Shen Council anywhere near them." Mentally, he added to Erran, *We're about to move. I'll meet you back here in a few hours. If I'm not back...*

Understood.

Ishelle gave a reluctant nod, then stood as well.

"Then let's go and speak to Driscin," she said quietly.

Davian glanced around the tunnel, more inclined to take in his surroundings this time.

"You're sure we need to use this?" he asked Ishelle.

"I wasn't joking about us not being too popular right now," said Ishelle. "Driscin's not supposed to be letting me go anywhere; he had to lie to get me out of the Tol without someone noticing. He said that we should avoid using any of our abilities, too—everyone's on edge about Augurs right now. I don't *think* we'd be assaulted if we were seen using them, but..." She shrugged.

Davian blinked. "We just *saved* them."

"And you really think that they'll just smile and thank you after what Rohin did to them? After what he's shown them that we're capable of?"

Davian swallowed, acceding the point with a nod. It shouldn't have come as a surprise; over the years, he'd seen plenty of regular people fear him purely because he was Gifted. The Gifted having the same reflexive reaction toward Augurs was disappointing, but far from a shock.

They walked for a few minutes, the only sound the echoing of their footsteps and at one point, the sound of rushing water from one of the branching tunnels. It wasn't long before they were emerging into Central Ward, drawing their red cloaks a little tighter as they made their way through the streets. It was evening and there was a chill in the air, so having their hoods up didn't look too unusual.

"Where are we going?" murmured Davian, nodding as nonchalantly as he could to two Gifted as they passed. The Ward was quiet as this hour, but far from deserted.

"It's not far. Follow me." Ishelle struck off to the east, and Davian had to hurry to keep stride.

They walked for a couple of minutes, until Ishelle suddenly emitted a low curse.

"Keep walking. They're watching Driscin's office," she muttered. "To our left."

Davian frowned, forcing himself not to physically turn, but instead reaching out with kan. Sure enough, two forms stood in the shadows at the corner of one of the structures, motionless but clearly alert.

"Too late to use a time bubble. They'd notice for sure," he murmured. "Is there a back way?"

Ishelle nodded. They kept walking until they were out of sight of the watchers, then ducked around and came at Driscin's office from the next street over. This time, there didn't appear to be anyone to avoid.

Ishelle tapped lightly on the door, the knock a sharp and precise rhythm. There was a pause, then the door opened and Driscin was peering out, looking more at their surroundings than at them.

"Come in. Quickly," he said, nervousness underpinning the urgency in his tone.

Once they were inside and the door was shut again, Driscin gestured them into chairs and collapsed into his own.

"They realized that you'd left," he said heavily to Ishelle. "Things are..." He shook his head, then sighed and turned to Davian. "She's all right?"

Davian inclined his head in affirmation, unsurprised by the question. "Rohin's influence is gone."

Driscin breathed out, visibly relaxing. "I'd assumed so, but it is nice to be certain. Now—we need to start talking about how to bring Rohin back to one of the cells. It's the only way to convince the Elders that you weren't working with him," he added, seeing Davian open his mouth to protest.

"*What?*" Davian frowned at Driscin. "They cannot seriously believe that."

"Deep down, they probably don't—but it's less about the truth and more about fear, at the moment." Driscin's expression was grim. "Most of them never fully grasped just how powerful you are before now; when they first proposed the Amnesty, their assumption was that you would all be coming here for training. Now that they know what you're already capable of, they're terrified, and they want to do something about it."

"Fates," muttered Davian. "Sounds familiar. You'd think that the last twenty years might have given them a bit of perspective."

"It's human nature," observed Driscin, a slight chiding note in his tone. "And I don't know the full story, but what I've heard of what Rohin made some of them do..."

Davian nodded slowly. "So we can't look to them for help."

"You can't look to them *at all*," emphasized Driscin. "If they catch you, they'll try to lock you up in one of those cells. Honestly—if you hadn't taken that stone dagger with you, they'd be figuring out how and when to use it right now."

Davian and Ishelle both stared at Driscin. "What are you saying?" asked Davian eventually. "That we need to run?"

Driscin nodded.

"I'm saying that you need to gather your friends and head for the Boundary. I can handle the Council, and I think that they will eventually come to their senses—but right now, I've never seen any of them so shaken. They survived five years of siege safe behind these walls, and Rohin came in here in a *day* and took over. They won't be rational about this for a while." He took a slip of paper from his desk and handed it to Ishelle. "A letter of passage. It says that due to the urgency of your mission, you have the Council's full permission to travel without being accompanied by Gifted, and that we will vouch for anything you need to do."

Ishelle's eyes widened as she scanned the paper. "You and Elder *Dain* signed this?"

"Don't worry. It's a good copy of his signature." He shrugged at Davian's look. "Nobody's going to be able to prove that he didn't sign it, and it's better than you two being considered outside the bounds of the Amnesty."

Davian nodded as Ishelle carefully folded the paper and pocketed it. "Thank you," he said quietly.

"What I said about being able to handle the Council is only

true if they get Rohin," said Driscin seriously. "I'm assuming that you have no way of holding him prisoner indefinitely anyway, so..."

Davian sighed. He didn't like the idea of giving the Augur back over to the Council, but it was by far the most logical option. "How should we do it?"

"The amulet is still preventing him from using any of his powers?" When Davian nodded, he continued. "The safest way would be via the Augur entrance, then. Just leave the door on the Tol side unlocked so that I can use it. Say, at midnight tonight?"

"We can do that," agreed Davian quietly.

"Good." Driscin released a long breath, evidently relieved that he hadn't encountered any opposition to the plan. "In that case, you should go. You may have made it in here without being noticed, but the Council's been keeping a very sharp eye on me. Especially since they realized you were gone," he added with a glance at Ishelle.

Davian hesitated. They were leaving the Tol; in some ways the question he was about to ask felt irrelevant. But he still wanted to know.

"Before we do," he said quietly. "Did the Council know about the attack on Ilin Illan a month ago? Did they have foreknowledge of it?"

Driscin stared at him for a long moment, utter silence in the room.

Then he nodded. "Yes."

Ishelle's eyes flashed, and she spoke before Davian could open his mouth. "And you never told me? Never tried to warn people?"

"To what end?" Driscin leaned forward. "Shel, be reasonable. This was a vision from the old Augurs, and many of their visions never came to pass. It was either wrong, in which case there was no point starting a panic, or right, in which case nothing we could have done would have prevented it."

"What about all the people who died outside of Ilin Illan, though?" asked Davian quietly. "What about preparing the city?"

Driscin grunted. "How? We're talking about something that we weren't even sure would happen, let alone when," he said irritably. "Some of the things in the vision hinted that it might be   383 real—Shadows, Gifted wearing Shackles, some of the physical changes to Ilin Illan over the past twenty years—but that was all we had to go on." He shrugged. "Lyrus and his group sometimes seemed to give it more stock than I would have, and I've wondered since if he might have known something that I didn't. But all the vision indicated was that there would be an attack, that it would be repelled, and that the Gifted would help. We didn't even know which *direction* it was coming from, let alone who the enemy was."

Davian frowned, but he felt his shoulders relax a little. The explanation was far from assuring, but at least Driscin was telling the truth.

"Why not just make the visions public, though? Give people some warning?" pressed Ishelle. "Perhaps they wouldn't have listened, but you could at least have *tried*."

Driscin sighed. "Think, Shel. You're a smart girl. If Tol Shen had come forward—even as recently as a few months ago—and announced that they had a vision from the old Augurs suggesting that there would be an invasion, what would have happened?"

Ishelle was silent for a moment, then scowled. "It would have been given to Administration to investigate."

"And they'd wonder why we were suddenly so interested in this one specific vision. Which would have inevitably, at some point, led to them trying to determine if we were harboring an Augur ourselves," concluded Driscin grimly. "It's easy to say what we should have done in hindsight—but at the time, we'd have been risking too much to warn people about something that may not even have come about."

Davian exchanged a glance with Ishelle, then nodded reluctantly. Driscin had been truthful throughout, and he made some fair points. It was enough for now.

"I have one thing I'd like to ask before you go, too," said Driscin suddenly, eyes narrowing. "How many of my memories did you take?"

Davian winced. "Ah. Erran only removed those from when you met him, and our figuring out of the real plan," he quickly assured the older man. "You shielded everything else when he took those memories, so he wasn't able to Read you."

Driscin looked far from satisfied. "I find it difficult to believe that I would have agreed to that."

"It was your idea," said Davian firmly, ignoring the look of amusement from Ishelle that Driscin fortunately did not seem to notice. "It was the only way that we could think to get Ishelle to—"

"Fine," interrupted Driscin irritably, still not looking convinced but evidently resigning himself to believing the explanation. "Next time..."

He trailed off at the scratching of feet on stone from outside and glanced toward the door. "Did anyone see you come in here?" he asked in a low voice.

Davian shook his head. "I don't think so."

Before Driscin could reply, there was a sharp rap on the door. The Elder gave Davian a dark look, then waited expectantly; Davian stared back in puzzlement until Ishelle grabbed him silently by the arm, dragging him over to the corner and closing her eyes.

Driscin watched, then nodded in satisfaction and headed for the door as another knock came, the impatience in its rhythm unmistakable.

It took a second for Davian to realize what Ishelle was doing, but he released a slow breath once he did. She'd made them invisible. As long as neither of them made a sound, whomever had come calling on Driscin at this hour wouldn't know that they were there.

Driscin swung the door wide to reveal Elder Aliria, her expression dark. Beside her, a young man only a little older than Davian stood nervously, eyes darting around the inside of Driscin's study as if expecting to be attacked at any moment.

"I hear you have company, Driscin?" Aliria's voice was ice.

Driscin frowned at her, his puzzled expression looking totally natural. "What? No." Davian grimaced as a minor stab of pain shot through his temple, but he just squeezed his eyes shut for a moment, maintaining his motionless silence.

"I saw them go in." The young man, whom Davian vaguely recognized but could not name, had an insistent note to his voice. "It was only a couple of minutes ago, and it was definitely them. I'll swear to it."

"Where are they?" Aliria asked Driscin. There was anger in her tone, but something more, too. Something darker.

Driscin peered at the redheaded woman with a mildly confused expression on his face. "Who? I've been working on my report for the past hour or so." He gestured, looking vaguely indignant. "You can come in and see for yourself if you wish. It's right there on the table."

"He's lying," the young man spat. He pushed his way rudely past Driscin, Aliria quietly joining him inside. "They're still in here somewhere," he continued, scanning the room and starting to peer behind various pieces of furniture. Davian went stock-still, suddenly glad that Ishelle had dragged him against the wall. The Gifted never came within ten feet of them, though, focusing his efforts on the chairs and desk at the other end of the room. By the time he finally gave up—Driscin watching him with a mildly embarrassed expression—his cheeks were red.

"That's enough, Symin," said Aliria after a few long seconds of awkward silence. "Perhaps you were mistaken." She paused. "Or perhaps they have already left."

Symin scowled, but reluctantly made his way back outside. Aliria moved to follow him, then hesitated, lowering her voice.

"He saw someone come in here, Driscin," she said flatly. "He may be an idiot, but he's not delusional. If you are helping them..." The cold threat in her tone was unmistakable this time.

Driscin didn't let his gaze waver. "Fates, Aliria. I was affected by Rohin, too. Don't tell me that I'm going to have to put up with this every time someone walks past my door."

Aliria studied him. "The Augur escaping is still on your head," she eventually said grimly. "Don't expect to get much leeway anytime soon."

She gave him a final glare and shut the door.

Driscin leaned against the door frame after it was closed, releasing a long, soft breath. Then he glared around at where Davian and Ishelle had been, raising his hands to his lips. Davian almost chuckled at the incorrectly positioned look, but the meaning was clear enough. Driscin was ensuring that Aliria hadn't loitered.

Then he made a couple of gestures in the air, and Davian saw lines of Essence settling into the walls. He was Silencing the room.

It wouldn't last—only until the Essence decayed—but it meant that it was safe to finally make some noise. He released a breath with an audible sigh.

Driscin's head swivelled toward them, his eyes focusing as Ishelle dropped her invisibility.

Davian glanced at Ishelle, half expecting her to make a quip about Driscin's acting, but the young woman just nodded to the Elder. "Thanks," she said quietly. She looked across at Davian. "We shouldn't wait around."

Davian inclined his head, concurring. "Will you come north to help us, if the Council eventually allows it?" he asked Driscin.

Something passed between Driscin and Ishelle, though Davian wasn't sure what. Then Driscin nodded slowly.

"At some point," he conceded. "But while the Amnesty is in effect, I should stay here. If a new Augur showed up tomorrow..." He shook his head at the thought, then gestured to the door. "Go. Be careful on the way out, though—Aliria may have believed me, or she may not have. Either way, I doubt it will take long for her or one of the other Elders to decide that they need to watch my back door, as well as my front."

"Should we use our abilities this time, then?" asked Ishelle.

Driscin hesitated, then grimaced and shook his head. "No. Not unless you can get all the way to the passage without stopping," he said. "If they spot you walking around, that's one thing. But if someone sees you appear out of nowhere—with the way things are out there at the moment—you're likely to get a blast of Essence in the back before you know what's going on."

Both Augurs nodded reluctantly, then made their farewells and slipped out the door.

They hurried toward the main street, hoods up again, only to skid to a halt as they rounded the corner.

A dozen or so Gifted were gathered a little way down the street.

The woman at their front turned, her eyes lighting up when she saw them, evidently guessing who they were despite their concealed features.

"Hello, Augurs," spat Aliria.

Chapter 27

"I think they're onto us," murmured Ishelle as the entire group of Gifted turned to face them.

Davian gave her a half-amused, half-irritated look as he tried to quickly assess the situation. "Thoughts?"

"It's not like they can stop us," observed Ishelle softly, "but let's try to negotiate first." There was hesitation in her tone, a nervousness that was unlike her.

Aliria continued to stare furiously at them, and Davian shivered. "All right," he said dubiously.

They pulled back their hoods and walked toward the group, Davian doing his best not to look concerned. "Elder Aliria," said Ishelle gently. "Please. We just want to leave."

"Of course you do." Aliria's words dripped with naked hatred. "You *murder my husband*, and then you want to *leave*."

"That was Rohin," said Davian angrily. "We're not responsible for his actions."

"I'm not talking about what he did. I'm talking about what *she* did. Look at her," snarled Aliria, as the Gifted moved threateningly around the two Augurs. "She knows who's responsible."

Davian glanced at Ishelle, his heart dropping. The dark-haired girl was staring grimly at Aliria, but the blood had drained from her face.

"None of us are responsible for things done under Rohin's control," said Davian quickly, recovering himself. "*Nobody* had a choice in their actions while he was here."

"Except you," said the Elder, her eyes flashing. "*You* managed, but not *her.*" She shook her head. "You both need to come with me. The Council has requested that you stay in the Tol until they can determine *exactly* what happened—and the Amnesty doesn't allow you to leave without their permission. So I will use force if need be." Her expression said that she would be perfectly happy to do just that.

Davian shook his head. "I am sorry for what happened to Elder Dain," he said gently, "but—"

He cut off as Ishelle let out a cry next to him, a flash of white light accompanying her crumpling to the ground.

Davian immediately stepped out of the flow of time, spinning to see a baton glowing with Essence descending toward his own head. Two men had sneaked up behind them as Aliria had talked. Ishelle was still falling to the ground; Davian couldn't see any blood, but he didn't think that his friend was conscious.

He stepped to the side and swung an elbow, smashing his assailant in the cheek. The impact hurt even in the time bubble, and he knew from the way the man's face crumpled that he'd broken bones. Davian stepped over to the other Gifted and punched him in the stomach. The man was still beginning to double over, his weapon—clearly a Vessel of some kind—dropping, as Davian crouched beside Ishelle's form, quickly checking her injury. It was minor, he thought, and she was still breathing, but the impact had knocked her unconscious.

He released his hold on time.

There was a moment of utter silence, Aliria and the others gaping at them. Davian wasn't sure if they were shocked that attacking an Augur had worked, or that attacking two of them hadn't.

He felt his expression twisting. He'd put up with Aliria and the rest of the Gifted's disdain and mocking since he'd arrived, then had risked his life—risked *everything*—to help save them. Perhaps he hadn't expected to be showered in gratitude, but *this*?

This was too much.

He ripped some Essence from one of the men standing next to Aliria and used it to toss two others backward, letting them fly like rag dolls across the street and slam hard into the walls opposite. A half-dozen more Gifted sprang into action and tried to stop him with lines of Essence of their own, but Davian immediately, easily sliced through their efforts with a kan shield.

He stepped outside of time again, anger crystallizing his efforts. He walked into the middle of the crowd, using Essence-enhanced arms to grab them one by one and throw them as hard as he could away from Aliria. The nature of his altered passage through time meant that the force he used was exponentially magnified; Gifted flew through the air away from him until only Aliria herself was left.

He positioned himself back in front of the still-sneering Elder, then let time crash back into him. Behind him, beneath the crashing thuds of falling bodies, he could hear Ishelle groan as she began to stir.

Aliria took a faltering step back as she gazed around in horror at her moaning, defenseless support, but her lip curled as she turned back to Davian.

"If you're going to kill me," she said, face drained of blood, "just do it."

"Kill you?" Davian gave her a look of half-bewildered contempt, his rage still fresh. "Aliria, I'm *not. Going. To kill you.*" He said the words with as much frustrated emphasis as he could muster.

Then he looked around for the first time, the worst of his anger evaporating as he took in the carnage he'd just created. The Gifted—the ones still conscious—were groaning on the ground some twenty feet away, several of them looking as though they were nursing broken limbs. And Aliria was staring at him as if he were about to murder her, despite what he'd just said.

He swallowed. He'd been frustrated, true, and the attack had angered him—but when had he ever let his temper get the better of him like that? Not since he'd learned how to use his abilities, certainly.

He could have, and should have, just grabbed Ishelle and escaped. Aliria and the others here had been in the wrong, but their actions stemmed from the fear that Rohin had left them with.

Trying to teach them a lesson, after what they'd just been through, had not been the right choice.

He shook his head, taking a deep breath and forcing himself to calm. "I *am* sorry for what happened to your husband," he added more quietly, "but we are *not* responsible." He glanced across at Ishelle; the other Augur blinked up at him dazedly, then looked around at the destruction he'd caused with increasingly wide eyes.

"Fates," she muttered, voice rasping a little. "You certainly know how to negotiate."

Davian gave a small, slightly panicked laugh. "We should go before we have to do any more of it," he said.

Ishelle gave him a wry nod of acknowledgment, then allowed him to haul her to her feet.

As Aliria watched, Davian formed a new time bubble, and they headed for the passageway.

⁂

Erran and Fessi leaped to their feet as Davian staggered into the room, supporting Ishelle on one shoulder.

"What happened?" Erran exclaimed.

"Davian tried to talk his way past some of the Gifted," said Ishelle weakly.

Davian snorted, giving Fessi a nod of greeting as he eased Ishelle into one of the chairs. "The mood in the Tol...well, let's just say that we're leaving as soon as we can," he said drily. He glanced out the window at the night sky. "First thing in the morning. I don't think Driscin can give us much more of a head start than that."

"He's not coming with us?" asked Erran in surprise.

"He's going to try and bring the Council around. However long that will take." Davian cast a glance at Ishelle. "He gave us a signed letter of passage. I think that's all we can hope for, at least for a while. After what happened at the Tol tonight, I half expect the Council will say we've violated the Amnesty."

"No." Ishelle shook her head. "They won't make it public, no matter how furious they are. They won't admit to the Assembly that they don't have us under control."

"She's right," Erran agreed immediately. "Shen worked hard to get where they are. They're not about to throw that away." *She's definitely better?* came Erran's voice in Davian's head.

Definitely.

Erran relaxed somewhat, and he turned to Ishelle. "I'm Erran and this is Fessi, by the way."

Introductions were quickly made, and then Davian turned to Fessi.

"How's Rohin?" he asked quietly.

"Gagged, tied up, and still has the amulet on." Fessi's voice betrayed no hint of pity as she nodded to the adjoining door. "He's in there. What does Driscin want to do with him?"

"We're handing him over tonight." Davian frowned at Fessi's grimace. "What?"

"I'm not sure that's the best plan. I Read him." Fessi's tone was direct, no embarrassment at the fact. "He's met Scyner. I think he might have been sent here by him."

Davian blinked, taking a moment to process what she'd said.

"This prewar Augur from Ilin Illan?" Ishelle's voice contained more than a hint of skepticism. Davian had told her what Asha had told him, but Ishelle hadn't really believed it.

"Yes," said Erran. He met Ishelle's gaze steadily. "He killed our friend, and he manipulated his passage through time to do it. He *was* an Augur."

Ishelle blinked at the intense certainty of the statement, then inclined her head in acquiescence.

"You say he sent Rohin here?" Davian asked into the silence left by the exchange. "Why?"

Fessi's frustration was evident in her expression. "I'm not sure. The amulet makes him difficult to Read, and I only got flashes. But it was *definitely* him." Fessi's voice was harder and colder than even Erran's had been a moment ago. Davian believed her.

"Did you find out anything else?" asked Ishelle.

"Nothing that makes much sense. You're welcome to talk to him though." She gestured at the door.

"He's gagged?" Ishelle asked.

Fessi nodded, expression softening for the first time as she heard the nervousness in Ishelle's voice. "We didn't want to take any chances."

Ishelle nodded back, looking relieved and then...something else. She didn't say anything, but her eyes suddenly held the promise of violence.

Davian stood before Ishelle could move.

"Maybe it's best if I talk to him," he said quietly. "Even if the amulet somehow stops working, he can't influence me."

He walked to the door and opened it, staring into the dimly lit room beyond.

His stomach churned as he took in the Augur sitting hunched against the far wall.

Rohin had been a prisoner for only a couple of days, but he looked a shadow of his handsome, confident former self. Ugly bruises marred his face and arms, and the young man actually cringed farther back into his corner when he saw Davian's silhouette in the doorway.

Davian stared for a long few moments, then turned back to Fessi. "Did he try to escape? Give you trouble?"

Fessi just shook her head, never breaking eye contact with Davian.

Davian hesitated, then stepped inside, shaking his head as Ishelle made to follow.

"We need information," he said softly. "Not revenge."

Ishelle's eyes flashed. "I can control myself."

"He's still more likely to talk to me." Davian blocked Ishelle's path calmly. "Perhaps later."

Ishelle's frustration was evident but she eventually nodded sharply and stepped back, allowing Davian to shut the door.

The young man on the floor stirred, and Davian shivered as he turned. His eyes were haunted, hollow and unnaturally red. Not from tears, though. It was as if the very life was being sucked from him.

Davian reached down and carefully removed his gag.

"You," Rohin whispered, raising his hands to his neck, brushing helplessly against the golden device that had melded to his skin.

"Me." Davian crossed his arms. "Or would you prefer to spend more time with Fessi?"

"Please." Rohin's voice was hoarse, containing none of the silver it had the last time Davian had heard him speak. "Please no." There was genuine terror in his tone.

Davian swallowed the sudden bad taste in his mouth, walking forward to sit on the sole chair opposite Rohin. "If you help me, I'll stop her from coming back in here."

Rohin gave a mewling laugh, the sound edged with madness. "If I help? I thought you were the righteous one."

Davian stared at Rohin. "Fates. You are the last person who

should be talking about righteousness. Don't think that this isn't a measure of justice." He shook his head in disgust, though whether it was at Rohin or what had been done to the young man, he wasn't entirely sure. "Why did you go to Tol Shen? Was there something more to it than... what you did?"

Rohin gave a bitter laugh. "I was trying to save you."

There was dead silence as Davian looked blankly at the prisoner. "*What?*" he asked eventually, unable to keep the incredulity from his voice.

"You want to know why I came here?" Rohin's tone gained a hint of desperation. "I already told you. It's because I saw it. I saw what would happen at the Boundary." He met Davian's gaze. "Maybe you'd like me to tell you about what I was dreaming of *every night* before you put this thing on me. About the monsters that come from the north in their thousands. The way they tear through our cities. The blood and the screams and the uselessness of everything we do to try and stop them." His hands trembled. "They're like a wave, and we're a speck of sand on the beach. We're annihilated. *Annihilated.* The only way to avoid death is to avoid them. Do you understand?" His tone became pleading, and to Davian's shock there were tears in his eyes now. "I've *seen* it. I've seen the end of the world over and over and *over*, and I will never be able to get those images out of my head."

His red-rimmed eyes held Davian's gaze for a few long seconds, intense and full of conviction, before he dropped his head again.

Davian gaped at him in silence. He'd expected defiance, arrogance, maybe even penitence. Not this, though.

"So you didn't come here because of Scyner?" he asked eventually, not knowing how to respond to Rohin's claims.

Rohin shrugged, not looking up. "The old Augur? I can only tell you what I told your friend," he muttered. "He wasn't affected by my ability, and he suggested coming here. Said I'd be safer here." He gave a short, bitter laugh at that. "I should have stayed at Decis. It wasn't much, but at least everyone did what I asked. Fates know that it was better than this."

Davian grunted, his distaste for the young man reasserting itself. "The days of people doing as you 'ask' are over," he said grimly.

He probed further for a while, trying to elicit more responses   395 from Rohin, but the injured Augur had evidently decided that he'd said enough. Eventually Davian shook his head in disgust and left, shutting the door firmly behind him and ordering his thoughts as he turned to the other three, who were watching him expectantly.

"He says he's Seen the Boundary being overrun," said Davian absently to their questioning looks, still trying to sort through his feelings. "Says he was trying to 'save' us."

"We should kill him."

Davian paused for a moment, sure he wasn't hearing correctly. He turned to stare at Ishelle, who had uttered the words. "What?"

"You heard me." Ishelle's expression, for once, held nothing but ice. "The Gifted can't be trusted with him. What if his influence is still lingering for some people? What if someone is careless and he escapes? Or—and trust me, this will be suggested at some point by someone in the Council—what if they decide that they can *use* him?"

Davian shook his head slowly. "No." Ishelle opened her mouth to protest, but he cut her off before she could say anything. "*No.*" He wasn't going down that road.

"Are you willing to take the blame for anything he does if he gets loose again?" asked Ishelle angrily.

"So you want to kill him because it's expedient," Davian responded bluntly.

Ishelle flushed. "It would be safest."

"So would killing everyone who opposed us. Everyone who stood in our way. Or Controlling them," observed Davian. "Why don't we just do that?" He almost laughed at the nervous shuffle from Erran in the corner, but the situation was too tense to show any mirth.

He turned to Fessi. "And *you*," he said coldly. "You tortured him."

"He had information on—"

"*I don't care.*" Davian let heat into his voice now. "We have to be *better* than this. Don't you see? The way that the Gifted have been treating us, the way everyone fears us, is *justified* if we take this path."

396   "You can't speak to us like that," said Erran angrily.

"Can't I?" Davian turned on the other young man. "You think you're above hearing hard truths about yourselves? Or don't you care about your friend? Don't you care that she's doing this?"

"And do you think you're so much better?"

"I'm NOT!" Davian shouted. "I've *killed* people, Erran. But where does it stop? What gives us the right to act this way? Our abilities?" He was abruptly reminded of a similar conversation with Wirr, what felt like a lifetime ago now. "We can't start mistaking what we *can* do for what we have the *right* to do." He scowled at the others and took a deep breath, calming a little even as he shook his head in disgust. "It's three against one, clearly— so I suppose I couldn't stop you from becoming murderers, if you were absolutely bent on it. But think on what I've said. Fates, please think on it hard."

He left, hands shaking slightly as he shut the door behind him. Had he gone too far? They all needed to work together if they were going to seal the Boundary... and yet, he knew he couldn't have let what was being suggested, nor what had happened to Rohin, go without remonstration. Rohin was a monster, but Davian wasn't going to let him turn the rest of them into monsters as well.

Suddenly exhausted, he made his way to one of the other small rooms that they'd rented and lay back on his bed, closing his eyes for a moment and trying to ease the pounding frustration in his head.

Eventually, despite having no intent to do so, he slept.

Davian shrugged away the scaled hand of the dar'gaithin as it marched him forward, the pathway ahead glinting where the soot from the low-burning torches did not fall.

"You fear this less than you should," the creature observed.

"Funny," responded Davian quietly. "I was about to say the same to you."

Internally, he frowned. It was his voice, but there was a disconnect. He hadn't consciously said those words.

He kicked at the metal underfoot as he walked. "Why here, Theshesseth? Darkstone everywhere in this cursed city, but in 397 these hallways, metal that never rusts. To what purpose?" Again, that strange disconnect—evident while walking, but even more so when he spoke. He felt oddly queasy, disoriented. It was hard to focus, but he slowly registered that he was somehow a passenger in his own head.

The creature rasped, and Davian realized that it was laughing. "Your time in the Mines has not sated your curiosity?"

Davian didn't respond, just stared at the creature levelly. The rasping faded, and the snake did not say anything for a moment. Trapped inside his own head, Davian watched its sinuous, swaying movement with horrified fascination.

"I do not know," it hissed eventually, reluctance saturating its voice.

They walked on in silence. The walls gleamed where they were not coated with grime or, occasionally, dried blood. He glanced over his shoulder, observing with curiosity the line of clear steel that the dar'gaithin's tail left behind them. Its movement along the metal surface created a constant scratching, grinding sound, heavy scale against metal. This place had definitely not been built with these creatures in mind.

Eventually they began climbing a long set of winding stairs; before long the flickering light of torches gave way to smooth Essence, and the metal underfoot became increasingly clean. By the time they reached the top—a good ten minutes of walking, though to Davian's surprise he didn't seem to find it much of an exertion—every surface was shining. Spotless.

"You really need to tell whoever cleans up here about those stairs," he said to Theshesseth, sounding relaxed. "It's much nicer up here."

The creature gave him another glance, this time clearly in irritation. Davian watched him curiously.

Then he understood.

This, here, was a vision of something that would happen to him. Which meant that his confidence when this actually occurred was likely coming from knowing what was up ahead.

Theshesseth opened a large pair of doors and Davian, unbidden, strolled into the room beyond.

The chamber was dazzling. Walls, floor, and roof were made of finely cut, intersecting pieces of steel, with lines of blue Essence pulsing and flowing in the minute spaces between. The pieces of the floor in front of him rippled as he walked forward, presenting him with a smooth path to the center of the room, though sloping upward at the sides so that he could not easily change course.

Davian walked forward nonchalantly, observing the dozen others already in the room, ignoring the prickling sensation that came from turning his back on the dar'gaithin. The twelve rose as one as he entered, inclining their heads in unsettling symphony as he came to a halt in the center of the room.

Davian gave them a tight smile. "Gassandrids," he said in mock greeting.

The dozen faces staring back at him did not move even a fraction in response to his jest.

"Time has passed, Davian," said a woman on the left.

"We had hoped it would give you the chance to reflect," said a gray-haired man to the right.

"The chance to reconsider." The child standing in the middle. Her brown hair came down to her waist. She couldn't have been older than ten.

Davian yawned and stretched his arms in front of him, idly observing the veins as they stood out starkly against muscle. "Reconsider what?"

"You know of what we speak." Another man, this time younger, dark eyes flashing as he spoke. "Do not treat this meeting lightly, Davian. We will send you back."

"We have told you what is at stake," said the woman who had first spoken.

"When the lines were drawn, you stood on the side of Shammaeloth," intoned a woman to the right.

"You fought for slavery."

"You fought for tyranny."

"You fought for destruction." The final speaker, a distinguished-looking older woman, gazed at him unblinkingly. "We gave you the opportunity to do what is right."

Davian said nothing for a few moments, staring around at the various faces.

"Is there any order?" he asked suddenly.

Silence for a few seconds.

"Order?" It was the small child again, tone puzzled.

"When you speak." Davian rubbed his chin. "I can't figure it out. Are you choosing people at random? I mean, what about this fellow over here? He's said nothing the entire—"

He grunted as a blunt force smashed across the back of his shoulders, forcing him to his knees.

"Impertinence, we can ignore. Waste our time again, though, and you will be punished," said one of the men.

Davian growled, the throbbing pain of the blow something he knew would last for some time. From the corner of his vision, he could see Theshesseth giving him a suspiciously satisfied look. "I keep telling you. I don't know who she is," he snarled to the group. "I never had any contact with this 'Shadraehin.' I can't tell you what she looks like, or sounds like, or smells like, or..." He stuttered back to his feet. "You see what I'm saying?"

"We know," said the old woman standing next to the child. "We also know that you know those who can tell."

"You're talking about Asha?" Davian could hear amusement in his voice. "Isn't that the entire reason you want the Shadraehin, though? So that she can tell you where Asha is?" He shook his head. "I'm confused. So you want me to find Asha so that she can tell you what the Shadraehin looks like, so that you can find the Shadraehin in order to make her tell you where Asha is?" Davian sighed. "I think you're making that process needlessly complicated. Possibly some circular logic in there. You really need to—"

Another blow, this one even harder than the first. Davian groaned, shaking his head to rid himself of the black spots dancing in his vision.

"You can go back." A woman to his left was speaking now. "To a time when you know where she is. A time when she would not be so guarded."

Davian took a few moments more to recover, then raised an eyebrow. "Unless something's happened to the Boundary— ilshara, whatever you want to call it—I'm not entirely sure how you expect to get me to Deilannis," he said weakly.

"We can send you back from here."

"Here?" Davian barked a laugh. "When you split up that mind of yours, Gassandrid, I think you forgot part of it."

The man nearest to him moved with blinding speed; before Davian could react he was being slammed up against a glimmering steel wall that had risen from the ground for exactly that purpose.

"It can be done. Little is impossible for the dead," whispered the man. His breath smelled of rotting meat, and up close, Davian could see that his eyes were hollow. Empty.

"I'm sure that's comforting to your puppet here," choked Davian.

The man growled, releasing Davian and letting him slide back to his feet. "You will go back to Ashalia Chaedris. You will mark her; physical contact will echo across time, and the sha'teth will find her."

Davian snorted. "Even saying that I believe that's possible. Which I don't," he added firmly. "There is nothing you can threaten me with. I know you cannot kill me."

"Cannot?" Though the child in the center spoke, all twelve arrayed before him smiled, at the exact same moment and in the exact same empty, joyless manner. "Your head will be on a pike soon enough. Do not mistake prudence for inability, traitor."

"Let's find out if that's true, then," murmured Davian.

Everything slowed.

Davian—inside his own head—observed in astonishment. He hadn't simply tweaked his passage through time. This was akin to Fessi's ability: everything around him was all but motionless, frozen.

Davian spun, grabbing a long scale from Theshesseth's neck and ripping it out in one smooth motion, an odd popping sound as he did so. He moved quickly around the front of the dar'gaithin and coldly, clinically, stabbed the creature in the eye.

Time was moving so slowly that black blood from the wound was only just beginning to seep outward when Davian turned, focusing on the men and women arrayed in front of him. The steel floor was inclined at an impossible angle, but Davian turned to the leftmost man, draining him of Essence in an instant and then going to one knee, slamming his hand against the cold metal plate. Lines of blue shot out from where he touched it; as *the Essence drained away, suddenly the metal plates forming the incline began to shift—relatively slowly, though he knew that they had to have been moving incredibly fast for everyone else.*

The floor beneath the eleven—the twelfth was now a pile of dust—dropped away, leveling out with the steel that he was standing on. Moments later, concern and shock registered on everyone's faces as they began to fall.

Then something changed. Though time evidently still flowed around him—the geyser of black blood continued to creep its way out of Theshesseth's face—the others in the room were suddenly moving faster. Still not as fast as Davian, but close.

Several landed, catlike, on their feet, but the rest were unbalanced enough to stumble and slip to the floor. Davian dove forward before they could recover, slashing left and right with the dar'gaithin scale. Bright red blood appeared on each neck that he cut, the scale razor-sharp everywhere but the dripping black root where he held it. The acid burned his hand, but he ignored it.

A redheaded man—one of the ones who had landed on his feet—sprang at him from the left. Davian moved to the side and caught the assailant by his left arm, spinning and hurling him with all his strength. The arm that he was gripping snapped, the extra force of Davian's relative passage through time—plus, apparently, the increased strength of his muscular arms—doing the damage. The man flew gracelessly through the air, tangling with an older woman before colliding hard with a steel wall and sliding to the ground in a heap.

Davian snatched more Essence and slammed his palm into the ground again; the floor rippled once more, snapping upward beneath the feet of a man and a woman rushing toward him. He watched in horror as the plates kept rising after the two had lost their balance, pressing them against the roof with incredible force.

There was an unpleasant squelching sound. When the steel floor lowered again, only bright red viscera remained.

He turned to face his next opponent, only to hesitate.

The young girl stood in front of him after having finally regained her footing, eyes wide as she watched him.

The hesitation was evidently all Gassandrid needed. Without warning, the floor beneath Davian twisted; he tripped as chains emerged from the steel, rising up and wrapping around his torso. They burned; immediately Davian's sense of Essence was lost. He roared, trying to free himself, but his restraints were too strong. Too thick.

The moment he realized, he forced calmness upon himself. Closed his eyes. Breathed.

Let time wash over him again.

There was utter silence for a few moments.

"Wonderful!" The redheaded man who had been thrown to the far side of the room stood, straightening his misshapen arm with a slight grimace. There was a flash of Essence and he flexed his fingers, the break healed. "Your progress is impressive. Better than I could have dreamed."

Davian kept his face smooth, not rising to the bait. "I'm glad you approve."

The child in front of him brushed her clothes, though there was no dust in here, no grime to speak of at all. "Tomorrow, Davian. Tomorrow you will go back and you will meet with Ashalia Chaedris." She placed a hand against one of the steel plates; it pulsed with blue light for a moment and then part of the wall slid aside, revealing another doorway.

"Aniria. Please escort our friend to his new accommodations and then clean this up," she said, satisfaction in her tone.

Aniria—a slave girl from the looks of it, a stunning young woman wearing an embarrassingly small amount of clothes— entered the room with head bowed. Her surrounds, evidently, were not unusual enough to throw her. "Of course, Lord Gassandrid."

She took Davian's bloodied hand, ignoring the dar'gaithin scale in the other, and calmly led him to the exit.

"That must have been quite a performance," she murmured once they were through. "But I have to admit, I am curious. Why the charade? Why allow them to send you back?"

"Because you said that you owed me nothing," Davian replied softly. "But I don't believe that is true anymore. My name—my real name—is Davian."

He glanced over his shoulder.

"Now figure out a way to get me out of here, Nethgalla."

Davian groaned as he woke.

It had been a vision, not a dream; he knew that from the moment he opened his eyes. He frowned, trying to commit as many details as possible to memory, even as he puzzled over the fact that it had happened. He hadn't had even a glimpse of the future since Deilannis—not since Malshash had repressed the ability. Why now? What had changed?

He lay there for a few more moments, thinking. Driscin had said that the vault entrance was supposed to remove all influences from someone's mind. Could that have been it?

The sound that had woken him—a knock at the door—came again. Remembering how he'd left things with the others, Davian grimaced, then swung to his feet and opened it.

All three of the other Augurs were waiting outside.

Davian frowned at them. "I still haven't changed my mind since—"

"You were right." Ishelle said the words bluntly, but she was clearly speaking for all three of them. "We had a long talk about everything, and..." She gestured irritably. "You're right." Davian raised an eyebrow at her, and she scowled back at him.

Davian repressed a smile but nodded; it was as close to an apology as he was going to get from Ishelle. He glanced at the other two, seeing contrition in their eyes. Or Erran's, at least. Fessi was staring at the ground, but whether it was from remorse or something else, he couldn't tell.

"Then we're all agreed?" he asked quietly. "Rohin goes to the Tol tonight, and we leave tomorrow?"

The other three nodded.

Davian breathed out, unable to contain his relief. He wasn't sure *what* he would have done, had the others chosen otherwise...but he didn't need to worry about that now.

He smiled, even the darkness of his vision temporarily receding as they began to talk about organizing horses, provisions, and everything else that they would need for the journey.

It was finally happening. They were going to the Boundary.

Chapter 28

Wirr shook his head as he watched Asha pack.

"I don't think you should go," he said quietly. "It's too dangerous."

Asha paused just long enough to roll her eyes at him, then continued her task. "I'm going, Wirr," she said firmly. She brandished the Veil at him. "I can look after myself."

"You can't use that in Deilannis," pointed out Wirr.

Asha shrugged. "Then I'll need to use my wits to survive, just like everyone else."

"So dangerous," said Wirr immediately, shaking his head solemnly. "So, *so* dangerous."

He ducked as Asha threw her cloak at him, giving her a grin. It faded quickly, though. "You haven't been there, Ash," he said gently. "If you had, you wouldn't want to go. Let me ask Master Kardai or one of the Gifted to find the information you're looking for. They'll be willing, I'm sure."

"I have to go myself." Asha had made up her mind. "They're trying to find ways to seal the Boundary, maybe a weapon to use against whatever's coming... and from what you and Davian told me, the longer that they stay there, the more dangerous it will be. They're not going to waste their time researching the Shadows for me." Not to mention that she had no desire to reveal her dizzy spells to either Master Kardai or Wirr.

Besides, she'd already told Wirr about what she'd been through over the past few days. He knew as well as she did that there were too many unanswered questions. That, combined with the

Assembly still preventing her from openly looking into anything to do with the Shadows, meant that ignoring this opportunity would have been foolish.

She sighed at Wirr's still-unhappy expression. She appreciated her friend's concern, but she also felt that she understood the dangers well enough. Taeris hadn't been thrilled with the idea of her going to Deilannis, either, though his argument had at least held more weight—that it made it difficult to justify her position as Representative when she decided to leave the city for such long periods.

Even so, her mind was made up. She was getting increasingly concerned about whatever was happening to her and the other Shadows; that, along with what she'd seen in the catacombs... she couldn't just let it lie. There was too much going on that none of them understood.

"At least let me go through more of my father's notebook before you leave," said Wirr. "What if it has the answers you're looking for?"

Asha shook her head. "I hope it does, Wirr, but it will still be here when we get back. The party heading to Deilannis leaves at noon. This is my only opportunity."

Wirr growled, evidently frustrated, but before he could continue arguing there was a quiet knock at the door. Asha looked up, surprised to see the princess standing at the entrance to her rooms.

"Princess Karaliene," said Asha, dipping her head formally. "What can I do for you?"

Karaliene walked in, shutting the door behind her and cheerfully waving away the show of respect. She knew that Asha was a friend of Wirr's, and had spoken informally to her a number of times. "No need for proprieties, Ashalia. Actually, I'm mostly here to speak with Torin before I leave, but it's convenient that you're here as well." She turned to Wirr. "Have you told her about your...guest?"

Wirr nodded; Breshada's appearance had been something that he and Asha had discussed at length that morning. "She knows." Then he peered at his cousin. "Wait. You're going somewhere?"

"North—not as far as the Boundary, but visiting some of the

areas affected by the Blind. Father's reputation isn't all it could be up there right now, and it's important for them to see that we're—" She stopped as Wirr suddenly held up his hand, frowning across at Asha.

"Are you all right, Ash?" he asked.

Asha waved her hand at him, indicating that she was fine. Another bout of dizziness, though this one at least felt less severe than previously. She shook her head to clear it.

"Just tired," she said with a frown. She looked up, giving a reassuring smile to both Wirr and Karaliene's concerned expressions. "A little light-headed. I'll be fine." She turned to Karaliene. "Sorry. You were saying?"

Karaliene studied her worriedly for a few more seconds, then nodded. "I'm leaving for a while," she summarized to Wirr, brushing a strand of flaxen hair back from her face. "But the reason I'm here is actually Ashalia's upcoming journey. It occurred to me that perhaps one more could be accommodated in her group."

Asha and Wirr both stared at her blankly for a moment. Then Wirr's brow furrowed as he understood.

"Oh. No," he said slowly. "That won't work."

"Why not? Weren't you saying just yesterday how hard it was to find Gifted who might be willing to help? The Representative here may not *technically* be Gifted, but I'm assuming she has a requisite knowledge of the basics." Karaliene shrugged. "Besides, there are already too many who know that Breshada is here, and Ambassador Thurin's people are good at their jobs. If you don't get her out of the city, it's only a matter of time before he finds her."

Asha hesitated as she saw what Karaliene was getting at.

"She's right," she said reluctantly, still trying to blink away the dizziness from earlier. She didn't like the idea—not even slightly—but she could immediately see why Karaliene had suggested it. "It doesn't sound like Breshada wants to learn anything complex, so I can certainly teach her. And we're all going to be armed, so if she has a red cloak, there's no reason she'd stand out." She nodded slowly. "Besides, Taeris has been struggling to find people willing to go to Deilannis. It's not as if she'd be taking someone's place."

Wirr scowled at the ground for a few moments, evidently trying to think of a reason why the plan wouldn't work. "I'm not sure it's a great idea to send her *closer* to Desriel."

"She'll still be safer than in the city," pointed out Karaliene. "And as a rather big bonus, not directly connected to us."

"And she won't actually try to hurt us," added Asha, the statement a half-question.

Wirr shook his head slowly. "No. She gave her word. For a Hunter, that's like being bound by the Tenets."

"It would give us more of a chance to find out about whomever it was that gave her that sword, too. Whether it was Caeden, or if there's some other link that we haven't put together yet," added Asha. Wirr had spotted the connection with the name Tal'kamar as soon as Asha had told him of her recent conversation with Taeris.

There was silence for a few seconds as Wirr thought. Eventually, he sighed.

"Very well," he said with a reluctant nod to Karaliene. He turned back to Asha.

"Time to see if she's amenable to a journey, then."

Asha glanced around the alley, but nobody passing by in the nearby street was paying her any attention.

She took a deep breath, glad that the dizziness of earlier had passed. She would have to go and visit Brase once again before leaving, see whether he or any of the other Shadows had experienced the same thing. For now, though, she was glad to have a clear head for the slightly unnerving task at hand.

This section of the Upper District was not yet fully rebuilt, and most of the crowd were workers going about their business, too focused to worry about someone entering a building that was structurally sound but abandoned. She used the key Wirr had given her and unlocked the side door to the Administration building, slipping inside and shutting it quickly.

She turned to find a knife pointed at her throat.

"Breshada, I presume?" said Asha carefully, ignoring the sudden pounding of her heart and cautiously raising her hand, pushing the blade away from her face even as she held up the key that she'd used. She met the gaze of the dark-haired woman behind the knife. "Prince Torin sent me. It was too risky for him to come personally at this hour."

Breshada scowled at her, lowering the dagger but clearly keeping it at the ready. "And how can I trust that is true?"

"You saved he and Davian at Talmiel, though you didn't know he was the prince at the time. You killed two Hunters to do it. Then you saw him speaking to the ambassador and followed him to his parents' estate, where—"

"Enough." Breshada sheathed the blade. "Your point is made, servant. What is it that you want?"

"I'm not a servant, and you need to get ready to leave." Asha kept her voice smooth and calm, despite Breshada's tone. "There's an expedition leaving the city at noon, and we're going to be a part of it." She reached into her satchel and tossed Breshada the red cloak that she'd brought.

Breshada caught the garment, frowning at it with clear distaste.

"This is not what was agreed," she said slowly.

"You'll be a lot safer on the road than here. There are no Administrators coming with us, and we'll be passing mainly through areas that were affected by the invasion. Nobody's going to bother looking at us twice."

"I came here to learn how to stop myself from using Essence," growled Breshada. "Will a teacher be accompanying us?"

"I'll be teaching you."

Breshada stared at her blankly for a long moment, as if not understanding the words.

"You are a Shadow. You are..." She gestured dismissively. "No. I do not see how this will be of any assistance."

Asha felt her jaw clench, but she breathed out. "You don't want to use Essence, so you don't need a sparring partner—just the theory, which I've already learned. I know more than enough for your purposes."

The former Hunter stared at her stonily. "And if I refuse?"

"Then I am unsure how much longer Prince Torin's protection will be extended to you," said Asha impatiently.

She regretted the words immediately, inwardly remonstrating

with herself for her loose tongue as Breshada's eyes went wide with anger and her hand moved to grasp Whisper's hilt. No matter the vows Breshada had given Wirr, the woman was still a murderer.

There was a sudden, odd hush as the Hunter smoothly drew the long blade.

Asha kept her breathing steady as she slipped her hand into her pocket, touching the Veil there. She didn't activate it yet, though. No need to give away that particular advantage unless it was absolutely necessary.

Breshada, though, had frozen. Rather than following through on her aggression, she was just...staring at Asha.

Then, to Asha's astonishment, she paled.

Slowly slid the blade back into its sheath.

There was silence for a few moments as the two women stared at each other, Asha blankly, Breshada looking suddenly uncertain.

"You have the mark of Marut Jha Andral," she eventually said softly. "You have held one of the Blades."

Asha blinked at her. "I don't know what you're talking about," she said cautiously, relieved to find that her voice was calm and steady. "But can I take it that you're not about to attack me, now?"

"Attack you? Bah." Breshada waved away the suggestion dismissively, though her eyes never left Asha's face. "You *do* have His mark, though. The sigil of a bear, plain on your forehead, visible the moment I drew Whisper. There was no mistaking it." She shook her head, then abruptly sat, gesturing for Asha to do so as well.

Asha felt her frown deepen but she accepted the offer, positioning herself opposite Breshada. Whatever the woman had seen, she'd evidently decided to accept Asha's presence.

"The mark of Andral means that you have wielded one of the Blades." Breshada sighed when she saw Asha's blank expression. "The five Blades, forged by the God of Invention himself? Of these, Whisper is one. The others are Thief, Knowing, Sight, and Fate."

Asha went cold. She'd never heard this legend before—unsurprising, as it was clearly part of the Desrielite religion—but she did recognize one name.

"Knowing?"

"As Whisper takes life, Knowing takes the mind." Breshada cocked her head to the side. "Was he the blade you wielded?"

Asha licked her lips. Isiliar had used the word, she was certain.

And it could explain how Asha had known the way out of the catacombs. Maybe the intense, strange dream she'd had, too.

"It doesn't matter," she eventually said softly.

Even as she said the words, though, she suddenly made another connection.

The names she'd heard in the catacombs—Isiliar, Alaris, Meldier, Wereth, Andrael, Tal'kamar. They weren't *quite* the same, but...she knew why they had been so familiar now.

Isil. Alarius. Meldier. Werek. Andral. Talkanor. All names from the Gil'shar pantheon.

All names of Desriel's Nine Gods.

"If you do not wish to speak of it, then so be it." Breshada hadn't noticed Asha's stunned expression. "Nonetheless. Perhaps you will be an acceptable teacher after all."

Asha shook her head, focusing on the other woman again. "Then...you'll come?" She wasn't sure what the similarity in the names meant—if anything—but for now, it didn't matter. If the sigil Breshada had seen was enough to make her receptive to the journey, then that was enough.

"I will come." Breshada said the words magnanimously. "Where are we going?"

"Deilannis."

Breshada cocked her head to the side. "Deilannis?" she repeated. She laughed softly. "Perhaps I accepted too soon. It is death to go there."

"Prince Torin traveled through it just fine."

There was silence. "And I have few options," Breshada eventually added softly, saying what she knew Asha had been thinking. She nodded slowly. "So be it."

"Good." Asha did her best not to show her relief. "Meet us on the north road, out of sight of the Shields. It will probably be late afternoon when we arrive. There will be a half dozen of us, but only a couple will know who you are." She hesitated. "So make sure you wear the cloak."

Breshada's lip curled and she looked as if Asha had just forced acid down her throat, but she nodded again.

"Then I will see you on the north road, Ashalia."

She stood, indicating that the conversation was at an end, and Asha gladly made for the door. Breshada's aggression seemed to have vanished, but Asha was no less uneasy about being alone with her.

She finally allowed herself to relax a little again as she left the Administration building, rejoining the flow of city traffic with no one giving her a second glance.

There was only one more stop to make before she left.

Brase brightened as Asha walked into the library.

"I was beginning to wonder if you'd forgotten about me," he said cheerfully.

Asha smiled back. "I can't stay for long. I'm leaving on a trip in less than an hour," she said. "I just came to find out whether you had any...incidents, this morning."

Brase's smile faded. "This morning? No," he said slowly. "And I was with the others sorting books for most of it. I don't think either of them felt anything, either." He looked at her, concern on his face. "What happened?"

"I'm not sure." Asha sighed. "I'm using the 'I'm just tired' excuse so much, sometimes I forget it's actually possible that I could be too tired." She chewed her lip thoughtfully. Even as she said the words, she didn't really believe it. She'd slept well enough the previous night, and her bout of dizziness had felt suspiciously like the other times, if somewhat less severe.

Brase grunted. "Are you sure you should be traveling, then?" He hesitated. "Perhaps you should have someone who knows what's going on along for the journey...?"

Asha gave him a rueful smile. "Thanks, Brase, but Deilannis isn't somewhere I want to drag anyone who doesn't need to be there. It will be dangerous, and even if I thought I could arrange it somehow, I couldn't do that to you—"

"I was actually talking about Reubin," interrupted Brase, nodding toward the dolorous Shadow trudging slowly between shelves on the other side of the large room. "And you *know* he's always up for danger."

Asha couldn't help but cough a laugh, the sound loud in the quiet of the library. She shook her head, flushing slightly at some of the irritated looks from Gifted studying along the wall. "Try and keep track of when it happens while I'm gone," she said quietly once she'd sobered again. "I'll do the same. I'm curious to see whether distance or location makes any difference."

They spoke for a few brief minutes longer, but soon enough Asha was making her apologies, hurrying from Tol Athian again before she ran into one of the Council or another Elder who would try to waylay her.

She breathed a sigh of relief as she emerged back into the Upper District, then headed straight for the palace.

It was time to leave.

Chapter 29

Wirr settled down at his desk with a sigh, flipping open the hefty notebook to where he'd left off.

After seeing Asha off on her journey, he had only an hour before his next appointment. Even so, he forced himself to spend the first half of that wading through more of the crimes committed by the Gifted, unwilling to risk his missing something important. His father had investigated thoroughly, and had spared no detail in his recording of evidence and eyewitness accounts. Wirr didn't recognize any of the names of the accused, but he could feel his father's frustration and anger emanating off the pages.

He could understand it, too. The injustices Elocien described were utterly horrific, unthinkable... and yet for every one, there was copious amounts of evidence to show that it had actually occurred.

Finally, he came to what appeared to be the end of the list. Exhaling with relief—reading through those pages had been draining—he moved on to Elocien's next page of notes.

> *By now, you will understand why you decided to make this stand against the Augurs—but doubtless are also wondering how such a thing could be possible. For several months, though I quietly searched for a solution, I wondered much the same thing.*
>
> *I was traveling through the Middle District three months ago when a young blond-haired woman,*

very beautiful, somehow slipped past my retinue and caught my arm, claiming that she could help me. At first I took her for a commoner out for her own gain, and demanded that she leave. But she then said that she wished to speak of my efforts against the Gifted.

Worried that others may overhear, and wondering how she could know such a thing, I quickly arranged for her to meet me back at the palace, where Kevran and I had a conversation with her inside a Lockroom. During that conversation, she claimed to have a means for us to fight against the Gifted—a way to nullify their powers. Ancient Vessels from a time long past.

Kevran was skeptical, but there was something in the way the woman spoke that convinced me to pursue the matter. She was articulate, calm, certain that the devices she was offering would enable us to succeed in our purpose. She refused to say how she had obtained them, though, or to explain how she could possibly have been able to come by them in such large quantities. In fact, she refused to give us even a name. This caused us no end of misgivings, but we also knew that if either the Augurs or Gifted had any suspicions about us, they would simply have organized for us to be Read. Given that, logic dictated that this was not a trap, so we chose to proceed.

We wondered at the time—and still do, for answers have not been forthcoming—if the woman is from Desriel, perhaps even an agent of the Gil'shar. They have ever been wary of the Gifted's power here, though they fear to challenge it. And there have often been rumors of such devices being stored within their sacred treasuries—enough to prevent the Assembly from ever doing more than verbally condemning the extreme attitudes of their religion.

Wirr's heart leaped, and he scanned ahead as his father went further into his own conjecture over whom the woman might have been. Elocien seemed focused largely on Andarra's enemies—Desriel, Nesk, even the Eastern Empire—but there was no mention of the Boundary or anything about the north. Elocien and Kevran had apparently tried to have the mysterious woman followed—several times—but without any success.

Wirr skimmed forward a page.

Our first offering of proof finally came almost a month after that first encounter. When we walked into the room in which the meeting was set, I immediately feared that we had been betrayed; three Gifted sat against the wall, two of whom I knew by name— Amin and Cirea, both powerful men. Though they were bound with rope, I also knew from experience that such simple restraints would be no match for them once they decided to be free.

The woman was waiting, as always, liking to arrive well before the arranged time. Kevran immediately began questioning her about the prisoners, and though he remained outwardly calm, I knew that he was panicking as much as I.

Yet despite our concerns, the woman was relaxed. She walked over to Amin and pulled back his left sleeve. To my astonishment, his entire forearm was encased in black metal—perfectly molded to the arm. Amin appeared to be in no extra discomfort due to the casing, despite his emotional state evidently swinging between terrified and furious. He recognized both Kevran and I at once, of course, and as soon as his gag was removed, demanded his release. The consequences he cited were beyond severe; truth be told, so accustomed was I to deferring to his kind, I almost complied.

Yet after weathering the worst of his verbal barrage, I came to realize something: that the words were empty, spouted by a man whose impotence was evidenced by his lack of action. The woman, after gagging her captive once again, explained calmly that the devices covering the men's wrists were called Shackles. Whilst they remained attached, the Gifted's abilities were rendered inert.

To prove her point—much to my and Kevran's dismay—she proceeded to demonstrate this truth by repeatedly slapping Cirea in the face. When I asked her to stop, she did so, but her point had been well made. Cirea was distressed, shamed, furious—but unable to react.

The woman went on to explain how these devices functioned, as well as to provide some of their history. She claimed that they were of High Darecian design, originally intended to be worn around the neck; however, she also stated that placing them on the neck, while working similarly under most circumstances, could be unreliable on some individuals. She strongly urged us to use Shackles only on the wrists of the Gifted. This would unfailingly cause what she called a "contract" to be formed—which in turn meant that only the one who applied the Shackle could then remove it.

When the woman announced that she had thousands of these devices, both Kevran and I were immediately skeptical. But she promised to show us where they were stored, as well as to demonstrate other, similarly powerful weapons to which she could give us access.

In the excitement of seeing the potential of what she was proposing, it was only when it was time to leave that it occurred to me that the three Gifted still captive were a problem. When I raised the issue, the woman had a simple solution.

She drew a knife from her belt and before Kevran or I could stop her, she had slit all three Gifted's throats, apparently immune to their muffled, fearful whimpering.

That image still haunts me, as I know it does Kevran. I have seen executions before, but not like this— and especially not the deaths of Gifted. So be aware that while your cause is just, this is very much what *you have in store for the future. It was disturbing, and brought home the reality of what we were talking about in a way that had never truly hit me before.*

It was also, I realize now, the tipping point. From that moment, neither Kevran nor I could turn back. We were complicit in the murders of—

Wirr flinched as a massive crash echoed from somewhere outside his room.

He sat up straight, wide-eyed, staring around as small puffs of dust drifted down from the roof. Then he pushed back his chair and made to stand, only to grip the side of his desk as another thunderous roar split the air.

It hadn't been his imagination. The entire building was shaking.

Hurriedly stuffing the notebook into a drawer and slipping the Oathstone into his pocket, he dashed for the door as faint screams began to reach his ears. In the hallway outside, various servants and members of the nobility were staring around in confusion, flinching at each new tremor, evidently with as little idea of what was happening as Wirr.

"Sire!" Andyn's expression was tense as he spotted Wirr, breaking away from his urgent questioning of a passer-by.

"What's going on?"

"I don't know." Andyn flinched at another crash. "But may I suggest that we don't find out?"

More screams sounded, these ones clearly from toward the front of the palace. There was a woman's voice shouting something at intermittent intervals, too—louder than any of the other cries that Wirr could hear, amplified somehow—but the words were muffled, disjointed.

Wirr hesitated, then shook his head. "Sorry, Andyn."

With a gesture for the other man to follow, he set off at a dead run toward the disturbance.

The hallways were filled with people now, some just milling about anxiously, others sprinting in the opposite direction of Wirr and covered in a layer of what appeared to be white grime. Wirr yelled at those running to stop, to tell him what was going on, but they barely seemed to even register his presence. To a person, they slipped straight past him and did not look back.

There were fewer and fewer people as he neared the palace entrance, until finally the last few hallways were completely deserted. Heart pounding, Wirr slowed to an uncertain jog, Andyn keeping pace and focusing warily on the way ahead. The shrieks of pain and fear were much louder now, and there was a veritable chorus of them.

Wirr rounded the corner to where the entrance to the Green Hall sat just past the main foyer of the palace, at first not register-ing the unusual amount of light in the passageway.

Then he skidded to a halt, a chill running down his spine.

The Green Hall—and the foyer beyond—were...*gone*. In their place now was just a swirling, angry cloud of white dust, flicker-ing beams of sunlight filtering through it and into the gaping pas-sageways beyond. Pieces of masonry still crumbled and scattered as they fell from the upper floor of the palace, hinting at the pos-sibility of complete collapse.

Away from the thickest of the haze, Wirr could see that the entire front of the palace had been torn outward, chunks of shat-tered stone lying as far as a hundred feet away. To his horror, he could see splayed limbs and splashes of deep red where some of the larger pieces had fallen on people.

Dazed, he focused again on the white cloud.

In its midst, silhouetted and features impossible to make out, stalked a lone woman.

The panicked cries continuing to cut through the air, seem-ingly coming from everywhere at once, finally dragged Wirr's vision upward. His breath caught as he realized what was causing the beams of light that penetrated the dust to shift and flicker so violently.

The flailing, frantically shouting figures were dangling in mid-air above the dust cloud. To a person, they were suspended as high as the palace roof. Perhaps even higher.

And there had to have been at least a hundred of them.

"I know you are hiding here. I *know*. Better, easier, quicker if you face me, but I will tear this building apart to find you if I must!" The furious shout emanating from the figure within the white cloud resounded in Wirr's ears painfully, clearly amplified somehow. The words were breathless, edged with mania. "I will tear your *friends* apart if I must!"

She gestured and a high-pitched shriek was quickly cut off as one of the silhouettes in the air was ripped in two, blood and viscera spattering to the ground amid a renewed desperation in the cries above. "Do you see the consequences for your actions, Tal'kamar? Do you yet regret them?" She gestured and another silhouette separated and fell in several places with a series of wet thuds. The woman didn't turn to look, didn't even appear to notice it had happened. "Are you such a coward as to let those who hide you suffer in fear and humiliation and agony? *Where are you?*"

The last was delivered in a frustrated scream; another motion from the woman resulted in a new section of the palace's facade ripping away with a shuddering roar, flying upward and outward, scattering massive chunks of stone across the gardens beyond. Some of those boulders smashed into the people suspended in the air; the chorus of panicked, despairing screams grew wilder as more blood began raining lightly to the ground.

Wirr made himself ignore the terror coursing through his veins at the sight, crouching with Andyn behind what was left of the passageway wall and trying to assess the situation. Tal'kamar. The name was coming up over and over again. Was it actually Caeden whom she was after? The woman was powerful—more so than anyone Wirr had ever seen, except for perhaps Caeden himself. There was no way that he could beat her head-on, but there was also no way he could stay hidden and just let this continue.

He and Andyn both flinched at a noise behind them, twisting to see a dozen Administrators led by Pria rush around the corner, only to come to a horrified halt as they took in the wreckage of the palace and the squirming, hovering shapes that blocked out the sun.

Wirr motioned for them to stay where they were and hurried over to his second-in-command. Pria gave him a dazed nod, for once displaying none of her usual displeasure at his presence.

"What...?" She gestured at where the Green Hall had once been.

"I think it's just one person. A woman." Wirr swallowed, looking at the weapons that the group was carrying. "You have a Trap?"

Pria nodded. "Already activated."

Wirr grimaced as he glanced behind him at the floating figures, still suspended high in the air. "Apparently that doesn't work against her, then."

"We also have Shackles. And blades," added Pria quickly.

A severed limb ricocheted off the nearby passageway wall with a wet thud, and Wirr took a deep breath. They had surprise on their side but other than that, there was no way to improve their odds.

"Shut off your Traps again. I'll distract her, attack her with Essence. I should be able to. This counts as the defense of Andarra to me," he added grimly. "You circle around, wait for your opportunity. Just...do what you can. We can't let this go on."

"No." Andyn shook his head firmly. "I'll distract her. You—"

"Rushing her wouldn't be enough." Wirr cut him off bluntly, indicating the struggling bodies high above. "You'd be up there in a moment, Andyn, and then she'd forget that you even existed. If we want to get her attention, someone needs to land at least a couple of blows." He shook his head, even as his stomach churned. "You want to protect me? Go with the Administrators. Get to her before she gets to me."

Andyn gritted his teeth. "Someone really needs to explain the meaning of 'bodyguard' to you, Sire," he said in frustration. He didn't argue, though, much to Wirr's relief. He saw what the situation called for, too.

Pria stared at Wirr for a long moment, then inclined her head in what was close to a respectful nod. She murmured something to her companions, and then they and Andyn hurried away.

Wirr crept back to his original vantage point. The woman stalked back and forth within the cloud, occasionally screaming more challenges toward the shattered palace. Wirr focused, then gathered everything he could into a single, sharply compressed ball of Essence and blasted it at the pacing silhouette.

The white dust burst from the path of his attack, exploding upward and outward, clearing the air between himself and the woman.

A good three feet before it hit her, the Essence simply vanished.

The stranger turned and for one long, helpless moment he locked eyes with her. She had red hair still visible beneath an outer coat of white, and her red-tinged emerald eyes bore into his.

Then he was being hoisted into the air as well, his stomach dropping away as he rocketed upward. The back of his head glanced off a jutting piece of the shattered roof and he flailed dazedly, spinning, for several nauseating seconds unable to get his bearings.

When his vision finally cleared, he was hovering only a few feet in front of the woman's wild-eyed gaze.

"Do you know where he is?" she asked softly.

Wirr groaned, then coughed as fine dust crept into his lungs. "Who?"

The woman squinted at him. "Your Shielding is better than most. Better and sharper and cleaner and..." She shook her head with a thoughtful frown. "But not enough to lie. Not to me. You recognize the name."

There was movement behind the woman, and he spotted Andyn, Pria, and the other Administrators sprinting silently toward them, weapons at the ready. "You're right," he said weakly. "I know where he might—"

It didn't work. The woman gestured behind her without even looking, and Andyn and the Administrators' charge came to a gentle, confused halt as they began looking around blankly.

"Release your Shielding, then. Let me see for myself," she said over the continuing terrified cries of those above.

Wirr stared at her in horror for a few long moments.

Then, slowly, he shook his head, doing his best not to flounder as he rotated slightly in midair. Perhaps she would only look through his mind for information on Tal'kamar...or perhaps she would Read more. He knew the details of every plan Andarra had in place to protect the Boundary. He'd been practicing his Shielding for exactly this reason.

The woman's expression grew dangerous, and she cocked her 423 head to one side as she gazed up at him and then back at the group behind her, evidently noting the matching cloaks.

She gestured lazily at Andyn, the only one in the group who stood out. The bodyguard's eyes snapped up, suddenly, painfully aware again. He locked gazes with Wirr, expression more confused than anything else.

His head crumpled inward in an explosion of red viscera.

"*No!*" screamed Wirr helplessly, thrashing against his invisible restraints as the remainder of Andyn's body slumped to the ground. Around him, the Administrators didn't react at all to the grisly sight.

"So. Perhaps I should tell these to kill one another, now?" the woman asked softly, seemingly unaffected by Wirr's shock and fury. "Or just command them to tear out an eyeball each? They will, you know, should I ask."

Wirr bared his teeth, breathing heavily as he tried to comprehend what had just happened, but said nothing. The woman watched him for a long moment, then shrugged.

Behind her, each of the Administrators began reaching for their own eye.

"STOP!" screamed Wirr desperately.

The Administrators paused, frowning.

They slowly lowered their hands again.

For the first time, Wirr's captor looked surprised. She turned to gaze at the Administrators, brow furrowing as if she were now concentrating.

The Administrators stared at her blankly. Nothing happened.

She twisted back to Wirr, her attention fully on him this time. "How?" Her voice hardened. "*How?*" She shook her head and then, without turning away, made an almost dismissive gesture.

Behind her, Pria and the other Administrators gasped and crumpled to the ground.

Wirr gazed at them, numb. He didn't need to see the sallow, wrinkled skin or glassy eyes to know that they were dead. Isiliar had drained the Essence from them, just as Davian had to Ionis. Just as Caeden had to the Blind.

"Isiliar!"

The deep voice cut through the simmering cacophony of pleading calls, moans, and shouts drifting down from above. Wirr turned his head to see a powerfully built man striding toward them through the dust, his gaze fixed on the woman.

"Do not, *do not* try to stop me this time, Alaris," snarled the woman called Isiliar. "I have been thwarted enough. I have suffered enough. I have waited *enough*." There was fury in the words, but also something more—a thread of despair.

Faint hope blossomed in Wirr's chest.

"Is," said the man gently as he came closer, slowing in his movement forward and holding out his hand as if approaching an easily startled animal. "He's not here."

"I followed him this far," snarled the woman. "He must be—"

"Is, look at me. *Look at me.*" The man's deep voice was quiet but commanding. "I am better at this than you, and I am not lying. He *was* here, but he found a way to hide his Trace. He is long gone."

"No. No, no, *no*." There was desperation now. "We need to end him. We need to finish this. It's not just for me. If we give him a chance, just a *chance*, he will—"

"You're killing people, Is. Innocent people. Look around. They don't know what they're doing," the man called Alaris said quietly. "That is not you. That has never been you."

"Perhaps it is, now," muttered Isiliar, shaking her head violently as if to wrestle Alaris's words from her ears. "Perhaps this is what he has made me. A monster just like him."

"You are gentle, and kind," said Alaris, so softly that Wirr could barely hear him. "You are just and strong. Perhaps he has made you forget that, Is. But he has not remade you." He took another step forward, tentatively laying a hand on the redheaded woman's arm. "We are not supposed to be here. You want to stop him? We need to do the right thing. We need to go home."

The woman stared at him for a long few moments, then looked around. For the first time, she seemed to take in the devastation of her surroundings.

Her face crumpled, and tears quickly began carving rivulets in the dust on her face.

"Oh, El. El, I'm so sorry."

The man held her as she wept, cradling her head against his chest.

"It's all right, Is," he said gently. "It's not your fault."

Then he carefully, almost lovingly, slid the darkly pulsing dagger he'd been concealing into her back. Through her heart.

Wirr barely had time to realize what had happened before he plummeted to the ground; behind him he vaguely heard a chorus of shrieks as everyone else who had been hovering—much higher than he had been—dropped as well. Even Wirr's impact with the white stone paving left him bruised and dazed; he groaned as he slowly caught the breath that had been knocked from him, rolling and carefully rotating the arm that he'd fallen on. It was painful, bruised—but nothing was broken.

When he looked up, both Alaris and Isiliar had vanished.

He just lay there for a long moment, then forced himself to his feet as he registered the moans and weeping behind him. He squinted through the gradually clearing dust, staggering a little as he took in the scene.

Bodies were everywhere. Some lay still—unconscious or dead, he wasn't sure—but others writhed in evident agony from where they had opened gashes or snapped bones from the fall. He resisted the urge to use his Essence on his own pains, instead forcing himself forward into the thick haze of white.

He wasn't sure how much time passed next. Wherever there was an injury that looked life-threatening, he did his best to heal it. He didn't have much Essence left after his attack on Isiliar, though, and before long, he could barely stand.

It was only then that he caught sight of the familiar form, lying motionless at the base of a shattered staircase.

His heart dropped and he stumbled over, dropping to his knees and rolling Deldri gently onto her back, almost weeping at the extent of his sister's injuries. She was alive, but her breaths came in shallow gasps. Her left arm was bent at an unnatural angle, and her clothing was shredded and bloody down her entire left side where she'd fallen hard against a jagged piece of rubble.

Wirr closed his eyes and healed as much as he could, but he knew that it wasn't enough.

426

"Help!" His voice was only one in a chorus of similar cries, but he was desperate, didn't know what else to do. He stood, only to fall again. He'd given too much Essence, and his own injuries were taking a toll. He grasped his sister's hand in his own, holding it tightly. "I need help here!" he called again weakly.

A dozen other voices echoed his plea into the ruins of the palace.

But nobody came.

Chapter 30

Davian stretched, then flicked a card atop the discard pile.

Ishelle and Erran scowled at him. Fessi didn't move for a moment, then leaned down so that she was looking into his eyes.

"You're cheating," she announced.

Davian shook his head firmly. "I'm just better at this than you three."

He yelped in surprise at a sudden stinging pain in his earlobe. He raised his hand and rubbed at the spot. "Not funny," he said, his slight smile betraying the words. He addressed the comment to Fessi. It didn't look like she'd moved, but she was the only one who could have done it so smoothly.

"What?" Fessi asked with an innocent look, while the other two grinned at him.

Davian snorted, then grinned back. Erran had picked up the cards at the last town they'd passed through; the purpose of playing was, ostensibly, to practice both their Reading and Shielding. It was difficult to concentrate on the game, masking the cards in his head even as he looked at them. Lockboxes were all but useless, as information was near impossible to shut away while you were taking it in. It was an interesting but difficult exercise.

However, it was also, Davian was vaguely surprised to find, fun. Despite the ulterior motive, he hadn't sat around with friends and played a game in…certainly not since he'd left Caladel. Not even in the months leading up to that, with all his studies gradually overtaking more social priorities. There was laughter, teasing, mock competitiveness. It felt good.

It felt...*normal.*

It had been two weeks since they'd left, and so far things had gone surprisingly smoothly. No one had stopped them, no one had recognized them as anything but a small group of travelers.

Fessi yawned again, dark circles under her eyes as she threw down the remainder of her cards in mock disgust, lying back and staring up at the starry, cloudless sky. "I need some rest anyway. How far away do you think we are?"

"Less than a week," said Ishelle. She shook her head. "Terrifying though that is. We shouldn't even have been able to make it to Ilin Illan by then."

Davian silently nodded his agreement. They had all helped to alter their passage through time and even with consistent breaks, including an extended one around noon each day, they were still covering more than twice the distance he would have thought possible.

His, Ishelle's, and Erran's contribution to the process had been all but meaningless, though, despite their relative proximity to Deilannis now. Fessi did most of the work, eating voraciously and ultimately collapsing a couple of hours after they stopped each night. She would sleep solidly while the rest of them took shifts keeping watch, despite her constant protests that she wanted to help in that regard, too.

It wasn't long before Fessi's distinctive snoring began to emanate from slightly away from the fire, eliciting the usual amused looks between the other three. They continued to play quietly for a while longer, but soon enough the game petered out, the desire to train gradually overcome by the natural physical tiredness that even fortifying their bodies with Essence could not stave off completely.

"So we've decided to share our visions amongst ourselves, correct?" asked Erran suddenly, studying the fire intently.

Ishelle and Davian glanced at each other. "For now. If we think it's a good idea," said Davian. There was no one with them who could act as Scribe, now that Davian's ability had returned—and it was important that if one of them foresaw something relevant, they all knew what might be coming. They were each privately recording what they saw, too. As always, much of it was irrelevant, inconsequential—but they had still agreed that anything significant should be shared.

"I think this one might be a good idea," said Erran. He glanced over at Fessi, whose breathing was slow and steady. "It wasn't much. I didn't recognize the region, but it was dry and open—desert, basically."

Davian thought for a moment. "Somewhere in the Isles?"

Erran shook his head. "No sand. Just hard ground, nothing alive. You were there, and Fess was there. I didn't see myself or Ishelle." He rolled his shoulders. "They didn't have the helmets, but I'm fairly sure that you were with some Blind soldiers," he added softly.

Davian shifted uncomfortably. "We were prisoners?"

"Yes. You were the only two that I could see, too," said Erran.

Davian accepted the statement with a nod, trying not to get too anxious at the concept. "Anything else? Any way it could somehow be related to my vision from a couple of weeks ago?"

Davian had told the others what he'd Seen just before they'd left Prythe; his fight against the multiple Gassandrids in the shifting room of steel, and his brief conversation afterward with Nethgalla, were still often on his mind. A few months ago, he would have just chuckled at that latter name being the same as the fabled Ath's. But after Deilannis, after Malshash had confirmed her existence...

That was all still conjecture, though. There had been little to tell him where or how far into the future he'd Seen, and since then, he'd had only two brief visions of the day ahead. Nothing more.

Erran gave him an apologetic look. "Not that I noticed. As I said, it was brief." He glanced over again at Fessi's sleeping form. "I just...I don't think it's the best idea to tell her. Not right now. She doesn't need anything extra to worry about."

"She's driven," observed Ishelle quietly.

"You cannot begin to imagine. She hides a lot of it, believe it or not." Erran shook his head. "She knows that sealing the Boundary is important, but her real goal is Scyner. When she finds him..." He trailed off.

Davian frowned. He knew what had happened, of course—knew that Kol had been killed by Scyner, and that the dead Augur had meant a lot to Fessi. He could understand her determination to seek revenge, he supposed, even if he couldn't approve.

"You think telling her what you saw could do more harm than good?"

"I don't know *what* it would do. She's ... changed, these past couple of months." Erran rubbed the back of his head wearily. "So have I, I suppose—but not as much as her. She's pushing herself so hard; if she finds out that she ends up as a prisoner ..." He shrugged. "It could be years away, anyway."

Davian nodded slowly. "We won't mention it," he said quietly, echoed by Ishelle.

Ishelle, sitting next to him, suddenly yawned. Then she stretched out and shuffled around, laying her head in his lap.

Davian sighed, shifting slightly so that her head slipped onto the grass, a little more roughly than he'd expected but not so hard that it would have hurt. After their first week on the road, Ishelle had seemed to regain some of her former humor—including, unfortunately, the pleasure that she took in trying to make him uncomfortable.

He rolled his eyes at Erran, who was grinning at him, then looked down to see Ishelle giving him a dirty look.

He shrugged cheerfully at her as she rolled into a sitting position again. "I've been meaning to ask," he said, suddenly reminded. "Is Asha still at Ilin Illan?" Ishelle had previously made physical contact with Asha, and thus was able to track her. Davian didn't ask about her too often—if nothing else, he didn't want to endure the constant teasing that he received whenever he did—but it was nice to know that she was well.

Ishelle grimaced, brushing bits of twig and grass from her long dark hair, then closed her eyes. "She's not," she said after a moment, eyebrows raising a little. "She's heading north. Not toward us, exactly, but definitely north." She yawned again, indicating that was all that she could be bothered to tell him. "Anyway—it's a nice night," she observed cheerfully. "I think I might go for a walk."

Davian echoed the yawn, nodding and grateful that for once, it appeared that he wasn't going to be mocked for asking. "Thank you. And be careful out there," he added, more from habit than any real concern. They were far from any town, but the road was hardly one along which he expected to see many dangers.

Ishelle disappeared into the trees, and for a minute there was only the crackling of the fire and the occasional whickering of a restless horse. When Davian eventually looked up from his reverie, he saw Erran watching him with a curious expression.

"What?" Davian shifted. "Did I do something?"

Erran smiled, shaking his head. "You really can't see it, can you." It was a statement rather than a question, clearly one that amused him.

"I don't know what you're talking about."

"Ishelle." Erran gave him a pointed look.

Davian stared at him and then snorted, shaking his head. "She's done that from the moment we met," he assured Erran drily. "She knows it makes me uncomfortable. Fates, it took almost a month on the road with her before I learned how to ignore it properly without blushing. But it doesn't mean anything."

"Fates but it does." Erran leaned forward. "Did you not see her expression just then? Or every time you ask her to tell you where Asha is?"

Davian frowned. "I know she doesn't like it, but..." He shook his head slowly. "I think you're wrong—but even if you're not, what can I do?"

Erran sighed. "Fess and I were talking about it the other day, and I'm not sure that there's anything you *can* do," he admitted. "She knows it's not going to happen. But...you could be gentler with her, sometimes. She puts on a front, but she's still got emotions. She didn't just go for a walk because she suddenly felt like it."

Davian grimaced, heart sinking. He wasn't ever going to change his mind about Ishelle—he was certain of that—but she was still his friend. Had he been hard on her without meaning to be? He hated the thought that he'd hurt her.

"Maybe we should go after her?"

Erran grunted. "Give her a few minutes. If she's not back by then, perhaps *you* can go after her." He shrugged. "Might be an opportunity to actually talk to her. Clear the air without anyone else around."

Davian winced, but nodded.

433

There was silence for a while after that, until eventually Davian stirred, earning a brief nod from Erran.

"Go easy on her," the other Augur reminded him quietly.

Davian inclined his head in acknowledgment, then headed away from the light of the fire. His eyes were slow to adjust as he wandered along the road, heading in the direction in which he'd seen Ishelle go. They weren't in a forest, exactly, but the area in which they'd stopped to make camp was reasonably thickly wooded, and the campfire was soon lost to view.

Starlight guided his way well enough—the trees weren't close enough to blot out the sky—but after a while he pushed through kan, extending his senses ahead of him. There were a lot of trees, a few vague outlines of nocturnal creatures creeping through the undergrowth—but no signs of Ishelle.

He frowned; he'd expected to stumble across her fairly quickly. They all knew not to go too far from the camp at night. Even if they thought an area was safe, there was never any reliable way to be certain that the road was free of danger.

He rolled his shoulders uncomfortably as he pushed on farther. Something was amiss, though he couldn't put his finger on what. He paused in the middle of the road, closing his eyes.

There was the faintest sound, coming from all around him. A nearly inaudible hum, little more than a vibration on the air.

And everything else was silent.

He pressed on nervously now, using kan again to search for any sign of Ishelle. His footsteps crunched as he trod on dry ground and twigs, but even that sound seemed muted.

Then, finally, up ahead he caught the faintly glowing outline of a person.

Ishelle was sitting on a fallen tree and leaning her back against another, facing away from the road and staring out into a clearing. He exhaled, the tension in his shoulders easing as he approached, despite the awkwardness of the situation.

"Ishelle?" He stepped forward hesitantly, releasing kan as he came within sight of her, though she was only dimly outlined in the starlight. "You've been gone a while. Are you all right?"

Ishelle didn't move, and Davian sighed. "Look, I'm sorry

about earlier," he said quietly, stepping around in front of her. "I think…"

The words died on his lips.

The finger-thin, jagged spikes that had pierced Ishelle's body were more than two feet long, the wicked black barbs slicing through her stomach, arms, and chest where they nailed her to the trunk. There were four of them inserted at different angles, each one glistening in the silvery light, globules of dark, viscous liquid congealing and dripping slowly onto the ground in front of her.

The humming vibration, soft only moments before, was suddenly thunderous.

Davian pushed back the shock and flinched around, a blur of motion from the corner of his vision the only warning he had. He threw himself to the ground as an enormous shape whined through the space in which he'd just been standing, the high-pitched droning sound grating on his ears.

He rolled, looking around wildly, his breaths coming short and sharp from sudden terror.

There was nothing.

Davian gritted his teeth, forcing his limbs to unfreeze and stumbling to his feet. The hum grew louder again. He searched the skies desperately, biting back a cry as he spotted a dark mass against the starlight. It was gone in a moment, though.

The buzzing was all around him now and he broke into a faltering run, skin itching from the expected attack, scrabbling desperately for kan that was suddenly impossible to grasp. He was almost across the clearing when something moved in the shadows beneath the trees opposite.

He skidded to a halt as the sha'teth emerged in front of him.

He tried to push through kan again, tried to snatch at Essence to defend himself. Nothing happened; whether it was from fear or for some other reason, he couldn't tell. He changed direction, moving to the left this time, angling away from the creature as it shot toward him with its unsettling, unnaturally fast gait.

The sha'teth gestured and a bolt of Essence split the night, sailing over Davian's shoulder. He stumbled on a root underfoot as the light flashed past his eyes, then fell as the humming, whining sound filled his ears.

In his heart, he knew he was dead.

He pressed his eyes shut against the horrific, all-encompassing sound and reached out for kan again. This time he grasped it.

Immediately, he forced the flow of time to bend around him.

He rolled to see the sha'teth towering over him, its movements not as slowed as everything else. Directly above Davian, silhouetted against the starlit sky of the clearing, was...*something*. He caught a glimpse of black shapes. Blurring wings and glowing yellow eyes. Rows of what looked like spears, riblike but protruding from each body, glistening with black ooze.

Motion. The sha'teth leaned down, a cold, white hand grabbing him by the foot. Davian tried to kick it away, but it was of no use.

The sha'teth pulled and pivoted, sending him airborne.

Davian landed in ungainly fashion, the air knocked from his lungs as his chest bounced on the ground and his shoulder slammed into a thick-trunked tree. His vision blurred from the sharp, grating pain of rough bark slicing across his skin and he lost his grip on time; suddenly the thunderous buzzing filtered back into his consciousness, punctuated by whining shrieks that sounded even angrier than they had before.

Everything passed in a haze after that. He could see the ground next to the sha'teth had suddenly sprouted five spears, all oozing black in the dim silvery light; it took him a long moment to grasp that it was exactly where he had been lying just a moment ago. The sha'teth had somehow extended its shadowy blade and was leaping through the air, impossibly high as it slashed gracefully at things that Davian couldn't quite make out. There were wet thuds. More furious whining, humming noises, but suddenly distant.

And then silence.

When he finally got up the energy and nerve to raise his gaze again, he was alone.

He slowly, stiffly dragged himself to his feet, every muscle protesting as he flexed cautiously. Nothing was broken.

His gaze traveled to Ishelle's body, still pinned to the trunk on which she'd obviously been sitting when she'd been attacked. Her eyes were open, staring ahead blankly. The only movement was the ever-so-slight rise and fall of her chest.

It took a moment for Davian to register what that meant.

Injuries forgotten he sprinted over, skidding to his knees in front of her, barely daring to believe what he was seeing. But it wasn't just an illusion, the shifting shadows of the trees. She was breathing.

He gazed at her with a mixture of terror and hope. The spears were thin, perhaps the width of his forefinger, but they had gone clear through her body where they'd struck. None in the face or neck, none through the heart. Stomach, though, for two. Right shoulder. Left thigh. Each one clearly coming out the other side of her body, pinning her to the wood behind.

He reached out to grab the first; he knew that it was dangerous but if he was going to heal her, he couldn't do it with those still in her body. He paused with his hand only an inch from the weapon, though. Large, slimy globules of black were still seeping from it—not just from its tip, but everywhere along the shaft. There was an acrid smell in the air, too.

He drew his hand away again, then carefully siphoned off some Essence from the surrounding forest and looped it around the first spear. To his surprise the Essence didn't seem to connect or dissipate; rather it appeared to simply slip off, unable to touch the black substance.

Davian frowned, refusing to let his rising panic get the better of him. He concentrated, delicately weaving kan to guide the Essence into something closer to a sheet, sliding along the spear and then closing over the far end. Gritting his teeth, he *pulled*.

The spear slid free, leaving a black trail of muck—but no blood, apparently—in its wake.

Davian was halfway through breathing a sigh of relief when his heart skipped a beat. Ishelle was motionless.

She'd stopped breathing.

Desperately now, Davian set about removing the other spears. He didn't know if it was the right thing to do, but he couldn't think of any other way to heal her. Each came out more easily than the last, until finally Ishelle's limp form slumped face-forward to the ground, her body finally freed.

Davian knelt beside her, hands shaking as he rolled her onto her back. There was no breath, no sign of life.

Just like Ell.

The thought came unbidden and suddenly Davian was light-headed, reliving the wedding he'd never had. Reliving what he'd gone through, and then what he'd done to try and undo it all.

He growled, shaking his head vigorously to get the images out of his head. Ishelle wasn't Elliavia.

But he still remembered what Malshash had tried to do to save her.

He began drawing Essence from everywhere that he could, letting it drain into Ishelle, the threads many and intricate as he directed them. He could sense more than see the wounds begin to close; he knew that he should probably try to get more of the black ooze out of her before doing so, but even if he'd had the means there was simply no time.

Still Ishelle didn't breathe, didn't open her eyes. Panic began to set in as Davian took more and more Essence, snatching it from everything living for as far as his senses could reach. There were no people around, of that he was certain. Animals, though, he had no compunction about draining. Not if it meant saving the life of his friend.

He snarled in frustration, tears beginning to form as he began to run out of sources. It was just like Ell. He'd been here before. He'd already lived this, and the two pains began to mingle, to become one.

He was losing again, and nothing that he did mattered. He wasn't good enough, wasn't strong enough.

He'd failed.

He sat back, spent, dizzy, blinking tears from his eyes.

With a choking, racking gasp, Ishelle sat up.

Chapter 31

Asha rode in silence, the warmth of the day pleasant as the group made its way steadily east.

They were more than halfway through their journey, and there had been few obstacles to their progress thus far. In fact, aside from an unusual sense of fatigue since they had set out, as well as the occasional bout of light-headedness—worrying signs, but nothing approaching the severity of the episodes in Ilin Illan— Asha's biggest problem thus far had been boredom. She was accustomed now to rising before dawn, studying, assisting with her duties as Representative throughout the day. Steady though their current pace was, the monotony had begun to wear on her nerves.

It didn't help that nobody in the group appeared to be terribly interested in talking to her. The three Gifted—Charis, Tyrin, and Lue—who had volunteered for the journey rarely spoke more than two words to her, keeping to themselves and looking at her sideways when they thought she wasn't watching.

Then there were the other two in the party, the ones who stood out and seemed as isolated as she. Breshada just rode along silently, adjusting her red cloak every few minutes as if its touch against her skin was like acid. The other Gifted didn't know who she was, but their few attempts at striking up conversation with her—one in particular by Tyrin, who had clearly shown a little too much interest—had ended in consistently sullen glares from the group.

Breshada had been far from friendly toward Asha, too, though her tone at least usually conveyed the slightest edge of respect when they spoke. The former Hunter had endured two short lessons on how to control Essence since their journey had begun, both of which had resulted in her walking away, under the guise of disgust but Asha suspected probably out of frustration. The concepts were not difficult, but Breshada hadn't grown up with them, either.

Laiman, on the other hand, had been perfectly genial and friendly to everyone—and said absolutely nothing of consequence. Whether it was a result of the many years he'd spent close to the king, or whether it was something else entirely, Asha couldn't say. The man was wonderful at small talk, but as soon as the conversation began to drift toward anything important, he would deftly steer it away again.

His presence continued to puzzle Asha. Despite what she'd overheard in Elocien's office after the battle—despite knowing that Taeris and Laiman had some sort of connection that they were keeping from everyone else—it didn't make sense, him being here. Officially, he was along because the Assembly had wanted someone that could reliably report back to them on the journey, and Laiman had been the easy choice. He was well liked, intelligent, and actually willing to go.

There was more to it than that, though, Asha was certain. She just wished that she could figure out a way to find out more without revealing what she already knew.

It was midday when the group traveling in the opposite direction came into view.

Laiman stiffened immediately when he saw them, and Charis cursed under her breath. There were five blue cloaks that Asha could see, and each one of the oncoming Administrators appeared to be armed.

"Be calm, and say nothing," Laiman said to his companions in a firm tone. "We have every right to be traveling, and I have the documentation to prove it. It will be fine."

They had already had some minor trouble with Administrators on the road—at one point they'd been stopped for an entire hour, purely because the Administrator in charge had found it amusing to inconvenience them. But it had always worked out.

Laiman received a few reluctant nods, and they pressed forward.

As they approached, Asha saw the lead Administrator eyeing them suspiciously.

"Halt!" he called as they came within earshot. He dismounted as they followed his command, indicating that they should do the same.

"Who's in charge here?" he asked, the casual superiority of his tone already setting Asha's teeth on edge.

"I am." Laiman pushed forward, producing a slip of paper from his pocket. "Laiman Kardai, adviser to King Kevran Andras. I have his signed permission for this party to be traveling." It wasn't technically necessary anymore—the law regarding the restriction of Gifted movement had been removed close to a month ago—but word of such changes sometimes spread slowly to the countryside, and was often accepted at an even lazier pace.

The Administrator waved Laiman forward impatiently, evidently unimpressed by his professed credentials. He glanced over the paper with a sharp eye, then looked up and scanned the rest of the group.

When his gaze fell on Asha, he paused, expression darkening.

"This does not cover your having a Shadow in the group," he said grimly.

Laiman frowned. "It doesn't specify," he observed. "But this is *Representative* Ashalia Chaedris. She is here on behalf of Tol Athian. The king is completely aware that she is part of this journey."

"But your note here does not *say* that," said the Administrator. There was a sudden tension in the air, and Asha felt her heart drop. The Shadows had left Ilin Illan without permission or warning, and there *was* a general command to apprehend any rebels if they were spotted. But she'd assumed that Laiman's note, and the word of those in the party, would have been more than enough to justify her presence.

"What's your name, Administrator?" asked Laiman quietly.

The man focused back on Laiman, looking caught between surprise and anger at being talked down to. "Kolis."

"Well, Administrator Kolis," said Laiman, "I am telling you

that Representative Chaedris is allowed to travel with us. I am also telling you that our journey is time-sensitive; we cannot afford to be delayed, and we will not move forward without everyone. We have been stopped by several Administrators already during our journey, and none of the others have taken issue with the Representative's presence."

Asha slipped off her horse, making sure to keep her head high and her gaze straight as she approached the two. As often as not, appearance mattered in these situations as much as legality. The more it looked as if she didn't believe that she would be arrested, the more likely it was that she wouldn't be.

Kolis watched her with a sneer on his lips as he replied. "It is irrelevant. We have been charged with detaining any Shadows that we come across, and returning them to Ilin Illan for questioning." His eyes got a dangerous glint. "And in the event that they resist, we have full authority to use force. Deadly force, if necessary, rather than let them get away."

"That isn't true, actually," said Asha. She did her best to appear calm, composed despite the obvious threat that these men were posing. "The Assembly granted you the right to question Shadows, and to bring them to Ilin Illan in the event of violent noncooperation. There was no mention of killing."

"She would know. She was there," added Laiman.

Kolis shrugged. "I can only tell you what my superiors told me," he said softly. "And *they* say that Geladra Andras herself sent down the order. So I will not be dissuaded, Master Kardai. Are you going to tell her to come quietly, or do we need to exercise force?"

Asha's breath suddenly shortened as a wave of dizziness hit her; she gritted her teeth as her vision swam and she stumbled a little, using every ounce of control not to go to her knees. She cursed inwardly. This was the *worst* possible time for one of these attacks.

Kolis and Laiman were both staring at her, but before either of them could say anything, another voice came from behind her.

"There's no need for this. I'm sure that we can come to some sort of arrangement."

Breshada pushed forward, a cheerful smile on her lips. She

was accustomed to dealing with Administrators, Asha realized through her dizziness with no small amount of trepidation. She was accustomed to them *liking* her.

Kolis glanced at her in surprise for a moment, though it was clear that he took in her red cloak more than her confident posture or the long sword hanging by her side. "Involve yourself in this, bleeder, and we'll be taking you in, too," he said dismissively, turning back to Asha.

The astonishingly powerful blast of Essence struck Kolis in the chest, lifting him from his saddle and slamming him with sickening force into the trunk of a nearby tree, accompanied by the meaty snap of at least one bone breaking.

There was a horrified silence, broken only by Kolis's moans as he writhed in pain.

Then there was shouting as the Administrators all scrambled for their weapons, screaming at the Gifted to back away even as one of them activated a Trap. Asha turned to see Breshada shaking with anger but wide-eyed, looking shocked at what had just happened.

"It was an accident!" Asha shouted, trying to make her voice heard above the others. Her light-headedness, thankfully, seemed to have passed again. She exchanged a desperate glance with Laiman, who had his hands stretched outward in a calming motion.

"She is under arrest," snarled one of the men as the shouts finally quieted again, producing a Shackle and brandishing it at them. He glanced across at Kolis, who was slowly getting to his feet with the assistance of another Administrator. The man's arm was jutting at an unnatural angle. "Release her to us immediately."

"It was an accident," repeated Asha in frustration. "She has the Mark, so the Third Tenet would have stopped her if she'd actually been trying to harm anyone. It *couldn't* have been deliberate!"

"Or it's another reason to wonder whether we've been told the whole story about these new Tenets," gasped Kolis bitterly, finally regaining his breath. The words were strained, spat out between gritted teeth as he dealt with the pain of his arm.

Laiman stepped forward. "We can heal that for you—"

"Do you think I'm a fool?" choked Kolis at the king's adviser. "None of you are touching Essence while we are here."

Both sides stared at each other, silent for several tension-filled moments. Then motion to Asha's left made her turn.

Breshada was glaring at Kolis venomously, but to Asha's surprise was also raising her hands.

"I surrender," she said loudly. "Under the condition that the rest of this group is allowed to proceed unhindered."

Kolis's lip curled. "Very well. Toss your weapon aside."

"Only once they have departed." Breshada stared at Kolis boldly.

Kolis thought for a moment, then gestured with his good arm in disgust. "So be it." He glared around at the others in Asha's party. "Go. Leave before I change my mind and have you *all* arrested."

Charis, Tyrin, and Lue needed no further invitation, turning and heading down the road without even looking to see whether Asha and Laiman were following. Perhaps they were too accustomed to obeying Administrators, but Asha couldn't help but cast an appalled glance after them.

"No." She wasn't sure why Breshada was sacrificing herself, but she wasn't about to let it happen. "It was an accident, and I will vouch for her."

"An *accident*? If she does not have control over her abilities, then she should look like you. Your vouching for her means nothing," sneered Kolis.

Asha closed her eyes for a moment. Took a deep breath.

She drew her sword.

"Then we have a problem," she said quietly, ignoring Laiman's panicked look. "Because you're either going to leave, or you're going to have to fight a member of the Assembly. And I don't care what your orders are—that won't go over well with your superiors."

Laiman hesitated, then gave Asha a frustrated look before stepping over to join her, reluctantly drawing his own blade. "You can add King Andras's adviser to that," he said heavily. A little way down the road, Asha saw the retreating Gifted turn as they heard the exchange. Breshada was watching Asha with surprise, but she made no move to draw Whisper, much to Asha's relief.

There was a long, tense silence as Kolis stared at them, wide-eyed and clearly furious, even through the evident pain of his cradled arm.

"Do not think that this will be ignored," he said eventually, cold certainty in the threat, gesturing curtly to another Administrator for assistance as he awkwardly mounted his horse again. "I will report this through the proper channels, and there *will* be consequences."

Before they could respond he jerked his head toward the road, and the Administrators were riding away.

Asha breathed out, then turned and winced at Laiman's glare.

"It wasn't her fault," she said grimly, ignoring the three Gifted as they sheepishly began making their way back toward them. She turned to Breshada, who was watching her intently. "Why did you surrender?"

Breshada shrugged. "Men like that are careless. They think that once a Gifted is Shackled, they are no longer a threat." There was a dangerous glint in her eye, and suddenly Asha understood.

"You were going to kill them?" she asked in horror.

"I was going to escape. Whether they died would have been up to them," said Breshada calmly.

"How? They had a Trap *and* a Shackle *and* they would have taken Whisper from you."

"It doesn't matter now." Slowly, reluctantly, Breshada dipped her head toward Asha. It wasn't much—an acknowledgment, a small sign of respect. From the Hunter, though, it was as good as an embrace.

Asha returned the gesture. Breshada *had* stuck up for her, when she'd had no particular reason to. If Asha's actions had helped gain some traction with Breshada, then perhaps this incident hadn't been entirely bad after all.

She turned to find the entire rest of the group staring at her. Flushing, she waved them away with a mildly irritated gesture. "Let's keep moving," she said brusquely. "I don't know why they acted that way, but there's no good reason to hang around and see if they come back." She stared after the Administrators worriedly, then turned to Laiman. "Do you think he was telling the truth? About Prince Torin's mother?"

Laiman frowned. "I hope not. It spells trouble if he was," he admitted. "But regardless of what Duchess Andras has or has not done—the Administrators are angry. They feel betrayed, vulnerable. In a few short weeks they have gone from being in complete control of the Gifted, to having one of the Gifted giving them orders. Not to mention the discovery that the Shadows—the one group of people in the world who might hate Administrators *more* than the Gifted—are now armed and completely unaffected by the Tenets."

He rubbed his forehead. "They're probably traveling in packs like that for safety, as much as for convenience. They're scared, and that makes them dangerous. We've been lucky so far. We'll need to keep an eye out for any others we encounter along the way. Try to avoid them if we can." He paused, then focused on Asha, leaning in and lowering his voice so that only they could hear. "Are you...all right? You looked like you were going to pass out for a moment back there."

"I'm fine," Asha assured him quickly, not elaborating.

Laiman frowned, but eventually just nodded; Asha busied herself by holding Laiman's horse as he got back on, as much to keep her mind off her frustration as to be helpful. There was still a long way to go to Deilannis.

She just hoped that things would be a little smoother from here.

The group was quiet as they made camp for the evening.

The Gifted had all worn mildly ashamed looks since the confrontation with the Administrators; though Asha knew that their willingness to give Breshada up was mostly an ingrained reaction from many years under the old Tenets, she didn't try to assuage their guilt. Laiman was off by himself for once, staring worriedly at the road ahead, the incident still clearly concerning him.

She couldn't blame him for that, really. There would doubtless be some unpleasantness stemming from it when they returned to Ilin Illan.

After a while she found herself alongside Breshada, who had appeared introspective over the past few hours. Asha looked

across at her, wondering about starting a conversation.

"Why?" asked Breshada suddenly, not looking up from where she was erecting a tent.

Asha paused, then glanced around to ensure that the question was actually directed at her. There was no one else nearby.

"Why what?" she asked.

"I know you surely consider me...a burden," said Breshada slowly. "You have no love for me and you owe me nothing. So why speak up, why save me?"

Asha squinted at her for a moment, seriously considering the answer.

"Because they had no right to take you. What you did was an accident," she said slowly. "And..." She sighed. "You probably don't want to hear this. But like it or not, you're one of us now."

Breshada didn't say anything to that for several seconds, continuing to work at her task. Asha was just beginning to wonder whether that was the end of the conversation when the other woman finally spoke again.

"You need to learn how to hold that sword of yours," she said abruptly. "The way you wave it around like some sort of a toy is an embarrassment."

Asha blinked, not responding for a moment.

"Is that...an offer?" she asked cautiously.

"It is a statement," said Breshada gruffly. "Watching you wield a blade makes me uncomfortable. It is like...watching a child who has never seen water deciding that they can swim. As there is the possibility that it will happen again, and as I do not wish to cringe in such a manner again, I will teach you."

Asha kept a straight face. "As I don't wish for you to feel uncomfortable, I accept."

Breshada studied her for a moment, then snorted, though Asha thought there was the slightest hint of a smile on her lips. "Dawn, then," she said.

Asha grimaced. "Dawn? Surely sleep would be better to—"

"Dawn," said Breshada firmly.

Asha hesitated for the briefest of moments; she was already more tired than she was used to and sorely tempted to refuse. But it felt like Breshada was reaching out, extending an olive branch.

"Dawn," she agreed heavily.

Chapter 32

Wirr made his way uneasily through the palace corridors, which were as empty as he'd ever seen them.

It had been four days since Isiliar's attack, but those still residing within the palace walls moved as if the shock of it had not yet faded. He could relate to that. This was his home, even more so than the Tel'Andras estate; for his whole life, no matter his political enemies, this had always felt like a place of at least physical safety. Aside from perhaps the two Tols, nowhere else in the entire kingdom was supposed to be as well-defended as here.

Yet now, the hammering and sawing from the front of the palace was a constant audible reminder of how little that had mattered against Isiliar. Repairs were proceeding apace, but nothing here would ever be as it had.

Wirr reached his destination—far enough to the back of the palace that the sounds of rebuilding were relatively faint—and took a deep breath. As heavily as recent events were weighing on him, he always tried to show a more positive side while he was here.

He pushed open the door and smiled with as much cheerfulness as he could muster at the room's two occupants.

"Tor!" Deldri's face lit up as she spotted him from her seated position in her bed. On a chair nearby, Dezia matched her smile.

"Prince Torin," Dezia said politely. "I was just getting to know your sister."

"Sorry," said Wirr as he sat down next to her.

Deldri stuck out her tongue at him. "I was just asking Dezia 449 whether she knew anything more about your mysterious dark-haired girl from a few nights ago. Everyone's still talking about it, you know. You may as well come clean."

Wirr snorted. By "everyone," Deldri meant her and her friends; the attack on the palace had all but wiped the incident from everyone else's memories. Still, he didn't feel the need to point that out to her. "There's nothing to tell. Trust me."

"Please." Deldri gave him a stern look, then turned to Dezia conspiratorially. "Are you sure you don't know anything? From the way he was talking on the way here, there's clearly *someone* in the palace who he's interested in."

Dezia raised an eyebrow. "Is that so?" Despite her straight face, Wirr could see the amusement in her eyes.

Wirr pointedly ignored her. "How are you feeling today, Del?" he asked.

Deldri sighed, looking disappointed that he wasn't going to engage in the topic. "Like I don't need to be in this bed anymore."

"You were badly hurt," said Wirr immediately. "You have to—"

"I know, I know." Deldri rolled her eyes at Dezia. "He thinks I'm an idiot sometimes."

"Sometimes?" asked Wirr.

He grinned as he easily evaded Deldri's mock-irritated swipe, the expression not entirely forced this time. His sister didn't remember anything of the attack or getting injured—whether because of her injuries or simply the trauma of what she'd seen, he didn't know. Either way, he was grateful. She'd been through enough without having to live with memories like that.

"I *am* fine," said Deldri eventually, giving up on trying to hit her brother. "Your friend Taeris did a good job; I'm just a little stiff. You can barely even see the scars."

Wirr nodded, sobering, doing his best not to show the pain he felt at the words. Deldri had only been here at the palace because of him.

Taeris had found them both, eventually, in the aftermath of the destruction—healed them, as well as any others that he could manage. Dras Lothlar had helped, and other Gifted had arrived soon after.

Even so, many had not survived the injuries they'd sustained from the fall.

"Just...rest," he said quietly. "You don't need to be up and doing anything, so take the time to recover properly. There's no rush."

Deldri sighed. "Have you seen Mother yet?"

Wirr shook his head, a little grimly. Geladra had arrived two evenings after the attack—she'd come as soon as she'd heard, presumably—but they hadn't crossed paths yet.

"I know your uncle has," observed Dezia drily.

Wirr grunted. The king had, thankfully, been kept well toward the back of the palace during the attack, and Wirr had been working together closely with him over the past few days. Kevran hadn't gone into the details of his meeting with Geladra, but he'd been in a distinctly foul mood after seeing her.

Deldri scowled. "*She* should go and see *Torin*. I told her that," she added to Wirr.

"I bet she took that well," said Wirr.

Deldri just shrugged, indicating that she didn't care much what their mother's reaction had been.

They spoke for a while longer, but soon enough the physician stopped by to check on Deldri, shooing Wirr and Dezia from the room.

Wirr sighed. "I have a meeting with Taeris. I should probably head there now."

"I'll keep you company," said Dezia cheerfully. "I want to hear all about this girl you're so interested in."

"Well...you remember that dinner with Iria Tel'Rath?" asked Wirr as they started walking, wincing as he earned a sharp punch to the arm.

Neither of them said anything for a few moments, and then Dezia looked across at Wirr, expression serious now. "So how are you?"

Wirr shrugged, a little awkwardly. "No complaints."

Dezia came to an abrupt halt, locking eyes with him. "Really?"

Wirr grimaced, then nodded apologetically. They had ascertained each other was safe after the attack, but hadn't really had a chance to talk since.

"It's...going to take a while," he admitted after a moment. "I didn't like Pria, but fates know she didn't deserve what happened. And Andyn..." His voice caught, and he swallowed a lump in his throat. His bodyguard's death had hit him harder than he cared to admit; he'd felt a bond with the man, and the grief of his passing was still painfully sharp in Wirr's chest whenever he allowed himself to think about it. "I liked Andyn. A lot. I know he was just doing his job, but..."

"He was your friend, too. It hurts," finished Dezia gently, nodding. She glanced around, then gave him a quick squeeze on the arm.

They walked for a while in companionable silence.

"Have you heard from Aelric lately?" asked Dezia eventually. "He mentioned that he was heading down to Miorette to do something for you, but I expected him back by now. Especially since he would surely have heard about what happened."

Wirr came to a sudden stop, closing his eyes and groaning. With everything that had been happening, he'd completely forgotten about Aelric.

"He's not back yet?" When Dezia shook her head, giving him a questioning look, he sighed. "Aelric asked me to give him an excuse to go. He said that there was a personal matter that he wanted to deal with, but he didn't want you coming along." He rubbed his forehead. "He wouldn't tell me the details, but he mentioned that there might be trouble. He was worried you'd put yourself in danger if you found out."

Dezia leaned back, not taking her eyes from Wirr. "So there's a good chance that he's gone and done something stupid," she said flatly.

Wirr looked away. Her gaze was one of hurt and disappointment.

"I'm sorry—I should have said something. I..." He rubbed his forehead, wanting to make excuses but knowing that there weren't really any legitimate ones. "It was a bad decision."

"It really was." There was an undeniable element of anger in Dezia's evident concern for her brother, though she was still calm. "You knew that he was doing something dangerous, and you didn't tell me."

"Yes," acceded Wirr quietly.

Dezia continued to meet his gaze. "Did he say anything about where he was really going?"

"Variden," said Wirr. "He wouldn't say why, though."

Dezia thought for a few moments. Then she paled.

"Telemaki. Devarius Telemaki lives in Variden."

Wirr looked at her blankly. "Who's that?"

"The man leading the group who backed Aelric for the Song," Dezia said softly.

Wirr took a moment to realize what she was saying. Then his heart dropped, and he inwardly cursed himself for not finding out more. Aelric had deliberately lost his final match in the Song of Swords, costing those who had backed him a fortune.

He understood why Aelric had asked him to lie now. There was no way that Dezia would have stood by if she'd known where he was going.

"I'll send some men to make inquiries," said Wirr quickly.

Dezia shook her head. "No. You need everyone either here or in the north," she said reluctantly. "I'll ask around. I know some people who might be able to find out what's happening."

"Can I help?"

Dezia was silent for a long moment.

"Not for now," she said eventually, hurt still thick in her tone. "I know you were doing what you thought was best, Wirr, but..." Her jaw clenched a little, and he could see her keeping in the emotions. "We should talk about this later. When I've had a chance to process it."

Wirr hesitated—he didn't want to let her leave with this unresolved—but after a second, he nodded.

"If you need me to do anything—anything at all—just let me know," he said softly. "I'll send word if I hear from him."

Dezia inclined her head, then left without another word.

Wirr sat down at his desk with a heavy sigh, flipping open his father's notebook once again.

He needed something to take his mind off what had just happened, and this was the most constructive way that he could think of to distract himself until his meeting with Taeris. He'd been reading more of it in every spare moment he had been able to find over the past few days. It was a fascinating read in and of itself—but since Isiliar's attack, he'd had another, more pressing interest.

He hadn't really remembered the oddity of what had happened until yesterday. The day after the assault, his only concern had been to ensure that everyone he knew—which was quite a large group, here in the palace—was all right. Aside from Deldri, those closest to him hadn't been caught in the attack, but there were plenty of others who had been affected. Many of those were allies, and some he even considered friends.

Yesterday, though—as he'd been considering what to say at a memorial for those who had died—he had thought again about Pria and the other Administrators. Not how they'd died, necessarily, but how they had seemed to resist Isiliar's Control.

How his desperate shout had appeared to interrupt what she had been trying to make them do.

The more he'd thought about it, the more certain he'd become. It might have been his imagination—or it might have been Alaris, interfering before he had revealed his presence. But it had *seemed* related to what Wirr had yelled out to them.

He closed his eyes, going through his logic again. A simple shout wouldn't have been enough to break Control—of that much, he was certain. *If* he'd done something—*if*—then it had to have been because of his relationship with the Administrators.

It *had* to be something to do with his being Northwarden.

Wirr knew that that alone wasn't it; he'd given plenty of orders to Administrators in the past that they hadn't even pretended to obey. He had almost given up trying to figure it out, when another factor had occurred to him.

He'd still had the Oathstone in his pocket.

Wirr rolled the Oathstone around in his spare hand as he flipped forward through the pages of Elocien's notebook. He hadn't let the sliver of stone out of his sight since he'd realized the possible connection. It *had* been strange that his father had kept it hidden away in his safe. Perhaps this was why.

And if so, it was surely detailed somewhere within these pages.

He'd continued reading for most of last night, but the notebook was thick and his father had gone into enormous amounts of detail, evidently wanting to ensure that no important information was left out after his memories were removed. Much of the book described various secretive meetings with the mysterious blond woman, including several—often violent—demonstrations of Traps, Shackles, and other Vessels that Wirr was now unwelcomely familiar with.

This morning, though, he had been reading for only ten minutes when a new passage caught his eye.

> *It was only our meeting three weeks ago—the one that ultimately led to the writing of these pages—that finally answered the last of our lingering questions.*
>
> *We had often wondered to our mysterious benefactor whether we would be able to coexist with the Gifted, should our coup be successful. Though the weapons demonstrated to us thus far were certainly effective, they were still weapons—a path to victory, perhaps, but not to an ultimately peaceable society. The woman had promised us answers to this problem several times, and this was the encounter in which we finally saw the future that she envisaged.*
>
> *Just as she had several times before, she had taken two Gifted captive in order to demonstrate her devices to us. As usual the men railed against us as soon as they recognized Kevran and I, demanding their release. However, as I came to realize later, their threats no longer unsettled me. Having seen others of their kind brought low in similar fashion, I no longer feared or hallowed their authority as I once had.*
>
> *After gagging the men and engaging with us in a discussion regarding the logistics of distributing her weapons to the outer regions of Andarra, the woman produced a small black disc, little larger than the size of a thumbnail. She pressed it against one the Gifted's necks; to my surprise the man appeared to be immediately, completely paralyzed.*
>
> *She then un-Shackled the other Gifted, telling him plainly that there would be no mercy shown should he*

455

resist or refuse her commands. The Gifted, of course, disregarded the woman's warning, clearly even now unable to believe that a non-Gifted could resist him. She was prepared for the eventuality, and the Gifted's screams as he endured his punishment are something that I will be grateful to no longer remember.

Once she was certain that the man would not resist again, she commanded him to direct a small trickle of Essence into the device on his colleague's neck. Upon doing so, the paralyzed Gifted began to convulse, and black lines the likes of which I have never seen appeared everywhere on his face, as if his very veins had been corrupted by darkness. It turned my stomach to watch, but despite my and Kevran's protests—the process appeared not unlike torture—the woman assured us that it was necessary.

She continued until the process was complete, whereby the paralyzed man fell unconscious. She then proceeded to kill the Gifted who had used Essence, but left the unconscious one alive, his face now marred almost beyond recognition.

She calmly explained to us that this procedure rendered the Gifted permanently unable to use their powers, but—besides the initially unpleasant process, and some associated memory loss—did them no lasting harm. Though at first Kevran and I were enthused by this prospect (if not the distasteful method of its execution), the woman warned us against considering it a blanket solution. She felt—and upon reflection, we agreed—that the Gifted would never peaceably coexist if they were forced to entirely, permanently forego their powers. This, she assured us, was better kept as a deterrent: a punishment less dire than execution, but awful enough to the Gifted that it would undoubtedly keep them in check.

She followed this by explaining that there was yet another device which would not only be exactly what we needed, but would restrict the Gifted in a far more
efficient way.

It was at this point that Jakarris himself walked in.

*When I saw the head of the Augurs enter that room—
the black-veined Gifted still slumped on the floor, next
to the bloodied corpse of his peer—I felt certain that
we were dead men. Even knowing Jakarris only from
afar, as with all the Augurs, there was no doubting who
he was.*

*Yet to my and Kevran's astonishment, Jakarris pro-
ceeded to greet us in a friendly manner, quickly assuring us that he knew our purpose and was in fact there
to assist. He explained that he had thus far concealed
his involvement because he wished to be certain of our
commitment and discretion before revealing himself.*

*Though this will undoubtedly be shocking news to
you—and still is to me—I believe that Jakarris's intent
is genuine. He gains nothing by pretending to support
our cause, and has had more than enough opportunity
to betray us since that meeting. I know it will be hard
for you to trust him, and I do not suggest wholeheart-
edly doing so. Still, I urge you to remember these facts.*

*Regardless—the discussions in that meeting were
particularly terse at first, neither myself nor my brother
believing that one of the Augurs could truly be involved
in plotting their downfall. Jakarris sensed this—or perhaps Read us—because he eventually insisted on elaborating upon his position.*

*What followed was as strange a tale as I have heard;
even now, I am unsure whether it could possibly be
true. Kevran, certainly, is more than skeptical. Yet
Jakarris appears to believe. Ultimately that is what will
drive his actions, and therefore is all that matters.*

*Jakarris's claim was thus: that the Augurs have long
known about, and passed down knowledge of, a danger inherent to their abilities—one that poses a very
great threat to all people. Each generation of Augur as
far back as he could trace has, he believes, willfully chosen to ignore this danger. He was reluctant to go into
detail, but when pressed, insinuated that the Augurs'*

mere continuing existence could ultimately result in the end of the world.

I imagine that you will laugh as you read that last sentence, as I did when it was first said to me. It is a grandiose claim, yet do not doubt: Jakarris trusts in it, heart and soul. He says that he intends to sacrifice himself, once all other Augurs are dead—and I believe that he will. Thus, I am not necessarily certain it is even important whether what he says is truth or insanity. Either way, he is firmly on our side.

After this explanation, it was hard to consider Jakarris's following statements seriously—and yet, the wealth of weapons he and the woman have produced still provided a compelling reason to listen.

The two of them proceeded to tell us of the final device that they had found for our rebellion: something that they believed could truly allow the Gifted and everyone else to form a new social hierarchy, without fear of an eventual uprising or retaliation from those who were usurped. Jakarris claimed that this device could bind the Gifted—all of them!—to rules of our choosing, and could optionally bind others to an entirely different set.

I immediately inquired as to why we did not utilize this device immediately, and ensure an all-but-bloodless coup. Jakarris and the woman made several salient points regarding this: the most important being that if we were truly not doing this merely for power—if we cared about the success of our revolution not just for next year, but for the next fifty—then we could not use this device as a means to conquer.

I protested, initially, but when Jakarris asked me how enslaving the Gifted in this way would make us any better than they are now, I could not provide an answer. And when Kevran pointed out that we would not impose harsh restrictions forever, the woman inquired as to at what point we thought it would be "safe" to remove them. A year? Ten? Once everyone who had once been in power had died of old age? She and Jakarris insisted that for there to be any kind of balance, the Gifted had to willingly submit to whatever rules were decided upon. Otherwise, the fighting would never truly be over.

It was frustrating, but I eventually conceded the validity of their arguments—though not before Jakarris indicated that he and the woman would not provide the device to us until they felt it was appropriate anyway.

After that, discussion turned to its possible uses. There were several that Jakarris proposed, but the one that resonated with Kevran and I was the concept of a policing force: a group of non-Gifted people in charge of the Gifted, dedicated to keeping them in line and also protecting them from any lingering backlash after the coup.

When I pressed for more details about the device, Jakarris remained vague, though he seemed happy to boast of its history. He said it was Darecian in origin, used originally by their greatest commander two thousand years ago, against the northern invasion by Aarkein Devaed himself. The claim was no less outrageous than others he had already made, and is irrelevant so long as the device works, so I refrained from openly scoffing. After all we have seen over the past six months, who can say? Perhaps there really is some truth to it.

Finally, though, Jakarris got to the true reason he had decided to reveal his involvement to us. Whilst he conceded that the Augurs have been distracted as they deal with their own problems—something which Jakarris refused to discuss, incidentally—they have still been having visions. Specifically, a few days prior, two Augurs had independently implicated both myself and Kevran in plotting against them.

Though this revelation was obviously terrifying, Jakarris says that there have been enough false visions of late that the Augurs have decided to organize a Reading of us to provide proof, rather than risk further *inflaming tensions with the populace by simply arrest-ing us. Kevran and I both panicked at this news, imme-diately wondering if we should move up our timeline for the coup, but Jakarris had a better solution—the reason for which I am now writing this account.*

He explained that he has the ability to remove all of our memories related to our dealings with the woman, as well as anything else that might appear particularly disloyal. Kevran and I both initially argued against this—the idea of losing memories was far from a pleas-ant one—but ultimately, the logic of Jakarris's plan won out. As far as our efforts have already come, we are not in a position to successfully launch an attack. This, realistically, is the only way forward.

To temper our concerns, Jakarris suggested that I write and Notarize this account, assuring me that he will take part in the verification himself, and that he can keep its specific contents safe from whomever else is present with him for the process. It is a risk, but I think perhaps a necessary one—otherwise, I am uncertain I could fully trust these words, regardless of whether they are written in my own hand.

Wirr frowned, reading a little further and then flicking for-ward a few more pages, but...that was it. Some final thoughts, exhortations to believe in the righteousness of their cause, but otherwise the end of his father's lengthy account.

He clenched his fist in frustration. It was interesting, even enlightening information—but not enough. The reference to the Darecian commander could perhaps be related to what had hap-pened with Isiliar and the Administrators, but it could equally be inconsequential. It was too little and too vague to be useful.

His shoulders slumped and he slid the notebook into his safe, locking it again with a sigh. He'd read it again later, perhaps, before giving it to Taeris—see if there was anything he'd missed, try and find if there was some important detail that he'd skimmed over. He didn't hold out much hope, though.

Shaking his head, he stood and grimly headed to his meeting with Taeris.

❦

Wirr flicked the door to Taeris's office shut behind him, then slumped into a chair.

The scarred man looked up from his desk with a mixture of concern and amusement at the entrance. "Rough morning, Sire?"

Wirr shrugged wearily. "Something like that."

Taeris sighed, pushing aside the papers he'd been reading. "My news isn't going to improve anything, I'm afraid."

Wirr's heart sank at his tone. "What now?"

"It's your mother." Taeris grimaced. "You know she's here, I assume?"

Wirr nodded, frowning.

"I haven't confirmed it yet, but…rumor has it, she's going to challenge for your positon."

"*What?*" Wirr stared at Taeris disbelievingly for a few moments, then suddenly shook his head, relaxing slightly. "Wait—no, she can't. She's an Andras by name, not blood." He knew the laws surrounding the leadership of Administration better than anyone, and that was a requirement that could not be circumvented.

"Your sister is, though," observed Taeris.

Wirr felt his brow furrow as he leaned forward, putting together what the other man was saying.

"So…she thinks that she can use Deldri to…what? Take the position, but then she acts as a kind of regent until Del's old enough?"

"Something like that." Taeris rolled his shoulders, clearly uncomfortable at having to deliver the news. "I haven't gone into the legality of it yet, but…these sort of rumors get discredited fairly quickly when there's no possibility of them being true. And if it *is* within the bounds of Administration's legal framework, then you need to start thinking about being friendlier toward your people."

Wirr closed his eyes. He wasn't certain, but he suspected that it *was* possible. "If it comes to a vote, Taeris, there won't be any point. You could put a dar'gaithin up against me and it would win in a landslide," he said heavily.

"And yet we both know the kind of things that your mother would press for if she was in charge," said Taeris quietly. "I know that you feel like you haven't been making an impact, Sire, but don't for a second underestimate the difference that your being Northwarden makes. You are the champion of the Amnesty, the only reason that it passed and the only reason it is still in effect. Your presence, your voice, has been the only thing stopping Administration from pushing back *viciously* against the progress that we've made in the Assembly over the past month—and your mother has the political capital to change that."

Wirr straightened, nodding slowly and taking a deep breath. "You're right," he said bleakly. "I'll talk to her."

"As soon as possible," urged Taeris seriously. "Head her off now, and this problem goes away."

Wirr just gave another grim nod in response. It wouldn't be pleasant, but this wasn't something that he could ignore.

They spoke for a while longer, Taeris updating Wirr on the Athian Council's response to Isiliar's attack—which, dishearteningly, echoed many of the other responses thus far. Though Wirr and Taeris had both tried to explain that Isiliar was linked to the Blind, they had little to go on and no real proof. Instead, most survivors were convinced that Isiliar had been a rogue Augur, crazed and bent on extracting some sort of personal vendetta. Everything that she had said during her attack backed up that claim, and Ambassador Thurin—who had been one of those whom Isiliar had attacked, though he had survived the resulting fall with only minor injuries—had championed the idea.

The resulting mess meant that ultimately, what Wirr had hoped would at least be a wake-up call for the Assembly, had instead managed to begin turning political opinion sharply back against the Augurs.

Eventually, Wirr's meeting with Taeris began to draw to a close. Wirr made to stand, then paused.

"Before I go, there's … something I wanted to ask you about. Probably a strange question, but …" Wirr sighed, shifting uncomfortably at the memory. "Once an Augur has started Controlling someone. Is there any way you know of to stop it?"

Taeris frowned. "You mean for someone other than another Augur?" He shook his head. "No. I don't think so."

Wirr hesitated. He didn't know whether it was a good idea, revealing to Taeris what had happened—but without Davian around, Wirr doubted that there was anyone else who would be able to help.

Grimly, he told Taeris about the Administrators. How his desperate shout had appeared to interrupt what Isiliar was making them do.

"It might have been nothing," he concluded, the same thing he'd told himself several times already over the past few days. "And it might have been Alaris, I suppose. But it *seemed* related to what I said."

Taeris leaned back, studying Wirr.

"Well, you're not an Augur," he eventually said drily, "so I think we can discount that. And a simple shout wouldn't have been enough to break Control." He thought for a moment. "*If* you managed to interfere with Control, then it must have been to do with your being Northwarden."

Wirr nodded, unsurprised that Taeris had come to the same conclusions as he. "There was one other factor," he said quietly. "It was pure coincidence that I even had it on me, but..."

He slipped a hand into his pocket and produced the Oathstone.

Taeris gazed at it for a long few seconds, frowning. "You had that with you during the attack?" When Wirr nodded again, he leaned back thoughtfully.

"Well. This could be...interesting." The Representative nodded slowly. "I have some things I need to see to first, but meet me in a couple of hours in front of the Middle District Cells. And bring your Oathstone."

Wirr frowned. "For what?"

Taeris smiled, and Wirr felt a sliver of unease at the look in his eyes.

"Experimentation," the scarred man said quietly.

Chapter 33

Asha slid into motion, blocking the blow from Breshada's blade.

It was steel borrowed from one of the men, of course; even Breshada, for all her bluster, had no intention of training with Whisper. Still, there were no training swords, and over the past few days Breshada had moved from stepping through forms to attacking with a reasonable amount of force. Asha thought that the other woman was probably skilled enough not to hurt her if she made a mistake. Probably.

The clash of steel echoed across the open, vibrantly green plains, brightly lit beneath the midday sun. Asha stepped back and continued to move, not breaking form, despite the incessant tug of the weariness that she still constantly felt. Breshada watched her and then gave a slight nod, lowering her weapon.

"Better?" asked Asha.

Breshada made a noncommittal gesture. "Not worse."

Asha restrained a smile; it was as close to a compliment as she would get from the Hunter. Though they were certainly still not friends, getting up so early each morning to train over the last week—as well as occasionally, like now, practicing further during breaks in traveling—had formed a bond of sorts, a mutual respect. There was no longer any bite to Breshada's insults, and Asha could clearly hear the difference between her speaking to Asha, and her speaking to any of the others in the group.

At an unspoken signal they sat, Asha quickly draining the water she kept on hand. Despite the day not being overly hot she was sweating, exhausted, while Breshada seemed to barely be breathing hard. Asha's fitness was improving, but she doubted that she would be Breshada's equal even in that regard anytime soon, if ever.

She glanced at the blade hanging from Breshada's side. "So how *did* you get Whisper?" she asked, as casually as possible. She already knew what Wirr had told her, but given the apparent connection to Caeden, she'd been waiting for an opportunity to inquire. Laiman had tried asking a few days ago, and Breshada had told him in no uncertain terms that it was none of his business. He'd only stopped pressing when he'd realized that she looked ready to use the blade on him.

Breshada stiffened at the question, not looking at her. There was silence for a few seconds.

"A long story," she said eventually.

There was nothing more forthcoming, and Asha knew better than to press. Breshada was still standoffish in their interactions, but Asha felt as though her brusqueness toward her was a matter of form now, rather than any actual personal dislike. Still—there was no need to push her luck. They were nearly at Deilannis, but she would have the entire journey back to find out more.

"We should go over the Draw principle again," Asha said quietly. She hesitated. "I know you don't want to, but it would be far easier to explain if you were willing to draw just a *little* Essence. You wouldn't even need to use—"

"No." Breshada's tone was firm.

Asha sighed. "Without the practice, you're going to keep running the risk of drawing it accidentally—it's amazing that you haven't done it again, actually. It's no different to if I wanted to learn how to use a sword, but refused to actually pick one up. You can teach me theory all you want, but it's never going to make me any good at it."

Breshada scowled. "And if the only way to learn was to cut off your own arm?"

Asha swallowed a snarky reply. The same conversation, the same result. Breshada wasn't stupid—far from it—and she'd managed to avoid further accidents since the incident with the Administrators, but that didn't mean that it wouldn't happen eventually.

466   "You will have to choose sooner or later, Breshada," she said

softly. Breshada was still absolute in her belief that touching Essence was an abomination, an affront to the Nine Gods. Asha had tried to find out more about the specifics—she didn't know much about Desriel's religion at all, if she were being honest—but Breshada was always closemouthed on the subject.

Still, it was an argument that she had already presented enough times for Breshada to know well; for now, it would have to be enough that the other woman was at least reminded of the reality.

"Theory it is then," Asha said ruefully after a few moments of silence.

They spent the next half hour going over some of the most basic mental techniques for the Gifted. Breshada had picked them up quite quickly, reciting back various principles with relative ease. Whether she was simply a quick study, or whether her time as a Hunter had already taught her some of this, Asha wasn't sure. Still, by the end, she felt as though they had made progress.

They rejoined the others, and soon they were on their way again, the dull roar of the Lantarche's violent white waters a constant accompaniment to their journey as they followed the edge of the deep canyon through which it ran. The Menaath Mountains—which they had been skirting for what seemed like forever—were still visible across the border on their left, but they had receded a little, even as more mountains had risen to their right. The area in between that they were traveling through, though, was flat and open.

They were, according to Laiman, getting close to Deilannis now.

Asha found herself slightly apart from the group as they rode, with only the king's adviser keeping pace with her. They proceeded for a couple of minutes in silence before Laiman stirred in his saddle, giving the slightest of nods toward Breshada.

"You have an interesting relationship with that one," he said abruptly, quietly enough that for a moment Asha thought that he was talking to himself.

Asha shrugged. "I think anyone who has a relationship with Breshada has an interesting one with her," she observed lightly. Laiman knew Breshada's real identity, as Wirr had let him know what was happening before they had left. He was the only other one in the group who did, though.

467

"Perhaps." Laiman allowed himself a slight smile, finally switching his gaze to Asha. "But you two are forming a bond. Unusual, given your...unique circumstances." He hesitated. "May I offer you some unsolicited advice?"

"There's no way I can answer that question without getting the advice, so go ahead."

Laiman's smile widened, and this time he looked genuinely amused. He sobered quickly, though. "It is simply that you should be cautious. I know a little of the Gil'shar, and what they believe..." He shook his head. "People like Breshada do not easily change. If ever."

Asha shifted. "People like Breshada don't often find themselves in her situation, either," she observed.

"Hmm." Laiman turned his gaze back to the overgrown road ahead. "Perhaps. I do not suggest stopping your lessons. Just... do not let your guard down."

Asha nodded, though her mind was already elsewhere. This was the first serious conversation she'd had with Laiman. Perhaps the man was finally relaxing.

"Have you had many dealings with the Gil'shar, over the years?" she asked casually.

Laiman shrugged. "On and off."

Asha waited, but nothing more was forthcoming. She snorted softly. "You're a wealth of information, Master Kardai," she said drily.

"Please." Laiman gave her a displeased look. "If you want answers, why not simply ask?"

Asha was silent for a few moments.

"Very well," she said eventually. "Let's start with why you're here."

Laiman gave her a puzzled look. "The king wanted a representative of his—"

"We both know that's not true," said Asha quietly. She watched Laiman's face carefully. The others were all still far enough ahead, well out of earshot. If she was ever going to bring this up, now was as good a time as any. "How do you know Taeris?"

Laiman shifted, but still looked confused. "Taeris Sarr? He's

468

the Representative for Tol Athian, and I'm an adviser to the king," he said in bemusement. "Our paths cross now and then."

Asha grunted. She was tired of this—tired of being suspicious, and not feeling as if she had much choice in the matter. "You can do better than that, Thell," she said in a low voice.

Laiman's posture and expression didn't change, but Asha was watching closely enough to see the flicker of shock in his eyes.

"I don't know who you think I am," he said slowly, "but you're mistaken."

"Then you won't mind if I start asking around, referring to you by that name?" asked Asha.

Laiman stared at the ground for a long few moments as their horses clopped along, the slightest tightening of his jaw the only sign he had even heard.

"Here and now is not the place for this discussion," he eventually said softly. "Ask me again once we're finished in Deilannis. We're not more than an hour away now." He looked up at her, and she could see that it was the best he was going to offer.

Asha hesitated, then gave a reluctant nod of acknowledgment.

Laiman watched her grimly for a second, then spurred his horse to catch up with the others without saying another word.

Asha lay on her stomach alongside the others, shivering as she looked down through the gap in the trees into the mists of Deilannis.

Davian and Wirr had both described the place to her—but the city, surprisingly, felt closer to Wirr's version at first glance. The way in which Davian had talked about it, Asha had assumed that Wirr's image of it was colored by the assumed loss of his friend. But she realized now that Davian had spent weeks there, had grown less fearful of the mists.

It wasn't hard to see that the fog was far from natural. Even from this distance the thickness, the way it clung to the faint outline of buildings as if to conceal even that from sight, sent chills down Asha's spine. There was something unsettling about the entire picture. Something that stirred a deep-seated unease in her.

"What are we looking for?" she asked Breshada quietly. The Hunter had gone on ahead as they had approached the rise overlooking the city and had immediately cautioned them to leave their horses behind and approach quietly.

"Wait," was all Breshada said.

A few moments later Asha spotted the motion, and from the sharp intakes of breath from beside her, she could tell that Laiman and the other Gifted had as well.

Slithering out from behind a series of large boulders down below—close to the beginning of the long, supportless white bridge—was a dark figure, relatively small from this vantage point but still easily discernible. Its black scales drank in the early afternoon sunlight as it glided across the gravelly ground, leaving a long, dark furrow in its wake.

A few seconds later there was more motion and the first figure was joined by two more as they emerged from behind a curtain of foliage.

"Dar'gaithin," murmured Laiman, dismay evident in his tone.

"We should just wait for them to leave," said Charis, adjusting her red cloak nervously. Mutters from Tyrin and Lue echoed the sentiment.

Asha shuddered as she watched the purposeful movements of the creatures. "I don't think that's going to be an option."

Breshada dipped her head in acknowledgment. "They are standing guard," she confirmed. "From what I have observed, one patrols, whilst two stay nearby the bridge."

"There must be a way to get past them," said Asha, brow furrowing as she studied the monsters below. The incline down to the flat area in front of the bridge was steep, and they would need to use one of the paths cut into the hillside to descend—but those appeared at regular intervals along the cliff, including one or two stairways in the distance that could well be out of sight from below. It was getting onto the bridge itself that was the problem. "Can we sneak by?"

"There is no way to reach the mists without being seen," said Breshada. She touched Whisper's hilt lightly. "But there are six of us. If we time our attack, take the two by surprise, then we can

deal with them."

Laiman shook his head, glancing at Breshada's blade. "I'm sure you're very good with that thing, but the rest of us combined wouldn't stand a chance against even one of those creatures. They are bigger than they look from up here—nine, ten feet tall—and fast. Powerful. Their scales act like armor, not to mention absorb Essence." He gazed down at the bridge worriedly. "I actually think Ashalia's suggestion is our best move."

Breshada glared at him. "And how do you propose such a thing?" She shook her head. "Our only option is to strike, and strike hard."

"Or we could just turn around," said Lue quietly. "I know this trip is important, but if we can't even use Essence against those things..."

There was a long silence.

"What if we could distract the two at the bridge? Draw them away?" Asha swallowed, suspecting that she was going to regret suggesting this. "If they were chasing one of us, surely the rest would be able to get to the mists before they returned."

"Suicide," said Laiman immediately, and even Breshada nodded her agreement. "They're too fast."

Asha hesitated, then reached into her pocket.

She reluctantly drew out the Veil.

"I have this." She touched the silver torc to her arm.

She heard a gasp from at least one of the Gifted, and both Laiman's and Breshada's eyes went wide as they just stared at the spot from which they would have seen her vanish.

"A Vessel?" asked Laiman softly as Asha deactivated the Veil again.

"You can move about freely as long as it's activated." Asha shrugged at his expression. "I know, but I didn't really want to give it back to Administration."

Laiman stared at her dazedly for a few more seconds, then shook his head wryly. "I can imagine." His gaze moved from Asha's face to the Veil and then back again, and suddenly there was a flicker of understanding in his eyes. "That won't work once you're on the bridge, though," he added.

"I will use it," said Breshada abruptly. "With such an advantage, I can certainly kill all three."

Asha frowned. "You don't have to risk—"

"Distraction is not a bad idea, but in this scenario there are too many variables. What if only one of those guarding the bridge pursues? What if it takes too long to lure the two away, and the third returns? Or if you cannot lure them far enough, and they still see us crossing the bridge? If they have the patience to guard and the intelligence to patrol, then we cannot assume that they will be easily fooled." Breshada said the words flatly. "Not to mention that if we do not deal with them now, we will have no choice but to do so on the way back." She locked gazes with Asha. "Sometimes, the most direct approach is best."

"She's right," said Laiman quietly to Asha as she hesitated. He stared down through the trees as the sole dar'gaithin set off again, its patrols appearing to be at consistent intervals. "I don't much like it, either, but your Vessel will give Breshada an enormous advantage. It's this or go home, and I haven't come this far just to turn back."

"Then it is settled," said Breshada before Asha could protest.

Asha paused for a long moment, then reluctantly nodded and handed the silver torc to Breshada. She'd had it for so long now, it felt strange to think of being without it . . . but Breshada's analysis had been accurate.

And—invisibility or not—she wasn't exactly *upset* that she didn't have to encourage two armored, nine-foot-tall snakes to chase her, either.

"All right," she said quietly, taking a deep breath as she studied the steep hillside in front of them. "Let's figure out how to do this, then."

Asha's heart lurched as one of the dar'gaithin that she could see stirred, turning its head and staring in the direction from which the third creature was now overdue to appear.

She and the others hadn't moved from their position at the top of the cliff, but Breshada had activated the Veil and vanished down the nearest set of stairs close to half an hour ago. The Hunter had decided to deal with the patrolling dar'gaithin first, and the creature's continuing absence suggested that she had

succeeded.

Suddenly there was a spasm of movement down below as one of the dar'gaithin flailed backward; it was hard to tell at this distance but Asha thought that she could see dark, viscous fluid spurting from one of its eyes. Its companion stared at it for a split second and then whipped around wildly, tail lashing out with blinding speed as it swung at the air, backing desperately toward the bridge. A few seconds passed, and then the second dar'gaithin's head snapped to one side.

It fell, twitched a few times, and then lay still.

As Asha and the others watched, Breshada blinked into view at the entrance to the bridge, calmly wiping her blade on the nearby grass. Then the Hunter looked up, giving a showy bow in their direction.

"I think she's telling us it's safe," said Laiman drily.

They cautiously picked their way down the crumbling, overgrown stairs, soon rejoining Breshada at the bridge. As Asha approached, the Hunter cheerfully tossed the silver torc to her.

"Simple," was all she said, a note of satisfaction in her tone.

Asha gave her a wry smile, pocketing the Veil and then shivering as she gazed at the scale-covered bodies lying motionless nearby. Breshada's blade had taken one of the monsters in the mouth, and the other in the eye; every other inch of their bodies was covered by the dark, heavy scales that Asha immediately recognized from her encounters with the Blind.

"Let's not delay," said Laiman, sounding as uneasy as Asha felt as he eyed the corpses. "The sooner that we're away from here, the better."

No one objected, and they started quickly across the smooth white bridge. The thundering of Lantarche below was loud here, even with what looked like at least a hundred-foot drop to the white, churning waters below. The bridge was wide but it had no railings; despite the polished look of the stone underfoot, Asha was relieved to find that it provided a comfortable amount of purchase as she walked.

They soon reached the thick, enveloping mists, Asha shuddering as the air suddenly felt heavier, damp and harder to breathe.

They had been in the fog for less than thirty seconds when someone gave a shriek of terror.

The scream was quickly joined by another panicked shout; before anyone could react, both were abruptly cut off. There was a blur of distorted motion toward where Lue and Charis had been walking up ahead, and for a moment, Asha couldn't make sense of the confusion of silhouetted shapes in the white murk.

Then something was rolling toward her along the ground, not properly visible until it was only a few feet away.

Charis's decapitated head stared sightlessly to the side, the trail of blood it had left nearly black against the cold white of the bridge. The base of her skull had been caved in, the blow that had killed her probably the same immensely powerful one that had ripped her head from her shoulders.

There was only chaos after that.

Everyone was yelling, but the murky fog and then, somewhere, Breshada drawing Whisper muted the sounds, making everything happen in a surreal hush. Dar'gaithin—Asha wasn't sure how many, but she thought there were only a couple of the creatures— flitted around the bridge, blurry silhouettes whose tails cut through the mists with blinding, horrific speed.

Asha shakily drew her blade as a red-cloaked body went airborne past her and over the side of the bridge. Then a massive, sinuous shape emerged from the mists ahead, the dar'gaithin's gaze bright and greedy as it fixed on her.

She made herself remember what Breshada had taught her. Stayed calm. Balanced. There was no running, not from this. Attack, and hopefully the surprise of someone resisting, was her only hope.

She lunged forward, her blade streaking toward the creature's mouth, the largest of the three possible targets.

The dar'gaithin reacted, moving slightly to the side, quicker than she could possibly have anticipated.

Her strike screeched off the side of its face, not even scratching the creature's light-drinking armor.

A moment later its tail was slamming into the small of her back, and there was a sickening crack as something broke. She felt her blade spin away into the abyss as she flew through the air herself, landing with an explosion of breath several feet away and
sliding even farther.

There was more numbness than pain; she tried to stop her momentum as she skidded, but her legs weren't responding.

Instead she slid, painfully slowly, over the edge of the bridge.

Shouting and twisting desperately, she managed to snare the very edge with her right hand, then swung and grabbed on with the left as well. She tried to pull herself up but her legs still wouldn't move, and there was nothing further on which to grab.

As she hung there, her grip started to weaken.

In the background, the shouts had stopped, and she could see Breshada's dim outline as the Hunter wrenched her blade from the face of one of the monsters. Had she managed to kill them?

"Help," she gasped, though the wind had been knocked from her and it came out as little more than a wheeze. *"Help."*

Movement registered to Asha's left, and she turned her head to see Laiman staggering through the mists. He saw her, and their eyes locked.

For a long, horrifying moment, the king's adviser hesitated.

Asha's grasp on the bridge slipped farther; Laiman came to a decision and scrambled toward her, skidding to his knees.

It was too late. As Asha desperately tried to will her muscles to move again, to reach up and grasp Laiman's outstretched hand, the last of her purchase was suddenly gone.

She fell.

Chapter 34

Wirr steeled himself, then knocked at his mother's door.

It would have been an understatement to say that he wasn't looking forward to this meeting; Geladra's outright hostility at the Tel'Andras estate was still fresh in his mind, and Wirr had no reason to think that she would be any less difficult to deal with here. He knew all too well that he couldn't afford to put it off, though. If Geladra gained control of Administration, it would be an unmitigated disaster for the Augurs—and subsequently for Andarra. What had already been an unpleasant personal conflict was now far more than that, and there was no way he could avoid it.

The door opened, and there were a long few seconds of silence as Geladra saw who it was.

"Torin," she said eventually, reluctantly moving back from the door. "Come in."

Wirr entered. "We need to discuss what's going on," he said without preamble.

Geladra gestured for him to sit. "So you've heard, then." She sat opposite, seeming just as wary and tense as she had been at the Tel'Andras estate. "To be honest, unless you're here to step aside, I'm not sure that there's much left to say."

Wirr pushed down an immediate flush of frustration, maintaining his outwardly composed demeanor. "I know that things are not exactly well between us, Mother, but we cannot let that spill over into affecting something as important as the running of the country. At least be willing to talk about this. I don't want to fight, and I certainly don't wish to place Deldri in this position." He said the words calmly, matter-of-factly, trying to convey the truth of the situation rather than sound accusatory or aggressive. He hesitated, then took a deep breath. "But I should also say from the start—my stepping aside is *not* going to be on the table."

He held her gaze, doing his best to project his determination. Since Taeris had told him of his mother's intent, he'd had a short amount of time to consider what it really meant to him. How he felt about the possibility that he might no longer be Northwarden. Despite his difficulties in dealing with Administration, his position had never been seriously in doubt until today . . . and this current situation had crystallized something in his mind that he had not, perhaps, fully acknowledged before.

Northwarden was *his* role now. Administration was *his* organization. He'd worked hard to reconcile who he was with this new position, had thought at great length about how he should lead, and had been painstaking to make sure that all of his decisions were the right ones given his mandate. He'd been unwavering in his commitment and had fought bitterly to put his father's legacy to its best uses, no matter what anyone else believed.

And as Taeris had said, what he was doing here was making a difference. Difficult, perhaps—but *good*.

There was no way that he was going to simply give it all up.

Geladra watched him silently, and from the tightening around her eyes, Wirr thought that at least some of his resolve must have shown through. She said nothing for a few seconds.

"I don't want this either, Torin. But I cannot trust you," she said eventually. "You still won't speak out against the Augurs, despite you and your sister nearly *dying* after that woman attacked. Why? Simply because you are friends with one?" She shook her head, looking strangely ill at ease. "It is too suspicious—and even if it wasn't, you are too late. The call for a vote is in motion and I have made certain that the process cannot be stopped, even if I . . . mysteriously change my mind. So if you're here to do whatever it was that you did to me back at the house, then get it over with. But it will do you no good." She stared at him with an odd touch of defiance in her expression.

Wirr gazed back blankly. "What I did to you?"

"Don't act as if you don't know." Geladra glared. "You forced me to let you leave with Deldri. I don't have any proof, but I *know* you did *something.*"

Wirr felt a chill as he processed the words, not responding for a moment. He thought back to that night, those few minutes after he'd opened the safe in his father's office.

He'd just found the Oathstone—and he'd been holding it when he had told his mother to let them go.

He swallowed, paling. If word got out about something like that...

"I haven't said anything. I want to see you removed from Administration, not lynched," Geladra added, watching his expression closely. "I don't even believe that you *think* you are doing the wrong thing, Torin—but after living with the bleeders for three years, you are naturally blind to their lies. That is why I am doing this. I will not let you destroy everything that your father worked so hard for, everything he risked, just because you have faith in the wrong people."

Wirr flinched at his mother's almost absent use of the derogatory term, jaw clenching.

"Destroy it?" He shook his head. "Father *wanted* this. He *died* for this!" His scowl deepened but then he gritted his teeth, taking a couple of deep breaths. Anger wasn't productive here, nor was pride. "Please. Come and work *with* me. Let me show you the same reports that I see from the north. We can discuss it. We can figure this out without throwing Administration even further into disarray than it already is."

Geladra hesitated, then shook her head.

"No. It's too late. Perhaps if you had come to me with that offer a few weeks ago...but now, you're only asking out of desperation. You cannot win a vote and you know it." She leaned forward, expression earnest. "The people you have been listening to are not good people, Torin. Please, just step down and—"

Wirr couldn't keep his frustration bottled up anymore.

"They're *not good people*?" He gestured in bemusement. "You don't even know them! Fates...you're...you're so sure that the Gifted and the Augurs are going to start acting as they did twenty years ago, that you refuse to even *consider* that perhaps things   479 have changed. I *know* that they didn't do the right thing back then. But that doesn't mean Administration gets to do the wrong thing *now*."

Geladra weathered the outburst in silence, waiting until Wirr was finished. Then as Wirr frowned in confusion she rose, walked over to her desk, and unlocked a drawer. From within, she drew out a bound leather book.

For a moment Wirr thought that it was his father's notebook—the cover was similar—but before he could make the accusation, he saw that one was much thinner and well worn, the look of a tome that had been read many times.

Geladra paused, then handed the book to him.

"What is this?" he asked with a frown.

"Your father's journal from a few years ago. Not like whatever it was you took from his safe, I assume"—she grimaced at that—"but a day-to-day record of everything in Administration. Where he had to be, what he had to do. I found it hidden behind the bookshelf when I was going through his things, after…" She gestured, swallowing. "A day or two before we had to leave for the funeral. It was covered in dust. Had been there since the last entry, I'd say."

Wirr opened it with a frown, seeing immediately that the handwriting was identical to that in the notebook from the safe.

He began flicking through. The information jotted down seemed unimportant—names and dates of meetings, a few personal observations on Administrators, but nothing of real interest. He felt his brow furrow.

"I don't see—"

"Keep going," his mother said quietly.

Wirr flipped a few more pages, then hesitated. The content of the notes hadn't changed, but the penmanship looked…off. Elocien's hand was usually neat and flowing, the mark of a man carefully schooled from birth. This was an approximation of that, but messier. More haphazard.

"The handwriting's changed," said Wirr slowly.

"It varies from page to page," said Geladra, "but what you're really looking for are the notes in the back. Beyond the first blank pages."

Wirr cocked his head to the side, flicking forward until he spotted the first of the scrawls that his mother was talking about.

Concerned I am being Controlled.

Wirr's heart lurched and he shook his head as he read the words again. They were the only ones on the page. Mouth suddenly dry, he flicked forward again.

An experiment. Short sentences don't trigger the blackouts.

Nothing for two pages, and then:

A longer experiment. Trying to talk to someone about this fails every time. The blackouts are getting longer and when I am conscious, I find it difficult to concentrate. Effect seems less when I'm alone at my desk. Perhaps he only takes over when threat of being revealed is high.

"This..." Wirr's voice shook as he looked up, seeing genuine sorrow in his mother's expression as she watched him. And something else, too.

Cold, contained fury.

"You should finish it, Torin. You should understand what these people you're so quick to defend are capable of."

Wirr slowly, reluctantly turned another page. This time the text was a block, scrawled but still clearly in his father's handwriting, a stark contrast to some of the earlier penmanship.

My time lucid is less and less. Memories are fading, too. This is the only way I can keep a record. There are things in this diary, meetings and decisions I do not remember making. Conversations that I've had confirmed that I was there, that I made those decisions and issued those orders. These are decisions I do not agree with. I cannot say as much though, else the darkness will come again. I think it must be the boy. I remember taking him in, but nothing beyond that. I told Administration that he was dead, but it seems likely that he is the one influencing me. I think he knows when he is losing control, but if I stay quiet and do nothing, he does not know that I am aware. My intent is to leave this diary hidden, then inform someone of its whereabouts. If someone is reading this, do not let on to me that you know. Watch my actions. Find those close to me who should not be.

Wirr swallowed, then flipped forward again. And again.

That was the last entry.

He said nothing for a long while as he stared at the empty page, trying to comprehend what he'd just read.

The final dated entry was from a little over three years ago. Back when his parents had been together.

Just before his Gifted-hating father had changed his ways, covered for him, sent him to Caladel.

He felt as though he were going to throw up.

"Of course, this is not the worst thing they have done," said Geladra quietly. "But then, you already knew that. You helped the Tols cover up what happened in Decis."

"Decis?" Wirr stared at her, still dazed, then frowned as he registered where he'd heard the name. "Those people claiming that an Augur Controlled their entire village?"

"Those people who came to you for justice for exactly that," said Geladra. "I had my own sources look into it, and they've verified enough to say it's true. The Tols scoffed, and the Houses decided that it wasn't worth the effort." She paused. "But that's what they do. *You*, Torin—*Administration*—*this* is why you're supposed to exist. To protect people. But you didn't. You didn't even *meet* with them."

Still disoriented as he tried to process the news about his father, Wirr shook his head, uncertainty suddenly assailing him. Elocien, it seemed, hadn't intended for him to be here at all... and maybe this was an example of exactly why.

For a long, gut-wrenching few seconds, he found himself doubting everything he'd done since becoming Northwarden. Wondering whether his mother was right.

Wondering whether he was a fraud.

Then he saw his mother's expression—too pleased at his shock, too smug at what she assumed was her point being proven—and everything that he'd learned over the past month began to reassert itself.

He'd been put off-balance plenty of times by Administration since taking this position; in all of those cases it was his appearance that had mattered most, not how stunned or confused he was really feeling.

He swallowed. Straightened his back. Pressed down his distress, and made himself carefully consider what his mother was saying.

He shook his head.

"No," he said, relieved to hear that his voice was clear and steady. "If you had compelling evidence—which *they* did not, incidentally—then you should have come to me." He said the words softly, grimly, holding his head a little higher and looking Geladra in the eye as her triumphant air faded. "I do not like dismissing accusations, Mother, but I made the best decision I could with the information that I had. You cannot blindfold me and then berate me for not seeing what is going on. If there was a clear case for investigation then the lack of one is *your* doing, not mine."

Geladra blinked, looking taken aback. She was silent for several seconds.

Then she stood, flushed, and snatched his father's notebook back from him.

"I have absolutely no desire to show people this. It will ruin your father's legacy—all of it, not just the past few years," she said grimly. "But do not think I won't sacrifice that if it's the only choice left to me." There was bitterness in her tone, but also resignation. She had hoped to shock him into standing aside, and now she was angry that her attempt had failed.

It was his cue to leave, and Wirr knew it. He stood, still stunned at what he'd learned about his father, heart heavy as he walked to the door. He thought that he could understand where Geladra was coming from, now; really, it was hardly surprising that she found it so difficult to trust anyone associating themselves with the Augurs. It didn't excuse what she was doing—and her existing, unreasonable antipathy toward the Gifted had undoubtedly made her behavior far worse—but at least it all made a little more sense to him.

He stopped just outside the door, something else occurring to him. He turned back to face Geladra.

"*I'm* not being Controlled, you know," he said quietly. "I'm making my own decisions."

Geladra watched him for a moment.

"Well. You have all the facts now. So I suppose we shall see," she said, her voice harsh with emotion.

Then she shut the door in his face, leaving him to deal with his shock and devastation alone.

⚬✼⚬

Wirr was silent as Taeris led him through the large gates and into the Middle District Cells.

The prison was deceptively small on the outside, its plain white facade barely larger than a house, though its steel gates and windowless, starkly utilitarian form betrayed its purpose. Once inside and allowed entry by the warden, a single, claustrophobically narrow flight of stairs—again constructed from the smooth, flawless white stone that typified the Builders' work—descended for close to five minutes until they eventually reached an expansive lower level, which was comprised of a grid of long, well-lit corridors that housed a multitude of secure cells.

Taeris looked across at Wirr as they started along the passageway.

"We'll figure it out, Sire. With your mother, I mean," he said. His words echoed along the quiet corridor. Though everywhere Wirr looked was lined with barred doors, most of them were open; despite the size of the prison, only a few of the cells down here were currently occupied.

Wirr just grunted in response, saying nothing for a while. He hadn't gone into detail regarding the meeting with his mother, nor had he told Taeris the revelation about his father. Quite aside from how painful the knowledge still was, he needed time to process the ramifications before he could decide who to trust—if anyone—with it.

"Whatever happened to those people from Decis? The ones who told us that an Augur had been Controlling their village?" he asked suddenly.

Taeris frowned at the question. "They were sent away. Remember?

It was impossible to verify what they were saying, and giving it the legitimacy of an investigation was only going to stir up trouble, politically speaking." He shook his head dismissively. "I cannot say whether they were lying, but I think it was for the best."

Wirr grimaced. "But what if they *weren't* lying? Now that I— Administration—have dismissed their claim, where else could they possibly go to get justice?"

Taeris gave Wirr a vaguely bemused glance.

"These are extraordinary times, Sire," he said eventually. "Their accusation may well have been genuine, but there were several dozen other complaints, quite similar in nature, that I guarantee were not. If things were different, then yes—we would treat them all seriously. Right now, though? If we give credence to one, then we give credence to all. We have to investigate. We have to give each allegation our attention, commit men and hours and judges and..." He gestured tiredly. "All of which would be an ongoing process which affects the very delicate perception of the Augurs. If we suddenly dedicate half of our resources to investigating whether they're criminals, you know that it will take the Assembly all of two seconds to distance themselves. We'd be risking the Amnesty, Sire. Risking our one chance to seal the Boundary."

Wirr took a deep breath, nodding. Taeris wasn't saying anything that he hadn't known, but it helped to hear it from someone else.

Taeris watched him for a moment, then sighed. "I don't know what your mother said, but don't let her get inside your head. Your position is hard, Sire—perhaps harder than anyone else's in the Assembly right now. But you've been making the best decisions that you can, and you've been doing a remarkable job. I don't say that lightly, either. So don't start second-guessing yourself now."

Before Wirr could respond, Taeris brought him to a halt and gestured, pointing through the long bars of a nearby cell. Wirr swallowed as he examined the prisoner within, who was watching them silently from the back of the small stone room.

It was hard to believe that it had been less than two weeks ago that this man had tried to kill him.

"You," sneered the man suddenly as he recognized Wirr. "I

suppose you think you're brave, coming down here to face me from behind those bars?"

Wirr glanced at Taeris, who just nodded.

Wirr took a deep breath, putting a hand in his pocket and grasping the Oathstone tightly.

"I came to ask you who arranged to have me killed," he said quietly.

The bald assassin stared at him for a long moment, then barked an obnoxiously loud, mocking laugh.

Wirr kept his face smooth, waiting until the sound had died. "Tell me who arranged to have me killed."

"I don't know. Vanni was the one who dealt with them. She's the one who told us about it, who organized everything. She never said who gave her the job, and we never asked."

There was silence for several seconds once the "gray" Administrator had finished, and Wirr felt a chill as the man gaped at him, eyes wide.

"What in all fates?" the prisoner whispered, blood draining from his face. He wasn't smiling anymore. "Guards! GUARDS!"

"No one is coming to help you," said Taeris as the shout was swallowed by the silent hallway. "That's what happens when you try to kill the prince."

The bald man stared at him for a moment, then started to yell again, though this time there were more curses than pleas.

Wirr closed his eyes.

"Be silent," he said.

The would-be assassin immediately stopped yelling, though his eyes were even wider now. He scrambled backward until he was pressed against the far wall of the cell, his breathing heavy and panicked, opening and closing his mouth but no sound coming out.

Wirr gazed at the terrified man in horror.

"Fates," he muttered to himself, shuddering. It was that easy?

"Fates indeed," murmured Taeris, watching the man in fascination. "It looks like a binding. He knows what he's doing, knows that he doesn't want to do it—but he can't help himself."

Wirr frowned, tearing his eyes away from the prisoner. "Like the Tenets?" He'd never heard the term "binding" used before.

"Exactly like the Tenets." Taeris nodded thoughtfully. "We know that the Oathstones are connected to the main Tenet Vessel. Your unique relationship with it must allow you to create new bindings, somehow. A sort of... localized Tenet, I suppose you'd say," he clarified, seeing Wirr's confusion.

Wirr shook his head in disbelief. "If that were possible, my father would have said something to me. *Someone* would have known."

"Your father wasn't Gifted. He couldn't change the Tenets by himself, so he very well may not have had this ability. Or even been aware of it." Taeris said the words absently, his gaze drifting back to the cowering man in the cell. "I wonder. Did the binding take effect because he could hear you, or was it because you were directing the command at him?" He turned to Wirr. "Go to the end of the passageway—out of his sight and out of earshot. Then tell him to say something to me."

Wirr shifted uncomfortably. "Is that necessary?"

"We need to understand how this works, Sire. And we cannot test it on anyone else, because if a real Administrator ever learned of it..." He looked at Wirr pointedly.

Wirr swallowed, thinking again of what his mother had said. "True enough."

"Although," mused Taeris as if he hadn't spoken, his enthusiasm evident, "perhaps you could command someone to never speak of something. Or to forget it entirely? I wonder." His eyes shone as he considered the possibilities.

Wirr flinched, stomach churning. He wasn't sure how he would have felt about this even yesterday—but now, after what he'd just learned about his father? He didn't want this. He didn't want anything to *do* with this.

But he knew that he couldn't just ignore it, either.

The following hour was as long a one as Wirr could ever remember. Physical proximity or being audible wasn't necessary for a command to work, so long as Wirr said it out loud and was thinking of someone specific. More precise directives worked better, as—like the Tenets—there seemed to be a degree of interpretation to them being carried out. Instructions to forget a set period of time, or specific events, appeared to work as well. Those memories clearly weren't erased, though; when the prisoner was told to remember them again, he was able to do so immediately.

It went on. A newer command would take precedence over a contradictory older one. Instructions—if they were laid out clearly enough—could be conditional, complex, triggered by other events. Taeris even figured out that Wirr could direct the man to follow orders that he had no memory of receiving—leaving him with no clue as to why he was acting a certain way, but still unable to prevent himself from carrying out the instructions.

By the end, they had answered a lot of the immediate questions surrounding Wirr's ability, as well as extracted the names of several Administrators who knew about the recruitment of more "unofficial" ones. They also, much to Wirr's horror, discovered that the bald man had been responsible for countless unreported crimes against the Gifted over the years—most of them covered up thanks to his commanding his victims to silence via the Fourth Tenet.

Even with those revelations, Wirr felt a little emptier with each new test. Perhaps he did need to know how this worked, and perhaps this man was deserving of everything that was happening to him. It didn't change how dirty manipulating the prisoner made him feel.

When the man had finally finished relating the last of his crimes, Wirr shook his head in disgust as he and Taeris moved a little distance away, to where they couldn't be overheard.

"Let's tell him to forget that we were ever here, and then to confess all of what he just told us to the warden," Wirr said quietly. "I've seen and heard enough."

Taeris nodded slowly, still staring at the bald man through the bars. He was outwardly calm, but Wirr had noticed his gaze holding steadily more heat as the would-be assassin had listed his wrongdoings. "I'd like to test the longevity of these bindings at some point," he said absently. "There's no way of knowing when—or if—they will eventually wear off. Tell him to forget, and I'll come back in a few days, then perhaps a few weeks after that. We'll see if he remembers any of this."

Wirr nodded, taking a breath to issue the command, when Taeris suddenly held up his hand.

488   "There's one last thing that we need to check."

"Which is?" asked Wirr wearily.

"Ask him to hurt himself."

"What?" Wirr stared at him. "No."

"We need to understand how far this can be pushed," said Taeris. The words were delivered calmly, but Wirr could hear the underlying ice in them.

"We don't need to know if it can be pushed that far, because I'm never going to tell someone to do that," replied Wirr grimly. "He's going to *hang* for what he's done, Taeris. I despise him as much as you do, but…" He shook his head. "That sort of punishment isn't for us to mete out."

"It's not about punishment. It's about understanding limitations."

"We both know that's not true," snapped Wirr.

"You need to be willing to take these extra steps, Sire." Taeris locked gazes with him. "This is a powerful advantage only if you understand its capabilities. Think about it. You can win the vote against your mother with this!"

Wirr stared at him in disbelief. "Are you listening to what you're saying?" he asked. "You want me to bind *all the Administrators*. Or at least all the ones who matter. How can I do that, in good conscience? How could I possibly call myself a leader if I simply force them to follow me?"

"Are you listening to what *you're* saying?" Taeris's patience was clearly running out. "How can you call yourself a leader if you do not, Sire? Administration will turn against all of our efforts if you're not in command—and if that happens, I'm not sure whether this brave new world that we're trying to forge will last." He rubbed his forehead in frustration. "Fates, you know them better than most. They still don't believe that Devaed is responsible for the attacks—don't believe that there is anything worse than the Blind and perhaps a few wild animals on the other side of the Boundary. How could you possibly let that foolishness cost lives—potentially even the country—when you could so easily make a difference?"

Wirr paled under the onslaught of words, but shook his head stubbornly. "Where would it end, Taeris? Don't we have a responsibility to do what we know is right?"

"This is just like at Gahille." Taeris face was a mask, but Wirr could see the tightly controlled anger behind it. "You want to do the right thing, but you don't want to do the *necessary* thing. And all it does is put others in danger." He leaned forward. "I say this not to embarrass, but to explain, Sire. It is a sign of a *weak leader.*"

Wirr clenched his fists. "So imposing my will, just because *I* believe something, is the sign of a strong one?"

"It is when you *know* it's right," said Taeris quietly. "You've seen enough to know the truth. They haven't. Besides—you call it imposing your will, and say that it's immoral. What do you think politics is, at its core?" He gestured. "Others will impose their will by threats, or by information, or by trickery, or with gold, or reason, or sheer charisma. They take advantage of what they have, Sire. None of them would hesitate for a heartbeat, were they in your position."

Wirr shook his head angrily. "I don't want to be like them, Taeris."

"And yet you *have to be.* It's the only way to win. Your father knew what it would take. Your father died for this. Your father—"

"That's *enough!*" Wirr shouted. "You don't know anything about my father! *Be quiet!*"

Taeris opened and closed his mouth silently at Wirr for several moments, eyes widening.

They stared at each other in steadily growing horror.

"You...you can speak now," said Wirr awkwardly.

Taeris let out a gasp, as if he'd been holding his breath.

"Well." The scarred man licked his lips, staring at the ground as if suddenly afraid to meet Wirr's gaze. "That...changes things somewhat."

Wirr slumped against the nearby wall. "Sorry."

"Not your fault." Taeris hesitated, then took a deep, shaky breath. "I was going to say this anyway—once we leave here, you can't keep that Oathstone on your person. All it would take is for one misworded comment..."

"I know. Fates, I know."

There was silence for a long few moments, and then Taeris sighed.

"I...am sorry, Sire. About what I said. I overstepped. I still think it's important for you to think long and hard about it, but...I can't force you to do anything." He gave a nervous laugh. "Unlike vice versa, I suppose."

"I understand why you brought it up." Wirr shook his head. "I just...we have some time left before the vote. At least a week. I have to at least *try* to win legitimately."

Taeris grimaced at that, but didn't protest. He eventually rolled his shoulders. "Well. At least you have someone else to test it on now."

Wirr smiled slightly, raising an eyebrow at the scarred man. "Who's to say I haven't already?"

Taeris blinked, then glared at him. The slight upward curl of his mouth indicated that he didn't mind the attempt at levity, though.

They talked for a little longer, but soon enough Wirr was giving the prisoner his final instructions, grimacing at the blank, mildly confused look that came over the man's face. He and Taeris quickly walked away before the bald man registered who they were.

The trip back was filled with awkward silence, Wirr finding himself uneasy about saying anything in case it came out as an order. The only real conversation came when Taeris mentioned his father's Notarized notebook again; after a short consideration, Wirr agreed to let him read it once they were back. There was no point in hiding the information it contained from Taeris.

Mostly, though, he found himself thinking about what Taeris had said in the prison. Wirr didn't want to do as the Representative had suggested...but he could also see his point.

There was little chance that he could legitimately convince any of the Administrators to vote for him. Almost none, in fact, especially while his mother had the evidence that she did. The task ahead of him was more than daunting.

But he still had a little time. He had to try.

Dezia was waiting for him when he got back to his rooms.

Wirr swallowed when he spotted her. He'd been trying to give her some space since she'd found out about Aelric.

"I heard about your mother and Administration," she said quietly as he approached, giving him a small smile of greeting.

Wirr nodded. "I tried talking to her earlier. It...did not go well," he said ruefully.

Dezia gave him a sympathetic look, but something in her eyes told Wirr that she hadn't simply dropped by to discuss his problems. He opened the door and they stepped inside.

He shuffled his feet awkwardly as Dezia shut the door again. "'Zia," he said softly. "Look, I know what I did—"

"I forgive you." Dezia stepped forward, lifting his chin up gently until his eyes met hers. "You were an idiot—there's no denying that—but there's not a malicious or deceitful bone in your body, Torin. It's one of the reasons I love you."

Wirr blinked at her for a few seconds, running the words over in his head a few times to make sure that he hadn't misunderstood. He broke into a slow, wide smile, his heart unclenching for the first time in a week.

"I love you, too," he said quietly. It was true, and to his surprise, he wasn't afraid to say it.

Dezia grinned at him, cheeks flushed, and a wave of emotion swept over him. He took a half step forward, caught up in the moment.

Dezia held up a hand, stopping him.

"Let me finish." She was still smiling, but there was sadness to it now, too. "I know that you need as much support as you can get right now, especially given what's happening with Administration. And I *want* to support you." She bit her lip. "But, Wirr... I've found some leads on where Aelric might have gone. And they take me south."

Wirr's smile faded, too, as he understood. For the first time he noted Dezia's plain but functional attire.

"You're leaving," he said in dismay. He closed his eyes. "You're going after him."

"I am." Dezia's tone was firm.

"Where?"

"He was spotted in Variden. That's where I'm heading." She shrugged slightly. "If he's not there anymore? I don't know."

Wirr swallowed. A large part of him wanted to talk Dezia out of what she was doing—if Aelric was in trouble, the last thing he wanted was for her to get involved as well—but at the same time, south was probably the safest direction in which she could go at the moment.

"Any idea what happened to him?"

Dezia hesitated. "He was seen talking to a man...I didn't get a name, but the description was familiar. It sounded like Tela del na Gurn."

Wirr shook his head. "I don't know who that is."

"Another of his backers." Dezia nodded grimly as Wirr winced. "There's not much doubt. Idiot's in trouble."

Wirr shifted. "I can send men with you. Contact Administrators there. We can—"

"No, Wirr." Dezia said the words gently, affectionately, but she shook her head with conviction. "We both know what it will look like if you use Administration resources to conduct a manhunt for your friend. You can't afford that. I've thought it through, and this is the only way."

Wirr gritted his teeth. "You can't go by yourself."

"I can and I am." Dezia gave him a rueful shrug. "I don't much like it either, truth be told. But...all I'm doing is looking for him. And if it does come to more than that, I can take care of myself."

Wirr took a deep breath. "I know." He leaned forward. "If you find him, though, and I can help in any way..."

Dezia nodded. "I'll find a way to contact you. And I'll come back as soon as I can."

There was silence, Wirr finding his gaze suddenly locked with Dezia's. There was no telling when they would see each other again.

He stepped forward. Cupped her face in his hands.

Then he kissed her, gently at first but with increasing ardor as she responded until eventually they broke apart again, flushed and grinning foolishly at each other. For a few blissful seconds, Wirr completely forgot what they had been talking about, his heart lighter than it had been in a long, long time.

Reality came back to them both too soon, though. Wirr gave Dezia's arm a gentle squeeze as his smile faded.

"Be careful, 'Zia," he said quietly.

"You too." Dezia smoothed back her hair, then raised an eyebrow at him. "By the way—the next time we see each other, I *do* expect you to still be Northwarden."

Wirr gave her an amused look. "I'll see what I can do."

Dezia nodded seriously. "And if you could resolve this whole 'Boundary' situation while I'm gone, too..."

Wirr laughed, only to be interrupted by another quick, passionate kiss.

Before he could react, Dezia was breaking away again and slipping out the door.

Wirr stood there silently for a while after she was gone, emotions roiling. He wanted more than anything to go after Dezia, to go with her. This was his fault, at least in part. If he'd been honest with her from the start—or even just pressed Aelric on what was really going on—this entire situation may never have come about.

Eventually, though, he sighed and compelled himself over to his desk, trying to decide where best to start with what came next.

He had a lot of Administrators to talk to.

Chapter 35

Caeden shivered as he stared across the long, railless white bridge.

It paled in comparison to some of his other memories, now, but remembering the last time he was here still unsettled him. The confusion, the white haze all around, the vague forms of the others behind him as they raced desperately out of the city. The shrieks of the creature, and then the feeling of despair as they'd collapsed on that smooth stone surface and realized that Davian and Nihim were no longer with them.

As he made his way toward the bridge, though, he quickly found himself more concerned with his purpose for being here. Nethgalla. The woman who had stolen his wife's face, stolen her memories. Even knowing only what he did, the thought made his heart beat faster with reflexive fury.

He knew that he couldn't let his emotions get the better of him, though. He needed to get in, retrieve the Siphon from Nethgalla, and leave again as quickly as he could.

Shale shifted underfoot as he walked along absently, and the cliff behind him cast a shadow over both him and the bridge. The mist across the chasm was thick as it twisted and swirled, thinning farther out where the light still struck, just enough to hint at the buildings beneath.

He didn't notice the dark shapes lying near the start of the bridge until he was all but on top of them.

Caeden froze as he took in the two black-scaled masses on the ground; his breath caught and he stayed motionless for several long seconds, watching warily. When neither of the figures moved, he cautiously crept forward again.

His tensed muscles relaxed a fraction as he finally saw that the dar'gaithin were indeed both dead. What had happened here? The ground was churned up around the corpses from where their tails had scarred the soft earth, but there were no other signs of violence. Everything was eerily still, the only sound the lonely thundering of water far below.

Glancing around nervously, he hurried onto the bridge.

He found the first of the bodies as soon as he entered the mists.

In horrified silence he picked his way through the barely visible scene. Dark blood was spattered everywhere, stark against the cold white of the stone underfoot. One figure that he spotted was entirely headless, its red cloak indicating that it had been one of the Gifted, while another—also red-cloaked—stared sightlessly up into the swirling white, its limbs mangled and neck at an impossible angle to its body.

Had this been the party from Ilin Illan? He'd deliberately slowed his pace over the past week, hoping to recall as much as he could before he had to face Nethgalla, and had eventually been overtaken by what he'd suspected was the group that Karaliene had mentioned. They had passed nearby while he'd been stopped for a meal a couple of days earlier, but he'd decided against making his presence known to them. It would only have resulted in complications.

Swallowing, he pushed cautiously onward. Two more dar'gaithin lay slain a little farther along, similar to the ones he'd seen just before. He gazed at the heavy black scales and powerful-looking bodies with a steadily increasing sense of dread. Was this the last of them? Who had won this fight?

Had anyone even survived?

Caeden hesitantly stooped down, touching a finger to one of the thick lines of blood nearby.

It was tacky. Drying, but far from old.

He shivered. It didn't really change anything, but it certainly didn't fill him with confidence, either.

He squared his shoulders and stepped over the last of the dar'gaithin corpses.

Pressed forward nervously into Deilannis.

The city was silent.

To Caeden's surprise, once he had stepped off the bridge and started walking along the main road, his dread had actually begun to lessen. The feeling of familiarity that this place gave him was stronger than ever. In a way, it felt a little like coming home.

There was still fear, of course. Though the streets gave him a sense of instinctive memory that he'd not felt since the last time he was here, everything was still swathed in thick white, the fog rippling and curling around things as if alive. Occasionally he would think that he'd heard something and freeze on the spot, holding his breath. There was never anything there, though. In each instance, if there had been a sound, it had to have been the echo of his own footsteps.

Of the creature that had hunted them last time, or more dar'gaithin, there was no sign. He suspected—hoped—that there wouldn't be, so long as he kept quiet and did not use Essence.

Within an hour he was entering the Inner City, passing through an archway tall and wide. No piked skull adorned this entrance, for which he was thankful. Despite everything he'd remembered since, for some reason that still sent a shiver through him whenever he thought about it.

The mists began to thin as Caeden pushed forward, gray light bathing everything in monochrome. He walked for a while in silence, then abruptly pulled up, staring at a house off to the side.

It was two stories tall, displaying none of the smashed windows, crumpled doors or scarring from fire that blemished some of the other buildings in the Inner City. He didn't remember it from his last trip to Deilannis; he'd passed this entire area in a blind panic, barely seeing the road in front of him let alone what lay to the sides. Yet it felt...familiar.

He hesitated, then opened the door and slipped inside.

The passageway, the kitchen with its small table, the winding stairwell to the left...they were all unremarkable, and yet he felt strangely comfortable here.

This, he was sure, was what it must feel like to come home.

He moved slowly through the poorly lit house, checking

cupboards, trailing his fingers along railings that were unset-tlingly absent of dust as he climbed the stairs. It felt as though, if he could just find *something*—one single thing that was personal—then he would be able to trigger a memory of this place. Figure out why it was so familiar.

There was nothing, though. The house was perfectly clean, and perfectly empty.

When he went back downstairs, the creature was waiting for him.

He shouted in alarm as the black figure detached itself from the doorway, its eyeless face and gaping, sharp-toothed maw a horror even if there hadn't been close to no illumination in the room. Its skin glistened in the dim light, and a hole where its nose should have been twitched as it sniffed at him.

Caeden braced himself, instinctively reaching for kan.

"Tal'kamar," rasped the creature.

Caeden froze.

He stared at the being, muscles tensed to spring into action at the hint of a threat. But it didn't move toward him.

Instead, it bowed subserviently.

Caeden gripped the back of a nearby chair, steadying himself.

"You know me?" he said softly.

"Ilian di Tal'kamar," said the creature. *"Orkoth sa elid."*

Caeden closed his eyes. Concentrated.

You are Tal'kamar. Orkoth knows you.

He took a deep breath. He understood, could translate. That was a start.

"You are Orkoth?"

"Yes." The creature's—Orkoth's—voice sent shivers down Caeden's spine. It reminded him of how the sha'teths sounded.

"How do you know me, Orkoth?" Caeden had to think, but he knew the words in the creature's language. He compelled his muscles to relax, though he didn't take his eyes from the monster.

There was silence for a moment, as if Orkoth was thinking.

"You brought me. To guard."

Caeden frowned. "This house?"

"This city. Everything."

Caeden swallowed. This creature...it had attacked them,

attacked his friends. Killed countless people over the years, if Tae-ris was to be believed. "Why?"

"To delay. To stop tampering. To keep others safe." A pause. *"Another is in the Great Library. Waiting. She is not of here. She is of me."*

Caeden blinked. He needed time to focus, to process, but his fear—or at least unease—was keeping him from concentrating on anything else. "What do you mean? Who is waiting there?"

"Another," was all Orkoth said.

Caeden grimaced. "Do you follow my orders?"

"Yes."

"Then sit." He gestured to a chair. "Don't move until I tell you to."

Orkoth sat, erect and perfectly still.

Caeden frowned, watching the creature for a few moments. Then he sighed.

He was immortal. It was about time he started acting like it.

He swallowed his fear, sitting opposite the creature, though unable to remain entirely relaxed across from its chilling, eyeless stare.

"What are you?"

Orkoth cocked its head to one side, as if confused by the question. *"I am as you made me. I am..."* It growled suddenly, and Caeden leaped to his feet instinctively, sure that it was about to attack.

After a moment, though, he realized that it was a sound of frustration. The creature wanted to explain something to him, but was unable to put together the words.

Caeden couldn't restrain a shiver. He had *made* this thing? "What do you know of me?" he asked tentatively.

Orkoth shook its head, evidently becoming agitated with this line of questioning. *"What is necessary. You pulled me from the Darklands. This form is not pain. That is all you gave. That is all that is needed."*

Caeden swallowed. "The Darklands?"

"Where He rules. His attempt at...this." Orkoth gestured vaguely around itself, though Caeden wasn't sure to exactly what it was referring. Its voice was rising now, sounding panicked. *"It is black and pain and blood and fear and death and—"*

Orkoth screamed.

Caeden sprang to his feet, knocking over his chair in his haste to get away from the hideous, soul-piercing noise. He covered his ears with his hands but it didn't seem to matter; tears started streaming down his face, as if the sound itself carried more misery than he could bear.

It seemed to last forever, but as suddenly as it had started, it stopped.

Caeden gasped on the floor with his back to the wall, where he had crawled. He was shaking. Sobbing. That scream had shown him images, flashes of things that were all too like the memory that Asar had shown him back in the Wells. He knew that his mind was reacting, hiding what he had seen from himself, protecting him against the incomprehensible horror so that he would still be able to function. But just the aftershock was enough to turn his blood to ice and his legs to water.

Finally, slowly, he dragged himself to his feet. Orkoth still sat silently at the table, looking at him as though nothing had happened.

"Go," whispered Caeden hoarsely. He must have shouted at some point, though he didn't remember it. "Go and do not show yourself to me again unless I need you. I will call for you if..."

He trailed off, but he'd said enough. Orkoth rose and without another word, left the room.

Caeden stood there for a minute. Two. Five. Just breathing, trying to escape the crippling feeling of dread that had enveloped him.

Eventually though, finally, he managed to compel himself to stand. Someone was waiting for him in the Great Library? Nethgalla, then. It had to be Nethgalla. He would get the Siphon, and then he would leave this place as quickly as he possibly could.

He gritted his teeth, facing the door.

The memory hit without warning.

Caeden strode through the halls of the Arbiterium, ignoring the screams of the dying that echoed through the building.

Outside, the streets of Deilannis burned with a fire that needed no fuel, a fire that flickered green then purple then black in a ghastly mockery of what the flames should be. It was the fire of the Darklands, the fire these fools had allowed into their most powerful place.

All because he had come here.

He shut out the cries, ignored the desperate eyes, pushed away hands as they grasped pleadingly at the hem of his cloak. A hard bubble of kan protected him against the cleansing the Darecians had begun, prevented the weaponized city from draining the Essence from his very being. The High Darecians had been foolish to try this. Their Cyrarium—he knew that they had to have one, to power the Jha'vett—must not have stored enough. They were sacrificing their people, all of them, for fear of the man who wanted to save them. To save everyone.

He saw the kan traps in his path long before he reached them. He still didn't quite understand how the Darecians had managed to manipulate kan, though it made him wonder if what Andrael had believed was true. He hoped not. El only knew that men were not meant to have power such as he and the others wielded.

He drew Licanius, slicing through the kan barriers as if they were not there. The threads split and dissolved at the sword's touch.

When he smashed down the enormous iron doors and walked calmly into the hall beyond, a thousand pairs of eyes turned to him.

"Who is in charge here?" he thundered, his voice cutting through the fear of hundreds of voices. Silence fell like a blanket, until it seemed that everyone in the enormous room was holding their breath.

"I am." A man stepped forward, head high, blue eyes proud. "My name is Garadis ru Dagen. You may have murdered my ancestors, Aarkein Devaed, but this time you are too late. You are too late, Destroyer. We have won."

Caeden laughed bitterly despite himself. The sound echoed around the chamber, and he could feel the fear slithering into the hearts of every person present. They knew him. They knew him from the stories of their grandparents, who had passed down those stories from their grandparents before them. How he had crushed the Darecian Empire. How he had turned their people—all but

501

the brightest, all but the High—to dust and ashes. How he had brought the Darklands to their door, and never let it leave.

And so now, because of panic and fear and ignorance, they were destroying themselves.

"I did not come here to fight, Garadis ru Dagen. I wish no one here any harm. But even if I did—even if I were truly your enemy—this could never be a victory for you," he said in frustration. "Listen!" He flicked his wrists, amplifying the screams from outside, funnelling them and distorting them further to emphasize his point. "Do you hear what you are doing to your own people?"

Garadis grimaced, though his gaze remained hard. "It is a necessary sacrifice."

"Sacrifice?" Caeden's voice grew louder now, angrier, thundering around the room. People cowered before it as if it were a physical assault. "Do not talk to me of sacrifice, you foolish, arrogant man. Nine hundred years ago, I sacrificed millions of your people so that we could stand here today. I sacrificed my soul for this moment." His voice cracked a little. "You use the word and yet you never needed to do this. You think to stop me with this? You think that I do not understand your plan? I made your plan. I whispered in the ears of your best and brightest. I sent them on their journey south with Ironsails laden with food. I timed my attack so that they would not be there when the rest of your people died. My goal—my only goal—was to get you to build this place." He took a breath. "I lit the fire that burns in you, Garadis."

Others in the hall were moaning now, and Caeden knew they saw the truth in his words, could hear it in his fierce tone. Garadis though, strangely, did not cower. He stood straight and tall, meeting Caeden's gaze with a steely one of his own.

He was a believer, Caeden realized. A zealot. He truly thought that he had El on his side.

If only he knew.

"Perhaps you are right," said Garadis quietly. A new hush fell over the hall, a thousand people hanging on their leader's every word. "But you are still too late."

He held up something in his hand.

Caeden frowned. It was a torc, like those worn by princes in the north. Like the old Princes of Dareci, the Elect. But the metal was…odd. Blacker than it should have been. It glinted wetly in the dim light.

"We are no longer the people whom you destroyed, Devaed. We are willing to do all that is necessary, this time. We will go back. We will teach our ancestors. And when you come? We will be ready."

Before Caeden could react, Garadis slipped the torc around his neck.

There was uniform movement behind him, a thousand pairs of hands echoing the motion. Caeden stared in puzzlement as every Darecian in the room placed identical torcs to their necks.

For a few seconds, everything seemed suspended. Garadis watched Caeden with a smirk of self-satisfaction.

Then the first of the screams echoed around the hall.

Garadis spun, searching for the source of the sound, but immediately more shrill voices began to join the first. The wails were worse than those Caeden had heard outside, worse than the sounds of the dying. These were…changing. The screams modulated in tone and intensity, but more and more and more voices joined until the entire room became one elongated shriek.

He backed away in horror as he watched Garadis's face twist. The torc was growing, expanding, melding to the skin of his throat and disappearing down his shirt to his chest. The man dropped to his knees, as had all in the room behind him. A thousand bodies, writhing in agony, all screaming that disturbing, unending scream.

Garadis began to burn.

It wasn't an external fire, though, Caeden quickly realized. This was something erupting from inside of Garadis. It burned hot and red, not the fires of the Darklands like outside, not the cleansing fires of kan meant to strip away all Essence. If anything, this was the opposite. This was Essence in its purest form, extracted and made physical, glowing like the sun itself.

It burned Garadis. It burned his face, his forehead, crept along his hair. It spread beneath his clothing to his limbs, skin and muscle and bone all disintegrating beneath its touch.

And yet, Garadis did not vanish. He lay there, writhing. A body made Essence. A man made fire.

And behind him, his people—the last of the Darecians—were the same.

Caeden watched on in utter horror, his anger vanished now. He hadn't wanted this. He still didn't know how the Darecians had known he was coming, but he'd hoped to steal in like a thief in the night, use the Jha'vett and finish this war before any more blood had been shed. He was already responsible for so much pain—these people's pain. No matter how little time this reality had left, he couldn't be responsible for the end of their kind.

Whatever their kind even was now.

He rushed over and knelt by Garadis, bending down to touch him on the shoulder, not sure if it would hurt. It caused Caeden no physical pain, however the light contact caused Garadis to scream and buck wildly. Caeden snatched his hand away, but Garadis was already . . . dimmer.

Garadis looked up at him with still-blue eyes full of pain and rage and fear and hatred.

"Help us," he whispered.

Caeden closed his eyes, breathing deeply. It would be so much easier to just let these people die, then undo it all later. He would undo it all anyway.

But this time, something held him back.

"How?" he asked.

"We need Essence." Garadis's voice was little more than a gasp. "Kan is draining us, Devaed. I feel it. We must get away. This place is tearing us apart."

Caeden thought for a moment. He'd always been able to touch kan; if that was the cause of Garadis's pain . . .

His eyes widened.

"Hang on," he whispered.

He spent the next thirty minutes preparing. Weaving strands of kan together, melding and hardening and guiding the scaffolding, just as Andrael had taught him. It was among the most difficult of all kan devices, and as far as he was aware, he was the only one left who knew how to construct one.

504   He worked, and he did everything he could to shut out the

writing bodies and the unearthly, stomach-churning screams. Every second felt like an hour, and as he labored he could hear more and more voices die out. Could see less and less light filling the room.

When he was done, he turned to see less than a third of the Darecians remaining.

Those who had died were just…gone. Dissolved.

There was no time to lose, no time to explain. He forced kan down through the bowels of the earth, doing his best to avoid the complex machinery that the Darecians had somehow figured out how to build. Tapped into the shockingly large Cyrarium.

Essence pumped like blood along the line of kan and into the scaffolding.

The Gate opened.

Beyond the portal he could see the lava pits of Res Kartha glowing fiercely, though within moments the abrupt proximity to Deilannis began to drain their energy. He grabbed Garadis, closest to him and almost extinguished. The man tried to fend him off, to direct him to the others, but Caeden knew more than anyone the importance of leaders.

There was no time to be gentle. He tossed Garadis through the portal onto the hard rock beyond, wincing a little as the burning man rolled before lying still.

Caeden tore his eyes away, moving on to the next body. And the next. And the next. Even with all his Essence, his arms began to ache and his feet drag as he carried each body across the threshold. Some made it. Some dissolved at his touch, and others in his arms. There were tears running down his face, but Caeden barely noticed. The ones who made it through the portal appeared to be surviving. That was all that mattered. He could not have a single more Darecian life weighing on him, no matter the cause.

And then the last of them was through. Caeden dropped to his knees, exhausted beyond measure.

He stared through the portal at the bodies. A hundred, perhaps? A hundred left of a hundred million? He wept, wept as he had not since after he had created the Plains. None of the Darecians were moving, but he knew that he couldn't check on them. His touch, his very presence might destroy them.

He raised Licanius and sliced through the scaffolding.

The Gate vanished in an instant, Res Kartha blinking out of existence, leaving Caeden on his knees in the hall, alone. The Darecians' screams still seemed to echo from the walls, despite the silence.

Caeden sat there for what felt like hours, forcing a kan shield up against the draining effects of the Jha'vett. Eventually his Reserve refilled, slowly restoring energy to his dead limbs. He stood, then walked stiffly over to the simple stone structure that stood between the gray columns. A table made of a solid block of white stone, a few symbols inscribed on its surface. The vanity of the Darecians, there. A boast of how it would be a tool of vengeance.

The Jha'vett glowed as he approached it.

He closed his eyes and pushed through kan, searching for the scaffolding, the machinery underlying the device.

He nearly lost his grip on kan, so great was his shock.

The scaffolding was like nothing he'd ever seen before. Had even Andrael ever envisaged such a thing? Layers upon layers of thin kan strands, interacting with each other to form something of unimaginable complexity. A web of hard and soft kan, bends and flows to direct Essence, endpoints structured in such a manner that he could only theorize as to their purpose. He looked harder, and shook his head in wonder. Impossibly thin strands of Essence, almost unnoticeable, ran between the ones that he had initially seen.

He let his gaze wander. The machinery wasn't just in the stone block. It ran deep beneath the hall. It ran through the columns, in the air between. It stretched downward farther than he could see, for what looked like miles underground.

Two hundred years of work, built atop two thousand years of knowledge and unlike anything even the Venerate had seen. Caeden had helped Andrael as he had deconstructed the Ironsails, had been with him as he'd unlocked the secrets of the Cyrarium and the workings of the Gates—and yet, none of that came close to this. This was artistry and science and the most incredible brilliance the world had ever known.

506   And it had all been turned against him.

And soon it would not matter.

He closed his eyes, locating the endpoint that initiated the flow from the Cyrarium. That, at least, was familiar.

He paused.

He picked up one of the torcs that lay on the ground, the ones that had re-formed once their wearers had dissolved. At first glance it was a Vessel for creating a basic ilshara, a shield like the ones the Darecians had to wear around a Cyrarium. But this was...different. It was pure kan, harder, more complete. The wearer would be invulnerable to any sort of draining, but would be unable to actually use Essence, too.

He studied it for a while longer, but eventually concluded that the torcs alone were not responsible for what had happened. There had to have been an unexpected clash, a reaction to the wildly complicated kan running through the room, and to the fact that the wearers had all been High Darecians—had all had Reserves. Some sort of unanticipated feedback from the kan running through the city, probably, now that he thought about it. He would have to remove these devices, lest another unsuspecting soul attempt to put one on within Deilannis's boundaries.

But he understood now. The Darecians knew what El had told him: that only those able to completely protect themselves from the pull of kan in the Darklands would be able to use the Jha'vett. As one of the Venerate, he could do it on instinct. The Darecians, though, needed something to do the protecting for them.

They had miscalculated, probably in the rush to complete the process before he arrived.

It had destroyed them.

Caeden shook off the thought, focusing again on the Jha'vett. He knew that he should have trusted El, stayed the course, participated in the northern landings rather than giving in to his impatience and going on ahead...but what was done was done and there was no telling when, or even if, he would have another chance at this. Here in front of him, finally, was an opportunity to break fate itself. To undo all that he had done, to free El from time and go back to begin again in a world of limitless possibilities.

A world in which Elliavia had never died.

He gazed for a few long, contemplative moments at the Initiation endpoint.

He triggered it.

He watched as Essence began to stream through the room, flowing along lines of kan, twisting and turning, burning bright in some areas as power began to congregate, congeal and form something new. Black lines turned to gold, to red, to bright blue as phases began to activate. The entire room was filled with a spider's web of minute, intricate designs in a spectrum of glowing colors. It was beautiful.

Too late, he saw where his drilling into the Cyrarium had caused damage to the scaffolding.

Essence began to leak into the air, quickly sucked back down into the Cyrarium, but the damage was done. Lines of kan remained dark. To his horror, he realized that several smaller endpoints were missing. He'd cut right through them, not even seeing them due to their size. And the Gate had shorn through more. His use of Licanius more still.

There was a whining sound, the sound of power building and building but not going anywhere. Endpoints began to crack as Essence overloaded them.

Caeden flicked the Initiation endpoint, but it did nothing. This was not a process that was meant to be stopped.

He ran.

He ran past the columns, cursing his stupidity, his weakness, his pity. He ran down the long corridor, dazed and furious and horrified, his heart breaking at being so close and yet not achieving his goal.

Behind him, a mighty sound like a thousand buildings crashing to the ground. An explosion of light, throwing him forward, slamming him into a wall.

He knew no more.

Chapter 36

Davian rode alongside Ishelle, the warmth of the late afternoon sunshine beating down on his back.

"We should probably make camp soon," he observed quietly, stretching as he looked around. The road here was narrow, little used, though it showed signs of having been recently cleared. This forest was different from those he'd traveled through before. The foliage appeared to be struggling to grow despite the humidity; the lush colors he'd seen elsewhere were absent, few trees displaying many leaves and undergrowth showing as much brown as green.

Ishelle snorted, giving him a mildly irritated look. "We're almost there. I can keep going, if that's what you're concerned about."

"No. No, it's..." Davian sighed. "Fine. If you're sure."

Ishelle gave a satisfied nod. "It's been a week. There's no need to keep worrying about me. I don't want to hold us back."

Davian just nodded again, not saying anything. Ishelle did look better; her sickly, pallid hue had faded over the past few days and she sat up straight in her saddle, showing no evidence of damage or even stiffness from the spears that had pierced her body.

Still, he wasn't entirely sure that she had recovered—at least not mentally. Her behavior since the attack had been sharply at odds with her usual outgoing personality; more often than not she seemed lost in her own thoughts, focused elsewhere, needing to have her name mentioned three or four times before she even realized that someone was talking to her. She'd been sober, too, far more quiet than he'd ever seen her.

But that was to be expected, he supposed. He could relate in a small way. He'd been younger, admittedly, but it had taken him weeks to start feeling even close to normal again after he'd been attacked in Caladel.

"As long as you're sure," he said eventually, dropping the subject. They'd talked about it enough over the past week anyway, trying to understand what had happened. What, exactly, had attacked them, and then why the sha'teth had seemingly saved them from it. He suspected that Ishelle, as well as Erran and Fessi, remained dubious on that last point—but regardless of whether they believed him, there weren't many new conclusions to draw from the incident. The only certainty arising from it was that they needed to be constantly on their guard now.

They rode in silence for a minute, Erran and Fessi chatting quietly between themselves a little way ahead.

Eventually, Ishelle shifted in her saddle. "Do you believe we change the future?" she asked suddenly.

Davian frowned, silent for a moment as he considered the strange question. "What do you mean?"

"Do you think we're…making a difference?" Ishelle stared straight ahead grimly, her brow furrowed. "All of this. All of this effort that we're going through. The pain. If it's all inevitable anyway…"

Davian thought for a moment, then inclined his head.

"I talked about this once with Malshash—about inevitability. He said that our actions matter, and it was simply that what will happen, has already happened. We shape the future. It's just that *how* we shape it—the results of our efforts, our decisions—has already been determined."

Ishelle frowned for a few moments, then nodded slowly. "Like the story of Aphelas."

Davian looked at her questioningly; he hadn't heard the name before.

Ishelle saw his expression and shrugged. "Just something that Driscin told me once, to illustrate a similar point. Aphelas served as Augur to King Leorin's army. One day, he had a vision that he would be hanged for treason. In a panic, he fled. Because he fled, he was hanged for treason."

Davian nodded. "Exactly. It shows the future *is* affected by us...because us seeing it can actively shape it," he said slowly. "If Aphelas hadn't Seen that he was going to be hanged, he would never have been hanged." He fell silent again, wondering why Ishelle had brought it up.

Then he paled.

"Fates," he whispered. "Did you *know*?"

Ishelle said nothing, the silence a confirmation.

Davian shook his head, trying to process the information. "Why...why didn't you say anything?" he asked gently. "We could have—"

"Could have *what*, Davian?" Ishelle snapped, the tension suddenly back. She glared at him. "Could have gone a different route? Not headed for the Boundary? I didn't know the specifics of where and when. Would you three have not let me out of your sights?" She leaned forward, not looking at him. "What if you had done something to try and stop it, slowing us down, and then it didn't happen until later? What if what you did to stop it *caused* it to happen? How would you feel then?" Her voice was quiet, but there was heat in it. "I see you struggling as it is. I know you well enough to know that you wouldn't handle feeling responsible for this very well."

Davian flinched at that, not responding for a while. In some ways, he *did* feel responsible; his thoughtlessness had sent Ishelle into the forest in the first place. He didn't say that, though.

"You're right," he conceded eventually. "Sorry." He hesitated. "We should still be sharing these visions, though. I know it's hard, but you don't have to carry that burden by yourself. And even if we accept that these things will happen, we can still fight for what we *don't* know."

Ishelle thought, then sighed and gave him a reluctant nod.

"Just don't take that advice too literally, Dav, else you'll never have a spare moment," she said absently.

Davian stared at her, then chuckled. It was probably the first real quip he'd heard from Ishelle in the past week.

Ishelle gave a small smile back and looked like she was about to say more, but ahead Erran suddenly pulled up short, glancing back at them excitedly. Davian's gaze traveled farther along, spotting what Erran had in the steadily deepening gloom of dusk.

The road ahead—which had been directing them up an incline for some time now—widened out until it abruptly ended in a high gray wall. There was a lone gate visible, its iron showing signs of rust but evidently still functional. It was shut, the two uniformed men standing outside watching them suspiciously as they approached.

"One of the old outposts," said Erran, his tone relief and eagerness in equal measure.

Davian nodded his acknowledgment, urging his horse forward alongside the others.

They had reached the Boundary.

Davian exchanged a glance with Erran as they were ushered through the gates.

"Not what I was expecting," murmured Erran, taking in their surroundings as they walked along moss-covered cobblestone.

"It's a fates-cursed ruin," muttered Fessi.

Davian wasn't sure that he could disagree. Up close, the gray walls were less than impressive; time had clearly taken a toll on the masonry, with cracks evident and entire sections weathered away toward the top. From inside the gate, Davian could see that the surrounding forest had actually begun to encroach, with climbing vines covering some sections of the wall, and branches poking over the crumbling edges of others.

"Not exactly overflowing with people, either," observed Ishelle, eyeing the barren parapets.

Davian nodded concernedly. After Ilin Illan and the Shields, he'd expected these outposts to be bustling with Gifted and soldiers, men readying defenses and preparing for the worst. Everyone here looked alert enough, but there were too few to have any impact if the Boundary really did fail. Did Wirr know that it was like this? Why had he and the Tols not sent people flooding northward?

They passed through two more gates—each set into walls as tall and as crumbling as the outer one—before finally coming to a large central keep, a structure with multiple staggered platforms that allowed for viewing out over the southern walls and, presumably at the higher levels, north toward the Boundary. There had evidently been at least some work done to strengthen the fortifications here; they looked in better condition than those back the way they'd come, if not by much.

They were ushered inside, where a portly man in a captain's uniform looked up from the table as they entered.

"Welcome," he said with a nod, polite enough without being ingratiating. He frowned slightly as scrutinized the group, evidently not seeing what he was expecting. "Where is the Elder from Tol Shen accompanying you?"

"There were some issues at Tol Shen," said Davian, meeting the man's gaze. "Elder Throll was unable to make the journey, but he did give us this." He handed across the slip of paper that Driscin had given them. "I'm Davian," he added belatedly.

There was silence for a few seconds as the captain scanned the document, then reluctantly handed it back. "Muran," he replied with a small frown. "I'm in charge of this outpost, as well as the ones directly east and west." He hesitated. "I don't mean to appear rude, but this document's not exactly unforgeable. I don't know why you'd *want* to pretend that you were Augurs, but—"

Fessi appeared behind the middle-aged man, tapping him on the shoulder. Muran started, eyes widening when he turned to see who it was.

"Ah." The captain took a breath. "Right you are."

Davian gave him a slight nod, relieved to see that Muran was not going to be difficult. He hadn't expected it—the purpose of the Augur Amnesty was hardly a secret—but people's reactions were never a sure thing. "How bad has it been here?" he asked quietly.

Muran grunted. "The good news is that the Boundary hasn't completely collapsed. The bad news is...pretty much everything else." He gestured around them. "You've seen the state of what's here—that's not exactly unique. There's one of these keeps every few miles, and they're all the same. Would have been *very* good defenses a thousand years ago. Probably still could be, if we had the numbers to repair them. Or at least properly man them." He scratched his head. "Fates take me if I know what those fools in the Assembly are doing. Or the Tols, for that matter. After what

I've seen up here—after the reports I've sent to every fates-cursed official that I can think of—we should be getting *flooded* with soldiers and Gifted. Athian and Shen, especially, should be uprooting themselves and relocating here, but apparently the Councils are convinced that you lot will take care of things before it's too late." He sighed, shaking his head. "Sorry if that's news to you," he added belatedly.

Davian remained silent for a few moments, heart sinking. This was worse than he'd expected; he'd assumed that the Assembly would be treating the northern border with more respect after the Blind attack.

"You said there were outposts every few miles?" It was Erran, sounding dubious. "Would those defenses even matter if the Boundary actually fell?" He gestured outside at the encroaching darkness. "I mean, does being here even help as a lookout station? What if there are enemies getting through at night?"

Muran grunted. "You don't know much about the area, I take it."

Ishelle shook her head. "Nobody we've spoken to has actually been here."

Muran nodded and rose tiredly, beckoning for them to follow.

"According to the Gifted that Tol Athian actually bothered to send, these outposts were built in the hundred or so years after the Boundary was created," Muran said as they climbed the wide staircase that wound its way up the center of the keep. "The golden age of the Gifted might have been coming to an end, but fates take me if they didn't know what they were doing."

They reached the top of the staircase, emerging onto what was the roof of the keep.

Davian gaped.

Though the southern-facing side of the outpost had only a gradual incline, the northern side simply...dropped away. They were at the highest point for miles, and Davian swallowed as he understood now why the outposts had been placed so far apart.

The sheer cliff wasn't just at the edge of the outpost, but ran in an east-west line as far as the eye could see. The first hints of moonlight reflected dully off its smooth face where it curled around to the west, and Davian thought that the incline was actu-

514

ally inverted, jutting out at the top—surely impossible to scale. In front of them, from the outpost's north-facing gate, he could see a path leading downward, but it was thin enough to allow for only single-file traversal.

Several hundred feet below, beginning at the base of the cliff, was a plain—but there was no grass, no trees, or any signs of life whatsoever. Like an enormous desert it just stretched away, barren and unsettlingly uniform.

That was all secondary, though, to the staggering blue-white wall of flickering energy that illuminated it all.

For the first ten seconds Davian just stared in silence along with the rest of them, trying to comprehend it. There was nothing to use for scale but he knew immediately that it was enormous; from this distance and elevation he could see it curling away as it got higher, forming a dome. Energy pulsed and shimmered as it flew across the wall's surface; with enough concentration, Davian imagined that he would be able to watch a single streak of energy traverse miles as it raced from one point in the Boundary to another. The plains below, the cliffs, even the cloudy sky above were lit by the Boundary's radiance.

"Fates," breathed Ishelle.

"It's hard to take in the first time you see it. Especially like this, at night," said Muran quietly. Davian turned to see the man gazing out toward the light, almost as entranced as the others. "The stories tell you what it's like, but...they don't tell you what it's *like*."

Davian nodded silently. Then he squinted. Far, far below and in the distance, there were a series of small dots moving near the base of the Boundary. Some sort of small animal, perhaps?

"What's that?" he asked, pointing.

Muran followed his finger. "Patrol," he said confidently. He gestured to a looking glass mounted on the parapet when Davian gave him a dubious look. "You can check for yourself if you'd like."

Davian frowned, turning back to study the tiny black dots, utterly dwarfed by the shimmering curtain of light that silhouetted them. Those were people? He felt a chill as he reassessed his first impression of the scale of the Boundary.

Clearly the others were doing the same. "We're supposed to fix *that*?" whispered Fessi in a horrified voice.

Muran watched them curiously for a long moment, then sighed. "As you can see, day or night, our lookouts can tell if something gets through," he said quietly. "Back when all of this was built, even these cliffs were supposedly positioned and shaped by the Gifted. The only ways up them end at outposts; it's all designed to funnel attackers here. The areas in between cannot be scaled."

"So you don't think that anything has slipped through?" asked Erran.

Muran grimaced. "No doubt some things have," he conceded. "Sometimes one of the men will think that they've seen something, but it's gone so quickly, they don't even get a chance to spot it in the looking glass. I'd discount it as their imagination, except..." He sighed. "I try not to alarm newcomers, but I suppose it's best that you know everything. We've had men go missing. As well as independent, correlating reports of...creatures, I suppose you'd say. Monsters."

"We were attacked by something along the road, too," said Fessi. "Quite a way south from here."

Muran cocked his head to the side. " 'Something'? What did it look like?"

"There were a few of them. Flying creatures that fired long spears at us," said Davian quietly.

Muran nodded, looking unsurprised. "The Gifted up here call them "eletai." One gets spotted breaking through every few days—I've caught a glimpse of one myself. We try to bring them down, but..." He shrugged. "They fly, and they don't seem too interested in coming near us. Nothing we can do."

Davian exchanged a grim glance with the others. They'd conjectured that the monsters attacking him and Ishelle had been another of Devaed's Banes, but it was still chilling to have it confirmed.

Suddenly there was a flash from the Boundary, a ripple of light that emanated from a single point and spread outward. Moments later there was a low, growling, buzzing thunder on the air that pressed down for a moment before dissipating.

516   "Right on time," murmured Muran.

"What was that?" asked Fessi.

"We think they're testing it from the other side." Muran kept his eyes on the Boundary as there was another flash from a different section, accompanied by another thick rumbling that made Davian want to rub at his ears. "Trying to send more monsters through."

Erran frowned. "What happens to the ones that don't get through?"

"If it's anything like what would happen on this side? Disintegration." Muran shrugged at their questioning looks. "The Boundary seems to reflect projectiles, block them entirely—but it dissolves flesh. Birds mostly know to keep away, but occasionally you see one get too close."

Davian shuddered, gazing out at the sight. "How long does it take to get there from here?"

"Including the climb down...an hour, perhaps?" Muran nodded back toward the stairs to the keep. "I'll have some quarters made up—fates know that there are enough spare—and get someone to take you in the morning."

Davian hesitated. "I'd prefer to go now."

Muran gave him a dubious look, but eventually inclined his head. "If that's what you want. You'll just need to be careful going down the cliff path. The Boundary lights it well enough, but it's narrow."

"We *could* wait until tomorrow," Erran observed to Davian.

"The sooner we get an idea of what we're up against, the better." It was relatively early, and Davian wasn't tired. Besides, they wouldn't need to take turns at keeping watch tonight. That already gave them a few more hours of sleep than they were accustomed to.

Erran made a face and Fessi didn't look thrilled either, but eventually they each acceded with a nod. Ishelle, as she had been for most of the conversation, was still staring northward in fascination and barely responded.

Muran grunted. "I may as well take you, then," he said with a sigh. "Less grumbling than if I have to ask someone."

He started back down the stairs, and the others began to follow. Davian was just about to descend, too, when he realized that Ishelle hadn't moved.

"Ishelle?" he turned back, frowning as he watched the other Augur. She was still staring in rapt silence at the light of the Boundary, mouth slightly open, unblinking and looking unsettlingly intent. "Ishelle, we're leaving."

Still Ishelle didn't respond; brow creasing, Davian hurried back to her, putting a hand gently on her shoulder.

Immediately Ishelle flinched and turned, blinking in a moment of apparent confusion. "What?"

"Are you all right?"

Ishelle hesitated, then gave him a tired smile, shaking her head ruefully as she realized that the others had disappeared from the roof of the keep. "Just thinking. Sorry."

"You're sure?" Davian gave her a worried look, but Ishelle inclined her head reassuringly and there wasn't much more that he could say. They hurried back down a couple of flights of stairs and rejoined the others, eventually coming to the north-facing gate, which was thick steel and appeared far sturdier than the southern one through which they'd entered. Unbarring it with Davian's help, the captain led them out onto the cliff's edge.

A cold breeze whipped at Davian as they began their descent. As Muran had indicated, it was a slow, careful process. The path was only wide enough to accommodate a single person, but he was relieved to discover that a railing had been etched into the cliff face; though he never actually lost his balance, he kept his left hand firmly sliding along the hold at all times.

It took perhaps fifteen minutes to pick their way down. Being at the base of the cliff offered little protection against the wind, which if anything felt stronger down here. Moonlight and the cold illumination of the Boundary filtered through clouds of dust kicked up by the breeze, giving the scene before them an ethereal quality.

Davian shivered as they walked and that wall of fizzing, pulsing light grew larger and larger, filling his vision until he felt completely, utterly dwarfed by it. Just when he thought that he'd grasped the scale of it, they got closer, and the concept eluded him again. He'd thought the Shields at Ilin Illan were tall. He'd thought *Ilin Tora* was tall. It was all insignificant compared to this.

And the entire thing...shimmered. It was not the steady light of an Essence bulb, not the kind of light he expected from Essence at all. It was all energy but it...*rippled*, dancing and flexing with different shades, pulsing and crackling and swirling in constant movement and rhythm.

"It's amazing," murmured Fessi suddenly, the first of them to speak in a while.

Muran nodded. "I've been here for a month, and I'm still not used to it."

Davian swallowed as they neared the base of the barrier, noting how the ground for several feet approaching it was charred, completely black. The air here held a hint of that thundering, rumbling buzz that they'd heard earlier, as well as the sharp smell of being out before a storm. The ground was starkly illuminated by the cold light; dust swirled dramatically near the base, somehow emphasizing how empty the space really was.

He shivered again. For the first time, it occurred to him just how much *power* must be flowing through that barrier.

"What's that?" asked Erran, pointing.

Davian followed Erran's finger to a little way down the wall, spotting the square stone pillar. It was perhaps thrice his height and a few feet across on each face, standing right at the edge of the swirling blue light. Polished, it was reflecting the colors of the energy around it, but Davian thought that it was white. The entire thing was nearly impossible to see until they were up close.

"There's one every mile or so," said Muran. "They're all along the Boundary."

They moved a little closer, and Davian felt a chill as he spotted a symbol amid the flashing energy, pulsing steadily on the pillar. He'd known that it would be there—Taeris had told him so, what seemed like an age ago—but it was still unsettling to see it.

The wolf's head was exactly as he remembered it from the bronze cube that he'd been given at Caladel, exactly as it had been tattooed on Caeden's arm. He wondered again just what that meant. He'd thought of Caeden now and then during their trip, wondered how his friend was doing and whether he'd found out anything more about his identity. Often pondered what his true role could be in all of this, too.

Ishelle came to stand beside Davian, and he frowned across at her. She had seemed fine since they'd left the outpost, but now her expression was distant again. As if she was not focused on the Boundary at all, but something else entirely.

"Ishelle?" he asked quietly.

Ishelle blinked, then shook her head as if clearing it and turned to him, giving a soft laugh when she saw his look. "I'm fine, Dav. Really. Just...a little intimidated." She nodded toward the pillar. "Are we assuming that these are the Vessels that are keeping this thing going?"

Davian nodded slowly. "That's a logical guess." He glanced at the others. "Thoughts?"

Erran shrugged. "We're going to have to look at it sooner or later."

Davian nodded again, then closed his eyes and *pushed* through kan, extending his senses toward the pillar and hoping desperately that the simple act wouldn't affect anything. For all his training, all his study, he had no true idea of what was or wasn't wise to do here.

His heart dropped as he took in what no natural vision would be able to see.

Kan was *everywhere*.

He examined it despairingly, trying to comprehend the vast, complex workings of the strands. The network stretched left and right, upward and downward farther than Davian's senses could reach in any direction. A layer of black lines and edges covered every facet of the wall of light, and there was even more—impossible to properly make out—farther inside.

More worryingly, that network was *confusing*. He probed along its edges, frowning, trying to understand the purpose of all the different elements that he could see. Here a hard curve of kan, presumably to assist the flow of Essence that appeared to come from deep underground. There a soft barrier, a buffer of some kind. An overflow mechanism, Davian thought, designed to soak up any extra Essence in case of a surge. Hard barriers to encapsulate the Essence, to stop it from decaying.

Then there were the parts that he didn't understand at all, could not fathom why they existed. Strands of kan that looked more like the tendrils he would use to Read someone. A section that seemed to be designed to affect time itself somehow, though to Davian's eye it appeared inactive, dormant.

520

It was delicate, intricate machinery. The sort of thing that one didn't tinker with unless one absolutely knew what they were doing.

Worse, he didn't think that they *could* tinker with it. There was no layer of hardened kan that he could *see*—he could examine the mechanisms easily enough—but that surely meant that the protections were simply hidden. More complex than a simple shield, and probably more dangerous.

He withdrew his senses, glancing at the others. Erran had his eyes closed and was evidently still inspecting the wall of energy. Ishelle was sitting on the ground, staring at the light with a fixatedly irritated expression. Fessi was off to the side, looking at a different section of the wall entirely.

Davian rubbed his forehead, glancing over at Ishelle. "I can understand some of the parts. Or I *think* I understand some of the parts. But how they all fit together..."

Ishelle snorted. "It looks like nonsense to me. Like someone tried to take all of our different abilities and jam them randomly into a wall."

Erran stirred. "That's about the impression I get, too," he agreed grimly.

Fessi wandered back over, shaking her head at their questioning looks.

"It's like..." She shook her head again, lost for words. "It's more complex than I'd imagined anything using kan could be. There have to be a hundred different elements in there, all used for different purposes... and all working together to create this." She gestured to the wall, tone despondent.

Davian nodded slowly. "Remember, we don't necessarily need to understand *every* aspect of it. We only need to figure out why it's getting weaker."

"Is that all?" said Ishelle drily.

Davian forced a smile. "It sounds like a lot, but we always knew it was going to be a big task." He felt overwhelmed, too, but it wouldn't help to show it. They needed to stay motivated. "At least we have an idea of what we're up against now. Let's head back, get some sleep and start fresh tomorrow."

The others didn't look convinced, but nodded.

Davian gestured to Muran, who had taken a seat a little way off and was watching them curiously. "Time to go back," he said, tiredness suddenly crashing in on him. "We'll be getting up early in the morning."

He glanced over his shoulder at the immense, thrumming wall of energy.

"We have a lot of work to do."

Chapter 37

Asha gave a wracking cough as she came awake to the thunderous, echoing roar of water crashing against rocks.

She forced her eyes open, though she barely had the energy to do even that. The roof above her, not more than six feet from her face, appeared to be natural stone. She turned her head slowly, blearily registering that everything in the cramped cave was illuminated by the flickering flames of a small fire to her left, which also appeared to be the only thing staving off the otherwise frigid air. She was lying on damp stone, near naked; her entire body was cold, sore, her muscles barely able to move. For a long few moments she couldn't bring to mind what had happened, how she had got here.

Then she remembered. The dar'gaithin. Dangling from the bridge. Laiman, hesitating, trying to save her too late.

The seemingly endless fall, followed by...nothing.

She managed to lever herself up onto an elbow, gazing around dazedly. Her clothes, she saw, had been carefully laid out by the fire. Beyond, she could see the cave entrance, which was mostly submerged by the pool that finished only a body's length away. In the slim gap visible between the water and the roof of the opening, a permanent haze of white hung where the Lantarche—she assumed it was the Lantarche—was smashing into the rocks beyond, causing the deafening roar that resounded constantly through the enclosed space.

She shook her head, exhaustion seeping through every pore as she tried to grasp what was going on. As painful as moving was, she didn't seem to have any injuries of note. Remembering the dar'gaithin's attack—that sickening, crunching snap as something in her back had given way—she cautiously wiggled her toes. Bent her knees. Pushed experimentally with her feet.

She breathed out. Her legs seemed fine.

Her vision swam as the sliver of energy she'd managed to summon finally gave out, and she laid her head back against the stone. Suddenly, across the flickering flames, a figure that had previously been hidden in the shadows stirred.

Breshada leaned forward so that her face was illuminated as she watched Asha, concern in her expression. The Hunter's lips were moving, but the thundering of the water drowned out whatever she was saying.

Asha stared at her blankly for a few extra seconds, but everything started to fade again.

She slept.

⟞⟡⟝

This time, when Asha woke the pain was almost entirely gone.

She rolled to the side, staring at her new surroundings. Another cave, this one larger, no water in evidence but with multiple dark, looming entrances and a set of stairs cut into its side. The stairs led upward into a tubelike passageway that was lit by lines of Essence, the light that was leaking out from its entrance the only source of illumination in the cave. The crashing of the Lantarche was still audible but far more muted here, and the air was slightly warmer, despite there being no fire now.

Across from her, back against the smooth cave wall, sat Breshada.

"Welcome back, Ashalia," said the Hunter quietly, observing Asha's waking.

Asha sat up slowly, scrubbing at her eyes as she looked around. "What...what happened?" She was clothed again, she realized, and her garments were blessedly dry. "Where are we? I remember the bridge, and then..."

"We are below Deilannis." Breshada pushed herself to her feet, looking strangely irritated. Uncomfortable, too. "You fell into the Lantarche. I followed."

Asha stared at the Hunter bemusedly as she was helped to her feet. "You *followed*? How? That drop had to be hundreds of feet. How...how did either of us survive?"

"I used Essence to lessen the impact." The words were short, sharp, as if Breshada were forcing them between her teeth.

Asha shook her head. "But that would have taken..." She looked at the other woman, a chill unrelated to the temperature running through her as her eyes went wide. "And you healed me, too. I didn't imagine that injury to my back, did I?" She swallowed. "How strong *are* you, Breshada?"

"I do not wish to speak of it." Breshada's discomfort made sense now, and it filtered through to her voice, too. "What is done is done. You are alive. Let us leave it at that, and be on our way."

Asha nodded dazedly, not knowing what to say. If the past couple of weeks with Breshada had taught her anything, it was that deliberately using Essence—any amount of it—would have been incredibly difficult for the young woman. Not on a practical level, perhaps, but without doubt on an emotional one.

"Thank you," she said softly. Evidently Deilannis's limitations on using Essence did not extend to down here; she wanted to find out more, but Breshada's expression indicated that that was not an option. Asha glanced toward the stairs. "So this is...a way up to the city?"

"Presumably." Breshada shook her head. "I have not yet searched upward."

Asha rubbed her forehead. "How did you even find this place?"

Breshada shrugged. "Werek's own luck." She gestured toward the multiple tunnels leading from the cave. "Or perhaps not. As you can see, ours was not the only entrance to this room from the Lantarche. I am uncertain as to why—these passages seem to serve no function, except perhaps to funnel fresh air—but I have scouted along some of them, and they all appear to emerge at intervals along the river."

Asha stared at the looming, near-circular mouths of the tunnels, frowning. "I suppose we should start trying to get back, then. Find the others." If any of them were still alive, of course, though she didn't say that out loud.

They started up the stairwell. The stairs were wide but looked strangely weatherworn, despite the enclosed space; the passage-way itself was arched, the walls displaying the same scoured smoothness as the stone underfoot. For the first few minutes they climbed in silence, the rumbling of the Lantarche lessening and then finally fading entirely. The way was well lit but drearily uniform, a seemingly endless winding ascent of identical, gently rising steps.

After a while, Asha leaned against the stone wall. "Time for a rest," she said, a little breathlessly, wiping a bead of sweat from her brow. While her injuries were healed, she was still even more exhausted than usual after what had happened.

Breshada nodded briefly, to Asha's annoyance looking as though she had barely expended any energy, and came to a stop.

"Is it getting warmer?" Asha asked after her breathing had steadied, frowning. She'd initially thought that it was just from the exertion, but the stone under her palm felt heated. Now that she was stationary and paying attention, the air had an unusual dryness to it, too.

"It is," agreed Breshada, staring upward absently.

Asha followed her gaze for a moment, then shrugged to the Hunter and indicated that she was recovered enough to continue. They pushed forward pensively.

A low, thrumming growl, barely noticeable at first, gradually began to build in Asha's ears as they climbed farther. She exchanged a look with Breshada, who looked equally mystified; just as Asha was about to comment on the strange sound, the stairs leveled out onto a small platform.

Both women came to a stuttering, shocked stop.

The cavern they now overlooked was immense, clearly man-made, and perfectly spherical. Golden, pulsing Essence coated the walls; more energy crashed and flickered through the air, jumping between hundreds of identical diamond-shaped shards of glistening black rock that hovered in midair, rotating slowly around the blindingly bright pillar that cored the center of the enormous sphere.

Asha shielded her eyes from the light, squinting in disbelief as torrents of yellow-white energy streaked everywhere across the open space, dizzying and mesmerizing and terrifying all at once.

She blinked, forcing her gaze downward slightly. The platform on which they were standing was inscribed with hundreds of strange symbols, all glowing blue. A little distance to the left, much to Asha's relief, she saw that the stairs continued upward.

A sliver of light suddenly split from the pillar in the center of the sphere and crackled directly toward Asha and Breshada; they both flinched but rather than hitting them, the energy struck an invisible barrier in front of the platform, dispersing into a rippling wave and merging again with the walls.

They both gaped in silence for several seconds at the surreal sight, until eventually Asha shook her head.

"What is it?" she murmured. It reminded her a little of the Conduit in the Sanctuary—but this was bigger. *Much* bigger.

Breshada shifted uneasily. "I do not know, but we should not linger." The low thrum in the air was more intense here than it had been in the stairwell, but still quiet enough to hear over.

Asha nodded absently, wide-eyed as she continued to watch the chaotic dance of light. "Agreed."

They slowly, almost reluctantly tore themselves away from the sight, and started up the second flight of stairs.

Several minutes passed as they ascended, and Asha was just about to suggest another break when the stairwell abruptly ended, transforming into a long corridor. The lines of Essence did not extend past the stairwell, leaving the passage ahead completely dark.

Asha swallowed her trepidation—there was nowhere else to go—and followed Breshada into the murk, trailing a hand along the wall to keep her balance.

The passage twisted a few times, and then they were walking into a massive hall.

It was dark where they had emerged, the only illumination a small pool of light some distance away that highlighted what looked like a solid stone altar. Otherwise, thick gray columns were the only objects that broke up the cold, cavernously empty space.

Asha pulled up short at a flicker of movement up ahead, within the light. She motioned silently to Breshada, ducking behind one of the stone pillars and peering around it cautiously.

A lone figure was pacing around the altar, staring at it and muttering something that was inaudible from this distance. Asha felt her shoulders relax a little as she recognized the man, even if some of the tension remained.

"Laiman?" she called grimly, stepping out from behind the column and moving forward.

The king's adviser started, looking around with nervous eyes until he spotted Asha walking into the pool of illumination.

"*Ashalia?*" He gaped at her in disbelief. "And...Breshada as well?" he added dazedly as the Hunter joined Asha in the light. He stared at them, then gave a short, incredulous laugh. It was a sound full of relief. "How...?"

"Breshada saved me," said Asha, locking gazes with him coldly. She hadn't forgotten what had happened on the bridge. Laiman *had* tried to help her...but not before hesitating.

He'd considered letting her fall.

Laiman saw her expression and flushed, glancing away. "That is wonderful news," he said, with what sounded like genuine emotion in his voice. He swallowed and looked up again, his gaze earnest as he met Asha's once more. "I cannot begin to tell you how relieved I am."

Then he shook his head in vague bemusement as what Asha had said finally registered. "But...I still don't understand... how is this possible? After you fell..." He turned to Breshada. "The others were all dead. I assumed that you had somehow been thrown from the bridge when you killed that last dar'gaithin, too. But are you saying that you *went after* Ashalia? How did you survive the fall? How did you even get back up here?"

Breshada shrugged. "I did what I thought necessary. It worked. We found stairs."

"There's a massive space underneath the city," supplied Asha, with a wry look at Breshada. "A sphere, some sort of...enormous Vessel, I think. Absolutely *filled* with Essence. The stairs we found go right past it, all the way down to the level of the river."

Laiman rubbed his chin. "I see," was all he said, though his expression had become thoughtful.

Breshada glanced around, looking impatient. "What is this place? Why are *you* here?"

Laiman sighed, and his face fell at the question. "This building was supposed to house a weapon," he said, a little despondently. "Something that could defeat Aarkein Devaed himself. But all I could find was...this." He gestured at the altar. "My High Darecian is not particularly good, and it seems like it *could* be related, but...I am unsure."

"Perhaps something in the Great Library will tell you more," observed Breshada. She shrugged at Laiman's look. "I believe that Ashalia needs to go there also. It seems our next logical destination."

Asha inclined her head. "That's true." She glanced at Laiman. "Do you know the way?"

The king's adviser gave the altar one last, rueful glance and nodded slowly.

"Follow me," he said heavily.

Despite what Davian had told her, Asha couldn't help but be astounded by the size of the Great Library.

She gaped up at the vast array of books, more than a little relieved that they were finally inside and unscathed. The city had felt dead as they'd walked its silent, eerily clean streets. The fog had absorbed the sound of even their footsteps, and the longer they'd been in it, the more sinister it had seemed. Her skin still crawled with the feeling that they had eyes on them.

How Davian had ever felt *comfortable* here was beyond her.

Still, she couldn't help but be impressed by the library. Not the size of the building, necessarily—from the outside it looked barely bigger than some of the surrounding structures. But once inside, the sheer *number* of books was overwhelming.

Breshada clearly thought so, too. She stared around in consternation. "How?" she asked in horror. "How do you expect to find answers amongst so many? It will take months. *Years.*"

Laiman said nothing, but Asha followed his gaze, spotting the squat stone pillar in the middle of the room. It was unassuming enough, placed in among a smattering of desks, but Davian had told her its true purpose. Laiman, seemingly, knew it as well.

She strode over, leaning down to examine the Adviser. Davian   529 had said he'd drained it of Essence, used it to keep himself alive. She ran her hands over its surface.

If it was a Vessel, then she *should* be able to use it. She *should* be able to infuse it with Essence again.

She closed her eyes, letting the Vessel tap into her Reserve. For a moment, there was nothing.

Then she felt the Essence begin to trickle out of her, flowing into the Adviser. Not much, but as she stayed that way, she felt the energy begin to grow within the device.

When she finally opened her eyes again, there was a blue glow atop the pillar.

"Let's see if this is as easy as Davian said it was," she murmured to herself, taking a deep breath.

She focused. Began to think of the Shadows.

When she opened her eyes, a single blue tendril was drifting away from the pillar, slowly stretching outward.

She hurried after it, slipping through the nearest doorway and eagerly grasping the book upon which it came to rest. It was a thick tome, unwieldy.

She flipped it open. It appeared to be a collection of historical documents, copied from the originals, some of them notated.

It didn't take her long to find the entry that she was after.

An Account of the Shadow War

The following is a translation of a Silvithrian text, one of the few remaining after the Culling and subsequent burning of that great city. It is suggested that the Culling indirectly originated from the events described within, though that is pure speculation.

—MARSEIS DU VIREN TEL, THIRD ORDER OF AELINITH

After the Decree today; and being of sound mind despite the touch of the Taint; I am committing these events to the great Book in order that others who might follow may learn of these terrible events and understand the measures that we had to take. The Shadowbreakers have afforded me this opportunity out of respect, and I pray that those who come after may see why they chose the course that they did.

It has been near two years since Lord Serrin, once little more than a lowly stablehand and yet now Ruler of Silvithrin and its surrounds, first inflicted the Taint upon these lands. At the time we knew not of its origins, of course; though even then I can say with little doubt that we could not have stopped what was to come. I nonetheless think upon this time with an unhappy heart, knowing as I do the lives which could have been spared had my instincts been sharper, had I but paid just a little more attention.

I remember him even now as the young man who so willingly and astutely tended to my mounts, always ready with a quick smile, always seemingly happy and satisfied at a job well done. Was that all an act? Ostella and Mirius both postulate an external force at work, some evil that infiltrated and worked on the boy until he became what he is today. Of that, I suppose it is possible, but I cannot say for certain. Oft enough is darkness hidden beneath a bright exterior.

When young Serrin first began to show signs of the Gift, that marvellous ability that so few of our people have managed to cultivate since the coming of the Shalis, there was a great celebration within our halls. The boy himself seemed more bemused than excited, but nonetheless we set him to task with the best of our mages, knowing that such a talent could not be allowed to go to waste.

Nor was it! I myself was able to marvel at some of the feats the boy accomplished early on. I saw him near single-handedly turn the tide of the Battle of Gethrenius, a moment which set back Lither and his minions years of planning. Then, even I must concede that I loved him.

When the Taint first appeared, in the poorer sections of Silvithrin and in many ways little more than a rumor to those such as I, there was no suggestion of foul play, no way to divine a connection between it and *the young man whose power and fame grew so rapidly within these walls. Black marks on the faces of a few minor mages, holes in their memories from when they had first contracted the strange malaise. Murmurs of the deformity made their way to me, of course, but the fool I was in those days did not enough to investigate.*

Oh, I looked into the claims, of course. I investigated this strange sickness, visited those who were ill. It was not contagious, I was assured by our best physicians; and even if it were, it would be restricted to mages only, of which of course I am not. The dark veins on the face were disturbing, true, yet the men and women affected—there were only a few—seemed otherwise none the worse. They could not perform their acts of magic, of course, which was a blow to the kingdom in ways which were both upsetting and frustrating. But they did not appear to be in any danger, or even particular discomfort.

And so when Serrin continued to grow, both in power and in popularity, it was a subject for rejoicing. Where others were no longer able to perform, he stepped in. The more who were Tainted, the more he began to fulfill their roles. In the space of less than six months, he became the most important mage in all Silvithrin, bearing the burden of many of his fellow mages who had fallen.

Mishaeil was the first to come to me—the first, presumably, to notice that something was wrong. She was a fine adviser, one of my best, and I have regretted a thousand times not taking her claims more seriously. Perhaps if I had, she would yet live.

She warned me of a pattern to the way that the Taint was taking mages. She said that she believed it was spreading through deliberate means—perhaps an attack on Silvithrin by Lither. She even hinted at Serrin's growing power, both literally and figuratively, as a motive. And she noted the dangers if he should turn on us. The instantaneous damage to our infrastructure.

I did not believe that it was possible. My faith in Serrin, like so many others', was absolute.

I still remember the day that all of that changed. I awoke to the screams—the terrible, heartrending screams of men and women who knew that they were about to die. Even as I leaped from my bed, Thorvis arrived to tell me the news: that the Taint had taken every mage but Serrin, and that Serrin was claiming rule.

You know much of what follows, I have no doubt. At first I wondered at Serrin's decision not to execute me. Why risk an uprising? I may not have been universally loved, but the Silvithrians are a fiercely protective people, loyal to the patriarchy, and usurpers are rarely seen in a positive light. It wasn't until Serrin came to visit me that I understood.

"Why have you done this, Serrin?" I asked him as he entered. "You had everything a man could want. Wealth. Power. Privilege."

Serrin smiled at that. He was relaxed, but far from the madman I had expected, given the horrors that I knew he had inflicted upon some of the others to ensure that his will was done. No killings, from what I understood. But maimings. Removal of limbs, in many cases, so that his victims could not walk.

"Every man alive has had these things," he said quietly. "The beggar who has been given a piece of silver has had wealth. The slave who has been asked to complete a task has had power. The prisoner who has not been executed has had privilege." His eyes shone as he sat opposite me. "I desire not the things of this world that are a matter of perspective, Javahan. I desire not the things which will only increase my desire. I desire not the petty things of men."

"Then what?" I asked, though I had trepidation in doing so.

"Choice," he whispered. He stared at me for a long moment, as if willing me to understand. I thought I

saw something in his eyes, that day. A sadness at what he had done. A wish for someone to understand him.

But then he shook his head and stood, glaring at me. "You cannot comprehend the things happening here," he told me. "You were a king—neither good nor bad, corrupt nor moral. But you wasted your power. Now I will use it for something more."

The words hit true, and I felt shame at them. But still I refused to simply let him leave, my questions unanswered.

"What will you do with me?" I asked. "Execution?"

Serrin shook his head. "A waste," he said, voice stern. "No. You will become as the others."

He left without explaining further, not responding to my calls. It was not until the following day that I understood what he meant.

He came for me in the morning. I still remember the sun shining so brightly, the blue skies traitor to the moment. He paraded me out in front of the people, and I wept to see their faces.

For the Taint had spread. For every one person untouched, three wore the black veins.

I was taken to the Great Square, wherein many had gathered, purportedly at Serrin's urgings. There was a stage set up above the crowd's heads, and despite Serrin's claims, I felt certain that this was to be my public execution.

When we arrived, though, Serrin had me stand in full view of everyone. There was no axman, no gallows. Instead, he produced a small black disc, thin, not much larger than a man's thumbnail. He held it aloft, and its import was clearly lost on me, for the crowd groaned. Some shouted in protest, but they were quickly silenced.

That is my last memory of that morning. I am told that Serrin spoke for hours. I am told that I was moved from the Great Square back to the walls of the palace, where Serrin felt the large crowd would better be able to witness what happened to me. I have little choice but to believe what has been described to me, as I myself have no recollection of these events.

I awoke back in my cell, and though ostensibly nothing had changed, I knew that something was amiss. I was tired, unnaturally so. My lethargy could have been put down to the stressful events of the past days, but I knew that that was not the cause.

There was no mirror in my cell, but I had a basin for washing. My reflection in the water told me all that I needed to know.

It is a strange thing, to see your face the same and yet so markedly different. It is a hard thing to reconcile, and for some days my mind denied it. I forced myself to look at that reflection periodically, to remind myself both of what had happened and what it meant. Just as Mishaeil had suggested, the Taint was evidently not natural—though its purpose, at that point, I had not yet surmised. For while the lethargy was a discomfort, and the scarring of my face upsetting, I did not feel ill.

It was a week later that it was done to me, as it had already been done to so many.

I did not understand the purpose of the men entering my chamber at first; I thought, perhaps, that they were there to take me somewhere else. Even when a third man entered, holding physician's equipment along with a sharp blade, I had no inkling of what was about to transpire.

They forced Sleeproot down my throat, of course. I suppose I can be grateful for that much.

When I awoke to the pain in my ankles, I did not understand. It was only by moving the covers aside and seeing the true horror—the two stumps where my feet should have been—that I understood.

I am not ashamed to admit that I wept then, more so than for the marks on my face.

I was soon moved from my lone cell and into a great hall, filled with those just like me. We were well cared for, as these things go. Our meals were delivered, our linen kept fresh. We were provided tomes to read, writing and drawing materials, music, games of chance. Anything to distract us.

At first I, along with many of those in the same facility, believed that we were the only ones. That Serrin had killed the others. Mishaeil, El bless her, was one of those left to me. It was she who told me of the true nature of the Taint, and thus postulated that Serrin would likely have facilities such as ours set up all over the city. Her quick mind is likely what attracted Serrin to her in the first place, and thus also likely what killed her.

Mishaeil was not, at first, amongst those who had the Taint. She was little more than a girl, and served as a nurse for those like me.

It was she who kept me informed of the goings-on outside. She told me about Wereth and his men, those who were ultimately to become the Shadowbreakers, and their resistance. It was Wereth who first deduced that the Taint was feeding Serrin's power in a direct and measurable way. It was he who first realized that we had become nothing more than extra Reserves for the new lord of Silvithrin.

I still shudder at the memory of being told that for the first time, but though I wish it were not true, I am certain that it is. Wereth, according to Mishaeil, first uncovered the truth during an incursion against a group of Tainted loyal to Serrin. Serrin himself actively participated in defending the city in those early days, and was in the process of constructing a grand wall around it. When Wereth's attack came, it killed over three hundred Tainted soldiers in a single blow. His spies reported that Serrin's ability to lift the enormous stone sections of wall instantly became less, and he knew immediately of what had happened, if not the details. It was after this, of course, that Serrin chose to maim and lock away the Tainted in housing that allowed neither escape, nor the possibility of accidental deaths.

A week ago, Mishaeil brought word that Wereth himself was coming to this building to speak with me. Though I have no power anymore, I welcomed the thought, despite initially cautioning against the meeting, as his capture would surely mean an end to the resistance. Mishaeil was adamant that he had insisted, though, so I ultimately conceded.

Had Mishaeil not died that very night, I am uncertain that I would have agreed to Wereth's proposition.

But when Serrin came for her, lust in his eyes, she refused to let him take her. Despite her struggles, despite the furious shouts of protest from myself and others, he came and dragged her away to a fate that I have no desire to imagine. I know that she did not talk—she was too strong for that. But when Serrin instructed her bloodied body to be displayed to us—to emphasize the perils of disobedience, no doubt—I vowed that I would do everything in my power to fight him.

So when Wereth slipped in to speak to me three nights later, I told him that he had my blessing to kill everyone.

He explained it all, though I could tell the mere thought tore him up inside. The object of power that Serrin had somehow obtained—the Siphon, he called it—tapped into a person's store of Essence. Far more useful when applied to mages, whose stores were by far larger than regular people's, but still effective on those like myself. The lethargy, even occasional fainting that we all experienced at various times was from Serrin draining our very life force to supplement his own.

Wereth thought that there may be a cure for the Taint, a way to reverse its effects—but he could not know until he had the Siphon itself. I was wary of this, knowing of his ability as a mage, and warned him of the temptation that possessing such an artifact would undoubtedly bring. He assured me that he would never use it, and that if it came to it, he would die before ever taking on that power for himself. I believed him.

But the reason he had come to me, risked so much, was that he needed my permission. For he had tried, many times, to obtain the Siphon through other means, both direct and indirect. All had failed, and the only path left to him now was one that was difficult to countenance.

The removal of those who gave Serrin his power. The deaths of the Tainted.

Sufficed to say, with Mishaeil's screams still ringing in my ears, I granted him my permission. I included myself amongst those who were to die; I could not in all conscience condemn other innocents to a fate that I was not myself willing to face.

Wereth has given me leave to write this record in my last hours, with my assurance that none in the service of Serrin will read it before it is time. No one checks on the things that we do here; it is well accepted that we are no threat, not in our current state. I shall place this account by my bed, and sleep. It will be retrieved by Wereth's men after they have killed me and my companions in this place.

I find myself growing reflective as I finish this record of events. It is a strange feeling, to know one's death approaches. A stranger feeling, too, to understand that it is necessary, in the service of something greater.

For Taria, who Wereth says is safe within his camp but does not know of his plans: I love you. Please read what I have been through, what we have all been through, and understand that this was necessary. You do not need to stay, to see this fight through to the end, though I know that you will feel such an obligation. I am gone now, and all that matters is your happiness.

I pray that you and our daughter are well. I pray that you live a long and happy life, regardless of what else happens this night. I pray that you forgive me for what I have authorized Wereth to do, and that your memories of me are always fond.

And so I leave this record, which I swear is full and true. If blame is to fall for Wereth's actions, let it fall on me.

So says Javahan du Tel Vederan, True King of Silvithrin.

Asha put the book down, her hands shaking.

She moved across to a nearby mirror, looking at the black scars on her face and then touching them lightly, not saying anything for a long time.

"What did you find, Ashalia?" asked Laiman quietly.

Before Asha could respond, there was movement in the corner of her eye. She spun to see a vaguely familiar red-haired man standing in the doorway, eyes wide as he registered their presence.

"Who in fates are you?" he asked, a low panic to his tone.

Breshada moved before anyone else, striding toward the intruder.

Asha threw out her hand.

"Breshada! Wait!" She recognized the man. He looked more tired, haggard—but it was him.

The man who had saved them all at Ilin Illan. Davian's friend.

"His name is Caeden," she said quickly. "He's on our side."

Breshada stopped in front of Caeden as the young man watched her warily. Slowly, she shook her head.

"I know who he is," she said. "His name is Tal'kamar."

Breshada's face began to writhe.

Asha choked back a gasp as the woman stumbled and then steadied herself against a nearby table while the bones in her face and body cracked and shifted, muscles contorting and stretching, skin ripping and reforming and changing color. To the side, Asha could hear Laiman gagging at the horrific sight.

It was over within seconds. Breshada's hair was still black, but longer and not quite as dark. She was shorter, marginally slimmer. Her skin was olive rather than white, and her face now bore the black veins of a Shadow.

The Shadraehin looked across at Asha, giving her a slow smile.

"He is here to meet me," she said softly.

Chapter 38

There was utter silence in the room for several seconds.

Asha just stood, frozen, trying to understand what was going on. To her left, Laiman had taken a stunned step backward.

"Nethgalla," he murmured, horror in his tone.

The Shadraehin ignored him, smiling slightly at Asha's expression. "I told you that we would meet again."

"But..." Asha floundered as she processed what had happened, straining to put the pieces together. She knew the story of Nethgalla—everyone did—and Davian had told her of Malshash's claims.

That made it no easier to accept the reality in front of her, though.

How long had Nethgalla been Breshada? And...had she been the Shadraehin all along, too, then? She shook her head, thoughts racing, making connections. Could Davian's message to the Shadraehin have actually been to *Nethgalla*? And he'd been telling her where to find Caeden?

Only Caeden himself looked unsurprised by the display, watching with eyes hard and filled with...disgust? Rage? It was difficult to tell.

"This is between you and me, Nethgalla," he said grimly. "These two have no part to play. Let them go."

Nethgalla sighed. "No part to play? If you had your memories back, Tal, you would know that that is not true."

To Asha's side, Laiman shuffled nervously. Nethgalla glanced across at him and gestured; Laiman immediately, silently, crumpled to the ground. Asha quickly knelt beside him, relieved to see that he was at least still breathing.

"Having Thell Taranor to deal with too is more trouble than it is worth, though," the black-veined woman added quietly.

Caeden hesitated, casting an uncertain glance at Asha and the now-unconscious Laiman. Asha felt her brow furrow as she numbly tried to understand what the shape-shifter was saying. She knew who *Laiman* really was, too?

Asha stood again, trembling, though her primary emotion was still confusion. "What have you done with the Shadows?" she asked, a sick feeling in the pit of her stomach.

Nethgalla smiled at her expression. "They are safe," she assured Asha quietly. Her gaze traveled to the book that Asha was holding. "Safer than Serrin ever made them, and nowhere near as badly treated."

Asha stared at her in disbelief. "You *knew*?"

In response, Nethgalla turned a little to the side, gesturing again. Essence exploded from her fingertips but it dissolved immediately, doing nothing.

And Asha fell to her knees.

She shook her head in a vain attempt to clear it. It was just like the light-headedness she'd experienced in Ilin Illan, and then again on the road when they had clashed with the Administrators.

Nethgalla was tapping into Asha's Essence.

"But... you're a Shadow," she said dazedly.

"I have the scars of one," Nethgalla corrected her calmly. "This is the *form* of a Shadow. It is far from the same thing."

"Enough." It was Caeden again, tension threaded through his voice. "Nethgalla, I've come here in good faith."

"Good faith?" There was suddenly a dangerous edge to Nethgalla's tone. "You may have forgotten the Crossroads, Tal, but I have not. You tortured me, just so that you could better understand the Darklands. You took my ability for *ten years*." She shook her head, latent anger but also a hint of sadness in the motion. "Your good faith is not nearly enough anymore. I rather fear that you would take the opportunity to kill me, now, if it arose."

"Then don't trust me. Right now, I just need the Siphon."

Caeden's gaze shifted and he suddenly looked uncomfortable.

"And…I need to understand what it does. How to use it against the Lyth."

Asha stumbled back to her feet as Nethgalla hesitated, then reached into her pocket and withdrew a transparent sphere, engraved with symbols and about the size of the palm of her hand.

"You only had to ask," she said quietly. She walked two paces forward, placing it on the table between her and Caeden before moving back again. "It's yours."

Caeden frowned at her, evidently suspicious of how easily Nethgalla had relinquished the Vessel, before walking over and picking it up. Then he produced an object from his own pocket, holding it up to the sphere.

He flinched as the two were sucked together, snapping perfectly into place.

"What does it do?" he asked quietly after a few startled seconds.

"She can tell you," said Nethgalla, nodding to Asha, who had been watching with a growing sense of horror.

The Siphon. The device that she'd just been reading about.

"You can't use it," she said suddenly.

Caeden frowned over at her. "Why not?"

"Because it's connected to all of the Shadows." Asha's gaze didn't leave Nethgalla's eyes, and she saw that she was right. "It…draws power from them. From us." Her heart skipped a beat. Could destroying the Vessel free the Shadows, perhaps? "And right now, it gives that power to *her*."

Caeden paled as he understood, then glared at Nethgalla. "How could this possibly fulfill Andrael's bargain?"

Nethgalla shrugged. "With the companion Vessel that you just attached, you can bind the Lyth exactly as the Shadows have been bound. They will become external Reserves—and by their nature, Reserves are protected from outside interference. They will be unable to use their powers, but they *will* be free to leave Res Kartha." She looked at him steadily. "It is the perfect solution. It is the *only* solution."

"A solution which would hand their power to you," said Caeden softly. "This cannot have been what I intended."

"I don't think that you expected me to be quite so involved," conceded Nethgalla, expression smug. "But the core of the plan

remains. I simply took it further. Mitigated some of the risks."
She shook her head at his expression. "Don't look so dismayed,
Tal. I'm on your side."

Caeden frowned, and there was a long moment as he digested
what Nethgalla had said.

"What do you mean, 'mitigated risks'?" he asked eventually, a
note of trepidation in his tone.

"Specifically? The last generation of Augurs." Nethgalla rolled
her eyes at Caeden and Asha's blank stares. "Their presence has
always made the ilshara vulnerable, but perhaps fifty years ago,
they started experimenting with things that you had convinced
their forebears to leave alone centuries ago. They were taking
more kan from the rift than was safe, threatening the operation of
the Tributaries. I don't know whether that was a machination of
the other Venerate, or if the timing was merely coincidental—but
in either case, you were still stuck in Talan Gol. You weren't in
any position to stop them."

"So you just... killed them?" asked Caeden in horror.

"I warned them first, but only one was willing to listen." Nethgalla
shook her head in disgust at that. "So, yes—I ensured that they were
prevented from continuing to walk that path. And rather than letting
society collapse into chaos as a result, I made the best of the situation. I used the opportunity to prepare for this moment—to make
sure that we would have a way to strengthen the ilshara, *regardless*
of whether the Lyth agree to your solution." She stared into Caeden's
eyes, and there was an unsettling amount of emotion in her gaze.
"But more importantly than that? I have a way to *save* you, Tal. I
know how to seal the rift *without you dying.*"

Asha had heard enough. "You cannot expect us to believe that
you were trying to help," she snapped.

Nethgalla sighed again, glancing at her wearily. "I could have
forced every mage in your country to become a Shadow, Ashalia. That's what I *would* have done, had I been aiming merely to
supplement my own strength." She shook her head. "But I did
not, because there are bigger things at stake. I left most of the
Gifted—the strongest—to fight. It was only those who were too
weak, those not disciplined or intelligent enough, whom I ensured
would be put to a better use. And believe me when I tell you this:

there is no better use than keeping what is behind the ilshara from getting to this city."

Asha stared at her in disbelief, then turned to Caeden. "You cannot listen to her," she said softly. "If what she says is true, then she *started* the war. Her actions have caused thousands upon thousands of deaths, and destroyed the lives of countless more."

Caeden hesitated.

His hand strayed toward the blade at his side.

Before he could do anything, a black cloud of smoke erupted from the ground, arrowing up and enveloping Caeden's face. The young man clawed desperately at his mouth but it poured into him, choking him with darkness.

"You think to draw a weapon against me here? Here of all places, Tal'kamar?" Nethgalla said irritably. Her focus turned to Asha. "And *you*. You really wish to stop me?"

Her lips curled into a sneer, and she drew Whisper.

Everything hushed; Asha took a faltering step backward and fumbled at her side for her own blade, but she knew straight away that she was still too weak for it to be of any use. She watched with wide eyes as Nethgalla strode grimly toward her.

The woman stopped a few feet away, then tossed Whisper disdainfully to the ground at Asha's feet. Even the clatter of steel against stone was muted.

"You have no concept of what is going on here. Your life is a speck of dust compared to mine and Tal's. I don't need a blade to face you, Ashalia. You simply don't have what is required for this fight." She stared at Asha confidently. "I have watched you over these past few weeks, and you are soft. Not *weak*, perhaps—but you do not have the fortitude required to be here, either. You thought that you were friends with the Hunter, didn't you? Liked her? Thought that she'd had a change of heart? And yet I killed her before you even met her. Your nature is too trusting, and you are too *soft*." She smirked mockingly as Asha stooped and picked up the blade. "You do not have the—"

Asha stepped forward and rammed Whisper with all her strength into Nethgalla's stomach.

Nethgalla's face twisted in pain, the black cloud around Caeden dissipated and everything...*changed*.

Essence suddenly flooded through Asha, bright and hot, overwhelming. She reeled backward, gaping silently as Nethgalla fell away, Whisper's steel emerging from her stomach coated in red.

Asha felt the black lines on her face burning, but she barely noticed among the dizzying array of sensations. In front of her, Nethgalla's body was changing, bones cracking and shifting and reshaping yet again beneath the skin. She became slimmer, lighter.

When the transformation was complete, Asha found herself watching an unfamiliar, dark-skinned woman with pure white hair gingerly levering herself up from the floor. Like all the forms which Nethgalla chose to take, this one was markedly beautiful.

Her gaze traveled to Nethgalla's stomach. Though the ugly splotch of dark red remained on the shape-shifter's clothing, the wound itself had vanished, the flow of blood stopped.

"That. Hurt," said Nethgalla as she straightened, shaking her head irritably. Her voice was rich now, deep for a woman's. She looked at Asha, and to Asha's confusion a flicker of sadness flashed across her face. "I am sorry, Ashalia. I actually rather liked you."

Asha stared at her blankly. The torrent of power she'd felt rip through her still tingled, still hovered at the edge of her awareness, but too much was happening too fast for her to focus on it.

"Regardless," Nethgalla continued as if nothing had happened, turning to Caeden as the last of the darkness choking him dissipated, "Andrael's ridiculous weapon did its job and took my Reserve, so the Siphon is now bonded to Ashalia rather than me. If you want to seal the ilshara, she will need to find the final Tributary. The one that you set aside for Gassandrid, until he began to suspect and split himself. And then yourself until Asar..." She trailed off with a shrug.

Caeden stared at her for a long moment, then paled. "No." He shook his head fervently. "I cannot ask her—ask *anyone*—to go into one of those."

"And yet you will have to. She is the only one with enough power, now," said Nethgalla matter-of-factly. "Meldier is free. Isiliar is free. Cyr is still frozen somewhere in the south, true— but he is not enough. He cannot hold out forever. Neither would you be able to," she added, a chiding note to her voice. "Though I would hope that you are not foolish enough to try. You cannot stop them if you dedicate yourself to that, and there is no one else who will."

"What are you both talking about?" asked Asha, unable to keep the apprehension from her voice.

Nethgalla edged toward the door, not taking her eyes from Caeden. "I'll leave the explanations to you, Tal," she said. "But be aware: dar'gaithin have started to breach the ilshara. Tek'ryl, too. And the eletai are not only crossing, but finding more for the Swarm every day." Her expression turned grim. "Not that any of that will even matter if the ilshara falls entirely—if He is freed and allowed to reach this place. So *do not* delay."

She finally glanced across at Asha.

"What you are looking for is with the rest of the Shadows." Another flash of pity passed across Nethgalla's face. "You will be able to find them, now—but you'll need to do so quickly. I wish you the very best of fate, Ashalia."

Nethgalla gestured abruptly and black smoke burst from the ground again, this time forming an opaque wall, obscuring her from Asha and Caeden's view. It began to clear after only moments but even as Caeden took a couple of stuttering, frustrated steps toward the door, Asha could see the same thing that he could.

Nethgalla was gone.

Asha sat opposite Caeden, trying to take in everything that had just transpired.

She did her best not to think about Breshada's absence. Nethgalla hadn't been wrong about Asha liking the Hunter—or the woman she'd *thought* was the Hunter, anyway. Breshada had stood up for Asha, trained her. Saved her life. If the shape-shifter had been telling the truth, then in reality Breshada had been dead for weeks—but the pain was sharp and fresh nonetheless.

It wasn't too hard to focus on other things, though. Everything that had just happened, everything else that she'd just learned, was...overwhelming.

She glanced at the redheaded man sitting across from her, who was staring off into the distance silently, clearly lost in his own thoughts. Laiman was still lying unconscious nearby where he'd fallen; Asha had taken the time to ensure that he was still alive, but beyond that didn't really know what more to do for him.

"So," said Caeden as he caught her look, stirring. "It seems that there are some things we need to talk about." He studied her face curiously. "How does it feel?"

Asha absently touched her face again. She hadn't realized until well after the fight—not until Caeden had mentioned the physical change. Even now, the concept was too much to grasp; every time she remembered it was a stab of realization, a sudden wash of wondering whether she'd been imagining the whole thing.

She was no longer a Shadow.

"Disorienting," she finally admitted. She looked at the young man, shaking her head. "I know it had something to do with Whisper, but...I still don't understand how."

Caeden toyed idly with the sheathed blade. "I know this sword," he said quietly. "I remember Andrael showing it to me. It was his first attempt at creating this." He touched his own blade, hanging at his side. "Whisper takes the Essence from anyone it cuts. Takes all of it—including their Reserve—and transfers it to whomever did the cutting."

Asha frowned. "So...now I have Nethgalla's Reserve?" She shifted uncomfortably at the thought. Breshada's—the *real* Breshada's—transformation from Hunter to Gifted was starting to make much more sense, too.

"I think so. And if that Reserve is what the Siphon is linked to..." He nodded uneasily. "I'm not sure that I understand the specifics, but I can see how it could work."

"How would it change my being a Shadow, though?"

Caeden shook his head. "The Siphon was drawing from your old Reserve; perhaps when you added Nethgalla's, it somehow broke the connection. Perhaps the Vessel was built to make sure that it could never be connected to its own Reserve. Or perhaps it's something else entirely." He shrugged, giving her an apologetic look. "I'm sorry. I remember pieces about all of this, but... not enough."

"It doesn't really matter, I suppose," said Asha softly. Not for the first time, she glanced down at her left wrist, still vaguely relieved to see that it remained free of a Mark.

Then she closed her eyes, concentrating again on her Reserve.

It was there. Accessible.

Immense.

She stayed that way for a few seconds, trying to focus on the ocean of light. It wasn't just *her* Essence that she could sense. Smaller pools of energy slowly began to resolve themselves, subtle differences to each one. More luminescence here, a faster rate of pulsing there. Miniscule disparities, but just enough to determine that it was not all one mass.

There were hundreds of those tiny variations. Thousands, maybe.

"How do we undo it?" she asked quietly. "How do we free the other Shadows?"

Caeden shifted uncomfortably.

"We can't," he said softly. "At least, I don't know how."

Asha got to her feet, striding over to the Adviser and placing her hand on it determinedly. She shut her eyes, focusing on the Siphon.

When she opened them again, a single blue line was stretching out from the pillar.

Directly to the book that she'd read earlier.

She scowled, frustration welling up inside of her. "That can't be it," she muttered.

She tried "Serrin"; there were a few books on the man, but none that mentioned more than his battle with Wereth. She tried "King Vederan"; again, only brief mentions within historical texts. She tried individual words and combinations, specific things and abstract concepts. She tried for close to an hour.

Caeden watched her with sad eyes. When Asha finally came to sit back opposite him, he said nothing for a few moments.

"So it has to be you," he said softly. "Once I've bound the Lyth to this thing, you're the one who has to use the Tributary."

"What is it?" asked Asha, from Caeden's expression already knowing that she wouldn't like the answer.

Caeden shook his head slowly. "It imprisons you," he said softly. "I didn't understand it until recently, but...it drains your

Essence. Constantly. There are several of them, all designed to power the Boundary."

"The Boundary?" Asha stared at him in disbelief. "How can one person be enough to help with that?"

"You won't be one person," observed Caeden. "You'll be the entirety of the Lyth. Trust me. It will be enough." He hesitated, looking reluctant to accede the next part. "And even if the Lyth refuse this solution and stay in Res Kartha... Nethgalla was right," he admitted softly. "I think the power that you already have would be sufficient, at least for a while."

Asha shivered at the thought. Caeden might be right, though. The presence of Essence burned in the back of her mind, making it hard to concentrate. "So is that all?"

Caeden grimaced.

"It...damages your body, to ensure that the flow of Essence is constant. It will be painful. You'll sleep for some of the time, and other times you'll be in something called a dok'en. Like a dream, but..." He shrugged.

Asha's stomach twisted. "For how long?"

Caeden looked away. "For as long as it takes," he said softly. He shook his head. "I'm so sorry, Ashalia. If there was another way..."

Asha felt as though she was going to throw up. So *this* was why Nethgalla had tossed Whisper at her feet, taunted her. Why she'd taken Breshada's form. Why she'd gone to such lengths to protect her on the journey there, too.

She'd been intending this from the beginning, and Asha had played into her hands.

"Was she telling the truth? Can you sense where the other Shadows are?" Caeden asked.

Asha nodded absently. "Northeast." That was where the majority of them were, anyway. There was a sense of distance as well as direction, but Asha didn't yet have enough confidence to interpret that part of it.

There was a long silence.

"If I do this," said Asha eventually, reluctance heavy in her voice, "will it really help to seal the Boundary?"

550   Caeden nodded.

"I think so," he admitted. "I think one of the reasons that the Boundary has been weakening is that some of the people who were originally in Tributaries have been released. It only stands to reason that adding someone with your power would strengthen it again."

Asha swallowed, the weight of what had happened finally beginning to settle on her. There was excitement, true—she was free of being a Shadow, and that was far from something to lightly dismiss—but the responsibility that was now on her shoulders was immense.

With a heavy heart, she realized that it wasn't something that she could ignore. Wasn't something that anyone else could help her with, either.

Caeden glanced across at Laiman, frowning. "What about him?"

Asha sighed. She didn't want Laiman as a traveling companion, not after what had happened on the bridge. "I suppose we go our separate ways. I head north, and he heads…wherever he wants."

Caeden nodded slowly. "You're going to do it, then?"

"Do I have a choice?" asked Asha quietly.

Caeden chewed at his lip, his avoidance of the question answer enough. "I could open a Gate—a portal—for you, if that would help," he said eventually. "But it has to be to a place that I already know. Somewhere I've been before." He rolled his shoulders apologetically. "I have no memories that can get you further north, I'm afraid."

Asha sighed, nodding an acknowledgment. Then she hesitated.

"Could you open a portal to Ilin Illan?"

Caeden gave her a questioning look.

"Taeris gave one of his Travel Stones to the men who he sent up north. Get me back to Ilin Illan, and I *think* I can get straight to the Boundary," she said quietly.

"You think?" said Caeden dubiously. "It's a lot farther south if you're wrong, and it's best if I don't go with you. Now that I finally have these Vessels, I need to deal with the Lyth."

Asha hesitated, then nodded firmly. "I'm certain."

It took them only half an hour to travel outside of Deilannis—a necessary precaution, according to Caeden. The Gate could cause damage to the city, apparently, though Asha didn't really understand how.

Caeden made the entire journey with a still-unconscious Laiman slung over his shoulder, never once stopping to rest. Asha glanced occasionally at the king's adviser as they picked their way around the dar'gaithin and Gifted corpses on the long white bridge, then emerged from the mists and finally stepped back onto Andarran soil.

"Is he going to be all right?" she asked eventually as Caeden propped the man carefully against a nearby boulder. She was still furious at Laiman, but not so much that she wanted to see him come to serious harm.

"I checked him. Nethgalla doesn't seem to have done anything worse than draining a good portion of his Essence," Caeden said quietly. "He might sleep for another few hours, but I think he'll be fine."

There wasn't much conversation after that, with Caeden focusing on creating his portal. In all, it took the young man about an hour to construct it. Asha watched curiously as she sat next to Laiman, though to her eyes, very little appeared to be actually happening.

Finally, though, Caeden stepped back and glanced over at her, giving a cautiously optimistic nod. "Ready?"

Asha nodded, scrambling to her feet as Caeden turned back and closed his eyes. Abruptly, a blue ring began to form, twice a man's height and just as wide. It began to spin, ever faster, blue flames blurring together to form a single circle.

Caeden breathed out.

"Step through it," he said to Asha. "You'll be in Ilin Illan. I'll close it as soon as you and Laiman are through." He waited until she had acknowledged the statement, then produced something from his pocket. A small bronze cube with strange markings on it.

"I will do my best to find you all again once I am done," he continued softly, gazing introspectively at the metallic box. "Tell Karaliene what happened here. Tell her that Nethgalla is still alive."

Asha stooped, grabbing Laiman's still-limp form and slinging him awkwardly over her shoulder. He wasn't a large man, thankfully, but even so, she wasn't sure that she would be able to travel far with him like this.

"I'll tell her," she said to Caeden. She gave him a short nod. "Fates be with you, Caeden."

Caeden gave her a wry smile. "You too."

Asha took a deep breath, then stepped into the vortex.

Chapter 39

Wirr stared at the Oathstone as he lay on his bed, holding it above his head and turning it over absently as he thought about the day ahead.

Today he was addressing the entire leadership of Administration—his last such opportunity before the vote in three days' time. This was likely the meeting that would decide whether he'd be allowed to continue in his father's footsteps, or be relegated to little more than a spectator as his mother took control of the organization. The consequences of the latter he could still barely comprehend, could barely stand to think about.

In the last couple of days, around the many hours he'd spent with his uncle seeking advice, he'd had to fake more friendly words and force more smiles than during the past two months combined. He'd bargained, cajoled, pleaded. He'd been charming, he'd been strong, and he'd dealt with the veiled insults—and some not-so-veiled—as best he could in each situation.

But he'd done it all without the Oathstone, and he knew that it hadn't been enough.

He stared idly at that small black stone for a while longer, considering how easy it would be to just put it in his pocket and take it to the meeting today. A couple of quick instructions, and every high-ranking official in Administration would be voting for him—and telling others to vote for him—even if they didn't understand why.

He gritted his teeth, then rolled to his feet and shoved the Oathstone back inside the safe. He'd meant what he'd said to Taeris.

He dressed, then flinched at a sharp, urgent knock at his door. Frowning—it was still very early—he walked over and peered out.

For a long moment he didn't recognize the young blond woman standing in the lamp-lit hallway outside.

Then his breath caught.

"Ash?" he said, stunned.

He opened the door wide and allowed himself to be wrapped in a hug, dazedly returning the embrace. Over Asha's shoulder he could see an exhausted-looking Laiman Kardai, the man's face drawn and his gaze bleary. The king's adviser gave Wirr a vaguely rueful nod of acknowledgment as he caught his glance.

"Sorry to do this to you, Wirr," said Asha as she stepped back again, giving him a tired smile.

"But we need to talk."

⚜

Wirr leaned back, dazed, as Asha finished her recounting of events since she'd left.

He shook his head as he tried to take it all in. Caeden at Deilannis. The other Gifted in the group dead, as well as Breshada. Nethgalla—*Nethgalla*, someone who he'd assumed was only a tale—revealing herself to have been both Breshada and the Shadraehin.

And Asha cured. Friends or not, if she wasn't so self-evidently no longer a Shadow, he wasn't certain that he'd have believed any of it.

He glanced across at Laiman, expression hardening. The man hadn't said a word since Asha had begun, not even when she had described his hesitation on the bridge.

"Now," Wirr said grimly. "I would like to hear *exactly* who you are."

Laiman met his gaze. "I can explain, Sire," he said calmly, "but first I would like... assurances."

Wirr felt his expression darken; he opened his mouth to respond, only to be stopped by a voice from the doorway.

"There's no need for that, Laiman."

Wirr turned, surprised to see Taeris standing at the entrance. He frowned. "How did you know we were here?"

"I made certain that I would know immediately when Master Kardai returned." Taeris's gaze never left the king's adviser as he spoke. "It's all right, Laiman. If anyone had to find out, these two are probably the best we could have hoped for." He hesitated. "And...Prince Torin has uncovered information about Jakarris that you need to hear, too. It changes things."

Wirr's frown deepened. Jakarris—the man who had betrayed the other Augurs, who had helped start the war?

Laiman stared at Taeris for a long moment, brow furrowed.

"You're sure?" he asked softly.

Taeris just nodded.

Laiman said nothing for a while longer, then let his shoulders sag. He nodded reluctantly, waiting for Taeris to shut the door and take a seat, then gazing at the floor as he spoke.

"So. My name is Thell Taranor," he said softly, as if barely believing that the words were passing his lips. The mere statement made him look like he wanted to throw up.

Wirr and Asha exchanged a glance, and from Asha's expression, the name meant as little to her as it did to Wirr.

"Who *are* you, then? Why hide your identity?" Wirr asked.

"The Council has sentenced Thell to death," explained Taeris.

"*Why?*" asked Wirr again, this time with irritated forcefulness.

Laiman glanced again at Taeris, who nodded grimly.

"They know this much," said Taeris quietly.

Laiman sighed in acknowledgment. "It's complicated," he explained to Wirr and Asha, "but the foremost reason is that I am the one responsible for creating the sha'teth."

There was silence for a few seconds.

"You *created* them?" asked Wirr eventually in disbelief, not sure he had heard correctly. "How? Why? Aren't they...*old*?"

Laiman gave him a wry smile. "Yes. And no," he said quietly. "It's difficult to explain. They *are* old—ancient, in fact—but most of their existence has been spent...elsewhere. I only brought them here, into this world, just before the war began. Criminality amongst the Gifted was out of control, and the Council desperately needed a way to track down and stop the worst of those responsible. The Augurs were in disarray, so..." He gestured wearily, as if suddenly tired of the excuses. "That was my solution."

Wirr frowned. "So if you gave the Council what they wanted, why do they want you dead?"

"The problem was *how* I did it," said Laiman quietly. "The sha'teth are not human, but they need hosts. To be what they are, to have the powers that they have, they needed living bodies. Gifted bodies."

Wirr felt his stomach churn.

"You killed people to create them?" asked Asha.

"Not exactly—there are traces of them still in the sha'teth, but...yes. To all intents and purposes, those people are gone."

"So the Council wants you dead more to cover up their secret than to mete out punishment," Wirr said flatly.

"In part," acceded Laiman. He still spoke hesitantly, as if the words were being dragged from him. "But the Gifted that I used were also from amongst the most powerful that we had—all members of the Council back then. They volunteered, but only because I thought that they would still be themselves after the process. And nobody *knew* that they had volunteered, because I was trying to keep the entire thing hidden from the Augurs. I was...using knowledge that I shouldn't have had." He sighed heavily. "I tried to explain that to the rest of the Council, after it was over, but it didn't make a difference. As far as they were concerned, I'd forced five of their most popular members to become monsters."

Wirr said nothing for a moment, trying to take it all in.

"But you're not Gifted," said Asha to Laiman suddenly, voicing the most obvious oddity a split second ahead of Wirr. "You can't be. Surely someone would have realized by now."

"And you deal with Tol Athian all the time," added Wirr. "Are you saying that no one from the Council has recognized you, in all these years?" He frowned. "And, wait—didn't you meet my uncle *during* the war?"

Laiman held up his hand, giving Taeris a weary look before continuing.

"I *was* Gifted," he said quietly. "When the Council condemned me, I went to one of the Augurs—a man whom you apparently know about. Jakarris. He...changed me. I still don't understand how, but he took away my Reserve, changed my face and body. Gave me this identity as Laiman Kardai."

558

"That's not possible," said Wirr.

"I'm telling you that it is," said Laiman steadily. "It was El-cursed painful, too."

Wirr glanced across at Taeris, who nodded slightly.

Wirr grimaced; even with Taeris's confirmation, he was finding this difficult to believe. "Assuming that we take your word for it," he said eventually, shaking his head, "why would an *Augur* help you?"

"Jakarris helped me because of what I know—and it's also why I need to stay away from the Council's notice. Why I need to stay hidden at any cost." He hesitated, glancing at Asha guiltily.

Taeris coughed.

"I can explain this part," he said quietly. He shifted, meeting Wirr's gaze. "Before the war, I was studying at Tol Athian. I wasn't much past twenty and not really anyone of note: always competent enough, but far from amongst the brightest or strongest at the Tol. I'd started to research the Boundary—purely an academic pursuit at that stage. One day there was a knock on my door, and Augur Jakarris was on the other side."

Wirr felt his eyebrows raise a little. "You knew the old Augurs?"

"Knew them? Goodness no," said Taeris with a small smile. "Nobody did, really—especially nobody at my level in the Tol—which is why Jakarris being there was so strange.

"Once I let him in, he just...started talking. Told me that of all the people in the Tol, I was one of the few that he felt he could trust. He was offering me the opportunity to rapidly advance through the ranks of the Gifted—for a price."

"Which was?" asked Asha.

"Becoming a memory proxy," Taeris said quietly.

Wirr cocked his head to the side, frowning. "I've never heard of such a thing."

"It's not something that the Augurs really made public," said Taeris drily. "They had the ability to connect directly to other people's minds, and they often used that ability to pass information to one another—to impart instantaneous knowledge, without the receiver needing to take the time to learn it. It was the easiest way to quickly educate new Augurs. But it also, somewhat more rarely, let them use other people's minds to *store* information."

He took a breath. "That day, when we first met, Jakarris was furious. Someone—he didn't say who, but I'm fairly sure he suspected one of the other Augurs—had sneaked into his quarters and destroyed every scrap of research that he'd gathered over the course of thirty years. He didn't tell me what that research was all about, at the time, but it wasn't hard to see that it was important. He said that the only place in which the knowledge now remained was his mind, and that there was far too much of it for him to simply go about trying to record it all again."

Wirr felt his eyebrows raising; to his left, he saw Asha leaning forward. "So...you volunteered to have an Augur *store information in you*?" she asked in disbelief.

"He asked, and I agreed to it," corrected Taeris quietly. "I was very good at Shielding myself, and he'd decided that I could be trusted—especially, as it turned out, because he saw how critically I was examining the situation at the Boundary. He knew that I'd understand the importance of at least some of what he gave to me straight away. So I saw some of his visions. I learned some of the things that he'd studied, texts of histories that were forbidden even to the Gifted back then. It was...enlightening, to say the least."

Wirr leaned back, stunned. Now he understood why Taeris seemed to know so much more about the Boundary, about its history and the potential threat behind it, than anyone else at the Tols.

"So you have all this information still stored in your head?" Asha asked, looking as dazed as Wirr felt.

Taeris shook his head. "Not all. There was too much of it to simply expunge into someone, and Jakarris didn't want to risk it all in one place anyway. A third went to me, and the rest to two other Gifted."

He glanced across at Laiman.

"You were one of the others," Wirr realized softly to the king's adviser.

Laiman inclined his head, albeit reluctantly. "Yes." He grimaced. "And some of it—such as how to create or control the sha'teth, for example—is far too dangerous to simply write down. Taeris knows as much as I could explain to him, but ultimately? If I die, that information dies with me."

Wirr just stared for a few moments, trying to decide if he really believed everything that the two men were telling him. It *did* explain a lot. Not that it excused Laiman's hesitation on the bridge, of course—but it at least made a little more sense now.

"This is also the main reason that the Council is so mistrustful of me," added Taeris, with an apologetic look at Asha as he did so. "They've been wary of me for decades, ever since the sha'teth. I told them that Thell had been killed by the creatures, but I couldn't produce a body, and they knew that we were friends. And then..."

He rubbed his forehead. "With the knowledge that Jakarris had given to me, combined with my observations at the Boundary over the past decade, I *knew* that there was something terrible coming. Or at least strongly suspected it. But when I tried to talk to the Council about it, they wouldn't listen to me. Whether it was because of their suspicions over Thell and the sha'teth, or because they simply couldn't believe what I was telling them without corroboration, I don't know." He grimaced. "So five years ago, I got desperate. I lied. I lied about things that I'd found, falsified evidence in order to try and explain away how I had the information that I did. And they caught me. They said that at best, I was insane—and at worst, was trying to destroy the Tol. It managed to sharpen their suspicion that I'd had something to do with the sha'teth all those years ago, too." He laughed bitterly. "Hard to regain trust after something like that."

There was a long silence as Wirr and Asha processed the information. It was a lot to take in, and Wirr found his mind racing with questions.

Before he could ask one, though, Laiman spoke up again.

"So what is this new information about Jakarris?" he asked quietly, brow furrowed as he looked from Wirr to Taeris and back again.

"Prince Torin found a notebook of his father's. Notarized," Taeris added quietly. "It says that Jakarris was the one who betrayed the Augurs twenty years ago."

Laiman paled. "That's not possible."

Taeris grunted. "There's more. Scyner—the Augur who was working with the Shadraehin here—was the one who directed

Prince Torin to the notebook. And from what Ashalia has told me previously, he also claims to have killed all the other Augurs." Taeris's expression was grim. "I think it's entirely possible that Jakarris is still alive."

Laiman just stared at Taeris in steadily growing horror.

The next several minutes passed in a blur as the four of them slowly, carefully untangled what each of them knew. *If* Jakarris had hidden his old identity behind a new name—which seemed likely, as everyone would have recognized the name of one of the old Augurs—did that mean that Nethgalla was then the woman who had provided the weapons to the rebellion? She'd set herself up as the Shadraehin, had seemingly engineered the creation of the Shadows. It made sense.

"So Jakarris thought that the Augurs' existence was some kind of threat," said Wirr slowly, eventually trying to summarize what they had learned. "He worked with Nethgalla to organize the rebellion. When it started, he killed the other Augurs and then… went into hiding, I suppose, down in the Sanctuary. Nethgalla provided the rebellion with the ability to create Shadows, which gradually gave her more and more power over the years."

"Right up until she gave it all over to me," said Asha quietly. "She wanted someone who was able to seal the Boundary, even if Caeden failed to strike a deal with the Lyth—but she didn't want to be the one who did it." She swallowed, nodding at Taeris's mildly skeptical expression. "There is a *lot* of Essence there. I didn't think that there would be so much, but I suppose with the Reserve of every Shadow from the past fifteen years combined…" She frowned, shaking her head. "I'm still confused about Scyner, though. If he really is this Jakarris, then he had the opportunity to kill the other Augurs, too, not just Kol. But he said that he wanted their help."

"Perhaps they don't pose the same threat as the ones from twenty years ago," suggested Wirr.

Before anyone could say anything more, there was a sharp rap on the door. Taeris opened it with a frown, and Wirr's heart dropped as he saw Administrator Myles standing outside.

"They're expecting you soon, Sire," he said, peering in at Wirr.

Wirr swallowed, nodding. "Give them my apologies, Adminis-trator. I'll be there in a few minutes."

He took a deep breath as the door shut again, shrugging at the looks of Asha and Laiman. "It's…a meeting that I can't miss," he said wryly, not feeling like going into detail.

"Sire," said Taeris quickly, "are you going to…?"

"No." Wirr met Taeris's gaze steadily.

Taeris grimaced, his disappointment evident.

Wirr glared at him for a few seconds, then turned to Laiman. "I have to leave, but first, I need to know—have you actually killed anyone to hide who you really are?"

Laiman shook his head firmly. "Nobody else has ever come close to finding out. Ashalia was the first."

"What happened with the sha'teth…it was a different time, Torin," chimed in Taeris quickly. "A desperate time. And those who ultimately became the sha'teth *did* agree to it."

Wirr closed his eyes.

"Perhaps," he said quietly. He glanced across at Asha, who had been largely quiet. "I haven't entirely decided what to do, yet, but regardless—we're not going to tell the Tol. Not if they're going to want him executed."

Asha inclined her head in agreement, and Laiman audibly exhaled with relief.

Then he swallowed, leaning forward and looking earnestly into Asha's eyes.

"About the bridge. I…need to apologize," he said quietly. "I truly did not want harm to come to you, but in the heat of the moment…" He grimaced, shaking his head. "I am ashamed that the thought even crossed my mind, but it did."

Asha chewed at her lip as she considered the king's adviser.

"I'm not going to pretend that you've left me full of trust, Master Kardai," she conceded eventually, "but at least I now know the reason. If you had not tried to help me at all, this would be a very different conversation…but you did." She inclined her head. "Your apology is accepted."

Laiman gave her a relieved, grateful look. Then he straightened and turned to Taeris, some of his usual self-assurance—completely absent since the beginning of the conversation—finally appearing to reassert itself. "Once you've sent Ashalia north, we should talk further."

Taeris nodded, glancing at Asha. "The Travel Stones are charged. You can be there as soon as you're ready to leave."

Wirr frowned, wanting to protest, but Asha saw his expression and gave him a rueful shrug. "That's why I came back here, Wirr—it's the quickest way north. Whatever else is going on, I don't think that Nethgalla was lying about what I need to do."

Wirr looked at his friend worriedly for a couple of seconds longer, but there wasn't time to argue right now. He stood, stretching, the nerves that had faded to the background over the past half hour suddenly returning.

"Just don't leave until I've had a chance to speak with you again," he said grimly. He glanced at the Decay Clock in the corner, then sighed. "Fates. I really do have to go."

With a nod of farewell from Laiman and Asha, and a sympathetic look from Taeris, he slipped out the door and began walking toward the Blue Hall.

It was time to face Administration.

Chapter 40

Caeden pressed his hand against the wall, steadying himself as the heat of Res Kartha once again threatened to overpower him.

"Garadis!" he shouted again into the shimmering, red-tinged air, not sure if there was anyone to hear him, but not knowing any other way to make his presence known. He was nervous about this meeting—and not only because the Lyth would undoubtedly be unhappy about the way in which he wanted to fulfill Andrael's bargain.

He understood who they were now, understood at least part of his history with them. He had slaughtered their people in Dareci, created the Plains of Decay so that they would flee to Andarra and build Deilannis. Build the Jha'vett.

He had done this to them. He had destroyed them.

Caeden wiped more beads of sweat from his forehead he walked along the dangerously narrow pathways of Res Kartha. As much as he tried to dissociate himself from the things that he had done as Aarkein Devaed, it was impossible to avoid the deep, omnipresent guilt. Impossible not to feel the weight of his actions every time he remembered just how much suffering they had caused.

His thoughts were interrupted by the flicker of red light up ahead.

He came to a gradual, careful halt as a being that seemed made of pure fire strode toward him, heedless of the edges of the path that dropped sharply to the lava far below. It did not take long to recognize Garadis, the Lyth's blue eyes alight as he gazed at Caeden with a look of unsettling hunger.

"Tal'kamar." Garadis's deep voice boomed through the red-tinged cavern. "You have returned."

"I have. I have found a way to fulfill the bargain with Andrael," said Caeden quietly. "I know how to free the Lyth from Res Kartha."

Garadis said nothing for a few moments, but his eyes held a fierce joy.

"How?"

Caeden hesitated, then reached into his pocket. Drew out the Vessel that Nethgalla had given him, which was still attached to the one that he had obtained from Meldier.

Garadis cocked his head to the side for a moment, frowning.

Then the light died from his eyes.

"A modified Siphon?" He stepped closer and examined the glass sphere, a slow look of horror spreading across his features. "No, Tal'kamar. No. This is unacceptable."

"It fulfills the bargain that you made with Andrael."

"In letter, perhaps, but not in spirit." Garadis's words were a snarl now. "We allow this, and all our knowledge is for naught. Without Essence, we cannot create. We cannot fight. We cannot build, or experiment, or better ourselves, or ever be *close* to who we once were—let alone find a way to go back and fix the Jha'vett. We have waited *two thousand years* for *one* purpose. And this…this *solution*…denies it to us!"

Caeden closed his eyes for a moment, heart breaking at the pain and frustration and fury in Garadis's voice. He had done so much to these people already. He knew that it was necessary but this still felt like a final insult, one last betrayal, like grinding their faces into the dirt long after they had already been defeated.

"It is what it is," he said softly. "And it is the best I can do."

"It is the best you are willing to do. As it ever has been, Tal'kamar." Garadis's blue eyes glowed with undisguised rage, but his voice was burdened with bitterness and heavy regret. He gestured, and a portal appeared in the air next to him. "Come, then."

"Where are we going?" asked Caeden cautiously.

Garadis's eyes bore into his.

"To tell the others."

As he walked among the Lyth, Caeden couldn't help but feel intimidated.

The portal Garadis had opened had led to another part of Res Kartha, but this...this was unlike anything Caeden had seen in the pits. They were still underground, but gone were the narrow walkways teetering above rivers of lava, area after area of crumbling infrastructure. Everything in this cavern was in perfect condition, and the cavern itself was *enormous*. The walls stretched out for what Caeden thought must be miles—entirely visible thanks to the stunning, glowing patterns set into them.

Bright red lava flowed down everywhere onto each of the four main walls, but none of it was haphazard. Up close, the cunningly carved rivulets created a series of beautiful, intricate designs, each section of the wall a work of pure artistry. But as Caeden got farther away, he began to realize that those motifs also formed part of a larger whole—each one meshing with the designs next to them to produce larger pictures, all in glowing, pulsing red. Some of those larger shapes were symbols, unknown to him but not unlike those on the Portal Box. Others were startlingly life-like images, strange creatures or enormous faces that gazed down at the city below, their pulsing and shifting lines giving them the unsettling illusion of breathing.

The city surrounded by those walls was sprawling, carved directly from the bedrock; nowhere was there the hint of untouched, natural obsidian. The structures here did not have the elegance of the Builders, but instead managed to exude menace, everything a mirror-finish black set against the red of both the cavern walls and the city's inhabitants.

And ultimately, despite all the other wonders, it was those inhabitants who commanded most of Caeden's attention. Every time he walked past one of the burning men or women, he felt a combination of awe and deep shame. They were strong, bright, and beautiful, a far cry from the fading creatures that he remembered tossing through the Gate. And yet he knew this was not how they had always been.

Once, they had been better. They had been free.

As he and Garadis walked along the wide alleyways between buildings, the Lyth who spotted them began to follow—first only a few, but then more and more at each corner until finally they were trailed by a living, breathing beacon of burning light that made the buildings and streets all around them blaze like the setting sun against black night.

Caeden sweated as he walked; the dry heat of the city was akin to the inside of an oven, perhaps even hotter than the walkways elsewhere in Res Kartha. He stumbled a couple of times from dehydration as he tried to ignore the increasingly loud murmurs, the horrified whispers from behind of those who had seen him.

The Lyth knew him, and none of their expressions were welcoming.

"How many live here?" Caeden asked quietly, gazing around at the myriad buildings. The city would be able to hold thousands, perhaps tens of thousands—and yet, there were not a great many Lyth walking through the streets.

"Those you see. A few others," said Garadis softly.

Caeden frowned, certain he'd misunderstood. There were perhaps fifty Lyth following them now. "Only a few? Where are the rest?"

Garadis did not look at him. "Gone, Tal'kamar," he said softly. "We built this city in anticipation of our numbers swelling once again, but it was not long before we realized that we could not reproduce. The only thing we had was Andrael's Law. It was enough to sustain us few, but everyone else...eventually, they grew tired. They lost faith. They Freed themselves."

Caeden felt a chill as he understood. He bowed his head and said no more.

Finally they arrived at an enormous, open square, the stone underfoot polished black like everything else. A small section stood raised above the rest, and Garadis led Caeden onto this platform, turning to face the assembled crowd. Caeden copied him, feeling unsure of himself.

"Tell them," said Garadis quietly.

Caeden gazed at the crowd, resisting the urge to shield his eyes. Men and women watched him expectantly. Hungrily.

"I have found a way to set you free from Res Kartha," he said loudly. There were murmurs at that but most remained silent, evidently seeing that he had more to say. He waited until the noise had died down, then continued, "but it may not be the solution that you had hoped for."

He drew the glass sphere from his pocket, holding it up and bracing for the explosion of fury that he knew was coming. For a few moments, there was utter silence.

Then the muttering started, the Lyth in the square beginning to talk among themselves. It was low and furious, a rumbling rather than the outburst of anger that Caeden had expected.

This...this was worse, somehow. These men and women were the last of their kind, thousands of years old, and had hinged so many of their hopes upon this. He could hear the sharp sound of bitterness and disappointment in each word that was spoken.

Garadis watched with sad eyes, then motioned Caeden to the side.

"Wait here," he said grimly. "We will discuss. We will decide." He cast his gaze out over the square. "It will not be long," he concluded softly.

He motioned to the others, who trailed after him into a nearby building. None of the Lyth looked at Caeden, even glanced in his direction. The air was thick with sadness, frustration, anger and grief and despair. But it was...as if it were expected, an inevitability. As if his mere presence had forewarned the Lyth that this was how things were likely to end up.

Caeden watched them go, seating himself at the edge of the podium and then focusing on the surrounding city. It was hot and stark and as markedly beautiful as it was empty. A reminder, perhaps even more than Deilannis, of what he had taken from these people. What he had taken from the world.

As the last of the Lyth left the square, the memory clicked into place.

Caeden swung open the massive steel door.

Beyond was...nothing. There was a path—little more than a ledge—that extended perhaps ten steps beyond the door, out over a completely black abyss. The thin light from the hallway seeped inside, but beyond an impression of the walls that surrounded the doorway stretching upward and away, Caeden couldn't see anything.

He stepped forward, lowering his gaze and shielding his eyes. He knew this place. Knew what was coming.

He closed the door again, and knelt carefully.

"I am here, El," he said firmly into the void. His words were swallowed by the emptiness.

Light.

Caeden rocked back in pain and shock. The light was not merely bright; it seared his eyeballs and a fierce, ceaselessly burning pain echoed through his skull. He braced himself, knowing that moving—taking his hands away from his eyes—would only make the pain worse.

Tal'kamar.

The voice was…everything. Deep and strong, reassuring and soft, filling his every sense. The agony of his eyes was forgotten as he did everything that he could to focus, to comprehend.

He'd known that it was coming, and yet there was little he could have done to prepare.

"I am here, Lord." Caeden breathed the words.

It is done? The voice came from all directions, burrowing inside his head.

"Yes." Caeden allowed himself the smallest sigh of satisfaction, the slightest flicker of pride. "We saved them. We saved them all."

This is well. Your faithfulness commends you, Tal'kamar.

"We all know that if we follow Your instructions, Lord, then good things will follow."

And yet it is you who leads the way. It is you who trusts to the courses of action which I provide, who pushes the others when their own wisdom says that they must surely fail. It is you who shows the strength and conviction and drive for what is to come.

Caeden felt his brow crease, even as a thrill of pleasure ran through him. Accolades from El Himself were rare, but this one sounded as though it preceded something more. Something important.

"What is to come, Lord?" he whispered.

There was silence for a moment. **Would you say that the Venerate have been a force for good, Tal'kamar?**

"Of course," said Caeden with alacrity. "We have prevented deaths, suffering, disease, wars..." He shook his head. "Since You brought us together, since You began telling us what needed to be done, we have made a difference unlike any I had ever imagined. We are changing the world."

You are, *said El. His voice was soft and yet it pounded against Caeden's ears like a thunderclap.* **And with each action, you form a different future from the one Shammaeloth first planned when he left me here. Each time you place your faith in me, you nudge this world in a direction away from that which he envisaged. You have been warping the very nature of the slavery that he wished to enforce.** *A pause.* **And yet, it is not enough. This, still, is merely an altered certainty. A different prison, but a prison nonetheless."**

Caeden's heart dropped.

"You said that one day, the difference that we made would mean an opportunity to go back. To break you free. To begin again in a world without inevitability, without his influence." *Caeden shook his head, hearing the panic edging his voice.* "I still believe that, Lord. I beg of You, please, tell me that that vision of the future has not changed."

My words are promise, Tal'kamar. My words are truth. You need never fear that. *El's voice was calm, soothing.* **But it is still as I forewarned—the path that we take must be the one that best diverges from Shammaeloth's. This is no simple battle, no mere case of preventing evil. He broke this world, but he understood enough to leave some of its beauty. Some of its joy. He knew enough to realize that sometimes, beauty is a temptation, and joy is a call for inaction. He knows to use good for his own ends also, Tal'kamar. He knows how to turn our own hearts against us.**

Caeden nodded slowly. "I understand."

Do you truly? It is his most powerful weapon, and it is one that none of you have yet to properly face. In fighting it, the depth of your faith will be laid bare like never before. In fighting it, you will need to above all remember the truth that I have always told you—that I have told each one of you again and

again, because it is easy to comprehend but difficult to sincerely accept. Which is that while I offer you a choice, it is a choice of duality and nothing more. You are always doing his will, or mine. But never yours, Tal'kamar.

"I do understand that, Lord. I do." *Caeden put every ounce of certainty he had into the words.*

Then hear me. *El's voice was suddenly more intense and Caeden flinched; it was as if someone was shouting in his ear and yet the words were deep and compelling.* **Because the time has come for action, and you alone amongst the Venerate have the strength to do this.**

There was a warmth in Caeden's head and he gasped, trying to steady himself. Images flashed through his mind, knowledge of... something. A device. Enormous. Unthinkably complex, and yet he could see all of its workings, and understood them.

Five black columns.

A weapon, one more powerful and more deadly than any Caeden had ever seen, had ever conceived. A device created only to destroy, to drain life from miles around until nothing remained. Until every living thing within its radius was completely, utterly extinguished.

"Lord," *he said softly, the beginnings of tears in his eyes at the horror he was being presented with.* "This is... evil."

This is necessary, *said El.* **This pains me more than anything, Tal'kamar, and yet it is my will. It is the act that will drive the Darecians to begin their studies. It is the act that will force them to flee south, to find the entrance that Shammaeloth sealed and to try and break it open again.** *A pause.* **So. Do you see the truth of his great shield, now? Do you finally understand what you must accept, must overcome, in order to defeat him?**

Caeden shook his head, tears trickling down his cheeks now. "I... cannot," *he whispered.*

You can, Tal'kamar. This is why it had to be you—the strongest of all. Because the others will balk. Some will despise you, oppose you. Others will fear you. None will fully understand. *El's rich, resonating voice was full of sadness.* **I cannot and will not force you to take up this burden—as always, this is the only freedom I can give. But I ask that you look to the greater good. I**

*ask that you remember that all that is done will be undone. And
I ask that you never forget that these sins will be mine to bear,
not yours. Just as Gassandrid told you when you first met.*

Caeden trembled, and for once it was not merely from the
impact of El's words. "You ask much, Lord." He swallowed a
lump in his throat.

*I ask all, Tal'kamar. And still I urge you. I beg you. Change your
name, if you must. Divorce yourself from your actions. But become
the man the world needs, even if it a man whom you despise.*

Then, as abruptly as He had come, He was gone.

Caeden blinked away tears for several long moments, still
shaking. Eventually, though, he gritted his teeth.

"We are the blade," he reminded himself softly.

He stumbled to his feet. El was right—he couldn't tell the
others. Couldn't begin to explain to them what had to be done,
couldn't ask them to share such a burden.

But this thing, this one terrible thing. He would do it. He
would bear it.

"Just the blade," he whispered numbly to himself as he left.

Caeden blinked away tears as he came back to reality.

It took a long moment for him to collect himself—not because
of the naked impact of the memory, this time, but because of what
it meant.

This was why he'd created the Plains. *This* was why he'd become
Aarkein Devaed. The Venerate had come apart after he had fol-
lowed Shammaeloth's orders, with several of them—including
Andrael—unable to believe that he had been doing as instructed.
And then when Andrael had ultimately uncovered the truth about
Shammaeloth, it had resulted in the creation of Licanius.

Caeden just breathed for a while, staring vacantly, utterly shaken
by what he'd seen. It hadn't been a trick. The presence in that cavern had been...*overawing*. Not just intimidating or strong or
knowledgeable, but *incomprehensible*. And he'd felt that way even
back then, when he'd been at the very height of his own power.

He eventually rubbed his face, feeling a chill as he tried to grasp
what he'd learned. He'd killed for his beliefs. He remembered

it, remembered that feeling of *certainty* that listening to El had brought.

It was a hard thing to shake.

And yet, he'd rebelled. After doing everything that El had asked him to do, after driving the Darecians to Andarra and forcing them to construct Deilannis, he'd switched sides.

Part of him could immediately see why. He'd known from the moment that El had shown him the Columns that what he was being asked to do was wrong, against everything that he knew to be good.

But that other part of him...it couldn't help but wonder. Couldn't help but remember what being in El's presence was like.

His thoughts drifted back to his conversation with Nihim, that night before Deilannis. They'd talked of religions, of El—the concept of El as most people knew it, anyway—and of how they could reconcile the concepts of inevitability and free will.

Nihim had called it the natural arrogance of man to want complete freedom, total control over their own lives.

The Venerate described its absence as slavery.

Time passed as he contemplated; he wasn't sure how much but when he saw motion at the end of the square, he stood again, muscles groaning in protest. He stretched, watching cautiously as Garadis strode toward him, the tall man's blue eyes flashing amid the fire of his skin. Behind him, the rest of the Lyth gathered silently.

Garadis came to a stop in front of him, contemplating him for a moment.

"We have decided, Tal'kamar." He sounded like he was forcing the words out, though his expression remained impassive. "We accept—on one condition."

Caeden breathed out, meeting Garadis's gaze. "Which is?"

"That you take us to Dareci once we are done."

Caeden frowned. "Why?"

"Because we will be unable to do so ourselves," said Garadis quietly. "And because none of us have ever seen our homeland."

Caeden hesitated, then inclined his head.

"Agreed." It was a far from unreasonable request. Distance wouldn't affect the Siphon—he felt certain of that, though he wasn't sure why—and he knew that he could use the Portal Box to take them there. There could be some ulterior motive to Garadis's request, of course . . . but Caeden knew that he was able do it, and he didn't feel that he could deny the Lyth this. Not when he'd already taken so much from them.

Garadis looked neither pleased nor upset at his decision. "Then let us proceed."

"Now?" Caeden blinked. "You don't want time to prepare?"

"We have prepared for two thousand years, Tal'kamar. Two thousand years without being able to see the sky, without knowing the smell of fresh air. Without *freedom*." Garadis gestured. "We are ready."

Caeden just nodded dazedly, drawing the glass sphere from his pocket.

The process took less than half an hour, all told. The Lyth lined up silently, one by one allowing Caeden to press the Siphon against their fiery skin. Each one shuddered and then . . . *dimmed*. Not completely, but as they walked away, they glowed more with the light of dying embers than blazing flames.

Men and women passed him in turn, moving off to the side and watching in grim silence, until lastly Garadis stood before him.

Caeden held up the sphere one last time, then hesitated. Something had been plaguing him and he wanted to ask now, while he had the chance. Before it was done.

"Why do you never refer to me as Devaed?" he asked quietly.

Garadis cocked his head to the side.

"Because that is not who you are—and it never was. It is the name you chose in order to instill fear in us, the name you chose because you wanted to pretend that your sins were not yours to own. But when we speak of you, Tal'kamar, we speak of *you*— for better or worse. Whether destroyer or savior, we will never let you hide behind another name."

Caeden swallowed, nodding. He'd asked, and he had received his answer.

"Ready?" he asked quietly.

Garadis inclined his head.

Caeden pressed the glass to his skin, watching as the sphere glowed for a moment before suddenly flashing impossibly bright,   575 shining like the sun itself, as it had for each of the Lyth. Then, just as abruptly, it was translucent again.

Garadis's shoulders slumped as his skin faded to a deep red, though his eyes were bright as ever. He took a long breath and nodded to Caeden.

"It is done, Tal'kamar," he said softly. "Time for you to uphold your end of our agreement."

It did not take long to send the Lyth through the fiery vortex of the Portal Box; for all the beauty they had built in Res Kartha, none of them appeared to want to take anything with them. There was no rejoicing, no glad voices ringing out at their newfound freedom as the still-imposing men and women walked through the portal one by one. Many glanced at him before they disappeared into the flames, but their expressions were inscrutable, as if they had still not yet decided whether happiness or sorrow was the correct emotion for what was happening.

The square became increasingly still, until finally only Garadis remained. Caeden took a deep breath as the towering man stepped up to the vortex.

"I wish you all the best, Garadis," he said over the roar.

Garadis watched him for a moment, then inclined his head. "We will see each other again, Tal'kamar," he replied. "Fate has not finished with either of us yet."

Without another word and before Caeden could reply, he turned and stepped into the fire.

Caeden stood there for a few moments, then drained the remaining Essence from the Portal Box, deactivating it.

The vortex disintegrated. Utter silence fell.

He gazed out over the wondrous, entirely empty city, allowing himself to catch his breath and sort through his emotions. To luxuriate in his sense of achievement, however brief he knew it would probably be.

It was done. His purpose here, as difficult as it had been, was complete.

After a while, he sighed and reluctantly held the Portal Box out in front of himself again. Found the only face that he hadn't yet activated.

The sixth destination. The last one.

Maybe, just maybe, this was the end of the plan that he'd been blindly pulled along by for what felt like forever. Nervousness fluttered in his stomach as he considered what that might mean.

Before he allowed himself to think on it too much, though, he poured Essence into the bronze cube, still unable to help flinching back as the vortex exploded into existence again.

He stared grimly at the sight for several seconds, then steeled himself one last time and strode into the flames.

Chapter 41

Wirr tapped his foot nervously against the dais, looking around at the milling sea of blue cloaks.

There were at least a hundred men and women present. It was the largest group of Administrators he'd seen in one place before—including, he realized wryly, when he'd been officially inducted. That had been not long after the Blind's attack, though; many in Administration had still been busy in the city and surrounding areas, giving aid where they could. Perhaps their absence then hadn't been entirely due to who he was. Perhaps.

He sat on a dais at the front of the room, facing the crowd, giving him a good view of just how quickly the hall was filling. Every Administrator with any sort of rank appeared to be in attendance—from Mari and Tachievar, to captains he didn't think he'd even seen before.

He studied those people's faces, trying to get a sense of the room. Most wore scowls whenever they looked at him—that was far from unusual, though. Still. Was that a slight smile from Reanne? A brief nod of the head from Heth? Did Tachievar meeting his gaze mean anything, or was the man simply focused on what was happening? He'd spoken to them all over the past few days, and not *all* of the conversations had gone *awfully*.

His train of thought was broken as he spotted his mother making her way through the crowd, which parted for her respectfully. After a moment of watching her, he felt a jolt of unease.

In her hands was his father's notebook.

He swallowed, then restrained a frown as she stepped up onto the podium and sat in the chair next to him, despite in theory having no more authority than any other Administrator in this meeting.

"Son," said Geladra with a nod as she took a seat, ignoring the curious looks of seemingly everyone in the hall. She looked calm. He wasn't surprised, even if he did feel a flicker of irritation at her composure. She'd been at his father's side and dealing with attention like this for longer than he'd been alive.

"Mother," he replied stiffly, though he made sure not to look unsettled by her presence. There were plenty of Administrators in the room who might still be swayed either way, and he needed to project an air of confidence—not arrogance, but the look of a man who felt comfortable in his right to be there. He knew from both instruction and experience that, consciously or not, onlookers would pick up on that sort of thing.

"I'm disappointed to see you here," said Geladra, quietly enough that no one else would be able to overhear. She kept smiling, but her tone was ice. "I thought you might have stepped down by now. If what I showed you didn't change your mind, I don't know what will."

Wirr smiled back, trying to look as though the conversation was a friendly one. "What happened to Father was horrible, and I fully intend on bringing whomever did it to justice," he said, keeping his voice calm and low. "But it has nothing to do with my leadership. Perhaps if you had told me and I had done nothing, you'd be more justified. But you didn't." He shook his head. "You say I turn a blind eye to the dangers of the Augurs, and yet you keep it from me when they do something dangerous. That's the act of someone in this for their own ends, Mother—not someone who wants what's best for Administration."

Geladra stiffened a little at that, and she said nothing for a few moments.

"Perhaps you're right," she eventually said softly, "but it's not just about that, Torin. It's your entire focus. It's not your fault, but you've been indoctrinated by the Tol, and now you leap to believe anything that they tell you."

She shook her head. "It has led to your legalizing the existence of the Augurs again because you want to defend some ancient, impassable barrier that's stood for thousands upon thousands of years. It's led to you thinking that the Gifted don't need as much oversight as they once did. You're opening the door a crack for these groups, Torin—but that's all they need. And you evidently cannot imagine what things will be like once they get a foothold."

Wirr stared at her with a frown, trying his best to see things from his mother's perspective. Trying to understand where she was coming from.

"That's truly what you believe," he said eventually. "About the Boundary, I mean? Despite the Blind, you *honestly* don't think there's a threat?"

His mother just shook her head. "A threat? *Perhaps*," she said softly. "But a threat no greater than that posed by the Augurs. Or Desriel or Nesk, for that matter." She sighed as she saw the frustration in his expression. "However hard it is for you to grasp that," she added quietly, "it is twice as hard for me to understand how you can possibly believe in such nonsense."

She stood and moved back to a seat at the front of the crowd, the conversation over before Wirr could say more.

Wirr watched her go, thoughtful now rather than angry. His mother didn't intimidate him anymore. She was just like the rest of them—willfully ignorant, passionately believing in something because she surrounded herself with people who also passionately believed in the same thing. He knew the type, now—those who found it easier to listen to people who reinforced what they already thought, rather than actually considering the opinions of those who didn't.

He gazed out over the gathered faces and had a sudden moment of clarity.

Their opinions *were* born of ignorance. A willful ignorance, perhaps—one born of fear and anger ingrained over many years—but ignorance nonetheless.

He had no right to force them into changing their minds. But that didn't mean that they couldn't be changed at all.

And if they *were* changed, whether he had his position here wouldn't matter.

He squared his shoulders, sitting up a little straighter as the certainty solidified. Deep down, he'd still been thinking of the

Oathstone as a last-resort option—but despite Taeris's encouragement, using it *would* make him worse than his mother and the rest of them. They were acting from blindness, stubbornness, and stupidity... but for the most part, they at least thought that they were doing the right thing. If Wirr used the Oathstone, he'd be doing so with the full knowledge of his wrongdoing.

What his mother had just said had given him another idea. Riskier, perhaps. But one that he thought he could live with.

Taeris would be angry. His uncle would be angry. Fates, he might be angry at himself in a few hours.

But for the first time, it felt like the right choice. Like it was the right thing to do.

The crowd were finally beginning to take their seats, and the chattering voices quieted. Wirr stood, heart pounding. There was a low murmur as he took center stage, most of it sounding disapproving.

"I've met with many of you, these past few days," said Wirr. The noise died down completely as he spoke, the carefully designed acoustics of the hall easily carrying his voice. "I've done my best to explain my vision for what Administration should be. I know many of you believe that I am not right for the job because of what I am. Because I have this." He raised his left forearm, displaying the tattoo there clearly.

He paused, staring out over the now-silent crowd.

"But as I have told many of you—I think that this makes me the *best* person for the job. The *only* one for the job. Nobody here can understand the Gifted as I do. Nobody can better understand their potential, both for good and for evil. Nobody can better gauge their powers. You are welcome to feel differently, but I truly believe it to be so."

He paused.

"I've been wanting to tell you how to vote," he said grimly. "I was going to say that you should vote with your heads, not with your hearts. That you should forget about bloc voting and vote for the person who you think will be *best* for Administration. I was going to plead with you to forget about politics. To forget about prejudices, just this once." Wirr closed his eyes for a second. That had been his plan, if he'd resorted to the Oathstone—

the most direct influence that he'd felt comfortable with. It might even have worked...but it would have been a fine line to tread. And it may not even have changed the result.

"But." He gave a rueful smile out to the sea of Administrators. He still hated speaking publicly, but he had become much more comfortable with it over the past month. "I've learned some things this morning. Things that have changed my position."

He took a deep breath.

"We have an opportunity, right now, to travel directly to the Boundary. The Gifted are about to send people there via a portal. I've seen it work before, I can verify that it is real and that it is safe." He looked around the room. "I want to invite any of you— *all* of you—to come north with me. *This* is how confident I am of what is happening up there. If you accept, see the realities of what we face, and return *still* wanting me to step down? Then I will. And I will not challenge for control of Administration ever again."

He looked out over the crowd, feeling at peace with his decision. He desperately didn't want to give up the position of Northwarden, and he was still deeply concerned about the direction that Administration would take with his mother in charge. There were bigger things at stake, though. Geladra was blinded by her hatred for the Augurs right now, but he understood why, and she wasn't a fool— on at least a purely intellectual level, none of those in the room were. True, some could be almost as bad as Ionis in their irrational fear of the Gifted, and those would cause problems no matter the situation.

But everyone else? If they were confronted with what was happening up at the Boundary—if they saw just a single one of the monsters that the reports indicated were occasionally breaking through—then they would come around. They had to.

Ultimately, more than his position here, *that* was what mattered.

There was utter silence after Wirr had finished, everyone looking taken aback by his speech. At the front of the crowd, Geladra stared at her son for a long few moments. She fingered the book in her lap thoughtfully.

Then she stood and walked over to him as murmuring began to break out behind her.

"I want your word, Torin. Your oath as my son," she said softly, so that no one else could hear. "I want to know that this is a   583 genuine offer. That you're not just intending to use another Gifted trick on us, like back at the estate."

Wirr met her gaze steadily. "You have my word."

Geladra studied him silently.

She slid Elocien's notebook into a pocket.

"I'll go north," she said loudly. Her expression was grim, and Wirr could tell that she thought she was calling his bluff. She turned to face the rest of the room. "And I urge every single Administrator who can be spared to do the same."

The murmuring in the room increased to a rumble as she turned back to him. "I hope that you are serious about this plan, Torin," she said softly. "Because there is no way to retract it now."

Other than his mother's brief speech, there was no reaction from the room beyond everyone talking among themselves in low tones. They'd come here expecting a grand speech, probably promises from him about the direction in which he wanted to take Administration—but certainly not this.

Wirr gazed around at the crowd. He wasn't sure that he'd made the right decision—but it was done, and there was no time to worry about it now.

He motioned to Tachievar, who had come closest to replacing Pria over the past few days.

"Please find out who is willing to come north, and have them ready to leave in a few hours," he said to the tall man quietly. He glanced toward the door.

"I need to warn the Representative that we might have a few extras along."

Wirr shivered in the cool afternoon wind as he walked up to join Taeris and Asha, nodding briefly to the uneasy-looking group of Administrators gathered on the other side of the courtyard.

"Thank you for waiting," he said to Taeris, noting the steadily fading light. It had taken a little longer than he'd expected, organizing everything that he needed to before he left. While the trip north would be instantaneous, the journey back would take a few weeks, and there were several things that he'd had to get in order

before leaving.

Particularly, as he'd realized nervously, because when he returned it may not be as Northwarden.

Taeris just grunted in response, still looking displeased. He'd been frustrated with Wirr's decision not to use the Oathstone, calling it rash, foolish, and several other choice words. Eventually, though, he'd reluctantly accepted that Wirr wasn't going to change his mind.

"You've spoken further to Laiman?" asked Taeris eventually.

Wirr nodded. "I told him that I wanted him to tell my uncle the truth—all of it. They've been friends for years, and the news should come from him. But given Laiman's position, it's not a secret that I feel I can keep from Uncle."

Taeris nodded. "Laiman will appreciate the chance to explain himself," he said quietly. "They *are* friends, you know. That was never something he lied about."

The Representative sighed heavily as he contemplated the situation, then glanced at Asha, who was staring apprehensively toward the palace entrance. "You don't need to listen to Dras," he told her gently. "Your position will be here when you get back. No matter how long you're away."

Wirr raised an eyebrow at his friend, who shrugged. "He heard that I was leaving again. Told me that if I went, it was proof that I wasn't taking my responsibilities here seriously. Said that he would make sure I wasn't Representative when I got back," she said tiredly.

Wirr's expression darkened. "If there was time, I'd be having a word with him." He'd already considered seeking out the Shen Representative before leaving. He knew that Taeris and Laiman suspected Dras of having a hand in his uncle's illness during the Blind's invasion, and now that Wirr had the Oathstone, he had no compunction about forcing Dras to reveal any involvement.

Taeris nodded approvingly, evidently following his train of thought. "When you get back, Sire?"

"When I get back," agreed Wirr quietly.

He sighed, touching the stone in his pocket, reminding himself to be careful not to issue any direct orders. He'd considered leaving it behind, but he was about to travel to one of the most dangerous places in Andarra—with a group of people who didn't believe that there was any threat. He sincerely hoped that he wouldn't need to force anyone to do anything, but given that a situation up there could quickly become life-or-death, it seemed foolish to leave himself without the option.

Taeris glanced across at the Administrators. "So this is all of them?"

"Yes." Including his mother, there were only a dozen or so of the hundred who had been at the meeting—but it was enough. Their word would carry weight with the others. Regardless of whether Wirr remained Northwarden, he felt confident that Administration would finally begin taking the northern threat seriously once they returned.

He'd used the afternoon to try and convince a few others to come, too, but without any success. In particular, he'd targeted ambassadors like Thurin, who had previously expressed their skepticism about the Boundary. Convincing them—and potentially gaining allies in the Boundary's defense—would have been a very large bonus.

None of them had been willing to make the journey, though. It was disappointing, but Wirr didn't regret trying.

"Then let's not waste time." Taeris drew out the familiar smooth black stone from his pocket, motioning the group standing across from him to join them. They did so, if somewhat reluctantly.

"Wait!"

Wirr turned with a frown to see Karaliene emerging from the palace. She had a determined look in her eye.

"Kara?" Wirr gave her a confused smile as she approached. "I didn't know you were back!"

His eyes unconsciously flicked behind her; the princess and Dezia were good friends and often arrived together. No one else appeared, though, of course.

Wirr sighed inwardly. He hoped that wherever Dezia was at the moment, she was getting on well. Was safe.

"I'm going with you." Karaliene shook her head with a glare as he opened his mouth to protest. "Administrators are all well and good, but you need someone who can convince the Houses, too." She stared at him defiantly.

Wirr hesitated. "Does Uncle know?"

"I just spoke with him," Karaliene assured him, a little too quickly.

Wirr's eyes narrowed. "I'll rephrase. Did he say that you could go?"

"I didn't ask, because I'm old enough to make my own decisions," observed Karaliene testily.

Wirr exchanged a glance with Taeris, who immediately shook his head. "Don't drag me into it."

Wirr sighed, then shrugged.

"Then I suppose you're coming with us," he said with a small smile at his cousin.

Taeris waited until they were all assembled and then closed his eyes, pouring white energy into the stone as he held it away from his body. The Vessel began to pulse and a sharp line of light materialized in front of the Representative, expanding until suddenly it blinked out again, accompanied by a low gasp from the Administrators. A hole now hung in the air, revealing a plain, gray-walled room on the other side of the portal.

Taeris gestured. "Whenever you're ready." He reluctantly handed the black Travel Stone to Wirr. "You'll need to be the last to step through—the portal will close once the stone is on the other side." He hesitated. "Get it back here as quickly as you can, Sire."

Wirr nodded, slipping the stone into his pocket and waiting patiently as first Asha, then Karaliene, then his mother and the Administrators cautiously stepped through. Eventually, only he and Taeris were left in the courtyard.

"I have more questions for you and Laiman, Taeris," he said quietly, looking at the scarred man meaningfully. "A lot more questions."

"I know." Taeris inclined his head. "When you get back, I'll answer them. You have my word."

Wirr nodded, then braced himself and stepped through the portal, blinking as he was struck by how much warmer it was here. The opening behind him winked out.

The room was empty save for its new occupants, a table, and a few packs thrown in the corner, but it did have a window. He glanced at Asha, and they walked across to it together, gazing out.

Wirr gaped.

They were positioned at the top of a cliff, overlooking a massive stretch of flat ground. The distance, though, was dominated by an enormous wall of pulsing, shimmering energy. The size and scope of it were...staggering.

He glanced back at the milling Administrators, then turned to Asha, exhaling.

"I think we're here," he said quietly.

Chapter 42

Davian wiped a bead of sweat from his brow and made another notation on the page, forehead wrinkled as he tried to make sense of what he was writing.

"Why would it absorb Essence there," he muttered, following the link in his notation to one that Ishelle had made the previous day. "There's no danger if the Essence overflows there. It would just decay. It's an unnecessary addition."

He studied the page in puzzlement for a few seconds longer and then growled, head aching from the long process of trying to piece together the enormously complex mechanisms of the Boundary. It had been four days since they'd arrived, and already they had pages upon pages of notes filled with their observations and analysis. Or speculation, in many cases.

But, slowly, even some of that speculation was beginning to form a picture. A vague idea of what some of the most basic components of the foundational pillars were intended to do.

He glanced over at the others, who were illuminated by the ghostly light of the Boundary. They had taken to working late—until they were ready to drop from exhaustion, in fact. It was too far to constantly travel back and forth to the safety of the outpost. They took occasional breaks, chatting as cheerfully as they could given the grim nature of both their surroundings and task. The vast majority of the time, though, their energy was spent examining the various functions of the Boundary.

Davian stared again at the column rising out of the ground a good thirty feet away, glowing with the familiar symbol of the wolf's head. It was there as a way to ensure that none of the kan moved; the positioning of each element appeared to be as important as its actual function. He resisted the urge to edge in for a closer look. He'd figured out enough of what the Boundary was capable of doing to know better.

Suddenly there was a flicker of movement at the corner of his vision, and he froze.

The torrent of Essence flying between each pillar was always in flux, but now, for a few seconds, it just...stopped. The Boundary sputtered, its low thrum hesitating, the usually regular pressure against Davian's ears stuttering.

His eyes widened.

On the other side of the torrent of Essence, between the flickering translucent lines, were several figures.

For a long few moments Davian stared at the motionless silhouettes, who seemed as startled as he by the sudden increase in visibility. They were human in shape—he could make out that much—but beyond that, they were little more than dark outlines against the lighter background. Illuminated by the Essence, but features indistinguishable.

He shouted out to the others urgently, turning to make sure that he'd gotten their attention. The thrum resumed just as he did so and when he turned back, the figures had vanished again behind a wall of blue-white Essence.

"Did something happen?" asked Ishelle as she rushed over, the others right behind her.

"I saw...people. On the other side," Davian said grimly as the other two joined them.

Erran glanced toward the Boundary. "Are you sure?"

"Certain. The section here...it failed for a few seconds."

Silence met the statement, and the other three suddenly looked as nervous as Davian felt.

"We were about to call you over," said Erran suddenly. He gestured for the others to follow and then struck out for where he and Fessi had been standing, about a hundred feet farther along. "We found something."

Davian and Ishelle hurried after him. "Found what?" asked

Ishelle.

Erran's tone and expression indicated worry more than excitement. "Something you're going to want to see." He pointed to a section of the wall of light, which on the surface was no different from the rest of it. "Look there," he said quietly.

Davian closed his eyes and stretched out, pushing through kan and letting his senses take over. The wall wasn't as complex as the pillars; though a tangle of threads of kan stretched between the columns, the columns themselves determined those threads' functions.

Where Erran had indicated, though, there was...something. Something unusual. Davian frowned, peering closer at the kan construct. It was hard, shaped like an archway, a little higher than six feet.

And to the side, there was another piece of kan machinery. At first it looked like everything else that he'd been staring at for the past several hours.

Then he started.

The machinery wasn't nestled within the barrier, like everything else he'd seen. It jutted slightly. If he reached out, he would be able to access that kan device. Touch it.

Activate it.

"Fates," he murmured, focusing back on the archway with a sudden surge of understanding. He opened his eyes, turning to the others in astonishment. "Is that...?"

"We think so," said Fessi with a nod, eyes alight with curiosity. She stared intently at the spot where Davian had been looking, even though there was nothing to see without using kan.

"I think we just found a door."

Davian sat back, rubbing his eyes.

It was late now. At least two hours after Erran had drawn his attention to the kan anomaly. Fessi and Erran had eventually gone to look at other sections of the Boundary—to see if, perhaps, there were other similar mechanisms elsewhere—but he and Ishelle had done little else except study the strange structure. Every time he looked at it, though, he came to the same conclusion.

"I can't see what else it could be," he said quietly. "It seems simple enough. The kan that we can access can be pushed, shifted inward. That would block off the flow of Essence to the archway, leaving it clear to walk through." He rubbed his forehead. "Not that we should do that," he added drily.

"Why not?"

He turned to stare at Ishelle, who was frowning absently as she examined the structure. She looked up and shrugged when she saw his expression. "What if we're not making headway because we can't see the whole picture? What if whatever's wrong with the Boundary is actually on the northern side? I mean—if someone's really trying to bring it down, it makes sense that they're doing it on the side that they can get to."

"There's not much use in strengthening the Boundary if we leave a hole in it, though," observed Davian drily.

Ishelle rolled her eyes. "Obviously. But it's easy enough to see that the kan could be pulled out again. It's made to be shut as well as opened."

Davian grunted, examining the structure again.

"You have a point," he conceded eventually, "but doors can have locks, and the north was meant to be a prison. I wouldn't assume that because we can get in, we would be able to get out again just as easily."

"We wouldn't *all* go," said Ishelle, her tone indicating the obviousness of the statement. "Someone could stay here, keep watch, open or close the door if necessary." She sighed as she saw his dubious look. "I know it's *dangerous*, but let's face it. We're not here to enjoy ourselves."

Davian shook his head slowly. "I see what you're saying, but it seems too early to be taking a risk like that."

"Too early?" Ishelle gave him a cynical look. "Weren't you just panicking that the entire fates-cursed wall was about to come down?"

Davian snorted. It hadn't been *panic*. "I just think that we need to get a better understanding of what everything on *this* side does first," he said firmly.

Ishelle frowned, turning and staring again into the blue-white light of the Boundary. She said nothing, and for a second Davian thought that she was having another of the strange, unsettlingly long lapses in concentration that had struck her now and then over the past few days. He'd tried to bring up her distracted behavior a few times—they all had—but Ishelle continued to shrug it off, and seemed to be getting more irritated every time that it was mentioned now.

Eventually, though, she sighed and shook her head ruefully.

"Perhaps you're right. Just keep an open mind," she said quietly, unaware of Davian's concern. She covered a yawn. "Fessi and Erran can't be too far away anyway. It's probably time to start heading back for the night."

As if to punctuate her words there was a sudden *thrum*, followed by a thunderous crash that made Davian flinch, despite having heard it plenty of times before. Bright Essence flashed at various points along the wall as what they surmised were the Talan Gol forces—probably including eletai, from the elevation of some of those flares—flung themselves at the other side of the Boundary.

He shook his head to stop his ears from ringing. "Let's make a start," he agreed, glancing along the crackling wall. Those few faltering seconds from earlier were making him even more nervous. They hadn't seen anything get through since they'd arrived, but the Boundary needed only to fade again at the wrong moment for things to quickly become dangerous.

They began making their way back toward the outpost. As they walked, Ishelle cast a longing look over her shoulder at where they'd found the archway.

"You cannot seriously *want* to go through," said Davian, following her gaze.

Ishelle shook her head, not taking her eyes from the barrier. "I don't *want* to. But doesn't it make you wonder?"

"Wonder what?"

Ishelle shrugged. "Why, after creating such a thing—this enormous, important, last-resort barrier to stop their enemy—the Augurs would bother to put a *door* in it?"

Davian opened his mouth to reply, then hesitated.

It *was* strange. Surely it had been a risk. The Augurs two thousand years ago had supposedly created this from utter desperation, when there had been no other options left to them. Why leave *any* gap in their prison, even if it was one that could only be discovered by one of their own?

"You have a theory, I take it?" he asked eventually.

Ishelle shrugged. "Perhaps. The first step would be to find out whether the one we found is the only one."

Davian stared at her in bemusement. "Of course it isn't," he said slowly. "The Boundary's hundreds of miles around. What are the chances that we would stumble onto the only door? Just where we happened to be?"

"What are the chances indeed," murmured Ishelle, raising an eyebrow.

Davian felt his brow crease. "You're suggesting that it might have been deliberately placed there...for us?"

Ishelle shrugged again. "Alchesh took part in the creation of this wall, and he saw a long way into the future. To *now*, if we're going to believe everything that you claim to believe. Who's to say that he didn't also See us?"

Davian shook his head slowly. "Seems a little grandiose," he observed.

Ishelle gave him a wry look. "*You* think that we're trying to save the world from the greatest evil to ever be unleashed upon it. If you're going to believe that, I don't think it's too grandiose to think that my theory is at least a possibility."

Davian grunted, but conceded her point. The healing of the Boundary—or its collapse—would surely be a crucial moment in the future, though he'd been trying not to think of it in quite such terms. It *was* possible that it had been Seen long ago, he supposed.

"Well, we should know soon enough," he said, gaze wandering down the wall of light to the east. "That looks like Erran and Fessi. They'll be able to tell us if the next section is the same."

They slowed, allowing the other two Augurs to catch up to them.

"Any news?" Davian asked as they got within hearing range.

Fessi shrugged. "Nothing important," she said, sounding as tired as she looked. "Everything seems close to identical to here, as far as I can tell."

"Did you find another door?" asked Ishelle.

Fessi shook her head. "No door."

Davian grunted as Ishelle's eyes lit up. "It doesn't mean anything, Ishelle," he warned her quietly. "There could be one every few pillars. Or one for every outpost, even. It's not necessarily unique."

"But this makes it more likely," retorted Ishelle.

The others looked at them questioningly, and Ishelle supplied her theory on the kan archway's purpose.

"What if the Boundary can only be fixed from the other side?" she concluded quietly. "Even if that doorway wasn't specifically made for us, the Augurs clearly wanted to be able to get into Talan Gol for *something*. Perhaps it was their way of ensuring that if the Boundary needed fixing, it could be done."

"It's still thin," observed Erran quietly. He held up a hand defensively as Ishelle glared at him. "I'm not saying that you're wrong. But I don't especially feel like wandering into Talan Gol just to find out whether you're right, either." He shrugged. "Besides, I'd like to think that if I'd helped make the Boundary, and then Seen us in our current situation, I would have left us something other than a door." He gave Ishelle a pointed look. "Like, say, instructions telling us how to fix whatever's going on here."

Ishelle sighed. "I suppose," she conceded.

They kept walking, quiet discussions about the mysterious door and other mechanisms in the Boundary fading to silence as they got closer and closer to the long climb up to the outpost.

They were all trying to maintain an optimistic outlook, but it was hard to avoid the slow, creeping sense that they were in over their heads.

Davian glanced back toward the now-distant rippling wall of light as he started up the stairs. Today had been the first time that he'd really seen a sign of just how badly, how rapidly, the Boundary was decaying.

He suspected that it wouldn't be the last.

Davian nodded to the two guards at the northern entrance, frowning slightly as he entered the keep beyond.

The outpost was quiet—as was the norm at this time of night—but there was a pile of satchels in the corner that hadn't been there when they'd left. A few men were sitting around a table in one of the side rooms, playing cards. Davian poked his head inside, giving a friendly nod to the one who looked up.

"Do we have visitors?" he asked curiously.

"You do," came a familiar voice from behind him.

Davian turned, a huge grin splitting his face.

"Wirr?" He wrapped his friend in a fierce embrace, laughing. "Fates! *Fates*. I did *not* expect to see you here!"

"And you cannot imagine how glad I am to see that you're here," said Wirr. The young man beamed back at Davian, though he looked worn—somehow even more so than he had the last time that Davian had spoken to him, after the battle in Ilin Illan. "You have no idea how hard it's been to get information on what you've been up to out of Shen."

Davian winced. "There's a reason," he admitted wryly. "But we'll get to that. What are you doing here? Shouldn't you be… Northwardening, or whatever it is that you do now?"

"Finally, someone who has a grasp on my job description," said Wirr with a grin. "Yes, ideally I would be Northwardening. But there have been some…complications."

There was movement at the door, and Davian paused as a woman in a blue cloak swept into the room. Her gaze fell on Davian, the icy look in her eyes immediately wiping the smile from his face.

"A friend of yours, Torin?"

Wirr smiled, but Davian could tell that the expression was forced.

"Mother, this is Davian. Davian, this is my mother, Duchess Geladra Andras."

Davian immediately dipped his head respectfully. "It's very nice to meet you, Duchess Andras."

"Hmm." Geladra looked unimpressed, eyeing him for a few moments. "You're the Augur."

"I am." Davian straightened. "We've been studying the Boundary, trying to—"

"I know the story." Geladra's gaze swept past him, searching the room. "Tell me, Davian. Did you know my husband?"

Davian glanced at Wirr, who was looking uncomfortable. "I

met him briefly just before the battle in Ilin Illan," he said quietly. "I am sorry for your—"

"Don't." Geladra's words had heat to them. "Are there others like you here? Where are your keepers from Tol Shen?"

Davian stiffened, glancing askance at his friend, who gave him an apologetic shake of the head in return. Wirr looked mortified, at least. That was something.

"There *are* others," Davian said as politely as he could. "But unfortunately none of the Elders from Tol Shen were able to join us. We were given permission to travel here by ourselves, given the urgency—"

"So you've had no oversight." Geladra's expression darkened. "For all we know, every man in this outpost is being Controlled."

Wirr groaned. "I know Davian, Mother. I grew up with him. He would *never* do anything like that."

"And you. *You* should be the one who's outraged, not me." Geladra glared at her son. "These Augurs are here in clear violation of the Amnesty, and yet your *immediate* reaction is to say that it's all right? Take responsibility for your position while you still can, Torin." Her eyes took on a dangerous look. "I expect you to organize for me to have a word with these other Augurs as soon—"

"That's enough. I'm saying it's all right because I am exercising my judgment on the matter," interrupted Wirr, his tone cool and gaze steady as he said the words. Davian blinked; Wirr's voice held more commanding, calm authority than he'd ever heard from his friend before. "You will have your chance to speak with the Augurs, Mother, as promised. But for now, I would like to catch up with my friend. In private."

Geladra glared at her son, face flushed, but after a few moments spun on her heel and left.

There was an awkward silence following her departure, Davian staring after her wide-eyed. He eventually turned to see Wirr shaking his head.

"Fates," he muttered. "I'm sorry, Dav. That wasn't the way I'd hoped to greet you."

"Not your fault." Davian raised an eyebrow. "So things are... not going well?"

"Not even close. You?"

"Worse." Davian rubbed his forehead. "Definitely worse."

There was another silence, and then the two boys grinned at each other.

"Come on," said Wirr, his smile widening. "We can commiserate later, but first, I can think of at least one other person who's going to be happy to see you."

Davian, Asha, and Wirr sat around the table, the conversation still lively despite the late hour.

It felt like forever since the three of them had been together like this. It *had* been well over a year, Davian supposed—they hadn't had a chance to simply sit and talk like this since Caladel. Despite the situation, despite the grimness of their surroundings and what was to come, each of them wore smiles.

After everything that they'd been through recently, this felt good. It felt *right*.

Still, the underlying tension of what was going on around them was unavoidable. Much of their conversation had been taken up discussing all that had happened since they had last been together. Davian had insisted that Asha go first, spending most of the first hour dazed every time he saw her face, still finding it hard to believe that she was really no longer a Shadow.

Even that, though, was almost easy to accept next to what she and Wirr had been through over the past few months.

"Fates," he said, sitting back after Wirr had finished explaining what he'd found in his father's journals. "So you really believe that all of this—the war, the last twenty years—was just..."

"I don't know." Wirr shifted uncomfortably. "It at least seems likely that Nethgalla and Jakarris worked together to take down the old Augurs. And that Nethgalla set things up so that she'd gain strength from the Gifted being turned into Shadows...but then, that seems to have been mostly in service of stopping the Boundary from collapsing." He glanced at Asha, who nodded reluctantly.

Davian felt a chill as he shook his head, trying to process it all. "It's still a terrifying thought," he observed quietly. "It means that they willingly ruined tens of *thousands* of lives just to get to this point."

There was a somber silence after that.

"So we think that Caeden's name is really Tal'kamar, now? He didn't say anything else to you? Or to Karaliene?" Davian asked eventually. He'd thought often of their friend but so much had been happening, it had never been for long. "If he's remembered anything more, then he might have some answers."

Wirr shook his head. "You know everything that I do. You can ask Kara yourself, though, if you want—she's here somewhere. Just be aware... she won't react to you quite like my mother did, but she probably won't be entirely easygoing about you and your friends breaching the Amnesty, either." He stretched. "So have you and the other three made any progress since you got here?"

Davian sighed, nodding an acknowledgment at Wirr's warning regarding the princess. "We're not making *quick* progress, exactly—but we're learning more about how everything works up here each day," he said quietly. He glanced at Asha, stomach twisting as he thought about what she was intending to do. "I'm sure that we'll figure out a way to fix the Boundary before you need to use this Tributary device, though."

"Liar," observed Asha with an affectionate smile, though Davian could see her nervousness behind it. She shook her head. "Do what you can, Dav. But if I need to use it, it won't be anyone's fault."

"When will you start looking for the Shadows?" Wirr asked her.

"Tomorrow. First thing. They're to the east—a little way, but not too far, I think." Asha's tone was confident. "The sooner I find them, the more prepared we'll be if I do need to do something."

Davian and Wirr both grimaced at that, and Asha rolled her eyes at them. "I'll be fine." She looked at Wirr. "Honestly, I'm more worried about you at the moment. I still can't believe that you offered to step down."

Wirr shrugged awkwardly.

"I'm still hoping that I won't have to," he admitted. "But I need to convince my mother of the problem. I need to convince her that there *is* a problem. Otherwise, she's going to cause more than a little trouble for the Augurs." He gave Davian a concerned look. "The thing is... we think that someone may have been Controlling my father for the past few years. We found some things that he'd written in a journal, and..." He sighed. "The worst part is, I was angry to begin with, but now that I've had time to think about it, I'm conflicted. If it's true, it probably saved my life. But it's still a hard thing to just let go."

Davian gazed at him in horror. "I'm so sorry, Wirr," he said quietly. Beside him, Asha just watched, her eyes full of sadness and sympathy.

The conversation stalled for a few moments, but eventually turned to lighter things after that. For just a while, Davian forgot where they were. Forgot the pressure, forgot the frustration and nervousness and panic that pressed down on him every moment that he was working on the Boundary, and just enjoyed the company of his friends.

Too soon, though, Wirr glanced at the moonlit landscape outside the window and stood, stretching.

"Well. I'm off to bed," he said with a yawn. He gave the other two a mock-stern look. "Don't run yourselves into the ground."

Davian smiled. "You're starting to sound like Elder Olin."

"Then fates rest him, that man was wiser than I gave him credit for." Wirr yawned again, nodding cheerfully. "See you in a few hours."

He left, and there was silence for a few seconds. Davian shifted.

"I've missed you," he said quietly, a little awkwardly.

"I would hope so." The corners of Asha's mouth curled upward. "I've missed you, too, Dav."

Then she paused, giving him a gentle nudge with her shoulder. "I see that you still have my ring, by the way," she added, eyes sparkling as she nodded to the band of silver on his finger.

"Of course." Davian hesitated. "I know you said to hang on to it until the next time we saw—"

"No." Asha reached over, pressing her hand down firmly over his and leaving it there. "I like that you have it."

Their gazes met and Davian smiled, a contented warmth suddenly in his chest.

They sat like that, just talking, for hours more. In the background, guards came and went as they changed shifts, and outside the moon rose and then began to fall again. Davian knew, somewhere in the back of his mind, that he should probably sleep. He needed to be sharp when the morning finally came.

In the end, he just didn't care.

A good amount of time had passed when, midconversation, Asha's eyes went wide and she swayed in her seat, gripping his arm tightly to steady herself. Davian half rose in concern at the expression on her face, but Asha quickly shook her head and waved him back down again.

"I'm all right," she said softly, shaking her head dazedly. "I think..." She shuddered again. "I think Caeden is starting to bind the Lyth."

Davian watched her worriedly. "Are you sure?"

Asha grimaced, still holding on to his arm for support. "There was already so much power there, it's hard to tell. But...yes." She shivered. "Yes."

Davian watched her silently for a few seconds, heart heavy.

"Are you really going to do this?" It wasn't completely in context with their previous conversation, but the seriousness of his tone, and their surroundings, was enough for Asha to know to what he was referring.

Asha gave him a rueful smile. "Not much choice in the matter." She reluctantly released his arm, seemingly having adjusted to the abrupt influx of power.

"We'll see," said Davian. "There's still a chance that we can find a way to make it unnecessary."

"I hope you're right," Asha said softly, "but don't make promises you can't keep. If it's what needs to happen, then I'm ready."

Davian nodded slowly, heart wrenching as he gazed into Asha's eyes.

Then he leaned in, a little hesitantly until she smiled, lifting her face gently to his.

Time passed in an all-too-brief blur of long embraces and soft, happy conversation after that; when Erran and Fessi abruptly burst into the room, the first hints of dawn were showing outside the window.

"Davian! There you are!" Erran pulled up short when he saw Asha and Davian together, having the good grace to wince and give Davian an apologetic glance before continuing. "Ishelle's gone."

"What?" Davian straightened. "Where?"

"Toward the Boundary. She must have used a time bubble to get past the guards without them noticing. They only spotted her a few minutes ago. She's not far from getting there."

Davian frowned. "Maybe she couldn't sleep. She could just be getting an early start," he said slowly. He saw Erran's raised eyebrow and cursed. "Fates, you're right. That doesn't sound like her. And she *was* awfully interested in that El-cursed door last night." He leaped to his feet. "Let's go."

"You're not going anywhere."

Everyone turned to see Geladra in the doorway, several Administrators behind her.

Davian frowned. "We need to go after our friend," he said urgently. "She left, and we're not sure why."

"None of you should be going anywhere without supervision." Geladra's eyes were hard as she looked at the three of them. "I would hope that you will respect the rule of law enough not to resist—but if you do, we are willing to use—"

Suddenly everyone in the doorway appeared to freeze.

Davian blinked, then turned to see Fessi with a look of concentration on her face. "Good thinking."

"Thanks." She glanced at Erran, then at Asha, both of whom she'd somehow managed to pull outside the flow of time, too, despite not being physically in contact with them. "I probably can't hold a bubble of this size for long, so let's make this quick. What are we doing?"

"One of us has to go after her," said Erran.

Davian nodded his agreement. "Fessi's the only one who can reach her in time," he observed.

"And you're the only one who she'll listen to," added Fessi wryly. She shook her head. "She's been acting strange ever since the eletai. We should have kept a closer eye on her."

Erran grunted his agreement. "Fess, take Davian. You won't catch her if you have to account for two of us. It's not as if Geladra here has any proof of wrongdoing, or any way that she can hurt me if she decided to try."

Davian exhaled heavily, then leaned down and gave Asha a quick kiss of farewell. "I'll see you soon," he said with what he hoped was a reassuring smile.

Before Asha could respond, Fessi grabbed his arm, retracting the time bubble so it encapsulated only the two of them.

They started toward the Boundary.

"So. You and Asha looked like you were getting along," observed Fessi.

Davian gave her a dry look, and said nothing. They were setting a reasonable pace, though it was a quick walk rather than a run; they had discovered that it was more efficient for maintaining concentration to move at that pace, meaning that they could ultimately get farther, faster.

"Is that Ishelle up ahead?" he asked, squinting at the wall of energy. They were nearly there.

Even as he spoke, there was a flicker of movement from the Boundary.

Davian watched in horror as the light near the distant figure of Ishelle simply...*melted*, revealing the archway that had been outlined by kan. Through it, he could see more of the barren, cracked ground that they currently stood on. Nothing else, though. No enemies.

Ishelle walked through the entrance, and Davian held his breath.

There was the slightest flash—a purple glint of light that danced over the archway.

And then nothing.

Ishelle was on the other side.

"Fates," breathed Fessi. "We're too late."

"No we're not. Come on," said Davian, pushing forward again.

"What?" Fessi blanched. "No. We can't go through."

"Erran's still here if something happens, but we need to catch her. Something's wrong, Fessi. Ishelle may be impatient and reckless, but this is different."

Fessi said nothing, but her expression told him that she thought the same. Ishelle hadn't been the same since the attack, but she hadn't wanted to talk about it and none of them had pressed. They'd all put it down to it being her way of dealing with what had happened.

He saw indecision sweep across Fessi's face, along with a flicker of fear. Still, she squared her shoulders determinedly.

"Let's make it quick," was all she said.

They approached the archway and Davian pressed forward without hesitation, followed closely by Fessi. Energy pulsed and rippled around them, a roaring, thrumming torrent of motion and light, close enough to make Davian flinch back every time that there was a flicker brighter than he'd expected. The darkness of predawn was slowly beginning to brighten to a violent orange in the east, visible through the translucent wall all around them.

And then they were through.

Davian breathed out as they emerged into Talan Gol. "Ishelle!" he yelled as they finally got within hearing range, Fessi dropping her time bubble.

Ishelle didn't turn, didn't seem to hear him. He tried again and this time she glanced over her shoulder, frowning. Her eyes were distant, unfocused.

Then they cleared, and the blood drained from her face.

"What in fates in going on?" Ishelle asked in horror.

"We'd like to know the same thing," said Davian grimly. "But right now, we need to get back."

He turned, and his heart dropped.

The archway was filling with energy again.

He took a faltering step toward it, but he already knew that it was too late. Within moments, their exit was gone.

Fessi let out a cry as she saw what had happened, and Davian closed his eyes, trying to push through kan. To his horror, it seemed...slipperier, here. Far harder to grasp. He gritted his teeth, eventually getting a handle on the dark power, using it to examine the space where the archway had been.

The Boundary appeared significantly different from this side. There were more mechanisms, other mechanisms, but they were somehow obscured. Hazy to look at, as well as heavily protected. Completely inaccessible.

604   And the doorway—any *sign* of the doorway—had vanished.

He opened his eyes and reoriented himself, making sure that he was focusing on the right section of wall. They had *just* come through it.

But when he looked again, there was still nothing.

His stomach twisted. It made sense, he supposed. You didn't build a door into a prison and then allow it to be unlocked from the inside.

He turned to look at the two girls. Ishelle was watching him blankly, confusion still her foremost emotion, though fear was beginning to take more of a hold as she started to comprehend the situation. Fessi, though, had seen what he was doing and already knew what his expression meant.

"We can't open it?" she asked, her voice small.

Davian shook his head, fear slowly welling up inside of him as he contemplated what had happened.

"It's gone," he said softly.

"We're trapped."

Chapter 43

Davian stared into the Boundary, peering through the translucent blue-white river in a desperate attempt to see any sort of motion on the other side.

He'd been doing that for a couple of hours now—though it felt like longer. He, Fessi, and Ishelle had decided to take it in turns to keep watch, trusting that Erran would come looking for them at some point. There had been no sign of rescue, though. If Erran had come, the wall of energy hadn't been weak enough for them to spot him, nor to let them reach him mentally.

Davian stretched muscles stiff from tension, giving a nervous glance across to where Ishelle sat cross-legged on the hard ground. She was pale and drawn as she gazed vacantly into the wide-open wastelands of Talan Gol, which the dim rays of dawn now fully illuminated.

"How are you feeling?" he asked quietly.

Ishelle didn't respond for a moment, then turned and gave him a wan smile. "About as you'd expect." She rubbed her hands together absently, though the air was already turning warm. "Responsible. Myself, but...responsible."

"You aren't," said Davian quietly. Ishelle had been confused and terrified when she'd realized where they were, and a Read of her—with her permission—had confirmed Davian's concerns. She had gaps in her memory, black spots; to Ishelle's mind, one moment she'd been at the outpost, the next in Talan Gol.

Reading her had confirmed something else, too.

Kan was *much* harder to use here.

It had taken Davian almost a half hour to successfully make contact with Ishelle's mind, even with her as a willing participant. Whenever he tried to use the power here, for anything, it just…slipped away. Using kan in Andarra had been like handling ice. Here, it was as if the ice melted whenever he grasped at it.

"I should have said something sooner." Ishelle had turned back to her inspection of the surrounding countryside, though there was little to see. Just flat, cracked, baked, and lifeless dirt for… miles. A mountain range broke the horizon, but it was so distant that the shapes rising from the ground were little more than a brown, shimmering outline.

Davian wiped a bead of sweat from his brow, glancing east at the rising sun. It felt hotter than it should have, particularly as the light itself seemed wan, as if there were actually clouds in the clear blue sky. "Probably. But I'm not sure that it would have changed anything," he said quietly, privately berating himself again for not noticing that something was amiss sooner. Ishelle had admitted that she'd been having blackouts like this since the eletai attack—though never for anywhere near as long, and never waking to find that she was somewhere else. "We might have told you to rest a little more, but I can't say that we would have done anything that would have prevented something like this."

He was about to say more when Fessi abruptly appeared, breathing hard and looking utterly drained from the effort she'd just expended. She had volunteered to scout the vicinity for any threats, using her ability so that she could do so without being seen. Davian had no idea how she'd been able to alter her passage through time here at all, let alone for the ten minutes for which she'd been gone—but she had evidently managed. Her control over that ability continued to astound him.

"What is it?" he asked her worriedly, Ishelle turning to watch the other girl, too.

Fessi took a second, hands on her knees.

"Movement to the north. A *lot* of movement," she gasped out eventually. "I didn't get close enough to really make them out, but…I don't think they're human. And they're coming our way."

Davian's heart dropped and he rubbed a hand over his face, glancing once again at the Boundary. He'd been reluctant to leave this area, hadn't wanted to venture out into Talan Gol itself, in case Erran figured out where they were and found a way to reopen the door.

Now, it seemed that they didn't have a choice.

"We need to find shelter, then—somewhere to hide. And water," he added quietly, glancing again at the unusually warm sun.

Fessi gave the wall of light a reluctant glance, obviously thinking along the same lines as Davian, but nodded brusquely. "I haven't seen anything but if we head west, perhaps we can—"

"That direction."

Fessi and Davian both turned to Ishelle, whose brow was furrowed as she indicated a point slightly north of the rising sun.

Davian and Fessi exchanged a glance. "Why do you say that?" asked Fessi cautiously.

"There's something over there. Water. Shelter. A cave, I think." Ishelle shifted uncomfortably as she said the words, her tone becoming defensive as she looked up and saw their expressions. "I know how it sounds. I wish I could explain it, but I knew almost as soon as we got here. I didn't want to say anything, because..." She sighed. "Well, because I knew you'd look at me just like that."

Davian frowned at her. Ishelle *thought* that she was telling the truth, at least. He glanced at Fessi. "How much time do we have?"

"Not enough for a discussion," said Fessi. She gazed at Ishelle worriedly.

"We don't really have any better ideas," observed Davian, giving Fessi a slight nod to indicate that Ishelle wasn't lying.

The dark-haired girl hesitated, then sighed. "True enough," she agreed heavily. "Give me a minute to catch my breath, though. If we run into trouble, I want to make sure that I'm able to get all three of us away."

Davian and Ishelle both nodded. Ishelle glanced at Davian uncomfortably, then resumed her study of the wastelands as Davian and Fessi both watched her with a slight frown.

Davian eventually shrugged silently to Fessi, then closed his eyes, focusing. Kan was hard even to sense here and harder to use with accuracy once he eventually grasped it. Still, what he wanted to do now was basic enough.

He hardened kan, then carefully set a large arrow into the ground that pointed in the direction in which they were intending to head. He didn't think that Erran was foolish enough to open the doorway and come through, but if he did, then he'd at least have a general direction in which to start looking for them. Besides, Davian felt better leaving something behind to mark this location—there were no landmarks to speak of in the surrounding geography. If the door through the Boundary still existed on the Andarran side, finding this spot again might be important.

"I'm ready," said Fessi after a few more seconds. She paused. "If we see anything that we need to avoid, I can probably shift all three of us outside of time for...maybe a few minutes. After that..."

"If it comes to it, just do what you can," said Davian, receiving a short nod of acknowledgment from Fessi.

The three of them gave the Boundary one last, reluctant glance, and started walking.

They headed northeast, Ishelle taking the lead, though Davian kept a sharp eye on her. The sun was well above the horizon now, uncomfortably warm but still casting an unusually wan light. More than once Davian squinted overhead, trying to see whether the Boundary was responsible for filtering the sunlight. He was fairly confident that the energy formed a complete dome—otherwise, if nothing else, the eletai could never have remained contained for so long. But the sky above looked clear, not at all like the torrent of power visible at the edges of Talan Gol.

They pressed on until the sun was close to its zenith, the Boundary to Davian's left retreating farther and farther into the distance until finally it was no longer visible on the horizon. Once it had faded from view entirely, the journey was surreal: everything here looked the same, and only the position of the sun confirmed that they were not simply walking in circles. Everywhere he looked there was just dry, cracked ground and endlessly, unnaturally flat horizons, broken only by occasional distant shapes that may or may not have been hills. The sun beat down with desertlike intensity, its heat then reflected up at them again from the hard-packed earth.

They walked mostly in silence and the longer that passed, the more uncertain Davian became about his decision. He wiped more sweat from his brow and licked dry lips. These were truly wastelands, vast, not the desolate buffer that met the Boundary on the southern side. If Ishelle was wrong—and he knew that they were taking an enormous chance in trusting her in her current state—then they were in serious trouble.

There was something else, too. Something that he hadn't mentioned to the others yet.

There was absolutely no Essence here, or at least none that he was able to detect. Even the sunlight didn't seem to be providing the small amount of energy that it normally would, and his self-made Reserve, which he'd been carefully maintaining since they had left Tol Shen, was now running dangerously low.

Before long, he was going to have to start drawing Essence from his companions to survive.

"Up ahead," said Fessi suddenly, her tense tone startling him from his thoughts.

Davian slowed, squinting in the direction that Fessi had indicated. At first he didn't see anything except a small rise some way away.

Then his eyes widened.

It was only just visible, but there was now a cloud of dust billowing upward in the distance, drifting across the wastelands.

"I thought you scouted in the other direction," he said softly.

"I did." Fessi's brow was furrowed. "That can't be the same group that I saw."

"We're not too far." Ishelle looked over at them. "Five minutes at most. We're aiming for that hill."

Davian shook his head. "And if that army is coming this way? We should go around, maybe wait for them to pass. Another hour wouldn't be the end of us."

"Agreed," said Fessi.

Ishelle hesitated, then shook her head.

"There's more. More are coming from everywhere," she said softly. She pointed directly north. "In five minutes, we'll see another cloud, and then another. They're massing."

Davian blinked. "How do you know—"

"I *just do*." There was an immense frustration in Ishelle's voice, and she stared at them pleadingly. "I wish I understood this, too, but right now, you're going to have to trust me. There's no getting around them, Dav. Where we're headed is the best place to hide. Probably the only place."

Davian glanced at Fessi, who grimaced. "It's not far. And if she's wrong, I could probably get us away again."

Davian stared at the cloud of dust ahead, then came to a decision and reluctantly nodded his acquiescence.

They pressed on, this time with more urgency in their step, though Davian didn't go so far as to ask Fessi to use her ability just yet. The dull flat brown of the world was barely broken by the hill that Ishelle had pointed out; if they had not been heading directly toward it, Davian wouldn't have given it a second glance. Still, as they drew nearer, he realized that it was a slightly different color and texture to everything around it. Craggy and jagged rather than uniformly worn. A darker shade of brown, and not just because of the shadow that it cast.

He glanced across at Fessi, who was frowning as she studied it, too.

"What do you think?" he murmured. There was no one around to hear—no one for miles, as far as he could tell—but the eerie, lifeless silence of this place made speaking quietly seem appropriate.

"Whatever's creating that cloud of dust isn't far away," said Fessi grimly. She nodded to the north. "And Ishelle wasn't wrong about them having friends."

Davian inclined his head; he hadn't failed to spot the second cloud rising off to their left.

Soon enough they were in the shadow of the small but steep-edged hill, allowing Davian's eyes to adjust. There was indeed an opening, though it was barely wide enough to accommodate an adult's frame, and not much taller. The hole at first appeared natural, but he soon noticed that the ground remained perfectly flat as it disappeared into the darkness, unnaturally straight compared to the jagged rock everywhere else.

He paused, listening for a few moments at the entrance. There was an odd sound coming from the cave mouth—a sighing, as if a gentle breeze was blowing through it.

"We should get inside," said Ishelle. "That army's not too far
away."

She vanished into the narrow passageway.

Davian grimaced, exchanging another uncertain glance with Fessi before shrugging and following Ishelle silently into the murky opening. He concentrated as he walked, fumbling with kan a few times before finally grasping it, questing out for any signs of Essence—and therefore life—ahead.

There was nothing, though.

He quickly let kan slip away again, turning his full attention to the way forward. The tunnel was straight and so not completely dark, the light from outside filtering down far enough to see by. The atmosphere in here was not what he'd expected, though. Rather than cool shade, the air felt just as hot as outside—only muggier, damp and dense in comparison.

He frowned, pausing just inside the entrance to let his eyes adjust. Ishelle's form blocked most of his view, but beyond her he could already see the end of the tunnel, perhaps thirty feet ahead.

They hurried forward silently in single file, Ishelle stepping aside once she reached the end so that Davian and Fessi could join her in the space beyond. The light from outside still provided some illumination, if only just; Davian could make out the walls as they sloped away and thick stalactites on the roof, but little else. The back of the cavern was cloaked in darkness.

Davian shuddered. The sighing sound was louder in here, echoing around, though he still couldn't feel a breeze on his face. He stepped farther into the cavern, hand brushing against the wall.

He snatched it back immediately. The stone was smooth and stickily damp, as if the cave were sweating.

"There's something very wrong about this place," whispered Fessi.

Davian opened his mouth to agree—there was certainly something unsettling about it, far more than just the knowledge of where they were—but he shut it again as the sound of tinkling water reached his ears. He licked his lips, suddenly registering just how dry his mouth was.

"The stream's this way," said Ishelle.

Davian eyed her warily in the dim light. Unlike he and Fessi, Ishelle was moving around the space with confidence, walking without any apparent concern for stumbling over anything in the dim light. He didn't think that she was leading them into harm—and he wasn't sure that they had much alternative but to trust her, at this point—but it was yet something else to make him wonder what was going on with her.

He and Fessi followed Ishelle cautiously, their footsteps squelching unpleasantly in the silence.

After about thirty seconds—the light spilling from the tunnel behind fading and fading until they were walking in near complete darkness—a glimmer caught Davian's eye up ahead. After a few more moments, he realized that Ishelle was leading them toward another passage, this one angling downward.

"That's a torch," he said softly, nodding to the light, though he doubted either of the others would be able to see the motion. "Somebody's been here, Ishelle. Recently. What is this place?"

"I don't know." There was genuine frustration in the other Augur's tone.

Davian stretched out cautiously with kan again, but aside from the faintly flickering torch on the wall, there were still no signs of Essence. He sighed.

"Lead on," he whispered. "Just be careful."

They moved into the new tunnel and began descending, Davian gratefully taking a little Essence from the first torch that they passed, easing the ache in his muscles. The path went downward gradually at first, but after a minute became an increasingly steep incline. The rock underfoot was damp and dangerously smooth, seemingly that way due to myriad deep scratches that appeared to have worn away every rough edge of the surface. Davian kept one hand on the wall as he walked, close to slipping several times as his boots failed to find purchase. Ishelle stumbled once, too, with only Fessi seeming to handle the slope without any difficulty.

The eerie sighing sound from the cavern began to fade as the trickling of water grew louder and louder, much to Davian's relief. After another minute the corridor opened up, dropping away on the left to reveal a stream emerging from somewhere above, creating a small waterfall before running alongside the path. Davian could see by the light of a nearby torch that the water looked clean and pure.

"Careful," cautioned Fessi. "We have no way to know if—"

Davian and Ishelle both dropped to their knees, scooped up handfuls of water and drank them.

"It's fine," said Davian with a sheepish smile at Fessi. He shrugged at her look. "Honestly, I'm not sure how much farther I could have gone if it hadn't been."

Fessi sighed, but nodded and joined them. Once they had all drank their fill, Davian leaned against the wall and gave a satisfied sigh, ignoring the odd damp on his palm as he pressed it against the rock. After a moment, though, he stiffened.

"Quiet." He held up a hand to the other two. "Do you hear that?"

Echoing down the tunnel—in the same direction from which they'd just come—was an odd, harsh scraping sound.

And it was steadily getting louder.

Fessi grabbed Davian with one hand and Ishelle with the other, squeezing her eyes shut.

Sounds—the scratching from the passageway, the crackling of the torch, and the tinkling of water—vanished. Davian glanced at the stream, impressed by how gradually the water flowed now; he had to concentrate to really see that it was moving at all.

"Farther down?" he asked quietly.

Ishelle shrugged, and Fessi mimicked the gesture. "Not many options," she observed, voice tight from concentration.

They set off, walking swiftly. After a couple of minutes the path branched; upon closer inspection, Davian realized that the right-hand one was not another tunnel at all, but rather a short passageway into a large room. He motioned to the others.

"We'll be trapped," observed Fessi.

"But we can get out if whatever's coming goes past. Even if it doesn't, there's space to hide, and enough room to maneuver past if you can keep up the time bubble." He licked his lips nervously, all too aware that they wouldn't have put much distance between them and whatever was approaching. "It's a risk either way, but this at least gives us a chance."

Fessi grimaced, but inclined her head. Ishelle—who had, worryingly, started to get a distant look in her eyes again—blinked, and then nodded, too.

They hurried into the room. It was well lit by torches, though the air was stale, even more so than outside.

He felt Fessi flinch; he turned and almost let out an oath himself at the figure standing silently in the corner of the room.

"Fates," he muttered, shaking his head ruefully.

It was a suit of armor—arranged as if it were being worn, but clearly empty. Davian shivered as he took in the small black plates, the gapless helmet, the strange symbol engraved where the face would be. He'd seen enough of that image to last a lifetime.

He stumbled a little as Fessi released her hold on time, shaking his head at the disorienting sensation. He and Ishelle glanced at the other Augur questioningly.

"I'm all right. Just need a rest in case I have to get us out of here again," Fessi said weakly.

Davian nodded; they would have a few minutes until whoever or whatever was coming down the tunnel got close. He stared around the room in fascination. Aside from the armor, there was a chair and a desk against the wall, the lantern hanging over it burning steadily. Papers were strewn across the desk's surface.

In the other corner there was a small bed, unmade, and a bookshelf next to it. He frowned at the scene for several seconds and then strode across to the desk, leaning over it curiously to read one of the scattered sheets on it.

After a moment he beckoned absently at the other two, not taking his eyes from the paper.

> The eletai do not individually display the same intelligence as dar'gaithin or shar'kath, despite their humanoid appearance. Nor do they have the mindless instinct of tek'ryl, or the innate savagery of an al'goriat. They do seem to share the same vision enhancements, though, allowing them to see mostly by Essence rather than natural light—perhaps better explaining their "scent," as others have described it.
>
> I also believe that they understand instruction—or at least, the hive does. When I issue an order to one it will often not move, and I am uncertain if it has understood. Later, though, I will discover that another eletai has completed the task. Whether this eletai was more

*suited to the job, or closer, or it was simply that crea-
ture's turn to work—I do not know.*

*I have also determined that the creatures retain mem-
ories, and that some are very old. Today, as I made my
regular rounds attempting to communicate, most as
usual did not respond to my conversation.*

*However one eletai asked me a question. He—or
she?—asked after a man called Eradimicius. I had no
idea who this was, but I responded that he was well,
hoping to provoke further conversation. The eletai
seemed relieved, moving on to talk about its role in the
war. At first I thought it spoke of the War of Progres-
sion, some eight hundred years ago—making it very
old. After a few minutes, though, I gleaned that in fact
it spoke of Devaed's First Darecian War, waged almost
three thousand years ago. I have cross-referenced its talk
of the extraordinary machinery and weaponry which
the Darecians brought against the Venerate, and it is the
only match I have been able to find. Externally, though,
this eletai appeared no different from the rest. Does this
indicate a longevity that is for all intents and purposes
immortality? Or is it an effect of shared consciousness,
maintained long after the original assimilation has died?*

Davian stopped reading as the scraping sound that they had
heard before entered his consciousness.

He glanced across at Fessi, who had been reading along with
him, and then turned to find Ishelle.

His heart skipped a beat as he stared around the room with
increasing panic.

"Where is she?"

Fessi blinked, then looked around. "I . . ." She paled. "She was
here a moment ago."

The other Augur gripped his arm, dragging him silently away
from the entrance to the room. They ducked down behind the
desk, Fessi keeping her grip, clearly ready to step outside of time
at a moment's notice.

Davian's heart pounded, though how much of it was concern for himself and how much concern for Ishelle, he wasn't sure. Why had she left? Had she had another blackout? The scraping sound grew closer, heavy but constant, thunderous in the silence of the tunnels.

A few seconds later it stopped, just as it sounded as though it were outside the entrance to the room. Davian held his breath, not daring to move, unwilling even to wipe the beads of sweat that were forming again on his brow.

A moment passed. Another.

Then the grinding started again, this time disappearing farther down the tunnel.

Davian and Fessi didn't move until the sound had completely faded.

"What was that?" asked Fessi softly.

"I think..." Davian grimaced, remembering back to the vision that he'd had several weeks ago. "I think it might have been a dar'gaithin. That sound could have been its scales grinding against the stone. Which would explain the marks that we saw earlier, too."

Fessi ran her hands through her hair, and her voice shook a little as she spoke. "What now?"

Davian did his best to focus, fumbling until he grasped kan again. Back up through the passage, there was nothing for as far as his senses could stretch.

Downward, though, there was the faintest pulse of Essence. He caught only a glimpse of it, but it was enough; he and Ishelle had trained together too much over the past couple of months for him not to recognize her.

"The dar'gaithin—or whatever it was—is going in the same direction as Ishelle," he said grimly. He rubbed his forehead, sighing. "Ready?"

Fessi blanched but after a moment nodded resolutely, much to Davian's relief.

They exited the room silently, following the faint grinding sound as they started after Ishelle.

Farther into the depths.

Chapter 44

Asha stared pensively out over the north-facing wall at the pulsing form of the Boundary, occasionally glancing right to eye the rising sun with an increasing sense of dread.

Behind her, she sensed Erran as he rejoined her in her vigil. "Still nothing?" the young man asked as he leaned next to her against the outpost's parapet.

Asha just shook her head, straining to make out anything moving in the vast emptiness below. Davian and Fessi had gone after Ishelle hours ago; they should have been long back by now, either with the other Augur or to get help.

"How long do we just wait?" she asked quietly.

Erran scrubbed at his eyes with the palm of his hand. "The moment we go, Geladra and the other Administrators will try to stop us, regardless of what Torin said." He shrugged, glancing over his shoulder at the two Administrators standing a little distance away. They'd been watching them for more than an hour now, not trying to hide their suspicion. "They *can't*, of course, but that doesn't mean that our leaving won't make things more difficult for Torin."

Asha nodded grimly. Geladra had argued for a good half hour after Fessi and Davian had vanished from in front of her eyes, and only Wirr's eventual appearance and intervention had prevented the Administrators from trying to lock Erran and Asha in one of the outpost's lower cells.

Despite her friend's impressively calm assurance in diplomatically dealing with the Administrators, Asha could tell that Wirr was fighting a losing battle to convince his mother of the danger here. Captain Muran's matter-of-fact explanation of what he had seen since he had arrived, as well as the word of various other soldiers and some of the Gifted stationed at the outpost, had resulted only in dark, suspicious mutterings about Control and the Augurs' lack of oversight. Asha was beginning to doubt that Geladra *could* be convinced, without seeing one of Devaed's Banes with her own eyes.

Asha sighed, putting Wirr's mother from her mind for the moment. "You still can't contact them, I take it?"

Erran shook his head. "It's not too surprising. It can be hard over long distances, especially if they're not actively trying to communicate," he explained, though he wore a frown as he said the words. "It's much easier if they're attempting to make the connection, too. As far as I can tell, they haven't tried to do that."

There was silence for a few seconds and then Asha glanced back toward the Administrators. They were still watching closely, but weren't close to within hearing range. Even so, she lowered her voice.

"You need to tell Wirr about what happened. With Elocien."

Erran blinked, his entire body tensing as he understood what she was saying. "No."

"You can tell him, or I will." Asha met Erran's gaze steadily. "I'm sorry, Erran, but he's my friend. When he didn't know anything, I thought it was for the best. But I'm not going to lie to him."

"He'll kill me."

"He'll be angry," Asha conceded grimly, "but I know Wirr. He believes in what we're all doing here and he knows why you did it, even if he'll hate it. You may not trust him, but trust *me*. If you go to him first—if the news comes from you—then it will end up better for everyone."

"Even if you're right, Geladra won't be so kind."

"He would never tell Geladra." Asha said the words with confidence.

"Easy for you to say." Erran fell silent for a moment, clearly considering her words despite his objection. He nodded slowly. "But I suppose they're not exactly on the same page," he conceded

eventually.

"Just think about it. It doesn't have to be right now." Asha set her shoulders, staring grimly out over the empty plains below. "Davian and Fessi, on the other hand..."

Erran rubbed his forehead. "Agreed. Just be aware, I'm only able to do small jumps. A couple of minutes of walking at most, if I'm forming a time bubble for both of us. We'll only get halfway down the path to the bottom before they know we're gone."

Asha shrugged. "It's not as if they can catch us."

Erran flashed a grin, seeming as relieved as Asha to be finally taking some action. He turned to the Administrators, giving them a pleasant smile and nod as he took Asha by the arm in a cheerful, gentlemanly fashion.

The leaves falling from the trees suddenly slowed and the Administrators appeared to freeze, half scowling and half confused as they digested Erran's motion to them. Erran and Asha walked past them, then hurried through the northern gate and started along the steps descending to the plains below.

As he'd predicted, Erran needed a break about halfway down; as soon as time crashed back into them, Asha could hear shouts of anger emanating from above. She glanced back up the cliff, but there was no movement yet visible. The Administrators knew that they were missing, but hadn't yet had time to figure out where they had gone.

The next half hour was a slow one as they made their way gradually toward the Boundary, mostly in two or three minute bursts as Erran altered their passage through time, then rested for a minute in between. Behind them, Asha could see Administrators making their way after them down the cliff, but they were soon little more than dots. Erran's ability, limited though it was, meant that he and Asha were easily outpacing their pursuers.

Asha kept scanning the horizon for something—anything—that might indicate where Davian and Fessi had gone, but it was uniformly flat, broken only by the torrent of energy up ahead that took up more and more of her vision as they approached. Erran was silent for the most part, concentrating on getting them there as quickly as possible, but he clearly didn't see anything of importance, either.

Eventually they arrived at the very base of the Boundary, Asha rubbing her ears against the uncomfortable, constant thrum. She squinted up in awe at the shimmering, pulsing wall of blue-white energy, difficult to look at directly for too long even in the daylight.

"No sign of them." Erran was frowning as he gazed at the wall, too, though he appeared to be focusing on a specific point. "I could have sworn that Fessi was heading this way, but..."

Asha turned her attention to him. "What is it?" She could hear the worry in his tone.

"I just..." Erran's frown deepened. "Davian told you about the door that we found?"

"Yes."

"Well...I thought that this was where it was supposed to be. I was *quite certain* it was here, actually."

Asha was silent as she processed what Erran was saying. "You mean you didn't take us to the right spot?"

Erran hesitated, then slowly shook his head.

"No," he said softly. "I mean that I think it's gone."

Erran and Asha walked in silence, each lost in their own thoughts.

Asha occasionally cast a glance to her left at the Boundary, wondering again whether Davian had somehow found himself stuck behind it. Erran had repeatedly insisted that Davian and the other two would be all right, but he'd had no real reasoning to back up his confidence. Davian had last been heading for the Boundary. There had been a door, and now there wasn't one, and Davian and the others were missing.

Even if it was coincidence, it was too big a one for Asha to simply ignore.

"The Administrators have given up," Erran observed suddenly, breaking her from her reverie.

Asha looked over her shoulder, seeing only an empty, lifeless expanse behind them. For a while the Administrators had done their best to catch up to them, but Erran had continued using occasional bursts of speed to put more distance between them. Evidently it had been enough to convince Galadra's lackeys of the pointlessness of their pursuit.

"That's something, at least." The Administrators had hardly been a threat, but Asha hadn't wanted to lead them to where she and Erran were heading now, either.

She closed her eyes for a moment, concentrating, shivering a little at the sensation of so much power being so easily within reach. It had been a little like that ever since Deilannis, but after last night, everything...*tingled* whenever she focused, so much Essence now available that it was almost harder in any single moment *not* to use it. She wasn't even tired, despite not sleeping—instead she felt sharper, able to see farther, sense more than she ever had before.

She had no doubt that Caeden had managed to bind the Lyth to the Siphon. Which also, much to her discomfort, meant that there was no longer anything stopping her from activating the Tributary.

They'd been walking for a couple of hours now, following Asha's sense of where the Shadows were, angling very slightly away from the Boundary but still in the flat, desolate valley that lay between it and the towering cliffs to their right. Erran had insisted on coming with her after she had decided that it was time to find the Tributary, and Asha was grateful for the company.

Besides, she could hardly blame him. She'd never asked specifics about Erran's time Controlling Elocien—how much had been entirely Erran, how much had been merely his influence—but she couldn't imagine that his relationship with Geladra was anything but awkward.

Asha suddenly paused, inhaling deeply through her nose.

"Salt," said Erran absently. "I think we're near the ocean."

Asha glanced at him in surprise. Her geography was rough at best, but she'd thought that they were farther away from the coast than that.

"We're nearly to wherever the Shadows are hiding, anyway," she observed.

The air continued to cool despite the heat of the late afternoon sun, and soon Asha could easily identify the westerly sea breeze. She drew in a few deep breaths, closing her eyes for a moment as she walked. She hadn't breathed air like this since Caladel.

Before long she realized that the cliffs to her right were gradually sloping away. In the distance there was the shimmer of blue and she could hear the call of gulls, even spot the small black dots gliding in circles. After a few more minutes there was the gentle sound of waves crashing against the shore and the hard-packed dirt underfoot turned to shale, then gradually gave way to soft white sand.

They were at the ocean.

Asha stared at the Boundary in fascination as it continued seamlessly from shore to sea, plunging into the water. It didn't seem to form a physical barrier to the waves, though, which passed through it rather than crashing against its side. The low thrum that Asha had grown accustomed to was even louder here, and there were periodic blue-green flashes of energy from deep beneath the water, made more obvious by the sun sinking below the horizon behind them.

As they trudged through the sand toward the waterline, Asha felt her brow furrow. The Shadows were closer than ever...she could all but *see* them...and yet, her sense of them said that they were still eastward.

Somewhere out to sea.

"So...?" Erran had slowed, realizing that their path was leading directly toward the water. There were the ruins of what appeared to be a dock ahead, the pier itself gone but two stone pillars still jutting out of the sand. No boats, though, and nothing else of note.

Asha shook her head, squinting, trying to see if there were any signs of land a little farther out. She couldn't see anything, though. The Boundary pulsed and crackled as it cut through the water, concealing Talan Gol beyond but presumably following the coastline as it stretched away. To the right there was an empty expanse of beach, and off to the southeast, Asha could see the distant shape of land on the horizon where the coast curved back around. But the Shadows weren't in that direction.

She scowled as she reached the water's edge, pulling off her boots as Erran watched in bemusement. Then she took a few steps into the ice-cold water, peering eastward.

Nothing. Despite dusk quickly turning to night, visibility was all but perfect—and all it showed her was a blue, flat horizon.

"They're *here*," she said in frustration, gesturing out at the waves. "I can feel them, Erran. We should be able to *see* them."

"Oh." The uncertainty in Erran's voice was clear—it was irritating, but Asha could hardly blame him. "How...how sure are you?"

Asha closed her eyes and pointed. "There. A group of Shadows, the biggest that I can sense by far." There was another group to the southwest—the ones still in Ilin Illan, she suspected—and others scattered around the country. But this, *this*, was where Nethgalla had intended her to go. She was sure of it.

She opened her eyes again, trying to gauge the distance. It was perhaps a thousand feet from where they were standing, not too far from the Boundary itself, though clearly on this side of it.

Erran peered in the direction that she'd indicated, still looking dubious. Then he grunted.

"Wait. You're right. There *is* something out there," he said slowly. "I think...I think it's been hidden by kan. I wouldn't ever have noticed it if you hadn't told me where to look; it's close enough to the Boundary that it just looks like part of it. But...it *is* different from everything else around it." His frown deepened. "It's a long way out, though."

Asha hesitated, then unfastened her cloak.

Erran blinked. "Um..." He quickly turned away as Asha began unbuttoning her shirt. "What are you doing?"

"Swimming." Asha was a strong swimmer, and had spent plenty of time in the sea at Caladel. She grinned at Erran. "Don't worry. I'm not taking it all off." She hesitated. "Are you coming?"

Erran barked a laugh. "No. *Nooo.* Not my thing." He shook his head firmly, looking mistrustfully at the waves. Then he frowned, stepping up to one of the pillars nearby and squinting at it. "Just... wait for a moment though. You may not need to swim."

Asha paused. "What do you mean?"

"There's something here. A kan mechanism. Something that can be activated."

Asha swallowed. "Maybe just make sure that you know what it does before—"

A line of cobalt light bloomed in the water, accompanied by a sharp whining sound that made both Asha and Erran immediately cover their ears. Gulls from the distant cliffs took flight in the opposite direction and Erran staggered back, eyes refracting the cold, shimmering blue in the encroaching darkness.

The sound stopped and for a moment there was nothing but silence.

Then there was a crash as a torrent of water spouted into the air along the line of luminescence, flicking highlighted spray high into the atmosphere. Asha danced backward as waves crashed against the shore, drenching her to her waist and nearly knocking her off her feet. She barely managed to avoid being dragged off-balance by the undertow.

When she finally regained her footing enough to take in what had happened, she drew a sharp breath.

In the weak light of dusk, a glimmering pathway of smooth steel now jutted from the beach, stretching out as far as she could see over the water. It appeared to be made up of multiple plates joined together, each one faintly outlined by the glowing blue Essence that held it in place, though Asha had no idea how the path as a whole maintained its position. Despite it appearing to be solid and secure, it was connected only to the first pair of pillars; otherwise, it hovered a good couple of feet above the level of the water.

"Fates," muttered Erran, stunned. He turned to Asha, shrugging sheepishly.

Asha didn't respond, squinting at the glimmering pathway for a moment longer. It was clearly made of metal, yet it had emerged from underwater. It should be rusted, or at least discolored. Instead, it shone like a newly forged blade.

She approached it cautiously as she refastened the buttons on her shirt, then hesitantly put a foot onto the first plate.

It gave slightly beneath her weight and she flinched back, half expecting the bridge to collapse violently back into the water. The plate didn't fall, though; she exhaled and tried again, trusting her full weight to it this time. There was a strange, springy give to the metal, as if it were resting on a cloud of air—but it held.

She turned to issue a small, relieved smile at Erran. "It doesn't look like we'll have to swim after all," she observed cheerfully.

Erran eyed the bridge mistrustfully. "Maybe."

Asha rolled her eyes at him. "If that happens, I'll save you," she said drily. "I promise."

Erran snorted, but he eventually sighed and nodded. "I suppose we've come this far."

He cautiously stepped up beside her—grimacing in anticipation as he took his first step, though nothing untoward happened—and then they slowly started walking along the suspended metallic platform.

They made the journey in nervous silence, proceeding away from the beach for perhaps ten minutes, though it would have taken much less time had Erran not been so intent on keeping his balance. Asha couldn't blame him too much, though. As soon as they were away from the shore the wind picked up, whipping spray into their faces and causing the waves below to swell dangerously high. The white-tipped crests threatened to seep over the edges of the pathway at times, but thankfully the water appeared to evaporate just before it struck steel. The ground underfoot, Asha was pleased to find, was also surprisingly firm, with none of the expected slipperiness that she had been worried about.

Just as Asha was beginning to wonder if the bridge actually had an end, something up ahead began to shimmer.

"Erran." When the young man behind her didn't respond, eyes still firmly fixed on the path underfoot, she sighed. "*Erran.*"

"What?"

"Do you see that?" Asha wiped spray from her face, wind whipping her hair, the thrum of the Boundary still unsettlingly loud in her ears. Where there had been open space a minute ago, now there was...*something.* A dark shape, a shadow.

"I see it." Erran's tone was troubled. "We're headed straight for it."

They pressed on. The dark blobs up ahead gradually became solid, turning into rocks and beyond them, scattered trees.

A shore.

After another minute they were cautiously, disbelievingly stepping off the metal plates—between two pillars that looked identical to the ones on the mainland—and onto sand.

"There's an entire *island* here." Erran's tone was awed. "Hidden by kan."

He wasn't exaggerating, Asha realized as she looked around. This wasn't simply a small sand dune with a few trees. The beach stretched on, level with the Boundary, for as far as she could see. The forest was thick, and in the distance she spotted what looked very much like a mountain rising out of the late evening skyline.

There was a sudden crash behind them. Asha turned to see the metallic bridge beginning to dismantle, then plunge back into the ocean with the same whining sound that had accompanied its emergence.

Erran watched the scene worriedly, then hurried over to the nearest pillar. After closing his eyes and placing his hand against it for a moment, he breathed out.

"It's the same as the one on the other shore," he said. "We should be able to get back."

Asha gave him a relieved nod, then turned to examine the rest of the beach. There were no structures beyond those two pillars, no signs of life at all. Just the constant, eerie glow of the Boundary reflected in the swell of the waves.

She focused for a few moments, then gestured to Erran.

"The Shadows are this way," she said, pointing inland.

Erran nodded and followed her without complaint. They picked their way through the thick-treed forest mostly in silence, the increasingly distant ocean and their breaking of the undergrowth the only sounds. Night had properly fallen now; though the near-full moon had been quick to rise, Asha still found herself tripping over branches and unearthed roots. She vacillated for a few minutes but eventually tapped Essence, sending a tiny ball of light ahead of them.

"Is that wise?" murmured Erran.

Asha shrugged. "Better than breaking an ankle."

She frowned as they pushed on, noting strange patches of black-scarred foliage that had previously been hidden by the darkness. It was as if a fire had been lit among the trees in several different places, but had been extinguished again before it could do too much damage. She brushed her hand again a charred trunk, her fingers coming away dirty with soot.

She shook her head at the sight but moved on, toward what she suspected was the center of the island. The mountain that she had spotted from the beach was beginning to loom on the horizon, outlined by moonlight now. If they kept on in this direction, it wouldn't be long before they reached its base.

"Buildings," said Erran suddenly, voice low as he nodded toward moonlit stone rooftops visible through the trees up ahead. "Are we close?"

"Very." Asha turned her head to the side slightly. "They seem to be—"

There was a flicker of light from close to one of the structures and on instinct Asha dove at Erran, tackling him to the ground.

A moment later a thin, searing blast of red fire ripped through the trees at head height, instantly turning the peaceful forest into a crashing, roaring inferno. Trees collapsed around them from where the blast had shorn through their trunks; Asha rolled to the side as a thick burning branch hit the ground where she'd been a moment before.

She tapped her Reserve, for the first time not trying to limit the Essence that she drew.

A startlingly thick dome of energy sprang into existence around them, disintegrating more burning branches as they fell on it, the cocoon instantly lessening the intense heat. Asha grimaced as she looked across at Erran, seeing minor burns on his face even as she realized that her own arms had blistered, too. She drew a little more Essence, quickly healing the both of them, relieved that the heart-pounding rush of reacting to the ambush had mitigated most of the pain.

She glanced down as the angry skin on her arms smoothed and paled once again, heart sinking as she registered the black symbol forming on her left wrist. She'd managed to avoid taking too much from her Reserve since Deilannis, but there was no point in holding back anymore. Her Mark had returned.

Erran groaned, shaking his head vigorously and then levering himself up onto one elbow, staring wide-eyed at the inferno surrounding them. "Thanks." He gestured at some burning wood that had made it inside of Asha's dome, and the flames vanished.

Bolts of pure Essence were raining down on Asha's shield now. She scowled.

"It's the Shadows. They're using their Vessels," she said in frustration.

Erran grunted, squinting uncomfortably out at the carnage of the burning, flashing forest. "Any way that we can maybe ask them to stop?"

Asha took a deep breath, ignoring the distraction of the explosions around her and focused. She could feel the Shadows nearby—in fact she could actually see the dark, vague outlines crouching behind cover as they tried to rain down fire and destruction upon Asha and Erran. Within those outlines she could sense Essence, individual and bright. Connected to her.

She concentrated, then drained them until each figure had only a tiny amount left.

The forest fell eerily silent.

With a quick warning nod to Erran, Asha dropped her shield. The Augur closed his eyes; a moment later the crackling of burning wood vanished, the fires around them extinguished, replaced only by drifting trails of smoke in the moonlight, and the occasional crash as a weakened branch finally made its way to the ground.

Asha held her sleeve to her mouth, coughing amid the thick smoke.

"I'm not here to harm you," she yelled into the forest. She hesitated, then sighed. "The Shadraehin sent us."

There was no response, so she and Erran walked cautiously forward, Erran careful to suck the heat from the scorched ground ahead.

Eventually, there was a flicker of movement amid the gray stone buildings.

"Stay where you are!"

Asha cocked her head to the side. The voice was vaguely familiar.

"Shana?" She'd met the woman what seemed like forever ago, when she had first visited the Sanctuary back in Ilin Illan.

There was a startled pause and then the brown-haired young woman emerged, holding what was evidently a Vessel in front of her threateningly. Asha wasn't too concerned; Shana, along with the rest of the Shadows hiding nearby, no longer had enough Essence to attack them.

Shana frowned at Asha and Erran for a long few moments, and then her eyes widened.

"You?" She gazed at Asha's face in confusion. "But...
you're..."

Asha gave her a weary smile.

"Stop trying to kill us for a moment, and I'll explain everything," she said tiredly.

Asha and Erran looked around curiously as they were led through
the small village at the base of the mountain.

Eyes peered out at them nervously from doorways that spilled
lamplight into the street, the chaos of their entry no doubt having
woken most of the residents. The buildings here were universally
short and squat, made from simple gray stone, unadorned but
sturdy-looking. Off to the side, Asha spotted several small garden
beds that looked to be growing crops, and somewhere off in the
distance she could even hear a dog barking. The Shadows, she
was pleased to see, were not living in hardship here.

"Why did you attack us?" she asked Shana quietly as they walked.
The young woman hadn't said much at all since Asha and Erran had
arrived; despite Asha's offer to explain why they were there, Shana
had simply asked for them to follow her. They didn't appear to be in
any danger from the Shadows—Shana had even seemed reasonably
happy to see her—so Asha and Erran had obliged. The other Shadows had stayed behind, apparently to guard the edge of the forest.
Against exactly what, though, Asha wasn't sure.

The young woman rolled her shoulders at the question, giving
Asha a nervous glance. "There have been...*things*...appearing at
night over the past couple of weeks," she said uneasily. "Usually
from the same direction from which you came. They're dangerous;
we've lost a few people to them already." She sighed. "Someone
saw movement, and...well, we're not really used to having guests."

"Things?" asked Erran.

"Monsters." Shana shook her head. "They crawl up out of the
water. They look like scorpions, but...big. I've seen the stings
on their tails skewer a man clean through." She said the last part
softly, the memory evidently still painfully fresh for her.

Asha swallowed, exchanging a glance with Erran before turning back to Shana. "Should we be worried?"

The Shadow shook her head. "We've kept them back so far." She kept her gaze straight ahead, though, looking reluctant to talk about it further.

Asha bit her lip, then nodded, dropping the line of questioning for now. "How did you all get here?"

"The Shadraehin used a Vessel of some kind. Once the battle at Ilin Illan was over, he opened a portal from the Sanctuary to this island."

Asha saw Erran stiffen at the mention of Scyner, but she gave him a slight, cautioning shake of the head. Scyner had killed Kol, and both Asha and Erran badly wanted to bring him to justice for that. But making accusations now, causing trouble, wouldn't help their cause.

"So he made you all criminals," said Erran, unable to hide the disdain in his tone.

Shana shook her head defensively. "He *saved* us. Do you have any idea what would have happened, if we'd stayed in Ilin Illan? How do you think Administration would have reacted to our being able to use Vessels? Or everyone else, for that matter?" She glowered at him.

"And the children came with you?" asked Asha, heart skipping a beat as she was suddenly reminded of the Echo that she'd seen in the Sanctuary.

Shana's face twisted, but it was more in sadness than pain. "Almost all of them. When the Shadraehin realized that the Blind were using the catacombs, he did everything that he could to get our families out. He took on the Blind *by himself* so that they'd have time to escape. Nearly died doing it." She swallowed. "But...still. Not everyone got out."

Asha nodded, exhaling. Ever since her last trip to the Sanctuary, she had feared the worst for the children of the Shadows. Regardless of whether Scyner had actually saved them as heroically as Shana claimed, knowing that most of them had escaped was some of the best news that she'd heard in a while.

They walked on for a little longer, eventually coming to a building set apart from the others, right at the base of the mountain. Shana paused, then rapped on the door.

There was a stirring inside, and the door opened. The lamplight from inside spilled onto the path out front, silhouetting a figure that Asha immediately recognized.

The man stifled a yawn, then nodded politely to her and Erran, stepping forward so that his features were clearly visible.

"Hello, Ashalia," said Scyner.

There was dead silence for several seconds as Asha stared at the prewar Augur, heart pounding as she tried to assess the situation.

"Erran," she said warningly, placing a restraining hand on his arm. The muscles beneath her grip were taut; her friend had gone stock-still and was staring at Scyner with clenched fists, breathing heavily.

Scyner observed the two of them for a moment, then turned to Shana.

"Thank you, Shana," he said politely. "I can entertain our guests from here."

Shana nodded, giving Erran a wide-eyed glance before hurrying away.

Scyner—the man whom they suspected had once been called Jakarris—waited until the Shadow was out of earshot, and then turned back to them.

"Please, come inside," he said quietly. "I've been expecting you."

"You're a murderer." Erran hissed the words, jaw clenched. "You killed my friend."

"I am. I did." Scyner said the words calmly and directly, meeting Erran's gaze. "You can try to kill me now in vengeance— either failing and dying, too, or succeeding and putting the entire world in jeopardy. *Or*, you can put aside your hatred, and I can explain to Ashalia here exactly what she needs to do to save us all."

Erran clenched and unclenched his fists, not moving for a long few moments. Frustration and anger warred on his face.

Then he let his shoulders sag, his stance finally shifting. Becoming wary rather than aggressive.

Asha let out a breath that she hadn't realized she was holding.

"Good." Scyner nodded.

He turned and disappeared inside, beckoning for them to follow.

The inside of the building was only a little less stark than the outside: a single large room with a rug, a bed in the corner, and

633

a few chairs against the wall. Scyner sat, gesturing for the other two to follow suit. Asha took a chair but Erran stood by the door-way, eyes never leaving the older man.

Scyner sighed, but nodded an acknowledgment. He turned to Asha.

"Has Tal'kamar succeeded in binding the Lyth?"

Asha stared at him in surprise for a moment, then grunted and inclined her head. "If you were expecting us—or someone, at least—then why not tell the Shadows?" she asked irritably. "And what are these monsters Shana was talking about?"

"I didn't tell them because I knew that you, specifically, wouldn't be troubled by a few Shadows with Vessels. And nobody else was welcome." Scyner squinted at her. "As for the second question—do you know what tek'ryl are?"

Asha frowned, trying to remember the tales from the Old Religion. "Like dar'gaithin," she said eventually. "A cross between man and animal. But tek'ryl...they only attack ships?"

"That's how they're described in the stories. They're amphibious." Scyner's expression was one of distaste. "Bodies like scorpions, six legs but with a tail that lets them swim. They've attacked this island several times already, looking for the Tributary."

"They know that it's here?" asked Asha.

Scyner nodded grimly. "I'm not sure whether it's knowledge or instinct, but more and more have been getting through the Boundary, and they all seem intent on coming here. Once the Tributary is activated, it will create its own defenses against them, as well as against anyone or anything else that may wish to interfere with its operation. But until that happens..." He shrugged. "That's why we brought the Shadows here. They're the only group that we can actually depend upon to defend this place." He held up a hand, forestalling Asha's protest. "They know a lot about what's happening, now—why they're here, what's at stake. Not *everything*, but they're not doing this blind, either."

Asha shut her mouth again reluctantly. She didn't like the idea of the Shadows being used in this way, but they *had* seemed unsurprised by her ability to drain their Reserves. Perhaps Scyner was telling the truth.

634 Erran had remained silent thus far, his glare never leaving

Scyner. Now, however, his gaze had focused on something on the desk in the corner of the room.

Abruptly he moved, striding over to it, his expression appalled.

"What is *this* doing here?" He snatched up something small, brandishing it at Scyner. An amulet, gold, depicting an eagle with widespread wings.

"I took it from the boy you put it on, after I killed him," said Scyner. He appeared to flicker for a moment, and suddenly he was the one holding the amulet rather than Erran. "Do not touch it again," he added grimly.

Erran paled. "You killed Rohin?" He shook his head in confusion. "Why? He was harmless so as long as he was wearing this. And Fessi thought that you were the one who sent..."

He gazed at the amulet in Scyner's hand for a long, silent moment, expression turning to horrified understanding. "You sent him there so that you could get *that*?"

Scyner slipped the amulet into his pocket. "I saw only that he would eventually wear it, Erran. Not the...specifics of the problems that he caused at the Tol," he said softly, what sounded like genuine regret in his voice. "He was a monster—I realized as much when I took this from him. Of the Augurs that I have ended, him I regret the least."

Erran shook his head dazedly. "Why, though?"

"Because it is needed for what is to come."

Erran scowled at him. "Was Kol's death needed, too?"

Scyner rubbed his face tiredly.

"Do you actually *remember* what happened, that night with your friend?" he asked quietly. "I could have killed all of you then and there, had I wanted to. Perhaps I could have handled the situation better, but *your friend* attacked *me*. I came there wanting your *help*. Perhaps I tried to get it more forcefully than I should have, and perhaps I should have tried harder to make my defense non-lethal, but..." He shook his head. "El take it, boy. Are you telling me that if three Augurs attacked you, that you'd react calmly and carefully enough not to do the same?"

Erran stared at him silently, jaw clenched and eyes cold. "Fessi would still kill you if she were here."

"Then it is fortunate that she is not." Scyner held Erran's gaze.   635

"Now, are you going to let me show Asha what you both came here for, or do we need to settle this?"

Erran's lip curled in anger but Asha stood and stepped over to him, laying a hand gently on his arm again.

Erran took a long, frustrated breath at the touch, then turned to the door.

"Let's go and have a look at this fates-cursed Tributary," he said bitterly.

Asha paused in her ascent, turning away from the glowing ball of Essence lighting their path and glancing down at the peaceful scene below.

Behind her, she could hear Erran and Scyner both give small sighs of relief as they came to a stop, breathing heavily. The steps winding their way up the side of the mountain were steep, though at least well-made and showing no signs of decay; it had taken a good half hour of climbing but she, Erran, and Scyner were more than halfway to the peak now. Unlike when she'd been a Shadow, though, the physical exercise felt...wonderful. She should be tired—both from the lateness of the hour and the exertion—but instead she felt just as energetic as when she'd woken that morning.

She gave the other two a few moments to recover and gazed out past the moonlit rooftops, the gently swaying forest and the silvery ripple of waves beyond, staring at the shimmering blue-white curtain of energy stretching away as far as the eye could see. Even with the seemingly boundless power crashing around inside of her, she couldn't help but feel another flicker of doubt as she took it all in.

She shook her head as if the motion could clear it of the concern, turning to Erran. "Ready to keep going?"

Erran responded with a displeased grunt, but inclined his head.

They continued trudging upward in single file, winding their way up the side of the mountain until the treetops below began to look small. The closer that they got to the top of the stairs, the more anxious Asha found herself getting.

After what seemed like an age she finally steeled herself, then pushed up the last few steps and onto the peak.

She stood at the edge of the plateau, squinting in the moonlight at the surrounds. There was perhaps a hundred feet across to the other edge of the mountain, though the space in between had clearly been smoothed, flattened so that it was easy to traverse. At the northern edge of the plateau stood a small stone pavilion, composed of a multitude of meshing, curving shapes, enclosed on all sides except its northern face.

Asha walked toward it, not waiting for the other two to catch up. The radiant light from the Boundary illuminated the inside just enough to see.

It was entirely empty, except for the Tributary.

Asha's steps faltered as she approached the jagged metallic-and-black mass, straining to see the specifics of it as it glinted at her from the shadows. She placed a foot on the first step of the pavilion, then flinched back again as Essence sprang to life around the structure's edge, lighting everything clearly.

As she fully took in the device for the first time, she couldn't help but shiver.

Bathed in the pure white glow of the pavilion, the Tributary gazed back at her with polished black eyes, its maw encompassing the coffin-like opening, jagged steel teeth looking ready to snap shut over it at any moment.

"Is that a wolf's head?" Asha asked in disbelief.

"Yes," confirmed Scyner quietly from behind her. She turned to see him staring up at the metallic monstrosity. "It is a signature, of sorts. Long ago, all of the Venerate bound themselves to an agreement. Weapons made using kan were appearing, and they wanted to be certain that none of their own number were responsible." He gazed at the threatening mass of steel. "This is Tal'kamar's sigil," he added softly.

Asha swallowed. Caeden had made this? She stepped closer to the menacing device, which at twice her height towered over her. Then she squinted inside the coffin-like section, noting the hundreds of tiny holes in the back. "And those are for..."

Scyner hesitated.

"Needles," he said eventually. "They pierce your skin, force your body to draw Essence to heal itself... but the Tributary takes away most of that Essence before it can be used. It creates a constant flow of energy, no matter whether you're conscious."

Asha felt her breath getting shorter, the first true vestiges of panic setting in. "And will I be? Conscious, I mean?"

"No." Scyner shook his head firmly. "Every month, you'll be woken briefly for something called the Shift—kind of a recalibration of the Boundary—but that is all. The rest of the time you'll either be asleep, or your mind will be in a dok'en."

"A dok'en?"

"You'll be...somewhere else. You won't feel the pain," said Scyner.

"How do you know all of this?"

Scyner shrugged. "You know with whom I've been working."

Erran, who had finally caught his breath again, stared at the device and then back at Asha again in horror.

"No." He shook his head firmly. "No, I can't let you do this, Asha. This is...sick." He stared defiantly at both of them.

"I don't think that I have much of a choice," said Asha softly.

As if to punctuate her words a strange, high-pitched shrieking noise suddenly cut through the ever-present thrum of the Boundary, sending a shiver down Asha's spine.

She turned northward, watching wide-eyed as the Boundary... *rippled.* For a moment the cold Essence turned translucent; she caught a glimpse of distant, lifeless cliffs towering over the ocean in the moonlight before the wall of energy abruptly snapped back into place, solidifying again.

She tore her eyes away from the scene, gazing again at the Tributary.

"Wait. Just wait." Erran put a hand on her arm. "Davian, Fessi, and Ishelle might still be in Talan Gol. If you do this, you'll be sealing them in there."

"You think I haven't already *thought of that*?" Asha realized that she'd raised her voice but she didn't care, all the tension and heartache that she was feeling at the moment suddenly released into the words.

"There is a greater good to think about," interjected Scyner.

Erran rounded on him. "You stay out of this!" he snarled.

Scyner blinked, but eventually held up his hands in a defensive posture and inclined his head. "As you wish. But whatever he says cannot change what is happening," he added to Asha.

He held her gaze for a few moments, ignoring Erran's scowl, then stepped outside.

Erran moved closer to Asha, lowering his voice. "Let me go back to the outpost. I can stay in contact with you via mental link. Let me try and make contact with them again before we do anything that we can't undo." He looked her in the eye. "You have a perfect view of what's going on from up here. If you need to activate that thing…then I understand. But I can tell you right now that if you leave Scyner and I as the only Augurs in Andarra, then we're in trouble." He smiled weakly at her.

Asha hesitated, then nodded slowly. She was wary of being convinced too easily; there was nothing that she wanted to do less than to step into that device. But Erran was right—she could see the Boundary well enough. As long as she was here, she could act at a moment's notice.

"You *tell me* if I need to seal it," she said softly. "No matter what. I want Davian back and safe, but I won't be responsible for more people dying."

Erran released a relieved breath, nodding.

"Just don't do anything until you hear from me. No matter what *he* says," he said grimly, casting a dark look out the entrance at Scyner. "See you soon."

He vanished.

After a few moments Scyner stepped back inside the pavilion, looking grim.

"You're risking the lives of everyone by delaying." Asha wasn't sure what, if anything, the man had overheard—but he'd clearly gathered what she had decided to do.

"My friends are missing, and we think that they might be in Talan Gol. I couldn't live with myself if I didn't give them a chance to get out." Asha found that her voice was steady. "But if I need to do this sooner, then I won't hesitate."

Scyner studied her, then gave a single nod of acceptance. "Very well."

He turned away to face the cold luminescence of the Boundary, breathing deeply.

"Then we wait."

Chapter 45

Wirr leaned against the north-facing parapet, pretending not to see his mother's irritated-looking approach from the corner of his eye.

He continued gazing out over the brightly lit wasteland, his absorption in watching the vision-filling dome of the Boundary only partially put on. In the little time since he'd arrived, he already felt as though it had weakened. Faded. Was that his imagination? In the distance to the west he could see another patrol returning, thankfully with the slow, determined walk of men with a purpose but without an urgent message.

"What can I do for you now, Mother?" he asked as Geladra came to a stop beside him, not looking up, knowing that his cynicism came through in his tone but too tired to care.

"You can tell me how you intend to deal with your Augur friends. And the Representative who helped them," Geladra said, barely concealed anger thick in her voice. "They don't have any right to be taking actions without proper supervision, and—"

"*Fates*, Mother." Wirr turned, sighing. "Are we really still doing this? I don't trust the Augurs, but I sure as fate trust Davian and Asha. I trust them more than I am *ever* likely to trust you, given how embarrassingly emotional and vindictive and *petty* you have been about this entire thing."

He grimaced as he fell silent. It was harsher than what he'd meant to say, harsher than he'd wanted to be. Regardless of the truth of the statement.

Geladra flushed, not responding for a moment.

"You think that me being angry over your father's Control—his murder—is *petty*?" she eventually asked disbelievingly.

Wirr closed his eyes.

"When it makes you more interested in vengeance than saving the fates-cursed *country*? Yes." He turned now, facing her. "Maybe you're right, and maybe I'm more conflicted about it than you are, because it probably saved my life. But that's not a bad thing. If anything, it gives me perspective."

Geladra's eyes flashed. "Don't you talk to me about *perspective*. You've just let—"

Whatever she was about to say was cut off by an abrupt, overwhelmingly loud whining screech that echoed from all directions at once. Wirr and Geladra both flinched and Wirr's heart dropped, argument forgotten as he turned to look northward.

The Boundary flexed, rippling like rain on calm water.

Then it became thin. Translucent.

Wirr felt the blood drain from his face as he could suddenly see beyond the barrier, into the vast wastelands beyond. It was impossible to make out specifics from this distance, but the dark mass that broke the dusty horizon was unmistakable.

There were figures lined up behind that curtain of energy, waiting just beyond in Talan Gol.

A *lot* of figures.

They were quickly lost to view again as the Boundary flickered, flashed blue and then solidified. Wirr caught movement to the side as Gifted and soldiers from around the outpost began rushing to the top of the wall, staring out northward, each one silent and wearing expressions of varying alarm and fear. Karaliene emerged from the keep, too, spotting him and Geladra and hurrying over to join them.

Geladra's frown changed slightly as she nodded to Kara, watching the people around them. Even she, angry as she clearly was, could pick up on when others were genuinely nervous. "What's happening?" she asked, gaze returning to Wirr.

"I don't know. I've never seen it do that before." Wirr turned to Captain Muran, who was standing nearby, having been one of those to hurry to the top of the wall. "Captain?"

Muran licked his lips nervously, not taking his eyes from the

Boundary. He shook his head. "This is the first time that's happened since we arrived."

He said no more, and Wirr joined him and everyone else in watching the pulsing curtain of blue-white light in the distance. The silence was eerie as they stared out over the expanse, as if everyone present were holding their breaths. Thirty seconds passed. A minute.

A low murmur started along the wall as tensed muscles began to ease, and a few people turned away. Geladra frowned northward a moment longer, then opened her mouth to say something to Wirr.

Another shriek split the air.

This time the Boundary just...faded. Not everywhere, but sections of it went so clear that for a heart-stopping moment, Wirr wasn't even sure it was still there.

Everyone along the wall spun back to watch as explosions of light started everywhere along the near-invisible barrier, accompanied each time by odd, whining thrums of released energy. Wirr watched in horror as he realized that those bursts were from distant figures throwing themselves at the Boundary, disintegrating in violent flashes of Essence. Farther to the east a series of brilliant explosions rippled higher up on the dome, though he couldn't specifically see what had caused those.

He squinted toward the more distant detonations for a moment, but gasps from next to him drew his attention back to the ones closer by.

Some of those far away figures hadn't stopped when they'd hit the Boundary, hadn't evaporated in flashes of light like the others.

They had kept going.

There were several moments of stunned silence as everyone on the wall processed what was happening. Dark silhouettes were streaming through the Boundary now, fighting past the cascades of explosions and into Andarra. Motionless forms began to collect at the base of the wall of energy, where people or creatures—Wirr couldn't tell which—had clearly fought through, only to succumb to whatever injuries they had sustained in the process. But even with the casualties, there were perhaps four hundred figures now sprinting toward the cliffs, and tens more were breaking through with each passing second.

"You should go." He turned to his mother, tone urgent. "You won't be of much help here. You and the other Administrators need to get out."

Geladra was frowning down at the scene, pale but curious. She shook her head.

"I've seen the defenses. This outpost is impregnable," she said confidently. "You brought me up here to understand the threat, but I cannot see how those men down there could possibly get past these cliffs."

"Those may not be men," Kara observed to her quietly.

Wirr nodded in frustrated agreement and glanced east again, but the flashes in that direction had stopped. For a moment he fancied that he could see something darkening the sky, but if there was anything there, it was too distant to make out. "And it's not just here. They have eletai—creatures that *fly*, Mother."

Geladra snorted, though Wirr could at least see an element of uncertainty in her eyes now. "So you bring me up here to observe the threat, then don't want me to see just how dangerous it is?"

Wirr stared at her in disbelief. "You *still* think that I'm trying to fool you?" He balled his hands into fists, shaking his head. He wanted nothing more than to walk away right now, but he knew that he'd regret it if he let his only surviving parent stay in danger simply because they were stubborn. "Fine. Watch." He licked his lips, touching the Oathstone in his pocket. "But the *moment* that you realize just how dangerous it is, you and the others must leave. You are to just get on your horses and *go*."

Geladra studied her son's face, seemingly not feeling the binding taking effect, but perhaps for the first time understanding just how serious he was. "Very well."

Wirr gave a sharp nod, turning away. It was the best that he could do for now.

"Prince Torin!" It was Captain Muran, breathing heavily, evidently having just returned from another part of the wall. "We could use your help. At that speed, they'll be here in ten minutes."

Wirr nodded, gazing out pensively toward the Boundary. It had solidified again but explosions of light still thundered, the enemies beyond clearly hoping for a repeat of its abrupt weakness.

"Let me know what I can do." He turned back to his mother.

"Perhaps you should gather the Administrators. You'll want to be ready to—"

Movement caught the corner of his eye. He turned, frowning, as the first warning shouts echoed across the keep.

The sky to the east had turned black.

He squinted, his mind taking a moment to comprehend exactly what he was seeing. When it did, his heart dropped and he turned to his mother, clasping the Oathstone again.

"Get out of here. *Now.*"

The swarm of eletai was a minute away, maybe less; they'd used the sun to conceal their presence until they were close. Wirr got only the impression of wings blurring and black sharp-edged blades glistening.

He focused upward, building a charge of Essence within himself and aiming at the lead creature. Some nervous archers had already loosed a couple of shots but they were well short; not knowing exactly how big the creatures were made judging their distance difficult. The rest of the archers, Wirr was relieved to see, had assembled in disciplined fashion and were being overseen by Muran, shading their eyes as they gazed upward, but none having yet drawn.

His mother wore a scowl but was hurrying reluctantly away, compelled by his words. She would doubtless have some hard questions for him later, if they both lived long enough for her to ask them.

He turned back, holding his breath as the first volley was let loose by the archers. Arrows sang with an eerie whistle as they sliced through the air.

Many connected with the first of the eletai, and there were some scattered cheers as a couple of the creatures faltered and then spun toward the ground.

Wirr waited for a moment and then began firing blasts of Essence into the sky, imitated by the several other Gifted who had taken up positions behind the archers. The air was abruptly filled with fizzing, blinding bolts of power streaking upward, exploding wherever they made contact.

And then there was chaos.

Wirr gasped as the Gifted standing next to him rocked back,   **645** a thin black spear suddenly protruding from his neck. Blood spurted across Wirr's shirt as another glistening black spike ripped through the man's shoulder, dripping viscous dark ooze as the red-cloaked man collapsed, eyes rolling into the back of his head.

A body crashed into him, forcing him to the side as more spears sliced silently out of the sky at where he'd been standing a moment earlier, so thin that they were barely visible. He stared dazedly as Karaliene scrambled to her feet after diving on him.

"Thanks," he gasped to his cousin.

She nodded, hauling him up as screams echoed around the courtyard, archers beginning to fall before they even got their second shot away. Thin black projectiles were raining down everywhere now; a few Gifted tried to raise Essence shields to deflect the spears, but the eletai weapons sheared straight through them. Wirr scrambled for cover, watching in horror as he saw a couple of the eletai make it to the courtyard. Those black spears were embedded in their bodies, protruding through the skin like ghastly broken bones; once they were close enough the creatures chose not to fire them but rather used them as blades, spinning and slicing and tearing at anything that moved.

He caught motion to his left and spun to the side, just in time to see two of the needle-like black spears arrowing toward his face.

They froze in place.

He yelled as he fell backward, wide-eyed, not understanding what had happened until he saw Erran standing a couple of paces away. The Augur's face was pale and drawn; from his expression, Wirr could tell that he was expending an enormous amount of concentration to include both him and Karaliene in the time bubble.

"Go," Erran gasped. "I'll follow."

Wirr nodded, then turned to the courtyard. His mother had made it most of the way to the southern gate, but eletai now blocked her path.

He frowned. She should have been turning to run—she'd be dead in moments, otherwise—but she didn't appear to be changing course.

"Fates," he muttered, a chill running down his spine as he realized what was happening. He turned to Erran. "We need to get my mother."

"There's no time, Tor," said Karaliene softly.

Erran followed Wirr's gaze, then squeezed his eyes shut. Wirr felt certain that the Augur was about to agree with Karaliene; the chaos in the courtyard looked a hundred times worse than it was even up here.

Eventually, though, he just nodded.

Karaliene grimaced but didn't resist as they snaked their way through the near-frozen madness, Erran keeping one hand on each of their shoulders, half leaning on Wirr as the strain of whatever he was doing clearly continued to take a toll. Wirr's stomach churned as he hurried past a soldier falling backward, blood spurting in slow motion from the hole in his chest where an eletai had just skewered him.

They descended the stairs, then made their way over to Geladra. She was staring wide-eyed at an eletai rearing up in front of her, mouth open in what was undoubtedly a scream even as she tried to push forward.

Erran nodded to Wirr, who grabbed her by the arm.

Geladra's shriek of fear was piercing as it entered the bubble.

"Mother!" Wirr forced her to meet his gaze, trying to calm her. "We need to go."

Geladra stared at him for a moment, panic still clouding her vision. Then she looked around in bemused wonder, slowly beginning to breathe again.

"You're...doing this?" she asked Erran.

Erran just nodded grimly. "But I'm at my limits. We need to get out of here."

Wirr turned to the exit, then blanched. Eletai had completely swarmed it, making it impossible to get out the southern side.

Erran saw the same thing; with a groan he nodded back toward the entrance to the keep, where the door was smashed in but currently unguarded. Time began to stutter around them, frozen one second and then a moment of everything happening at full speed, making Wirr's heart stop every time. There was no doubt that if they couldn't get free of the courtyard now, they wouldn't leave alive.

Wirr, Erran, and Karaliene all began heading for the keep but Geladra pulled in the opposite direction, nearly wresting herself free of Wirr's grasp.

"What are you doing?" hissed Erran to her.

Wirr paled as he understood. "You don't have to leave anymore, Mother. Come with us."

Geladra instantly reversed her direction, falling in step with he and Erran. She didn't say anything, but Wirr could see from the way that she looked at him that she'd figured it out.

"I'll explain later," he muttered to her as another leap forward in time sent a spear gliding across their path, forcing them to skirt it awkwardly.

Once through the door they allowed Erran to lead them down a narrow flight of stairs, into the depths of the keep. Wirr hadn't been in this section before, but he noted with some relief the narrow passageway, which with his broad shoulders he almost had to turn sideways to fit through. The larger proportions of the eletai wouldn't allow them down here.

There was a warping of the air around them as Erran sagged a little, and suddenly the torches on the wall were flickering and stuttering in regular motion again. From up above there was still the occasional muffled shout, but for the most part the outpost had fallen eerily silent.

Wirr and Karaliene quickly supported the Augur as he stumbled. "We can rest," Wirr said quickly. "Those creatures can't get down here."

Erran shook his head grimly. "The dar'gaithin can, though. I saw them on my way here. Hundreds of them got through." He took a deep breath, straightening. "It didn't look like there were any more coming from the other side of the Boundary—at least for now—and I cannot imagine that they'd bother much with the outpost beyond passing through it, but they're still going to be here soon. You need to stay hidden for a few more hours at least."

Wirr paled, but nodded.

They pressed on, soon enough coming to what looked to be the outpost's cells. They hurried inside, Wirr relieved to see that the sturdy steel door was able to be barred from the inside.

Geladra slumped to the ground, back against the wall, looking dazed and exhausted. "What *were* those things?"

"Eletai." Wirr didn't see the need to elaborate. He turned to Erran. "Where's Asha? And Dav?"

"Asha's getting ready to strengthen the fates-cursed Boundary, I hope," said Erran grimly. He hesitated. "Davian...we think he might have been stuck on the other side. That's why I'm here. To try and make contact before Asha seals everything off again."

"*What?*" Wirr's heart dropped. "Fates. These things are getting through. You need to let her know to seal it *now*."

Erran shook his head.

"Fessi's out there, too. And Ishelle," he said grimly. "We can't assume that Asha can keep the Boundary up forever—and fates know that I can't fix the El-cursed thing on my own. If they're stuck out there, then we need them back." He held up his hand as Wirr opened his mouth to argue. "This reunion's been fun, but I don't have any more time. I have to go."

Wirr gritted his teeth, but nodded. Even if he'd wanted to stop Erran, he knew that he couldn't. "You tell Ash to seal it as soon as you can," he said grimly.

Erran gave a short nod and turned to go.

"Wait."

It was Geladra. Wirr turned to see his mother had stood again and was watching Erran narrowly.

"Was it you?"

Erran blinked, then flushed, suddenly looking flustered. "I...I don't know what you mean."

"It *was* you, wasn't it." Geladra's eyes were wide as she gazed at Erran, a mixture of fascination and rage in her expression. "I didn't notice it at first, but just now...I can see it in your mannerisms, see it when you look at me. I can *see* it." There was cold certainty in her tone.

Erran frowned, feigning confusion, but the flicker of guilt in his eyes told Wirr the truth.

His mother evidently saw it, too, because she took an angry step forward.

"He killed your father, Torin." She looked at Wirr expectantly.

Erran licked his lips, glancing from Geladra to Wirr. More than anything else now, he looked sad.

"I have to go. Davian and Asha are depending on me."

Wirr stared at him for a long moment. He glanced at Karaliene, but his cousin's expression was inscrutable.

Finally, he nodded.

"I couldn't stop you anyway." He held Erran's gaze.

Erran inclined his head, ignoring Geladra's cry of protest. "Don't come out until you're sure it's safe," he said grimly.

He vanished.

There was silence as Geladra stood there, glaring at her son, trembling with pure anger.

Eventually, she just turned away.

There was stony, nervous silence for a while after that. The sounds from up above had ceased now.

After a minute Wirr walked over to the door, shutting and barring it. If there was anyone else coming, they would be able to hear them and let them in... but he didn't think that there would be.

He slid slowly to the ground, back against the door, the horror of what had just occurred above finally dawning on him. Not just the immediacy of the death and destruction, but its implications.

Even if Asha sealed the Boundary straight away, there were too many creatures that had gotten through. Loose in Andarra, they would cause devastation, wreak havoc for years to come. Decades, maybe.

Wirr swallowed. Was Dezia still in the south? He hoped so. And then there was Deldri, his uncle... everyone that he cared for, really.

They were all in danger now.

He exchanged a glance with Karaliene, seeing the same grim realization on his cousin's face.

Neither of them said anything though. There would be time to worry about the bigger picture later.

If they were lucky.

Closing his eyes, he settled down to wait.

Chapter 46

Caeden steadied his breathing as he slipped silently behind one of the massive black pillars that lined the hallway, allowing another patrol to pass by.

After coming through the portal, he'd emerged...here. Into the middle of an enormous hall that was completely empty, completely silent. Assuming that the men he'd subsequently seen marching through were not looking for him, his arrival had seemingly gone unnoticed.

He took another slow, calming breath and looked around. Torches were mounted on every side of each square column, though much of the light was absorbed by the muting black of the stone itself. It wasn't obsidian like Res Kartha, polished and smooth and beautiful. This was as if everything had been charred, smeared with ash, though when he brushed it lightly with his fingers, nothing came away.

He wasn't sure how tall the hall was—he couldn't see its roof—but a hundred paces away there was a doorway leading outside, evident thanks to the wan light filtering through. He moved cautiously toward it, ears sharp. He'd already had to avoid two other patrols since he'd arrived. He wasn't sure what would happen if they spotted him—or, in fact, if they were even patrols—but he wasn't about to take any chances. Until he understood exactly why he was here, he wanted to remain as inconspicuous as possible.

Reaching the entrance, he emerged onto a wide, completely deserted balcony that overlooked a sprawling city below. Caeden moved cautiously to the railing, peering over. He was standing at least two hundred feet above the city, but he didn't think that the structure itself was that tall; rather, it appeared to be set into the side of a steep mountain, from which the stones of the building—and all the buildings below—seemed to have been taken.

He shivered as he gazed down at the city, the dark stone and unnaturally pale light giving everything a hazy, shadowy look. Caeden squinted up toward the sun, which was close to its zenith. There were no clouds to speak of but it was still strangely weak, filtered, despite the oppressive heat.

He frowned, trying to determine where he was. The streets below were quiet but far from abandoned: in many sections he could see bustling crowds, no different to many other places that he'd been in the past.

His gaze shifted to his left, where an entire quadrant of the city appeared to be empty. He frowned as he studied the thick, spiked wall that cordoned it off.

That was definitely unusual.

Within the abandoned section, jutting out from among the smaller buildings, he spotted a tower. It was a tall and thin square column—probably room enough inside for a stairwell, but not much else.

He remembered the moment that he saw it.

Caeden sat atop Seclusion's third and tallest tower, staring pensively out over Ilshan Gathdel Teth.

The fortress-city beyond Seclusion looked different here than it did from the Citadel. There it was entirely visible, naked, laid bare by its design. Here it was more mysterious, chaotic, the view of some streets blocked by buildings, the careful layout obfuscated by angle. That wasn't surprising though. The Builders hadn't built this tower, hadn't built any of the warren of structures that adjoined Ilshan Gathdel Teth. They'd never anticipated a view from this particular vantage point.

"So you are set in this detour of yours."

Caeden twisted to see Asar standing a little way into the top-most room of the tower, arms crossed as he leaned against the doorway, like Caeden looking out on the city below. His expression was absent, a little wistful.

"Yes." Caeden said the words more confidently than he felt, rolling the ring around his palm again before holding it up, examining it. Three silver bands twisted together, flowing but irregular. A reminder of why he was doing this.

Asar watched him sadly. "And when you have determined that it is not possible?"

Caeden glared at him. "If."

Asar shook his head. "The Darecians were driven by dreams of revenge, Tal, and their theories sprang from that desire. This hope of changing things, of creating limitless realities, was always a fantasy. Albeit a compelling one," he added softly.

Caeden was silent for a moment. "You are very probably right, and yet I cannot go farther until I am sure. I've already been made to kill..." He gestured, swallowing. "I will not take one more life until I know everything that I can."

Asar hesitated.

"Nobody and nothing made you do what you did, Tal. Inevitable or not, you chose to believe. You chose to follow. You chose to act."

Caeden flinched at the rebuke. "I take ownership of my actions," he said defensively. "But it does not mean that I—"

"That's not what you need to do, Tal'kamar," Asar interrupted gently. "You know this. The true evil is always in the reason and the excuse, not the act. I was fooled. I was angry. I wasn't thinking. I had to do it, else worse things would have happened. It didn't hurt anyone. It hurt less people than it would have if I hadn't. It was to protect myself. It was to protect others. It was in my nature. It was necessary. It was right." He said the words softly. "We have both been alive long enough to know that evil only wins when it spreads. It can cause destruction, it can cause death—but those are consequences of its nature, not its victory. Not its goal. The danger of evil, the purpose of evil, is that it causes those who would oppose it to become evil also." He looked Caeden in the eye. "And that, my friend, is what happened to you."

Caeden paled under the weight of the words, but nodded. The

crushing guilt settled again on his shoulders, his chest, his head. As it did each and every day.

Asar stepped forward, gripping Caeden's arm firmly. "I say this only because you asked me to," he said quietly. "You said—"

"I know. To not let me deflect." Caeden gave him a tight smile. "I know."

Asar watched him for a long moment. "My original question stands. Once you have been to Deilannis this last time, will you finally act?"

Caeden nodded slowly.

"I will go through Eryth Mmorg." Here, at the very peak of Seclusion, was perhaps the only place where he could utter these words aloud and not fear being overheard. "I will take Licanius. Kill Meldier and Isiliar, retrieve the Siphon. And then when I have bound the Lyth, I will use the final Tributary to make sure that the ilshara does not fall before its time." He said the words softly. This was a plan that had been a long time in the making, but he despised it no less because of that. "After that, it will be up to you to seal the rift. I'll give you Licanius, but you will have to kill the others, as well as any Augurs in Andarra who are old enough to have come into their powers. Then Cyr. And lastly, the both of us."

Caeden felt sick as he finished. It was a final evil to oppose evil, a failure of conscience even if they were victorious—and yet even Asar had conceded that the cost of inaction here was too great to bear.

They could not pretend to a moral imperative, this time. They were choosing the darker path because they feared the consequences of not. It wasn't something to feel good about or to be proud of. It simply...was.

"Good." Asar watched him grimly. "But you're still thinking about what Alaris said, aren't you?"

"Yes." Caeden saw no need to deny it. He and Asar had not always been friends—not always even allies—but they had a bond founded on trust, on openness. "His arguments are hard to refute."

"I would say that they cannot be refuted," said Asar. "He is arguing from a position of belief, Tal, as are you. You are both intelligent men, and there are no flaws in either of your lines of reasoning. If there were, then we would not be in this situation."

Caeden shook his head, allowing his frustration and indecision to creep onto his face. He could do at least that much here, where no one else would see. "He and the others are all just so... certain. So *certain*, even after..." He gestured. "We're not just talking about anyone, either, Asar. These are the best of us. These are our friends." He grimaced. "And they all think that we are wrong."

Asar raised an eyebrow at him.

"You already know my response to that," he said quietly. "I love and respect them just as much as you do, but that doesn't—and shouldn't—change anything. We have more perspective than that. 'The people with whom we are friends should never affect our morality; rather, our morality should affect with whom we are friends.'"

Caeden smiled slightly at the quote, but nodded. Asar was right. They'd both lived long enough to see how people—societies, even—could succumb to mob morality. The desire for acceptance, the desire to feel like they were fighting for some-thing... too many were willing to base their beliefs around such shallow things. It was rarely about what was actually *right* or *wrong*. Such influences were understandable, but they were unquestionably to be avoided.

"Still," he said softly. "I would like, just once, to be certain." He motioned outward, over the city. The gesture included every-thing beyond, too, as Asar would know full well. "I would give anything just to *know*."

Asar was silent for a long moment.

"You are not alone there, Tal," he eventually sighed. "But we knew one day that we would die. Then we knew that we were alone, unique. Then we knew that there was no one out there that was more powerful than us." He shook his head slowly. "Then El found us, and we knew that we were on the side of good. We knew that we were doing the right thing. We knew that we were protecting people and fighting to save the world. We knew that our actions were not our own, that we were merely "the blade." Each time, we *knew* these things." He paused, then walked for-ward, sitting on the edge of the wall next to Caeden. "Certainty is hubris, Tal. It is arrogance and bluster and those who claim it deserve nothing but to be mocked."

Caeden let his silence concede the point. He'd known the answer, hadn't really expected to be told anything new. He'd just needed to hear it again. To be reassured that he was not alone in the pain of his doubt.

They were silent for a time, just watching the people of Ilshan Gathdel Teth scuttle like ants below, going about their daily business. At one point he thought that he saw movement deep in Seclusion itself, but as soon as he opened his mouth to point it out, it vanished. He settled back again, trying to decide whether it had simply been his imagination. No one had seen anything in Seclusion for years, but men and women nonetheless disappeared beyond its gates regularly.

Asar glanced across at him, evidently spotting that he was still troubled.

"Do you ever wonder why He chose us, Tal'kamar?" the white-haired man asked quietly.

Caeden blinked. "Because without us, the rift would have closed. Without us—and now without the Augurs, too—He would have had no way to escape this world. He gave up a great deal of His power, but He did it to serve His own ends."

"That's why He chose someone." Asar gazed out over the city contemplatively. "But He could have chosen the Venerate from amongst those who lusted for power, or from those who would have happily killed for him no matter the reason. We both know that there have always been enough of those people in the world." He shook his head. "Instead, He chose from amongst those who wanted to do good. To be good."

Caeden was silent for a while.

"There's a purity of purpose to redemption, I suppose," he eventually said softly. "To being able to undo the things for which we hate ourselves. Especially when we are told that it is in the service of the greater good."

Asar grunted, nodding. "The lesser of two evils, or the greater good. Get a good man to utter either of those phrases, and there is no one more eager to begin perpetrating evil."

656 The sun was beginning to cast long shadows across the city,

and Asar stretched, his contemplativeness evaporating with the light. He offered his hand to Caeden, who allowed himself to be pulled to his feet.

"Once we leave Seclusion…"

"I know." Caeden hesitated, then embraced the other man. His camaraderie with him was as strong as any of the others, save perhaps Alaris. Without Asar, Caeden was unsure whether he'd have had the strength of will to continue. "He is getting too wary; this will have to be the last time. I know that it will be a long wait, but I need to send you back to the Wells. I'll contact you if Deilannis changes anything."

Asar gave a tight nod.

"A century is not so long to be patient," he said softly. "We lit this fire, Tal, and we are the only ones who can put it out. That is more than enough motivation to get me through."

He disappeared down the stairs.

Caeden took a long look out over Ilshan Gathdel Teth, and followed his friend into Seclusion for the final time.

Caeden's vision cleared, and he felt sick to his stomach.

After all his protests to himself, all his denials, it was true. Part of the plan—*his* plan—had been to kill the Augurs.

Not to mention his friends and himself.

Asar had lied to him in the Wells, feigned ignorance, claimed that he didn't know the details…but Caeden could immediately see why. Simply explaining their intentions would never have been good enough, not for this. Had Asar tried, Caeden would probably have fled the Wells and never returned.

But that was something that Asar had understood from the beginning—that without his memories, without context, there was no way that Caeden would ever have accepted the truth.

Even now, he wasn't sure that he could.

He swallowed; so much of it was coming back now, it was overwhelming. He remembered struggling with the concept of yet more killing, the refusal to admit that it could possibly be necessary…and then, finally, a breaking point. The reluctant acknowledgment that there was no other way. He didn't recall the specifics, exactly—not in the same way in which he'd been reliving other moments from his past. This was more just…the knowledge that it had happened. A general recognition that it was a decision that he had made, simply the way that things had been.

He leaned against the railing, taking a deep breath. A hundred years ago. This memory had been by far his most recent, near two thousand years after the creation of the Boundary. He'd still been pretending to be loyal to El despite the others' mounting suspicions, walking an impossibly fine line between trying to stay safe and trying to convince his friends of the truth. He had delayed for longer than he should have in that pursuit, taken more risks than were strictly wise in the hope that even one more of them would eventually change their mind.

None of them had, but he had never regretted trying.

As he peered down at the black stone buildings below, there was suddenly more. This city was deep in northern Talan Gol, and it had been his home since El's invasion—Aarkein Devaed's invasion—had ground to a halt. He'd only ever meant to be here for a few years at most, the Boundary merely a means of delaying their progress so that he could settle his growing unease about El's plans before pressing on. But the more he had investigated, the more that Andrael's words had seemed less and less those of a madman.

And then El had acted. He had restricted the Venerate to Talan Gol, announcing that despite Caeden and Gassandrid's ability to create Gates, none of them were to leave without His permission. He had given them plenty of reasons as to why, and as always they had made indisputable sense…but it had nonetheless increased Caeden's doubt. The more he had considered the situation, the more it had seemed that El simply did not want the Venerate away from His influence.

The more it had seemed that He did not want them traveling to Deilannis before He could get there, too.

Caeden frowned, nodding slowly as he stared down at the black stone buildings and took a deep, shuddering breath. It was coming back. There were still holes in his memory, but they were *holes* now. Gaps between the things that he remembered, rather than the other way around.

He straightened again, glancing around back at the palace. The

Citadel, they called it here in Ilshan Gathdel Teth. Home to the Venerate. They hadn't built it; it had been taken in their last great push, their effort to reach Deilannis. The Darecians had known that they were coming, though; their Ironsails had spotted them more than a hundred miles offshore. They had had hundreds of years to prepare for his and the other Venerate's invasion, and they had used that time well. Spreading fear of him, even if at that point they hadn't known his true name. Building weapons here in the north, ones that he and the others had been forced to deal with before searching for their objective. Laying traps. Hiding their great accomplishments deep underground.

But it would never have been enough, if not for the Boundary.

Caeden frowned. He'd always had doubts, but something had changed after the beginning of the Andarran invasion. Sometime after what had happened with the Jha'vett in Deilannis, he'd *given* the surviving Andarrans the secret to creating the wall of energy, even if they never actually knew that it had come from him.

He closed his eyes, breathing deeply. The air here was more stale than in Andarra, hotter and danker and heavier than anywhere outside of the ilshara. It was familiar, though. Every lungful brought back more memories.

After a few moments he shook his head, touching the blade at his side for reassurance. There was a lot to sort through, a lot to understand—but now wasn't the time. The others, if they were here, would undoubtedly have detected his entry into the city. The Portal Box gave off too much energy for them not to have noticed.

Still, as he peered cautiously back into the main hall of the Citadel, there was nothing. No movement. No one rushing to detain him.

He thought for a moment and then hurried back inside, through the hall and down a set of winding stairs to the left. He briefly checked the way ahead with kan to ensure that he wasn't going to run into someone on the journey down, grimacing at the amount of effort it took to even grasp here.

The spiraling staircase took him nearly to the ground; he emerged onto a short, steeply inclined street, the ground underfoot solid ashen rock.

"Tal'kamar."

Caeden stiffened, then turned to face the man who had evidently been waiting for him.

"Meldier." Caeden met the older man's gaze steadily, trying not to show the panic that was flashing through him. "You made it back."

Meldier eyed Caeden warily. "Once I was free of the Plains, Lethaniel found me easily enough."

Lethaniel. One of the sha'teth. Like Echoes but more self-aware, able to act of their own will and able to use kan. Capable of things that not even the Venerate were able to do. Caeden had given them a new set of bindings, turned them to the Venerate's side after the Gifted had created them. He'd had to, in order to excuse yet another journey across the Boundary.

He'd managed to build some safeguards into those bindings. Not many, though.

Meldier clearly saw the recognition in his eyes because he immediately took a step back, hand going to the hilt of his blade.

"And you have remembered." He cocked his head to the side. "I have not raised the alarm with the others, because I wanted to have this conversation with you first. So, Tal'kamar? Are you still so certain that you are on the right side?"

Caeden hesitated.

For all that had come back to him recently, despite everything, Caeden knew that he had never felt *certain*.

"No," he said softly.

Meldier betrayed a flicker of surprise, though he eventually nodded.

"Honesty," he said quietly. "Good. You are more...*you* than last we spoke, then." He remained wary, though. "Does that mean that you are reconsidering?"

Caeden shook his head slowly. He could have tried to deceive Meldier, could have tried to get close enough to use Licanius without a fight...but Meldier was too wise by far to fall for something like that.

And more importantly, Meldier had been a friend, once. Even if Caeden had thought that it would succeed, he wouldn't do that to him.

"I remember El telling me to create the Plains." Caeden watched Meldier closely. "He did it so that the Darecians would come here, find the rift and try to use it. Put machinery around it that could break it wide open and release him."

"That was never in dispute, Tal." Meldier held his gaze. "He did it because it was the only way to change the fate of this world." He swallowed, his expression earnest. "The things I said to you on the Plains . . . El knows that I was angry, but they remain true. I am not angry that you did as El asked—I am angry that you are trying to make that act be without meaning. You cannot take the weight of the Plains upon yourself, Tal. This prison was made to make our actions inevitable, and even in following El, we are only doing His will rather than Shammaeloth's. We are the blade, Tal'kamar. We are not the hand that wields it."

We are not the hand that wields it.

Caeden felt his muscles tighten at the phrase. Meldier must have seen something in his eyes because he stepped back, suddenly looking afraid.

"You're wrong." Caeden walked forward, abruptly feeling more sure of himself. "We *are* the hand, Meldier. These *are* our choices. Maybe El is right and Shammaeloth has usurped his creation in order to make every action inevitable. Perhaps we really are all just cogs in the machinery of El's prison. But he convinced me to kill *millions*, and he ultimately did it by offering me something that I desperately wanted." His voice shook slightly. "Even if I was always meant to make that choice—even if Shammaeloth or God or whomever we want to say set all of this into motion exists—it was *my* choice."

Meldier scowled. "You shoulder blame where none is due, Tal. If I take a bird, clip its wings, and toss it from a cliff—is it then the bird's choice to fall? Because that is what has been done to us. Our every moment from birth has been guided, prepared, set up in such a way as to ensure a very particular outcome. And choice is *meaningless* if it cannot affect the outcome." He shook his head. "If you truly remember—then how can you doubt Him? Doubt His power, doubt His story?"

"I do not doubt his power." Caeden clenched his fists. "And perhaps he is even a god, Meldier. But he is not one we should be following. He is *not* one who can be trusted."

Meldier said nothing for a few moments, then sighed heavily. 661

"Then it is decided," he said regretfully.

He drew his sword.

"I don't want to fight you." Caeden stepped backward, half drawing Licanius from its sheath. "We were friends, Meldier."

"Friends. Enemies." Meldier smiled sadly. "We have known each other for thousands of years, Tal'kamar. We are men. We have been both."

Caeden grimaced, his heart dropping. "I still don't want to do this."

Meldier watched Caeden sadly. "Then don't."

He gestured.

Five enormous, twisting columns of kan erupted from the ground in a circle around Caeden, hundreds of thick black threads entwining to create each one. They hurtled fifty feet into the air, towering over Caeden before the sharp-edged tips curled back downward.

Streaked toward Caeden in an unthinkable torrent of dark energy.

Caeden snatched himself from time, breathing hard as he watched the tentacles inexorably reaching down toward him. Even with Licanius in his hand, kan was hard to control here, and those grasping threads were going to be on him in moments. This wasn't something that Meldier had simply conjured—not here, not with how difficult it was to handle kan in the first place. This was something that he'd planned, knowing that Caeden would eventually come to Ilshan Gathdel Teth.

This was a trap.

Caeden stepped forward, slashing desperately with Licanius at the nearest column, his vision all but filled by the wall of writhing kan. Even as the black lines dissolved and Caeden saw Meldier standing calmly beyond, the first tip of another of the columns touched him.

He gasped as the kan drained into him, cold and dark and insidious.

His time bubble dissipated and the remaining three columns flooded into him, too, though there was no pain. He stood for a moment, frozen, waiting for something more to happen.

"What did you do?" he breathed eventually, reeling. The kan was just sitting there inside him, like ice flowing through his blood.

"Did you think that we wouldn't prepare for you?" Meldier asked grimly. "You might have stopped some of it, Tal, but it wasn't enough."

He vanished.

Caeden stepped out of time again, acting on pure instinct, spinning as Meldier's sword came slicing toward the hand that held Licanius.

Pain ricocheted through his head.

It had happened the moment he'd touched kan, he knew, but he snarled and ignored it as best he could. He threw out a quick blast of Essence at Meldier's face but the other man didn't bother moving; the bolt dissolved before it got within a foot of its target.

Caeden gritted his teeth. Even with Licanius, it was taking every ounce of his concentration to move past the pain and grip kan, to keep the flow of time at bay.

Meldier pressed forward, faster than Caeden now. How the man was managing that level of control without Licanius, here beyond the Boundary, Caeden had no idea.

The Venerate attacked again and Caeden defended desperately, so focused on keeping Meldier's thrumming blade from his skin that he didn't have enough time to respond with either kan or Essence.

Meldier finally eased up, eyes cold and frustrated as he stepped back. He clearly hadn't anticipated that Caeden would last this long.

Caeden suddenly knew what he was about to do and threw out a web of suppressing kan, but the knives tore through his mind again and he was too slow. A blazing bolt sizzled into the sky, illuminating everything within miles a heavy, burning orange.

He cursed. There wasn't much time until the others got here.

He knew that running was probably the best course of action now.

Instead, he attacked.

Meldier's eyes went wide as Caeden let his instincts take over. Ignoring the furious pain in his head, he stretched out his palm; pulsing needles of Essence began streaming from it, swarming as if alive, surrounded by minute, delicate strands of kan. Meldier threw up another barrier but this time the attack sliced through it. Meldier screamed as several of the needles struck his face, blistering wherever they touched. One hit him in the eye in an explosion of viscous fluid and he stumbled backward, almost falling.

Caeden only had time for a sliver of relief before Meldier straightened, his vision already healed.

Caeden's heart dropped. Even with Licanius, the constant, near-unbearable pain meant that he didn't have long before time would wash back over him, and this would all be over.

Meldier gestured and an arrow of twisting kan flew toward Caeden. Caeden knew that if it reached him it would burn through his mind; moving on instinct alone he met it with a creation of his own, not a simple shield but a complex, multilayered arrangement that smashed into the spiraling kan and altered it.

Meldier screamed again, but this time it was more than simple agony.

The other man fell to the ground, eyes wide and suddenly terrified, his spinning defenses vanished. "No," he choked as Caeden let time crash back into him, then moved forward to stand over his opponent. "Please, Tal'kamar."

Caeden gazed at Meldier, a deep sadness heavy in his chest.

He stepped forward to use Licanius, and the movement saved him.

Pain lanced through his back as the blade swung from behind scored deep, raking along his shoulders. He fell, Licanius slipping from his grasp, noting almost absently that Essence was not rushing to heal the wound as it should have been. He collapsed on top of Meldier but was aware enough to smash his elbow into the man's face, then rolled to the side the moment that he hit and snatched Licanius back up again.

He got only the impression of flashing steel before his right arm burned with a deep cut; he growled as he came to his feet, stumbling a little. Meldier was still on the ground, unconscious from Caeden's last blow.

His vision cleared enough to see Isiliar, red hair wild, her eyes wide and blade dripping blood.

Caeden staggered, holding up a hand half in warning, half in petition. "Isil—"

Before he could even finish her name the Venerate was moving forward, teeth bared, sure and smooth despite the mania behind her stare. Her blade flicked out just as he forced his way through the pain in his head and regained his control over time, scrambling backward as Isiliar's blade scored a deep, sparking mark in the black stone wall where Caeden's head had just been.

Then Isiliar was upon him again, and Caeden knew immediately that he was no match for her. Whatever advantages Licanius gave him were nullified by the screaming pain that echoed through his head as he touched kan. Just like in Alkathronen, it was all he could do to fend off her blows. His back burned; small cuts began to appear on his arms, his chest, his face as Isiliar's blade whirred forward again and again and again.

None of his injuries healed now.

Sweat stung Caeden's tired eyes but he was unwilling to blink in case he gave Isiliar an opening; he gasped for air as he fell steadily back against the onslaught, Licanius growing heavier and heavier in his hands. Against Meldier, Caeden had at least felt capable. Not confident, but still with the slim hope that he might emerge from the fight alive.

There was no chance for such optimism here.

After what seemed like minutes Isiliar finally broke off, snarling with frustration. Caeden didn't even have enough energy to try and press the attack, simply grateful for the momentary respite as he desperately sucked in lungfuls of air. It wouldn't last long, though. Isiliar was rushing, almost manically eager to finish him, trying to end the fight with every blow. If she had been her usual, methodical self, he would already have lost.

From the steely aspect that was creeping into her fury-filled gaze, he suspected that she knew the same thing.

He stumbled backward a little, wiping his forehead with a sleeve. The worst part—even through the pain and fear—was that he understood the raw rage in her eyes...and he couldn't blame her. Whenever he looked at her, he saw the broken reflection of the woman that he had trapped in the Tributary two thousand years ago. The friend whom he had betrayed, and so utterly destroyed in the process.

Isiliar lifted her blade once again, stepping forward.

"Isiliar. Please. Please...forgive me for what I did," he wheezed at her as he held his blade up to defend once again.

Isiliar froze.

"Forgive?" she breathed in disbelief, the word a curse on her lips. "*Forgive?* No. No." There was silence as she shook her head dazedly, and there were tears glistening in her eyes. "El take you, Tal'kamar. *This* is my forgiveness."

She stepped back, gesturing in the air, and Caeden suddenly knew what she was doing.

Feeling sick to his stomach, he reached deep past the pain one last time and grasped at kan.

Another complex structure. Another counteraction. He knew exactly what it would do this time, knew that he'd designed it precisely to fight Isiliar. This was her terrible weapon, the one that she didn't think anyone could beat.

They released their creations at the same time.

A wall of flame raced toward Caeden. Met his kan. Paused.

Reversed course.

Swept inward.

Consumed Isiliar in a torrent of fire and screaming and blood.

Caeden could feel tears in his eyes as he staggered over to her. Isiliar's skin was charred, blackened. She was sobbing through cracked lips, and her eyes rolled upward to meet his.

Caeden knelt down beside her.

"I am so sorry, Is," he said softly. Her eyes, for the first time, were not full of hate. Regret, perhaps. But no longer madness. "I wronged you, and..." He swallowed down the lump in his throat. "I wronged you."

Before she could regenerate, he gently drew Licanius across her throat.

He collapsed beside her body, everything a haze of pain and grief, for...a minute? Two? Thousands of years of life, and he had just snuffed it out. Tears flowed freely down his face as he looked at Isiliar. He knew, somewhere in the back of his mind, that the danger was far from over—but the emotional and physical toll was too great. Whatever Meldier had done to him seemed to be restricting his healing, slowing it. He could feel everything knitting back together but it was not going anywhere near fast enough.

Finally he dragged himself to his feet and tried to stumble forward, but it was too much. He was losing too much blood. His vision swam and he collapsed again, resting his hand against a nearby wall. He grasped for kan but Licanius, for some reason, didn't help this time. Behind him, he could hear something moving, someone groaning. Meldier.

He tried to turn, squinting in the garish orange light still hovering high above.

Dark energy crashed into the base of his skull, and he knew no more.

Chapter 47

Davian covered his mouth, restraining a cough as he tried not to breathe too deeply of the dank stench of the tunnel.

The smell had gotten steadily worse as they'd gone deeper, air ripe with a thick, unidentifiable sweetly sick tang that burned his lungs. Beside him, Fessi maintained her grip on his shoulder but was using her other hand to press a cloth against her mouth, looking ill.

They moved carefully forward, wary of every turn in the increasingly narrow passageway. This part of the tunnel system seemed natural rather than hewn; only the ground underfoot was smooth, scratched and worn from what appeared to be constant traversal. The only light came from the sliver of Essence that Davian maintained in front of them, a tiny ball that barely showed them what lay a few feet ahead.

Partly that was due to caution, but it was also because Davian had very little Essence to draw on. With no torches, no plants, no energy anywhere around—*and* kan being so difficult to grasp—it was, quite simply, the best that he could currently do.

After a few minutes of tense silence, a split in the tunnel revealed itself.

"Which way?" Fessi asked.

Davian closed his eyes. The Essence light vanished as he reached out with kan; the power was too difficult to handle here to do both at once. After a few moments he was able to make out Ishelle's Essence signature, pulsing faintly off to their left.

"Down here," he said grimly, gesturing to the entrance that led toward their friend.

They pressed on, barely breathing as they crept forward, only too aware that the dar'gaithin would be somewhere nearby, too. But there was no movement, nothing to give them cause for alarm. The bowels of Talan Gol were damp, hot, and silent.

After a few more minutes of walking, Davian finally let out a long breath as he spotted light up ahead.

He extinguished his ball of Essence and nodded toward the opening in the tunnel. The light was bright, even from this distance. "Another way outside?"

Fessi frowned, squinting and shaking her head. "We're too far underground," she said quietly. "That has to be Essence."

They crept forward until they reached the entrance, then both stopped in stunned silence.

In front of them was another huge cavern, completely bathed in a hot, hazy yellow glow.

And it was draped in lush green life.

Fessi let go of Davian's shoulder for a moment, and time crashed back into him as he stared. What appeared to be a permanent haze of rising steam hung over the thick, vibrant jungle that stretched away below them. Bright flowers poked out from among the willowy, waist-high grass and lofty trees, though these trees were unlike any Davian had ever seen. Broad leaves that looked to be at least a foot long glistened as they beaded with sweat. Thin, patterned trunks supported foliage that seemed too heavy for its wiry branches. Everything rustled and moved, though there was no breeze to speak of.

Davian quickly siphoned some of the life from the nearby foliage, replenishing his artificial Reserve. Beside him, Fessi caught her breath, then rested her hand on his shoulder again. Everything slowed.

Davian wiped a bead of sweat from his brow, noting that the damp heat in here was even more stifling than in the tunnels. He shook his head dazedly. This was in complete contrast to everything that he'd seen outside, everything he'd seen since entering Talan Gol.

"She's really somewhere in here?" murmured Fessi, dismayed.

Davian nodded, seeing immediately why she was concerned. The undergrowth was impossibly thick below, the only visible path through it looking narrow and winding. They wouldn't be able to see more than a few paces ahead once they climbed down amid the trees. Using kan would help, but it seemed that dar'gaithin couldn't be sensed that way. If there was trouble waiting for them, they may not know until it was far too late.

"How much longer can you keep us outside of time?" he asked quietly.

Fessi hesitated. "A few more minutes. Maybe."

Davian grimaced, but nodded. "Let me know if you need to rest."

They clambered down the short incline and into the jungle. Davian did his best to use kan to scout ahead, but it was all that he could do to keep a fix on Ishelle's position. They crept forward, doing their best to disturb as little of the foliage as possible as they moved.

After a while, Fessi cocked her head to the side.

"Do you hear that?"

Davian paused and then nodded, frowning. It was an odd buzzing noise, low and constant, nearly unnoticeable.

The two Augurs pressed on, the strange noise growing louder and louder as they drew closer to Ishelle's position.

"She's just up ahead," said Davian eventually, whispering despite there not being any evidence of anyone else around.

Suddenly the trees gave way to open space, and both Davian and Fessi stopped dead at the edge of an enormous clearing.

Though the sight had been hidden by the close-set trees, the air here was dark with flying bodies. Gray-yellow wings blurred as eletai hovered and darted everywhere in jerky, violently agitated movements. Davian flinched as a fight suddenly erupted in the air not far from them, eletai claws scratching and blades ejecting from bodies until one fell in a spray of viscera, quickly hidden by the long grass.

On the ground, moving with calm purpose, were several dar'gaithin. Davian shivered as he watched one slither to the spot in which the eletai's body had fallen, retrieving it and carrying it carefully over to a stone table a little distance away. Several more eletai were on other tables. Some were motionless, while others writhed weakly.

"There," said Davian suddenly, pointing.

Ishelle was crouched not too far away at the edge of one of the stone tables, out in the open, somehow thus far undetected by both the eletai and the dar'gaithin. She was gazing in silence at the scene, her eyes wide with horror.

Fessi and Davian moved around the edge of the clearing and then dashed toward her; despite everything outside of their bubble moving in slow motion, Davian couldn't help but flinch every time one of the eletai buzzed close, their protruding black blades flicking dark bile into the grass whenever they abruptly changed direction.

Fessi and Davian reached Ishelle, and Fessi placed her free hand on the Augur's arm. In a moment, Ishelle was moving at the same speed as them.

"Ishelle." Davian kept his voice low; even in the bubble, he had no idea how sharp these creatures' hearing was. "What in *fates*—"

"Wait. Just wait." Ishelle turned to Davian, but her gaze was distant. "Can't you *hear* them?"

Davian and Fessi exchanged a concerned glance. "Ishelle," said Fessi softly. "It's incredibly dangerous here. We need to get away."

Ishelle didn't respond.

Davian grimaced and then cautiously, tentatively reached out to her mind with kan. Under normal circumstances he would never think of doing so without her permission—but there was clearly something wrong, and they didn't have time to follow proprieties.

He almost flinched back from the contact straight away. Ishelle's mind was . . . scattered. Disordered, more chaotic than any other mind he'd ever touched before. It was as if she was connected to a thousand different voices, all communicating with her.

He took a deep breath. Concentrated.

How do we get across? It was Ishelle's voice, frustrated, yelling into the noise.

There were a hundred different answers at once.

You cannot.

The ilshara cannot be passed.

To try is death.

But as many whispered back a different response.

There are doors. Secrets and doors and tunnels and gates.

We can show you. We can take you.

Wait. Wait and it will be gone forever. Wait.

Telesthaesia. While it is this weak, Telesthaesia will work.

Then suddenly the sense that a thousand pairs of eyes were on him, and all spoke in unison.

One intrudes.

He gasped and broke the connection as Ishelle blinked, shaking her head as if coming out of a daze. She went pale as she looked around, then back at Davian and Fessi.

"How did we get here?" There was an edge of panic to her tone. "Davian, I *don't remember coming here.*"

"Stay calm." Davian didn't know how reassuring his tone was, given how nervous he was himself at that moment, but couldn't think of what else to say. He and Fessi both took an arm and began pulling Ishelle back into the forest. "Let's just get out of here, and we'll worry about…whatever this is later."

There was movement above them but Davian didn't pay it any attention; with the swarm of eletai everywhere, one was bound to eventually fly overhead.

Ishelle pushed him aside too late.

A gleaming, wetly black blade came slicing down, scoring along his shoulder and down his arm in a blazing, fiery trail of agony. Another blade caught Fessi across the back; she screamed as the time bubble collapsed and everything snapped into regular motion again. Davian stumbled to the side and against one of the viscera-covered stone tables, his hands suddenly covered in the gooey yellow liquid.

Immediately the thrum of eletai overhead increased a thousandfold, drumming violently into his head. He felt dizzy, and not just from the pain.

He forced himself to focus, snatching some Essence from the foliage nearby and using it to heal the wound before it could bleed too much. He did the same for Fessi, then helped her to her feet.

"Get us outside of time again," he said to her urgently.

Fessi closed her eyes, then went pale and shook her head in a panicked motion. Davian's heart dropped. Whether it was from fear or from some other problem, Fessi wasn't able to use her ability.

The buzzing sound suddenly intensified, and Davian looked up to see hundreds of eletai had ceased their irritated, jerky movements and were now drifting.

Coming toward them.

"You are not here."

The words came from behind Davian; he turned to see the eletai on the table—its organs still visible—had somehow woken and was staring right at him. There was horror in its eyes as well as its tone. "You are not here."

"You are not here." The words came from another eletai high above.

"You are not here. You are not here. *You are not here.*" The air was suddenly filled with the whisper, over and over and over again, stunned and fearful and angry. The eletai in the air burst into motion, flying upward in a cloud, away from Davian and the others. They hit the roof; Davian thought that he could see them clawing at it, as if desperate to escape.

Davian and Fessi didn't watch for long; the unsettling commotion had attracted the attention of several dar'gaithin, which were slithering their way rapidly toward them. Fessi grabbed one of Ishelle's hands and Davian took the other, together forcing her to move, retreating into the jungle once again as the strange refrain chased after them.

"You are not here," whispered Ishelle as they ran.

Davian restrained a shiver as he looked across at his friend. Ishelle's expression had been vacant again but she suddenly snapped back to alertness, looking a combination of terrified and determined, shaking off his hand and pouring speed into her step.

They reached the exit to the cavern unhindered; a quick glance behind them showed that even if the dar'gaithin had spotted them—and Davian wasn't sure how they could not have—then they weren't pursuing. The Augurs slowed as the twists and turns of the narrow tunnel meant possibly running into other oncoming enemies, and Davian eventually brought the other two to a halt, pulling them to an out-of-the-way corner and with some difficulty managing to form an invisibility mesh around them.

Fessi realized what he was doing and gave him a tired nod.

"What in fates is going on?" she whispered, the question directed as much at Davian as it was at Ishelle.

Davian just shook his head in bafflement, but Ishelle looked at the ground.

"I...I can feel them," she said softly. "The eletai. I can sense them. There's...something seriously wrong with me."

The other two were silent as they stared at her, trying to comprehend what that meant.

Eventually, Davian shook his head.

"We need to get you away from here. *Far* away from here," he said grimly.

"I agree, but...I don't see to where unless we can figure out a way back across the Boundary," said Fessi.

Ishelle shifted uncomfortably.

"There is a way." She hesitated. "The eletai told me."

Fessi gave her a skeptical look, but Davian nodded to her in confirmation.

"I heard it, too," he said quietly. "I don't know whether it can be trusted, and not all of them seemed to agree, but...she's right."

"Telesthaesia." Ishelle said the word quietly. "That was the way that they seemed most certain would work. That's how we can get back."

Davian and Ishelle exchanged glances. "What does that mean?"

"It's armor." Ishelle sighed. "Telesthaesia is what they call the Blind's armor."

⁂

It took them twenty minutes to creep their way back to the room near where they'd first entered the underground warren.

The armor, much to Davian's relief, was still there—though a laborious search of the room showed that it was the only set. Twice during their rummaging they'd had to conceal themselves as dar'gaithin slithered by, but none appeared to register that anything was amiss, and none entered.

After a while, Davian sighed and looked at the others ruefully.

"It looks like there's just the one." He rubbed his face tiredly. "One of us will have to wear it. Get across and see if the door's still there." He didn't really believe that it was, but it was important to stay positive.

"And if it's not?" asked Fessi quietly.

"Then we find some more of the Blind. We *take* their armor." Davian did his best to sound confident. "For now, one of us should wear it. It's easier than carrying it, and it's not particularly heavy."

"I'll wear it." Ishelle shrugged awkwardly. "We know it blocks kan, so maybe..."

Davian and Fessi both nodded, immediately understanding. If the armor blocked kan, it might just stop the eletai from communicating with her, too.

It didn't take long to equip the armor to Ishelle; it was quite light, and remarkably flexible despite the hardness of the scales. Davian shivered as Ishelle put the last piece on. If she added the sight-blocking helmet, she would be indistinguishable from the countless attackers that he'd fought atop the Shields at Fedris Idri.

"Are you going to be able to move?"

Ishelle tested her limbs gingerly, then nodded. "It might get a little warm once we're outside, but I'll manage."

They made their way once again along the passageway, Ishelle surprisingly quiet despite the armor. As they approached the dark upper cavern, though, a chill went through Davian.

There was an angry buzzing coming from up ahead.

He paled as they reached the entrance. Dark shadows flew everywhere in the dim light; what he'd initially mistaken for stalactites were gone, the eletai that had evidently been asleep now awake and just as active—as agitated—as those below.

"*You are not here,*" came a faint cry from above, repeated mournfully by others.

He glanced at the others.

"Fessi, are you able to..."

Fessi hesitated. "I...think so. Not for long, but I think so," she said weakly, her injury from the eletai attack evidently still affecting her.

She grabbed both his and Ishelle's arms; suddenly the whining hum faded and the jerky motions of the shadows overhead slowed.

"Let's go," she said with a tired nod.

Their journey through the cavern was a tense one; Davian flinched and ducked several times as creatures buzzed close, but none actually seemed to notice their passing. Ishelle, thankfully, remained lucid throughout.

They finally reached the far end of the cavern and broke into a slow jog, heading for the blindingly bright light of day up ahead.

When they reached the entrance, though, Davian's overwhelming sense of relief was short-lived.

"Fates," muttered Fessi in horror.

A short distance away, along the great flat valley, an army marched toward the Boundary.

Davian swallowed as he took in the sheer scale of the force from their slightly elevated position. There were *thousands* of them. Eletai darkened the sky to the west, but down on the ground were even more monsters—dar'gaithin and something else, distant, crawling on all fours in a scuttling, insectlike motion.

And among them strode people, soldiers wearing the Blind's armor. Telesthaesia.

Davian watched the soldiers for a long few moments, a sudden, faint flicker of hope breaking through the dismay. As bad as this situation was, at least they knew where they could find other sets of armor now. Other chances to get back.

"We need to warn everyone." Davian turned to see Fessi staring out over the mass. "This army won't reach the Boundary for another few hours; we can get there in two if I can get enough rest." She glanced at Ishelle. "One of us needs to get back across. To tell Asha that she needs to seal it *now.*"

Ishelle shook her head. "We need two more sets of armor first."

Davian's stomach churned as he thought it through.

"Fessi's right. We can't risk getting caught just to save ourselves—not when one of us can already make it back. The two of us who stay will just have to figure out something else," he said quietly. "If that army gets through, it won't much matter which side of the Boundary we're on."

There was silence as the two young women processed that thought.

Eventually, Ishelle nodded.

"Then let's get moving," she said heavily.

Chapter 48

Asha shivered as a frigid breeze gusted along the small plateau, transfixed by yet another fluctuation of the Boundary across the water far below.

Flashes of bright green and yellow burst deep underwater, small explosions that she knew were probably more of the tek'ryl that Scyner had told her about trying to get through. A heart-stopping moment of translucence allowed her to see beyond the shimmering curtain of energy, into Talan Gol itself, though it quickly faded to cold blue and white again. Not that there was much to see. A coastline comprised mostly of cliffs. Barren land. What looked like the ruins of a single structure, perhaps a lighthouse, though it was distant enough that she could barely make it out.

She shifted, trying to make herself more comfortable. She was perched on the top stair of the pavilion's opening, her back to the darkly glinting mass of steel that lay waiting in the shadows. Scyner had already shown her how to activate it, and she'd otherwise forced herself to examine it closely, to do her best to understand its function and prepare herself for what was to come.

It hadn't helped. The sight of it still only brought home just how little time she had left.

"We cannot afford this delay."

Asha glanced to her right, over at Scyner, who was pacing back and forth even as he warily watched the display below.

"As long as the Boundary is still holding, we're waiting until I hear from Erran," said Asha firmly, a phrase that she had repeated more than once over the past several hours.

Scyner sighed, still staring out over the water. "Your friend, the prince. He is part of the defenses, at least?"

Asha blinked, surprised by the shift in conversation.

"He is," she said slowly.

"Good." Scyner continued to gaze northward. "And he brought the Gifted with him?"

"There are *some* Gifted at the outposts," Asha said slowly. She hesitated. "Not enough, though."

Scyner scowled at that, and Asha watched him for a long few moments.

"You're Jakarris, aren't you?" she said quietly, statement more than question.

The Augur paused, for the first time since she had arrived looking taken aback.

"It's Scyner now. I left the name Jakarris behind long ago," he eventually said softly. To Asha's surprise, there was a note of regret in his voice.

"So you knew what Torin would be able to do with the Oathstone."

Scyner gave her a mildly irritated look. "Of course I did. Even if we prevent the Boundary from falling here, Andarra is eventually going to need someone to coordinate its defenses. Someone who doesn't have to worry about all the ridiculous politics that have plagued the Gifted since... well, since even before my time." He shook his head ruefully. "He needs to actually *use* his ability for it to be of any worth, though."

Asha frowned at him.

"When we met in the Sanctuary, and you sent me to find out what Elocien was doing..."

Scyner snorted. "I foresaw Elocien Andras's son using Essence more than twenty-five years ago, Ashalia. So yes. I already knew." He shrugged wearily at her expression. "Getting the Vessels was a priority, but so was finding out what the duke knew about his son's whereabouts. We were... concerned, when Prince Torin disappeared. To be honest, Ashalia, I understood the importance of his role far more than I did yours at that point. I wondered about you, of course—your surviving the attack at Caladel, and then Aelrith's decision not to kill you. But at the time, you were mostly a convenient means to an end."

Asha shook her head at that, not knowing what to say. Every time she learned something new about what was going on, it felt more and more like she was just a piece being shifted around a game board.

There was silence for a while after that. It was midday and while the sun beat down, the stiff and constant sea breeze more than removed any warmth that it held; Asha rubbed at her arms absently, lost in thought as she gazed out over the precipice at the curtain of energy.

Was Davian still trapped in there? She hated the indecision that that question pressed upon her. Deep down, she knew that Scyner was probably right: the sooner the Boundary was reinforced, the safer that everyone would be. But if she was going to sacrifice herself for the indefinite future—years, perhaps—then she couldn't do it without at least giving Davian a chance. She had to trust that Erran would let her know when things became too dire to hold off any longer.

And a part of her—a very small part—still hoped for a way out, too. That they would find another way.

She stared down at the waves, the troughs seeming darker as the wind at ground level evidently started to pick up.

Then her brow furrowed and she leaned forward, focusing.

"Scyner," she said quietly, tone urgent.

Scyner glanced at her, then walked over and followed her gaze down to the water below. After a few moments, he grunted.

"Wait here," he muttered. "If they look like they're going to break through, you use that fates-cursed machine—no matter what. They won't be able to stop it once it's activated."

He vanished.

Asha watched worriedly as more dark shapes joined the ones that she'd spotted in the water, visible almost as far out as the Boundary, arrowing with alarming speed toward the beach. They looked small enough, but she knew that was only due to the distance. For her to be able to see the creatures from here—and underwater, at that—then they had to be big. Bigger than a full-grown man, at least.

From her vantage point she could see the beach where she and Erran had arrived, the bridge no longer there but the pillars that marked its beginning still visible. Her heart lurched as glistening monsters started slithering out of the water and onto the golden sand, moving quickly toward the trees.

Closer by, several Shadows were running through the black-scarred area that she and Erran had traversed last night and moving into the forest, while others hurried to take up defensive positions among the buildings nearer to the base of the cliff. She spotted Scyner striding around, pointing urgently, directing the Shadows to various points that were clearly intended to defend the path up the cliff. Everyone moved with alacrity and purpose and though it was impossible to tell for sure from this distance, there didn't appear to be any panic in the Shadows' ranks.

She flinched as the far edges of the forest suddenly sprouted gouts of flame outward onto the beach and into the oncoming mass of dark, crawling shapes, the sound of explosions reaching her ears a moment later. The Shadows controlling the fire-throwing Vessels didn't need to aim; they clearly had enough to cover a wide swathe of land.

Still, even as distant, high-pitched shrieks filled her ears and some of the black shapes stilled, others were making it through to the tree line.

One by one, the gouts of fire faded.

Asha watched in horror as more and more of the creatures slithered up from the water, moving at an uncomfortably quick pace over the open ground and vanishing into the trees. There were bursts of light from within the greenery and many of the trees began to burn, but after a while some of the Shadows—far fewer than had initially run into the forest—stumbled out toward the village, waving their hands desperately at their comrades.

"You need to do it now."

Asha started at the gasping voice behind her. She turned to see Scyner, the left arm of his shirt gone, blackened edges indicating that it had burned off. His hands were on his knees as he tried to catch his breath.

"They need help." Asha didn't take her eyes from the scene below. "They'll die."

"Then they'll die." Scyner looked her in the eye. "The vast majority of your power comes from the Lyth now. Once you're in the Tributary and its defenses activate, it won't matter what happens to them. I'm sorry, but there's just *no time*."

Asha watched the chaos below, heart pounding. She didn't need to trust Scyner to know that he was right. The defense of the Shadows was turning to panic as they began to realize that they were about to be overrun.

She stood and twisted, looking into the murk of the pavilion at the glinting steel of the Tributary. Felt cautiously at the power flooding through her veins, begging to be released.

Then she scowled, turning back and nodding toward the village. "I'm going down there."

"No."

Scyner's expression told Asha all that she needed to know. His patience had run out.

Asha closed her eyes, focused on Scyner's pool of Essence, and drained him just as the man vanished.

A moment later the Augur appeared again halfway toward her, eyes wide and skin pale as he collapsed to the ground, a look of utter shock on his face.

"Forgot that I could do that, didn't you," murmured Asha coldly, stepping over his prostrate form as he slipped into unconsciousness. She'd made certain earlier to check that Scyner was truly a Shadow, and with the two of them the only ones on the plateau, it had been easy enough to isolate his Essence. Asha knew that he wouldn't be out for long—she'd been careful not to take too much from him—but it would be enough.

She hurried to the top of the path down the cliff, flinching at every new explosion, the sounds of screaming and panicked yells becoming more and more audible. There were still sporadic bursts of fire and energy directed into the forest, but they were becoming less frequent, and she could sense that the Reserves of the Shadows around her were running low. Even going downhill, there was no way that she could reach the base of the mountain in time to help.

"Time to see how strong I really am," she muttered to herself.

She tapped Essence.

The torrent of energy suddenly at her command was almost too much; she flailed for a second and then funnelled some—a tiny drop of her Reserve—into her body. Strengthened her arms. Legs. Torso.

Everything.

She leaped.

She shrieked with a mixture of alarm and delight as the jump took her much, much higher and farther than she'd anticipated; after several terrifying, exhilarating seconds she finally landed—thankfully back on the steps—accompanied by the sharp shattering of stone beneath her feet.

She paused for a moment, breathing hard, though more from thrill than effort. There had been a slight jarring sensation, but the impact hadn't otherwise hurt, almost making her wonder whether the three-foot-wide crater in which she now stood had already been there.

She glanced over her shoulder, wide-eyed.

She'd covered half the distance down in a single jump.

The excitement that Asha felt quickly faded as more yells from below reached her ears, and she saw that the tek'ryl were at the edge of the forest now, close to overwhelming the Shadows. She picked an empty point in the middle of the village and leaped again, hurtling to the ground in a dizzying streak of speed and bright-white light.

Staggering only a little on impact, she hurried toward the forest, soon coming up behind the terrified-looking Shadows. Shana, she quickly spotted, was amongst them; despite the determined look in her eyes, the woman's entire left arm was blistered and red.

Asha grabbed her good arm, commanding her attention. "Is there anyone left out there?"

Shana's eyes widened as she registered who was talking to her. "What in fates are you doing down here?" she said between gritted teeth. "You need to get back up there!"

"Is there anyone else in the forest?" Asha repeated calmly.

Shana hesitated. "There might be." Her voice was thick with worry and pain.

Asha gave a single nod of acknowledgment, then strengthened her body with Essence again and *pushed* herself forward.

The village blurred away as she covered the ground between it and the edge of the forest in a single leap, skidding to a halt as she approached the first of the close-set trees and leaving a long furrow in the dirt as she did so. Fires starkly lit some sections here, while the rest remained gloomily shaded by both smoke and the thick leafy canopy overhead. Shadows twisted and flinched everywhere, and in the distance, she could hear a chorus of desperate shouts.

She was about to leap in the direction of the noise when an alien, chittering sound to her left made her spin.

Her heart lurched.

The tek'ryl was *enormous*, much bigger than anything she had envisaged. Its glistening black scales still dripped with sea water as it stared at her with dead, entirely red eyes, elongated pincers bigger than broadswords snapping menacingly either side of its unsettling gaze. It was only ten feet away; a barbed tail was suddenly curled over its head, poised and quivering, ready to strike.

It rushed forward at her, all muscle and scales and horror.

Asha flicked Essence at it.

There was a blinding burst of light; much of the energy was absorbed by the tek'ryl's armor but the rest caught the small, unprotected areas of its body with full force. The creature *launched* into the air, smashing clean through tree trunks as it spun and flailed helplessly, reaching as high as the treetops before crashing back down a good fifty feet away into the middle of one of the dying fires, motionless once it came to an ungainly halt. Even through the debris, Asha could see that its legs were mangled, its head entirely caved in from multiple violent impacts.

She stood stock-still for a moment, shocked, staring with a combination of astonishment and relief.

"All right," she muttered to herself, a little dazedly.

Another pleading shout reached her ears, and she pushed herself into action again.

The next few minutes passed in a blur of motion as she sped among the trees with increasing assurance, hurling tek'ryl away from Shadows as they desperately retreated, healing those who had been injured and ushering everyone that she could find back toward the relative safety of the village. Despite the danger, she couldn't help but feel a thrill, an exhilaration as she dashed through the wild, burning chaos of the forest. The tek'ryl were nothing to be feared—not for her. Today, she was a fury of light and power and speed.

Today, she was unstoppable.

Finally, though, there were no more shouts, no more panicked calls for help. Asha tossed aside a few more tek'ryl—they seemed to keep on coming, no matter how many she dispatched—and pushed herself forward once again, motions more confident now as she leaped her way back to the village.

The surviving Shadows had gathered in a crowd, murmuring among themselves. Silence quickly fell and they watched on with wide eyes as Asha skidded to a halt in front of them.

"Is everyone safe?" Asha asked Shana, a little breathlessly.

Shana just nodded, staring at Asha. "Anyone still out there is dead," she said softly. "But most made it back. Thanks to you."

Asha inclined her head and opened her mouth to respond, but suddenly more flashes of fire erupted from the front line of the buildings. She turned, grimacing at the sight of a new wave of tek'ryl scuttling out from the trees.

A low moan passed through the assembled Shadows. For each tek'ryl burned by the defenses, two more now took its place.

"We can't stop them," said Shana, the horror and despair in her tone echoed in the frightened murmurings of the others.

Asha ignored the statement and stepped forward, motioning for the defending Shadows to stand down as she moved in front of them. Still more tek'ryl were breaking from the forest, a sea of the unsettling scorpion-like monsters scuttling with chilling speed toward her and the Shadows.

Taking a deep breath, Asha once again tapped the immense power within her. Focused it, this time.

Pushed it outward all at once.

A blinding white blast of energy erupted from her hands, expanding into a massive wave of power that swept inexorably forward.

Everything it touched simply...*disintegrated*. Trees were reduced to ash that whipped around on the thunderous gust of wind that accompanied the wave; rocks liquefied to glowing red and sand turned to glass.

There were no audible shrieks, no evidence that the monsters had been caught in the blast. But when the air cleared, only a mile of flat, molten rock and ash lay between them and the now-bubbling, frothing ocean.

Then there was silence. No more screams of panic from the Shadows. No more shouts of command from anyone.

Asha turned to see that everyone behind her had stopped.

They were all just watching her, wide-eyed.

Asha felt a chill as she turned back to look at her handiwork. The ocean in the distance bubbled and steamed, and now several badly disfigured black bodies began floating to the surface, along with countless fish and other sea life. Boiled alive. It was more devastating than anything she'd seen before, more devastating than all the power of all of the Shadows that had been unleashed at the Shields two months ago.

But this still hadn't drained her.

This hadn't been an *iota* of her power.

She turned to Shana, who cringed beneath her gaze. The other woman didn't look *afraid*, exactly. More...intimidated. Still, Asha flushed a little at her reaction.

"I'm going back up there now. I'll use the Tributary," she said grimly. "But you don't need to stay here once I do. It has its own defenses."

Shana hesitated, then shook her head.

"I'll ask the others," she said quietly. "But this is still more than we have elsewhere. We have a purpose, here. A home."

Asha grimaced, but inclined her head. She didn't have the time or desire to argue.

She ignored the lingering, awed stares of the Shadows and made her way slowly back up the cliff, just walking this time, the hundreds of eyes on her back like a physical weight as she made the long climb. Finally reaching the top, she moved past Scyner's still-prostrate form, every muscle tensing as she stepped into the darkness of the pavilion.

She swallowed as she approached the Tributary, eyes slowly

adjusting to the dim light. It looked more menacing than ever, angular steel and black polished surfaces everywhere. Inside, she could see the tiny holes where she knew the needles would emerge, piercing her skin and forcing her body to draw on Essence to heal.

Slowly, reluctantly, she stepped inside. Turned to face the pavilion entrance.

Asha.

Asha flinched, then held her breath.

Erran? The voice in her head had been faint, but she recognized it.

I've made contact. They're in Talan Gol like we thought, but they're on their way back. They think that as long as the Boundary is still weak, they might be able to get through. A pause. *But...they're only just ahead of a massive army, apparently. So you need to get ready. Sorry.*

Asha took a deep breath. Not good news, exactly—but Davian was alive. That was more than just something.

Tell me when.

I'll do better than that. I can bring Davian into the conversation. Another pause. *In fact, I think...I think I can show you exactly what's happening here. Wait a moment.*

There was nothing for several seconds, and then Asha gasped.

A heartbeat ago she'd been staring grimly outward from the Tributary.

Now...now she was at the Boundary.

It was the strangest sensation: she could still move her limbs but they had no effect on what she was seeing. She had no ability to direct her vision. But she was *there*, standing exactly where Erran stood, watching as the clearly weakening wall of energy shimmered and faded and flexed.

And beyond, through the increasingly translucent curtain, she could see three distant figures hurrying toward her.

Ash? Davian's voice was thick with tension. *Are you all right?*

Dav! I can see you! Asha almost laughed with relief. *I'm probably safer than you right now.*

Probably. A pause. *We have a set of Blind armor and...and we* think *that it will let us pass through the Boundary without getting hurt. At least, as long as it's still weak.*

Asha's smile faded and her heart all but stopped as she processed the words.

One set? she repeated.

Yes. Davian's tone was heavy. *And not much time to use it.*

Asha—or rather, Erran—squinted. Behind the three figures approaching the Boundary, there was something else. A dark line that she'd initially taken to be just the horizon.

But it was getting bigger.

You're not going to be the one crossing, are you, said Asha softly. She knew that it was true even as she said it—knew it from Davian's tone, knew it from knowing him. If there had been two sets of armor, he'd have been the one demanding to stay behind.

He was an idiot like that.

Ishelle's already wearing it. She has some sort of connection to the eletai. If they get across, she might be useful to you. If she stays here . . . He trailed off, but his voice indicated that he didn't want to think about the consequences.

Asha felt desperation rising in her chest. If she was going to do this—if she was really going to sacrifice herself to this purpose—then she at least wanted to know that Davian was safe. *But—*

This is the way it has to be. Not a decision we reached lightly. He hesitated. *There are more Blind coming. Maybe we can ambush a couple, get their armor before too many get through.*

Asha swallowed. *Of course.*

He was lying. She knew it, could tell from his tone. He'd always been a terrible liar.

She didn't say anything.

There was an interminably long silence, the vague outlines of Davian, Fessi, and Ishelle moving urgently as the darkness behind them grew steadily larger.

Finally, abruptly, an armor-clad form appeared, emerging from the wash of energy, sparks of blue and white flying off the black plates as the figure collapsed on the Andarran side with a cry.

Erran ran to help them up—Asha moving involuntarily with him—and removed their helmet.

Ishelle's forehead had blistered and her skin was red from burns, but she was awake. Breathing.

Asha's heart sank. Despite what Davian had just said, there had been the briefest moment when she'd thought that it might have been him. That the other two might have somehow convinced him that he was more vital than they.

Is she all right? It was Fessi, voice shaking.

She's fine, Fess. A little...singed, but fine, said Erran. *Now we need to—*

Ash. They're too close, and there's too many of them. Davian's voice cut through whatever he was trying to say. *You need to do it now.*

What? No. We can still find a way. It was Fessi, her voice panicked.

There's still time, agreed Ishelle, clearly conscious enough to participate in the conversation.

Davian—his features visible now as the Boundary faded even further—stared across at Erran and Ishelle, but Asha could tell that he was talking to her.

There isn't. His voice was quiet, calm. Certain.

Asha felt tears forming in her eyes. *We'll see each other again.*

Wait! Fessi and Ishelle spoke in chorus, fear in their tones.

Asha kept her eyes locked on Davian. He slowly nodded, then raised his hand in farewell, not looking behind him at the charging mass that was close enough now to make out individual figures.

She reached out blindly, felt around until she found the point that Scyner had indicated to her earlier.

Placed her hand on it.

The needles were not as painful as she'd expected as they slid gently into her body; there was a strange, surreal sense of removal as Essence burst forth from her, trying to repair the damage even as it was being caused. She sighed as—still looking through Erran's eyes—she saw power flicker and then spring to life, thickening, slowly obscuring Davian and Fessi until they were just silhouettes.

The approaching mass flooded over them, around them, concealing them from view.

The Boundary screamed and shivered as bodies crashed into it in explosions of dazzling light, then thickened to an unbroken
curtain of blue and white.

Whole once more.

Erran's vision was suddenly gone, replaced by the seal of the Tributary forming around her, leaving only a small window through which she could see the pavilion entrance. Across the water, the Boundary gleamed in the dusk. Strong. Solid.

Unbreakable.

Asha drank in the sight as everything became hazy. She held back tears as the pain suddenly intensified, gritting her teeth and embracing it as best she could.

The darkening blue sky outside slid away as a something solid and heavy started grinding its way across the entrance to the pavilion. Within moments it had finished with a booming echo, sealing her in. Only the eerie blue light of the Tributary remained.

And then that faded, too.

Chapter 49

The outpost was eerily silent as Wirr slowly made his way between bodies, numb as he checked the next for any sign of life.

There was none, just as he'd assumed. The deathly stillness, the scarred stone and splashes of red, all spoke of nothing but death for anyone who hadn't been able to take refuge below.

For anyone except him, Karaliene, and his mother.

Still, he moved to the next motionless form, knelt beside them and gently checked for a heartbeat. He had to try. As little choice as there had been, and as hard as they'd fought, part of him couldn't help but feel the weight of these men's and women's deaths.

Had some of them still been alive as he and the other two had cowered below? Could some have been saved if they had acted differently, stayed up here a little longer?

He straightened again as he registered the pair of open, sightless eyes gazing in horror, then glanced out the smashed northern entrance, reassuring himself once again that nothing had changed. The Boundary still pulsed in a single, comfortingly solid curtain of blue and white.

They were far from safe, but this wasn't the end. Not yet.

He swallowed as he gazed at the wall of energy, remembering again how it had been restored. Even in that success, he had mixed emotions.

"Torin."

Wirr looked around, grimacing as he saw his mother watching him uneasily. He knew that it wasn't just their surroundings, now, not entirely—and he wasn't sure that he could blame her. She knew that he could utter a command, and she would be forced to obey. That wasn't something that anyone could simply ignore.

"What is it?"

"We need to leave." Geladra's eyes were tired. "We need to get back to Ilin Illan. To warn them."

Wirr bowed his head for a moment, biting back the cynical, frustrated urge to ask whether she was satisfied that the threat was real now. The carnage around them was reproof enough.

"I know." He gazed across the courtyard. There were corpses everywhere but it was worst at the southern gate; the entrance was all but clogged with bodies, evidence of how many men and women had broken, desperately tried to flee the rain of death. "A few more minutes. I just want to be sure."

Geladra sighed, but inclined her head. She glanced over toward Karaliene, on the opposite side of the courtyard, bent over yet another motionless form as she checked for life. "A few minutes. No more," she said softly. "We need to get you both as far from here as possible. Now that the Augur's gone, we have no way of escaping if those creatures come back."

Wirr acknowledged the statement with a brief nod, stomach lurching again as he considered the possibility. He didn't think that the dar'gaithin or eletai would return—they had no reason to—but he barely had any Essence left in his Reserve as it was. If any did come back, or if he and the others encountered some on the road before he'd had a chance to recover his strength, then they would be all but helpless.

How many had made it through before the Boundary had been restored? Two thousand? Three? And perhaps half as many eletai? He felt a violent chill at the thought. Even if the creatures scattered, there were enough of them to cause terror and panic on an unprecedented scale for years to come.

And too many in one place—if they had any semblance of cohesion or organization—then they would be able to tear any one of Andarra's cities to the ground.

He closed his eyes for a moment, steadying himself against the horror of the thought. The Boundary was sealed, but they hadn't won a victory here today. Not even close.

694 "What are you going to tell Administration?" he asked eventually.

Geladra hesitated.

"I will convince them of the threat." His mother looked him in the eye. "But that's not what you're asking, is it?"

Wirr said nothing.

Geladra sighed again. "I don't know. I need time to think about it. But whatever this power that you have is...it's wrong, Torin."

Wirr's heart sank. "I haven't used it," he assured her firmly. "I could have commanded everyone to vote for me, but I didn't. I did the right thing. I've done the right thing ever since I learned of it."

"You have," conceded Geladra slowly, to Wirr's surprise a note of pride in her tone. "But can you guarantee that you'll continue to do so? When it came down to it, you forced me to try and leave. I know why you did it, but it nearly killed me."

Wirr rubbed his forehead wearily. "So you don't trust me with it?"

"I didn't say that," said Geladra quietly. She waved her hand around at the destruction of the outpost. "You have made your case, Torin—this is a danger beyond anything that I had imagined, and these monsters are..." She shuddered. "I...I've been wrong. About you. I still don't agree with a lot of the things that you've done, but this is real, and that at least deserves a conversation." She said the words slowly, and Wirr could tell that the admission came hard for her.

He considered her for a moment and then inclined his head, breathing out. It was a start.

His mother sighed. "It *doesn't* mean, however, that I should just ignore what you can do. Because there will always be arguments which you have no other way of winning. And one day, there might just be a cause that will tempt you too much." She saw his expression and shook her head in frustration. "I'm not trying to make a comment on your character, Son. I'm making a comment on *people*. I don't know a soul alive who could resist using that sort of power forever."

Wirr looked away. He hated to concede the point, but he knew that there was at least some truth to what she was saying.

"This is something that we should probably talk about later," he eventually said softly. "I'll go and tell Kara that we're leaving."

His mother nodded, looking vaguely relieved; Wirr wandered across the courtyard, stepping carefully to avoid treading on 695 splayed limbs or pools of sticky red. Karaliene's expression was somber, distant, as she gently closed the eyes of another corpse, then carefully doused it with liquid from a decanter.

Wirr frowned as he watched her; she'd already done the same with several other bodies in the courtyard, as evidenced by empty flasks set over to the side. "What are you doing?" he asked.

Karaliene turned in surprise, evidently not having heard him approach.

She hesitated.

"We can't leave them like this," she said eventually. "I know we have to go, but...if we can't bury them, then we can at least make sure that they're not left for the animals. We can give them some dignity in death."

Wirr grimaced as he understood. "A pyre?"

"Something like that." Karaliene's gaze pleaded with him. "There are only a few inside. If we put them all out here together in the middle of the courtyard, it won't damage the outpost."

"Not that it was much use to begin with," observed Wirr heavily. He sighed, but nodded; the outpost hadn't exactly been heavily manned, so it was not going to be an enormous undertaking. "All right. But let's be quick."

It was grisly work, and his mother was far from pleased by the delay, but with all of them pitching in it didn't take long. When the last of the bodies had finally been dragged from inside, Karaliene quickly began emptying the remainder of the decanters, evidently wanting to be done here just as much as Wirr.

He wrinkled his nose as he leaned against the southern wall; the midday sun was already going to work on the corpses, the smell permeating through the sharp tang of alcohol. He gazed at the sight, despite part of him wanting nothing more than to close his eyes and block it out. Black spears jutted everywhere from the corpses, though there seemed to be less of the glistening barbs than there had been initially. He and the other two had been cautious not to touch them. There was no telling what poisonous qualities the black slime on them held.

"I think that's all," he said to his mother, who was facing him, her back turned to the gruesome sight. "We're going to have to travel cautiously. We have no idea what these creatures will do now that they're free to roam. They may keep heading south, but they may equally settle nearby and start preying on anyone and anything that comes by. We should..."

He trailed off with a frown.

Just behind his mother the pile of corpses shifted again, definitely not his imagination. Karaliene was at the opposite side of the courtyard, pouring out the last of the alcohol.

"Kara? Are you seeing—"

It all happened in a moment. A man emerged from underneath two other bodies, and Wirr's eyes widened as he looked at what he first thought was a survivor that they'd somehow missed.

He took in the black eyes, the strange, jerky movement and the protruding lumps beneath his shirt far too late.

The man—if that was what he even was now—extended his hand toward Geladra.

A dripping black blade ripped from his wrist, slicing out through skin in a spray of blood and then plunging clean through Geladra's back until it extended out of her chest. Geladra barely made a sound as she collapsed.

Wirr stood frozen as the attacker turned to him, but from behind, Karaliene was quicker. She had already lit one of the torches on the wall in preparation; she snatched it from its socket and hurled it at the man, who still dripped with the alcohol that he'd been doused with earlier.

The man exploded into flame.

Wirr grabbed his mother's prone form by the arm and dragged her toward the exit, quickly helped by Karaliene as the half-human creature screamed and flailed, stumbling back into other bodies which then also began to catch. The mound of corpses began to writhe and Wirr felt bile rise in his throat, quickly forcing it down again and concentrating on getting his mother clear.

Once they were far enough from the gate, Wirr dropped to his knees, carefully laying his mother's body on the ground. He knew before he checked what he would find, though.

The blade had pierced her heart. Geladra's eyes were open and sightless, and she was not breathing.

Wirr choked back a sob, pouring the last of his Essence into her, searching for any sign of life.

Nothing happened.

He sat like that for a minute. Two. Longer; he wasn't sure how much time had passed when a hand on his shoulder finally startled him from his grief.

"I'm sorry, Tor, but we...we need to burn her, too," said Karaliene softly. "We can't let her come back as one of those... *things*."

Wirr nodded in tired, grief-stricken acknowledgment. He didn't understand how, but it was clear now that those black blades were more than mere weapons.

Slowly he dragged himself to his feet, then picked up Geladra's body. It felt lighter than it had before.

He grimaced at the intense heat emanating from the courtyard, holding his breath and pressing forward until he was right at the limit of the temperature that he could withstand. As gently as he could, he laid his mother's body so that it stretched across an already-burning corpse, watching for a few moments to ensure that it caught.

Then he retreated, dazed and numb, to stand beside his cousin. They watched as the flames rose higher, visible over the top of the walls now.

Karaliene began to sing.

Wirr didn't know the song and barely took in the words but it was a shimmering, haunting dirge. When she was done, there was silence for several seconds.

"Thank you," said Wirr eventually. "That was beautiful."

Karaliene nodded absently.

"One of my favorite songs," she said softly. "I just wish that there were happier times to sing it." She laid a hand gently on his shoulder. "We're going to figure out how to stop them, Tor."

"I know." Wirr swallowed a lump in his throat as he watched the flames. "I know."

After a few more moments they turned in unspoken agreement, starting slowly down the southern road, leaving the distant pulsing blue-white light and the closer, crackling red of the blazing pyre behind them.

Epilogue

Despite the waning of the weakly refracted sun, Davian sweated as he trudged across yet another desolate, endless plain.

He gave a tired glance to his left. Fessi looked as exhausted as he felt, dust mixed with sweat streaked across her face from where she'd been wiping it, unable to hide the dark circles under her eyes and a hollow, vacant stare as she shambled along. Davian knew that she was forcing one foot in front of the other, ignoring the blisters, pressing down the surreal moment-to-moment panic of what they were going through. He'd been doing exactly the same for the past six days.

He grimaced as he stumbled on a protruding rock and the black-armored soldier behind him clamped his shoulder, preventing him from falling. He suspected that it was from a desire for speed, not any sense of compassion. The three Blind who had been tasked with taking them on this journey had not abused them, exactly, but nor had they cared for their injuries or listened to their pleas to slow down.

"Not far now, Runner," a low voice said in his ear. Davian turned to look at the helmetless man. A long, ugly scar traced its way from lip to at least his ear, possibly running farther but disappearing under a mane of long red hair. His expression was... if not sympathetic, then at least understanding. "Then you'll get some time to rest before the Arena."

Davian just nodded, unsure to what the soldier was referring, but unwilling to show as much. They all called him and Fessi "Runners"; the Augurs were clearly prisoners, but beyond that their captors appeared to have no idea that they had come from the other side of the Boundary. There had been no reason to think anything of the sort, he supposed; there was no evidence that they were capable of crossing, and nothing about their appearance was drastically different to any of the other people accompanying the would-be invasion force. Even the language here—slight accent aside—was the same.

He took a deep breath and pushed forward once more, reminding himself again that their current position was still better than what he had been expecting. When the Boundary had flared back to life and Andarra had vanished from view, his sense of kan had dropped away to almost nothing, and he'd been certain that he and Fessi were dead.

Then the dar'gaithin had streamed past. Ignored them, started throwing themselves at the Boundary instead, bursting into smoke and light the moment that they made contact. The two Augurs had stood stock-still, holding their breaths as hordes of the monsters had rushed by.

It hadn't taken the Blind soldiers following long to spot them, though. And without meaningful access to kan, there had been little that they could do to resist capture.

He glanced across at Fessi again, wincing as she turned, displaying the new scars on the side of her neck. Those had been carved there by one of the soldiers. The same had been done to him; he could still feel the combination of burning pain and irritation on the right-hand side of his neck. Fessi's was a mass of partially-dried blood, and he assumed that his was the same, but they had clearly been marked with a specific symbol. He still hadn't been able to tell what it was, though.

How are you holding up? It was difficult to make the mental connection here in Talan Gol, even right next to each other, now that the Boundary was at full strength. It *was* possible, though. They had been severely beaten when they had first started trying to converse normally; after that, the extra expenditure in concentration seemed well worth it.

Silence for a few moments, then, *Tired. Sore. But my connection to kan is slowly improving. A few more days, and I think I might be able to do something useful with it.* Fessi's expression didn't change at all and she didn't look in Davian's direction, but she sounded happy to be talking.

He could understand that. The long days of silence left only time for thinking about their situation. About what was surely coming once they reached their destination, wherever that might be.

Good. Same here, I think. They'd agreed not to attempt escape unless it was either absolutely necessary, or they had a good chance of succeeding. These men didn't know that he and Fessi were Augurs, and in fact appeared to think that they were relatively harmless. They weren't bound, weren't being especially mistreated. A failed escape, however—an indication that they were something out of the ordinary—could very quickly change all of that.

He was about to say more when they suddenly crested a rise in the terrain, and Davian nearly stumbled again. This time, it was from surprise.

A hundred feet from where he stood, the desert abruptly ended—and rather than more of the same dry, cracked brown ground stretching out for miles, the land ahead was *green*. Not just with a little grass, either. The road ahead ran through neatly cultivated fields, which eventually gave way to forest in the distance. In the reedy afternoon light, Davian could tell that the vegetation was thick and lush, the crops well tended.

The redheaded soldier gave him a gentle shove, pushing him forward once more. "Told you we were almost there," he said. "Don't try anything."

Davian licked his lips and nodded, suddenly uncertain. So much of Talan Gol was the same, it had made the past week feel like a single moment that would last forever.

This was a stark reminder that their journey had an end.

They walked on for several hours, until long after the sun had died once again below the horizon. All three soldiers carried torches for evening travel; though there were no clouds, the constant filtering haze overhead meant that the silvery moon rarely provided enough light to see by, and starlight was all but nonexistent here. The landscape passed by in shifting black shapes, more mysterious and unsettling now that they were no longer traversing open terrain.

Despite yet another long, hard day, Davian found himself feeling physically better than he had in some time. The change in their surrounds had provided him with at least one positive—he no longer needed to take any Essence from Fessi. He'd hated having to do that, even with her permission, even in the tiny amounts needed to supplement what he'd managed to siphon from torches and campfires during the evenings. However, up until now their captors' constant wearing of Telesthaesia, combined with the utter lack of any other life during their journey through the wastelands, had left him with little choice.

Just when Davian thought that it must be time to stop for the evening, he saw the torches dotting the wall in the distance.

He swallowed as they drew closer, the scope of the city before him—it was clearly a city; no walls were built so high or so wide to accommodate less—intimidating. It was difficult to tell in the dim light but he thought that the stone here was all black, rough-hewn and jagged but also solid, well maintained. Shadows moved atop the hundred-foot-tall walls, which were periodically lit by flames that looked more like bonfires than torches; beyond, in the distance, he could see specks of light moving where the city climbed toward the peak of the sharp slope on which it was built.

"How does it feel to be back, Runners?" sneered the soldier walking behind Fessi, evidently mistaking the astonishment on their faces for fear. He was an older man with graying hair and a thick beard, and had been by far the most unpleasant of their three captors.

Neither Davian nor Fessi responded.

As they made their way to the looming gate at the end of the road, Davian cast a quick sideways glance at Fessi. The other Augur had kept her composure well since the moment they'd been captured, but now...something was off. It was obvious in the hesitant way in which she was walking, the vaguely concerned look on her face as she studied the walls in front of them.

What's wrong?

It's probably nothing. Fessi didn't stop studying the city ahead, though.

There were two men at the gate, though neither wore armor nor any discernible uniform. They were waved through, Davian and Fessi receiving glares from the strangers but nothing more.

The way ahead was well lit given the hour. The streets were bright with torches, revealing black stone everywhere; even the roads were a basalt-like rock, worn smooth from traffic. It was easy to spot a distinctive architectural style to the city: everything had sharp edges, jutted, the shadows emphasizing the jaggedness of their surroundings.

The few people still walking the street at this hour appeared perfectly normal, though. A couple of men swayed slightly, evidently intoxicated, while a woman glanced in their direction but promptly hurried the opposite way. There was what sounded like a strange, rhythmic music emanating from one of the buildings along with the low murmur of voices, but otherwise everything was quiet.

Davian looked up. Looming over them at the city's peak was an enormous black palace, visible only thanks to its outline against the hazy moon and the array of torches along its walls. More torches lit the way up a steep cliff to its gate: a single staircase that looked uncomfortably narrow, given how it stretched at least a hundred feet into the air.

They pressed on for a while. Davian did his best to take note of landmarks along the way—the giant bell tower with the strange inscription written down its western side; the field of stone swords surrounded by flowers; the odd, man-size sphere in the middle of an empty square with pulsing lines of blue Essence running jaggedly across its surface—and tried to fix their positions in his mind relative to each other and the omnipresent, looming palace atop the cliff. He didn't know if they would get a chance to escape, but he wanted to be able to find his way back if the opportunity arose.

He glanced across at Fessi again after a while, noting with concern the growing unease in her expression. He'd tried a couple of times since entering the city to communicate with her, but whether because of how difficult kan was to use here, or because Fessi was too distracted, the other Augur hadn't responded.

"We're here," announced the gray-haired man suddenly.

Davian stuttered to a halt, swallowing as he studied the structure in front of which they had stopped. It was an enormous, windowless tower, its stone facade bleak and dark, the only entrance a narrow passageway lit by flickering torches. Men in the black armor of the Blind—though, again, not wearing the vision-covering helmets—were positioned at regular intervals around its perimeter, most of them staring at Davian and Fessi suspiciously.

It wasn't hard to guess the building's purpose.

Fessi. Davian focused as hard as he could now, trying to get a response from the girl. *Do we want to try and get away before they lock us up?*

There was no response for a few seconds, then, *I don't think I have enough control yet.*

All right. Davian licked his lips nervously as they were shoved toward the entrance, then ushered through the tight passageway until they emerged into a long room with a solid-looking iron gate at the other end.

A handsome black-haired young man with pale skin rose from behind a desk as they entered, studying Davian and Fessi critically.

"Runners?" he asked, tone slightly weary, as if the concept were something of a boring one.

"Evening, Keeper. Caught them near the ilshara, of all places," said the gray-haired man.

The man—the "Keeper"—grunted, looking mildly more interested. "Further than most," he observed. "They'll have to go in the lower level. Lord Gassandrid has asked for exclusive use of the upper."

The soldier with the long scar frowned. "Why's that?"

The pale-skinned man hesitated, then leaned forward, lowering his tone conspiratorially. "Special prisoner. They're not saying much, but there are rumors. He's been here for almost a week."

"For a week? When was the last time someone made it..." The scarred man's eyes widened. "*Oh.*"

The Keeper just nodded, evidently satisfied that the soldier had understood his meaning. He walked over to the gate, fishing some keys from his pocket and unlocking it.

"You know where to go?" When the gray-haired man nodded impatiently, the Keeper opened the gate, allowing the soldiers to prod Davian and Fessi through.

They had been walking for about a minute when they first heard the screams.

The sounds seemed to be coming from only a single source, but they echoed unsettlingly through the stone hallways, soft at first but gradually increasing in volume and intensity as Davian and Fessi were prodded farther inside. There wasn't just agony in the cries, either.

They were full of desperation. Of complete and utter hopelessness.

Davian shivered as they came to the top of a dim stairwell leading downward, glancing across at Fessi. To his horror, he could see that her hands had now begun to tremble, and the blood had drained from her face.

We'll be all right. He continued looking at her, trying to catch her gaze. *We just need to rest for—*

Suddenly there was a hand on his shoulder, and Fessi was standing in front of him.

"I'm sorry." She looked grim, terrified. "I can't extend this to two of us; I can't even hold it much longer for myself. Ducking down here is the best I can do." She nodded to the passageway off to the left and started pulling Davian urgently along behind her.

Davian allowed himself to be towed away from the near-motionless soldiers, heart pounding. "Why now? What's going on?"

"It's here. This place. I recognize it. I...I can't be here." Fessi just shook her head, clearly panicked by something. "I can't hold this. I'm so sorry. Fates with you, Davian."

Before he could react, she let go of his hand.

There was a blur of motion as Fessi sped away; apparently even pushing the limits of her ability, she couldn't move fast enough to maintain complete invisibility here.

Davian gaped disbelievingly at the retreating figure, then spun around as shouts erupted from behind him. He was alone, but he and Fessi hadn't made it far enough away.

His captors could be upon him again in a matter of seconds, and he doubted that they'd be so casual about his imprisonment next time.

He ran.

The screams were still echoing unnervingly down the hallway; 705

he found himself sprinting toward them, having nowhere else to go if he wanted to put distance between himself and the confused yells of the soldiers.

He slowed as he came to a junction in the corridor, risking a glance behind him. There was still no sign of his pursuers, but their angry voices were louder, and he thought that their shouts had been joined by others now. He ducked left, then grimaced as he was faced with only a stairwell leading upward.

There was no time to vacillate; he took the winding stairs two at a time, gasping for air as he reached the next level of the prison. The seemingly unending screams were piercing now, sending ice through his veins every time that they rattled off the walls.

He slipped through the doorway in front of him and then stuttered to a horrified halt, bile suddenly in his mouth as he took in the scene.

He had emerged into a large, semicircular room that was well lit by both torches and hanging lanterns. One of its two occupants stood in its center: a large man with his back to Davian, having apparently not noticed Davian's entrance. He held a long blade that glistened wetly with blood, while another one hung sheathed at his side.

Pinned against the wall was another man, this one facing toward Davian, though his blank gaze didn't seem to register Davian's presence, either. Thick, dark chains emerging from the stone were wrapped tight around his chest and limbs, suspending him slightly above the ground.

Davian couldn't see that the man had any physical injuries, yet there was blood...*everywhere*. Drenching the prisoner's clothes. Spattered on the wall. Pooled thick on the stone floor, along with what looked suspiciously like a pile of severed body parts.

The sight was grotesque enough that it took Davian a few seconds to register the familiar face, haggard and twisted in agony though it was.

"Where is she, Tal?" Caeden's torturer spoke softly, but the words sounded rote. As if this was a question that he'd already asked hundreds of times. "I promise you that even after what you did to Is, this is only happening because you've left us with no choice. So just tell us where she is, and this will stop."

"I don't know, Meldier," rasped Caeden, his voice desperate. He choked back a sob. "It's the truth. I don't remember."

The man called Meldier stepped forward and with one smooth motion, calmly cut off Caeden's right arm.

Another hoarse, furious, desperate scream resounded through the chamber, louder and more terrible than anything Davian could have imagined. He stumbled back, watching in wide-eyed disbelief as Meldier coldly slammed his hand down onto the gushing open wound. There was a blinding burst of Essence and Caeden cried out again, but the sound was muted in comparison to his first shout, this one more of an anguished moan.

When the light faded and Meldier finally took his hand away, Caeden's arm was whole.

Davian swallowed down his urge to retch, his lips curling to a snarl. Both men were too engrossed in what was happening to spot him, but he'd seen more than enough.

He closed his eyes, taking a deep breath. He'd only be able to step outside of time for a few seconds, here, but he couldn't— *wouldn't*—let this go on.

He fought with kan for a few moments, then let time flow around him and ran forward. The large man didn't hear Davian coming, didn't even turn as Davian grasped the hilt of the sword at his waist.

Everything froze.

Davian nearly lost his grip on kan, so surprised was he by how suddenly easy it was to grasp. He drew the blade free, heart pounding as the light from the torches began to bend and swirl toward it.

This wasn't just a blade.

This was the one that he'd seen Caeden use at Ilin Illan.

He gasped, shaking his head as he tried to get to grips with the dark power now seeping through his veins.

"Who are you?"

Davian's gaze snapped up to see Meldier looking at him, hands outstretched in a display of calm surrender. Behind him, Caeden was still all but motionless, expression frozen in a rictus of pain.

Davian took a hesitant step back.

Meldier had managed to step outside of time, too. Perhaps not as well as Davian—his voice was a little slow, his eyes a little behind as they tried to focus—but he was clearly able to manipulate kan. Manipulate it incredibly well, given where they were.

"It doesn't matter." Davian held the blade steady, adjusting his grip slightly. He was a long way from a true swordsman, but Aelric's memories gave him a good deal of confidence with the weapon. "Let my friend go."

"Your *friend*?" Meldier barked a laugh. "*Tal'kamar?*"

"Yes."

The laughter quickly died. "Do you know who I am?"

"I don't care."

"You should." There was an unsettling force behind the man's words, which boomed in the surreal silence that surrounded them. Then Meldier cocked his head to the side. "But...you are not from here, are you? Not if you can use Licanius."

Davian motioned with the sword, trying to look confident. "I'm not interested in talking. Let Caeden—Tal'kamar—and I go, or I'll use this."

Meldier said nothing for a moment. If Davian hadn't been keeping time at bay more effectively than the other man, he might have missed the flicker of fear in his opponent's eyes.

"Do you even know who he is?"

"I told you. He's my friend." Davian's jaw clenched. "That's all that matters to me."

Another silence, and then suddenly Meldier threw back his head and roared with laughter.

"You don't!" He subsided to a chuckle, shaking his head. "Oh, El. He didn't tell you." He lowered his hands, as if suddenly deciding that Davian wasn't a threat. "This man that you're so eager to save, to protect? Your people know him as Aarkein Devaed."

Davian stared blankly, the words taking a few moments to sink in.

Then he laughed.

"That's..." He shook his head. "I don't even know how to respond to that." He stepped forward threateningly. "Now let him go."

Meldier scowled. "It is the truth. I can prove it."

Suddenly the chains on the wall behind him rippled, turning from thick metal into what looked like a dark, smoky glass.

And then Caeden was blinking at Davian, mouth open, as if not comprehending what he was seeing.

"Dav?" He struggled against the chains, eyes suddenly wide. "Dav, get out of here!"

"Not without you."

"Touching." Meldier shook his head. "Now tell him, Tal'kamar. Tell him who you really are."

Davian frowned as he saw panic in Caeden's eyes. Followed by regret.

Followed by shame.

There was an interminably long silence, and Davian's heart dropped.

"No," he whispered eventually, dazedly, taking a confused step back. Even holding Licanius, his grip on time almost slipped.

Caeden took a shuddering breath. "You once told me that when I got my memories back, that no matter what I found, I'd have a choice." He squeezed his eyes shut. "I...I *was* him, Davian. I was Aarkein Devaed." He opened his eyes again, staring at Davian. Pleading for him to understand. "But I'm not anymore. I realized that I was on the wrong side, and I erased those memories because I wanted to get away from them. I can *never* make up for the things I did...but I want to do the right thing now." He gasped as the chain around his throat suddenly shifted, tightening. "If you believe anything, please believe that."

Davian felt light-headed as he stared at the blood-soaked man pinned against the wall.

There had been no black smoke from Caeden's mouth.

"So now you see." Meldier's voice was calm. "Words are easy, but the truth? Your *friend* is a murderer. Your *friend* is responsible for *literally millions* of deaths, and he will kill you, too. What is happening to him here is not one one thousandth of the punishment that he truly deserves." He held out his hand, palm upturned. "You are on the wrong side, boy. Give me Licanius, surrender of your own free will, and you will be treated well. In fact, I can promise you safety. You have my word."

Davian shook his head. Everything felt off-balance, surreal.

Meldier was speaking truthfully, too.

Eventually, though, he again registered the blood that was

everywhere. The disgusting, glistening mass of disfigured flesh beneath Caeden's feet.

He tightened his grip on Licanius.

"Caeden." He felt his brow furrow as he took a long, steadying breath. "You fought them."

Caeden looked up, a flicker of hope in his eyes.

"I did," he said softly.

"You saved us at Ilin Illan. You helped Asha strengthen the Boundary." Davian nodded slowly, mostly to himself, a small seed of certainty growing. "I remember that conversation, too. I know you. I *know* you, and...I meant what I said back then." He licked his lips, then met Caeden's gaze. "You *are* my friend, Caeden. I believe that. So tell me that you're really on our side, and let's go home."

Before Caeden could respond, Meldier acted.

The calm the large man had been displaying vanished in a frustrated snarl as his blade whipped out, slashing with stunning speed toward Davian's head.

Davian's instincts—or those he'd been given by Aelric—took over. He moved to the side smoothly, avoiding the blow.

Stepped forward.

Rammed Licanius as hard as he could into Meldier's chest.

The big man's eyes went wide in shock and disbelief; he stumbled and then collapsed backward, the motion wrenching Licanius from Davian's grasp. Time crashed back into Davian and he gasped, staggering from the abruptness of the shift.

When he was able to focus again, Meldier was motionless on the crimson-soaked stone floor.

Distant shouts—unnoticeable while he had been outside of the flow of time—penetrated up the stairs and into the chamber, now, too close and too loud.

Panting, the shock of everything that had just occurred quickly beginning to set in, Davian scrambled over to Meldier and yanked Licanius from his chest. He closed his eyes, focusing.

To his horror, kan still eluded him.

"It won't work that way for a while." Davian turned to see Caeden, his face twisted in a grimace of pain. The chains had faded from black glass back to metal again, though they now somehow looked even tighter than they had been. "I think it uses all of its power when it kills one of us," the redheaded man concluded heavily.

"It doesn't matter. We need to go." Davian shut the door to the stairwell and hurriedly barred it, then dashed over and yanked at the chains holding Caeden in place.

They didn't move.

"How do I get these off?" he asked desperately. The shouts were louder now. Coming up the stairs.

"You don't." Caeden met Davian's gaze steadily. "Dav, they're looking for Asha. They know that she's the one who's stopping the Boundary from collapsing. They...they got her name from me, but that's all. I didn't give them anything else." He took a deep breath. "I think I know how to end this, but you're going to have to trust me."

Davian flinched as there was a rattle at the door, followed quickly by a series of crashing thumps as whoever was on the other side tried to break it down. "What do I need to do?"

"Get Meldier's sword. Not Licanius." Caeden's breaths were short and sharp, the redheaded man evidently just as anxious as Davian as a sudden splintering sound came from the entrance. He gave a single, tight nod once Davian was holding the plain steel. "Now you have to cut off my head."

"*What?*"

"I can't die, Davian. I'll come back elsewhere. In a different body." Caeden stared at him, expression willing him to believe. "I will come for you, but you *have to trust me.*"

The door collapsed off its hinges and men poured into the room.

With a scream of frustration and anger and confusion, Davian swung.

The Wells of Mor Aruil were silent as Caeden slumped into Asar's chair, staring contemplatively at the black splotch of dried blood on the carpet and wondering again if he'd done the right thing.

Five days. Five days since he'd woken...wherever it had been. A different body, probably a different land. The latter hadn't been much of a problem; he'd had the Gate underway before nightfall, and open before he'd even felt the need to sleep. It had been more than a relief to return here, where he knew that there would be silence and solitude and familiarity and a chance to finally rest.

The former had been... unsettling, though, for a while.

He'd almost settled on accepting his new body—too tall, hands too large, skin too pale—when he'd realized that he could just shape-shift back. It had been harder than he'd expected, though, even with his disquieting memory of the village in Desriel to tell him how to do it. It was, he'd vaguely recalled, one of the skills that he had always lacked.

Still, after two days of trying, he'd been successful. There had been pain, but only briefly. And it had been worth it to feel *himself* again.

Now, though, there were no more excuses.

He had to figure out a way to keep his word to Davian.

He shook his head slightly as he reflected, mind straying back to those last, terrifying moments in Ilshan Gathdel Teth. Davian had sided with him. Saved him.

He'd done that, *knowing who Caeden really was.*

Perhaps Davian had seen no better choices—but the decision still mattered to Caeden, even more than he'd expected it to. It said something about the side that he'd chosen, the people who he had decided to trust. That one act had given him more confidence, more resolve, than he'd had since the moment that Asar had shown him who he really was.

He straightened and took a slow, determined breath. It was time to find a way to save his friend.

The memory hit him without warning.

Caeden shook his head again, still hazy from the explosion of the Jha'vett.

Around him, Deilannis burned—not with the ghastly flames of the Darklands now, but with something else entirely. Something he'd never seen before. Red energy glittering with odd specks of yellow burned in every crack and divot, ran through every stone, the city seething and writhing despite there being no obvious physical damage to the Arbiterium itself.

As his vision finally found some focus, he stuttered to his feet at a sudden flicker of motion.

A little distance away, somehow, the doors to the Arbiterium were opening. Everyone in there should have been dead and yet as he stared, a single figure emerged.

The man looked around, his face lit red in the ethereal light. Curly black hair framed a narrow face. Two separate scars marred his features and as he turned, Caeden saw a third cut deep into his neck.

He frowned, his confusion now complete. It was Alaris's sigil, the mark of the Shining Lands.

The stranger spotted Caeden, and for a moment there was something complex in his expression. Relief? Fear? Resignation? They were all there and all gone in an instant.

Caeden scrambled to his feet as the muscular man came toward him, stopping only when they were face-to-face.

"Tal'kamar. Aarkein Devaed." The stranger's eyes never left him; he appeared unperturbed by what surrounded them.

"Yes." Caeden's gaze flicked to the entrance of the Arbiterium, but no one else followed. They were alone, it seemed.

The man let out a long breath. "My name is Davian. I have used the Jha'vett to come here, now, to deliver you a message." He paused, for the first time looking hesitant. "It is ... something that you need to hear. Something which only a friend can tell you."

Caeden stared at him in disbelief.

"The Jha'vett is broken. What you see are the consequences of it breaking." He shook his head cynically. "But let's say I humor you, stranger. What message does my friend bring that requires him to travel through time itself?"

"That you have been deceived," said Davian, looking unperturbed by Caeden's tone. "That no matter how much it hurts, you need to recognize that El is not who he says he is. You need to accept that you are on the wrong side of this fight ... and that you always have been."

"Is...that all?" Caeden sneered. "Is that the best that you have to offer? 'Change sides?' Just like that?" He laughed bitterly. "I fear that you have come a long way for no reward."

"That is not all," said Davian quietly. "You also need to accept that it is your fault. It is your fault, and there is no undoing it."

Caeden stiffened despite himself. "You'll have to do better than—"

"You alone." Davian paused, but only to draw breath as Caeden gaped at him. "You killed your friends and loved ones. You destroyed a civilization and sent the scant few survivors on a path that led to yet more destruction. None of this can be undone. None of the lives that were lost can ever be brought back."

"Enough," said Caeden. Nobody spoke to him this way.

"You slaughtered innocents. You hid behind the names Aarkein Devaed and El, but it was always Tal'kamar—always you," pressed Davian. "You lie to yourself about what you truly believe, and you do it over and over and over every single day because you are afraid of admitting to what the alternative means."

"Enough." It was a snarl now, a promise, but Davian refused to heed it.

"You need to accept that your wife is dead and that she cannot be brought back. That Elliavia is dead and that you will never see her again. You need to do this, because your selfishness has already cost the lives of more good men than there are stars in the sky. Your selfishness, Tal'kamar. Not your blindness, nor your arrogance, nor your good intentions. Your utter contempt for anyone but yourself."

"That's not—"

"Listen to me, Tal'kamar! You are at fault! You and you alone! You shield yourself from what you've done, you justify and justify and justify but you know deep down that it is NOT ENOUGH!" Caeden was trying to talk over him but Davian plowed on, forcing his words through. "For all that you've been given, you are fearful and weak and cowardly! For all you have lost, you have not learned! It's not fate and it's not love and it *was never, ever because you thought that you were doing the right thing! You know this! You know this better than—"*

"ENOUGH!"

The world was red, a blur. He knew he was reaching for Licanius. Knew he'd drawn it. Knew he'd swung.

An impact.

The heavy thud of something dropping to the ground.

Caeden's vision cleared.

The stranger's severed head gazed sightlessly to the side, mouth agape as if still trying to utter more accusations. A few paces away his body had slumped to the ground, dark red blood fountaining in spurts from his neck.

Caeden stared for a long few seconds, hands shaking, rage still gripping him.

"You're wrong." He addressed the words to the lifeless head. "You're wrong."

Who had this man been? Caeden didn't really believe that he'd come through the Jha'vett, but he'd known more than most, more than anyone should have. Known exactly what to say to prod at all of Caeden's fears, all of his insecurities. A lone survivor of the High Darecians, perhaps, seeking a quick end after the destruction of his race? It didn't really fit, but it was also as good as any other answer that he could come up with.

He crouched beside the body, searching it. Nothing but the simple band of silver on Davian's finger. Caeden hesitated for a long moment, then pocketed it. It was a Vessel—one of minor power—but more importantly, it was tied to the dead man. If he ever chose to find out more about this puzzle, it could be useful.

He made to walk away, then scowled. His rage at the stranger's unprovoked words still burned, hot and steady.

Death wasn't enough. Not for this.

He snatched up the severed head by its hair, ignoring the trail of blood as he began to walk. The Door of Iladriel was not far.

Sometimes, examples had to be made.

Mounting the head on a steel pike was grisly work, but he'd done it plenty of times before and it did not take long. He barely noticed as the red of the city around him began to fade, replaced instead by a thick fog. It was odd, given the heat, but he ignored it. It did not interfere with what needed to be done.

His rage cold now, he set the head at the apex of the Door. A reminder for the Darecians—for whoever had sent this man, if anyone actually had—that there were lines that should not be crossed. Accusations that should never be made.

He frowned a little as he stepped back, observing the results of his work. It felt less satisfying than it should have.

Then he scrubbed absently at the traces of blood still on his skin, suddenly tired.

"Such a waste," he muttered in disgust at the head. "What other outcome could you possibly have expected?"

He turned abruptly. Walked away.

Let the steadily encroaching mists hide the sightless eyes of the foolish stranger from view.

Acknowledgments

As always, my first acknowledgement has to go to my wonderful and always-supportive wife, Sonja. Her constant willingness to read (and reread, and reread) full drafts, and give constructive feedback on each in an encouraging way, is vital to my writing process and is a blessing that I will never take for granted.

Next, a huge thanks to my editors, Will Hinton at Orbit and James Long at Little, Brown. Both have been a pleasure to work with, and I've been thrilled that their visions of what this story should be are so closely matched to my own—their input has been invaluable not only for making these books better, but in generally sharpening my writing skills for the future. Thanks are most definitely also due to my agent at Janklow & Nesbit, Paul Lucas, whose excellent advice and hard work over the past couple of years have taken me to the wonderful position in which I find myself today.

My beta readers were once again a great help on *Echo*—everyone involved in the process devoted a great deal of their time and energy to give me feedback (often on a deadline), and each ended up shaping the book in some way. In particular, Nicki, Chiara, Aiden, Jeremy, and Dean provided extremely valuable contributions. I could never leave the indomitable Balthazar out of these acknowledgments, either—excellent work, Thaz.

Finally, a special thanks to all the readers who took a chance on *The Shadow of What Was Lost* when it was newly self-published all the way back in 2014. Between its success taking me by surprise, the birth of my first child, and the transition to traditional publishing, it will have taken me almost three years to get this book released—a long time, even in the world of epic fantasy!—and I can't overstate just how much I've appreciated everyone's ongoing enthusiasm, support, and (most of all) patience during the wait.

Glossary of Characters

Aarkein Devaed (ARE-kine deh-VADE): A powerful Gifted whose invasion of northern Andarra two thousand years ago resulted in the creation of the Boundary. Considered by the Old Religion to be a figure of great evil, strongly associated with Shammaeloth himself. Also see *Caeden*.

Aelric Shainwiere (AIL-rick SHAYN-weer): Ward of the king, brother to Dezia. A talented swordsman who, for political reasons, deliberately lost the most recent final of the Song of Swords held in Desriel.

Aelrith (AIL-rith) / The Watcher: One of the sha'teth, who was once commonly seen by Shadows in the Sanctuary. Now deceased.

Aganaki (ag-an-AH-key): The Eastern Empire's ambassador to Andarra.

Alaris (al-ARE-iss) / Alarais (al-are-ACE) / Alarius (al-ARE-ee-us): One of the Venerate, and former king of the Shining Lands. Considers himself Tal'kamar's friend.

Alchesh Mel'tac (AL-chesh MEL-tack): The first Augur. In legend, driven mad after seeing too much of the future. Soon after the creation of the Boundary, he warned of its eventual collapse and Aarkein Devaed's return. Though his visions were initially considered reliable, after several hundred years without apparent threat from Talan Gol, his writings were dismissed by the priests of the Old Religion and struck from canon.

Aliria (al-IRR-ee-ah): One of the Elders at Tol Shen. Wife to Lyrus Dain.

Andrael (AN-dree-el) / Andral (AN-drahl): One of the Venerate. A talented inventor. Creator of the five Named Swords, which were forged for the purpose of killing the other Venerate. His deal with the Lyth forced Tal'kamar to erase his own memories in order to reclaim Licanius.

Andras (AN-drass): The royal line of Andarra.

Andyn (AN-din): Wirr's bodyguard, assigned due to rumors of an assassination plot after Wirr inherited the position of Northwarden.

Asar Shenelac (AY-sarr SHEN-eh-lack) / Tae'shadon (TAY-shah-don) / The Keeper: One of the Venerate. Meets Caeden in the Wells of Mor Aruil in order to help restore Caeden's memories.

Asha (ASH-uh) / Ashalia (ash-AH-lee-uh): A Shadow. Childhood friend of Davian and Wirr, having grown up with them in the Gifted school in Caladel. Turned into a Shadow by Ilseth Tenvar in the aftermath of the attack on the school. Made Representative for Tol Athian by Elocien Andras, who also had her secretly take on the role of Scribe for the Augurs Erran, Fessi, and Kol.

Astria (ASS [sounds like "mass"]-tree-ah): A woman from Caeden's past, who was murdered and replaced for a time by Nethgalla.

Ath (ATH [sounds like "math"]), The / Nethgalla (neth-GULL-uh): A creature of legend, known for her ability to take the form of others.

Brase (BRAZE [sounds like "raise"]): A Shadow working in the library at Tol Athian.

Breshada (bresh-AH-duh): A Hunter who mysteriously saved Davian and Wirr from two other Hunters in Talmiel. Wields Whisper, one of the Named Swords.

Caeden (CAY-den) / Tal'kamar (TAL-cam-are): After waking with no memories in Desriel, Caeden eventually discovered that he had deliberately erased them, primarily in order to fulfil Andrael's bargain with the Lyth and obtain the sword Licanius. After travelling to the Wells of Mor Aruil and meeting with Asar Shenelac, he remembers that he once called himself Aarkein Devaed.

Cyr (SEAR): One of the Venerate. Assisted Aarkein Devaed in the destruction of the city of Silence.

Daresh Thurin (dah-RESH THOO-rin): The Desrielite ambassador to Andarra.

Dastiel (DAS-tee-el): A Shadow working in the library at Tol Athian.

Dav (DAV [sounds like "have"]) / Davian (DAY-vee-en [sounds like "avian"]): Grew up an orphan in the Gifted school at Caladel, where he became childhood friends with Asha and Wirr. An Augur.

Deldri Andras (DELL-dree AN-drass): Younger sister of Wirr, daughter of Elocien and Geladra.

Dezia Shainwiere (DET-zee-uh SHAYN-weer): Ward of the king, sister to Aelric. Talented archer whose romantic relationship with Wirr must be kept secret, due to her lack of an official title.

Diara (dee-ARE-ah) / Diarys (dee-ARE-iss): One of the Venerate.

Dras Lothlar (drass LOTH-lar): The Representative for Tol Shen. Suspected by Taeris and Laiman to have had a hand in the king's strange illness during the attack by the Blind.

Driscin Throll (DRISS-kin THROLL): An Elder at Tol Shen. Mentor to

Ishelle. Formerly part of the sig'nari, and attempting to locate and train the newest generation of Augurs.

El (ELL): The benevolent deity of the Old Religion.

Elliavia (ell-ee-AH-vee-uh) / **Ell** (ELL): The murdered wife of Malshash. Her name is sometimes shortened to Ell, pronounced the same as El.

Elocien Andras (el-OH-see-en AN-drass): The former duke and Northwarden. Father to Wirr and Deldri, husband to Geladra, brother to King Andras. Killed by an Echo during the battle for Ilin Illan against the Blind.

Erran (EH-rin [sounds like "Erin"]): An Augur who worked in secret at the palace for Elocien Andras. Later, revealed to have been Controlling Elocien for the past two years.

Fessi (FESS-ee [sounds like "messy"]) / **Fessiricia** (fess-eh-REE-sha): An Augur who worked in secret at the palace for Elocien Andras, alongside Erran and Kol.

Garadis ru Dagen (GA-ruh-diss rue DAY-gen ["GA" as in "gash"]): The leader of the Lyth. Struck a deal with Andrael in which he agreed that the Lyth would guard the sword Licanius, in exchange for the promise of eventual freedom from Res Kartha.

Gassandrid (gass-AN-drid) / **Gasharrid** (gash-AR-id): Considered the founder of the Venerate. The first to reveal to Tal'kamar the inevitability of the future, and suggest to him the reasons behind it.

Gawn (GORN [sounds like "thorn"]): One of the Hunters whom Breshada killed in Talmiel in order to save Davian and Wirr.

Geladra Andras: (gell-ADD-ra AN-drass): Wirr's and Deldri's mother. Elocien's widow. A former Administrator who despises the Gifted.

Havran Das (HAVE-ran DASS): A merchant in Ilin Illan, used as bait by Alaris to lure Caeden into an ambush by the Blind.

Iain Tel'An (ee-AIN tell-AN): A young nobleman from Ilin Illan who is interested in courting Asha.

Iria Tel'Rath (IRR-ee-ah tel-RATH): Daughter of Lord and Lady Tel'Rath. Suggested as an appropriate romantic match for Wirr.

Ishelle (ish-ELL [sounds like "Michelle"]): An Augur, originally met by Davian on the road to Ilin Illan prior to the Blind's attack on the city. Has been under the tutelage of Elder Driscin Throll, with the full knowledge of Tol Shen's Council, for the past two years.

Isiliar (iss-ILL-ee-are): One of the Venerate. Driven insane after she was imprisoned in a Tributary by Tal'kamar.

Jakarris si'Irthidian (jah-KARR-iss see-er-THID-ee-an) / **Scyner** (SIGH-ner): An Augur from before the rebellion, now a Shadow. Killed the other twelve Augurs at the beginning of the rebellion twenty years ago. More recently, posed as the Shadraehin to the Shadows in the Sanctuary. Killed Kol after attempting to blackmail Kol, Fessi, and Erran into helping him.

Jin (JINN): The Shadow who first introduced Asha to the Sanctuary. Killed by Aelrith.

Karaliene Andras (KA-rah-leen ["KA" as in "carry"] AN-drass): Princess of Andarra. Daughter of King Andras, cousin of Wirr and Deldri.

Kevran Andras (KEV-ran AN-drass): King of Andarra. Brother of Elocien, father of Karaliene, uncle of Wirr and Deldri.

Kol (COLE [sounds like "pole"]): An Augur who worked in secret at the palace for Elocien Andras, alongside Erran and Fessi. Killed by Scyner.

Kolis (KOLL-iss): An Administrator who attempts to interfere with Asha's journey to Deilannis.

Laiman Kardai (LAY-men CAR-dye) / Thell Taranor (thell TAR-ah-nore): Chief adviser to King Andras. Asha discovers a mysterious connection between him and Taeris when she overhears a conversation between the two of them after the battle with the Blind.

Lethaniel (leth-AN-ee-el): One of the sha'teth.

Lyannis (lee-AHN-iss): A young nobleman from Ilin Illan who is interested in courting Asha.

Lyrus Dain (LIE-russ DANE): An Elder at Tol Shen, and the leader of the Council there.

Malshash (MAL-shash): An Augur. Davian's mentor during his sojourn to the past in Deilannis. Husband to Elliavia. Is able to shape-shift, an ability which he claims to have temporarily stolen from Nethgalla.

Marut Jha Talkanor (MAHR-ut JAH TAL-can-or): The Desrielite God of Balance.

Andan Mash'aan (AHN-den mahsh-AHN): The commander of the Blind army that attacked Ilin Illan.

Meldier (MELL-deer): One of the Venerate. Imprisoned in a Tributary by Tal'kamar.

Muran (moo-RAN): The captain in charge of the outpost at the Boundary.

Narius (NAH-ree-us): An Elder at Tol Shen.

Nethgalla (neth-GULL-uh): See *Ath*.

Nihim Sethi (NIGH-im SETH-ai): The priest who accompanied Taeris, Davian, and Wirr to Deilannis. Killed by Orkoth.

Orkoth (ORE-koth): The creature from Deilannis that slew Nihim. Appears to obey orders from Malshash, and has been instructed not to harm Davian.

Paetir (PAY-ter): A warlord from Caeden's past, who attempts to ambush the Venerate using kan-enhanced weaponry.

Pria si'Bellara (PREE-ah sih-bell-AHR-ah): Administration's current second-in-command under Wirr.

Renmar (REN-mar): One of the Hunters whom Breshada killed in Talmiel in order to save Davian and Wirr.

Reubin (ROO-bin): A Shadow working in the Tol Athian library.

Rill (RILL): Captain in charge of the guards at the Tel'Andras family estate in Daran Tel.

Rohin (ROE-in): An Augur who arrives at Tol Shen after the Augur Amnesty is announced.

Scyner (SIGH-ner): See *Jakarris si'Irthidian*.

Serrin (SAIR-in): A Gifted from Caeden's past who uses the Siphon to enslave Silvithrin.

Shadraehin (SHAH-druh-eh-heen): The leader of the "rebel" Shadows living in the Sanctuary. Originally thought to be Scyner, later revealed to be a mysterious woman.

Shammaeloth (shah-MAY-loth): The malevolent deity of the Old Religion.

si'Bandin (sih-BAN-yen): A minor House in the Assembly.

si'Danvielle (sih-DAN-vee-ell): A minor House in the Assembly.

si'Veria (sih-VER-ee-ah): A minor House in the Assembly.

Tachievar (TACK-ee-eh-var): A senior Administrator.

Tae'shadon (TAY-shah-don): See *Asar Shenelac*.

Taeris Sarr (TAY-riss SARR): A Gifted. Face heavily scarred. Currently the Representative for Tol Athian despite a contentious relationship with Tol Athian's Council. Accompanied Caeden, Davian and Wirr during their escape from Desriel via Deilannis. Present three years ago at Caladel when Davian, as a child, was attacked. Has been researching the degradation of the Boundary for many years.

Tal'kamar Deshrel (TAL-cam-are DESH-rel): See *Caeden*.

Thameron (THAM-err-on): An Elder at Tol Shen. Appointed by Tol Shen's Council as Scribe to the Augurs.

Thell Taranor (thell TAR-ah-nore): See *Laiman Kardai*.

Thil (THILL): An Elder at Tol Shen.

Torin Wirrander Andras (TORE-en weer-AN-der AN-drass): See *Wirr*.

Tysis (TIE-sis): One of the Venerate. Killed by Andrael during the destruction of the city of Silence.

Vhalire (vah-LEER): One of the sha'teth, mentioned to Asha by Aelrith during their encounter in the Sanctuary.

Wereth (WHERE-eth) / Werek (WHERE-ek): One of the Venerate. Creator of the Siphon.

Whylir (WILL-eer): The Narutian ambassador to Andarra.

Wirr (WEER [sounds like "beer"]) / Torin Wirrander Andras (TORE-en weer-AN-der AN-drass): Gifted. Northwarden. Prince of Andarra. Brother of Deldri, son of Geladra and Elocien, cousin to Karaliene, nephew to Kevran. Secretly sent to the Gifted school in Caladel by his father, where he met and became friends with Davian and Asha. Due to his lineage and ability to use Essence, he was capable of changing the Tenets by himself.

Glossary

Absorption endpoint: A common element of kan machinery that absorbs Essence.

Administration: An Andarran organization dedicated to uploading the terms of the Treaty with the Gifted. Led by the Northwarden, members are bound to the Tenets via Oathstones, by which they receive a red Administrator's Mark on their forearm.

Administrator: A member of Administration.

Adviser: A Vessel in the Great Library in Deilannis, used to locate texts about specific subjects.

al'goriat (al-GORE-ee-at): One of the five Banes led by Aarkein Devaed during his invasion of Andarra.

Alkathronen (al-KATH-ron-en): The last city of the Builders. Also connects each of the Builder's various wonders via portals.

Alsir (AL-seer): A small town in Andarra.

Andarra (an-DARR-uh): The country in which Davian, Wirr, and Asha reside. Originally spanned the entire continent north of the Menaath Mountains before Devaed's invasion two thousand years ago. Now bordered by Talan Gol to the north, and Desriel and Narut to the west.

Arbiterium (arr-bit-EER-ee-um): A structure in Deilannis, in which the Jha'vett is housed.

Assembly: The Andarran legislature.

Augur (AWE-ger): People who have the ability to use kan to Read and Control minds, manipulate time, and see into an inevitable future.

Augur Amnesty: An amnesty passed by the Assembly in response to the attack by the Blind, removing the death penalty for any Augurs who are willing to undertake the task of sealing the Boundary.

Banes: In Andarran legend, warriors led by Aarkein Devaed during his invasion that were mixtures of men and animals, and all but impossible to kill.

Blades, five: See *Named swords*.

bleeder: A derogatory term used by the Andarran populace to refer to the Gifted.

Blind: The invasion force from beyond the Boundary that attacked Ilin Illan. Known for their unusual helmets, which completely cover their eyes.

Boundary: The enormous wall of Essence to the north of Andarra, which encapsulates all of Talan Gol.

Builders: The mysterious race who constructed Ilin Illan, Alkathronen, and many other wonders.

Caer Lyordas (care lee-OR-das): Castle from Caeden's homeland.

Caladel (CAL-ah-dell): Town on the southwest coast of Andarra, where Davian grew up. Formerly home to one of the Gifted schools run by Tol Athian.

Conduit: The enormous cylinder of constantly flowing Essence in the Sanctuary.

Cyrarium (sear-AIR-ee-um): A massive storage container for Essence.

dar'gaithin (dar-GAY-thun): One of the five Banes led by Aarkein Devaed during his invasion of Andarra. Taller than a man and snake-like, armored with black scales that absorb Essence.

Dareci (DA-reh-kai): The enormous capital of the Darecian Empire. Destroyed by Aarkein Devaed. Now known as the Plains of Decay.

Darecian (dah-REE-see-en): Refers to the long-vanished race that came to Andarra a thousand years prior to Devaed's attack. Extraordinarily advanced and powerful Gifted.

Daren Tel (DAH-ren TELL): The area in which the Tel'Andras family estate is located.

Darklands / Markaathan (mar-KAH-thahn): The realm beyond the rift in Deilannis, from which kan is drawn.

Decis (DECK-is): A small village in Andarra.

Deilannis (dye-LAN-iss): Long abandoned, mist-covered Darecian city straddling the border of Andarra, Desriel, and Narut.

Desriel (DES-ree-el): Hostile country to the west of Andarra. Governed by a theocracy that believes that Essence is not for mortal use.

Devliss (DEV-liss): The river that separates Andarra and Desriel.

Disruption shield: A complicated shield of kan designed to protect an Augur from both physical and mental attack by other Augurs.

dok'en (dock-EN): A device used to create the illusion of a physical area within someone's mind, which can then also be accessed by others.

Door of Iladriel (ih-LAD-ree-uhl): Archway in Deilannis, the official entrance to the Inner City.

Echo: A being originating from the Darklands that utilizes a dead person's body and memories.

eletai (ELL-eh-tie): One of the five Banes led by Aarkein Devaed during his invasion of Andarra. Wasplike creatures that can fly and act with a hive intelligence.

Elhyris (EL-here-iss): A country from Caeden's past.

endpoints: Common mechanisms within kan machinery that serve a pre-defined purpose.

Eryth Mmorg (EHR-ith MAWG): Also known as the Waters of Renewal. Located in Talan Gol.

Essence: Energy, the life force of all things. Used by both the Gifted and Augurs.

Fate: See *Licanius*.

Fedris Idri (FED-riss ID-ree): The sole pass into Ilin Illan. Cut from the heart of the mountain Ilin Tora by the Builders, with three defensive walls known as the Shields.

Finder: A Vessel that detects the use of Essence.

Freed: The Lyth's term for when one of their number willingly leaves Res Kartha, resulting in their death.

gaa'vesh (gah-VESH): The derogatory Desrielite word used to describe the Gifted.

Gahille (GAY-ill): A town that the Blind completely razed on their march to Ilin Illan.

Gate: A construct of kan and Essence that allows instantaneous travel between two physically distant points.

Gifted: People who have the ability to wield Essence, their own life force.

Gil'shar (gill-SHAR): The governing body that controls all aspects of life in Desriel. Members are considered to have been appointed by divine selection.

Ilin Illan (ill-INN ill-AHN): Capital of Andarra. Accessible only via the difficult-to-navigate Naminar River or through Fedris Idri.

Ilshan Gathdel Teth (ILL-shahn GATH-del TETH): A city in Talan Gol. Home to the remaining Venerate.

ilshara (ill-SHAH-rah): A type of shield, used to protect individuals against being drained of Essence when working with a Cyrarium. Thanks to similarities in their design, the term is now commonly used by the Venerate and others to refer to the Boundary.

Initiation endpoint: A common element of kan machinery that allows a device to be triggered.

Ironsails: A type of ship used by the Darecians.

Jha'vett (jah-VET): Device in the center of Deilannis that draws Essence from every part of the city. Designed by the Darecians to allow time travel.

kan (KAHN): The power used by the Augurs. Drawn from the Darklands.

Kharshan (CAR-shahn): Gassandrid's homeland.

Knowing: One of the five Named swords. Stored by Tal'kamar in the Tributary with Isiliar. Used, and subsequently hidden, by Asha in the catacombs beneath Ilin Illan.

Lantarche (lan-TAR-ka): The massive river that flows around Deilannis and forms much of the border between Andarra and Desriel.

Licanius (lie-CAN-ee-us): One of the five Named swords, also known as Fate. The only weapon that can kill one of the Venerate.

Lockroom: A room that is specially shielded to prevent all kinds of eavesdropping, even by Gifted or Augurs.

Lyth (LITH [sounds like "myth"]): Powerful beings composed almost entirely of Essence and currently trapped in Res Kartha as a result.

Mark: A symbol – a man, woman and child enclosed in a circle—which signifies being bound to the Tenets. For the Gifted, this symbol appears in black on their left forearm when they first use Essence. For Administrators, it appears in red on their right forearm when they are bound to the Tenets using an Oathstone.

Mor Aruil (more ah-RUE-ell): A network of underground tunnels, once used by the Darecians as conduits to draw Essence to the surface. Inaccessible except via a Gate.

Named swords: The five swords created by Andrael in his attempts to find a way to kill members of the Venerate. Also known as the five Blades in Desrielite religion. Individually, the swords are known as Whisper, Thief, Knowing, Sight, and Fate.

Narut (NAH-rut): Small country to the north of Desriel and northwest of Andarra.

Nesk (NESK [sounds like "desk"]): Hostile country to the south of Andarra.

Northwarden: The head of Administration. An inherited position, currently held by Wirr.

Oathstones: Vessels that are used by Administration to bind new Administrators to the Tenets.

Portal Box: The small bronze cube that originally led Davian to Caeden. Created by the Lyth, it enables a portal to be opened to any of six pre-set destinations—one destination for each face of the cube.

Prefects: See *sig'nari*.

Prythe (PRITHE [sounds like "tithe"]): City in the south of Andarra. Neighboring Tol Shen.

Res Kartha (rez CAR-thuh): The home of the Lyth. The only place in which they can currently survive, due to their susceptibility to kan.

Rinday (RIN-day): Region that was attacked by Paetir long ago.

Scribe: The person responsible for collating and reading through each Augur's visions of the future, and then determining if there are any that corroborate each other.

sha'teth (shah-TETH): Creatures originally used by Tol Athian to hunt down and kill Gifted criminals. No longer under the Tol's control.

Shackle: A Vessel that, when worn by a Gifted, prevents them from using Essence.

Shadow: A Gifted who has been stripped of their ability to use Essence. Signified by dark veins marring the face.

Shalis (SHALL-is): Serpentlike race that trained Caeden to use Essence. Now extinct.

shar'kath (shar-KATH): One of the five Banes led by Aarkein Devaed during his invasion of Andarra.

sig'nari (sig-NAR-ee): The name given to the Gifted who served directly under the Augurs before the rebellion. Also known as Prefects.

Sight: One of the five Named swords.

Talmiel (TAL-me-el): Town on the Andarran side of the bridge that crosses the Devliss River. Talmiel's bridge is the only official inland crossing between Andarra and Desriel.

tek'ryl (TEK-rill): One of the five Banes led by Aarkein Devaed during his invasion of Andarra.

Telesthaesia (tel-es-THAY-see-ah): The Essence-absorbing armor worn by the Blind. Telesthaesia helmets completely block the wearer's vision.

Thief: One of the five Named swords.

Thrindar (THRIN-dar): Capital of Desriel.

Time endpoint: An element of a kan-powered device that deals with the manipulation of time.

Tol Athian (toll ATH-ee-en): One of the two remaining major outposts of the Gifted. Located in Ilin Illan.

Tol Shen (toll SHEN [sounds like "pen"]): One of the two remaining major outposts of the Gifted. Located next to the city of Prythe.

Trace: A sample of a person's Essence, potentially allowing them to be tracked.

Treaty: The treaty signed between the besieged Gifted and the rebellion fifteen years ago, resulting in the end of the war but the submission of the Gifted to the Tenets.

Tributary: A device designed to hold one of the Venerate. It uses needles to cause persistent injuries to its occupant's body, in order to generate a constant and uninterruptable flow of Essence.

Variden (VAH-rid-en): A town in Andarra.

Veil: A Vessel that allows its user to become invisible.

Venerate: An immortal group of Augurs, originally brought together by Gassandrid with the aim of freeing the world from fate.

Vessel: A device that stores and/or uses Essence for a particular purpose.

Whisper: One of the five Named swords. Currently wielded by Breshada.

Zvael (zeh-VAY-el): The name of the people from which Gassandrid originated.